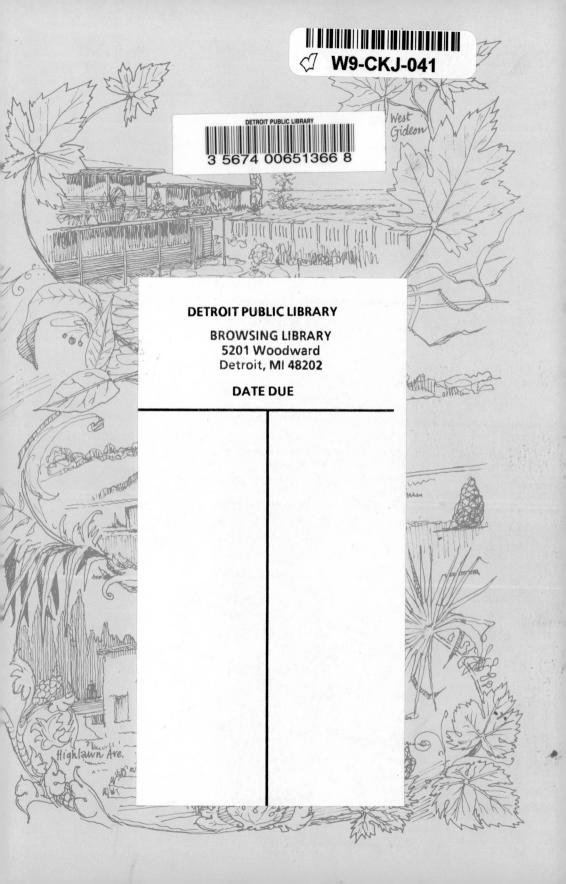

GOLDENEYE

GOLDENEYE

Malcolm Macdonald

Alfred A. Knopf   New York
1981

THIS IS A BORZOI BOOK
PUBLISHED BY ALFRED A. KNOPF, INC.

Copyright © 1981 by Malcolm Macdonald
All rights reserved under International and Pan-American Copyright Conventions.
Published in the United States by Alfred A. Knopf, Inc., New York, and
simultaneously in Canada by Random House of Canada Limited, Toronto. Distributed
by Random House, Inc., New York.

Library of Congress Cataloging in Publication Data
Ross-Macdonald, Malcolm.
Goldeneye.
I. Title.
PR6068.0827G6   1981   823'.914   80-23235
ISBN 0-394-5118-2

Manufactured in the United States of America
First American Edition

For Petra
A girl in 2, 134, 521

PART ONE

1919-1920

Three generations of Scottish stock
come to life as they come to terms
with their humanity in this evocation
of immigrant life in western Canada.

1

It began at the waterfall, over the hill, beyond sight of the little croft. Catherine often went there to wash herself all over, where her father wouldn't see her. His eyes were always on her, ever since her mother died. He wouldn't stop looking at her. In the wash-house, his eye was at the knotholes. When she crossed to the byre or hung out the wash, he gazed on her from slant corners or beyond the blind glass of the windows. Since the mother died there was no peace from him.

Catherine had gone to the waterfall that evening, not to wash, but to let Huey MacLintock kiss her. But her father had spied them out. Not idly was he nicknamed An Dóiteán—the great fire. He nearly killed poor Huey. She thought he would kill her, too. But instead he fell to his knees in the torrent of white water and threw his arms around her in a hug that begged her understanding—and so much else besides. But she could not forgive, nor give, nor understand.

She ran from him, from his everywhere eyes. She ran from herself, fearing herself. She fled that whole country. It was the spring of 1919.

She had no idea Scotland was so big. The long, anxious miles the train had brought her from Fort William were a revelation. And Glasgow was reassuringly huge. Yet her memory of the old, sepia-toned globe in the corner of the schoolroom at Strath told her she had not yet travelled a measurable fraction of the earth's surface. Its alien vastness began to frighten her. If Uncle Murdo had not left her the money for this voyage, if Uncle Murdo were not waiting for her in Canada, she would turn around and go home.

No! There was one thing she feared more: her father. She feared his anger, his angry, devouring eyes, his angry, burning hair, his fiercely freckled brow and cheeks, his furious possession of her . . . his implacable love. Fear of him had driven her here, this bright embarkation morning.

Fear of his merciless, loving eyes harried her down over the cobblestones and granite setts, down through grime that all the rain in Scotland would not cleanse, down through the bleary daybreak, down to the tardaubed quay, where the promise was all of North America.

HECTOR was the name around the vessel's stern. She was a salt-stained cargo carrier with room for ten first-class passengers and as many steerage as could be packed in without revolt. Below her name ran the legend JOHN BROWN—GLASGOW. In a way, then, *Hector* was at home here. *In what way?* Catherine wondered. *In the same way as me.* She stepped hesitantly up the gangplank.

"We sail in two hours," a seaman told her. He sounded oddly reproachful.

Catherine looked puzzled; two hours—surely that meant she was in good time?

"The rest of your baggage," the man explained. He looked at her battered suitcase, then at her face. "Is that all?"

"Aye."

He shrugged. One less worry. "Female steerage is on the deck below this. Up forrard. Ye may walk on this deck in the hours of daylight and the forrard well deck at any time, but only when the hatches are battened. If the covers are off, you stay clear. Ye'll see Mrs. MacEuan, the stewardess, for a berth."

She thanked him and went to the companionway. MacEuan. A good Highland name. There were MacEuans in Strath; one farmed near Beinn Uidhe. *Petty, vindictive, small-souled informers!* The memory of her father's judgement rolled in like thunder from the lowland hills around Greenock and Gourock, where *Hector* lay, waiting for the seaward pluck of the tide.

Catherine was weary. Her joints ached. Soon she could rest for ten days —perhaps more.

Two women, who might have been gentlefolk in better days, were walking arm in arm around the forward well deck. The hatches were uncovered but no one told the women off. Another seaman was signalling down the last few bales of some late cargo—sealskins? Hides? The giant dried leaves of some plant? Even their colour was indeterminate. The man eyed her, frankly admiring, as she passed. He spoke, but when a Glaswegian speaks he sounds merely as if he is clearing his throat. She did not understand one single grunt in that machine-gun rattle of glottal stops.

"Whisht!" she said. The safest reply.

His admiration—or, rather, the open and honest joy of his admiration— frightened her. She was used to the hooded glance, the pinched and furtive inspection. Only one young man had hacked his way through those thickets of shame. Huey MacLintock. "You are beautiful, Catherine," he had said. And she had run to the secret place on the far side of Beinn Uidhe, where she kept hidden a fragment of a looking glass, to see what "beautiful" was. For that, her father had nearly killed Huey MacLintock. For that, Huey

MacLintock was now bound for Canada, too. Somewhere. On some other ship. There had been no time to see him before he left.

Mrs. MacEuan was a good soul, and a careful judge. Catherine, who had expected steerage passengers to be treated like cattle, was surprised at the woman's smile, her pleasant greeting, her unhurried air. In fact, the stewardess could not at once decide whether Catherine was genteel or rough. The first half-dozen genteels went into the six-berth cabin; the roughs and the rest went into the mess.

"Would you be coming from these parts, Miss Hamilton?" she asked. It was the first Highland voice Catherine had heard since she had run from home.

"I would not, Mistress MacEuan. I would be coming from Strath, in Inverness."

"You are welcome, so." Mrs. MacEuan led her to the six-berth cabin and gave her pride-of-place on one of the two upper berths. As Highlanders they dropped naturally into the Gaelic. Mrs. MacEuan told Catherine that her cabin companions were two Sassenach ladies, Mistress Wharton and Mistress Jones, widows since the Great War, and a Lowland-Scotswoman and her daughter (she called them Sassenachs too) who were joining a brother on a farm in Canada; the husband was in the male-steerage mess. Their name was Wilkie.

"And don't be worrying yourself. We'll find a good person for the sixth berth," Mrs. MacEuan promised. "Did you ever go to sea before?"

"Only for the lobster creels."

The image hit her with a sudden, visceral intensity: the wickerwork and the trapped crustaceans shimmering upward through the dark-green-blue-black sea, bursting through the roof of their world in a foaming of light. And other images: the black peat soil of Beinn Uidhe in her hands, squeezing from it the golden water. She would never see and do these things again—yet, such is the curse of memory, she could never cease to see and do them.

"Are you quite well, Miss Hamilton?" Anxious eyes looking at her.

"I was not feeling altogether well these days that went past, Mistress MacEuan. But I'm well to be on this ship, and well to be going where she is going."

She leaned against the rail, her back to the grim little port, and opened her Bible, seeking an omen. The sun rose above Glasgow, away to the east, but could not struggle through the smoke. A fan of its red fingers spanned that half of the sky. *Red of a morning . . .* no, that was not the Word of God. Not an omen.

Psalms. Good—her favourites. Psalm LV. *Give ear to my prayer, O God; and hide not thyself.* . . . She knew it. Her eye fell down the page, seeking the word *wanderer . . . wandering . . . wander.* It was there, somewhere. It *was* an omen!

And I said, Oh that I had wings like a dove! for then would I fly away, and be at rest.

Lo, then would I wander far off and remain in the wilderness.

I would hasten my escape from the windy storm and tempest.

Destroy, O Lord . . .

It was not the sort of omen she wanted. Her unsatisfied eyes slid across to the neighbouring column. Psalm LVI.

Thou tellest my wanderings: put thou my tears into thy bottle: are they not in thy book?

When I cry unto thee, then shall mine enemies turn back: this I know; for God is for me.

She sighed. The omen was good.

A darkening fell across the book. Her body flinched, preparing to meet her father, for his was the only shadow ever to dim those pages. Her ears were ready to hear him say: "Get some work into your hands, girl!" Her eyes, when they lifted to his, would see that ginger fierceness; his brows would burn red, his freckles scream.

The darkness resolved into a skirt, a pleasant face, a smile. "So you're for Canada, too!" Bewilderment must have lingered in her own face, because the woman frowned and said, "Miss Hamilton, is it not? I'm Mrs. Wilkie."

Catherine hugged her Bible to her and, smiling now, nodded. She told the woman: "Yes, I'm going to Hawk Ridge in Saskatchewan, to join my uncle, Murdo Hamilton, and his family."

Murdo, who had said, "For the love of God, girl, if you stay here that man will be killing you—or worse!" Murdo, who had left the money for her passage with Mistress Menzies, the postmistress in Strath, and the letter for the Immigration.

"We're going to my brother-in-law in Dauphin, Manitoba. Iain Wilkie. He has a farm there."

Catherine, damned with a camera's memory, saw it on the map of central Canada that she already carried in her mind. *L. Dauphin* to the northeast, *Riding Mt.* to the southwest, a mottling of pools above it, interspersed with grass tufts, thus   . What sort of land was that? Like the sedge marsh at Camas Mor?

"That would be the very edge of the settlements," Catherine said.

"You know it!"

"Only from the atlas."

"They say it's as well to go through New York as Halifax. There are terrible strikes in Winnipeg and they may spread across Canada."

Catherine could not imagine a strike. Untended lobster creels . . . the kine not milked. It was not possible.

"The ticket agent said the ship bound for Halifax would not be good," she told the woman.

"They were telling us the same. Wilkie says it's just that they would be getting a bigger commission from the owners of this ship."

There were so many things that made no sense—strikes . . . commission. What were they all? Her legs and arms ached from the walking and carrying. But she didn't want to go below and rest. She wanted to watch Scotland slip away. She wanted that camera in her head to capture the last possible memories of hill and island, cloud and water.

Mrs. Wilkie's daughter joined them, a lively, gap-toothed girl of six or seven. "Colin says the—"

"Who's Colin?" her mother interrupted.

"A sailor. Colin says the decks'll be going round and round soon," she told them.

"Not the decks. The propellor."

"He says we'll be seeing Arran and Prestwick and Ayr and everything."

"Aye," Mrs. Wilkie said heavily, meaning it would be no pleasure to her. "I doubt we will."

The little girl's mistranslation of the sailor's words was close to the truth, though. The *Hector* was hardly out into the Firth of Clyde before it seemed to Catherine that the decks were, indeed, going round and round. She knew then that she was about to be a dreadful sailor. She had rowed through storms to save the lobster creels, and her little boat had tossed like a cork. But she could not take the slower, queasier motion of these big decks.

She went to the door where the companionway led down to her cabin, but one whiff of that warm, oily air, overlaid with traces of steam and burning coal, was enough to send her to the leeward rail (and to send her breakfast even farther). Empty, she felt easier. She faced the wind and drew deep lungsful of the sea air. She yawned a hundred times and wiped the damp skin where the breeze pushed the water from her eyes back horizontally. The dried salt of those tears was silky to touch; but the dried salt of the seawater, thrown up in a stinging spray from the bows, was tacky.

She did not know that she was really very ill. Her seasickness masked the fever. The sea wind and the cold spray chilled her skin, which would otherwise have burned. When she watched the coast of her homeland tilt and jerk as it receded, she thought it was a side effect of her heaving innards. And it was the same with the blackness that crept in and seeped up and stole down across her field of view.

All day she endured the misery, shrinking from the touch of her clothing, boiled up by her fever, chilled by the wind, smiling wanly in return at smiles from fellow sufferers (as she thought them), refusing all suggestions of food.

"It would be best," Mrs. MacEuan advised.

"I will be fine the morn, Mistress MacEuan, just fine," Catherine promised.

That night she was one of six groaning sufferers, all of whom prayed they might be "just fine" come the morn.

Three of them were—the two war widows and the little girl, Mina. It was Mrs. Wharton who first realized that Catherine had been stricken by something far more serious than mere seasickness. Even Catherine understood it by then as she blinked out on a world where fact and delirium mingled with baffling promiscuity.

A thermometer burned under her tongue. There was a worried man looking at it. There was ice in bags all about her; it burned, too.

She was in another room, alone except for a smiling woman who dabbed her brow. Every joint ached; even the act of breathing hurt her ribs.

For long periods she left the ship and wandered again over the crofts and glens of Bienn Uidhe.

A man with bright freckles and burning eyes watched her in the bathhouse. Those eyes watched her at the breadmaking. They watched her stooping to gather eggs . . . milking . . . tying the lobsters' claws with deft loops of string while his ginger-freckled hands clamped them firm.

The dusty road was an almost blinding white against the black dresses of the two women, who leaned toward each other and flayed the moral state of the population with unsmiling joy. Child Catherine, who could not hear a word, knew every word they spoke. Their talk was of sin, which she did not then understand.

A young man ran away from her, away from the waterfall, down the glen. She could not see his face but she knew it well—and knew it was stained with tears. She even knew that the tears were of rage, impotent rage.

A man with bright freckles and burning eyes silenced the whole kirk congregation with his shout: "Lewd! Lewd! Lewd! Ye're all damned! Whosoever looketh on a woman to lust after her hath committed adultery with her already in his heart. Will ye take your hellish, hoorin' eyes off her and keep them off!"

A young man was pleading with her, urgently.

She stopped using the bathhouse and took to bathing in the burn where it cascaded down the glen—and where an overhang of rock gave shelter from those piercing eyes.

A young man stood by that cascade and put his lips to hers; he detonated all her sense: "Catherine, you are beautiful." Veins of an unsuspected fire branched through her body, shining a sudden light of meaning on a hundred puzzling prelections, or sermons. At last she understood sin. Delicious childhood ended; the grown-up world was there instead, beckoning without inviting. Fear-ridden, unforgiving. And delicious, too.

A young man ran away from the waterfall, down the glen.

A man with burning eyes shouted, "Lewd! Lewd! Lewd!" He held the young man high over his head. The young man was petrified and did not struggle. The older man sought this way and that among the gravestones, looking for one sharp enough to impale the young man or break his back. The minister and people leaped upon him and bore him down before he could kill the young man.

"For God's sake, Ian—it's your own wife's grave you're desecrating!" the minister shouted.

A young man ran away from her, down the glen.

She and the man with the burning eyes tended a sick woman. The stillborn child was wrapped in sailcloth outside. There was a monstrous, unspoken fear between them that the sick woman would die—for her departure from that house would place intolerable strains on the two who would be left. She, Catherine, did not know it; but he did. And the fear it put on him was passed on to her, though she did not understand it.

A young man put his lips to hers—and then she understood the fear. His lips detonated all her understanding.

The sick woman died and the piercing eyes of the freckled man screamed at her: "Lewd! Lewd! Lewd!" Those eyes harried her through two summers and three eternal winters. "What is it that's come upon you?" she asked, weeping. "Why are you never kindly to me as you were before she died! What is it I've done?"

A young man put his lips to hers, and inserted fear in place of that question. He detonated fear. She feared beauty and how it kindled men. She feared men and how they kindled her.

The burning eyes watched her everywhere.

A young man ran away from her, away from the waterfall, away from the glen. He was crying, too.

"I do believe its over," a voice said.

Catherine was too exhausted to turn and see who spoke. Half of her still wandered in the nightmare lands.

Later—it could have been minutes or hours—she opened her eyes and actually managed to look about her. The nurse saw the movement.

"Are you going again?" she asked, and answered herself with a smile. "No. I think this time you'll stay with us."

Catherine frowned. *"Hector,"* she said.

"That's it! Och, ye'll be just fine. Mrs. MacEuan has good friends here in New York. You'll likely stop there. She's away now to make the arrangements."

There were so many questions Catherine wanted to ask the nurse. Deep inside herself they seemed important, but as they struggled to the surface, to that part of her mind where they were assembled into words, their importance drained away. The very act of searching for the words (and not always finding them) seemed to rob the questions themselves of meaning.

It was not a side effect of her illness, though her exhaustion made it easier to lie passive. She had always been so. At school, in the kirk (especially listening to prelections), on the farm, out in the little boat, the impulse to ask questions had often stirred her, but rarely to the point where they survived translation into words. Usually, if she stayed silent, people or life itself would provide the answers.

A prattling child, the daughter of a rich and rare holidaymaker in Strath, had once come out to the lobster creels. "And why do you tie their claws?" she had asked. Moments later a yet-to-be-tied lobster gave her a painful nip. Then she had cried; but even through her tears she had forced the words, "Why did he pinch me?"

Catherine had never asked the first of those questions because the answer was immediately obvious. The second was just as obvious but not so immediate; it had taken nineteen years of living to understand that life itself was brutal and would bide its time until it saw the chance to hurt.

So time answered all questions, as young Huey MacLintock's kiss that evening in the glen—and the unsuspected passions it had exploded within her—had told her all she had ever wondered about the power of sin, and her father's obsessive vigilance, and his lunatic anger in the kirk . . . and why his eyes never left her face and body.

"You know you had the Spanish flu," the nurse said. "You're lucky to be alive. It's killed millions." She said it the Glasgow way: *moo-yuns,* which Catherine did not understand.

The words lodged in her mind and sank; one more unasked question— did they blame her for the death of this other passenger with a name like Moe Yuns? She looked around her.

The nurse saw the movement. "It's the sick bay. Really it's the first class. We had to turn out Mrs. Fawcett, puir thing! She must have looked forward for months to being seasick and pampered for the whole crossing. Och, she wasn't too pleased, I dare tell you!" She laughed.

While the nurse changed the sheets, Catherine sat, palsied with weakness, on a chair. It was of heavy red mahogany, held to the floor with a large brass hook. She felt an impulse to take a cloth and fetch up the rich shine on both, wood and metal. Polishing a thing was one way to possess it and be at home with it. She knew as much from polishing the kirk benches and her father's carver chair.

"A wee walk to the heads?" the nurse suggested; and she helped Catherine to the lavatory at the end of the passage outside. In the looking glass there she was not beautiful.

Back between the sheets Catherine felt their crisp softness and had a sudden vague memory of waking here a hundred times when the sheets grated like sandpaper and her joints and bones had flinched at the very touch. In this new world, a universe away from Beinn Uidhe, the memory was enough to justify the sin of lying there, no longer ill.

The nurse put a thermometer in her mouth, but told her she already knew it would read normal. Then she gave Catherine a shrewd, sidelong glance; her tongue lingered on her lip before she asked, "And who's Huey? Is he the same as MacLintock?" She expected the deadpan face but was astonished that her fingers felt no change in the girl's pulse. This lack of response embarrassed her. She had wanted to provoke a blush, a little teasing, a warm, giggling confession, and a heart-to-heart. She herself yearned for a young man who was half a world away.

Now she had to rise above this petty failure. "Such goings on!" she said. "And here was me thinking Highland life was all rain, mist, work, and whisky! I never heard of such capers! Talk about the Highland Games!"

Catherine, understanding this sudden flood of banter (though she could never have put that understanding into words), rewarded her at last with a blush and a small, voiceless laugh, enough to release the woman.

"Go on!" the nurse said as she took out the thermometer. "Who is he? Is he your young man?"

"I don't think so."

"You mean you don't know?"

"He was kissing me once."

That was all Catherine had intended saying but, somehow, the rest poured out. She listened to herself with surprise. "My father burst his head open with his fist and was standing on him in the burn until he thought him drowned."

The professional reasserted itself inside the nurse when she saw Catherine's agitation. "There now! Dinnae fash yourself now. Lie quiet till Mrs. MacEuan returns."

It was an easy order to obey. Outside ordinary people were doing all sorts of ordinary work. She heard the slopping of a water-filled pail, someone scrubbing a deck, someone (the same?) whistling, a clatter of china and cutlery, a sea gull, the deep, mechanical throb of a winch, a shout. . . .

One day, soon, she would have a pail to slop, a cow to milk, a song to sing as she worked. But for the moment it was glory to close her eyes and let the sounds become as alien as the sea. Untroubled sleep was such a luxury.

Hours later she was awakened by Mrs. MacEuan, who was trying so hard not to wake her. Their eyes met. Catherine smiled and stretched.

"So it's yourself at last!" Mrs. MacEuan beamed as she came over and felt Catherine's forehead. "There were times we gave you up for lost."

Catherine smiled again.

"Well, you're silent enough now!"

"Was I talking in the fever, Mistress MacEuan?"

"You may say so!" The stewardess stared at her until Catherine grew uncomfortable; but it was some internal argument that consumed the woman. At length she said, "Well, if I would be washed ashore at Strath, I daresay I'd not be scorning the help of your heretic hands. A Free Kirk blanket's as warm as a nun's, I'm thinking. And Free Kirk soup's as nourishing."

She leaned forward to straighten the sheets and, for the first time, Catherine noticed the crucifix that hung about her neck. She wondered at the blasphemy—that anyone could wear such a thing merely in the way of jewellery.

2

"Would you be knowing the cuckoo?" Mrs. MacEuan asked. "Which lures the other birds to care for its young and abandon their own?"

Catherine had never been in a motor car before. Because she was so weak they were taking a cab from the pier on the West Side, up in the thirties, to the convent just off Washington Square. The rumble of the motor and the speed it produced excited her.

"I was hearing one once," she answered, "but never saw one."

She had no idea what a convent was and had not asked when Mrs. MacEuan had promised to leave her in the care of one. She hoped it would not cost much. But of course it wouldn't. Wasn't Mistress MacEuan herself a Highlander?

"There's something of a cuckoo in you," Mrs. MacEuan said. "I never saw an Immigration official so helpful."

"Everyone was kind," Catherine said. "Especially yourself, Mistress MacEuan. I will not be forgetting."

The older woman looked at the pale, earnest face of the younger, seeing all its innocence and vulnerability on display there, and wished, not for the first time, that she could somehow stay behind when the ship sailed, and nurse this woman-child through her convalescence, and see her safe to . . . what name had she babbled in her fever? Hawk Ridge.

"Aye—a cuckoo," she murmured.

"There's black folk here," Catherine said in amazement. "Are they heathens?" She thought of all the pennies gathered at the kirk for missions to the black heathens; but the descriptions brought home by the missionaries did not tally with what she saw of New York.

"They are not. They would be good Christians, after their own way. And you must not call them black, nor niggers. They are Negroes."

Catherine nodded and stored the fact away. She was, she realized, already growing used to novelty. When she had left home, stalking and crawling down the glen in the moonlight, she had lived between two fears—the fear of her father, dwindling; and the fear of the great unknown world, looming. But Glasgow had blunted the edge of that second fear and, in a strange way, had made New York seem less alien, too. Not that Glasgow was the more foreign of the two, but her experience of it had followed so soon upon that moment when she had burst out of her little Highland world. It had been so much more immediate, the sensation so much more raw. Nothing would ever be quite as unnerving again. She had to look out of the cab window and say, almost aloud, *foreign* city, *foreign* land, *foreign* people, *foreign* ways, before even part of that exciting terror would return.

Mrs. MacEuan left her at the convent door as soon as the woman in black opened it. There was a hurried conversation between the two before she turned to Catherine and, giving her an awkward hug, set off down the flagstone path to the high and massive garden door that led out onto the street. Catherine began to repeat her thanks.

"Whisht!" Mrs. MacEuan said and passed out of view. In that second while the street was visible, a young man, one of a laughing group of three, poked his head in and shouted, "Hey, chicken! Don't waste it!"

The woman in black snorted, wearily rather than in anger. "Come in, child," she said. "I'll show you your room."

Catherine felt at ease at once. The house was so simple. The croft had been simple, too, with its whitewashed walls and stone floors—just like here. But unlike here there had always been oilskins and sou'westers, boots, twine, pensioned-off lobster creels filled with the turf, knives for sharpening . . . all the bric-a-brac of a small croft; here a single flower petal would have been out of place. If she ever owned a home, it would be as spare and simple as this.

As they threaded their way through corridors and up two small flights of stairs, the woman in black explained that her name was Sister John, that Catherine ought by rights to be at the girls' refuge but that, seeing as she was convalescent, Mrs. MacEuan had brought her here "because we're after being a nursing order, d'ye see?"

Catherine, thinking she did see, said, "Yes. She was kind to me. And so are you. I have little money."

"Bless you, child. A prayer's as good. And sure, did you never hear of casting bread upon waters?"

Catherine answered at once, not like a child serving up a lesson but as if it were everyday conversation, *"Cast thy bread upon the waters: for thou shalt find it after many days. Give a portion to seven, and also to eight; for thou knowest not what evil shall be upon the earth."*

Sister John turned and looked at her. "Lord bless us!" she said admiringly.

"Are you from Scotland, too, Mistress Sister John?" Catherine asked, embarrassed enough to want to change the subject.

"That I'm not. Can't ye hear I'm from Ireland?"

A small warning bell rang in Catherine's mind. Ireland was a papist land—though there were good Presbyterian souls there, too. "I was never in that place," she explained. "I was never away from Strath before."

"Are your parents alive at all?"

"My mother would be dead, but my father lives—An Dóiteán."

"Sure that's an Irish name. It means the big fire."

"I know. It was a scholar of the Gaelic from Ireland gave it him. He was in Strath, collecting the language, and he had an argument with my father. Everyone has an argument with my father. And before that time his name would be An t-Sradag, which means the spark. And the scholar said it wasn't fierce enough altogether for him and he should be called An Dóiteán—the big fire. And so he was from that day."

"And is there great fire in his arguing, child?"

"There's great fire in *him* and in all he is doing."

"Then he's well named so."

"His brother, my uncle, where I'm going, is called An Sionnach."

"That means the fox in our Gaelic," the sister said.

"And in ours," Catherine told her.

And thus they found they had two languages almost in common.

Her room was a bare, simple cell; a paradise it seemed.

"We eat at six, after the Angelus," Sister John told her. "Will you rest until then? You'll hear the Angelus bell, here and from the old cathedral."

"I am not tired, Mistress Sister John. It would not be rest but idleness. Have you no work for my hands?"

"Call me Sister only. There will be time enough for work, child. You're much weaker than you think, you know. But—ah, sure—a little walk in the garden would do no harm."

A vestibule led to a lobby between house and garden. In an arched niche at one end was a statue of a lady in biblical dress holding a baby. A lamp burned before it. Sister John knelt a moment and prayed.

A horrified realization began to dawn on Catherine. When Sister John rose again she asked with bated breath, "What would that be?" nodding at the statue.

"Faith, child!" Sister John laughed. "And you who know the scriptures backwards. Isn't it the Virgin and the Christchild—what else could it be . . ."

Her voice tailed off in perplexity as she saw the horror flood into the girl's face.

"But—you're—you're—" Catherine whispered, taking a step back.

It was monstrous. She was trapped in a house of superstitious idolaters. The "prayer" she had just witnessed was one of their loathsome, obscene rituals in the service of the Antichrist himself, the Scarlet Devil of Rome. She backed away into the lobby.

"What is it, child?" Sister John asked, going toward her.

"No! You're papists!"

There were good Christians in Strath who would cross the road rather than meet a papist, or move house rather than live in the same street as one.

Within the hour her fever had returned. The doctor visited her twice that night and they even debated sending for a Free Kirk minister. But by morning she was almost back to normal and the danger had passed.

It was Sister John who nursed her by day. She alone had heard that cry of *papist;* she alone understood what troubled the girl and, as soon as Catherine was alert again, she told her that they'd considered sending for a Free Church minister. "So, you see, it's not your soul we're after at all. Sure, I think God has that article safe in His keeping already—and who'd dare to go stealing from Him!"

Later she told Catherine that if she really wanted to go to a place of her own faith, it could be arranged the minute she was fit for moving. Catherine remembered the enigmatic words of Mrs. MacEuan. She smiled at Sister John and said, "A nun's blanket's as warm as one from the Kirk."

"Warmer," Sister John said stoutly. "Though we'd say it's from charity and you'd think it's from the hellfire, no doubt."

Catherine giggled.

Sister John, emboldened, said, "Will I take off me shoes now and show you the cloven hooves on me?"

Catherine laughed.

Sister John gave a conspiratorial glance behind her and leaned low over Catherine's face. "Wait while I show you!" She gently eased back her starched wimple at her forehead. "If you look good and close, you'll see where they cut the horns out of me when I was no more than a babby."

Catherine laughed until a fit of coughing intervened.

Sister John spoke a lot about her childhood over those days of Catherine's recovery; the two women learned how much they had in common. Both came from crofts, though Sister John swore her family's was no more than a *sheskin*—a marsh. Both families eked out a meagre subsistence from cows and sheep with lobster and inshore fishing. Both cut turf for winter firing. Both told the time by the shadow of the door post on the kitchen floor.

None of this reconciled her to Sister John's papism. Instead, the nun became two quite different people—on the one hand the cheerful countrywoman and competent nurse, full of the authority of good sense, and, on the other, a poor, deluded soul, a victim of superstition and idolatry, limping through her days on the crutches of ritual incantations only half understood, and needing bells and beads to keep her incomprehension in order. Even her name, *John,* seemed as sinful as putting a woman into trousers.

That rich holidaymaker's daughter who got nipped by the lobster had also been possessed by a strange heresy: her family were Jews. Catherine (at that time only ten years old) had believed the Jews were an ancient, extinct people, like the Hittites or the Philistines—preserved only in the Bible. The little girl told her they had the same God as the Christians but didn't believe Jesus was His Son.

"But that's wicked," Catherine told her. "How can you persist in such wickedness when the Word of God Himself is telling you otherwise?"

And the little girl had said, "Well, *I* know Jesus was the Son of God, but it's just that *we* don't believe it."

Somewhere at the back of her mind Catherine had similar hopes of an equally ambiguous conversion of Sister John. Whenever the nun rattled away at her beads, charging like a charabanc through her *Ave Mariagratia-plenadominustecumbenedicta . . . fructusventristui Jesus,* Catherine pointedly took out her Bible and read to herself, imagining that her attitude would show the poor deluded woman how easy it was to commune directly with God—that no one needed beads and rituals. Only toward the end of her time in that house did she come to understand that those dreadful practices gave the nun as much solace and strength as she herself derived from her own Free Kirk faith; then, like a good tourist, she marvelled.

After a week the doctor allowed Catherine out into the garden. Sister John had to go back to her regular nursing in the hospital and they could find only an hour or so together each day. They spoke no more of their past, only of the future. Sister John wanted to go and nurse in Africa; New York wasn't at all to her liking. "There's too many Irish here," she said. "Sure I'd as liefer stay at home as come to this city."

She wanted to know all about Murdo Hamilton—the uncle Catherine was to join—and his wife Mary and their sons, John and Ian. And how old were they all? So young! He wasn't long married then. And how long had he the farm? Two years! Well, it wouldn't be paid for yet. And what a great help she'd be to them—sure, wasn't she already only a marvel here at the convent, never leaving off with the polishing and cleaning only someone made her stop.

And then, with a shy, sly wistfulness, quite different from her manner with other questions, she asked was there a young fellow in it?

"I don't know," Catherine said; but she blushed now, enough to encourage the other.

"Go on, why else does a young woman leave home! I'm sure it's a fellow."

"Young Huey MacLintock was kissing me the once, and he ran away to Canada," Catherine told her.

"Lord love us, was it that bad!"

"An Dóiteán was nearly killing him first with his fists, then in the burn."

"And so you ran away from him. Is that it?"

"It is."

Catherine ventured no more. There was a silence that she found easy, but Sister John fidgetted all the time and finally came out with, "Well, for all the gossip that's in you, you'd as well be a Carmelite."

Catherine wanted to tell her more but thought, *How can I?* She did not fully understand her father's obsessive vigilance. If she had felt that Sister John might be able to explain it, she would have risked stumbling through the thickets of her own bewilderment, but she knew there was no hope there. The nun had called her own father "an aisy man—and, faith, with fifteen children at his heels what else might he be!" How could she, from that teeming, intemperate Irish *boha,* more of a tribe than a family, even begin to understand the intense, loving hatred of the silent croft, where it was A Terrible Thing to Fall into the Hands of the Living God, and the Devil lurked in every shadow and cranny? Turf fires, the heather, the sheep, and the roaring of the sea . . . shared memories of these could not bridge such a gap.

So she spoke instead of the summer and the harvest time, when even her father, An Dóiteán, grew so exhausted that to lie in the headlands amid the wild flowers was no sin. And the picture she drew was so sharp and alive that Sister John did not feel cheated.

"Ah, 'twill be a gray old place when you're gone, child," the nun said.

3

New York, the second time, was a stark surprise. She had lived in the city for three weeks with no sense of its being there at all. The few skyscrapers that loomed above the convent walls were mere stage scenery; her world had become that quiet, simple house of whitewash and stone (desecrated only by the graven images of saints and the Virgin).

On the way to the front door, after a leavetaking with the Mother Superior, Sister John began to tease. "Ah, 'twill be a grand thing to get out me horns and tail again. Sure, we only took them off to deceive you. And wasn't I lost without them."

Catherine longed to throw her arms around the woman and hug her, but was too shy. The conflict brought a tear to her eye, though she was not at all miserable. "I'm sorry," she said. "I couldn't be thinking you're right, of course. But nor would I be thinking you're bad anymore."

"Well that's grand, so," the nun said. "Just grand." She stood a little apart; her eyes, too, were clouded, though she was used to human severance and the deprivation that followed. "You'll be writing to us."

"I will." She thanked her and said goodbye in Gaelic: *"Tapadh leat, a phiuthar chòir, agus guma math a theid leat."*

After that, and knowing Sister John's eyes were on her still, she did not find the streets half so alien. At the corner she turned and waved; the nun nodded back and closed the gate. She was alone once more. It was Tuesday, late afternoon; she would be in Hawk Ridge by noon on the Sabbath.

She was proud of the route she had worked out, with the help of time-tables borrowed by the priest. She was destined first for Buffalo, then to Detroit and on to Chicago, where, after a twelve-hour wait, she could catch a train bound for Winnipeg via Minneapolis—but she would change at Grand Rapids north of Minneapolis for a train to Minot and then over the border to Moose Jaw, Grand Junction, and Hawk.

She left from Grand Central. She could have gone two dollars cheaper from Weehawken in New Jersey, but this way she would see the Niagara Falls, which everyone said would be worth the extra money. There were so many different railroads and alternative trains that it had required a whole morning of figuring. Every minute of the day a train arrived from and departed to somewhere in New York.

It was already dark by the time her train emerged from the underground portion of the tracks, beneath Park Avenue, so her first impression of suburban and rural America was of a shimmering panorama of lighted windows that gave way to patchworks of dark and more distant light and finally to long stretches of dark with only the occasional group of glowing pinpoints.

She read her Bible for a while. Then she read and reread her train schedule, repeating to herself all the names—Yonkers, Ossining, Pough-keepsie . . . (for she had copied them all down whether the train stopped there or not, and whether the time of its passage was day or night). Then she walked up and down the train, envying those who could afford the Pullman sleepers. She ate a "hot dog" (having been assured the meat was not actually canine in origin) and washed it down with water from the coolers. She had calculated that if she ate for under $1.25 a day, her $75 ought to last to Hawk. The fares to Grand Junction would mount to $67.10, some $20 of which had already gone on the ticket to Chicago. The budgeting was tight, with no allowance for overnights even in the cheapest sort of rooming house, and certainly nothing to spare for sleeping cars. But reclining seats were "no extra charge" and somewhere between Fonda and Little Falls she fell asleep in one. Twice during the night the conductor straightened the shawl with which she had covered herself.

The conductors, it seemed, were a new order of chivalry devoted to escorting unaccompanied women safely through the maze of the railroad network. All the way to Canada she was handed on from one to the other like royal freight. A new conductor came on at Buffalo, just before daybreak —a small, round, cheery Negro. Almost his first task was to make sure of Catherine's welfare.

Last night at Grand Central she had realized the train was longer than the Highland Railway train that had brought her most of the way to Glasgow; but now she saw just how much longer. Even on a fairly lazy curve she could see both the locomotive and the car at the tail; she had to keep looking from one to the other to make sure they indeed belonged to the same train.

She was at breakfast as they came to a brief halt at Niagara Falls. The edge of the gorge concealed the foot of both the American and the Canadian portions, but the sight of such vast torrents of water pouring endlessly over the edge of the escarpment was awesome. She had seen the Atlantic in some fairly impressive moods off the Highland coast, but nothing to match this for sheer spectacle. The thunder, even at this distance, was frightening.

A young man sitting opposite her spoke. "Ten million years ago they were way down near Lake Ontario," he said. He had been fidgetting ever since he sat down, obviously dying to strike up a conversation. Having broken the ice he blushed and looked down. "Or is it ten thousand?" he added. "No, I guess it must be ten million."

"A long time ago, anyway," Catherine said.

He laughed immoderately. "Sure is."

The silence that always adorned Catherine returned. He looked desperately at the landscape, as if some other natural wonder might rescue him. "Yes," he said, sucking in air. "A mighty long time ago."

The train began again. Still no new wonder offered itself. He was reduced to staring at her plate. "Don't you like bacon?" he asked.

"It's cut too thin," she said. "And overcooked." But she ate it all the same. Like all Highlanders she knew the value of a good breakfast; she could last through to the evening and then top up with another hot dog.

"More coffee?" the attendant asked.

To her own surprise she answered, "Yes, please." She had never tasted coffee before. The aroma had been marvellous and so, too (after the first few bitter mouthfuls), had been the drink itself.

"It's good coffee." The young man was pleased to find some positive peg for yet another attempt.

"It would be the first I've tasted," she told him.

"Ever? In your life?"

"Aye."

"Hey!" He was intrigued—interested beyond the mere desire to talk to her. "Where've you been?"

So she told him. And after that, talk was easy. His name was Hyman Amoils and he was on his way to Chicago, to study the conservation of paintings and objets d'art at the Art Institute. She knew nothing about art except that it was vaguely wrong—at least, in the eyes of the Kirk; but she also knew that other, by no means bad, people did not share that view. Once a new dominie had come to the school and had begun to teach art (which meant drawing copies of jugs and flowers and leaves and such things); but the minister had put a stop to it.

"D'you like art, Miss Hamilton?" Hymie asked.

Greatly daring, she made the first statement in her life that ran directly counter to the expressed views of a Free Kirk minister. "I'm thinking there would be no great harm in it," she said.

He was both puzzled and delighted, and pressed her to explain.

"Gee! You mean you never were in an art gallery? You never saw a painting? *Ever?*"

"Where would I? We do not bow down before graven images."

"Of course not." He retreated at once from this potential minefield. It was a move she did not then recognize as essentially American, for in the Highlands she had left, as in the prairies that lay ahead of her, there was not the same need to tolerate a hundred alternative points of view. In both places there was the Word of God and there was Error—and that was that.

"Still," he said. "Never to have seen an original Rembrandt or a Titian! Gee, I'd love to watch you go round a gallery for the first time. To see the masterpieces of the world as an adult! You—you're not stopping over in Chicago, are you?"

She shook her head and was surprised to note that he was blushing; she had not seen a man at the next table grin and wink at Hymie, and punch the air, attaboy-style.

They left the diner together. Her car was nearer than his, and when he saw the seat beside hers was empty he asked, "Would you mind if I came and sat there?"

"I would not."

Quite the reverse. She was delighted. It was a delicious freedom to sit like this with a handsome young man and talk about anything they wanted, and only God looking on—who would know its innocence and not need to have it demonstrated with parades of modesty and avoidance exaggerated to the point of melodrama. The tendons at the back of her knees twitched with impatient excitement while she waited for Hymie to return.

A new thought struck her. She alone had decided he was fit company.

No one else, no dominie, no elder, no general opinion had decreed they might sit side by side and talk. She alone. And that's the way it would be from now on. Less reassuring was the knowledge that her company would be sought after, or shunned, on exactly the same principles. She searched for the pale ghost of her own reflection in the window and used the illusion to rearrange curls that were no more than a dim suffusion of auburn over the passing landscape (and that were, in any case, already perfectly arranged). Did Hymie like her, she wondered? And why? Still, it was nice that he even appeared to.

He returned with a book, *Les Trésors du Louvre*. "Seeing these is nothing like seeing the paintings themselves," he warned. "But this is the very best Swiss colour gravure, so it'll give you some idea. The Louvre is one of the great art galleries of the world, in Paris, France. D'you speak French?"

"I do not."

"Good. The language won't distract you, then. Go on. Look at them." He gave her the book.

It was a revelation to her, so marvellous it almost hurt her eyes. There were landscapes you could swear you'd be able to walk in, with all the beauty of real landscape held forever, and without distractions such as breezes and sounds and movement. There were bowls of fruit and flowers—marigolds and old-fashioned roses with dewdrops trembling on the petals, grapes with the bloom still on them—and arrangements of game—pheasants and hares and salmon—so sumptuous you didn't want to turn the page. And *people!* All the varieties of people—not just short and tall or fat and thin, but mean or jolly, proud or modest, sly or open, worried or confident. Some of them were so real it seemed rude to be staring at them.

And some were not so real—or were real in a different way. There was one by a painter who signed himself Breugel MDLXVII—a horrible painting, really—showing six deformed and crippled beggars cavorting pathetically on the grass, surrounded by brick walls with one arched gate, impossibly far away in the distance leading out into a beautiful landscape. You couldn't say it was realistic—you'd never take it for a photograph—yet, at the same time, you'd swear you'd seen every one of those beggars—somewhere . . . sometime.

"You like that?" Hymie asked.

"I wouldn't be saying 'like'—but . . ." She couldn't think of the word.

"I know what you mean."

"Why would he be painting such a thing?"

"Ah—there's a lot in that picture. You see how they're all in different hats? That's a peasant's hat and that's a king's, and there's everything in between—soldier, merchant, bishop, and so on. Look at it one way and you can say it's a carnival. But look at it another and you can say those six beggars stand for the whole of society. Maybe Breughel's saying the whole of his society was crippled or useless."

"Maybe?" she asked. "Why 'maybe'? Is he or is he not?"

"Both."

She shook her head in bewilderment.

"Sure!" he insisted. "Art's like that. Everything can have two . . . three . . . four . . . a *dozen* meanings. And they're *all* correct at the same time."

A week earlier Catherine would not have had the slightest idea of what he was talking about. But now (especially after her most fundamental belief about the equivalence of papists and devils had been eroded, leaving her exactly halfway between that belief and its opposite) she could just begin to glimpse how two or more apparently contradictory things could be simultaneously true. And the painting, which was both a straightforward view of beggars at a carnival *and* an attack on Breughel's society, became an easy way for her to understand that plurality of truth.

There were some paintings of naked people. She turned those over quickly.

He was amused. "You don't like looking at them?" he asked.

"There would be no two ways of looking at *that,*" she challenged, turning back to the one she had just skipped.

It was Giorgione's *Le Concert Champêtre,* doubly shocking because its foreground portrayed two clothed men and two naked women.

"Try this way," he said, and turned the painting upside down. "The nude is a landscape of the human body. The painter sees it as he sees any landscape. Look." He flipped forward to Rembrandt's *Flayed Ox.* "A landscape of a carcase." He turned back to Mantegna's *Crucifixion.* "A landscape of grief. Do these nude men on the crosses offend you?"

She did not answer.

"Or this?" He turned to the Avignon Pietà, with its near-naked Christ.

Because she was reared in a religious tradition absolutely void of imagery—even the symbols of the cross being frowned on—she found herself looking at it as a painting, not as an icon. Its stark beauty overwhelmed her, and for a moment, before its religious content struck her, she saw exactly what he meant in saying that all paintings are landscapes of something.

She refused his offer of lunch, being shocked that he would believe her capable of incurring such an obligation. While he was away she feasted yet again on the treasures of the Louvre, looking especially at the dozens of utterly different images of Christ, both as an infant and as a man. After some while it occurred to her that she had not once wondered which was the *real* Christ—a problem that would have struck her forcibly before Mr. Amoils had undertaken to begin her visual education. Now she understood that each one was in its different way the real Christ.

To cross the river between Windsor and Detroit the train rolled straight onto a ferry. She stretched her legs then and squandered ten cents on a coffee and sandwich. The boat and the water were disappointingly *un-*reminiscent of the sea, the water being fresh (and not so fresh as all that).

"Goodbye, Canada," he said.

She gave him a puzzled glance.

"Ever since Niagara Falls," he told her. "That was Ontario. Didn't you notice the Customs people?"

She looked back at Windsor, surprised now that she had spotted no difference. People in Strath had always spoken of Canada like a second home; but America was supposed to be really foreign.

At Detroit he bought a *Chicago Tribune,* which he read dismissively—but thoroughly—as far as Kalamazoo. "Seems there's a lot of this Spanish flu in Canada," he said. "Where are you headed—Saskatchewan?"

"Aye."

"There's a lot of it there, too. They say if it goes on like this, it'll kill more people even than the war."

She told him then all about her Uncle Murdo and Aunt Mary, and the little boys, and the farm, and all the work there'd be, and about her old home at Beinn Uidhe (but not about her father and Huey MacLintock), and how she had had the flu herself on the voyage over, and her convalescence among the Sisters of Mercy. And the train fairly flew over the rails to Chicago, where they arived at ten o'clock that Wednesday night.

The cars had been reshuffled in coming off the ferry at Detroit, so that hers, which had started out in the middle of the train, was now near its head. They had pitifully little way to go before they reached the street, and even then the conductor came between them before they could properly say goodbye.

The conductor took her to get her ticket—an "immigrant special" through to Grand Junction, Saskatchewan. It saved her ten dollars. Then he showed her to the platform where her train would stand from eight next morning, two hours before departure.

"Be sure now and tell the conductor Julius Williams said he was to take real good care of you," he said with gruff warmth. Then he gave her the address of a Christian girls' hostel near the station.

She thanked him and went out onto the street, just in case he was still watching. Actually she had no intention of wasting money on a bed—even though, thanks to her immigrant special, she now had it to waste. It would be no hardship to her to stay up all night. She could doze the whole of to-morrow on the train.

In fact, even if she had a bed, she was sure she'd never sleep tonight. The excitement of being in this great new country was just beginning to grip her. She had now travelled for a night and a day—enough to go by train the length of Britain and back—and still she was hardly more than a third of the way to Hawk. She, who had only weeks ago been staggered at the size of Scotland!

She walked up the foot pavement and turned to re-enter the station by another door, where she immediately ran into Mr. Amoils.

"I thought so," he said, grinning broadly.

"You thought what?"

"You ate almost nothing since breakfast and now you're going to sit around the station all night. Correct me if I'm wrong."

"I'm not tired."

"You're short of funds, am I right?"

"I have enough."

"Listen, everyone in this country was an immigrant once—or is de-scended from someone who was. Like I told you—I came here when I was nine. So we *know*. Let me loan you some. It's no disgrace here."

She was too confused to answer. She liked him. She saw he meant it kindly. But nothing would induce her to accept money from a stranger. And she could think of no way to tell him that without hurting him. At last she said, "My head's too full. I'll sleep on the train tomorrow."

His manner changed at once. "Know what?" he said. "I kind of feel that way, too. Mind if I keep you company?" When she frowned he added, "No funny business, I promise. But you honestly can't hang around the station. You'd be arrested."

"What for?"

"Just take it from me. Lesson One for an immigrant girl." His blush told her not to press her bewilderment. "And you know what Lesson Two is?"

She shook her head.

"Never turn down the offer of a meal—on account of you don't know where the next one's coming from."

He made it sound almost a duty.

They checked their bags and then found a modest German establishment on 13th Street, right by the station. There, over a leisurely two hours, she had her first taste of Aalsuppe, Sauerbraten mit Knödel, Apfelstrudel, and a sip of Liebfraumilch.

She had never been waited on before her breakfast on the train and now dinner—not even for a cup of tea and a scone in a cafe. It seemed a dangerous luxury. She kept feeling she ought to get up and help the waiter. Hymie was even easier to talk to now than he had been on the train. He gave no personal confidences and he asked none of her. All his talk was commendably abstract—"Life is. . . . A person ought to. . . . One must never. . . ." She copied his style and discovered within herself a treasure house of hitherto unexpressed beliefs, waiting his key in the door. She learned that she had "always" felt one ought not to act out of fear or ignorance but out of knowledge and understanding. Especially of oneself.

Hymie talked of many things that she only half grasped—science, politics, psychology. . . . Not that she minded. She enjoyed the way their eyes kept meeting, and his obvious pleasure in looking at her face—all the things they could say without words.

Yet when, in a fit of bravura as they left the restaurant, she took his arm and thanked him, she felt him flinch. It surprised her into letting go and saying sorry. Then he was embarrassed. "I'm the one to say sorry," he told her, taking up her hand and putting it where it had been before. "I didn't mean to shake you off."

"Then why did you?"

"Scared, I guess."

"Of *me!*"

"Kind of."

She squeezed his arm to show how silly it was. He squeezed back and laughed at himself. They strolled past the train depot and up into Lake Park, where the lights, being more distant, were softer. An amber moon hung overhead, showing almost every leaf on every shrub and tree.

"What scares you about me?" she asked.

She didn't really want to know—in fact, she didn't believe him; but she wanted to hear him talk about her.

He laughed but did not answer directly. She asked what was funny.

He sighed. "Think of all the millions of words that were ever written and spoken about men and women. Poets, writers, preachers, doctors, philosophers, psychologists—everyone. If I were to answer you properly, I'd have to try and boil all that down to one or two sentences. I'm laughing at the impossibility of it—and at the fact that, if you ask me again, I'll try the impossible."

"You said scared of *me*," she reminded him.

"You're relentless, you know that?"

"I'm not. I just think it's foolish to be scared of me."

It was not precisely what she had meant to say, but the words were out now.

"All men are just a little bit scared of all women. Didn't you know?" he asked.

"But what for?"

He was silent so long she repeated: "What for?"

"It would be so much easier to tell you if we'd only just met. If this was breakfast at Niagara again. I'll never forget that, Cath. Will you?"

"Of course not."

"But suppose I wasn't a man. Suppose I'd been another girl, your age, travelling alone. Suppose everything else had happened just like it has done, including that meal we just ate and this walk we're now taking, arm in arm. Would it be the same?"

She said nothing.

"Isn't there a special, extra pleasure in what has happened since Niagara Falls just because I'm a man and you're a woman?"

Quite suddenly she was aware of her heartbeat—strong and fast, as when she had had a fever. Because she did not understand it, she was afraid. And then she thought she understood what he had meant when he spoke of fear.

"You know what I'm talking about?"

"Aye," she said.

"What?"

"Sin."

He raised his hands to his temples as if stricken. "Aiee!"

"What ails you?" she asked.

"What ails *me!*" He stopped abruptly and turned to face her—or, rather, turned her to face him, gripping her by the shoulders. "Is this sinful?" he asked. "Does this feel like a sin?"

She knew the proper answer to the first question: *Yes.* But the honest answer to the second was *No.* The contradiction silenced her.

"You are lovely," he said in a much gentler voice. "Is it sinful merely to be lovely?"

His head and hers were close but she could not say which of them had moved. Their lips touched softly and, just as softly, they parted. "Sinful?" he asked.

Half her innards were pulled into a sudden vacuum. She threw her arms around him and hugged tight. His hand cupped her chin and forced her head upward. He kissed her again, more urgently. He kissed her many times, until the urgency dwindled and the act became merely pleasant. Then he broke from her and put an arm around her waist. They resumed their walk. She was glad of the movement as a mask for the trembling that still afflicted her.

"Which do you trust?" he asked. "The conventional wisdom you've been fed from childhood up? Or your own feelings? Surely you feel it's no sin?"

"Look at the waves," she said. "They're as big as the sea."

They were an oily yellow under the moon.

"It's a big lake. I guess you're no talker, huh? Is it because you think too little or too much?"

"Or not at all!" She laughed.

"Oh, you *think* all right." He pointed to a Greek-style building on the fringe of the park. "That's where I'll be working." He kissed her again. "Every time I look out of the window, I'll think of you now."

She was thrilled, but kept it from him.

They walked for miles, up over the river and along the shore to the Breakwater Carriage Drive and Lincoln Park. He said that if she stayed in Chicago, he'd surely fall in love with her. Later he said he was probably a little in love with her already. She didn't care much for that talk but she enjoyed being kissed and hugging herself tight against him, so she provoked him into it as often as she could. It was nice, too, when he ran his hands from her shoulders down to the small of her back. There were other parts she wanted him to caress, but he didn't try. She would have stopped him, of course, if he had; but she was disappointed he didn't even try.

This contradiction was something new she learned about herself that night—just as, when he had asked her, "Do you mind?" about keeping her company, she had felt both pleased and resentful; she wanted the decision to be his, not hers.

For a long time they sat in silence and watched the waves curling over; the setting moon behind them picked out the troubled water ever more strongly.

On their way back downtown, in the darkest hour after moonset, they passed a man so hugely fat he could hardly walk. As he wheezed and waddled by, the oceans of lard that wreathed his face contorted in a spiteful grimace. "God damn!" he spat in a venomous tenor. At the corner of the silent street they came to a house with an open door. Framed within, a blue silhouette against the dim interior light, stood a nervous, angular woman.

"Pay no heed, sir," she said, inclining her head toward the elephantine mass, which had progressed a bare yard further. "He can't bear for folks to see him, the way he is. This is th'only time o'day he can take a walk."

Catherine was so moved to pity by this encounter that in her fatigue she cried. Hymie hugged her firmly until they were out of the woman's sight. Then he kissed the tears off her cheeks. "You're beautiful inside, too," he said. "Oh, Cath! Stay here. Stay in Chicago and be in love with me. Please!"

She didn't want him to say things like that so she withheld any response.

Then he laughed. "We're crazy, you know that?"

She sniffed her salt-laden nostrils clear.

"Laugh," he commanded.

She shook her head. "It's sad. But it can't be helped."

"Well, I hope we meet again, a long time from now. We'll laugh then."

They watched the waterfront revive as the longshoremen came on with the bleary dawn. They dodged freight trains that crawled, ding-ding-ding-ding . . . through the streets to and from the piers. They downed a ravenous breakfast in a teamsters' diner by the Illinois Central subdepot. Then he got a shave and a shoeshine while she went for a wash and brush up. And then it was time to part.

The kiss, in the heedless bustle and noise of the station, had none of the magic of the moonlit lakeshore in the wee small hours. Perhaps it was just as well. At the last moment he produced a plain-wrapped package. "I know how you feel about taking things from total strangers," he said. "So this isn't a gift, it's a payment. It's something I owe you. It's a thank you. It's my poor way of saying thank you to you for being so—for being—" Possibly he had prepared a longer speech; but all he could now say was, "—for being Catherine. Promise not to open it until the train's moving."

There was a lump in her throat. "I have nothing for you," she said.

"Does your uncle know you're in America? Shall I cable him for you?"

"It will be cheaper from Grand Junction."

"Dammit, Cath, I'm asking for your address."

She told him. Then she realized she did have a present for him. In her bag was a sprig of Beinn Uidhe heather. She broke off a small portion and gave it to him. He made her spell out *Beinn Uidhe, Strath, Inverness,* while he wrote it down. "Your past is your present." And he laughed.

By the time the train pulled out she was fast asleep. She did not open the package until they were almost into Minneapolis. It was *Les Trésors du Louvre.* She hugged it to her and laughed. People around her in the car laughed, too, her joy was so infectious.

4

From Minneapolis through Grand Rapids to Minot the landscape was progressively drier. It was a night-long, day-long journey from rolling green farmland through maple woodland to dry prairie. Saskatchewan was to prove drier still but she did not then know that. The land was often featureless—dead flat to the horizon, a vast cloth of gray and pale-green grass with never a tree or a house in sight. Were it not for the occasional telegraph line or boundary fence she could have believed the whole country uninhabited. A woman told her that Saskatchewan had hundreds of miles of the same sort of emptiness. She began to wonder if she would ever grow accustomed to such plain monotony.

"The Badlands are worse," the woman said. "But if you go over the border from Minot, you'll miss them. That's pretty country round the Cypress Hills. Where are you headed?"

"Hawk. The farm's called Hawk Ridge. That could be a hill?"

"It could be the *only* hill! Is that Battleford way?"

"It would be in that corner of the province, aye."

"There's hills around Battleford. But Hawk—I don't know."

No man or woman had ever known this land—just life-accidental bits of it.

At Minot, where they changed over to mountain time, there was a six-hour wait for the westbound. She fell in with a family of five bound for Moose Jaw. The eldest boy, about thirteen, took out a pocket notebook and began to make detailed drawings of the track, switch points, levers, signals—anything to do with the railroad. The younger two, boy and girl twins of about eight, were fretful. The mother was near the end of her tether, Catherine could see. She offered to take them for a walk.

She had never looked after children before and so was a bit nervous. But it proved to be the saving of her, for, when Kit and Wal (as they called themselves) suggested a game of I Spy, and she said she didn't know how to play, they were amazed enough to go into the whole business of her education. By the time the train came she could play I Spy, Hangman, Don't Say a Word, and several more. Because the games were new to her she played them like a child—and so discovered the secret of minding children.

From Minot into Canada she travelled in an old "colonist" car, full of wicker seats on swivels and heated by an upright stove—a pot-bellied affair known as a Quebec heater. Each phase of this marathon journey was like a step back in history. By the time she reached Hawk, she felt, New York would be five days behind her and a century ahead. What made the journey not just bearable but absorbing was the host of pleasant, good, interesting people she met.

But it was one of those nice people who stole her last fifteen dollars.

It was now four o'clock on Sunday morning and she was at Grand Junction, almost a hundred and fifty miles from Hawk, with nothing but a handful of loose change, $1.37 in all, about her. How the man (she was sure it was that man) had taken her money was a mystery. He had been such a cheerful, talkative fellow—a canned-meat salesman on his way to Moose Jaw. He had shown her the different American and Canadian bills, using a mixture of hers and bills from his own wallet. She was sure he had given hers back but then he (or someone) had seen exactly where she kept them. She did not discover the loss until she came to buy her ticket onward from Grand Junction.

The night telegraph clerk obviously didn't believe her story; he was most unsympathetic and unhelpful. Not that he could have done much, anyway. At Moose Jaw they had said there would be a connection from Grand Junction at least to Saskatoon and Edinburgh (the name itself was comfortingly homelike), where she would have at most two or three hours to wait for the Hawk local. But now the clerk told her that the strikes in Winnipeg and the Spanish flu everywhere had turned the schedules inside out, and not only was there no train onward to Edinburgh, he couldn't even say when one might run. He might know more firmly in a couple of hours.

She sat in the dim, cold, empty waiting room—for Grand Junction was far from grand—longing for a bath and some clean clothing, and tried to sleep. But the benches were hard and every ring of the telegraph and every movement from the clerk's office next door jerked her back out of her dozing. So around half past five she opened her bag, intending to get out her Bible. But her eyes fell on the Treasures book and she found herself taking up that instead. She thought of Hymie and his kindness and all the friendship they might have known and she was greatly comforted.

Around six the day clerk came on. She decided to see if he would prove more co-operative. As she rose to her feet, she fanned the book slowly to its front and then noticed for the first time that there was some writing on its flyleaf. "To Miss Catherine Hamilton," it read, in a beautiful calligraphic hand, "with great respect from her friend, Hyman Amoils." She began to weep. And that was the condition in which the new clerk found her.

He could not have been more different from the other. Where the night

man was young, he was old—close to retiring. He was friendly and concerned—and radiated that unobtrusive confidence which comes from having
seen and heard and done everything connected with the railways. Best of
all, his name, too, was Hamilton—Graeme Hamilton—though his speech
was as North American as anything she had yet heard.

He took her next door, where he built up the Quebec heater to a goodly
blaze. On it he fried her three of the tastiest eggs ever laid and put them on
top of four rashers so thick that an American would have made four rashers
out of each. And the coffee was the best she had tasted and smelled since
leaving New York. But he still had no idea how she would reach Hawk,
beyond the unhelpful remark that she'd have done better to go through
Regina. "But," he said with a grin, "something will turn up. Let's just hope
it makes a noise mighty like a train."

He had been a conductor on the C.N.R. back in the 1880s, before the
line was even halfway across Manitoba. He'd been on the trains that had
carried most of the first-generation settlers onto the prairies and told her
many a tale of those times.

When he was a boy of ten, the physical markers of the Canada–U.S.
border finished at a God-and-man-forsaken spot on Lake of the Woods and
began again on a forlorn ridge above Waterton Lake in the Rockies, almost
nine hundred miles away. He saw the surveyors and their escort of foot-
soldiers and cavalry come through the Red River Valley at Pembina, when
Winnipeg itself had been little more than Fort Garry. His father had been a
Highlander, like hers, and had taken a half of one of the 800-acre sections
that had been doled out for a time when Manitoba was first opened for settlement. But the border, with its mile-by-mile markers, soon reimposed the
discipline of the square-mile (or 640-acre) section used throughout the mid-
west and western plains.

It imposed other disciplines, too. It imposed the Law of the Great
Mother on refugee Indians who were astonished and delighted to find white
men who did not speak with forked tongues or use a friendly backslap to
mask the knife's penetration between the shoulderblades. It imposed that
same Otttawa-based law on gunslingers, gamblers, and whisky traders who
were equally astonished (but less than delighted) to find that the men who
were created free and equal included Indians and Métis, even though no
written constitution might say so. Catherine had no idea what "gun law"
meant but she accepted his word that the iron markers along the 49th
parallel, and the handful of Mounties who patrolled the wide, empty land to
the north of them, had stopped its spread from America.

"Civilization's a grand thing," he said. "Maybe a person has to see it, before and after, to appreciate it. Like me. I saw it before and I saw it come

and take root. There's an inborn decency in folk that only needs a touch of civilizing to bring it out. Even in Americans. I've seen gunmen *glad* to leave their guns behind and come up here—when there was still ranches here, before the winter of oh-six showed them just what makes Saskatchewan so different from Kansas."

He told her more homely, personal stories, too. One of his jobs was to dream up names for the halts that were built every ten miles or so along the track.

"I gave the names to MacGregor and Douglas and Kelso and Peebles and Glenavon," he said. "But I thought it wouldn't be right to transfer the whole of Bonnie Scotland here—loch, stock, and whisky barrel, you might say. I'd beg names off any passenger who'd give them me. I mind a young English lassie, no older than yourself, who came to see her brother at Stonewall. She gave me Cromer and Kendal. And a Russian it was who gave me Odessa. Aye, there's a tale hangs by every name."

Catherine understood then that everything around her in this her new home—all the roads and houses and telegraphs . . . everything—had been built during this man's lifetime. By him and others like him—men and women like her Uncle Murdo and Aunt Mary, the latest pioneers. How different it was from Strath, where there were stones put in circles by men who, according to the dominie, had lived before Christ, and where the tales that once had hung by the names of places were long gone from folk memory.

Around eight o'clock he tried Saskatoon again for a list of the day's movements, but none could be given; they might have word for him by ten. Then at nine thirty an unscheduled train came down the line from the direction of Moose Jaw. The clang of its bell and the shuddering roar of its cylinders carried a long way.

Mr. Hamilton flagged the driver down, had a brief conference with him, and then came back to Catherine. "Your luck's turned," he told her. "These are damaged box cars headed for the repair shop at Edinburgh. I'll break out some straw in the best of them and you can set yourself there nice and snug. And by two, two thirty you'll be in Edinburgh. Meanwhile, I'll try and get a message to your folks in Hawk to come and meet you or fix the fare, but just in case, you'd better take these." He held out five dollars.

If his name had been anything but Hamilton, she would have demurred. But a clan is a family writ large and to refuse would have been to deny their shared kinship. He did not need to tell her it was a loan; she did not need to promise its repayment. "No hurry," was all he said. She thanked him and climbed aboard.

"Goodbye now," he called after her. "Sorry if I was a mite mouthy."

The broken box car creaked menacingly with every swaying of the track but otherwise it was, in Mr. Hamilton's words, nice and snug. She sat in the straw, opened her bag (which was by now even more battered than it had been in Glasgow) and eyed her Treasures. Then she remembered for the first time that this day was the Lord's and so took out her Bible and read the whole of the books of Proverbs and of Jonah.

For all that she was young and hale, she was fairly jolted and crippled by the time the train pulled into Edinburgh; a heap of straw on a board floor is not the same as even a poorly upholstered seat. She limped awkwardly onto the platform. The clerk was peering out of his office, surprised that this particular train hadn't rolled straight on to the siding in front of the repair shop. Then he saw her and hit his forehead as if to say, "Of course!" He ducked back inside and reappeared almost at once, holding a piece of paper. Catherine waved a thank you to the driver, who waved back and opened the valve. The train pulled slowly out and coasted to beyond the switchpoint, where it reversed into the siding.

"You're Miss Hamilton. Miss Catherine Hamilton," the clerk said.

"Aye." Her throat was choked with straw dust; she made several husky sounds before she got out the word.

"Message for you." He held out the piece of paper.

She must have seemed somewhat blank for he then quoted it, as if he thought she could not read: "Miss Catherine Hamilton is to come to Goldeneye."

"Would that be the name of a place?"

"Yes, miss. Ten miles short of Hawk."

Goldeneye! In her weariness she was light-headed enough to invest the name with all the allure of some fabled city of the Orient; like Samarkand and Cambaluc, it was worth the privations of a voyage halfway around the world just to see it and die. *Goldeneye . . . Miss Catherine Hamilton is to come to Goldeneye!*

"Was it my uncle sending this?" she asked. "Murdo Hamilton of Hawk Ridge?"

"No name. Sorry. Came from the Goldeneye depot."

Did he talk like that from sending so many telegraph messages? she wondered. "And my fare? Did they. . . ?"

"Paid to Goldeneye."

"And the next train?"

"Only train today. Six o'clock this evening. Through train from Saskatoon. Be in Goldeneye by eight."

She went into the waiting room and stretched out full length on one of the benches, too tired to wonder for long what this change of destination might mean. Yet she could not sleep—or no more than fitfully. The bench was so hard, and she was afraid of falling off it. She considered walking over to the siding and climbing into "her" box car, with the lovely soft straw (as now, in hindsight, it seemed); but she was too exhausted to make the move.

At five the clerk asked her if she'd like some coffee. Before she joined him she took a stroll along the platform and looked about her for the first time. In every direction the land was flat to the horizon.

Immediately behind the station building was a straggling lot filled with farm machines—weeders, ploughs, seed drills, combines, and balers. The village of Edinburgh itself was all to the southwest of the station, beyond the branch to Goldeneye. Only a single-storey brick building with the unmistakable lines of a school was visible from where she stood.

Beyond the farm machines, separated by a dirt road built on a welt of a ditch half full of water, rose the gaunt and already familiar outlines of a grain elevator, two silos, and a water tower. Far out over the prairie two other towers broke the skyline, marking the track of the railroad. As benchmarks, they had little competition: two small buttes on the northern horizon, a snake of aspen and a taller growth of the ubiquitous wolf willow lining what must be a river, a few stands of aspen and silver birch around the sloughs, a shelter belt of something that looked like a European larch—the first she had noticed in North America—near a homestead and obviously cultivated. And that was it.

Where were all the people? Whom did these railways serve? Who bought the machines and fetched their grain to these elevators? She did not then know how closely a soddie homestead blends with the prairie from which it is, after all, cut. The chequerboard of new-ploughed land broken by the brown-turning-to-green of winter wheat was the only evidence that man roamed beyond the narrow strip of the C.N.R. tracks.

"Hey!" the clerk called.

She turned and went to his office.

The clerk spread her a feast of wheat crackers and Karo syrup. The sweetness and the coffee revived her miraculously. He looked her up and down admiringly—but not as a woman. A farmhand rather.

"Your uncle will be mighty glad to see you," he said.

"I hope so!"

"You look as if you and work are no strangers. Were you ever on a farm before?"

"I was. I was born on one. I was never off it until a month back."

"Plant potatoes? And lift them? Vegetables?"

"Aye. And tend cows. And sheep. And set lobster creels. And cut the turf. And brew and bake. And card and spin and weave."

The clerk laughed. "He surely will be glad, I tell you! You're better than gold in the bank. And he's been spared the raising of you, too."

Catherine smiled, pleased. But part of her began to wonder just how selfless her uncle's "gift" of a hundred and fifty dollars had been. She would work off the debt, of course. But then—would she have a wage? This brief journey from New York had given her more insight into the value and importance of money than all her nineteen years at Beinn Uidhe. Not for nothing was her uncle known as An Sionnach—the fox.

"Yes, ma'am," the clerk was saying. "Murdo Hamilton is a smart fellow! While his neighbours make do with English orphans not worth much more'n their keep, he gets you over."

"Help would be scarce in these parts, then?"

"*These* parts! Coast to coast you could say."

As a canny Scot she stored these facts away.

The only train of the day was moderately full—at least to start with. Folk were very friendly. Soon there could hardly have been anyone in the carriage who didn't know that the niece of Murdo Hamilton of Hawk Ridge had arrived. Many of them were Scots, Highlanders like herself— but not, she thought, eager for news of home. "Home" was here now, and they seemed more keen to talk about the new life than the old. As she caught the spirit she felt more welcomed among them than she would have believed possible; she, too, had much to forget—or at least to leave behind. Many of them repeated the clerk's observation that Murdo was a shrewd and lucky man. In a way, that was also welcoming. Even if her uncle, during his visit home to Beinn Uidhe, had seen her intolerable relationship with her father, An Dóiteán, and had used it to his own advantage . . . well, isn't that the way of all people, family or not? At least she was wanted here and there was work for her hands.

The stations were roughly at ten-mile intervals. Knuckle, Westward Ho, Montparnasse, Five Pines . . . at each of them the train emptied a little until, by Dry Hole, only a handful were left.

A woman, a Mrs. Mudie, a neighbour of Murdo's at Hawk Ridge, said it was one of the nicest spots in the whole prairie, with good views, a big windbreak of trees that was coming along just fine, and it was less troubled with flies in summer than other places. She'd been away at her daughter's in Regina, so she couldn't imagine why there had been this message to leave the train at Goldeneye.

Only one station, Furs Platt, remained; no one got on or off there.

At last it was Goldeneye. She took her leave of Mrs. Mudie, with promises to cry-in anytime in the passing, and stood waiting on the platform. Four or five others got down, too, but made at once for the way out or to those who were waiting for them. Soon she and one other person, a man, not her uncle but of her uncle's age (as far as she could tell) were the sole figures on the platform. The train began to pull away.

The man turned and came directly toward her. He was tall and moved easily, lifting his hands in welcome; but his smile was diffident.

"Miss Hamilton," he said. His accent was Dundee-Scots, overlaid with the merest trace of North American. He was in his forties, older than her uncle.

"Aye." She half lifted her hand, not being sure whether he wanted to shake it or take her bag.

He did both, shaking her hand warmly between both of his, and lifting the bag from her side before she could stoop for it. "I am Dr. Macrae," he said.

"Doctor?"

"Aye." He walked quickly ahead of her. "Come you to the car, I have something to tell you."

She was sure it was bad news. She ought to have suspected it when the clerk handed her the telegraph message at Edinburgh. The false security of the long journey, the chivalrous protection of the conductors and all but one of the clerks, the relief at being well and truly beyond her father's reach— these had lulled her normally vigilant nature. She must gather her wits now, and quickly—else, in her tiredness, she'd go to pieces.

"It's about my uncle, Murdo Hamilton," she said. "Was he sending you here, Dr. Macrae?"

"In a manner of speaking, aye he did."

"Is he not well?"

The doctor opened the passenger door. "Please, Miss Hamilton."

She got in. The inside smelled of new leather and pipe tobacco. He put her bag on the back seat and went round to his door. Curly light-brown hair stuck out from under his deerstalker hat. He had a generous mouth and kindly eyes.

"It isn't just your Uncle Murdo," he said when he sat beside her. "It's the family, I'm afraid. It's all four of them."

"Are they dead?"

"Three of them are alive still—the two bairns and your uncle. But your Aunt Mary, I'm sorry to tell you . . . it's this Spanish influenza. The *grippe*. It's got to us at last."

"I was struck with it myself on the ship. I was near to death."

"And recovered! Well that is good news—you'll have the immunity now."

"Where are they?"

"I'll take you to them. Hold this lever here and when she fires push it back to there."

The touch of his hand as he took hers and demonstrated, the human contact of it, was a marvellous comfort. She was not alone. Even the simple act of following his instructions and moving the lever as the motor came to life was pleasing. In an obscure way she knew she had passed from outside something to the inside of it. The long journey was finished. This was not the last mile of the old life, but the first of the new.

"Well, you're either very brave," the doctor said, "or even more tired than you look."

Tired, she thought. Or numb, rather. This awful news ought to have floored her; she ought to be sick with worry for her uncle and the two boys, and full of apprehensions for herself. If this news had reached her in New York, that's exactly what would have happened. But the journey had changed her—so that although she *was* worried and apprehensive, there was beneath it all a solid conviction she could cope. If the very worst happened, she'd cope.

"I'm not too tired," she said.

"Good. Good. We need a nurse. It's the worst epidemic I've ever known. They say it's the worst since the Black Death."

Her mind tidied up the passing townscape, visible as no more than dimly lighted windows. Later, when she saw its straggling dirt roads, timber-siding houses, ditchbank paths, and boardwalks, it was quite a shock.

"A man at Grand Rapids was telling me it has killed more folk than the Great War itself," she said.

"You had a good journey, Miss Hamilton? Uneventful, I hope."

"Aye." She smiled to herself in the dark.

"Really?" His face, backlit from the headlamps, creased in sardonic amusement. "The Western Highlands must have excitements unknown to us poor folk from Angus."

She had met many friendly, fatherly men on her journey, but none had filled her with such ease as this Dr. Macrae.

5

The "hospital" was a haybarn behind Dr. Macrae's house on the western outskirts of Goldeneye. The hay was piled outside under tarpaulins and the barn was full of mattresses and the sick—thirty-two of them when Catherine arrived, and more were turning up every day. The doctor had no time to pay home calls, except to the very old and the very young. Everyone else had to be brought in here. A low wall of hay bales separated the men and the women.

Not that there was much to be done for them beyond regular dosing with aspirin or phenacetin. Those with the catarrhal form also had to be given steam inhalations. But this makeshift isolation hospital was more of a public-health measure than a therapeutic one—an attempt to curtail the spread of the epidemic.

"Uncle Murdo?" She knelt beside him. "Uncle Murdo?"

There was not the slightest flicker of a response. His breathing was rapid and shallow; he was bathed in sweat.

Dr. Macrae stripped off the single coverlet, picked up a towel and began to fan him with it, like a second in a boxing bout. "Get another towel and do the same," he told her.

Catherine, who had never seen a naked man before, was shocked—or, rather, felt the first stirrings of shock. They would have grown if Dr. Macrae had been in the slightest degree awkward or apologetic; but his vigour, and his assumption that she would do exactly as he bade—which, indeed, she did—quelled the feeling. She stood facing the doctor, fanning until her arms ached, and glancing from time to time at those parts she had never seen before.

"His fever's running away from us," the doctor said. "Help me get him into that bath."

A large enamel bathtub, brimful of cold water, stood at the end of the hay-bale wall, directly beneath the storm lantern. Dr. Macrae grabbed Murdo under the armpits, she took his ankles, and between them they man-handled him awkwardly to the tub. As they lowered him in, the shock brought him back to consciousness. At least he opened his eyes, though they rolled this way and that without immediately fixing on anything.

The doctor kept his eye on his watch. "Bring me that sheet," he said. "I don't want him wet in this dust and hay."

"Uncle Murdo," she said, after she had done as she was asked. "It's me, Catherine. I came like you said I should. Uncle Murdo?"

She looked at Dr. Macrae. "Go on talking," he said. She continued to speak her uncle's name and to tell him in various ways that she had arrived at last. Her voice seemed to calm him—or perhaps it was his falling temperature. His eyes stopped rolling and settled on her. "Catherine!" he whispered huskily. "Is that yourself, girl?"

"Aye, Uncle. It is myself at last."

"Catherine." It was a whisper now.

"Aye?" She put her ear close to his mouth.

"He must come out now," the doctor said.

She started to move away but Murdo's hand flashed up in a starburst of water. "Hissst!" he said urgently.

Both doctor and girl put their ears close to his lips.

"I doubt I'm done," he said.

"Why, man . . ." Dr. Macrae began some encouragement.

But Murdo shook his head angrily, twice as urgent. "Aye. I doubt I'm done. But listen now. The homestead is proved up. The debts are paid. The place is for Mary and the boys. If they die, it's for you, girl."

So he did not know about Aunt Mary.

"You'll not be dying, An Sionnach." She used his Gaelic name, The Fox, to remind him of all the things he had to live up to.

"Do you hear me?" Murdo insisted.

"I hear you." He was not satisfied until they both repeated it.

"Quick now, out with him!" Dr. Macrae said.

They heaved him out and onto the sheet.

"What's that girl doing here and that man naked?" A deep but female voice spoke from the darkness beyond the door.

The doctor paid no attention; Catherine suddenly felt the shame she would have felt earlier but for his briskness.

"Dry him," Dr. Macrae commanded. Then to the unseen woman he added, "She's more right to look on than you, for he's her uncle."

Catherine obeyed him, but flinched from the inspection she knew was in progress from beyond the pool of light.

"It's not decent, James. You should have more sense." A tall, slender, fair-haired woman stepped into the barn. Her face was thin and drawn; she was plainly exhausted.

"Whisht, woman!" the doctor told her. "The man's near gone with the fever and you worry about the revelation of what the good Lord gave him in the first place."

"Then you'd be Miss Hamilton?" the woman asked. "Miss Catherine Hamilton?"

Catherine, still dabbing the towel over her uncle's chest and stomach, nodded and smiled.

"And I'm Mrs. Macrae, yon man's wife whenever he remembers the fact."

"Now dry the part you've been avoiding," the doctor told her impatiently. "If you're to help me nurse them and these others—and until they mend I don't see what else you may do—you'd best get accustomed to it." He turned to the woman and his smile belied the coldness that had seemed to be between them, "Was there more phenacetin?" he asked.

She held forth a jar of tablets. "The last," she said.

"There'll surely be some tomorrow. Give me three for him now and see to Mistress Seton."

Listlessly she obeyed. Watching their movements, Catherine suddenly saw how exhausted they both were. "How long have you been at this?" she asked.

"Help me get him back to bed. We may have overdone the cooling. I think we'll spare the medicine a wee while."

They carried Murdo, unconscious again but not in high fever, back to his mattress.

"I forget," Dr. Macrae answered her question then. "At least a week."

"Thirteen days," Mrs. Macrae called from a dark corner of the barn.

"Without sleep?" Catherine was appalled.

"We sleep out here. We wake every so often and do a round. There's plenty of help in the day—and usually at night, too. Just tonight we're unfortunate."

Catherine was suddenly wide awake and full of energy. What had she done these weeks past, she told herself, except rest and sleep? Her own tiredness, which had seemed overwhelming down at Edinburgh, was trivial compared to the exhaustion these two must be feeling.

"Well, you'll sleep tonight," she said. "Tell me what I must do and what I must wake you for, then away to your bed with both of you."

"Are you not tired yourself?" he asked, taking the thermometer from Murdo's armpit. "Better," he said when he had read it.

Mrs. Macrae joined them. "She knows how tired or not she is."

"It's not three weeks since she had the flu herself," he told her impatiently, as if she always came with only half the story and he was tired of always supplying the other half.

"Och, then she's immune!" His wife was delighted—and suddenly very friendly toward Catherine. "We usually have help, day and night, but then so many are down with it. Miss Carmichael died and Mistress Seton is gey poorly. But someone will come. It may be lonely country but you're never short of a neighbour's help."

"She's hardly fit herself," the doctor still protested. "Anyone with half an eye can see that."

Catherine laughed. "Call me a neighbour. I'm fit enough to see out the night."

"Have you supped, Miss Hamilton?" Mrs. Macrae asked suddenly.

Catherine, caught between her hunger and her wish not to inconvenience these people, hesitated. It was answer enough.

"You be telling her what to do, James," his wife said, "and I'll bring a bite for us all. And then we'll try to remember how to sleep."

The two boys, John and Ian, tossed restlessly but their fever was not high. "They're over the worst of it," Dr. Macrae said. "I have no great fears for them." He showed her Mrs. Seton and three other patients, all men, whom he considered to be on the danger list. "Last week it was four women. Three died." He smiled grimly. "The Reaper is more even-handed in sickness than in war, you see, Miss Hamilton."

"Have you bairns of your own, Dr. Macrae?" she asked.

"If this one gets worse, he'll need a steam inhalation. D'you know how it's done?"

"I do not."

"I'll show you." He took a simmering kettle from the kerosene cooker and poured it out. "Always keep two or three on the go. You may refill that from the tap beyond the door."

"Bairns," he repeated when she returned with the full kettle. "Margaret's a bairn still you might say. She's fourteen, but wild and young. Helen's away. Married and away, with a bairn of her own expected in the fall." He showed her how to use the tincture of benzoin. There was difficulty with one of the patients, but they got him up on one elbow, from where he could just manage to inhale. The other two were easier. The doctor looked around, seeking something but not finding it. "There was one other thing I had to tell you, but I've forgotten it," he said. He sighed and gave up. "Too tired!"

Mrs. Macrae came back with cold beef and potatoes, and apple pie to follow. She had a whole can of coffee, which she stood in the midst of the three kettles on the cooker, where it would keep drinkably hot without stewing all night. Coffee had already become something of an addiction for Catherine.

Moments after bedding down they were asleep. Catherine swilled the plates at the tap and laid them back in the basket. The cold water on her arms was as invigorating as the coffee and made her long for an all-over wash. *And why not?* she thought.

She did a round of the beds and then, taking soap and towel and a change of clothing from her bag, she slipped outside to fill a pail of water. Then she went into a crooked hollow between two tarpaulin-covered ricks where, out of sight of the barn but still well within earshot, she slipped off all her clothes.

The cold water was gorgeous. She was reminded at once of bathing by night in the waterfall at Beinn Uidhe. She finished by tipping the bucket all down her.

When she towelled herself dry she felt flakes of skin and grime rolling like dough away from her; every pore tingled. And her clean clothes seemed of silk—though she never had felt silk in her life. It was just a name for everything smooth and soft and luxurious. Her body glowed with freshness as she stepped back into the barn. She left her old clothes soaking in the pail.

Toward four the minister came with another patient, a Mrs. Carmody, badly taken. He introduced himself as the Reverend Lennox. Catherine felt dreadful at having to stir Dr. Macrae; she marvelled at how quickly he came awake—not knowing what years of night calls kept such alertness at the very threshold of his slumber. Within minutes of admitting the woman and doing a quick, satisfied round of the others, he was back in bed and asleep once more.

Just before eight her uncle's temperature began a new climb beyond 104°, and she had to waken the doctor yet again; this time Mrs. Macrae woke, too. "God bless you, Miss Hamilton!" She smiled. "One more such night and I'll be myself again. Did Margaret call yet?"

"I've heard nothing, Mistress Macrae." She and the doctor were fanning her uncle with towels.

"If she's overslept again . . ."

But at that minute there was a loud ringing of a bell—something like a school bell. It came from the house, which Catherine could now see about three hundred yards away through some trees—a large, imposing building of stone.

"That means the porridge is made. We'll away and collect it," Mrs. Macrae said. Her husband nodded, meaning he could manage alone. "Sleep well, Miss Hamilton," he called after her.

Catherine picked up the basket with last night's crockery; also her dirty clothes, which she put back in the pail after tipping out the water.

"Yes, I thought you'd changed." Mrs. Macrae's voice was warm with approval.

"I had a wash all over. I hadn't the chance since I left New York."

"Oh, you came that way. It's as well, I often think. Here, let me carry one of those."

"No. They balance just fine. Maybe you have a tub I can wash these in?"

"Of course. Of course." She laughed. "They can join the mountain."

Cleanliness was obviously one way to Mrs. Macrae's heart. In daylight her good looks were striking. She owed them mostly to her high, delicate cheekbones and large eyes. But there was a reserved quality about her, even when she laughed. Catherine felt it would take a long time to get close to such a woman.

Emerging from the orchard they had a good view of the whole of Doctor's House. To Catherine, from her small Highland croft, it seemed vast. How could anyone ever use such space? It was even bigger than the manse at Strath. She had never seen such a lawn before. It was like cloth. She had to set down the basket and touch the grass with her knuckles before she could believe it.

"The original timber house is still inside," Mrs. Macrae explained. "That's how the windows are so deep. We added the stone just before the war. And the new roof, which was marvellous. It gave us another whole floor. It's the only stone building for fifty miles."

A young girl—Catherine assumed it was Margaret—watched them sauntering over the back lawn. Her eyes were vigilant, her lips pinched; she gave an impression of surliness. Yet as soon as she opened her mouth to speak, her whole face brightened. "Miss Hamilton! Welcome to North America, Goldeneye, and my porridge—in increasing order of importance," she called out. One hundred percent Canadian.

"My, but you're chipper this morning," her mother answered. "How do you know this is Miss Hamilton?" She turned to Catherine. "By the way, this is our daughter Margaret."

"Mistress Noakes was here with another dozen each of Easton's Syrup and Bynomalt."

"Oh good! No more aspirin or phenacetin?"

"Nope! She also told me all the gossip and I mean *all,* and that's how I knew who Miss Hamilton was, but did *you* know the minister was out until gone four this night?" She lapsed into a delicate Aberdeen-Scots accent, obviously parodying Mistress Noakes. "And did you know that when Jack Hill set him down from his buggy, he *fell* to the ground. And got up and fell *again* on the path. Such carryings on! It's going to be even more fun

than the book of Old Master paintings they found in his study when he forgot to lock the cupboard." She turned to Catherine, her eyes brimming with
comic scorn. "It was full of shameless, neekit weemin in their birthday suits
and without any clothes on and standing there in front of the camera as bold
as Jezebeels!"

Catherine laughed—but, remembering her own *Trésors du Louvre,* not
entirely easily. She recognized the sarcasm in Margaret's repetition of what
Mrs. Noakes must have been saying; but she was Highlander enough to take
the first accusation seriously. "The minister," she said. "Would that be the
Reverend Lennox?"

"Aye." Mrs. Macrae looked at her in surprise.

"He was here this night that went past. At four o'clock. He came with
Mrs. Carmody. He was sober enough then."

Margaret and her mother looked at each other and burst into laughter.
"I'm sorry, Miss Hamilton," Mrs. Macrae said at length. "It's just that we
never take seriously *anything* Mistress Noakes may say. She has a tongue on
her the woodpeckers might envy."

Catherine was, if anything, more shocked now. "But to accuse a minister of religion of drunkenness!" she said. ("And," she might have added,
"to make a jest of such an accusation!")

"We'd best get that porridge out to the barn." Mrs. Macrae pushed past
Margaret and into the kitchen. "Come in, Miss Hamilton. Everything's
hugga-mugga, I'm afraid. The two girls we had working here are both
down with it."

She was not exaggerating, the way some women do to excuse the fact
that they have neglected to do the spring cleaning during the past half hour.
There was, as she had said earlier, a mountain of washing to be done, and
crockery going back many days. Catherine itched to be at it. "I'll soon clear
all this for you," she said.

"You'll do no such thing, young miss. You'll go directly to bed. Margaret—show her Helen's old room. And then come and help me up with the
porridge." She turned to Catherine. "Take a bowl yourself up with you."

"And who'll carry the Easton's and the Bynomalt?" Margaret asked.
"They have to take that with the porridge."

"That's right." Mrs. Macrae was at a loss.

"I'll carry those things," Catherine said. "I'll sup my porridge up there
with everyone and then Margaret can show me the bed. For which I'll thank
you now."

And so it was done.

Catherine, who took nothing but salt with her porridge, and would never sit to eat it, was nauseated at the very idea of mixing it with syrup or malt extract; she was glad no nun had thought of that during her convalescence.

Murdo's temperature was down to 102° again but Dr. Macrae was plainly worried at his lack of progress. "We just must get more aspirin," he said.

On their way back to the house Margaret said, "What if he dies?"

Catherine felt at home with such directness. "I will mind the boys."

"But you can't run a homestead."

"I never tried."

"You know Mary Hamilton has a sister, Irene? Married an Englishman called Kirby. They live over to Micah, about fourteen miles beyond Hawk Ridge."

"My uncle was never telling me that."

"Well, it's true. They came and saw to her funeral last week. Said they'd mind the boys if they were better before their father."

"Did they hear of me?"

"Gee, I don't know."

When they were nearer the house Margaret went on, "If the Kirbys take the boys, and you don't want to go with them, I guess I could just about talk my folks into letting you come here."

Catherine laughed at this artlessness. "I guess you just about could!" she said. Her Scots accent gave the Americanisms a strange ring.

Margaret pouted. "I don't like girls my own age. I think they're silly. I wish you'd come and stay here."

Catherine linked arms with her, enjoying the contact. It was the sort of gesture she had been unable to make with the nun in New York. "You miss your sister, Helen," she guessed.

"I miss Burgo more."

"Burgo?"

"My brother. He's just started medical school at MacNair."

So Burgo was what Dr. Macrae couldn't remember last night; it showed how tired he was, to forget his own son.

"You wouldn't like Burgo," Margaret went on. In a stage whisper she added, "He isn't a very nice person."

"Oh?"

"He's too big for the prairie. Helen and I sometimes wonder if the whole of Canada is big enough to hold him. You know how children play with little wooden building blocks?"

"No."

"Or pebbles . . . or twigs. Anything small like that."

"Och, aye."

"Not Burgo. Nothing smaller than a tea chest for him. And real logs."

"That doesn't sound bad."

"Except he'd break it all up as soon as he had it built. We'd play with it three minutes and then he'd say he was bored, and break it up."

"I had ne'er a brother nor a sister."

Margaret laughed. "But why are we wasting my time talking about him when there's all of me just standing here? I know you'd much rather hear about me. Just ask. I'll tell you anything. For instance, this is the way up to Helen's old room."

Catherine eyed the chaos of the kitchen and hesitated to follow Margaret up the stairs; the girl came back and grabbed her officiously. "You're not to touch it. That's a local ordinance, now."

No wonder Mrs. Macrae had called it Helen's *old* room. Helen must have taken every last personal thing with her when she left. But for the rug on the floor and the faded floral chintz of the curtains it might have been a nun's room.

"Och, it's just beautiful," she told Margaret, who looked about her in amazement, as if she had missed something vital.

"What's so beautiful?" she asked, abandoning the search.

"No fuss—no fash. I like simple things."

Margaret drew breath. Catherine saw the girl was trying to think of something clever to say, but nothing occurred to her. "Right," she said. "Sleep well. I'll bring you a cup of coffee when I get back from school. Or tea?"

"Coffee!"

She had feared that Margaret's question—what to do if Uncle Murdo dies as well?—would stop her from going to sleep. But it did not. Instead it woke her up early in the small hours of the afternoon.

What would she do? The farm would need a man. That was certain. Well, she would just have to find one and marry him, then. There is a saying in Gaelic: A man with two cows will soon find a wife; with four cows, the wife will find him.

True, the farm would not be theirs; it would belong to her cousins, John and Ian. But she and her easy-got husband could take a share of the profits—all fairly proportioned—and save to buy a place of their own when the two boys were old enough for their inheritance.

The sin of lying awake but idle began to oppress her. She rose, dressed, and went below to begin the mammoth task of washing up and seeing to the laundry. Halfway through the dishes she realized that the water for the laundry ought to be heating. She scouted around until, in an outhouse, she came upon the copper, with a built-in fireplace. Obviously it was a long time disused; they probably sent all their laundry out, like the doctor in Strath. But who'd take it in now, with all the sickness upon it? She filled the copper with water and kindled a fire.

The unaccustomed smoke caused a commotion among the ravens. Their racket, in turn, brought Mrs. Macrae halfway down the orchard, where the plume curling from chimney brought her running the rest of the way. But as soon as she saw Catherine, by now back at the dishes, she understood.

She leaned breathless against the doorpost and shook her head in friendly reproach. "Why are you not fast asleep in your bed?" she asked.

"I woke up," Catherine explained.

"At least you could lie and rest."

"In idleness!"

"Aye." Her voice implied it was no terrible thing. "In idleness."

"It's an abomination."

Mrs. Macrae was nonplussed.

"It would feel wrong," Catherine translated.

"Really and truly?"

"Aye."

"Do you never sit still? Never? Just looking at the birds . . . or the clouds? Or just daydreaming?"

"Of course not!"

Mrs. Macrae snorted a single laugh. "Well, Miss Hamilton, either I'm bound for hell or you've got a lot of life to catch up on." She looked at the dishes and sighed. "So I guess it's no good even commanding you to go back to bed."

Catherine smiled. "There's but ten commandments I'll obey."

"So be it." She grabbed a towel and began to dry the glasses and cutlery. "If you're determined to do the laundry, too, we'll let the fire you lit die out. That old place hasn't been used since . . . oh, three or four years. We've the hot water in pipes, now. I'll show you."

It was a miracle. They had an entire room just for washing clothes and linen! And it was all mechanical. The water was heated from a wood stove in the scullery and you let it out through a hose into a tub. And the tub had a tight-fitting lid with a paddle underneath connected to a crank handle on top, with a gleaming ebony knob. And you put the dirties in the hot water, shook in the soap, which was cut into thin flakes, put down the lid, grasped the knob, and cranked the handle this way and that, through three-quarters of a circle. You cranked a hundred times for very dirty, sixty for moderate, forty for lightly soiled—and that was it! The worst of the washing was done. Only the rinsing was left to do by hand. You could lift things out, one by one, with wooden tongs, in great wreaths of porridgy steam, and feed them into a mangle with rubber rollers that squeezed everything nearly dry, with far greater pressure than the old wooden mangle Catherine was used to. And if a button turned the wrong way, or a knotty tangle wouldn't go through, you could punch a plate on the top and the mangle would spring apart and you could pull the half-wrung article out with no fash at all. And there was a tray at the bottom you could tilt forward or back—forward to spill the cool rinsing water down into the drain, or back to send the hot washing water back into the tub. You started with the cooler things, like wool and art silk, and you let some of their wringing water out down the drain to make room for hotter water for the cottons and linens. For the linens you added two kettles of boiling water. Mrs. Macrae sorted everything into tubloads in order of temperature and, gratefully, left her to it.

Catherine sang all the way through the washing. Canada, she thought, is surely a paradise for women with such everyday miracles as this. What man in the old country would ever dream of lightening a woman's load with such marvels?

Margaret came home after school and said, "Oh, I was going to do that." But later she gave the lie to herself when she said, quite truthfully, that there were twenty or more neighbours who would gladly have helped with the work but her mother was pernickety about whom she let in her kitchen. She meant it as a compliment to Catherine.

6

That night there were five patients fewer. Two had died, four had gone home, only one new case had been admitted. No aspirin or phenacetin had arrived. The companies were making the stuff as fast as they could but the pandemic had created a world shortage.

The doctor had an arrangement with a Mr. Ah Wong, who had a cafe in the town. Each evening around six he came up with a great, steaming tureen filled with a pork casserole or a chicken hotpot and two baskets of baked potatoes. The doctor and Mrs. Macrae stayed on until this meal was finished and then bedded down as before. Once again, this time with Catherine and the doctor's wife as witnesses, Murdo repeated his verbal will and testament.

"He must have told us half a dozen times already today, poor fellow," Mrs. Macrae said.

"He doesn't know about Aunt Mary?"

"He did know. He knew last week, but he's forgotten."

At least the boys were over the worst. Whenever they woke during the night she read to them from the Bible—the adventure stories, like Jonah in the whale, or Joshua at Jericho, or Joseph sold by his brethren—and it soothed them. She read to other patients, too—whatever was their favourite text. Dr. Macrae woke once during the night, quite spontaneously, and sat awhile listening to her reading from the Psalms to an elderly man who, earlier, had been running quite a fever.

The doctor took the man's temperature and then tapped her Bible. "Bless my soul if it's not better than aspirin," he said and went back to his bed.

On the third day Murdo died. They sent word to his brother- and sister-in-law, the Kirbys, at Micah, who replied they had sickness and could not travel to the funeral. The following morning Murdo joined his wife in a four-grave plot in the burial ground, where several dozen mounds of new-turned soil gave mute testimony to the power of the "grippe."

John and Ian, who had recovered well enough to be allowed up for a few hours the day before their father's death, were griefstricken—not once but a dozen times a day. In between, their childishness and their boyhood asserted itself and they pushed each other, and quarrelled, and giggled at trivia. Catherine was astonished that they showed no curiosity over what was to become of them. Perhaps at seven and four you take protection for granted. Though she was sure she never had.

The question, what was to become of them, would not leave her alone. She knew that the answer lay with her. She had come out here, already in debt to her uncle, intending to work it off and then begin a new life; well, now she could do both at once. Somehow.

She kept remembering that Huey MacLintock had run away to Canada, too, after An Dóiteán had nearly killed him. But where? If she could find him, he could marry her, and they could manage Murdo's farm and bring up the boys to it. And a family of their own, of course.

She wrote to her father, in English, to show him she really had begun afresh:

Dear Father, I am deeply sorry to tell you your brother Murdo died yesterday forenoon of the grippe. He lies at peace in the Presbyterian burial ground in Goldeneye. His wife died before of the same and I am to see to the two boys and the farm. Your daughter, Catherine.

To save the postage she slipped this letter inside another, to Mistress Menzies, postmistress at Strath, asking the whereabouts of Huey MacLintock. Next day, after she had slept, Dr. Macrae got out the car and said he'd drive her and the boys over to Hawk Ridge—not to settle in but to get more clothes for the youngsters, renew the arrangements with the neighbours to look after the livestock, and generally give Catherine an idea of the size of the place and of the burdens she now proposed to take upon herself.

The drive, about twelve miles, gave her the first real experience she had yet had of the prairie—except for glimpses from the train. The sheer flatness of the landscape was still astonishing to her. It made the skies so vast. All her life some part of the sky had been cut off by mountains or coastal hills. Only once, on a boat trip with her father, when they had passed out of sight of land, had she moved under skies so infinite. Perhaps if she hadn't been below decks all the way over the Atlantic, she would have been more prepared.

On this day the sky was made to seem even larger by the bewildering variety of cloud it contained. To the east were long rashers of blue, powdered with light, fleecy streaks, white and gold in a sunlight that somehow failed to reach Goldeneye. To the north, the cloud formed a pearly, warm gray with colder gray dabs upon it. In the south it looked like rain, where streets of sloping, inky-blue plumes were marshalling. But the western sky, in front of them, was filled with swirling shapes, making ragged tunnels outward and upward into vaults of sulphur yellow across which were dragged startling black splotches of cloud; it was impossible to determine what was near and what was far.

The thaw was not long past so the sloughs and coulees were full. Half the sky seemed to have fallen in smithereens upon the land, wherever the water lay. For a mile or two from Goldeneye, the soil was poor, a collection of sandy dumps, drumlins, and kettleholes, left by the retreating glaciers of the last ice age. Nearer to Hawk were the true plains, scoured smooth by those same ice sheets, their clay since turned to a dark, rich loam that, some say, is the best farming soil in the world. Sods cut from it to build the soddies—the pioneer houses of the prairie—were so thick with tangled roots that not even the heaviest rain, driven horizontal by the fiercest storm, could penetrate them.

Distances were deceptive here because the air was so clear. *Crystal* clear said it precisely. The horizon, three miles away, was as sharp as a telegraph line not that many yards away. The railroad to one side and the fence on the other took their directions from a textbook on perspective and vanished at a point as delicate as a pinprick, exactly on the flat disk of the horizon. At that same point, the pale dirt of the road pinched to nothing.

When Goldeneye was no more than a huddle on the skyline behind them, the doctor stopped and switched off. They all got out. Over the pinging of the car, where the hot points were cooling, came the relentless soughing of the wind. It did not buffet and slack. It did not even rise and fall. It was as devoid of variation as the plain over which it thrust so steadily—not so much a wind as a moving layer of the atmosphere, dredging the prairie, twisting every blade of the new wheat, combing the tight wool of the buffalo grass. It furled the sloughs as in a child's drawing.

It carried with it the scents of all it touched, blending them, losing the dark musk of wolf willow amid the pale hay scent of prairie wool, cured on the stem. The rich aroma of new-turned earth mingled with the sharp, alkaline tang of clay, each hiding the other.

"Smell that!" the doctor said.

She smelled it all, and distinguished nothing; she felt only its uniqueness. She had not the plainsman's knack of tucking herself into this kind of wind, tricing up to it as a condor braces itself to the mountain thermals before it plummets into a launch. Her head was tall on the column of her neck; her fine, auburn hair streamed out behind her. The wind burnished her skin; the sun gleamed in her eyes. For no other reason than that she was *there,* she felt happier than at any time since leaving home—perhaps than at any time in her life.

Dr. Macrae glanced sidelong at her and was shot through with regret for his youth that had had no such girl in it, and with envy for some unknown, and certainly less worthy, young man who would feel no such regret.

She gave him a smile so dazzling that he started guiltily, fearing she had read his thoughts.

"Can we take that can on the runningboard and pour it down this gopher hole?" John called from about ten yards out.

"Certainly not! That's top-grade petroleum spirit, I'll have you know."

They all got back in. Dr. Macrae swung the engine while Catherine repeated the trick with the advance-retard lever, but then he came round to the passenger door just as she was starting to move over. "Go on," he said. "You stay at the wheel. Let's see what sort of driver you make."

"What!" Her jaw dropped. She stared at him with incredulous delight.

"Go on!"

After five miles on a dead straight, dead flat road, and after imagining several times that she had left the gears behind in mangled heaps, like a mechanical dung (in her first, clutchless changes), and after demonstrating that this "petroleum spirit" was more probably kangaroo's milk (when she half-grasped the working of the clutch), she made quite a tolerable driver. And if the prairie had truly been endless and the road had led to a real, rather than an artistic, infinity, she could have gone the tankful. But Hawk Ridge—a trifling fifty-foot fold in the land—was Lesson Two: What to Do in a Stall.

"Enough for one day," Dr. Macrae said as he pushed the button that let down the sprag that stopped them from rolling back downhill. "I'll show you how to swing her now. It's my belief that a woman who can't swing a car isn't going to be much use in these parts five, six years from now."

The road, which had run parallel to the C.N.R. track all the way from Goldeneye, divided just before the crest, one road going on to Micah, still hugging the track, the other veering north and then northeast along the ridge, toward the farm. The small township of Hawk was clustered around the fork.

They stopped at the post office to collect any mail that might have come for Murdo. There was an Eaton's mail-order catalogue, two letters from the Grain Association, a fob watch returned from repair in Saskatoon, some chintz samples for curtains, a circular from the Goldeneye Burns Society, a brochure for a stationary-engine generator. . . . "Oh," the clerk said, "and a letter from Chicago for Miss Catherine Hamilton. That you, miss?"

Delighted though she was, she was even more annoyed that she could not suppress her blushing.

"Will you not read your letter?" Dr. Macrae asked when they were back on the road again. He chewed his smile and avoided looking at her.

"I will, later," she said.

"I have a nightmare about letters put aside for 'later,'" he answered. "When I open them they begin, 'Meet me at the depot at two o'clock the day after tomorrow . . .' and I look at the date and I realize that's today."

Though she knew the letter from Mr. Amoils (who else could it be from—especially with that beautiful calligraphic hand?) would say no such thing, she opened it then.

I cannot forget you, it began.

She stopped reading. Her heart beat violently. This was a Love Letter—something she thought never to receive—something she associated with a world she would never move in.

I cannot forget you. I know it is probably useless to write and tell you these things. You have perhaps already forgotten who I am. Even if you haven't, you are there in the middle of the prairies, beginning a new life, which is what I am doing here amid the skyscrapers of Chicago. How can our paths ever cross again when our differing ways of life are so far apart?

Yet I cannot forget you. I go to sleep at night remembering your loveliness. And when I wake in the morning your beautiful face is all I hope to see. Actually, that's just shorthand, "your beautiful face." *All* of you is beautiful. You are a beautiful person. A *good* person. Your goodness is so much rarer than you know.

I knew it within a hour of meeting you. You are so radiant with that quality only the blindest fool could miss seeing it. I know I asked you to stay, and you said nothing. So why do I write now?

You see, I imagine myself many years from now hearing in some very roundabout way that you arrived at Hawk Ridge and found things very different than you expected. There's someone there you don't get on with, say—or you just can't take all that wheat and sky. And there was a time when you'd have done anything to get away from it—even accepted an invitation (that's what this letter is) from the unmemorable, unprepossessing, un-anything fellow whose name you only remember because he wrote it in a book you're still (I hope) fond of. (That's why I gave it to you. I saw how much you liked it and foolishly hoped that, by tagging my name on its flyleaf, some of that liking might transfer to me.)

So here is the invitation: If now or anytime you find that things in Saskatchewan are not to your liking, there is here in Chicago someone who loves you sincerely, who misses more, far more, than he can ever express or even explain your goodness of soul and beauty of person, who (to be practical) would send you the fare were it five thousand dollars instead of less than fifty—and think one smile from you a hundred times too rich a repayment.

And now, dearest Miss Hamilton, smile sweetly as none but you can smile, tear up this letter, wonder for two or three days—perhaps even a week—what you may reply that will not hurt me too much, decide at last to write nothing at all, and then resume the all-too-easy business of forgetting entirely,—Your devoted, Hymie Amoils.

She folded the letter back in its envelope.
"Does it distress you?" Dr. Macrae asked.
"It sorely perplexes me."

He grunted but pressed no further. "A two-horse buggy has come this way and has not returned."

They were on the farm track now—a washboard road—and he was reading the spoor in the dirt.

Murdo, when new to the country, had unwisely built his soddy a furlong in from the road. His crofter's eye had tucked it snugly into the eastern side of a mound just off the backbone of the ridge. But six years of digging out through the snow to the road had shown him the sense of living like everyone else, only yards from the highway. As they made the turn they saw the frame of the new house Murdo had been building when the grippe struck.

The track led a lazy S through a windbreak—a small plantation of well-established cottonwoods and balsam poplars, the legacy—and now the only sign—of an earlier settlement. It emerged just where this shelter belt pinched in to form what, from a distance and in certain lights, looked like the prow of a ship. As soon as she saw the soddy, Catherine understood the urge that had made her uncle build here. It commanded a view of his entire half-section—320 acres stretching away to the north and east; and, beyond it, ten miles of prairie on the sunrise side of the house. In a land where even a child casts a tall and lonely shadow, he must at times have felt like a king up here.

A hundred yards beyond, where the ridge began to dip down to the plain, stood the windmill. It turned briskly in the breeze, marking the top and bottom of each stroke with a single clank of its worn pinion. Beside it was the barn and reservoir—or rezavoy, as she came to call it. Between there and the house lay a straggle of buildings—the piggeries, where a dozen or more pigs were squealing over the last of the feed that was fattening them against the November slaughter, a granary, an extra hay store, and the privy.

The car pulled up a little way short of the soddy, opposite a delicate whitewashed gate in a picket fence that protected a front garden which even a townsman would have considered small. Some dead foot-high maples and cypresses lined the path. They had been dying even as seedlings when the grocery store at Hawk gave them away with every two dollars' worth of purchases; only an extraordinary love had coaxed this foot of mortal growth from them.

The buggy whose spoor the doctor had seen stood unhitched in the yard. Two horses were half untacked in the paddock. So this was clearly no visit by help-out neighbours come to feed and water the stock.

"I wonder who?" the doctor mused.

A woman came to the door. As soon as the boys saw her they shouted

"Aunt Renee!" and ran to her. Dr. Macrae said, "Of course! Why didn't I think of that!" He went ahead. "Mrs. Kirby!" he said. "You've recovered well from yesterday's sickness, I see. Or was it your husband?"

The woman continued to hug the boys to her and pulled a glum face at them over the two tousled heads. "You shame me now, doctor. The truth is I've been to too many funerals already. I couldn't face it. But I was wrong, I know." She sounded as Canadian as Margaret.

She was a plump, short woman, darkly handsome, supple in her movements. Her face never seemed to rest but was forever hinting at some slight shift of mood—interest, concern, surprise, amusement . . . anything except solemnity or boredom.

"This is Miss Catherine Hamilton, your late brother-in-law's niece, just come from Scotland."

The two women shook hands. To do so, Mrs. Kirby had to take her right hand from behind her back and—with a guilty little smile—transfer the frock it held to her left.

"I was trying some of Mary's things on," she said by way of explanation. "Isn't that shocking!"

Mary had obviously been even more plump.

"I think it'll take in all right though. What d'you think, Catherine?"

Catherine was astonished to hear her own Christian name. "You'd not be wanting to let it out, Mrs. Kirby," she said.

"Call me Renee, there's a honey. Ed and me aren't over-fond of ceremony."

"Where is he?" the doctor asked.

"Making the inventory." She crouched down and pushed the two boys out to arm's length, her eyes looking at one, then the other, back and forth, never resting. "I guess we'll be rearing you two vagabonds now, so when the time comes we'll want to hand over everything that's rightfully yours, and then some." She near-knocked their heads together. "You don't get a word of it, do you! Who wants drop scones?"

"Meeee!" the boys shouted in unison.

She looked up at Catherine and the doctor. "They get some things, though," she said. "Like drop scones. Will you join us?"

"I thank you," Catherine accepted for both of them.

The soddy was, by soddy standards, luxurious. It had two rooms. A partitioned bedroom lay to one side of the entrance door, which opened into an everything-else room. A large, windowless food store had been cut deeper into the hill from the end that served as a kitchen. The walls of the all-purpose room had recently been daubed with a clay-sand mix and painted over with calcimine of a rather bilious pink. It was a fit place to stand off months of snow siege.

"Look, Cousin Cath! Look at us!"

The boys, who had vanished into their bedroom the minute they entered the house, came hurtling out, proudly wearing cloth caps that bore the legend *De Laval Cream Separators.*

"My!" she said. "Aren't ye two of the finest!"

"We got them cheap because of the advertising," John explained.

"And cleverest!" Catherine added.

Renee cooked the drop scones on a two-wick coal-oil stove. The smell of the burned kerosene took Catherine back to every Highland winter she could remember.

The scones were smeared with maple syrup and devoured as soon as they fell off the knife; but Renee was able to accumulate a small stack as the boys' appetites were appeased.

"We'll not wait for Ed," she said as she offered the plate around. "And so, Catherine, what'll you do now?"

The question implied something that would never spontaneously have occurred to Catherine—that she was now free of any obligation to her uncle and his family. According to her conscience a hundred-fifty-dollar debt was written in the Recording Angel's book and nothing so transitory as Murdo's departure into the next world could cancel it. There was thus a tinge of sin about the suggestion. She thought of the letter in her pocket and its wild, impossible offer—not now so utterly impossible. Dr. Macrae looked at her as if he, too, had a more than casual interest in her answer.

Renee saw her hesitation and moved the conversation back a pace or two. "Or what was on your mind when you came here to Hawk Ridge? This afternoon, I mean. Or did you know Ed and me was here?"

"No. We came for some more clothes for John and Ian—and to see the neighbours about the beasts."

"Yeah. But the future, I mean. . . . Did you think of staying on?"

"Aye. I thought I just might like to try to run the farm and bring up these two."

"Oh." Renee was not put out. She just had not considered the possibility. "Alone? By yourself?"

"Could I not hire the help needed?"

"Sure. All it takes is cash!" She giggled.

"Aye, but the farm is paid. There's no debt. Could I not seek a loan from the laird . . . ?"

"The *what?*"

"The laird. Who owns the ground?"

"Why, Murdo, of course. Or those two boys of his."

Dr. Macrae chuckled. "There are no lairds in Canada," he explained. "Not yet. But give it time—and you'll know them by their Kansas accents!"

"You might get a loan from a bank or one of the wheat merchants. That's true," Renee said. Then she sighed. "Well, here's a thing now! We just assumed that as next-of-kin we'd kind of take charge and rear them. Over to Micah, of course. But maybe they should stay here, where they were born and where they're at home. I don't know. We'll leave Ed to decide."

"Och, no!" Catherine said. "I just never thought of you—how could I? But they'd have a home with you—a proper home with a man at the head. No—they must go with you."

"But? You sound like you're winding up to an almighty howsomever."

"My Uncle Murdo was lending me a hundred and fifty dollars to come here. I must pay the debt."

Renee laughed richly. She obviously lived in a different moral universe from Catherine. "Listen, hon," she said, "if that's all that's heaping you, come and stop with Ed and me and take the weight of those two imps off my hands for a year. That'd sure wipe out the debt!"

She had begun this suggestion more in irony than in earnest—in the same spirit as parents say to their children, "If you want to ruin your life, go ahead and ruin it." But something within her was quick to notice that Catherine not only took her seriously but actually welcomed the suggestion; and that same quick something saw what a blessing it would be to have a spare pair of hands about the house, *free*. Guiltily she added, "Think it over."

"Good heavens, woman," Dr. Macrae exploded jocularly. "Would you be taking away the best nurse in Goldeneye!" He squeezed Catherine's shoulder in a gesture that was curiously man-to-man, or even colleague-to-colleague. "Why, Miss Hamilton, to be *wanted* suddenly—and by everybody. I'll warrant that's a change, eh?"

"There's Ed," Renee said.

The door was darkened. A slim, rangy, fair-haired man stood there, taking in the scene. He was moderately out of breath. Sweat beaded his brow.

"Doctor." He nodded toward the older man, but his eyes never left Catherine's. She knew as much because hers never left his, either. He was so handsome he hardly seemed real.

"Miss Hamilton," the doctor said. "Allow me to present Mr. Edward Kirby."

"Ed." His handshake was both firm and gentle. And lingering.

"Catherine," she was mesmerized into saying.

Renee knew exactly what effect her husband was having on the young girl. She watched not jealously but with pride.

"I will stay while you need me in the hospital, doctor," she said.

"You are a good person, Miss Hamilton." He looked at his watch.

7

Fiona Macrae was furious at this turn of events. To lose Catherine because of her family obligations to the boys and the farm was one thing; she could have reconciled herself to that. But to see the girl—who was the most efficient organizer and hardest worker she had ever come across (and those were lines in which she prided herself, so she was a very mean judge)—to see this girl turn herself into an unpaid nanny and housemaid, for people who needed neither, was intolerable. She was careful to keep her anger from Catherine herself, but she let her husband have it in full.

"You should have stopped it. You should have done something."

He smiled knowingly back at her (knowing, that is, how much angrier such a smile made her when she was already angry enough). "You do not understand the parsimony of the Free-Kirk Highland soul, my love. She needs—"

"Understand! Needs! I understand that the Kirbys have a gey fine unpaid housemaid they *don't* need. And we've lost the best chance we've had in ten years of building our hospital. That girl could—"

"We lost it, my dear, the moment Murdo Hamilton lent her that hundred and fifty dollars. It heaps her soul. Until she's—"

"Soul! You and all this soul nonsense. You ken right well we could settle that debt for her so she'd be free to— That girl has more competence and hard work in her than any dozen we've ever considered as suitable for the hospital. And now you've lost her."

His smile did not waver. "Lost is a relative term, my dear. We may lose her to gain her. Time will tell."

"Och, such fine confidence! It's the most maddening thing about you. 'Time will tell!' *I* will tell: We've lost her. You've lost her."

"To settle the debt for her would merely transfer the obligation, don't you see? It would not free her soul. She would do that by working out her year with us instead of with the Kirbys. *Then* she would feel free. And free to do what? Why, to stay or to leave. *Or to leave,* my precious. I don't want that. When she comes, I want her to come freely—not in obligation. That's why I say you do not understand the Highland soul."

"I understand that a bird in the larder's worth three in the glen," she said.

He could not resist repeating, "Time will tell."

She stormed out; moments later she met Catherine. "Men!" she said, and just managed a smile.

"Has he a moment to spare me, Mistress Macrae?" Catherine asked.

"Time? He has all the time in the world!"

Catherine went into the surgery, where the doctor was just starting to write up his notes. The hospital now had plenty of help each day from good folk who had themselves recovered during the first wave of the grippe, so the three of them were no longer worked off their feet—they even, Dr. Macrae thought wrily, had the luxury of time in which to quarrel.

"Was it aught I did that was upsetting Mistress Macrae?" she asked.

"Not at all. Take the weight off your feet, woman," he said. When she was seated he smiled grimly and added, "There are people who need anger. It nourishes them as you, I think, are nourished by silence and calm."

Catherine nodded and listened.

"We must pity them," he went on. "They cannot help it, but there is that small part of them which can never grow up. A demanding child. They drag a demanding child at their heels wherever they go. However mighty they become, there is always this squawking brat that dogs their path."

The hair of her scalp tingled. It was her father he was talking about. An Dóiteán. At first she had imagined he was explaining his wife's behaviour. But his steady gray eyes, fixed on hers, spoke of such depths of understanding that as soon as the memory of her father and his anger occurred to her, she *knew* the notion was in his mind, too.

"We must not indulge them, of course. But we must nourish them because, even though we do not share the need, we understand it. I believe it is an act of love. So is anger, of course. For them."

Once more she nodded. He was explaining why she had stayed on at Beinn Uidhe for the two years after her mother died—two years in the hell of her father's unreasoned, unremitting anger. It was An Dóiteán's love, that anger; and her staying had been hers. What else could have kept her at Beinn Uidhe where An Dóiteán's burning eyes never left off their merciless vigilance? Only love.

"You do not ask what nourishes me," he said.

"You need to help, I think," she said, not because she was especially perceptive but because she wanted help from him and so thought it wise to steer their conversation that way.

He saw through it, of course, and chuckled. "These days that went past," he said, making it easy for her, "I have accepted a great deal more help than I gave, Miss Hamilton."

"May I ask help of you now?"

"Of course."

"It's that letter I had yesterday." She passed it to him and said no more.

She watched minutely for any sign of condescension in him while he read. There was none. He looked up at her and smiled once or twice, but much as to say, "How marvellous this is for you!"

Even when he finished, when he had refolded the letter and passed it back to her, he smiled and his eyes had a faraway look. "How did you meet this young man?" he said at last.

Catherine told him.

"So you were in his company . . . what? Just the one day?"

"Aye."

He pointed at the letter. "Are you surprised at that?"

She understood he was not talking about the shallow surprise of receiving a letter but about the urge that prompted Hymie to write at all. She remembered Hymie's face then, vividly; his intense, dark eyes resting on her . . . and his kisses.

"No," she said simply.

"And no more am I."

"I ought to be."

"Ah! That's always quite a different matter." He became brisk. "Well, are both we and the Kirbys to lose you? Do you want help to go to Chicago? Is that it?"

"It is not."

"Then what?"

"I have the writing. It is not that. But I lack the words. I want you to help me write a letter with the proper words to make this man"—she tapped Hymie's folded letter—"come here to me and work the farm."

Dr. Macrae hissed out through his teeth and stared at her, mouth agape.

"Then the bairns need not go from their home to Mistress Renee. If that one wants help to rear but two boys, I'm thinking it's no work for her. I would need no help, except for the farm. And Mr. Amoils could be doing that."

The doctor laughed weakly. "A picture restorer!"

"Aye. You will be able to tell him"—she remembered the rail clerk's phrase—"that work and I are no strangers. And you will say what bairns he wishes he may have. And that I am thrifty."

He sank his head in his hands and shook it slowly. "Och, woman . . . woman! Do you not know the quality of men this land has already defeated?" He sighed, then he looked into her eyes. "You think anyone can farm? Just anyone?"

"Aye. Some better than others, I'm sure."

"I'm sure, too! Does it occur to you that Mr. Amoils has probably never seen a cow nor an ear of wheat?"

Now it was she who gaped at him.

"And do you know that he's a Jew?"

"How can you possibly be knowing a thing like that?"

"His *name*, woman! He could not be anything else. Just as 'James Macrae' could not be other than Scots."

She pondered that awhile. "He could yet be saved. He says he loves me. Then he will surely leave off his error and accept his Saviour for me if not for his own soul's sake? You will put that in the letter, too."

"Do you love him? Will I put that in?"

When he said "love" a picture of Ed came into her mind. She blinked it fiercely away and said, "I would not be knowing what that love is. I love as Jesus commands—that we love one another. I love John and Ian because they are my kin. I will find out what that other love is and then I will feel it for him. You will tell him so."

"I will not—not until you have considered the fact that Mr. Amoils probably knows less of farming than you know of the world. And, you may believe me, there is no greater gauge of ignorance than that! You will also consider the fact that his faith may be as dear to him as yours is to you."

"But his is false, and mine is true."

He merely shook his head.

Catherine, seeing it was no good pressing him, then said, "Very well. There is another young man who might suit better. Huey MacLintock. A crofter's son from Beinn Uidhe. He was kissing me the once. I will wait until I hear his address."

The doctor made one last try. "Is it the one burning ambition in you," he asked, "to be a farmer's wife? Does this great New World you've chosen hold nothing more than that?"

She could not answer. It was not simply that the question could never have occurred to her, she lacked the very basis on which it might even be framed. The farm was there. The boys were orphans. The need was obvious.

To question it, or even to put it in the context of alternative lives that might now be open to her, would be a kind of impiety.

She shrugged and rose to go. Almost as an afterthought she turned and asked him, *"Am* I . . . what that letter says?"

He grinned wickedly. "Ah . . . what does the letter say? I have forgotten."

She blushed. "Beautiful," she managed at last.

Chuckling, he rose and came around his desk to her, saying, "You cannot trust the word of Mr. Amoils, is that it? You think he is partial, eh? His opinion is tainted?" He put a hand behind her shoulder and propelled her gently toward the lamp. "You want the opinion of an old curmudgeon who could not possibly be partial in that way—so you think. Eh? Well, *are* you beautiful, Miss Hamilton?" He took her chin gently and turned her face this way and that, looking at her.

Watching, delighted at his good humour, she saw a puzzling change come over him, from playful to serious. He let down his hand, and stared, it seemed, into the very heart of her. "Do you suppose," he asked, "that you are a most ordinary person?"

"I do. Of course I do."

"Well, you are not. Think, woman—how the Catholic nuns took you in. How Mr. Amoils feels after one day of your company. How a railway clerk risks his pension to get you to Edinburgh. How we let you nurse our sick after two hours of knowing you. How Renee Kirby offers you a home after twenty minutes! D'you not see the pattern? D'you imagine we—all of us— spend our lives in such behaviour toward others?"

"I don't know." She was afraid to follow the thought because, as far as she could see, it had no conclusion.

"D'you even understand what I'm driving at?"

"You mean I'm a cuckoo?"

"A *what?*"

"The bird that makes the other birds take over . . ."

"Och, I see!" He laughed. "Well, I'd not be putting it like that."

"Mistress MacEuan did. She was the stewardess who took me to the papist house. She said I was a cuckoo."

"Aye, aye! That's a woman's view, no doubt. What we're all saying, Miss Hamilton—each in our different way—is that there's a rare quality in you. Mistress MacEuan may call it 'cuckoo'; Mr. Amoils says 'goodness'; I would not dare to name it, for I believe we have none of us seen it for what it truly is. But I'll give *you* a name for it."

She held her breath.

"Power," he said. "And here's what I'm driving at, Miss Hamilton. Until you understand it yourself, it should terrify you. Such power. At the very least it should terrify you into *not* writing proposals of marriage to young men you don't love." He smiled and squeezed her arm to soften the words but not, he hoped, the message.

With all her heart she wished her father could have been like Dr. Macrae. She had not the faintest idea what he was talking about, but he spoke with such sympathy, and radiated such a profound understanding of everything, that she accepted it as a kind of revealed truth.

Nevertheless, it was a very *abstract* truth. It did not in any way impinge upon her intention to write to Huey MacLintock when she knew his address, about marrying her and coming to share the work of Hawk Ridge. The farm, the boys, the go-forth-and-multiply imperative of marriage . . . these were facts against which, in her life at least, no mere abstract truth could prevail. Her faith, of course, was the greatest *fact* of all.

"But am I beautiful?" she repeated.

He saw he had both won his point and yet lost her commitment. "You'll pass," he said sadly. "Aye, you'll pass very well."

It was all she had wanted to know. To accept good opinions from good people was no sin.

On her way to Helen's room she passed Margaret. "You don't know how lucky you are to have such a marvellous man as the doctor for your father."

"Oh, swell! Is he in a good mood?" she asked. "I'll talk him into doing my math homework."

James Macrae thought about Catherine a long while before going to sleep that night. When he told her she ought to be terrified of this strange power of hers, he had meant also to convey that *he* was terrified of it. At first he could not say why. Because she threatened him in some way? Because he was attracted to her?

But—like all men—he was attracted to half the women he met. And the older he got, the bigger that half-circle grew. It couldn't be that—or not just that.

It was her ruthlessness, he decided—the same quality as sometimes frightened him in Burgo, his son. Burgo had a ruthless streak in him, too. But Burgo knew it; sometimes he would guard against it, sometimes he would rely on it—deliberately use it. Catherine did not know (did not *yet* know?) she had it.

Both had the power to frighten him. But which, he wondered, was the more to be feared?

8

It was June and the flies were at their worst. Almost too small to be seen, they settled in dense, biting swarms on any piece of uncovered skin and made life a misery. Ed lit a smudge in front of the door each evening to keep them out of the house; but unless you took a deep breath and practically stood in the smoke, it was only half effective. A wipe of coal oil, at least over arms and legs, worked better, but it didn't last. Wintergreen repelled them, but it burned the skin. Goose grease made it harder for them to bite, but it felt awful. In the end Catherine, like thousands before her, set herself to bear it. Renee's good humour was a help.

"Know what I like about the prairie, honey?" she asked once.

"July?" Catherine guessed. "When the mosquitoes go?"

"Apart from that."

"What?"

"The way everything's so individual. You can't say, 'He's a typical prairie man' or 'That's a typical prairie home'—or if you do, you'll be proved wrong. The land's the same for hundreds of miles. But the people!"

"I've met so few of them yet."

"Come harvest you will. Oh, the harvest is just my favourite time. But— what I was saying. About people. Now, you'd think Doc Macrae was just a typical plains doctor. But he's a rich man. Rich when he came here. And he lives in a stone house with piped water. There isn't another like it for fifty miles east and—oh—five hundred west, I guess. So how is he typical? And look at this place. Drive by and you'd say there's a typical prairie farm, on the prospering side." She laughed. "How many homesteads are run by Old Etonians, eh?"

"What's an Old Etonian?"

"Ed is. He went to Eton. Now ask me what's Eton."

"The mail-order."

"No! It's only the best school in the world. Next door to Windsor."

She remembered Windsor, where they crossed by ferry to Detroit. "Oh yes," she said.

"Where d'you think Ed got his perfect manners? In Canada? You wait till the dance, Saturday. You'll see manners!"

Catherine wondered how any school could be better than any other; surely twelve times twelve was a hundred and forty-four at all schools? But it was true that Ed had perfect manners. He always put the chair under Renee when she sat; and now John was trained to do the same for Rowena Carmichael, the young schoolteacher, who boarded with them; and Ian did the same for her. And Ed always sprang to his feet when she entered the room, until she copied Renee and Rowena, saying, "Don't get up, please," as she crossed the threshold.

She and Rowena agreed that Ed was just about the handsomest, nicest man ever. He insisted that the womenfolk should have a separate privy from the men and that they should have the soft tissue wrappers from the apples and oranges while the men used the coarser shiny pages from the old Eaton's catalogues. Catherine thought of him every time.

"That's what he wants, of course." Rowena giggled. "Don't let him catch you alone. He's a terror with women."

"How d'you ken that?" Catherine asked.

"Last spring. Behind the barn." She winked. "I swear I'd be there yet."

"Doesn't Renee mind?"

"Renee! She's so gone on him, and so proud of him, she'd probably lend him out if you just admired him enough and allowed how lucky she was."

When she and Catherine were alone, Rowena liked to unwind and be a mite girlish and forward; but in public she was highly conscious of her status as the community schoolteacher—the most favoured catch for any beau within twenty miles or more. She was the first one every eligible bachelor asked to the Saturday dance. Catherine, out of pride (for Rowena was a year younger), chose Webster Law as her beau. He was the only one who hadn't asked Rowena first and been turned down.

"He's a good partner," Rowena said judiciously, as if she had exhausted all his qualities a long time ago. "But on the way home his hands get mighty big. And that's not all!"

"What d'you mean?"

"Well—what happens after dances in Scotland?"

"I never was at one."

"You mean this is your first dance?"

"Aye."

"First *ever*?"

"Aye."

"Lordy!" She frowned and became serious. "Someone's got to tell you."

"What?"

"About men and loaded guns."

"Guns?"

Rowena hit her own forehead. "Be serious," she told herself. She peered quizzically at Catherine. "But it *is* serious. Men *are* like loaded guns. That's what my dad told me. D'you know about babies—where they come from?"

"Out of a woman's belly."

"Good! Out of *any* woman's belly. And any girl's belly, too. Out of yours or mine. And I'm talking about not getting them started in there in the first place. D'you know how they get started? How men start them?" When Catherine was silent she said, "D'you know what fornication is?"

"A sin."

"And it's also what men go to dances for."

"All men?"

Rowena sighed. "No. Not all men. But most of them. Webster Law, certainly. I don't want to spoil the dance for you, but it'd be worse if the dance spoiled your life. It's safest—just take it from me—it's best to treat them all as guilty until they prove themselves innocent. Especially Webster Law."

"I don't understand you, Rowena. Are you saying there will be fornication at this dance?"

"Not at it. After it. That's the thing, you see. *We* think the dance is the real fun of the evening. But they don't. For them the dance is a boring ceremony that has to be gotten through, for our sake. Because we like it. It's a sort of price they pay in the hope of getting their fun after—on the way home."

Catherine laughed with relief. "But the dance is only down the road at the Stensons'. What can happen in two hundred yards on the way back?"

"What can happen, my sweet, is that they'll take the short cut, which goes way out over someone's section. Now ask me what can happen in five miles!"

"Then I will insist on coming directly home."

Rowena shook her head. "That's called biting your nose to shame your face. Kissing's fun. And cuddling. Especially after dancing all night. And in June, too, out on the prairie, with the moon. The thing is to stop them from going further. They'll plead, they'll whine, they'll cry, they'll mock, they'll scold, they'll try to go just another inch and tell you you're the only girl in the whole country who won't at least do that, they'll tell you even the schoolteacher lets the fellows do *that*. Just don't believe them. Men would walk a hundred miles for the chance of it. And they'd tell any lie they think will help. The golden rule is never take off your drawers. And never let them get their hands inside them. To begin with, anyway."

"To begin with! I should think never."

Rowena smiled. "See how it goes, eh?"

It did not go at all as Catherine had either hoped or feared. The suggestion that there were certain circumstances ("advanced" ones, not for beginners like her) in which a boy might be allowed to get a hand inside her drawers appalled her. But it also tantalized her. The vein of possibility that Hymie had tapped with his artless question about whether she trusted conventional teaching or her own feelings now widened to quite a lode.

The fact that she had run away, so many thousand miles, and scraped so near to death, and met so many people, and was now surviving—and surviving well—all alone . . . these things had changed her. She was still a servant of the Lord, of course. And she always would be. She still sought to walk in the way of the righteous. But she was a different servant. A better one, because she was more sure of herself. So she was no longer quite so content to walk the path of righteousness merely at the order of her elders, in blind obedience.

She wanted to find the path for herself now—by testing its shadowed borders. She wanted to *know* good and evil, not simply to be told about them; and it was no longer enough to be told that the wages of sin is death.

And the serpent said unto the woman, Ye shall not surely die: For God doth know that in the day ye eat thereof, then your eyes shall be opened, and ye shall be as gods, knowing good and evil.

But that was the Garden of Eden, long ago. It was different today, out here in the prairie. She couldn't say how; she just knew it was different.

The reputation Rowena had given Webster Law coloured the whole night. He was wonderful to her. When he found she couldn't do two-steps, the lancers, polkas, and all the other dances, he didn't get impatient but taught her and built up her confidence until she could cut as good a path around the floor as any.

But Catherine kept remembering that all this pleasantness on his part was merely investment in a hoped-for reward after the dance. She wondered at his deviousness, for his behaviour was impeccable. She saw other girls having to hitch up their partners' hands when they casually inched downward. Webster never let his hand even reach the small of her back. When she danced with other fellows, they pressed up against her. But not Webster. If she pressed herself against him, he pulled apart and apologized. He actually seemed to enjoy the dancing, too. His act was very convincing.

At about four o'clock in the morning those who had early milking chores to do and twenty or thirty miles to go began to leave. The dance broke up over the next half hour. Rowena winked at Catherine on their way out to the buggies.

Webster did all the expected things. He said, "No point in going home to sleep now, is there?" And he drove the buggy off into the prairie. And he took her in his arms, and he kissed her. But that one most expected thing of all he did not even attempt. She imagined him trying it—in a confused way she almost willed him to try. And she wondered how long she was going to let his hand stay there before she pulled herself away and said no. But he didn't even look like starting. He talked a lot. Quite interesting talk, too. He was a good mechanic and he wanted to build up a car and tractor repair shop and agency. He was shooting coyotes every spare minute and saving the bounty. Every now and then, while he spoke, he kissed her, but it was just something to fill the silences—the way men sip beer when they get together and talk.

She took less part in the conversation than she might have done, knowing as she did that he was only trying to soften her up. At last he laughed and said, "I wondered what the schoolteacher saw in you. Now I know."

"What?"

"You're a great listener."

She said nothing.

"I knew it had to be something. Hoity-toity young ladies like that don't often choose friends who are prettier."

"D'you mean I'm prettier than Rowena?"

"About a million times. And far, far nicer."

A suspicion began to form. "Did you ever quarrel with her?"

"She quarrelled with me."

"What about?"

He wouldn't say. She pressed him.

"Whited sepulchres," he said at last.

He asked her to next Saturday's dance, which was at his folks' place about ten miles away. But she was still too unsure of him—and anyway she didn't want a regular beau. She said she'd already been asked, which was true.

Later, when she told Rowena what had, and hadn't, happened, the schoolteacher said, "Hell hath no fury like a man spurned."

But it didn't fit. Webster had been philosophical, not at all furious. Catherine began to glimpse, and to feel, the terrible confusions and compulsions that beset all relations between men and women. No one could be trusted—not even herself.

Rowena wasn't at the next dance. School finished that week and she

went home to Montparnasse. Ed decided that young John needed occupa-
tion so he bought in fifty head of cattle and ran them on part of his section
that he hadn't yet had time to fence. John, now eight, and one of the neighbour's boys, Tony Brady, a mature nine-year-old, rode herd all day. Ed and
the hired man, Haydon Evans, went down to help get them penned each
evening. It worked well enough to start with but later in the summer the
spring went dry and they had either to carry water or drive the herd for
miles—at a time when the harvest demanded every hour they could spare.
But Ed sold them then for a good price, so he was pleased enough.

"That's the curse of this country, Cath," he told her as they all rode back
from the stockpen at Micah. "Drought. People don't realize how close we
are to being a desert."

Ed took a great interest in her—even more so now that Rowena had
left. Catherine remembered what the schoolteacher had said about being
caught by Ed behind the barn and wondered if there had been anything between those two. There was certainly something between herself and Ed.
She couldn't help it. When he came into a room she had to look at him. She
was always aware of him. If she was milking the cows and he came into
the shed to look them over, no matter if she was at one end of the row and
he was way down by the door, there was a sort of electricity in the air. And
it got stronger as he worked his way up, saying each cow's name and running his hands over them, until he was right by her and looking—she knew
—not at the cow but at her bare arms and the rippling muscles as she
pulled, pulled, pulled the white jets from the udder. Just before he reached
her, she would sweep her hair over to the right, where it burst out in auburn
profusion from under her cap. Then she could literally feel the pressure of
his gaze on her exposed ear and her neck.

He was the same about her, too. She knew it. Their eyes met and lingered—like the eyes of creatures trapped in separate cages—far too often for
it to be accidental. But in all other ways his behaviour toward her was
meticulously correct. He took no chances, even when the chances were there
to be taken. Sometimes Renee would play the piano and Ed would teach
her new dance steps like the foxtrot, the waltz, and the veleta; but never did
he take advantage of it to give her an extra squeeze or a caress not demanded
by the dance.

He also taught her to drive the pickup, which she took to very readily.
Curiously, that was the only element in her relationship with Ed to make
Renee jealous. Renee said the steering jerked her arms out of their sockets;
and she never could master the crash gearbox. She got angry when Catherine
told her it was really easy.

However, the work of the homestead left little time to indulge any of these passions—anger, jealousy, or . . . whatever it was between her and Ed. "Lust" did not feel at all the right word. The whole outfit ran as close to self-sufficient as possible. They grew all their own vegetables, stored their root crops and canned or bottled their greens in crown and beaver jars against winter; they laid down eggs in waterglass, in pails; they made their own butter and curd cheese, which, at the height of summer, they kept in an old wicker picnic basket down the well; they kept their own pigs, fattening them for slaughter in the autumn; they shot whitetail deer in and out of season and smoked the joints in the smokehouse (they were the only folk around with such a luxury, but Ed swore he'd die without ham and other smoked meat); they bought in cordwood and cut and split it themselves. About the only thing they couldn't grow was apples and pears. They came by the barrel load, along with the oranges. Ed also got a dozen barrels of sour apples, which they pressed in a press his family had brought from England sixty years ago. From the juice they made a rough, potent cider that lasted from one harvest to the next.

When she looked at the work that had to be done each week, Catherine often wondered how they'd fit it all in. But when she looked back, she was amazed at how the memory of the drudgery faded (and a lot of it was just sheer drudgery) while the happy times, reading, dancing, or playing games, lingered on. No matter how much work there was, they always seemed to have time for those recreations.

Except when the harvest came round. Then they worked all eighteen hours, dawn to dusk—and longer if there was machinery to fix. All the men in the district pitched in and harvested one another's crops co-operatively, working generally from southernmost to northernmost in rear of the ripening wheat. They needed four big cooked meals each day, so the women were busy enough, too. Often Catherine ended up doing the "evening" milking past midnight. But, after long hours of cooking and carrying, and stooking the sheaves in moments that would otherwise have been idle, the milking was so peaceful and relaxing it hardly seemed like work at all.

That year Ed had planted a new variety of Red Fife short-season wheat. It had yielded well, up to sixty bushels on the best land; and even some of the older fields had given twenty. It was a good grade, too. He had a hunch the winter was going to be hard so he decided to thresh as soon as he could and get as much of it down to the elevators at Goldeneye as possible. That would leave Murdo's section at Hawk Ridge to thresh later. It was only two miles from the siding at Hawk.

On the last day of the threshing he began to worry about the casing around the fan. It ought never to have been fitted. It was warped from the start and now it kept coming loose. If it hit the fan at speed, there'd be metal everywhere and all hell to pay. He asked Catherine to take the pickup and go down to Sim Harris, the agent in Goldeneye, and get a good replacement.

Renee complained—as she did whenever Cathy drove the truck. It was much too late in the evening. Who was going to help get the supper? Who was going to put Ian to bed? Mrs. Law volunteered, so that finished that. Just as Catherine pulled away, Ed came running after her. "Come back through Hawk Ridge," he said. "We won't waste the trip. I'll get a lift over there with Pete Keller and we'll load up with that good hay of Murdo's."

Something in his demeanour told her this whole arrangement was a fake. The fan casing wasn't in danger of shearing. He could get that hay any time before winter set in. He was fixing for him and her to be alone together at Hawk Ridge—and doing it openly so as to disarm suspicion.

Nothing within her reacted to this knowledge. She felt neither fear, nor pleasure, nor surprise, nor anger. A strange fatalism scoured her mind—and her body. Even her body did not react. Instead, all her concentration was focussed on the immediate moment.

The day was the hottest of the year. She took the cross route to Goldeneye, which went either due east or south as it made sharp L-bends round the sections. She looked out for the landmark of the elevators, but the entire horizon had vanished. The whole distant landscape seemed made of liquid or fire. The heat peeled off flamelike shapes of land and shook them upward into the cloudless glare. The thermometer needle on the radiator cap was the only clear object in view. It climbed inexorably toward the red.

She had to be careful to keep out of the ruts made by the iron tyres of horse wagons when the road had been soft. They were only three inches wide. Now, baked to brick hardness, they would cut the truck's four-inch rubber tyres to flutters in half a mile.

Several times on that journey she thought she'd die of the heat. Unseen torches blew through both windows; the front windshield, too, was wound out horizontal on its quadrant but the heat off the radiator and bonnet only added to the torment. The sweat poured out of her but dried as soon as the air touched it. Two miles from the town the truck began to boil. Fortunately the Goldeneye River was not too far ahead. She coasted forward and stopped right above. There was nothing to do then but lift off the bonnet sides and let it cool.

The barely perceptible flow of the river was easily shouldered aside by low bars of clay and sand, overrun with dogwood and wild roses. Dragonflies like blue darning needles darted and hovered; tiny skaters rippled the surface. She took a can and slipped down the cutbanks, through thickets of aspen, silver birch, and wolf willow, whose dark, musky smell hung miraculously on the air, not cooling it, yet soothing and reviving her. It quickened all her senses and filled her with a strange, drowsy longing.

Without a second thought she slipped over the lowest cutbank and, fully clothed in skirt and blouse, sank beneath the water, risking the leeches. Warm as a bath, it felt cool that day. Cool fingers of it reached deliciously up her arms and thighs.

She did not linger but filled the can and returned to the truck. The boiling had stopped. She topped up and set off again. Before she reached the town, she was bone dry—even that part of the skirt on which she sat had dried out into the cloth of the seat.

She got Sim Harris out of the pool hall and he gave her the part, grumbling that Ed Kirby was a hen with one chick. Doc Macrae was in the pool hall, too. He came out when he heard her voice, delighted to see her again. He insisted she come home with him for a wee bite.

Both he and Fiona were keen to hear how she was getting on and what plans she had made for her future. She told them she hadn't heard of Huey MacLintock's address, but she still had hopes of marrying and farming Hawk Ridge and rearing her two young cousins. She'd been to enough dances now to know that finding a husband wouldn't be hard.

"Ed will be your difficulty," Fiona told her.

"Why?"

"A paid-up section, more than half of it broken to the plough, with farm buildings, two miles from the railway? Ed isn't going to yield that too easily."

"But he doesn't benefit. He says he'll put the profits to the children's account."

"Och, well . . ." Fiona's smile said she did not wish to trespass upon such innocence.

"Did you think more about being a nurse?" the doctor asked.

"Not until next spring," she said warily. "I've promised the year at Micah and I'm content enough, so I'll see it out."

"As a nurse you'd be equal with your friend Rowena Carmichael," he said.

"As long as you don't equal her in *all* departments," Fiona added darkly.

The sun was low in the sky when she resumed her homeward journey via Hawk Ridge; mercifully it was setting twenty degrees away to her left.

All the way there she thought of Ed and of what was going to happen. She was not in love with him. She knew that. She never daydreamed about him. Nor did the mere thought of him put her in a turmoil. But the sight of him did. Whenever he was actually there, in the room—even when he was behind her—or even when she could just see him, half a mile away, there was a special electric *something* between them.

But now this new thought, thrown in by Fiona Macrae, that Ed would fight her for Hawk Ridge, put a different light on it. He knew he had this power over her; was he using it not so much to get near her as to keep her from farming Hawk Ridge?

She backed the truck to the hay barn, leaving room for the doors to be opened, and sauntered off through the liquid heat to the northern point of the windbreak plantation. She knew (because Ed had told her) that her eyes, being precisely five feet above the ground, usually put the prairie horizon exactly 2.9 miles away. Hawk Ridge was fifty feet above the prairie—which pushed the horizon back to no more than 9.2 miles. But now that she had lived on the plain for months, this modest elevation seemed to bring half of Canada into view—until she looked east and saw, by the last direct rays of the vanishing sun, the Goldeneye elevators right on the sky-line. Northwest she could not see Micah at all, not even the great pall of dust that had hung over the thresher all day. But halfway between there and where she now stood she could see the dust of a buggy coming toward her over the Hawk road. Exactly four miles away. She knew that because there was a longitude adjustment four miles north of Hawk Ridge and the north-south fences started from a new base, so that they didn't coincide with the north-south fences on this nearer side of the adjustment line.

In less than thirty minutes Ed would be here. Still it meant nothing.

She lay down in the buffalo grass but the ground was hot and the air closest to it even more airless than at head height. She rose again and walked aimlessly over to the soddy, a movement that brought the illusion of a breeze. It was so rare for the prairie air to be still, she felt lost, like people in Niagara when the falls freeze solid. She sauntered around the soddy and up onto the bank into which it had been cut. Ed had done some fencing here this summer. He was going to fallow the land and then put it down to grass for hay, and pasture for the dry cows. He used the wire his cousin had sent up from Kansas, a whole carload, with wicked long barbs. She scratched her hand on it, trying to make herself feel something. Below, on the western skirts of the ridge was the cutting, where the C.N.R. line, having been deviated by the ridge, wound its way back to the appropriate section line.

"Hello!" That was Ed. Pete Keller must have dropped him at the turn-in. It was almost dark. "There's a storm lantern in the soddy," he said, making for the hay-barn door.

She lit the lantern before she brought it out. Its light was feebly local in the yard but much stronger in the barn. He reached down from the top of the hay pile to take it; the underlighting made his face satanic. "Back her in," he told her.

When she switched off he saw the spare fan casing in the back. "You're an angel," he said and reached the handle of his fork down for her to grab. She hardly needed to climb. His immense strength lifted her like a feather. "But you could have opened the door and let it cool off."

It was stifling in there—but it was stifling outside, too. Even so, she was on the point of apologizing when she saw it was just his excuse for stripping off his shirt. He grinned as he watched her, mesmerized by the sight of his naked torso in the lamplight.

"Better," he said, making it half a question. "Shame about you."

They threw down half a truckload and then jumped down to spread and consolidate it. He jumped first and then caught her. They stood a moment, eye to eye. *Now,* she thought. Her skirt, which had billowed up in her descent, hung on his belt. Slowly, giving the action great significance, he eased it off and let it fall.

Next time then, she thought.

Next time was when the truck was full. Again he jumped down first, parked his pitchfork in the corner, took hers and parked it, too, and then stood to catch her.

This time he did not push down her skirt. Her thighs fell in against the rough denim of his trousers. Her bare arms went around his bare body. And she lifted her face to his. Her heart began to pound briskly.

When she kissed him it was like no other kiss she had ever had. Not from Huey or Hymie—and certainly not from the boys after the dances. They were not even a kind of preparation for this magic.

Now she understood why she had not been able to think of this moment; if she had she would have thought—as with all her beaus—*I'll draw the line at that.* But now, even at this first kiss, she knew she would draw no line with Ed.

"Oh, Cath!" Ed broke the silence.

"Be careful with me, Ed." They weren't the right words. They sounded silly.

He seemed puzzled. "Did you never do this before?"

"Never."

His whole demeanour changed subtly. His hands, which had been gently easing out her blouse, came up to hold her head, moving it into the light. "I didn't know," he said. He kissed her brow . . . again . . . several times. "Are you sure you want to?"

She kissed his mouth, urgently, on the verge of anger. She did not want to decide. She had already decided.

He broke. "I wouldn't want you to—"

"Don't talk. Just don't talk." She shouted at him.

He heard the anger in her voice, saw the tears in her eyes. "All right," he said. "All right."

At once she was calm. She hugged him, flattening her breasts against his chest. His hands went inside her blouse. He raked fingernails up and down her back, sometimes barely touching, sometimes on the verge of pain. She copied him and then stepped away to let his hands come around the front.

Button by slow button he undid her blouse and eased it off. She wore no camisole or slip below; she was naked to the waist. She was ashamed to feel so shameless. He caressed her ribs, her stomach, her neck, her collarbone; he lifted her arms above her head and ran his nails down their undersides. Everything but her breasts. She moaned for him to hold them.

Suddenly he stooped and began to suckle her like a baby, first one then the other, changing swiftly. She heard little cries escape her. She held him merely for support, too enthralled to move.

He knelt, hands on her wet breasts, and began to kiss her stomach—or, rather, to run his lips, light as swansdown, over the soft sheen of hair. She eased down her skirt and drawers in the same hitch of her thumbs. His lips chased down the hem.

He spread out her skirt and blouse on the hay. She knelt upon them and undid his belt. His thing was huge—much bigger than the fever-lank thing she had seen on Uncle Murdo. It would surely hurt. And it would hurt him, too. She would disappoint him. She would be too small. She didn't know anything about herself. It was going to be awful.

She lay down and waited for it to be awful.

But he did not even try. Instead, when she was all worked up again and longing for him, no matter what the pain or humiliation, he gave her his thumb. He moved it around. He knelt half over her and suckled her breasts again, and moved his thumb.

There was a great rushing and a falling inside her. She knew something was going to happen. "No," she had time to cry. "I want *you!*"

And then she all melted and flowed together in an exquisite fire and she stopped breathing and cried "Oh" and gasped and couldn't breathe enough and pulled him onto her and got his thing into her hand and squeezed and the whole universe whirled around the dervish thumb; and hours of minutes later he gave a strange falsetto giggle and she felt her side was wetter than their sweat had made it.

"More," she said.

He kissed her.

"That wasn't proper, was it?"

He laughed. "You have a way with words. 'Proper'!"

"Are we going to do it properly?"

He sat up and showed her his shrinking thing.

"If we waited a while?"

He lay full length upon her and whispered in her ear: "Next time."

She relaxed. All she wanted was to feel him flesh to flesh and to hear "Next time."

9

There was a tin tray of chocolate fudge on a top shelf in the root store. It had been cooked in the tray and cut into the usual squares; but then it had been abandoned. Catherine had stolen one and eaten it months ago. It had a bitter tang, not unpleasant but not fudgelike. A week or two later she had eaten another . . . and then another. And so it had gone on. Over the months she had helped herself to a dozen or so. At last she felt she ought to own up, in case John or Ian got blamed.

She took the evidence to Renee and said, "I was helping myself to these ever since I was first here. I'm sorry. I ought to have asked."

To her surprise Renee went deep pink and said, "I know."

"Oh, dear! You knew it was me?"

"Who else! Once Rowena left and they went on vanishing."

"I'll pay you for them."

Renee, growing less flustered, laughed. "Of course not. Have fun, I say. But I meant to tell you—they're all right for married folks, who wouldn't mind a baby too much anyway. But you're taking a risk."

"A baby!" Catherine looked dubiously at the fudge. *A baby?* Where was the connection?

"I meant to tell you. But then I thought 'she knows what she's doing.' I hope you do, honey."

"I don't know anything. What has eating fudge got to do with being married and having babies?"

Renee stared at her. "Eating *fudge?* You mean you've been *eating* that stuff?"

"What else?"

Renee began to laugh. She laughed until the tears ran and her breath gave out. "Lordy!" she panted, sitting down. "Now I really am embarrassed. It never crossed my mind you were *eating* it." She screwed up her face. "What does it taste like?"

"Quite nice, if you don't like fudge too sweet. There's a sort of bitter tang."

"Quinine."

"You mean it's not fudge?"

"No, honey, it's not fudge." Renee chuckled. "I'll tell you what it is. There's no shame in it, I reckon. And if you were my younger sister I'd make darn sure and tell you. It's a pound of cocoa butter and an ounce of boric acid and an ounce and a half of tartaric acid—you know, like we use in the orangeade?—and a tablespoon of tincture of quinine. And you melt it in that tray in simmering water and stir it all together and then set it to cool. And when it's set you cut it like fudge. And" —she lowered her eyes and smoothed her dress— "you know how babies are made?"

"Aye."

"Well, if you want to have fun with your husband and you don't want to start making one, you put one of those up inside you first. Your body heat melts it and then it kills all his seed before it gets the chance to quicken you."

Catherine turned away to hide her confusion. "And you believed I was doing *that?*" *But not with Ed,* she thought or surely Renee would never be so calm.

And another thought was shrill within her: *It can be safe!* She was afraid the triumph would show.

Renee sprang to her feet and, standing directly behind Catherine, put her arms around her shoulders and rested her chin on her neck. "I'm sorry, honey. Truly. If I'd known you then like I do now, I'd never have believed it. But you know what they say about religious girls."

"No. What?"

"Never mind. Anyway, it was something Rowena said."

"About me?"

"Well . . . not *said.* Not in so many words. But she could say things without words. You know how she was."

"And she said I was that sort of girl?"

"Pretty much. I guess it's just as well she isn't coming back." She felt Catherine react. "Didn't you know?" She let go of Catherine and straightened a fold in the curtain. "Her folks are sending her on a trip to Europe—or that's the word they're spreading."

"Isn't it true?"

"Not the way some tell it—but then people have dirty minds, anyway. Me, too, I guess—suspecting you like that."

Catherine picked up the "fudge" to carry it back to the root store. "And it really works?" she asked.

"It seemed to. Then when Ed and me wanted to start a baby, about the time of the Armistice, and I stopped using it, and nothing started, I thought, oh well, we just can't have them anyway. But, knock on wood, I think I'm carrying."

"Oh, Renee—that's lovely for you, hon."

"Don't say anything when Ed's around. I didn't tell him yet. One more month without Our Friend and I'll be certain." She sighed. "Then, I guess, it's no fun for Ed until the spring. Poor fellow!"

And Catherine said, "So, if you've no need for these, I could still eat one or two now and then? I like them."

10

That fall the weather went by the book. Some years there was no early snow, no hot blast of a chinook to melt it, and no Indian summer. But that year brought all three—and the biggest berry harvest in memory. Renee and Catherine were bottling fruit and jam, jelly and juice for weeks. Then in November the first big snows came. All the cars had been put up on blocks a couple of months ago. Now the horse and cutter came into its own. Catherine had heard all the stories from the born plainsmen but none of them induced half the respect for snow that she derived from a minor incident in her own back yard. It didn't seem so minor at the time, though.

She went out to the privy one evening carrying a storm lantern. A gentle breeze drove a moderate fall of snow across her path. By now she had the prairie habit of tucking herself into the wind, so it didn't bother her. She marvelled at the silence of everything. Only the hiss of the flakes hitting the canopy of her lantern broke that eerie stillness.

She wasn't in the privy long, but even before she emerged she knew the wind had got up. It buffetted the door. And when she opened it she was almost choked by snow. It was falling so thickly she thought there must surely be more snow than air in front of her. It was drifting fast, too. The path was no longer visible.

She pulled her head right down into her collar and stumbled for the house. And she stumbled, and ran, and stumbled. The whole yard was enclosed by fences, gates, or buildings, so she knew she couldn't have strayed onto the prairie. Then she really would be as good as dead. But where was everything?

Moments later she came up against a brick wall. Her lantern showed a blackened slit that Ed had once tried to fool her was a rifle slit from back in the days of wild injuns. It was the wall of the smoke house. She had gone exactly ninety degrees off her intended path—in less than thirty yards!

If she had been thinking straight, she'd have hugged the wall and worked her way past the small hay store, the pigpen, the hay barn, the tractor shed, and then, by a short fence, to the back porch of the house. Two sides of a triangle. Instead she was so relieved to rediscover her bearings that she ran off along the diagonal and, a mile later, wound up at the cowshed, on the very opposite side of the yard from the house.

She had dressed for a brief dash across the yard and back. Her body was warm enough in her thick coat, but her feet—in carpet slippers—were numb. So, too, were her hands. The shed was warm from the kine. She slipped inside to regain her breath and get thawed.

"Cath!" It was Ed's voice, strangely muted, as if he were half a mile away.

"Here! In the cowshed!"

"Keep calling!"

She shouted *Here!* every couple of seconds until he lumbered out of the dark.

"Oh, Ed!" She flung her arms around him and hugged him.

"Thank God!" He hugged her, too. "Now d'you believe old man Purdue died in a snowstorm in his own yard?"

"I do."

They continued holding each other long after the relief died down.

"Ed?"

"Yes?"

"When?"

"When what?"

"It's been months now. Don't you like me?"

"Of course I do. My God, if only you knew!"

"Or did you just get what you want and now you can't bear me?"

He kissed her. The passion of it was his answer.

"When?" she repeated. "I know about that cocoa-butter stuff. I've got some. It'd be safe."

"Oh, Cath, it's torture. I long for you. But I don't want to lead you into such wrong. It's wrongdoing. Aren't you afraid—I mean, you're so religious?"

"I'm damned anyway. I've likely been damned since I deserted my father. Oh, Ed, I just want you so much."

"You're not in love, I hope. With me?"

"Of course not. I just want you."

He laughed ruefully. "I asked for that, I suppose. But I'm afraid of falling in love with you."

"Don't fash yourself about that. I'll leave if you do."

"We can't stay out here. The whole community will come searching."

"I'm not going back indoors until you say when."

He sighed. "Soon."

"But when?"

"Doc Macrae says Renee should rest an hour or two every afternoon. I'll send Haydon over to Hawk Ridge for something. And then we'll have time. Also I have to see the Zam Buk man."

"Why?"

"Never you mind. That's man's business. But I don't trust your cocoa butter."

Catherine did not like herself much that night. She even thought it might have been better if she had wandered out onto the prairie and died. But she knew she could not act otherwise. She was utterly in thrall to this new kind of experience. For the moment it was the most important thing in creation. She was truly in the mire of it now, and there was no turning back. If she was to get out, it would have to be on the far side.

The Zam Buk man, who also sold Sloan's Liniment, Dodd's Kidney Pills, and Hair Restorer, had a secret compartment in his suitcase. There he kept rubber johnnies to sell to the men. When Ed had secured his supply, he sent Haydon over to Hawk Ridge, and took Catherine up to the cowshed. There was a feed passage at the back of the stalls leading to the stables and provender at one end and the woodstore at the other.

From December on they went up there just about every week. Haydon couldn't always be sent away, but there were plenty of tasks to absorb him and keep his head down. They took awful risks but were never caught. The first time or two was painful, then uncomfortable, and then those moments were the sweetest and most glorious she had ever known.

Ed told her he was addicted to her and thought about doing it with her all the time. She thought he was just flattering her because in between times she hardly thought about it at all—or him (or not in that way). Even on the day itself, when he checked the weather and gave her a wink, meaning *today,* and all morning her innards would churn and her heart would go into brief racing spurts—even that had little to do with him; it was just her own body's private anticipation of its forthcoming experience.

She tried not to think about him at all, because when she did, it worried her. Specifically it worried her that she could like him so much as a person— a neutral—in one part of her mind; while in another part she could still have those romantic *ooh-ah!* feelings for him that she and Rowena had half-joked about; while in yet another part (or was that exclusively in her body?) she was ready at any moment to lie with him. Surely, she felt, her romantic feelings and her sexual readiness should at least mix together? But they didn't.

Still, Ed was the only one she would lie with. In winter, whenever the weather allowed, there were always dances, school cantatas, town jamborees, or socials of some kind going on. At Christmas they seemed to last all week; and, as there were at least five boys to every girl, she had a marvellous time. But she never let any boy take the slightest liberty. There were plenty of chances. A girl wasn't chaperoned on the prairie. There was a general understanding that if she acted bad and there was a baby on the way, there'd be a hasty wedding, and folks would look down their noses at her for a year or two (even redoubtable matriarchs who themselves had had bonny, nine-pound first babies three months early), and then they'd turn into decent folk, and the shame would wear off. So it was not unusual for a boy or a girl to spend hours alone in a cutter behind a loose horse. Catherine often did, but the action never went beyond light petting. Mostly they just talked.

She made a lot of good friends that way and had some fascinating conversations. She heard the tallest of tall stories, like the farmer who got caught up in a chinook wind and just made it into town in his cutter, galloping all the way, with frozen ice ahead and meltwater right behind. She grew attuned to that marvellous, dry, gentle prairie humour—like the other farmer who, under the guise of darkness, joined the Halloween pranksters and helped dismantle his own wagon and get it reassembled on the roof of his barn; and when they giggled and said, "Wonder how Ol' Tom's gonna get *that* down," he giggled right back and said, "Same way as we got her up, fellas!"

Webster Law (she'd worked around to him again) told her of a political meeting in his father's yard, when a Conservative came out to talk to a whole crowd of farmers; and he was standing on a trestle about ten feet in front of the manure heap. And he said he knew they were all busy men and he didn't want to waste any words, when Murph Hendy chipped in and said, "Back up a piece then, mister! We won't waste 'em."

Over that winter she was accepted into the community and became part of its tale-bearing, information-sharing network. That acceptance was a great balm to her conscience and helped her feel she was not really a bad woman.

Then she read in McCall's that "forty-one percent of bad women in one Toronto prison come from strictly religious homes." So that was what they said about religious girls. She didn't know what "percent" meant but even if it was just a fancy way of saying forty-one women, it still sounded an awful lot. She thought of those forty-one women, all of whom at one time must have gone to church regularly, read their Bibles, said their prayers—and it hadn't helped a bit. They were all bad women, and all in jail.

And did they all start by being bad with just one man—like she was with Ed? Did they then reason they were damned to perdition anyway and might as well be hanged for the whole sheep? Was that what she was risking? Whom could she ask?

The new schoolteacher was a cousin of the Wilsons, half a mile down the road, so she boarded with them, even though their place was really too small. But she didn't need any parlour for courting. She was a young widow, only twenty-two, who'd lost her husband just last fall in the most horrible threshing accident. Her name was Marie Wilson and she and Catherine soon became friends—which, seeing how close they lived, was pretty inevitable anyway. A couple of evenings every week Marie would walk over to the Kirbys' and sit and talk with Catherine while they darned socks and mended cuffs and turned sheets sides-to-middle.

Catherine asked her what "percent" meant, and Marie explained. Then she asked how Catherine had come upon the expression, and, too flustered to think of a lie, Catherine told her.

Marie smiled. "Why are you reading about bad women who started out religious? Are you afraid of turning into one? Because of your own religious upbringing?"

Catherine stammered, "Who can be sure, ever, I mean?"

Then Marie divined how serious a point this was for her. "Temptations?" she asked.

Catherine nodded.

"Boys?"

"A man. One man."

Marie studied her in a nerve-racking silence, nodding judiciously. "Why don't you marry?"

Catherine shook her head.

"Oh! That is serious."

"Yes."

"You just mustn't give way."

Catherine liked that answer. Most other women would have tried to get her to tell everything. But Marie was a self-contained woman. Even her own sadness she kept to herself.

A week later she said, "Shall I come and board here? Keep you company?"

"Och, would you?" Catherine was delighted—and she knew Ed and Renee wouldn't say no to the extra thirty dollars a month.

"I don't think my dear cousins will mind. And I'm . . . well—lonely, too. I mean we can lead one another not into temptation."

Usually teachers had their own rooms but Marie was adamant about moving into Catherine's. Often they lay awake into the small hours talking about everything under the sun—or, at that time of day, the moon, which, helped by the snow, could make the room as bright as day.

Their friendship wasn't deep; Marie confided no great intimacies— nor did Catherine. But it was nonetheless warm and undemanding. Friendships with boys—even with boys who knew for a certainty that she wasn't "hot," or with fellows like Webster, who would probably be offended if she made an advance—such pure friendships always had that edge of sexual possibility. After all, that was what made them exciting. But it wasn't relaxing. She could never completely relax with a boy. But with Marie it was the opposite. She was always relaxed.

Without Marie she would never have been able to tell Ed she wasn't going to do it with him anymore. Even then she backslid once, when there was a social at Hawk, and Ed, who had some Grain Association business to see to that evening, took her over there in the cutter. This ungainly vehicle looked like an outside privy on runners, but it had the supreme virtue of being windproof and containing a small charcoal stove. On the way home he pulled into the plantation at Hawk Ridge, without a word, and they spent a delicious twenty minutes in the snug warmth between their furs. But that was the one and only time.

To her chagrin, Ed seemed a mite relieved at her new decree. The strain of finding outwork for Haydon, and risking callers, or Renee's premature awakening, was beginning to outweigh the delights of the cowshed feedway. Also, she felt sure, Renee hadn't been able to hold out and had probably found ways to accommodate him without risking the baby.

Marie transformed Catherine's life in one other way, too; it would seem trivial only to someone who has not experienced life at forty below. Apart from the kitchen stove the only source of warmth in the house was a large wood-burning Eagle heater in the living room, which had tanks on the side for water. Ed always heaped it last thing at night and shut the flue right down. In the morning it was still going and the water was hot. By his decree, Catherine and Renee were allowed to come down for hot water, but only he and the boys were permitted to get dressed by its warmth. The agony of climbing into icy shifts and other garments when it was cold enough outside to freeze the spit before it landed was one of the greatest tortures Catherine knew.

Marie Wilson simply ignored the decree. Ed and the boys could gawp their eyes out for all she cared, or they could wait their turn. She was going to dress by the heater. Catherine gleefully joined her. Marie could have been a frump and a bore, it would not have mattered; that action alone would have redeemed her. Marie also taught her the old trick of parbaking potatoes in the oven before bedtime, then tipping them into the foot of the bed for the night. In the morning those same potatoes would peel and fry in half the usual time.

It would not be true to say they entirely avoided all confidences; they developed an oblique way of talking about them instead. The lesson in church one Sunday had been from Genesis—the passage Catherine had recalled when she first lay with Ed, where the serpent tempts Eve with the knowledge of good and evil.

That night Catherine said to Marie, "You're teaching knowledge all the time, hon, and the Church only exists to teach about good and evil. I never was understanding why it was wrong for Adam and Eve to learn about good and evil."

They discussed it a bit but Marie had no ready-made answer. "I must think," she said. But she knew that Catherine's interest in the answer was profound and personal.

Next night she asked, "When you were back in Scotland, before you came here, did you ever want to know about good and evil? I mean, did you think about it a lot?"

"Never."

"Why not?"

"Because I already knew. I mean, everyone knew. I heard it from the minister, and the dominie, and the elders, and An Dóiteán my father, and my mother while she was living. I just knew."

"The Garden of Eden is the Garden of Innocence. I think Scotland was your Garden of Innocence. You were content to accept the general authority on such questions."

"I was a child."

"Yes—well, isn't that what Adam and Eve were? Two naked, innocent children. I don't think they were the first man and the first woman. Not then. I mean, the whole thing's only an allegory, anyway. But even in terms of the allegory, they didn't become Man and Woman until after they were expelled. That's when innocence turned to just plain ignorance. That's when they had to work. To start learning."

"Yes, but what was it knowledge *of?* The tree of *what* knowledge?"

"You don't need to ask that, Cath."

"Each other?"

"Each other. About being a Man and being a Woman."

"So I still don't know whether it's right or wrong for *us* to try and get that knowledge. It was wrong for them. But is it for us?"

"They had a choice. They could have remained innocent. Do you think we have that choice?"

Catherine thought of Sister John in New York. "Nuns do."

"Would you like to be a nun?"

"They aren't bothered by . . . life."

"They have to work very hard. They have a hard discipline."

"I'm not afeared of that."

"What are you afeared of?"

Catherine thought awhile, rejecting the babble of confession that begged to be uttered. "Of always making mistakes. Never getting anything right. I sometimes think I'm going to make a awful mess of my life."

"What would you call a mess?"

"I never was thinking about it. Life was . . . just life. There would be a croft. There would be a man. There would be bairns. Life."

"Ah! But now you have a choice. You can do anything."

"Aye, especially make a mess of it."

"Are you glad you ran away from Scotland?"

"I can't always run away, though. It's like Snakes and Ladders. Running away is the snake. It puts you back."

"You've got serpents on the brain tonight! Anyway, I wouldn't call coming to Canada a *backward* step."

Catherine despaired of explaining it. Not because she was ashamed or embarrassed, but because she lacked the words. She hardly understood it herself. There was something in what happened back there at Beinn Uidhe —something she ought to have stayed and fought. If she had, and if she had won, she would be ahead; her mind, her knowledge of herself, her understanding of the perplexing undercurrents that seemed to move the whole of humanity, her soul—all of these would be more advanced, in some mysterious way, than they were now. But by running away, by not facing it, she had slipped down the snake and was back in some more primitive state of ignorance.

"What about a ladder?" Marie asked when she saw that Catherine was at a loss.

"Ladder?"

"What about getting married? That Webster Law would be a good man."

"I just can't seem to love him. I can't seem to love anybody."

"Nobody?"

"Just nobody."

Now it was Marie who was silent awhile. "That's maybe a good thing. D'you know the saying, 'on the rebound'?"

"No."

"If a girl's been engaged to a boy for years and then she breaks it off, or he does, often she gets married to someone else very quickly. And folk say, 'he got her on the rebound.' Those marriages aren't usually happy."

"But I'm not on the rebound from anyone."

"It doesn't have to be from someone you loved, I mean some boy. You could be on the rebound from Scotland even, or your home, or your old man—Old Dutch or whatever that is you call him."

"I see."

"I mean it was a big upheaval, that. Running away like that. Small wonder you're too numb or confused to love anyone right now. Believe me, honey, I *know*. If I felt myself falling in love anytime in this next year or so, I'd be mighty suspicious about it. So don't *worry*, huh?"

Tears welled in Catherine's eyes; she was glad of the dark.

"Or infatuation," Marie went on. "It's very easy to be infatuated with someone without loving him at all, especially some handsome, gorgeous young fellow." She gave a light laugh. "I mean, if Ed weren't already married . . . well!"

Catherine giggled. "Rowena and I used to talk about him a lot like that. I think I was what you said, infatuated, with him when she was here. We both were."

Marie giggled, too—something she rarely did. "And isn't it *lovely!*" she said. "Just pure make-believe."

"Aye!"

"Even though you know you'd rather die than actually, you know, *do* anything."

"Oh, much rather!"

They talked about Ed for a while, saying what it was they particularly liked about him—the tuck of his lips, the curl of hair just under his ear lobes, the dint in his jaw, and so on. Catherine amazed herself to be talking about him so impersonally, like a carving or some inanimate object.

Finally Marie said, "Don't go and be a nun, honey. Having a husband you love . . ." Her voice cracked. "Your very own, who loves you . . ." She began to cry, but still struggled not to show it. "It's . . . something."

Despite the cold, Catherine slipped out of her own bed and sat on the edge of Marie's. She stroked her hair and regretted they had not developed such intimacy as would allow her to get in and cradle her to sleep.

11

It was the Easter holidays and Marie was away when Renee's baby was born. A big storm that blew most of the week prevented Doc Macrae from getting through. It was a hard labour and a harder birth, but Mrs. Stenson came up the road and helped. She wasn't qualified but she'd helped several women, including her own daughter, when their time came. There were some who wouldn't have anyone else.

Catherine helped, too. Before she went into the room her heart had been up in her throat and she had trembled like a willow. But as soon as there was work for her hands, and comfort or encouragement to give, she was amazed at how calm she became. And even when Renee screamed, she hadn't gone to pieces but had tried to find the most practical way to ease the pain.

Mrs. Stenson said, "Is that true? Doc Macrae wants you for a nurse?"

"Aye."

"Then if you turn him down, you're a fool. You were born to the work."

Catherine knew it was true. Even from this one experience she could feel a sort of aptness in her for it. She could *care,* without going to pieces over pain or blood or anything.

The baby was a little seven-pound girl. They called her Kathrine.

"The family will think it's after Renee's grandma," Ed told her. "She spelled it with a *K.*"

"But we'll know who it's really after," Renee said.

She was left very weak for several days and Catherine had to do most of the management of her tiny namesake—everything except the actual feeding. That glorious transition as she put the baby to Renee's breast, and it went from lusty howling to instant contentment, making little grunts between sucks and swallows, filled her with a yearning for one of her own. How long would it be? she wondered. And whose? One night she put little Kate to her own breast and just for a few seconds she enjoyed the serenity of it. But then the trick was discovered, no milk flowed, and the howls were angrier than ever.

All that time Ed was banished to the schoolteacher's room—the one that had been Rowena's. Catherine brought her bed in and set it up by Renee's, so that she could wake up and be there instantly she was needed. For three days Haydon coped with the milking; but he had been reared on a ranch in Alberta and had only just accustomed himself to arable work. Handling the cows disgusted him and he quit, saying he'd leave as soon as the storm blew out. Ed coaxed him to take it back, but only by promising to do the milking himself. Renee thought it the joke of the year. But she saw it couldn't last too long, and she was feeling so much better now she told Catherine they could all go back to normal from tomorrow. That was the last night Catherine slept in Renee's room.

After the small-hours feed she was unable to go back to sleep so she took a candle into her room to get *Les Trésors du Louvre*. She had only just returned with it when she realized she had left the candle burning in her room. She went back and picked it up. She turned to the door and found it barred by Ed.

"Cath?" he pleaded.

"No, Ed."

She walked toward him. The candlelight, shining upward into his face, gave him the same satanic look he had had that first night, at Hawk Ridge. She caught the familiar smell of him. All her penned-back lust came flooding out. She could actually feel it in her veins, melting her flesh, drowning her will.

"No," she repeated. But he could see her eyes.

"We must," he said. "Oh, my darling, I want you so much."

Not his words, not his voice, but his moving lips spoke directly to her. She could not take her eyes off his face; she adored every part of it. The worship in his eyes was like a bondage.

She put down the candle and he lifted off her nightdress. In the frozen room she was on fire. She pulled his waistcord and eased his jacket and dressing gown back over his smooth, strong shoulders. His upraised thing, crushed between them, was a furnace. They slipped beneath the quilt on Marie's bed, then he was all life inside her and she all heat around him with her limpet thighs and arms.

In the after calm, when she realized that neither of them had taken precautions, she looked at the door, thinking *I must go down and use some fudge*. Renee stood there. Catherine would have screamed, except that Renee looked so unnaturally calm. For a moment, long or short she could not say, they were held thus, eyes locked.

Ed felt her sudden rigidity and began to turn. In ghostlike silence Renee drifted sideways, out of view. Ed saw nothing but he needed no telling who had been there.

"Thank God," he said. "It's out at last."

"What?" She could not believe it.

"We don't have to hide it anymore. I'll tell Renee that's how it's going to be now."

"Ed!"

"Don't worry about her." He rose and got back into his night clothes while he spoke. "She'll accept it. You'll get on well with her. Better than before, even. We'll all get on." He walked out quite jauntily.

When he was gone, she raced downstairs and put three ice-cold squares of "fudge" inside her. Then she lay face down on the carpet by the heater and put her backside high in the air to make sure it melted deep into her.

When she put it in that place she felt herself to be a foul, sullied creature. The fishwife stink of her was the malodour of corruption. Her body was vile. She was vile—a bag of tripes and blood, of deceptive beauty, built around a hole, a space that Ed and all men craved, a sink of iniquity. But even in the midst of this self-laceration, she could feel still the ecstasy, the overpowering sweetness of being clasped around him, open to the hilt of him.

She dressed, milked the cows, raddled the stove, put on the porridge, and woke the two boys. She cooked and served all their breakfasts. Ed went out to work, whistling.

She saw now. She would have to defeat it. She would have to subjugate her flesh and destroy those dreadful carnal lusts or they would finish her and she would become another percentage point in the women's prison. "You know what they say about religious girls!"

She had to run away, yet again, but not blindly. This time she'd run to somewhere safe, somewhere and to some work that would absorb all her energies. She went and packed her few belongings.

She took Renee's breakfast upstairs, left it outside the door, and gave a soft knock. No sound came from within.

The storm had blown over in the night. Doc Macrae came around eleven. Catherine showed him up to Renee and, by a natural conspiracy, both women behaved as if nothing at all were amiss between them. But when the doctor went back to his cutter, Catherine ran after him, threw her bag in the back and, sitting herself beside him, said, "I will be coming with you."

Their eyes met. She thought she had never seen eyes so full of wisdom. He was marvellous. He asked no questions. All he said was, "Aye. Aye. So." His tone implied he understood all. And forgave all. He was the father she had always needed. She had awakened from an awful dream.

She pulled the furs around her and looked out at the white-shrouded world, all crisp and new. The sun was out, the prairie sparkled. Everything was pure. The icicles on the bare branches of the shelter belt trees were melting. They fell upon the ice crust in an endless tinkling of fairy bells. The two horses arched their heads gracefully inward as they pulled. The steam of their breath wreathed between them and around Catherine with an almost aphrodisiac power. It made her do something she had not expected to do for months. It made her laugh aloud. She laughed at the purity of everything. It was a laugh of hope.

Two days later she got forty dollars in the post. There was no letter but she needed none. It was her past two months' wages. After she had repaid Mr. Hamilton's loan, she had put aside ten dollars each month in the Goldeneye Credit Union, in the boys' names. When it reached a hundred and fifty she'd send them the book and be clear of that debt, too. She added a further twenty from this forty. The debt was two-thirds paid.

She thought about Ed from time to time, or about what they used to do, and the old lust would seize her. Then she put her hand inside her bodice or under her skirt and pinched herself until she bruised—but where no one else would see it. In time, she was sure, this would cure her of that evil carnality. Already she was blotched red-brown-purple-blue-and-black from the knees up and the armpits down.

After a week at Goldeneye, her time at Micah began to seem like a nightmare in another country and another age. Then a cutter pulled up at the front door—an all-too-familiar cutter, but this time Renee was at the reins. It was a Saturday and Meg answered the call. Renee wouldn't get down and come in. She just asked to see Catherine.

When Catherine, her heart in her mouth, came to the door Renee didn't waste a moment. With a speed that took Catherine by surprise she hurled something at her. Catherine had the impression of a fluttering—a chicken, she thought; Renee was hurling a dead chicken at her. Then it struck her head with a solidity and hardness that no chicken could possess. Catherine reeled back indoors, crying out at the pain of the blow. Margaret, aghast at this violence, bent down to pick it up. "It's a book," she said.

By the time Catherine got back to the door, the cutter was already a hundred yards away. She knew what book it was before she even looked—*Les Trésors du Louvre*. In the conflicts and upheavals of her last hours at Micah, she had forgotten it was in Renee's bedroom.

"It's ruined," Meg said, holding up the two halves into which it had burst.

Catherine fitted them together and began to turn the pages.

"Oh, my God!" Meg said in even deeper horror.

Renee (who else?) had taken a blue indelible crayon of the kind used for marking the wheat sacks and had scrawled HOOR . . . LOOD . . . BITCH over every naked female in the book.

"God, why don't you cry?" Meg asked. "Shout! Yell! Take Dad's gun and go after her! *Anything!*"

But Catherine was looking at the disfigurement of all those women and she saw that it in no way differed from what she was doing to herself. She turned to Meg with a wan smile and said, "I couldn't hurt Renee, hon. I owe her too much."

She looked back at the spoiled nudes.

"But it's no answer," she said. "It's just another form of running away."

PART TWO

1924~1925

12

"Connie Rogers says the muskrats are building really high this year. Six foot, she said." Fiona spoke with a poisoned lightness of tone.

"They set an example to us all, my precious," James told her.

"The Mounties say the deer are coming south in abnormally large numbers, too," she persisted.

James pretended to be bewildered. "Can it be," he asked, "that you believe we are in for a hard winter, my love? Surely not—for when I say such things to you, you call it 'superstitious nonsense.'"

"And you yourself said you'd never seen the ponies' coats so thick."

"I didn't say never, I said not since nineteen-oh-six."

"And that was the worst winter in memory."

"Or could it be, light of my life, that you are trying, in your gentle, tactful way, to say you think Catherine and I should not be going to Micah?"

"What does it matter what I say?" Idly she untangled some strands of wandering Jew. "You'll do as you please, anyway."

"We'll look after our patients, anyway."

"So that they can maintain us in ungraded oatmeal, dubious bacon, and undersized pullets' eggs."

He laughed. "It's a diet that keeps us sharp, though."

"Sharp?"

"Aye—my wit and your tongue."

Fiona snorted, folded her arms, and looked out at the frozen landscape. "You don't think of me," she said.

"The whole town thinks of you, my dear."

"And well it might, since half of it is mortgaged to you!"

Still he laughed. "Conversation with you, my love, is like scattering seed in the tropics. Throw down anything, anything at all, and it grows." He put an arm around her shoulder and gave a hug. "You have a most fertile mind."

She grunted, trying not to smile. "Fertile . . . fertilizer . . . I can guess what comes next!"

"What comes next is a pleasant trot over well-packed roads to Micah. I'll telephone you the moment we arrive. And before we leave."

"D'you think she's right, James?" Catherine asked when they were on the road.

The ponies trotted smartly and the cutter sang over the packed snow. The sky did look unnaturally dark.

"We are not going to lose this baby," he answered.

"We could have caught the train."

He looked at the clouds. "That isn't snow."

She hoped he was right. He usually was. But she'd had enough experience now of prairie blizzards to know what utter folly it was to take chances. That first experience in the Kirbys' back yard had been only a foretaste. She'd been caught in far worse snows since then.

He cleared his throat. "Er—if Renee's baby decides not to join us at once, we'll have to stay more than just the one night."

"I'm no stranger there."

He said nothing. The silence forced her to add, "It's true Renee and I didn't see eye to eye."

"See eye to eye," he said in a surprised tone, as if it were a very novel way of describing the relationship he had in mind.

"All right. We loathed . . . or she couldn't abide me." She glanced at him out of the corner of her eye and saw he was staring straight ahead, smiling. *Damn him,* she thought. He behaved as if he knew everything— which he couldn't possibly do. "Look, she wants this baby, desperately. She knows I'm the best nurse she'd ever get (thanks to who taught me). She'll behave all right."

"Good for her, but, as a matter of fact, it wasn't Renee I had in mind."

Now she was silent.

"You know Ed's grandfather was the Earl of Dunmow?" he said. "In fact, he still is. He lives with that cousin in Kansas—the one who'll inherit the title. Did you ever hear the story?"

"There was some disgrace," she said. "Ed never spoke about it."

"There was no disgrace. There was pride and stubbornness—on a scale that was more Celtic than Anglo-Saxon."

"What happened?"

"I think it was back in the eighteen seventies. The earl went to India with the Prince of Wales. And the countess got into some sort of compromising liaison back in London. If everyone had behaved with tact and reticence, it would have blown over in a year or two. But the earl made such a pursuit of it that in the end he was forced out of society and had to come to America."

"Dear me! What a terrible fate!" Catherine laughed.

"It was the best that ever happened to him. He worked like a slave and became the first Kirby for about three hundred years to wind up richer than he started."

"Ed's the same."

"Yes," he said lightly. "Ed, too, is more Celt than Sassenach. He's not a forgetter."

"I am," she said. "It was four years ago. I've forgotten."

It seemed a lot longer than four years. Sometimes she looked back on herself as she had been only a month earlier and she felt a kind of retrospective embarrassment for the awkward, ignorant thing she saw. But that poor, bewildered creature of 1919! What possible link could there be between them? How had she survived—and come through it all so relatively unharmed? It was a human miracle. And the human master of it had been James. And, in her way, Fiona.

She had seen enough doctors by now to know they were basically of two kinds. One saw the practice as an ancient mystery, the mystique a part of the cure: "Take these magic potions and you'll be right as rain," they used to say. (Now it was, "Take these antidiuretics and your metabolic system will restabilize within the norms." But the meaning was the same.) The other saw the patient as the real doctor, and the doctor as no more than a midwife to the healing process. James was firmly of this second group.

"Never forget," he would tell her, "most of our patients aren't ill. They are well people who have the temporary misfortune to be sick. They will get better whatever we do. A minority—and, thank God, it's a small one—truly are sick. They are sick *people*. And they will die whatever we do, some within the day, some within years. But we cannot prevent it." And if his son Burgo was around—Burgo who was on the point of graduating, and who was just as firmly of the antidiuretics and metabolic-mystique school—he would add: "We must look after the first, for they bring us our reputation, and we must hang on to the second, for they are our bread and butter."

She was so won over by James's humanity she could not understand how Burgo could resist it. Burgo said it wasn't really humanity, it was cynical modesty. Sometimes he almost convinced her. He knew so much, and his enthusiasm was so great—for he was sure that in the next fifty years medicine was going to abolish disease and most disorders and make a good start on the more deep-seated hereditary ailments. But James, not by saying anything but just by being James, always prevailed in the end—to her mind at least. His was a wisdom that stretched right back to ancient times.

Over the years he had taught her much more than any prairie nurse needed to know—partly because she found that "anatomy" and "physiology," which sounded the dullest topics imaginable, were about the most exciting things in the world, and partly because he loved to talk shop and she was the only one with whom he could regularly do so. With Burgo he argued shop, but that was different.

That sadly misguided girl who had set out to pinch and bruise her body into submission was just one of the selves whose memory made her cringe. She now understood that God had devised a mechanism whose subtlety and grandeur lay far beyond the reach of such tinkering. It might once have worked for some ignorant, smelly hermit out in the desert, but the tree of the knowledge of good and evil had borne new fruit since then. And, as she had discovered, it was the hardest fruit to leave uneaten.

This new diet, coupled with the fascination of her work as James's nurse, both in his general practice and in his cottage hospital, absorbed her totally. From time to time she had offers of marriage, from the most eligible and well-thought-of bachelors and widowers in Goldeneye, and from all the country round. Many of them said they wouldn't object if, between babies, she went on nursing. A few even stressed how much they would welcome it. But, though she still thought she would get married someday, next year or the year after, and though the urge to have children was strong within her, none of it seemed pressing enough to make her break the status quo. Even with the men she liked or admired best, the thought of leaving James's company each day and going home to theirs was dismal. For the moment, then (and what a long moment it was proving to be), nursing, learning, and James gave her all she wanted from life. And if some true prophet had told her she would never marry, that all her days would be as these days now, she would have been content enough.

Some of this change in her outlook she owed to Fiona, who was, in many ways, an even more interesting person than James. Catherine longed to discuss her seriously with him, despite the intrusion it would represent; but he would never speak of her except in a lightly ironical tone. For instance, if Catherine said, "You shouldn't tease her so, James. You shouldn't say those things to deliberately provoke her," he would answer, "You think I should let her stew in the juice of her own misapprehension? Don't you see, woman, my perpetual challenge is all that stands between her and total severance from reality? She is a potential female Caligula. Her present sweet and gentle disposition is entirely my creation."

Fiona was the worst pessimist imaginable. She predicted failure, disappointment, disaster for everything. The cottage hospital would lose money. A new, rich patient would prove a bad payer. A good servant girl would leave at the least convenient moment, and they'd never get a replacement. The car would break down any day now. There was a funny noise in the water pipes. Everything she ordered from the Christmas catalogue would be substituted. James was hopelessly optimistic about everything. Next year would be worse.

Most of her venom was directed against men. At first, when Catherine had picked up a smattering of modern psychology, she thought it might be some kind of defence against them. Maybe Fiona was so attracted to them, subconsciously, that she had to belittle them and sneer at them every chance she got. But lately she had begun to suspect this explanation. The truth lay deeper. Fiona actually resented the whole biological necessity for the existence of men. Men thought only of themselves. She did not deny that they were the doers, the performers, the achievers in life. But they'd only do and perform and achieve for themselves unless women constantly prodded and goaded and sniped at them from behind, or somewhere safe. At heart she hated the prairie because it was man's country, where the traditional male virtues of courage, strength, endurance, and indifference to pain were vital to survival; and where women who were not long-suffering, self-sacrificing providers of meals, babies, and comforts might as well quit or (as some did, indeed) hang themselves.

Catherine suspected that if James hated doctoring, if he had to drag himself reluctantly to work every day and make a real sacrifice of it, Fiona would be happier. For instance, if he had had to drag himself from a warm fireside and a good book to make this cold, uncomfortable trip to Micah for what everyone knew was going to be a difficult delivery, Fiona would have laid out his coat and snow boots last night, and as soon as she woke up she'd have prodded James and said, "Don't forget you have to go to Micah today," and every half hour she'd have asked him when he'd be leaving. But because he loved the life, she felt he was in it only to please himself. So it was certainly not something to be encouraged by her.

If he had an interesting case and came home bubbling with it, she would say, "But when are we going to see our money?" Sometimes these sniping comments of hers became hilarious, as when once he came out of the lavatory and she, going in, asked, *"Must* you make such a smell in here?" Catherine, who had overheard the question, stepped back into her room and half-closed the door just as James went shuffling by, chuckling to himself. How he stood it half the time she didn't know. But her work brought her into many homes and showed her people at their most vulnerable and least guarded moments; she knew there were many marriages in the neighbourhood where the woman would have made her husband's life a misery if the husband hadn't been able somehow to shrug it off and carry on as if everything were rosy.

Of course, she saw many marriages of the opposite type, where the lord and master was beyond all criticism. But since that had been the pattern of her own home life up until the time her mother died, it somehow seemed more natural. She was constantly amazed at Fiona's recklessness. Doesn't she understand, she wondered, how easy it would be for James to take up with some other woman? There were other husbands who did just that. But to Fiona their perfidy was grim proof of her own belief in the basic selfishness and hedonism of men.

She wondered what Fiona's childhood had been, and what sort of a father she'd had. A weak, remote man, she guessed. Fiona hardly ever mentioned him but she did once let slip a revealing little fact. They were going through an old chest of clothes, looking out things to send to her daughter Helen for her children. Fiona picked up a pretty lace dress that a fourteen-year-old might have worn in the 1890s. "Oh, I remember this," she said. "Whenever my mother wanted some money or a little favour out of my father, she always dressed me in this and sent me to him to try and wheedle it out of him for us."

"Why you?" Catherine asked.

Fiona shrugged. "I had the knack. I knew how to get anything out of him."

By living in the same house as Fiona, Catherine was enabled to feel much more thankful for her lot in life than she might otherwise have been. And when that allotment included James's company for most of her waking hours, she realized how much there was to be thankful for.

13

She had not set eyes on Ed since that day she left Micah. Every time she had visited Renee—as nurse, of course, not as friend—Ed had pointedly been absent. But this confinement might take days. There was no purpose in Ed's trying to find activities that would keep him out of the house indefinitely. They had to meet again.

It was a shock. She had matured so much; he, not at all. The hunger in his eyes was exactly as it had been on that afternoon of their first meeting. His desire for her shouted so loud she was astonished that James did not react to it, if only to protect her. But he seemed not even to notice.

Whenever Catherine looked at Ed, she found his eyes upon her. And *why,* she thought, did she have to look? What terrible fascination did he hold for her still? Feelings she thought had died four years ago sprang up again within her, as vigorous as ever. Her stomach fell away and her heart raced exactly as it had done on those days when he had tipped her the wink. She needed to remind herself that she was *not* going to steal out to the cowshed, *not* going to take off her clothes, *not* open herself to him.

It was only because he was physically there, she knew that. The mere thought of him would never have such an effect—quite the opposite. And if she left Micah now and went back to Goldeneye, it would all die away again, at once, and she could live as virginally untroubled as she had these past four years. It was that electricity of his presence, the *pressure* of his eyes on her skin, her breasts, her body. Why did no one else seem to feel it?

Thank heavens she was once again safely in the little trestle bed beside Renee's.

Renee was behaving very differently. Perhaps it was because she was pregnant. Catherine had often seen how pregnancy could change a woman's nature. Or perhaps time had done more for her than it had for Ed. She didn't exactly gush with warmth, but at least she was relaxed and friendly.

Catherine left a small night light burning in the window recess, behind the curtain. She said her prayers and climbed into bed. As soon as she was settled, Renee said, "We ought to make it up, honey, for both our sakes."

"I'd like that."

"It's a long time over."

"Aye." After a pause Catherine added, "It never threatened your marriage, you know. Ed would never leave you, but I wasn't even trying to make him."

"I guess he was more to blame than you. Men will go for all they can get. Like the yard bull. It's only natural."

Catherine laughed. "That makes me more to blame, not less. But I wouldn't dispute it. I was to blame."

"Well, like I said, it's a long time over. Ed and me are really close now."

"I'm glad. It wasn't love, you know. It's just that he's so attractive and I was so juvenile. It was really stupid."

Doesn't she see? she wondered. *Is she just saying this so as to keep up her spirits? Or am I imagining it? Is the hunger I feel in Ed really only in me?*

She began to doubt.

Renee went on. "I'm sorry what I did to that book of yours, honey."

"You had every right."

"I had no right. It was mean. Bad and mean."

"It was just what I needed."

"Anyway, I got you another book. You know the *Family Herald,* when they gave away 'Welcome Home' and 'The Awakening'? Did you collect those? Anyway they offered this book, so I thought of you, and what I'd done, and I sent for it. It's on the shelf up there."

"Can I look at it now?"

"Oh, if you like." Renee's tone was casual but Catherine could tell she couldn't wait.

She found the book and carried it over to the night light. It was a collection of paintings by Rosa Bonheur. No substitute for Rembrandt and Rubens, of course, except in the currency of penitence and peace offerings. "Oh, they're lovely!" Catherine said. "I'll always treasure them." She sat briefly on Renee's bed and, leaning over, kissed her forehead. "Thank you."

Renee was flushed with the wine of righteous forgiveness. "Anyway," she said archly, "it's Fiona who should be worrying now, eh?"

She saw at once what a blunder she had made. "I was only joking, hon," she said.

"Not a very funny joke."

"Anyway, I didn't mean you, I meant him."

Catherine knew she should just tell Renee to hold her tongue, but for some reason she heard herself ask, "What d'you mean by that?" Her tone was icily formal but for the first time in this whole conversation she was aware of her heartbeat.

"Oh, it doesn't matter. I shouldn't have said it."

Catherine tried to sleep but could not. She knew from Renee's breathing that the same was true of her. At last she said, "What *did* you mean, hon?"

Renee was very guarded. "It's just the way he looks at you. I'll bet Fiona wishes he looked at her like that."

"What way?" She tried to sound scornful and disbelieving but could not keep her interest out of it.

"D'you mean you've never noticed?"

"Never. He's a very good friend, of course. The best I ever had. But . . . well, he's more like a father to me."

"Of course he is. It was only a joke."

"What way does he look at me?"

"Lookit, I was wrong, honey. I saw it wrong."

"But what did you *think* you saw?"

"Nothing. And anyway, if you're so certain-sure I'm wrong, why are you so interested?"

Hours later Catherine fell asleep still pondering that question.

Next morning the contractions began. But, after all their fears, it proved to be quite a normal delivery. By midnight Renee was cradling an eight-pound-six-ounce baby boy in her arms, exhausted and happy. They named him Edward James.

After breakfast the following day Catherine and James set out in bright sunshine to make a number of other visits in the area before returning to Goldeneye. They called home first to set Fiona's mind at rest.

"How was she?" Catherine asked.

"In tiptop form. She said the weather is going to turn for the worse."

Catherine surveyed the barely clouded sky and laughed.

"I promised we'd stay at Jeremiah's if it did."

"That was apt!"

Jeremiah Bell was the last of their intended calls that day, about ten miles north of Micah and farther away from Goldeneye. He had a poisoned foot that was slow to heal.

The cloud was thickening when they reached him, about midday. Catherine took off the dressing and poulticed the wound. James thought it looked a whole lot better. Jeremiah then put on some venison steaks and beans and they all sat down to a real bachelor feast. Once, Jeremiah told them, he had gone fifteen months there without seeing another Christian soul. That was back nearly twenty years, when Ed's father had the only farm at Micah, before that whole community sprang up. Now it was getting so he couldn't turn around without a knock on the door. Every *month* someone'd turn up.

But Ed was a good neighbour. He'd saved Jeremiah's skin last summer when he had a haunch of out-of-season venison in the oven and the Mountie dropped by about some quarantine on the pigs. And Ed just slipped into the kitchen and cut the meat up real fine, and threw in a can of tomatoes and some cheese and turned it into a kind of hot meat loaf—which he said was some Eye-talian canned stuff his cousin sent over from London.

" 'Course," Jeremiah said, "the Mountie knew exactly what it was but Ed just stared him out with those eyes of his and that fellow said nothing. Ed just got his way like that!"

Catherine was glad to hear she was not alone where the uncanny power of Ed's eyes was concerned.

They stayed jawing far too long. By the time they left, the sky was almost completely clouded over; the sun poked searchlights down here and there, making blinding splashes on the darkening snow. Before they regained the Micah-Goldeneye road, a uniform darkness overhung them. But it was exactly the sort of sky under which they had travelled out—the sky that James had correctly said did not mean snow—so they were not unduly worried.

Until the wind got up. And the first flurries began to fall. Catherine said nothing but she noticed how often James now looked up at the sky. The temperature was falling as fast as the wind was rising. Within an hour it would be dark—and that was by the almanac; out here, in reality, it was almost dark already.

They reached the Micah road and turned east toward Goldeneye. They went past the turnoff that led across country, due south to Hawk, going by Hawk Ridge, ten and eight miles away, respectively. She thought of suggesting they should take that road, not least because it would put the wind square behind them. But then she realized that if they were just looking for the nearest shelter, they ought to turn right around and head back for Micah, only four miles behind them to the west.

After a further mile eastward that was just what James decided to do. The wind was now so fierce it almost cut. The snow, which had been soft and fleecy to start with, was like salt or desert sand. Instead of settling it scoured the existing ice and snow, beginning to sculpt it to fantastic shapes.

"We'll have to turn back," James shouted above the roar of the wind and the hiss of the scouring snow. "You put on more clothes."

She sprawled back inside the cutter, glad of the minimal warmth from the little charcoal stove, and made her own preparations for survival. The wind might yet grow so fierce they'd have to abandon the vehicle, cut the horses loose, and walk with them to the nearest shelter. And she had no intention of trying to walk in a skirt. James kept a spare set of clothes in the back, in case of vomit, blood, or infection. As best she could in the confined—and now dangerously swaying—cabin, she wriggled out of her skirt and into his long woollen underpants (mercifully with integral socks) and trousers. She pulled her stockings over that and her snow boots over the lot. Then she wrapped a scarf around her head and face, leaving just a slit for the eyes. Then her fur coat and hood. Then mittens inside thick sheepskin gloves.

She was ready for the worst; at least she could be no readier. She emerged just as they came back to the Hawk turnoff.

The wind had risen still further. By now its buffetting threatened to overturn the cutter. "We'll never do four miles," she shouted. Her voice, filtered through the scarf, was pitifully inadequate; he could make out nothing she said.

"Turn here!" She pointed south.

In the very last of the daylight the ponies saw the turnoff. To them it represented escape, downwind. They were already inclining that way when the orders came to them via the reins and James's barely audible *hoo-ah!*

She reached over and grabbed the traces, jerking her head back. He understood and went inside to prepare himself for a possible walk.

The light was now so dim she could not be sure whether what her eyes saw was real or phantom. The little remaining illumination was so filtered by the snow it appeared to shine evenly from all directions—above, below, and every quarter. Nothing had mass. The ponies, if, indeed, it was the ponies, were a darker shade of dark in the gathering black. There was no point in trying to steer them. She just had to hope that the track, being more polished than the snowcrust over the prairie on either side, would remain discernible to the pair of them. At least, with the wind behind them, they were making spanking good progress. In a couple of miles they'd come to a section that was fenced; in fact, from there on, the road was fenced all the way to Hawk Ridge—at least on one side.

The danger then would be that the road would drift up and force them to cut or throw down part of the fence and make a detour through the field. Detours were where people got lost. And killed.

James came back just as they reached part of the road where the potholes were bad. The ponies grew nervous that the vehicle would shoot forward and cut their heels; they began to gallop. It took James almost a minute to get them back in hand. During that time Catherine could feel they had left the road and gone out over some unfenced section of the prairie. But to the right or to the left? The difference was vital. To the right, or western, side of the road most of the sections were fenced. If they had to get out and walk, they could follow a fence southward until they struck either the ridge or the railroad cutting. To the east of the road there was a lot of unfenced land still; and even if they found a continuous southward line, there'd be no ridge to aim at—nothing until they reached the C.N.R. track to Goldeneye, which was at least two miles farther than the ridge. In storms like this people had been found dead twenty yards—never mind two miles—short of safety.

She would not have believed it possible for the wind to rise yet further, but it did. It now began to buffet and rock the ungainly cutter in an alarming way. She did not see how it could stay upright much longer. They'd certainly never be able to turn east or west—which is what they would have to do when they reached the first fence.

But where was the first fence? Her memory for maplike things was unbeatable. Even now, five years later, she could see the pattern of the fields between Hawk Ridge and the longitude adjustment, four miles away. But north of that, the part they were now traversing, had on that hot summer's day been lost in the haze. She knew it only from the road; she had learned it not by seeing it all at once but by passing through it, spread out in time— and her memory for sequences was not nearly so good.

Then she remembered the coulee. Somewhere here, near to the adjust-

ment, a coulee meandered. In spring it carried the meltwater off to the
Goldeneye River; now it would just be a snaking depression in the flat landscape, marked by the bare trunks and branches of aspen and dogwood.
Where exactly was it, though? How far north of the adjustment? She just
couldn't remember. But its presence somewhere out there meant it was
foolish to go bowling along at this pace. Even if they didn't tumble over its
edge, they could get hopelessly tangled in the thickets.

She folded the scarf off her mouth and, putting her lips close to James's
hood, shouted. "The coulee! We must stop!"

He understood her at once and began to haul on the reins. At that moment the ponies struck a soft patch of snow, probably over a slough. The
runners sank at the front. The animals, plunging sideways in their search for
firm ground, spun the cutter athwart the wind. The leverage of the wind
did the rest. The whole vehicle lifted up beneath them, poised for a moment
as if it might fall back again, and then bowled over onto its offside corner
as, with a crack that resounded above the storm, the runners splintered and
broke. They were both pitched violently out into the snow.

How long they lay there, dazed, she could not tell; but by the time she
recovered her senses, flames were beginning to consume the cutter. The
charcoal stove had spilled its contents. The ponies, immediately downwind,
and still harnessed to the now unmovable vehicle, were thrashing and neigh-
ing in panic. By the light of the fire she saw that James was risking his life
to cut them free. Plunging hooves and rolling flanks threatened him every
moment.

As soon as they were freed they vanished. It was as if the storm had
simply plucked them up and borne them off. Not a sound would carry back
up that wind.

Where the flames hit the open air they flattened into a guttering roar,
creating little light, and a fitful light at that. No more than three or four
yards around was visible; the rest was a dark gray obscurity of driven snow,
not quite black.

Catherine stood and was bowled over at once. She had thought the
wind strong enough when they were sitting in the cutter. Now she realized
how much they had been sheltered. She rose again and, leaning at what felt
like forty-five degrees into the wind, made her way back to James. He was
rescuing some cord from the blaze. She tapped him on the shoulder. He
turned, saw her, and gave a wildly exaggerated nod of relief. He tried to
shout in her ear but she could make out nothing. Then he held up the cord,
pointed to his medical bag, and patted his chest.

She understood. He wanted to tie the bag around his chest with the cord. She had a better idea. She had wrapped her skirt around her, under her jacket; the belt was still in it. She put her hands inside her fur coat, parked the gloves in her armpits, and, after some struggle, worked the belt free. The fire was raging now, with tongues of flame carrying yards downwind. Quarantine posters were being peeled off, one by one, and carried away, still flaming, into the dark. Of course, the wind and cold would extinguish them in moments but the darkness swallowed them first, so the impression was of fiery rockets, streaking southward.

He saw the belt and nodded with the same degree of exaggeration. Only whole-body movements would communicate anything here. He raised an arm. She passed the belt through the handle of his bag and put it around his neck. Her by now numb fingers could only just get the tongue through the buckle. It needed his strength, too, to tighten it to even the first hole.

He, meanwhile, had made two running loops in the cord. One was already around his waist. He gestured her to step into the other and pull it up around her; out there a single divergent pace would be enough to separate them for good.

Awkwardly he jerked the loop round to behind her, gesturing that she was to walk ahead of him, where he would be able to shelter her, if only slightly, from the full might of the blast. She struggled into her thick gloves and swung her arms, trying to coax the circulation.

Without a backward glance at the cutter, now almost three-quarters consumed, they set off downwind into the dark. And it really was dark. Unthinkingly, because of the whiteness of snow, she had expected some light to persist, however faintly. But it was already as black as blackest night. She closed her fur hood right down over her face; there was no extra darkening.

But it felt wrong. The habit of a lifetime made her shrink back and stretch out her arms as if blindfolded. Her fantasy conjured up such impossible prairie features as trees, rock walls, bluffs, and ravines. She had no choice but to open the hood and peer out into the dark through the slit in her scarf. There was a just perceptible lightening of the world; perhaps it was the same fantasy. No matter. It felt safer to be walking with her eyes peeled.

And peeled was the word for it. The cold whip of the wind made them water. She had to keep squeezing her eyelids tight. In past winters she had felt the bristles in her nostrils freeze up—which was why she was wrapped in the scarf. Now her eyelashes were freezing together, too. She had to close her hood again and let enough warmth build up to melt them; then she'd just have to force herself to blink as little as possible.

Already she felt exhausted. And how far had they come? Two hundred

yards? A quarter-mile? Fifty yards, probably. Was there any point in counting? They did not seem to be in ordinary space or time. What time was it?
Between four and five, she guessed. And would they live? The exhaustion
did not seem like a premonition of death. She ought to pray to God for
deliverance.

But with James there, was that necessary?

That was an odd thought. And a wrong thought. She should ask forgiveness for it. She would. She most certainly would. When she got around
to it.

The cord went slack. James's hands were on her shoulders. "Eee?" he
shouted.

"Say?" she shouted back.

This time she made out: "Feet?"

"Fine!" And it was true. She was surprised at how warm she felt.
Weary, but not frozen. The cold was numbing her mind more than her
body. Her weary legs moved onward mechanically—left foot up, over the
crust, on the crust, through the crust, crunch down, shift weight, rolling like
a grizzly, right foot up, over the crust, on the crust. . . . The snow was too
cold to bind. It crunched and slithered away underfoot like a mixture of
gravel and powder.

She sang into her scarf. *For those in peril on the sea.* Her breath turned
to crystals. The whole world would freeze to crystalline. The crystals of her
breath glued the scarf to the pale, downy hair of her upper lip. To free it
she had to inhale deeply, slowly, and then, just as slowly, let it out into the
frozen wool. She pulled the scarf slightly looser, to prevent its freezing to
her again. How, she wondered, did James manage with his moustache? Perhaps it wouldn't be dangerous if only a moustache froze; after all, it couldn't
get frostbite.

She began to hallucinate bright lights. Did high blood pressure do that?
Or low? James would know. The wind, too, began to sing. Strange
whistlings at first, like an untuned radio; then choirlike noises, rolling loud
and soft, like a remote station. The lights and the choir began to coalesce.
They wove in and out at the edge of her vision and the limits of her hearing.
There was something enticing about them. They seemed to beckon her to
turn aside and follow; but when she moved her head to see them more
clearly they skipped to the new edge of her vision.

Had she turned toward them inadvertently? The wind was suddenly
buffeting her from a new quarter, over her left shoulder. Again the cord
went slack and James was at her side, this time to stop her. His voice was
even less clear, having to struggle out, no doubt, through festoons of frozen

breath on his scarf. But she managed to make out "Compass." There was a compass, and a flashlamp, in his bag.

She slipped off her glove and mitten to open the bag. She located the compass and the flashlamp but, not realizing how quickly her fingers had grown nerveless, she let both fall into the snow.

With a scream of fury she dropped to her knees, took off the other mitten, and began to scrabble wildly in the snow between his feet. He realized what had happened but still did not manage to avoid treading on one of her hands as he bent to help. When she woke up to the fact that she had felt the weight, but not the touch, of his boot, she realized that even if her hands located either of the missing objects, they would be unable to inform her.

"Fool! Fool!" she shouted. She opened her jacket and tucked her hands under her armpits to warm them back to life. The wind almost bowled her over. She sank her head deep between her shoulders and, deep in her fur, tucked herself into its blast. Four times she warmed, froze, warmed, froze her hands in that search. Once she thought she had found the lamp, but it turned into one of James's fingers, so cold it almost burned.

Then, when she was thawing out her hands for the fifth time, a sharp light, blinding in its intensity and certainly no hallucination, stabbed out upon the snow between them. James had found the lamp.

The compass was between her heels. She backed off it and was about to pick it up when he put a hand forward and stayed her. He turned it over, face up. The spirit in which the disk usually floated was frozen.

She grabbed it and thrust it inside her jacket. The cold of it was a torment but five minutes more of walking had thawed out the spirit and the compass was free again. She brought it out, no farther than the cavern of her fur. He had to poke his head inside to read it.

When he straightened, he took the lead. But he must have misread it. The wind was not now at their back. It was coming across from their left— what would be northeast if they were still headed south. What did it matter now which way they went? They'd wander in circles until they dropped. Her body was still cold from the compass; it would never grow warm again.

Again her scarf ice-welded itself to her, but this time she was ready and plucked it away before the join was bigger than a postage stamp. Did skin come away with it? Once the Goldeneye humorists had made poor Mr. Ah Wong lick a frozen tap at fifty-five below; he'd left the skin of his tongue and lips behind. She knew because she had changed his dressings for weeks.

After a plodding eternity they blundered into a fence smack across their

path. That was good news. All the fences ran either north-south or east-west;
so either they were on course or they had gone off by a full ninety degrees.
The compass confirmed it—they were on course. But the wind was now
nearly due east.

She did not realize—though James did—the implication of the change in
wind direction. It meant the storm was not moving away westward but was
enlarging and intensifying. So far they had driven and walked along what
ought to have been (with a north wind) the vanishing edge of a pretty
severe storm. Heaven knows what it had been like near to its centre; and
now Saskatchewan was about to find out, too, as the depression swelled.

They turned westward along the fence, happy for a moment to get the
wind behind them again. They were feeling their way along to the next
southward fence, which they found soon after. But their joy was short-lived
for they then had to turn broadside on to the wind, which was now very
nearly due east. It howled and roared about the opening in front of her face.
Even pulling the fur right down made no difference; the noise was frightening. She could not believe it was made by a mere inanimate force like the
wind. There had to be a spirit behind it, bellowing its glee. And the merest
whisp of it that penetrated through some temporary chink in the fur, as the
gale bowled her against the fence or into James (who now trod the path
down ahead of her), was enough to chill her even through the hood of her
jacket and her scarf.

The ground fell away at one point. Still hugging the fence, they
stumbled into a thicket of aspen. The wind changed the timbre of its shriek
as it whipped the saplings to a frenzy. Here at last was the coulee. It struck
her then that, instead of blundering over the prairie, they might be able to
follow the watercourse down to the river and so to Goldeneye itself. How
could she communicate the idea to James? The cutbanks might give them
some shelter, too. And where there was ice the wind would have scoured it
free of loose snow; the going would be a lot easier.

The objections occurred to her the moment she tugged at the cord: The
coulee could meander miles out of their way—even from this point either
direction, west or east, might be the one to bring them to Goldeneye, which
was southeast on a beeline. Also it could broaden into a wide, shallow
slough at any point, indistinguishable from the prairie all around.

She gave James a push to signal *go on*. He fell. At first she thought she
was the cause—that or a badger or coyote hole. But then she saw the lamp
was flashing. He was flashing it on his face—on and off, swiftly, urgently.
Something was wrong. She went down on all fours beside him to see what
it might be; but even then, if she had not been thinking of it earlier, she

would have missed it. His breath had frozen in his scarf, stuck to his moustache, then to his lips. James was choking to death on his own frozen breath.

She seized the lamp from him and tore open the hood of his jacket. A pencil-sized hole at the left corner of his mouth was all that remained. It could close at any moment.

What should she do? If she tore the scarf from him, she could take away half his lips. Half his lips? Half his *face*. But wouldn't that be better than dying? It was a meaningless question. Nothing would make her mutilate him. Then she knew what to do.

She lay on him, one potato sack on another, and pulled the hood of her fur coat down around them. The coulee banks and the aspen thickets gave some merciful shelter from the gale. She eased the folds of the scarf away from her mouth. Then she inhaled, put her mouth to the one open side, where his lips strained for air, and breathed slowly out. Then in again . . . out . . . in. . . . Her breath was a furnace between them. The scarf began to yield. The ice plate gave to the pressure of her mouth. She was sure she heard the wetness as he sucked it in gratefully.

He tapped her on the back to show he was okay now. She ignored it. He tapped again, thinking she had not felt it the first time. On and on she went, breathing into the scarf, growing dizzy with it. She worked her fingers into the folds of it, cracking the ice that was still thick in his moustache.

When it was all gone, she parted the folds of his scarf and put her lips to his. For the merest fraction of a second James resisted; then she felt his arms go around her. His hand clasped her head to his so that they were one. That hesitation, so brief—in a way so *un*surprised—and the violence of his capitulation was the first hint that he felt anything for her. His lips fell apart and he pulled her fiercely, ravenously, to him as his tongue thrust upward onto hers. It was all she had ever wanted.

Now they could die.

The numbness of her mind stifled surprise. Even the joy of what they were doing was curiously matter-of-fact and expected. It was as if a voice inside her was saying, "But of course! You've been in love with James for years. I'm sorry—I thought you knew."

Renee had known. Renee had seen it at once. Who else? Did Fiona know? There was simply no way of telling. It didn't matter, anyway. They weren't going to survive this storm. The only person who had to know was James. She could not bear him to die without knowing.

"I love you," she shouted into his hood.

She could not make out his reply.

"I've always loved you."

They stood and hugged each other briefly before setting off once more, southward, following the fence down into the shallow coulee and up again into the fury of the gale. It was even worse than before. More than once she felt that the wind had ceased to be made of air and had grown mighty fingers that nudged her with the force of a piledriver. Once they actually were bowled over by something solid—a great ball of Russian thistle, the tumbleweed of the prairie.

Toward midnight, as it seemed to her, they reached the end of the fence—or, rather, they came upon the next east-west fence. She made a cavern for James to check the time. He tried to keep her from seeing but she saw, all right. Six fifteen. It had taken ninety minutes to cover the previous mile. How many to go? She was waiting for the longitude-adjustment line, four miles north of Hawk Ridge. But they'd never make it.

Angrily she derided the thought. She flung her arms around him again. "We've got to live, James! My darling! We've got to live!" she shouted. Her voice was torn away by the blizzard. "We will. We will!" his arms answered.

That fence was not the longitude adjustment, for the north-south fence ran straight on through. Her disappointment was acute. It meant they had at least five miles to Hawk Ridge—even assuming they were to the west of the road. Otherwise they had at least seven miles to reach the C.N.R. tracks. What kept them going when they knew it was so hopeless?

The next mile took another hour: seven fifteen. That fence, too, was not the adjustment. So they still had at least five (or seven) miles to go. By now she was past mere fatigue. Each movement of her legs was—literally— a wonder. They seemed to have lost all their substance; they were not even like hollow tubes, but had faded away through every stage of exhaustion until they were no more than ideas—corporeal memories of what ought to be—phantoms, with nothing to contribute but real pain, real rebellion.

They did not stop to confirm their direction. Both felt that any check in their rhythm of pain would be their last. They climbed through the wire in the beat of four steps and plodded on. Some time later the wind moderated again. Then the temperature rose until (he guessed) it was "only" thirty below. But their relief was short-lived, for the new conditions brought a snowfall they could *feel,* even in the pitch dark, even swaddled as they were.

She would not have believed the going could have become harder— until it did. Now, instead of scouring the thaw-crust clean with its searing sixty-plus, the moderated gale began to pile the snow in their path. Each step became a plea to die, a plea from the body to be *allowed* to die.

Untold hours later they came to the end of the fence. The wind had dropped to a whisper but the snowfall was thick; it had already devoured half the fence. They could not continue. In open ground they could flounder off-line every other step. From here on their compass reading would have to be continuous. Except that there could be no "on" from here. Here was the end of their tether, which was their grasp on life, or on the future.

James huddled to read his watch. She did not care what time it was. "Ten past nine," he said.

They could hear each other speak now.

By the last flicker of his flashlight, as he returned it to his pocket, she saw it catch the barbs of the wire. They ought to mean something, she thought; but she was too exhausted for any sort of meaning to take hold.

This was the end. It did not worry her. She leaned against him. Contact with his body was now the only reality. Fleetingly she wondered where, exactly, they were.

She knew, in fact. That is, she was convinced she knew, if only she could stir herself to think. But the fatal lethargy of the cold was already stealing into her bones. The little shrew in the one last warm cavern of her mind, nagging her to think . . . *think!* . . . was an infernal nuisance. It was bliss to die. To die here . . . wherever it was. *Think!* To die with . . . what was his name? *Think!* With . . . him. This. The thing leaning against her. *Think!*

Everything was getting so light. Not pale. Floating. She was floating. He was floating. They were together. Always. *Think!* They would always be together now. They would haunt this stretch of prairie. *Think!* They would be its familiars.

Then she remembered those barbs. Wickedly long. The special wire Ed's cousin had sent up from Kansas! Ed had used it around the Hawk Ridge homestead that first summer. They were there! They were safe! Hawk Ridge was right above them, to their left.

But how could she have missed the adjustment line? It must have been the very first fence they came to. How could they have reached it without crossing other fences? Drifts? It must be that, unless someone before them had laid the fences flat.

No matter—they were safe. They were less than a hundred yards from the soddy her uncle had built just over the brow of this ridge. This fence, the eastward leg of it, would lead them to its very roof.

"James," she cried. "We're home!"

"Home!" he repeated.

"No. *Home!* Hawk Ridge. My Uncle Murdo's old place. It's just up the hill here."

"Home."

He was talking in his sleep.

"We can shelter there," she said, growing desperate. "Fire! Food!"

The elementals. No struggle could have been more elemental.

"Home," he said.

She turned him to face the hill. "Walk!" she shouted, not knowing if he heard.

She went ahead of him, tugging the cord almost angrily. When he failed to respond the anger became real.

She knew she had no hope of untying herself (for she had a vague idea of going up to the homestead for a shovel and returning to dig a way for him). She had to take him with her.

"James!" She pulled with all her little strength. He stumbled forward. She took a hasty step back, pulled again. Again he stumbled toward her. Another step back—but up the hill, the right direction. Another tug.

He fell.

"James! Oh, darling, please . . . *please!*" She stooped low over him. "Darling!"

He stirred. She took his arm and put it on one of the wires of the fence. With infinite slowness, infinite pain, he hoisted himself up. Her words reached him.

"Darling!" she repeated.

He stood.

"I love you," she said.

She was no longer alive. Not as herself. If he were not there, she would be dead already. She needed him in all ways, in every imaginable way. Simply to exist.

"I love you."

He fell against her.

She stumbled back against the snow, against the hill, but by super-human effort stayed upright. On he came. Back she fell. "I love you." On. Back. On. Back. Forever. "I love you." Forever. On.

Thus they stumbled up the hill, holding that single, central truth of their lives . . . their life . . . somewhere in that lurching space between them.

The full fury of the gale hit them at the hill crest. It felled them. She had not even the strength to clutch her fur coat about her face; how then should she find the strength to rise?

Yet strength she did not know she had managed to find some way into her muscles, goading her up, up, painfully up. The fence wire in her hand shivered with her weakness. As soon as she was up she fell again.

The wind roared. It shrieked its triumph, keened their wake, wove their winding sheet of snow.

Crawl!

She crawled. Her knees began collecting frostbite. *Crawl!* His body (his corpse?) slithered in her track. They were over the crest. The slope was down. *Crawl!* Her knees would not obey.

She rolled onto her back and dug in her heels. *Stand!* Horizontal, she stood. A surface snow-mole. The tug of him was still there. *Stand!* Another six inches.

She was no longer conscious when the fence gave out and she fell into the drift that had piled against the front of the soddy. His body fell after her. Perhaps it woke her, or perhaps it was the new silence. Or the splintering of the door as it fell inward.

Fate was kind at the last. Had they fallen on either side—a mere three feet or so, either way—they would have perished. But they fell from the roof of the abandoned soddy exactly where the snow had piled up an almost intolerable burden against the door, with its rusting hinges and nails. When it gave way, they and the snow fell indoors.

She awoke, dazed and drunk with fatigue, but knowing they had won. Somehow they had cheated that monstrous malevolent storm and, out of the endless prairie, battered their way through to this, the only haven they could possibly have reached.

She fought her fingers into untying the knot about her waist. The soddy was no longer lived in, of course, but it was used for cooking, and for the occasional overnight, when Murdo's half-section was being worked. And Renee and the boys liked to rough it there occasionally, too. So she knew there would be certain very basic amenities—a coal-oil stove, candles, matches, a few cans of food, maybe some forgotten potatoes or rutabagas, some oats for feed and for porridge . . . that sort of thing. She blundered toward the kitchen end of the all-purpose room.

The match found the candle, and the candle found the stove. Gratefully she shrugged out of her fur coat. The loss of it was like a grant of new muscles. She could actually drag herself around the room now instead of merely aiming herself where she wanted to go, and then wondering how she found the strength to get there.

James was lying mighty still. The sudden panic-thought that he was dead brought her hobbling to his side. But he was breathing. He was even smiling a little. Best, then, to leave him so, wrapped up in his fur, until she had some kind of fire going.

She fought the door upright again, first scraping aside the snow, then propping it with a broken lid off a seed drill that happened to be lying on the dirt floor nearby.

Then a discovery. The old Quebec heater was still there, and there was firing beside it. With the help of straw from the potato clamp in the root store, and a little coal oil, she soon had a great blaze going. Each of these return steps to civilization added fresh strength to her. The fire was best of all. She realized then how much of her exhaustion was due to mere cold. In a while she was no longer exhausted beyond endurance; she was merely exhausted.

It was time to get James out of his fur. It must now be colder inside there than it was in the room. She dragged him close to the heater.

She loosened the belt that held his doctor bag to him. Then she pulled off his coat. He stirred but did not waken. She fed more fuel to the heater; at least there was no shortage of that. She found some coffee, only a couple of months old, neither aromatic nor rancid—a neutral coffee, halfway to being undrinkable.

She smiled at the judgement, which came from another universe where there was warmth, and shelter, and money, and such things as supply merchants. Undrinkable? If it were ten years old, it would be nectar here, as long as it was hot.

While she waited for the snow to melt and boil in the pan, she turned out his bag. There was the water of life, *uisce beadha,* a leather-sewn hip-flask of whisky. She took a sip and let it burn her. Then a good swig.

She loved James. She always had. Too late to deny it now. She looked down at him and smiled. The cherub-boy who stared truculently out of the sepia-tinted groups in the family album was there still, etched now in gold and black by the roaring firelight.

It was wrong. He was married. Nothing could ever come of it. Nothing good, anyway. She read in the magazines of Jezebels who fastened on married men; how she hated them, those homewreckers. But Fiona asked for it, the way she treated him. Still—that didn't make it right.

The water boiled. She tipped in the coffee grains and took the pan off the heat. Never mind how old the stuff might be, its aroma was marvellous— everything that coffee had ever promised. James caught the whiff of it in his sleep and stirred. She sat beside him on the rug, leaned over, and kissed him, gently.

His eyelids flickered and fell open. She withdrew, wanting to see his whole face. There was something new about it, a boyish hesitancy. He sat up, slowly, groaning at the pain of it. He made it onto one elbow and blinked his gaze around the room. He looked at the fire, at the coffee, at her, and smiled, still only half believing—half *daring* to believe.

"I missed something," he croaked. He cleared his throat. "Who found us?"

"No one."

"You?" His tone said *surely not!*

She bent again and kissed him.

He relaxed. "Aye!" He chuckled. "I remember that."

"Tell me it's wrong, James. Say we mustn't. It's not too late."

He stared at the fire a long time. "I think it was too late the day you came." Suddenly he gave a yelp of pain.

"What?" she asked.

"Frostbite. My feet. Get some snow. Quick! In a bowl."

The snow that had fallen indoors with them had not melted. She scooped the bowl full and carried it to him. He, meanwhile, had struggled up onto a chair and was trying to get off his boots, which were leather with sheepskin linings. She knelt in front of him and had them off in no time, and his woollen stockings.

The relief of the cold snow on his raw-red, burning feet was immediate. When he was settled more comfortably she poured out the coffee. She held his to him in her left hand with the hipflask in her right, ready to pour. Her eyes put the question.

He chuckled. "Need you ask?"

She poured a good tot in her own as well. "It tastes different from Ed's," she remarked.

"His is Canadian muck, made from rye. It was bad enough before Prohibition, but now that the Americans'll drink anything, it's got ten times worse. It's 'whiskey' with an *e*. But *that!*" He took the flask from her and tipped a dram more into his cup. "Aye, this. This is malt. Whisky with a *whee!*" He held it forth. "Another taste yourself now?"

She held out her cup but did not take her eyes off his. "If it promises life, my darling . . ." she said. She did not want ordinary conversation.

When his feet had slow-thawed enough, she dried them on a sack and helped him back into his socks.

The bedrooms were empty except for a horse blanket, an ancient military overcoat of the kind known as British Warm, and two fur rugs. She brought them back to the other room, near the heater, which he had stoked again.

He put one rug on the floor; he picked the other one up uncertainly. There was space for it on the far side of the heater. His eyes questioned her.

She put her head on one side and smiled fondly. He gave the faintest shrug and spread it over the first. He climbed in between them. She spread the rugs over the top, the horse blanket to cover their feet, and rolled the

British Warm beneath the lower fur to make a pillow. All she took off were the overshoes and her boots.

She climbed in beside him, blew out the candle, and crept into his arms. It could only have been seconds before they were deep asleep.

She woke late the following morning and slipped quietly from the bed without waking him. Her muscles were in agony but exercise was their anaesthetic. She built up the heater and put some water on to boil. He did not wake until she took down the door and began to shovel the snow; she put the first lot indoors until she had made a dugway big enough to throw it out. The storm was still blowing.

"Here, I'll do that," he called and, groaning and wheezing, rolled out of bed and pulled on his boots.

"I'm pretty desperate," she said.

He looked at her in surprise. "Use the bowl."

She took it into the bedroom.

When they were eating their breakfast he said, "You're like Fiona. The thing is called 'washing-up bowl' so that fixes it in some compartment of the mind where it could not even be considered as a chamberpot. Once I fell asleep in the drawing room. She woke me up. Told me it wasn't a room for sleeping in. Wrong name, you see."

Catherine smiled; it sounded very like Fiona.

It was a good breakfast. She had found a pail of water-glazed eggs in the root store, along with biscuits, salt butter, cheese, several cans of English marmalade, other canned vegetables, and a ham. Ed liked to come over here and ski in the longer days of February and March; he obviously didn't starve himself. A spare pair of skis was behind the bedroom door, tied together, sprung over wood blocks. Two smaller pairs were beside them, for the boys.

"It's a strange thing about skis," James said. He pronounced it *"shes,"* which was then the way. "They're such an obvious mode of getting around, yet they've never caught on. Charlie Nilsson thinks we're insane."

"He and Ed are the only two you ever see on skis."

"Did you know it was a Hamilton who brought them to Canada? Only about forty years ago. Lord Frederic Hamilton. He brought the first pair. From Russia."

"Were you here then?"

He looked at her, shocked, and then laughed. "What did you do in the Flood, eh, granddad!"

She reached over and squeezed his arm. "I didn't mean that."

She was going to remove her hand but he covered it with his own and held it there. She shivered. "No," he said. "Of course you didn't. I was a boy in Edinburgh, then."

"Why did you come to Canada, James? I never asked."

"I bought a good practice in Aberdeen, when I qualified. Aberdeen in Scotland, I mean. I hadn't a notion of leaving. But Fiona was a Henderson. They're Campbells, you know, the Hendersons. And half my patients were Macdonalds."

Catherine drew a sharp breath.

"There you are, you see," he said. "You understand it at once. But innocent me! I didn't know such passions, such hatred, could still possess civilized people. Fiona warned against it." He chuckled. "But then she's always warning against *something*. The danger with being a Cassandra all the time is that people will ignore you even when you're right."

"Like we ignored her yesterday. Was it only yesterday!"

"Aye." He nodded ruefully. "It becomes a habit."

"How do habits start, James? Are we starting one?"

"I suppose we are."

"Just like that?"

"Tell me you won't," he challenged.

"No. You tell me."

His grin recruited hers.

"Just like that," he said.

But she persisted. "It can't be so easy. It doesn't feel right."

"Ah hah hah!" He laughed mirthlessly. "You Calvinists! How can God be so sure that mankind is wicked and sinful, eh? He *cheated!* He wrote the formula first." Then he took her hand, to force her attention. "Have no fear. It will end as easily."

She fell to her knees at his side and hugged him. "It will never end. I love you, and I always will."

"It will end just as easily."

"I don't know how I never saw it until yesterday."

"Did you not? I thought you always knew. D'you mean to tell me I've been admiring your self-control all these years for nothing!"

"Don't talk like that, James."

"Like what?"

"Supercilious." She had never used the word before. She tensed herself against his possible laughter. When it did not materialize, she went on, "I must be completely honest with you."

He stood and backed away from her. "Please!" His horror was a melodramatic parody. "Not honesty! Parents should never pray for an intelligent child. And lovers should never seek to engage in honesty."

He had used the word: *lovers!* It outweighed all his flippancy—which, she saw plainly, was just a disguise for his inability to cope with this new situation. The word was enough for her: *lovers.*

"You realize," he said, sitting again, "that while the storm lasts, no one will be looking for us. Fiona will assume we are at Jeremiah's. Jeremiah will assume we are in Micah. Ed will assume we got home."

"Ed will call Fiona to check," she said.

"She'll say we stayed at Jeremiah's. And he has no phone. No one can venture out in this, anyway."

"The ponies. Someone will see them. Then they'll know." She turned to him, wanting to salvage at least one tender or solemn moment. "We are already on borrowed time."

But he grinned at her portentousness. "We always will be," he said. "But don't worry. There may be years of it to borrow."

She smiled back, not really caring which of them prevailed in that sort of sparring bout. Then she began to undress.

14

Fiona knew. Catherine could tell. For a while she suspected it was her own guilt; but in the end she was certain Fiona knew. She behaved no differently to Catherine. She was as pleasant and confiding as ever. It was almost as if she were saying she did not especially value what Catherine was stealing— and, in any case, no two women of sense could possibly fall out over anything so trivial. James was only a *man!*

"Of course she knows," James said. "She's always known."

"Always suspected, you mean."

"No. *Known.* Just as she knows Helen's marriage won't last. Just as she knows Burgo won't work hard enough and will fail his finals. Just as she knows Margaret will come to a bad end. Just as she knows I have a hole in this sock, and even if I show her"—he slipped off his shoe and revealed: no hole—"she'll say, 'Well, you soon will have. I never knew a man go through socks quicker than you.' So that's how she's always known about us."

"But how awful to be like that," Catherine said. It was the first time she had thought that way about Fiona, who was usually much too positive in her opinions and too convinced of their rightness to evoke pity. "She's against herself all the time."

"You know very little about women!"

"Why?"

"Women don't sit down and work out what's in their own best interests and then go forth and do it. The formula"—he pointed at God above—"doesn't permit it. They do whatever makes them *feel* right. Whatever gives them that feeling of rightness and goodness. And what gives Fiona that feeling is proof of her own superiority. When she peeps in another woman's storecupboard and says to herself *How can she tolerate such disorder!* When she predicts disasters to show she's a step ahead of God— oho, He can't put one over her! When I exceed my quota of marital rights and she says, 'I wish you'd get a mistress.' When she says, 'No thanks, I only drink at Christmas.' All these things add to her feeling of superiority. *Her* universe is tidy. She's no foolish optimist about the future. She needs no alcohol or sensual titillation like other poor mortals. Once I withheld myself from her a month. A whole month! I heard her weeping in the bed beside me, but she would not ask—not even . . ." He reached forward one finger and stroked her forearm lightly, once. She shivered. "Not even that. It would be to confess a kind of dependence. And dependence is death to her. Superior, above it all, untouched by human frailty, immaculate. Those are the things that make Fiona *feel* good and right. And because she is a woman, she will pursue them to the death, in the very teeth of her own true happiness and real self-interest."

She knew very well he wasn't talking only of Fiona, but of her, too. All the things she was now doing—becoming James's lover, ignoring proposals from good and eligible men, running hard into this sterile, childless, marriageless dead end of love—these were precisely against "her own true happiness and real self-interest." Yet they felt so right—to love him and be loved by him, to make love together—that nothing would prevent her from behaving as she was.

This time she did not worry for her soul. She accounted it already damned. It was damned at birth with the curse that had driven Adam and Eve from paradise. The curse was renewed when her mother died and her father had begun to lust for her (she could face the truth of that now); and again when Huey's kiss had so fired her; and again and yet again with Ed; and a hundred times again, in the four solo years since Ed; and now she was damned once more with James. Her soul was so chipped with little deaths she had no hope of its weight in the final balance. What worried her this time was Burgo.

If she had been the sort of person who considered each action first, she would not even then have thought of Burgo. In all the four years—nearly five now—that she had lived at Doctor's House he had been, for her, the least important member of the family. Everyone in the Goldeneye community had at some time linked her and him romantically. But they had first grown to know each other in the long vacation at the end of his freshman year—or the ten days of it he had condescended to spend at home. That was in the time when the sense of her own corruption and unworthiness still heaped her. And he faced years of gruelling study. So from every point of view there was no possibility of romance between them. In any case, he had been promised almost from childhood to the lawyer's daughter, Mina Jeffcott; she was the one he took to dances and other festivities.

None of this had stood in the way of friendship, however. Over the years Catherine and Burgo had become almost brother and sister to each other, sharing their hopes and ambitions, their feelings and thoughts, and those confidences that teeter on the edge of sexual revelation—things that neither strangers nor intending lovers could possibly impart. In this way they had also come to share an odd sort of rapport. So now she was afraid that, within a very few days of returning home for Hogmanay (the Scot's New Year), Burgo would divine exactly what was going on between her and his father.

Even if Burgo didn't, Meg would. She was just completing her first term as a student of fashion and textile design at the Endowed Polytechnical College in the smoky heart of Selkirk on Lake Ontario. Burgo was at the MacNair Medical School on a hill to the west of the town. They shared a small apartment in Dunedin, once a rival to Selkirk, now that city's swellest suburb. Meg had grown up smart and knowing.

Catherine's spirit was absurdly elevated when, at lunch one day, Fiona said, "It'll just be the three of us at Christmas and Hogmanay this year."

She ought to have known Fiona better.

"Oh?" James said. "Have you had a letter?"

"No. But we can hardly expect the young folk to come back to us, to this nothing place beyond the edge of nowhere, year after year."

"Ah." He saw that she was flying the usual fustian kite. "You think Margaret will have discovered the fleshpots of Selkirk and will have led Burgo astray? Their shame will not face us, is that it?"

"You may mock, dear." Fiona was as unshakeably confident as if she really had had a regretful letter from Burgo or Margaret. "But if you're counting on their coming, well, I just hope you won't be disappointed. That's all."

They came, even Helen and Arthur and their three children, all the way from California. No one had expected them. Nor did anyone expect Burgo and Margaret to come by car—it was madness, an appalling risk (as James and Catherine could have told them). Everyone laid up their cars even before the first snow. But there it was, his own used Model T—very used. He and Meg had come by train as far as Saskatoon, where one of Burgo's lecturers, P. J. Hanafy, lived; Burgo had bought the car from him, intending to leave it on blocks until the summer. But then he had looked at the cloudless sky, called several weather forecasting centres, and decided he could do the trip in two or three hours without any risk. So they had climbed into all the furs they could scrounge and set off. It took only six and a half hours.

"We used two boxes of petrol patches," Margaret said. "I can fix a flat in ninety-four seconds—that's my best."

"And then it takes two hours to wash your clothes." Fiona gave her a token hug at an aseptic arm's length. "Look at you. I don't think even your father could get that dirty." As an afterthought she added, "And don't say flat, say puncture."

Burgo grinned his lopsided grin, which pushed his top lip out on the right like the peak of a military cap. He had curly dark-brown hair and a face that was too full of character to be called merely handsome. But interesting, Catherine thought. Even fascinating.

"Apart from that, Mom," he said, "did you *miss* her this term?"

Fiona, whose scolding was a mask for her joy at seeing them again, said, "Well, of course I did," in the same cross tone.

"Waal, gol' durn it!" Burgo parodied a toothless old-timer. "I guessh I jesh losh ma bet." He passed a cent to Margaret.

"A penny!" Fiona mimed chagrin.

He put an arm around to comfort her. "That's the trouble with you, Ma—you're not predictable enough for anyone to lay out good odds."

She pushed him away and, grinning furiously, led the party back indoors, where they met James, who had been seeing a "customer," as he called his patients. "Ah," she said. "Your father's woken up at last!"

Even Fiona joined in the laughter that followed this comment; it was a kind of gladness among them all that home was still the same.

No one asked Burgo where he'd got the money for the car. He wouldn't have given a straight answer anyway. Burgo always seemed to have money; not to be rich—he never did anything extravagant and was, in fact, somewhat abstemious in his tastes—but whenever a little spending was necessary, Burgo got by.

He worked most vacations—logging in Banff, digging new sewers in

Toronto, washing corpses in the Winnipeg city morgue . . . all kinds of hard, dangerous, or distasteful (and therefore well-paid) work. James, out of pride, had paid his tuition; Burgo had found the rest, also out of pride.

"Dad, I'm going to steal Cath for a half hour. Help me unpack, oke?" Margaret asked.

Burgo laughed. "Help? A newborn babe would be too strong to lift most of your clothes." He turned to his mother. "You should see them."

"I think perhaps I should."

"Anyway," Burgo went on, assuming a natural priority, "I want Cathy to show me the hospital."

"Which is where I should be now," Catherine said. "I'm not relieved until six." She was sure they could read her guilt—or soon would. She just wanted to get away.

"Oh, good," Margaret said, as eager for Catherine to see her new clothes as she was to prevent her mother from seeing them yet awhile. "I'll come too."

"One more and you'll outnumber the patients," James said.

Catherine finally got to see Margaret's clothes that evening. Burgo hadn't been exaggerating—they were mere whisps of things, mostly in art silk and crêpe-de-chine.

"Aren't I beautifully skeletal?" Margaret said. "I've *starved* myself to afford these. Look at this." She slipped it on.

It was a tube of green froth—Catherine could think of no closer description. Two shoulder straps, thin as laces, held its top just above her nipples—needlessly, since the dress they supported left nothing to the imagination. The froth finished just where her thighs began; beneath its edge peeped a brief cascade of autumn leaves in art-silk shades that not even the most gorgeous Canadian fall could match—violets, purples, magentas, and what Margaret called, apparently with approval, "the sickest, sickest greens!" The leaves reached only halfway to her knees.

"How much did it cost, Margaret?" Catherine asked.

"Practically nothing. I designed it myself, of course. Isn't it divine?"

She fished out another dress. "Here, you can wear this. You're almost skinny enough."

"No!" Catherine was appalled.

"Go on, don't be such a rabbit."

"I couldn't, Meg. Honestly."

Margaret held the dress against her, standing to one side so Catherine could see herself in the mirror. It wasn't so bad. Well—it *was* bad. It was dreadful. But not nearly so bad as Margaret's.

"Shall I?"

Margaret shrugged, "Only if you want to," she said cunningly. "Everyone ought to try anything once—just to see what it's like. How will you ever know who you are if you keep saying no to anything new?"

"Well . . . just for a moment." Catherine was now actually quite eager to see herself in one of the wicked dresses everyone was talking about. "And only if you lock the door." It struck her then as odd that she, convinced of her own sinfulness, had never wondered what she might look like if her outer garments frankly matched her inward state.

Margaret obliged. "Get out of that dreadful old frock," she said.

It was, in fact, Catherine's newest and proudest purchase: a sensible, below-the-knee dress which she had reseamed to drape, she thought, quite nicely. The frills just above the elbow were very fetching. She had bought it especially for this Christmas. The dress Margaret offered was, by contrast, a shapeless tube of black velvet (imitation, too) that exploded in a confusion of vermilion-red organdie, well above the knee.

Reluctantly, despite the locked door, Catherine took off her dress and stood, feeling foolish, in her camisole, knickers, and corselette.

Margaret howled with laughter at the sight. "Jasper! Do they still make those things!"

That annoyed Catherine. "Don't talk like that. You were wearing them yourself only six months ago."

"I know! Wasn't I a hoot! Come on—you can't wear this over those." She rummaged in her suitcase. "Here." She produced an elegant pair of crêpe-de-chine knickers with elasticated frills to reach halfway down Catherine's thighs. "That'll cover those awful garters."

"Suspenders," Catherine corrected.

"You get more like Fiona all the time. Garters . . . suspenders—either way they're awful."

Catherine changed knickers and then took off her camisole. Margaret put her head on one side and looked at her critically. "You're a bit of a dairymaid, aren't you! Hunch your shoulders forward and sink your chest right in. Put the dress on first."

Catherine obeyed. Her excitement began to return. But the sight of herself in the mirror was a shock. She had never actually seen a whore, nor (if there was any difference) a harlot, but what stared back at her from the looking glass was every inch her idea of one. She was about to whip the costume off again when Margaret came up behind and slipped three or four glass-bead necklaces around her neck—long ones that hung down several feet, black, amber, and scarlet—and put an eighteen-inch cigarette holder in her hand.

Catherine now looked (to her own way of thinking) such a caricature that she no longer frightened herself. She even gave a deliberately provocative sway to her hips, planting her free hand on one of them and bending the elbow forward. She shrieked with laughter at the effect.

"That's *it!*" Margaret joined in. "Now you're cooking with gas!" She grew thoughtful again—no one could switch moods quicker than Margaret. "But the details are wrong. Your hands are simply too Lord Lister and your hair went out with Maid Marian." She rummaged again. "This isn't exactly à la mode but we'll just invent a new fashion. I'm always doing that. My work is actually very much in demand, you know. Anton Neff came all the way from Montreal to see some of the things I've done. He's offered me a place anytime I want to leave. But I think I'm too immature yet. Anyway, I don't know that I'll take it. They say he pays awful low. I might do a lot better in New York or Paris. . . ."

She gabbled on while she helped Catherine into arm-length gloves of the same scarlet as the organdie. "Wouldn't a dinky little Cartier watch look *ravissant* just there!" And she scooped all Catherine's pale hair up into a black chiffon bandanna, which she bound very tight, hugging to Catherine's skull. "It just needs an orchid there." She touched her temple. "Did any man ever buy you an orchid, Cath? It's divine, I tell you. This'll have to do instead." With deft fingers she tucked in a smaller piece of red chiffon. She really was inventive, with a flair for getting an effect just right.

Catherine looked at the transformation of herself with a mixture of wonder and horror. She would never have imagined that the sensible Canadian nurse she saw daily in her mirror—in whom a great measure of Scots peasant lass survived—could so swiftly transform into this exciting, flighty, repellent, fascinating creature.

Even Margaret was a little taken aback. "Say, you ain't a bad looker," she told her. "Mebbe a bit honky-tonky with them boobles, but you can bind in a bit. Lemme paint your lips."

"No!" Catherine almost screamed. But even as she refused, she felt herself preparing to agree. Now she'd started this thing she knew she had to go all the way.

"Hold your damn tongue still!" Margaret swore as she worked.

"Sorry."

"You keep licking it onto your real lips—which I'm doing my best to lose. This is a work of art, you know, turning Perils of Pauline into Theda Bara." She sighed. "Virginity is so hard to lose."

Catherine looked at her askance and then burst into laughter.

"I mean," Margaret added crossly, "it's hard to *disguise.*" She was annoyed at having made such an unintentional joke. She stood back and admired her own handiwork even more intensely than she would otherwise have done. Then, suddenly devaluing it all, she became cool and business-like, throwing the lipstick casually onto her dressing table. "What the hell!" she sneered. "It's ghastly, isn't it? But men like us that way, so who are we to complain."

Catherine was fooled for a moment. She even began to think of cheer-ups. She was actually about to say, "Oh, no, Meg, I think it looks beautiful," when she caught Margaret's impish smile. Then she pulled back her hand to offer a punch.

Margaret skipped out of reach. "Come on," she said, excited again. "Do the Charleston. Like this."

Catherine, drunk now with novelty, picked it up much quicker than her inhibitions of half an hour back would ever have permitted. Margaret was a whole, breathless jazz band, booping and diddying the tune as she flashed her fingers, shoulders, eyes, and feet.

Wilder and wilder they danced. More and more frenzied grew their laughter. Catherine had never known such fun. Even the sound of some-one trying to open the door didn't slow them—after all, it was safely locked.

The door burst open and Fiona nearly fell into the room. Margaret, in her haste, had only half-shot the bolt.

The look of scandalized horror on Fiona's face was something both young women would remember for years. Margaret, always deeply under her mother's influence (and never more so than when she acted in open re-bellion against it), was starkly terrified. Catherine was simply more em-barrassed than she had ever felt before. So she kept her eyes on Fiona, which Margaret could not bear to do. Margaret therefore missed an inter-esting split-second drama in her mother's eyes. Catherine did not.

For half that fleeting instant Fiona intended to explode. The way she drew herself up, squared her shoulders, prepared to breathe in, all threatened an eruption of titanic size. But then something else must have occurred to her. Perhaps Margaret's terror or Catherine's discomfiture made her see things in a different way. At all events the pugnacity went out of her, to be replaced by a broad smile.

"Fancy dress!" she cried. "You clever things! You've done it so well! Come down and show everyone. They'll die!"

The two women had no choice then, reluctant though they were to follow.

Fiona, striding ahead, laughed in preparation. "I nearly had a fit! I thought you were serious." She turned round and narrowed her eyes at Margaret. "If it had been only you, young madam, I'd have thrown that fit. But Cathy! I didn't *know* you. Wait till the others see."

James was with a late customer but the others—Burgo, Helen, Arthur, and the children, Wendell, Eva, and Cameron—were all there. Burgo was playing Beggar My Neighbour with the young ones; their parents were skipping through back numbers of *McCall's,* borrowed from the waiting room. The children, seeing only two women in funny clothes, responded with amused surprise; they looked to the grownups to see how to take it from there. For a moment Burgo, Helen, and Arthur were as shocked as Fiona had been. Catherine knew it was a horrible mistake to have come down; she felt almost naked, and certainly cold. The below-the-waist opening at the back with its heart-shaped outline was a dreadful exposure— as if a monster flatiron had been left out in the snow and, when really chilled, pressed against her. She felt her flesh crawl with embarrassment and goose-pimples.

But the moment passed. Fiona's unusual gaiety infected the others; they saw then how they were expected to take it. Burgo gave a whoop of delight and sprang to the victrola, which he wound vigorously, already dee-dahing the rhythms of the Charleston.

"Margaret!" Helen laughed and turned to Arthur. "That girl—wouldn't you know it! And *you,* Catherine, of all people . . ."

"Where's your father?" Fiona asked. "He ought to see this."

The music began. Margaret dashed to her brother but he made straight for Catherine. "Let's cut this rug, sugar," he said.

Margaret turned at once to Arthur. "You own that spot?" she shouted, holding out her arms to him, all angles and straight lines, like a fashion plate. Bemused, but warming to it, he wove a path around the furniture and joined her.

The men, the music, the laughter of the children, Fiona's rare applause, all helped relax Catherine. The steps she had just mimicked upstairs with Margaret began to come back to her, helped now by Burgo, who proved just as expert.

But there was a difference. She and Margaret had danced together to encourage each other, to work up a bit of make-believe fun—in a way, just to enjoy the muscular violence of the rhythm and movement. With Burgo there was all that and something more. He could not take his eyes off her. They gleamed. They stared at her dancing feet, her flashing knees, her shimmying hips, her jellyfish breasts, her face . . . her eyes. Mostly it was her eyes.

Burgo had never looked at her in that way before—well, only fleetingly, automatically, the way most men did. Without thought. But this was different. Not automatic. Not unthinking. She could not help responding to it.

Also, Catherine suddenly realized, the costume was the perfect mask for her guilt—or, to be precise, for her fear that *he* would sense her guilt and guess its cause. The best place to hide a pebble is on the beach. Even the flirtation that was now obviously going on between her and Burgo—that was not *really* her, but the abandoned creature she was parodying in this ridiculous costume.

"I didn't know you could dance," Margaret shouted across to her brother in jerky, breathless fragments.

He was not so energetic and answered more evenly. "My interest in the art is anatomical."

Catherine, noticing where his eyes were as he spoke the words, grinned triumphantly. Then she blushed.

Burgo saw it but refused to share the embarrassment. He was so rarely embarrassed. "To be precise, my interest is arthrological." He mimed a sore back. "And if this gets any more hectic, it will be decidedly arthrodyniac and might even progress to being arthrolytic."

Margaret laughed. "We have to believe you, Burgo, dear."

Catherine was doubly excited now—by her own frenzied movement and by Burgo's eyes. Burgo! So sensible, so brotherly, such a man of the world—he could be chained like this to *her!* She could own his longing. She could provoke it, feed it, fan it. She could deny it to him. Or she could satisfy it. She knew such things now, how they showed themselves, how they worked. They didn't frighten her so much anymore. She didn't want to run away. Now, when she was excited like this, they didn't frighten her at all. Inside herself she felt a great relaxing.

The children caught the spirit of fun and joined in—not the Charleston but a wild, general-purpose dance that would do for Indians, cannibals, or Zulus. Eva, more conformist than her brothers, managed to work in the loose-ankle shake and the just-drying-my-nails movement of her hands. The boys wagged their heads violently and giggled as their eyes vanished upward into their sockets.

When Burgo rewound the machine and turned the record over, Margaret suggested a change of partners. He didn't even hear her (as it appeared), but returned straight to Catherine. She was exultant. Helen took up with Fiona and then the whole room was full of dancing, bouncing people, all laughing, all having fun.

In the middle of it Catherine's eyes swept past the door and zoomed back to fix on James, staring at her in horror. She froze. Burgo slowed down, looked over his shoulder, saw his father, and then carried on.

But the spirit had gone out of Catherine. James's look was so hurt, his face so filled with his sense of betrayal, that it recast everything she had done in a new light. The unspoken reproach she saw in his eyes became her own.

Burgo stopped again. Curiosity was now uppermost in his eyes. He looked questioningly at Catherine and then at his father. Then back to her, thoughtfully. She knew then that he had guessed. But that was absurd. Impossible. She wanted to vanish. To run away.

Everyone stopped, even before the needle ran—*shaa, shaa, shaa . . .*—into the playoff groove. Margaret, breathless, excited still, shouted, "Oh, Dad—you . . . *poop!*" She did not control it well enough to show she was belligerently joking; only the belligerence came through.

James rounded on Margaret, whom he had barely noticed until now.

Catherine turned to Fiona, the only possible saviour of this situation. Surely Fiona would step in with the same laughing cajolery she had used earlier to get the others to see the joke. But Fiona was silent. She smiled at Catherine, a strange smile of feline contentment, and turned expectantly to James.

"Your impertinence only compounds your stupidity," James said to Margaret.

But she was just one term too old to be talked at in that way. "Oh," she answered. Her nostrils always flared like a horse's when she was riled. "You think I can't say a lot worse than that?" she challenged. "You think I can't tell the *truth.*" Of course, Margaret knew nothing of what was going on between her father and Catherine; but she know how to fetch down a vaguely cosmic threat—and this time she had accidentally picked one that reached bone.

Catherine knew why James hesitated that fatal second. She knew why Fiona was the only one to laugh. She knew why she herself now stepped swiftly across the room—never more painfully aware of being what Margaret called a "dairymaid," but never more angrily cold within.

She gripped Margaret's arm, far harder than she would have gripped any other person. One had to. "Come on, Meg honey," she said calmly. "It's too cold for us to be dressed like this."

Margaret almost dug her heels in, but then gave way. Side by side they swept from the room to a chorus of disappointed *aaaaaws* from the children. Catherine did not look at James as they passed him.

"Tomorrow," Margaret said matter-of-factly while they went upstairs, "I'll fake a cable calling him to Loon Lake, or somewhere he'll have to stop overnight." She giggled but it triggered her fury at once. "God, I'd like to drive a grain truck over some people. I wouldn't bother tipping it either."

"Hey, easy!" Catherine said, as she would soothe a pony. "Hoa back! It's nothing."

Margaret now affected an aloof curiosity. "The funny thing is you'd expect Fiona to be the one to get mad. James is the easygoing sort."

"Why have you started calling them Fiona and James?"

They went back into Margaret's room; Catherine checked that the door was securely bolted.

"I'm trying to rearrange my attitudes toward them."

"That still doesn't say why."

As Margaret lifted her dress up over her head Catherine saw, by the light in her eyes, that she took this as a challenge. When her head emerged from under the leaves of "sickest, sickest green," she sighed nonchalantly and said, "When a shy, young country girl from a backwater like this blossoms into womanhood and the big city, it's a dangerous time, you know. If she limps along on the crutches we label 'father' and 'mother,' it's apt to give her . . ." She tired of the pose and fell into grumpy silence. She threw down her cigarette holder; she picked up a lipstick and threw that down, too, even more crossly. "If you want to know, Cath, it's apt to give her a pain in the ass. God, I hate my father. I *hate* him. Why can't he . . ." She couldn't finish.

Catherine had forgotten the compelling—even attractive—violence of Margaret's moods. She had also forgotten how to cope with them. You had to be quick. Fortunately Margaret cured this one herself. Her last outburst made her think a moment; then she added solemnly, "Or—as Fiona and you would prefer me to say—it gives me a pain in the arse."

Catherine, who would prefer no such thing, was shocked into laughing. Margaret joined her, but it was the sort of laughter that could so easily tip back into anger. She was right on that pivot.

"D'you know what I'm going to do?" Catherine said, to distract her. "I'm going back down there and I'm going to be charming to everyone. *Everyone.*"

She meant it was everyone's Christmas, especially the children's, and she wasn't going to be the one to spoil it. Margaret understood her to mean it would be a splendid way to score off James. "Yes," she gloated. "That's exactly what we'll do. There's something to be said for that peasant cunning of yours. Take that lipstick off, you look awful."

"It *is* off," Catherine protested.

Margaret laughed; Catherine had fallen for it.

Margaret babbled on. "I suppose it's really only because James loves me so much. He couldn't bear to see me in that cheap, tawdry rubbish. Did you notice that? Bet you didn't. He couldn't even look at me. That's why he looked at you instead. Or didn't you notice that, either? It's what Freud calls re—something. Re—re—?"

"Rejection?" Catherine suggested.

"Transference! I knew it began with an *r*. Or *almost*. Yes. He couldn't bear to see me so cheap-looking, so he transferred it to you. But I could see the disappointment in him. You wouldn't have seen it, of course. But I did. It was so moving."

Catherine had to look away, pretending she was checking herself in the other, longer glass. Margaret, with her silly dramatization of something that wasn't even true, or was the truth stood on its head, had exposed the nerve.

Later that night, alone again, she faced her own inquisition.

Helen had her old room back. Catherine had moved over to the cottage hospital, to the room she used when she was on duty.

She closed the back door and turned to face the cold, pure, snow-drifted world. There was a magnificent aurora, a great horseshoe of glowing drapery.

"We're safe awhile," James used to joke. "God has drawn a veil on His creation. And rightly so!"

What had happened tonight? She did not want to know. She wanted oblivion. She did her silent rounds. Only three patients were left. Mary Nairn, who had lost another baby, due home tomorrow, fast asleep. Young Frank Dale, who had lost half his left hand in an Indian-corn kibbler, fast asleep. And Old Fram—Widow Laframboise—who had lost her husband, a Métis, and had come back to her own white folks to die, fast asleep.

And what must I lose as the price of my sleep? Catherine wondered.

She turned up the steam radiator in her room and went down the corridor to run a bath as hot as she could stand. A trick to cheat insomnia. She did not want to think tonight. Had she forfeited James forever? There had been a moment, while they were all hanging up paper chains and coloured lanterns, when she found herself near him and everyone else out of earshot.

"Don't you ever do that again!" he hissed.

"You don't own me," she had stammered around the tacks in her mouth.

Such truths! The whole wonderful richness of him-and-her reduced to cable-ese, by anger, by time. He owned her respect, didn't he? He owned her will to please. He owned every longing of which she was capable. He owned her happiness. And if he did not own her body, he owned the giving of it. So what was the "me" she so angrily told him he did not own?

Her skin was all strawberry patches when she stepped from the bath— as it had been once when, in fascination, she had looked at her body in the mirror just before she douched the way James had taught her.

She wanted him so much. *Now.* Here. There was such safety in the assurance of her wickedness.

Her room was hot. She drew open the curtain, intending to let in some of the cold night. Automatically her eyes sought through the bare branches of the trees, coming to rest on his window. It was lighted still. For an instant Fiona stood silhouetted there; her silhouette reached up and drew the curtains closed with a flourish.

A message in mime—like a Christmas game? Had Fiona been standing there, waiting to see Catherine, waiting to make that gesture? Or had it been sheer chance?

And what about Burgo?

She had never been drunk. But she thought her confusion now must be very like drunkenness. There was a sense in her that something big had happened tonight. Something had changed permanently. To do with Burgo. He had always been outside that unseen network of loyalties, emotions, and memories that cocooned her and James; but now he was inside it. The shape was triangular.

She ought to be able to think about a change as important as that. Did she welcome it? Ought she to stop it? Push Burgo back outside? But her mind kept veering off it. Her heart raced; the beat of it made an uncomfortable flutter in her throat. What about Burgo? She could not concentrate. Instead her innards yearned for James.

Fresh from her bath, she could smell herself on her week-old sheets. They ought to have been changed today. James would love it if he were here. Fiona never smelled of anything but soap.

"Redheads," he said, "all redheads, from auburn like you to bright ginger, have a special smell. A musk. An aroma. A bouquet. Like cinnamon. Did you know that?"

His worship of her, his delight in her body, especially in those parts she had once loathed most deeply, had done much to restore her. What she could not love for its own sake she could enjoy for his—which was why she needed him now more than ever.

Sleep came to her eventually that night; and so did James. She awoke to find him kneeling at her bedside. He might have been there for hours, just looking at her. She could see nothing of his features—she could barely see his outline against the pale wall beyond. Instead of slowly surfacing into consciousness, she came wide awake all at once. She did not move but he must have heard a change in her breathing.

"Cathy?" he said.

"Tell me what to do, James."

"Are you miserable?"

"Yes." She lifted the bedclothes for him but then lost her nerve and kept silent.

"I woke up," he said. "I was shivering. It wasn't cold. I couldn't understand it. I wanted you—that's why I was shivering. But it was Fiona I put my arms around—or my hands. I put my hands round her hips. She always sleeps with her back to me. And she woke. She said . . ." He paused.

"Come in, darling," Catherine said at last.

He climbed in, slipping from his dressing gown in the same movement. He was shivering still though her room was hot. Catherine almost tore her nightdress in her haste to get it off. They made love in that same urgent misery, without finesse. On fire. He withdrew, as always, for his own climax. As always, she felt the pang of common sense; the world reclaiming her too soon.

"What did Fiona say?" Catherine asked when she had douched—for they took no chances.

"I don't know why I did it. Why I touched her like that. It was you I wanted."

"What did you say?"

He kissed her tenderly, her neck, her ear, her cheek, her lips, her chin. It was a postponement. Deliberately she withheld her response. Then he sighed and said, "What she always says. She told me for God's sake to get myself a mistress if I couldn't learn to control my hands at two in the morning."

His voice invited her into his body. She lay in the longing of his mind, felt his hands on Fiona, felt the irresistible desires surge through him, heard that chilling outburst, and was crushed—like him.

"Oh, James! Oh, my darling." She squirmed upward between the sheets, clutching his head to rest below her neck. He accepted the role and relaxed. "Why does she try to hurt you so? It can't just be her need to feel superior. It must be something more. Why does she do it?"

"I wish I knew. When she does . . . *consent*—on the few nights each month when she does consent—" He stopped and chuckled.

"What?"

"I'll tell you how I know. Most times, I'll kiss her good night and maybe touch her—like this . . . or here . . ."

Catherine said, "Mmmmm," and pressed those parts closer to him.

"Yes." He laughed. "Well, that isn't how she responds. On those nights when she isn't in a consenting mood, she gives a weary sigh and says—in exactly the same tones she used with Burgo when he came home all muddy from football—she says, 'Good . . . *night.*' That tone means *Men! You just can't help it, can you!*"

"And when she . . . consents?" Catherine was torn between wanting to know and not wanting to hear.

"Oh, then! Then I say good night and—I don't always caress her, too, you see—I say good night and she says, 'Good night?' with a surprised little lift in her voice. Then I know." He gave a single humourless laugh—a snort. "No woman with a gigolo has a better-ordered life. On those occasions she is actually very passionate. I used to ask her—where do you keep it in between? Why doesn't even the memory of it linger and make you respond to ordinary tenderness? How can you forget how marvellous it is?"

"What are we going to do, James?"

"Do?"

"I crawl with envy when you just tell me you put your hands around Fiona's waist." She knew he had actually said "hips," but she could not bear to re-create that image here in the bed between herself and him; did he notice, she wondered?

He put his hands on her hips and, though so recently satisfied, she longed for him all over again. "And I," he said ruefully, "behave like a child when I see you in . . . in what was only fancy dress, after all—in your case, at least." He removed his hands. "What are we going to do, indeed?"

"Grow up?" she suggested. She meant to tell him how hurt Meg had been, but her own fears were more important.

As if it were saying the same thing in different words, he echoed, "Grow apart?"

She threw herself about him, clinging like a frightened child. "No! I couldn't face that. I won't."

He caressed her gently, raking his fingernails down her spine, soothing her. *"Had we never loved sae kindly . . ."* he quoted.

She recognized the poem "Ae Fond Kiss," by Burns. "Go on," she told him.

"Had we never lov'd so blindly, Never met—or never parted, We had ne'er been broken hearted."

"Aye," she said. "There it is—*never parted.* That's all I ask."

"I cannot say you no." He gripped her arm in that man-to-man way, bracing her for bad news. "But it will be bleak."

She reached up and kissed him. *"The desert were a paradise, If thou were there, if thou wert there."*

15

"Hello. I thought you were going over to the Jeffcotts' today," Catherine said to Burgo.

"Well, it takes all thoughts to make a whirl." He grinned. "Let me tell you mine. I thought we'd take ponies and skates and mosey over to th'ole rezavoy."

"But my work?" she objected, knowing from his confidence that it was already taken care of. She tried to make her delight the sort it would have been on any previous holiday—warm and sisterly.

"I said all thoughts. My next thought is that since you now have only two patients—one of whom is at this moment over in the kitchen, helping Mom with the baking—Dad could hold the fort." His eyes and the hands he slowly extended to her bridged the short, teasing silence. "And he can."

"He said so?"

"He said so."

"Wheee!" She grasped both his hands and spun a couple of carrousels. "I'll go and put on my woollies."

She was halfway down the passage before she turned and came back to the door. "Meg's coming along, too, of course?"

"Of course." His wicked grin challenged her to show disappointment.

She welcomed this chance to get her relationship with Burgo back to where it always had been. But then, she realized, she ought not to have asked about Meg. It didn't matter whether Meg came or not.

She turned back to Burgo. "Meg doesn't *have* to come," she added.

"That's true," he said, with the same damnably knowing grin.

But he can't know, she thought. *Or he'd never even talk to me.*

Burgo always gave the appearance of knowing. Anyway—what did it really matter to her?

The day was overcast, with spotlights of sun forming leaning pillars to hold up the brightest part of the sky, far away to the south. Margaret had the ponies already saddled up.

"Hey!" she greeted them. "Are these fellows fat! Burgo, why don't you buy us a little airplane and we can come home weekends?"

"Well . . ." Burgo huffed as he checked the girths. "I've come within an inch of it, half a dozen times."

There was a silence, then Catherine put in the "But . . . ?" he was begging for.

"Can't seem to fix on the colour," he said solemnly.

The women laughed. Catherine wondered how he could make jokes like that, yet still leave you with the firm impression he could so easily buy an airplane—just as he'd bought the Model T.

When they arrived at the rezavoy (which was little more than a man-made slough, about thirty yards by forty, scooped out of the ground by mule shovels), Burgo took a horse collar from the haybarn, put it on his own mount, and attached it to a wooden scraper he'd devised many years earlier. He soon had all the snow scraped off and the ice was bare and smooth enough for skating.

Margaret was a superb skater, literally making circles round them. Catherine, who had learned to skate in her first winter here but had only made it through without a big blue dinner plate of a bruise for the first time last winter, was pleasurably surprised to find she was about as good as Burgo —or as he perhaps allowed himself to appear.

They had had enough while Margaret was still warming to it. They took off their skates and went over to the hayshed to boil up some chocolate, the essential finale to any skating expedition among the Macraes.

The rezavoy was actually built over a spring, so even in the depth of winter there was a steady pressure of water under the ice. James had connected the spring to a buried cistern in the hayshed and had put up a little half-kilowatt wind dynamo to energize heating coils around the edge of the cistern, just below the water line. Now, after a windy night, a careful scoop with the bucket could bring up hand-hot water that would melt many times its own weight in ice in the horse troughs. The arrangement doubled the wintertime utility of what James called his "ranch."

Their ponies, thinking this was feeding time for them (which would also have been catching-and-resaddling time), came eagerly over. Burgo scattered them with a hail of snowballs. Catherine joined in. When the ponies ran she was left with a spare missile, which she threw at Burgo. It burst on his shoulder, firing some snow behind his earflaps. He, too, had a spare snowball, but he pointedly dropped it, declaring a closed season on horseplay between them.

While he got the coal-oil pressure stove going, she scooped up a pail from the cistern.

"What d'you think of Meg?" he asked. "Think she's changed much since going away?"

"She's doing what she always wanted. And she seems to be doing very well."

He was surprised. "What makes you say that?"

"She told me about that offer of a job from Anton Someone in Montreal."

"Anton Neff? Did you believe it?" He saw her hesitation and went on, "D'you think it's likely that one of the country's leading couturiers would come to Selkirk, of all places, to see what a first-semester textile student is doing?"

Put like that, of course, it seemed most unlikely. Yet Margaret had made it sound so convincing. After all, this *was* the land of opportunity. Girls did get discovered "slinging hash in diners" (whatever that was—it sounded horrible) and were made into stars in weeks.

"The trouble with Meg," he went on, "is that she's always grown up out of balance. Lopsided. Her intellect and body way ahead of her emotions and her general understanding. Look at her now."

She was executing a faultless sequence of spins and leaps.

"She could skate like that, almost, when she was seven. Same with horseriding. And if ever we got in a scrape, she could spin tales that would get Mom and Dad so confused, they'd literally give up trying to sort out the blame. But emotionally . . . !" He shook his head.

"Emotionally," Catherine took up his word, "she's very dependent on Fiona."

He shot her a schoolmarmy glance. "Someone's been leaving bad books around. That doesn't sound like the Catherine Hamilton we all know and love."

She laughed. "Your father *is* taking an interest in psychology. A slightly scornful interest."

"Don't waste your time," he told her. "The future of medicine is where I'm going—pharmacology. Life is a chemical system. One day there'll be a chemical cure for every known disease."

"D'you think Meg's emotional dependence on her mother is like a disease?" Catherine asked.

The water began to sing loud enough to be heard over the small roar of the pressure burner.

Burgo gave it some thought. "It can't be healthy. Meg should learn to value herself for what she is, not for what approval she can get."

"She's very good at designing clothes. I don't know the first thing about it, but even I can see that."

"Keep telling her that, Cath. Your approval means a lot to her. If she hears it enough from you, she'll stop needing to invent visits from Anton Neff."

The water boiled. He brought the pan over to the cups.

Catherine called Margaret. She waved back but did not stop her gyrations.

"She'll let it go cold. Whatever she's doing she's got to do it to death," Burgo said. "She doesn't like reading novels because there's always a page that says 'The End.'" He watched Margaret and shook his head fondly. "She'll cripple herself for a week now. And then tomorrow, when you and I come back here, she'll say it's not fair."

There was such tenderness in his voice that Catherine felt a mild wave of jealousy for Margaret. She fought it. It was not the right feeling.

"Behaviour is so complicated," he said. "Take Mom and Dad. I'll bet there've been a dozen occasions these last years when you've wondered what keeps them together—why they never divorced."

"They're too God-fearing." Catherine was acutely embarrassed to be discussing James and Fiona like this.

"That's not the reason."

"I don't think it's at all right for me to talk about it." She wished he wouldn't fix her so with his eyes.

"Oh, come along, Cath. You're family now. You should hear Meg and me talk about them."

"What is the reason then?"

"They love each other too much. The way she snaps at him and grumbles all the time, and the way he just goes along with it and teases her and even creates situations for her to respond to—that's their kind of devotion. Isn't that weird? Or *outré,* as Meg says."

Why was he suddenly telling her things like that? They had never discussed his parents before, not in the vaguest terms.

She couldn't think what to answer. *Did* he know about her? And was he saying it didn't matter—it was a mistake—anyone could slip like that— just turn about and walk away from it. Here I am. Is that what he was working around to?

And would she? She had never thought of it before because there had seemed no alternative to James. He was so wise and good that, if he loved her, she could not be all bad. She loved him for that. Aye, and for more. For himself. For all the marvellous things he was. And because there was no one else.

But now? Was there Burgo as well? Was that what he was saying?

Margaret came over to join them. "I'd adore to go on and on," she said, "but I'd only ruin myself for tomorrow. Sufficient unto the day are the excesses thereof."

Catherine smiled *so there!* at Burgo.

"Gadzooks," he said. "She groweth up. Actually she could hardly share an apartment with me for three months without some of my amazingly suave maturity rubbing off on her."

Margaret bared her teeth at him. "La, sir!" she simpered. "I did but stay skating upon the frozen tarn betimes in hope that you'd go and roll Cathy in the hay, ya big lug!"

Catherine knew she ought to die of embarrassment at that suggestion. But in a curious way the very fact that Burgo was in it, too—and had been assigned the active role—insulated her from it. She did not need to react at all. She could leave it to him.

Burgo was furious. He stood with his fists clenched and glared at his sister.

Margaret was delighted. "It's not that I'm particularly fond of shotgun weddings, but the thought of four years in Selkirk, sharing an apartment with thee, dear brother, would be a lot sweeter if Cath was there, too."

Catherine was astonished at this. She turned to Burgo. "Four years? Aren't you coming back here to join your father when you qualify?"

He shot her a brief glance and then looked back at his sister, still angry. He raised the cocoa to his lips and sipped, without taking his eyes off Margaret. "She's rushing a lot of fences today." He lifted a warning finger and shook it at her.

When his hand fell back to his side, Margaret smiled and said, "Eftsoons his hand drops he." She turned to Catherine. "Hell, hon," she said. "I love you anyway. Why don't you come? Move in with us for my sake. And for your own. You could train to be a proper nurse. Meet horrible people like young bachelor doctors—good for nothing except marrying and paying off your bills. Whaddya say? Let's hold a pyjama party tonight and mull over all the good old days we haven't even had yet."

They did not go skating again until after Christmas. The festival itself was so busy, what with the cooking, the children, the washing up, the carol concerts, the church services, and the curling competitions on Boxing Day, that Catherine, Burgo, and Margaret hardly had any time together in between.

When work began again, and the hospital started to refill—with accident cases, mothers-to-be who expected complications as well as babies, flu victims (the ordinary kind these days), and convalescents from the main hospital in Saskatoon who wanted to be nearer home—Burgo rolled up his sleeves and pitched in. He said plenty of things like, "We ought to turn one of these rooms into a small path. lab. Just think what we could do with the advance diagnosis of things like diabetes and a whole string of renal and hepatic disorders." It seemed to give the lie to Margaret's hint that he was thinking of a career somewhere else.

James would grunt something that might have been agreement and say things like, "What I look forward to is the chance to do some real surgery when you're here permanently. All these distressing accidents we get—fingers off, hands severed, feet and legs crushed . . . I'm sure that quick surgery, within minutes if we can, could do a lot. We're so used to sending people down by buggy or on the train to Saskatoon—by which time it's so late all they can do is trim back and tie off—we've come to think that's the right and proper thing to do."

It promised a rare old clash of medical visions for the future.

The day of their second skate outing was brilliant, with just a few perfunctory whisps of high cloud in the sky. Margaret wanted to go to the Goldeneye River. She had developed a trick of skating herself up to hair-raising speeds, hurtling straight at a sandbar, and then, at the last minute, leaping clear over it, crashing through the bare twigs of dogwood and the wild rose bushes, to land, usually without a tumble, on the ice on the far side, where she would at once start to power surge her way forward to the next bar. But the other two outvoted her. It was the rezavoy again.

"Aha!" She grinned. "The lure of the hay, what?"

This time Catherine was much less embarrassed. Burgo chose not to hear. Margaret sighed. "It must be the way I tell them."

The pleasure of the golden midwinter sun kept Burgo and Catherine on their skates much longer this time. Even so, they left the ice before Margaret was halfway through her extensive repertoire. When she saw them go she fixed an evil leer on her face, folded her arms, and skated past them with one leg cocked. Burgo held a warning finger toward her.

"I didn't even *think* it," she shrieked back over her shoulder, adding a witch's laugh. Then she pretended to lose her balance and went into a long, impromptu, clever clowning sequence, trying to recover it. The joke and the embarrassment were both defused.

"What do they make of her?" Burgo laughed.

"Who?"

"Well, I meant the college, but anyone who hasn't watched her grow up —if, indeed, she has. What do you make of her?"

"She's marvellous company. Always so alive."

"She's just like that little mare she rides. Except I sometimes wonder if she knows the limits. I have a terrible fear that Meg will overdo something one day."

They walked in silence to the hay barn.

"Have the Jeffcotts gone away?" she asked.

He breathed in to speak, then thought better of it. He looked at her and gave a pensive grin. "Mina?" he said at length.

"Yes. Has she gone away?" Catherine now wished she hadn't asked the question. He made it seem so important.

"I don't know," he said, deliberately lightening it again.

She went to draw the water; the pressure stove was almost hot enough to pump. When she came back, he said, "I have put away childish things."

"Corinthians," she said. "Thirteen, eleven."

He chuckled. "I used to wonder, when I saw you buried deep in *Gray's Anatomy,* how it would be when you had learned it by heart. If I then said 'Recurrent Laryngeal Nerve,' would you immediately respond 'Cranial nerve—ten—fifth branch . . .' or whatever it is?"

The table in *Gray's* flashed before her: *Branches of the Vagus Nerve.* "It's the sixth on the right, ninth on the left," she told him.

He laughed. "You're amazing. No, but to get back to Mina Jeffcott, there never was anything real between us. Just family assumptions that went back years. Nothing real on my side, and I don't think on hers—though she was a bit dumpy about it when I told her we ought to look seriously for other . . . partners, shall we say? Last summer." He saw her face soften with contentment and wondered if she was even aware of it. He often wondered how self-aware women were. "Has Mina seemed upset this fall?" he asked.

"Her mother—and yours—are behaving as if it's still on."

"It's been sustained entirely by their hopes for the past two years. How has Mina been?"

"Not . . . heartbroken. I didn't know it was over. Nothing in her behaviour showed it."

"I think she was relieved. Once she'd got over the shock of hearing it like that—out in the open."

"I'll get the cups," she said.

He followed her. "Did you ever slap a man in the face?" he asked.

"No!" She laughed, wondering what foolery this was.

"I'm dying here to give you the chance." He caught her arm and gave a gentle pull, not enough to turn her but enough to ask her to turn.

She did.

And he was suddenly at a loss.

But she did not notice. Burgo was never at a loss. Instead she was confused and shy and awkward and embarrassed. "Oh, please!" She felt fifteen again—and dreadful. "I can't be funny and witty and serious all at the same time. Like you. I don't know how to do it." She smiled at him, shivering with sudden fright—at herself and at where this stumbling little speech was dragging them. "I don't know what to do," she said. None of these words were what she meant to say—or knew she ought to say. They were frightened idiocies that flew off the top of her mind before she could stop them.

He took up her hands and said, "I don't know what to do either. And I was the one who came out here knowing exactly what I was going to do."

He let the suggestion hang until she had to ask, "What?"

"I was going to kiss you," he said.

"I don't mind." She closed her eyes and pursed her lips toward him. It was easier than saying no. Saying no was like running away.

But he ignored the offer. He took her in his arms and laid his head against hers. "But there's too much friendship between us, Cathy. Don't you feel that? We've been too much like brother and sister—had too much ordinary fun together. It would be like beginning again. We're strangers in love—and old friends in everything else."

"Love?" The suddenness of the word shocked her.

"Yes, of course." He kept his arms about her but pulled his head away to look into her eyes. "I love you, Cathy. I think I've loved you for years, though I only knew it last summer. I've thought of no one else and nothing else but you ever since. It isn't just that I want to kiss you. I want to marry you. Be with you always. Have a family with you."

He could not understand the growing horror in her face.

"No!" She broke and ran from him. Then, having started, she could not stop. She ran for the railroad track and the path home.

That word had done it: love. She could not possibly love Burgo *and* James. It would be monstrous. All the wickedness she had caused and tasted up to now would be as nothing when set beside so vile a "love." Would it not be a kind of incest—the very fear she had run from in the first place? Dear God, was it to stalk her in one guise or another all her life? Would she run from it again, run to the ends of the earth, and there meet it yet stronger? Was it something in herself—did she carry it with her, like a bad seed, and cause it to grow, with tropic fervour, whenever she rested her guard?

All her instinct was to run, get away, flee this terrible mark. But the thought that she might span the globe and meet it at her landfall made her pause.

If not run, then fight.

If not fight, then submit. Endure.

Never! She would fight it. She would fight Burgo. She would fight even James. And once again, herself. She would defeat herself. Once and for all.

It took Burgo some little time to saddle both their ponies and make after her. She was almost home before he caught up.

"What's the matter! Did I say anything wrong?"

"No." She stopped.

"At least you can mount up."

She managed without help.

"Did I insult you, Catherine?"

"No, of course not. You're much too good for me. I wasn't insulted. You'd be insulted if I said yes." She was calm now that she knew what she must do.

"D'you really believe that? You think I'm too good! Or you're not good enough?"

"You don't know."

"Then at last I've found a flaw in you. I *knew* you just couldn't be so perfect."

His tone made her smile against her will. "What?" she had to ask.

"You're about the worst judge of character I've ever met."

"Just take it from me, Burgo dear. Take it as final. I won't marry you or anyone else. There are reasons."

"You love someone already."

"I'm not saying any more."

"I won't quit," he said quietly. "I'll pursue you in every way I know. I've imagined my life with you so often and so deeply I can't think of life in any other way. I love you, and you are going to love me. Dig in for a siege, Catherine. You've seen nothing of me yet. I'll wear you down like . . ." He looked about them. "Like the glacier that ironed out this land."

16

Each Hogmanay, Catherine wrote to her father. He didn't reply, but she understood. That year she did not write until after Burgo had gone back to MacNair. In fact, Burns night came and went, before she put pen to note-paper. Confusion over Burgo prevented her, of course—yet what did she

write in the last week of January that she could not have written in the first?
"Another good year . . . kept busy in the hospital . . . nearly killed in a
blizzard . . . Renee Kirby (she looks after my cousins Ian and John, remember—my first friends in Canada?) had a little baby boy at last . . . Dr.
Macrae got nearly a thousand dollars for his best palomino mare . . . I miss
the sea still, sometimes. . . . The work will be even more interesting when
young Dr. Macrae joins his father this fall. . . . How are things at Beinn
Uidhe?"

It was a story so emptied of emotional truth she wondered if anyone
would believe it. Yet wasn't the simple, placid life it portrayed exactly the
sort of thing she had hoped for in leaving home? Wouldn't the unambitious
wee thing who came here almost six years ago have loved such a life?

What would An Dóiteán say if he knew the truth? Once he had almost
had an apoplexy when he heard her hum a little tune on the Sabbath. How
could he even begin to comprehend wickedness on this scale?

She would have to give James up; she knew that. It would have to stop.
But not yet.

He came to her room two days after Burgo went back east. He brought
an oppressive mood with him. Their lovemaking was greedy, almost desperate. Afterward they lay apart in morose silence. A light in the house am-
plified the sparse movements of twigs in shadows on her wall. She tried to
find significance in the shapes, but saw none—or none that lasted. Everything was only half-glimpsed these days. Things flashed from darkness back
into darkness.

"I love you," he said.

She stopped breathing for a moment.

"I love Fiona, too. But I also love you."

"Yes."

"Do you doubt it?"

"Of course not."

"To love two people . . ." he began.

She waited for more and then said, "What of it?"

"Aye—what of it?"

Suddenly she realized he meant Burgo—herself and Burgo. And herself
and him.

"I don't know. What do I know of love at all? I've only ever loved you."

"Only?"

"Perhaps it happens to everybody."

"What?" he asked.

"Loving two people at the same time. How do I know?"

The bed shook. He was laughing silently.

"What's funny?" she asked.

"So you do love him."

"I didn't say that."

"Didn't you?"

She hadn't thought about it. Or, rather, she had forced herself not to think about it. She remembered when Burgo put his arms about her, when his head was close to hers. It had been a wonderful moment. But was that love?

"I want you to have a life of your own," James said.

"My life is with you. I told you that."

"A home of your own. Children of your own."

"With Burgo! I couldn't, James."

"Ahaa!" His body did not move, but his voice pounced on her from out of the darkness. "There we have it! You think it would be a kind of incest?"

"Well, wouldn't it?"

"Of course it wouldn't."

Part of her wanted his words to be true; part of her wanted to argue, to punish herself, because it would be so nice if what he said were true. Caught between these impulses, she said nothing.

"You and Fiona!" he said. "You have that same urge to hurt yourselves. You are sisters under the skin. I must have some special . . . some fatal attractant. You're a pair of moths and I your candleflame."

She had a momentary image of a moth excitedly burning to death. It was hard to believe the creature wasn't in ecstasy.

"You think," James went on, "that if you married Burgo and loved him and had children it would be like offering your neck up on the block. You've tempted God with me, with what we've done. And then, to find happiness with Burgo—that would be inviting His revenge."

She shrugged. "Believe that if you wish."

"And you will stay here until all our misery is absolute. Then you will be able to say to God, 'See! . . .'"

"Misery! You call what we've just done 'misery'?"

"You think there are no joys in hell? How could the torments be made unbearable then? How do you see black when all is dark? Och, no, woman —hell has its storehouse of joys well enough. So—as I said—when our misery is absolute, you can say to God, 'See! I have taken Thy revenge for Thee. No need now for Thee to do worse.' But d'you think you can cheat God, Catherine?"

"You know a lot about God suddenly."

He chuckled. "You thought *you* had that corner, eh? I know nothing of God—not even whether He exists or not. But if He exists, I know this. The worst sin—listen now, Catherine, don't try to turn it into something else—the worst sin is to seek to know His mind."

"I'm not seeking any such thing. I already do know."

"Ah, I was wrong. *That* is the worst sin: to know already. That's the knowledge Satan carried down to hell with him."

"I don't understand any of this."

"You will if you listen. Suppose, just for example, you commit a little sin—you tell a fib, say—and then, with one eye on God, you punish yourself: you forgo some small pleasure. Now God has *two* sins to forgive. A wee sin, like telling a fib, and a monstrous dark heinous crime such as the Prince of Darkness himself might shrink from—the crime of believing you know what punishment would be fitting in God's sight. You could destroy the world and be forgiven. Or you could take God's prerogative upon yourself and wantonly kill a single insect one second before it would anyway die a natural death—and for that you might be damned eternally. The mind of God is absolutely unknowable."

"But my mind is knowable. If I know I've done wrong, I can't just let myself go free!"

"Then God have mercy on you."

"But I can't."

"You must! You must go on—you must try to live as good and rich and happy a life as you can. You must let your sin go unpunished—by yourself anyway. You must beg God's mercy yet give Him every chance to *smite* you." He chuckled savagely. "But if you build your own hell, then you're setting yourself up in His business. There's no mercy for that. He's enjoyed the monopoly too long. It's my belief that Hell is peopled entirely by judges." He caressed her hair. "And silly girls who cut off their noses to spite their faces. That's why you must marry Burgo and build a home and bring us our grandchildren—and every day and every night, cry mercy as you stretch your neck on that block."

"No," she told him simply.

He said nothing.

"James?"

He breathed, as if about to speak. At last he said, "When I came here tonight, I hoped not to have to say this. I hoped to persuade you some other way. But now I must say it. This is the last time I'll come and see you like this. I will never come to your bed again."

She sat up and stared at him, a hunched figure in the dim, greenish snowlight. At first she was astonished, then angry. It was one thing for her freely to arrive at such a decision, but to have it thrust upon her was quite another. She ignored the faint voice of reason, telling her that he had as much right to cry halt as she; instead she took it as a challenge. She met it with another.

"You won't be able to do it, James. It means too much to you."

He cleared his throat, slowly, uncertainly—a sign in him of reluctant agreement. "I see. It seems I, too, must 'dig in for a long siege.'" He felt her stiffen at the quotation. "Aye. Aye. He told me, too. He told me you loved someone else. He asked me to tell him who it was. D'you know what that cost to his pride—Burgo, to ask me such a thing? Me! And when I told him I didn't know, he begged me to find out. You may not understand what measures of desperation this sacrifice of his pride reveals. But I do."

He might as well not have spoken. "Give it six weeks," she said. "You won't last out longer than that."

"And then?"

She almost said, "Then we'll see about 'measures of desperation'!" But her anger was a reminder, telling her she was not just some person trying to win a debate, she was a woman challenged by her lover.

"I won't yield," he said glumly.

"Six weeks," she repeated with a see-if-I-care brightness.

He heard the deliberate, unreal hardness enter her voice. His spirit sank at the thought of those awful, semiconscious, feminine weapons which would now, from this moment, be trundled out against him—and for months to come. A new cocktail of hormones was just beginning to leach out into Catherine's blood, irrigating her every cell . . . up through the blood-brain barrier as if it didn't exist, up into her brain, and down into her guts, forging a new alliance with but one purpose—to defeat his moral will, to bend it to his body's will. Body would call unto body. Hers to his. His to hers. Trojan horses. He would not know how to hide his longing; she would hide hers without effort.

And her body would know all the strategies—learned at that same effortless university. If it was necessary that her skin should glow—nothing easier: Squirt, squirt, little hormones, and peaches would bloom. If she must be happy in order to drive him mad—squish, squish, and she would hum irresolute melodies the livelong day. Her very breath would turn to per-fume for him.

And what hostages he had given her already: "I love the curve of your elbow just there . . . I adore that little curl, right at the angle of your jaw. . . ." She had a hundred of them. And a hundred times a hundred would be flaunted at him in an unrehearsed choreography that others would label prosaically "Changing a Bedpan" . . . "Dusting the Medicine Cabinet," seeing no aphrodisiac at all.

He began to sweat at the nightmare of becoming sixteen, all over again.

She turned her back to him, faking an early decline into slumber. "Six weeks." She yawned.

17

They both reckoned without Burgo. He wrote to her every single day. One of the strategies that had briefly flitted through her mind, when she first said "six weeks, and then . . ." was to kiss James openly in front of Fiona. She dismissed it, of course, realizing she'd have to be cleverer than that; but here was Burgo doing the same to her. A letter a day, in a small place like Goldeneye, where "Town Bull" Donaldson sorted every item of mail himself, was as good as a public kiss.

At least, that was how Goldeneye took it. She could hardly fail to be aware of her new status—higher even than a nurse's. When she went down the boardwalk she was greeted in a new way. Storekeepers, quadrupling their estimates of her future trading value, were four times as eager to serve her. Certain high-and-mighty women no longer condescended to her when she went with Fiona to the church circles, where it ceased to be "Mrs. Macrae and er . . ." and became "Mrs. Macrae and of-course-Miss-Hamilton-my-isn't-she-looking-well!"

Burgo surely knew his home town.

He also knew Catherine, better than she realized. She opened his first letter with a sinking feeling, expecting it to be full of unrequited love and misery. Not a bit. That see-if-I-care lightness of tone she was using on James . . . here it was coming back at her. Burgo was having a splendid time.

He read books. He saw movies. A couple of times he and one of the nurses ("a friend of many years' standing—you'd love her") (*so why not tell me her name?* Catherine thought angrily) took in a theatre in Toronto. He went walking up in the woodlands on the Niagara escarpment above Dunedin. (*Alone?* she wondered—as she was meant to.) He told her of a Bach recital in the church; of a Mountie raid he'd seen on a moonshiner in the nearby vineyard country; of a group of artists, friends of Margaret's, who led rich, hard-working, disorderly lives; of the Great Missaqua Valley World Fair and Quilting Contest—still ten months away—half of which (the quilting half) Margaret hoped to carry in triumph; of Lake Ontario in its many moods; of the excitement of the steelworks at night; of the big and little dramas of the hospital where he was intern.

Within two weeks she could have moved to Selkirk and dropped easily into his life, so well did she know it. Only in his third letter did he mention love. He told her she knew already he was in love with her and wanted to marry her—and she also knew it was why he was writing these letters. But, once said, it was said, and to keep repeating it would be boring, so he'd say no more. Promise.

After about a month of letters in which he faithfully kept his word, she found herself wishing he'd break it just a little. She didn't want a full out-pouring of devotion—only a word or two. He could say, "I'm beginning to miss you," or "Send me a photograph, I forget just how you look" . . . something slight like that.

Instead he wrote: "An amusing thing happened at the nurses' dance last Saturday night. One of the fellows here, whom I will call B—, because he thinks he's the bee's knees at diagnosis, was dancing with Gloria S—, a nurse on the male dermatology ward (not that it matters). First thing B— spots is that she's tall and thin. Then that her fingers are remarkably spidery —or 'they exhibited arachnodactyly' as our masters prefer us to say. What B— said was, 'Aha!' It began to look interesting.

"Two of the nicest things about Gloria S— had until that moment con-cealed the fact that her chest—the bony bits of it, anyway—was somewhat sunken. (Kyphoscoliosis to you and me.) The next piece also belonged to the same jigsaw: Gloria was not, he noticed, exactly the nimblest dancer on the floor. (Muscular hypotonia, I hear you muttering to yourself, dear Catherine. And you would be right.) (Have you got it yet?) (Try it on Dad —see if he does. This is the point where *I* got it—when B— told me after, of course.)

"The clincher was a sticky one. B— had to waltz her outside onto the balcony, hasten her behind a potted palm (actually it was a turkey trot, the corridor, and a water cooler, but you know how incurably romantic I am), kiss her, and get his tongue up against the roof of her mouth—all before the Dragon appeared, doing the slow handclap.

"He almost failed—failed to get his tongue on her palate, I mean. Not that she was unwilling, mind you. Surprised, yes. Unwilling, no. And not that the Dragon stormed upon them. But Gloria's palate was so *high!*

"That clinched it, of course: arachnodactyly; tall, slim build; kyphoscoliosis; muscular hypotonia; *and* a high palate. A child could work it out from there that she also has an auricular septal defect and aortic hypoplasia. So, grateful Gloria went along last Monday to the Cardiac Clinic, where every specialist in Ontario auscultated her, and ringed her delectable left breast with electrodes, and shouted with a single voice, 'Marfan's Syndrome!'

"But we're all worried about B—'s somewhat unconventional approach to diagnosis. You see—he's intending to become a gynaecologist!"

The effect of such letters on Catherine hardly need be imagined. She knew well that they were cunningly contrived to have exactly that effect—to make her curious about his experiences and feelings, longing for the next installment . . . to make her (by the very absence of any mention of the subject) think about his love for her and to imagine how enjoyable life with him would be . . . and, every now and then, to prick her jealousy a little (for even a woman who scorned her lover would be a *little* jealous to hear he was enjoying himself with another).

If it were as coolly calculating as that, she could have weathered it. But Burgo steered a faultless line between the sort of contriving that is legitimate in a lover, and the sort of outright manipulation that is not. Through every paragraph, even when he teased her and was therefore most at arm's length, there ran a tender good humour and a warmth for her. The "glacier" image of himself, plucked out of the unthinking air when he warned her to dig in for a long siege, could not have been less appropriate.

When the first few letters came she had, out of bravado, shown them to Fiona and James. It was a way of declaring how little they meant to her. By the time his purpose grew clear it was too late; a see-if-I-care posture had been struck and now had to be maintained. So both parents had unique front-row seats in their son's courtship of Catherine.

It was the salvation of James. If he had not known what pressures were coming on Catherine from Burgo, he would have cracked. When he told her he would not come to her bed again, he knew it was going to be tough. He'd helped alcoholics fight their addiction often. Twice he had helped a colleague throw off an opium habit. He knew what a screaming fight the thwarted body could put up. There would be nights when he would shiver with fire for her, when his nerves would stretch with the overwhelming genital urge that brings heroism to trenches, riots to prisons, and that gives the marching orders, in one form or another, to half of humanity. There would be times when he would neglect or postpone important duties for the merest sight or sound of her. Images of her would heap him.

In his youth, when he had courted Fiona, he had seen his love for her not as something entirely within himself but as a real *thing,* something "out there," an objective part of her—as much as her beautiful lips and lovely hair, which also played such havoc with his sleep and appetite. This delusion, which is the true blindness of love, is a young lover's protection; for when his feelings are not returned, as happened several times to James with other girls, he can say, "How unobservant she is" or "How much more percep- tive am I!" Age had stripped James of that protection. There was no adora- tion independently "out there," take it or leave it. He was alone with his longing. Take it—or take it.

But now, with the daily feast of Burgo's letters, he was in the extraordi- nary position of feeling primitive jealousy of his son as rival, alongside a most civilized gratitude to him as bringer of temporal salvation. The same schizoid, primitive-James/civilized-James yearned for Catherine as lover and longed for her as daughter-in-law.

It was still a battle, but at least it was genuinely "out there." It was ob- jective. If he chose how close to stand, it would be through self-discipline, not self-delusion (for how can you choose to stand this-close or that-far from something wholly within yourself!). As Catherine's six-week deadline drew on, he knew he would not break.

Time, and the enforced separation, changed her, too. James, after seem- ing theatrically light-hearted, then morose, had discovered the trick of behaving exactly as he had behaved to her before they became lovers. He was cheerful, witty, avuncular, wise, caring—and properly distant. It was maddening. Worse still, he could even talk about it with that same proper distance, almost as a medical and philosophical phenomenon.

She said to him once, "You remember how you said Fiona is so pas- sionate at those times, and then in between you wonder where she keeps the memory of it? It isn't a mystery at all. I think every woman would under- stand that. I don't miss you at all in that way. I thought I would, and I don't." She peered at him for signs of pain, not realizing until then how much she wanted to see him hurt.

But he would not oblige. His mask was that of a kindly judge. "Is that all you wish to say on the subject, Catherine?"

"What else is there to say?"

"Perhaps Burgo is right. We are all prisoners of our bloodstreams. Female hormones must carry the gift of amnesia."

"And yours?"

He smiled. "The gift of reticence."

She tossed her head. He became serious. "There will be pain my dearest. There *is* pain. But there would be so much more, one day, if we did not stop now. What you did with me was a small sin—a peccadillo. But what I did with you . . . it reeks to high heaven. I blighted your life. I stood between you and a husband, a family, a home."

"Well . . ." She did not know what to say.

He saw it. He saw she was on some knife-edge of decision, not consciously, perhaps, but at more important depths. Still in that same kindly tone, he said, "I am not the Great Love of your life. Only the first. You must leave me behind you and go on." He smiled. "Thank heavens for Burgo, eh?"

"Oh, shut up!" she shouted and stormed out, not truly understanding why he made her so angry. If only she had been the one to say *stop,* everything would be so different.

Maybe Old Fram, the Irishwoman who had married a Métis and had now come back to Goldeneye to die, overheard this or some similar exchange, or maybe she just guessed at what was upsetting Catherine. At all events she mentioned one day how the Great War had killed off a lot of young men. "Aye," she sighed artlessly, "many and many's the young woman will grow old and wrinkled on a damp pillow, thinking *if only . . ."*

"That may be true of the east," Catherine said, deliberately turning the conversation away from herself. "It certainly isn't true of Saskatchewan. I could pick among dozens. If I wanted."

Fram had made such good recovery in the cottage hospital that James, in that casual way which so maddened Fiona, had taken her on as a kind of resident working patient. She certainly earned her keep.

Fram returned to the subject when they were stacking dishes after lunch. "I wonder would it be worse now, never to have had a man at all, like you, or to have had one and lost him, like me?"

Catherine parried with, "D'you miss him a lot, Fram? You never talked of him much." She did not know how devious an old woman can be or she would never have provided such an opening, oblique though it was.

Always after stacking the dishes they sat down for a cup of coffee. Today, that was when Fram told Catherine all about her husband. It took three cups of coffee, in fact, because she, being Irish, could not see her late husband without also seeing the history of his people, the Métis. It was the Irish in her, too, which saw that history only in terms of the waste of a whole people and their traditions, of chances lost. This time the destroyers were not so much the Saxons, but, ironically, her own people and Catherine's—the Celts.

The Métis, offspring of the pioneer French and the aboriginal Indian, had never scorned and never been scorned by the European half of their parentage: the French, who were the most civilized of all the white colonizers. Laframboise himself had always maintained that the world would be a far more gracious place, and a better home for civilization, if the French hadn't killed off their aristocracy and then one another, leaving the rest of mankind to the philistine arrogance and exploiting efficiency of Saxon, Scot, and Hun.

Old Fram agreed. "Them Saxons practised on us Irish," she said. "Then they went out and did it to everyone."

Had it not been for Saxon brutality (as Fram saw it) the Métis could have bridged the two civilizations—those of the Plains Indians and the European settlers—and made the prairie a paradise. The Métis had farmed along the river fronts, like the first Québecois, and they had also hunted the plains, like the Indians. At those times they turned their stock loose to graze on great communal grasslands, inland of their riverside farms. It was a way of life that once prevailed from here to the Rio Grande, a system that suited the dry hinterland in a way that ranching and farming never would. The European, with his obsession for surveys, square-mile sections, barbed wire, and machines, had destroyed that balanced, endlessly self-renewing way of life as surely as his extinction of the buffalo turned the Indian into a hereditary mendicant. Two good, rich, many-sided cultures killed by a bad but single-minded third.

"And now we're after finding our way isn't best," she said. "We took a good land, but a hard land, and we used it wrong, and we're spoiling it."

She seemed to remember then that she was supposed to be telling Catherine about Michel, her husband—or Midge, as she called him. Midge had died twenty years back. There wasn't much he couldn't do, and even less that he had not done. In a way, his very richness of talents had been his downfall. Somehow, as the reminiscence went on, Catherine began to sense a parallel between Midge's failure and the destruction of that old, finely balanced farming system his people had evolved. Then she saw that Fram's earlier words had not been the ramble they had seemed. A preamble, rather. Fram considered the two were part of a single process of misuse.

"The land's alive," she said. "The plains breathe. And everything that lives has got one right use—a fit use—put for it there by God. Just one. Only one. And then there's a thousand bad ones, brought in by men. But, sure, we ain't so clever as what we suppose. We get by just so far, so we do. Then the tank's dry. The sod is dust. And the loan gets foreclosed." She rocked in her chair and sucked the dregs of the coffee through the grounds. Then she smiled at Catherine, a smile more compelling than friendly. "Same with people, me darlin'," she said. "One fit use for each of us, given by God. Anything else—it's just waiting for the man to foreclose."

She spat the grounds back into the cup and stared Catherine out. "Now you marry that Dr. Burgo," she rapped. "Hear me now?"

A few nights later, Catherine was awakened by a gentle knocking in the shave-and-a-haircut: two-bits rhythm James always used—with his own characteristic pause after "shave." She sprang to the door and had it half opened before she realized it would have been seemlier to stay in bed and call out to him to go away.

"Go away," she said, but it wasn't the same. He could hear the tremble in her voice.

"You were right," he told her. He sounded miserable.

"Right?" She wished she could see him, the passage was so dim.

"Aye. Six weeks you said."

Her heart beat like a water hammer. "You'd better come in."

"I tried," he said. She still could not see his face for he took her into his arms at once. "I can't forget you. I can't do without you. Oh, Cathy, Cathy, the very smell of you!"

His dressing gown was open. She felt his erection prod her stomach. The mechanical speed of his arousal affronted her. He seemed alien to her now, so long since last time.

But then he kissed her and his hands caressed her spine. His nails raked the shelf of her buttocks through her nightgown. Memories and suppressed longings stirred. As she began melting to him she felt also a surge of panic. It must not begin again! Now *she* could say halt.

She pulled away from him and held her arms and fingers outstretched, like hayforks, to ward him off.

"No!" she said.

"Oh, darling—please. I'll do anything you want. I'll even tell Burgo not to come back when he qualifies. There'll be no partnership. Just you and me."

"No!" He was frightening when he spoke so wildly.

"I'm cold. Let's go to bed."

"No, James. That must stop now." It cost her dearly to say it. The animal in her was already rioting in memory of nights when *no* had been a daylight word.

"Just one last time. Please, Cathy?"

"Well . . . if we do . . ."

"Yes!"

"No! If we do, we'll be lost. We'd be saying this six weeks of suffering was all for nothing."

"Suffering! You admit it then. You've suffered, too."

"Of course I have, James. I never said I'd stopped loving you."

"Oh, darling! Nothing matters but that. Love sanctifies everything."

He took one hesitant step toward her. "No!" she said more firmly than ever. "I really mean it now."

He collapsed. It seemed that only a reflex memory kept him upright. "Then pray for me," he said. "Pray I may have your strength."

I'll go, she thought. *I'll run away, yet again.*

He made to leave. At the door he turned to her for the last time. "And Burgo. What about him?"

"For heaven's sake!" she said angrily. "I'll marry him. Why am I so important, anyway!"

"I knew it." His voice was hollow with misery. "Ever since Christmas I've known you loved him."

By the time she had recovered from this stunning display of self-pity—stunning because it was so completely out of character—he was gone. She went unhappily back to bed and hugged herself into a cocoon of eiderdown and linen.

She wondered at what she had just said: "I'll marry Burgo." The decision had brought the most amazing sense of peace—more than peace, a terrible joy. The Peace of God. An exultation that was biblical. She was the prodigal daughter. She was laughter in heaven.

She tried to worry about James and his misery, but could not. If she could have seen him at that moment, she would not even have tried. For he, having done his round of the wards, was skipping through the snow, back toward the house, like a schoolboy.

18

The Niagara Escarpment runs almost fifty miles westward from the falls themselves, along the thirty-mile-wide neck of land between Lakes Erie to the south and Ontario to the north. From the top of the escarpment you can look northeast, over the smog of Selkirk, far out over Lake Ontario, to Toronto, where the western edge begins its eastward curve to form the long upper shore. Selkirk itself is partly obscured by the hill on which stands MacNair University. Between that hill and the escarpment lies a broad wooded valley, half-concealing the little town of Dunedin. Once a commercial rival to Selkirk, it is now a Garden of Eden dormitory to that much larger city. There, in Dundas Avenue, Burgo and Margaret shared an apartment.

For Catherine it was a kind of intoxication to stand again on ground that sloped and rose more than a few feet. Here was a landscape in which a "feature" like Hawk Ridge could easily get lost in anyone's back garden. Burgo's descriptions of it had been accurate but her mind had clad these hills and rocks with the heather and stunted trees of her native Highlands; the rich variations of bark and branch, of maple, oak, birch, and willow, came as a surprise. When she arrived at Selkirk train station her heart had fallen; after the keen, clean prairie, the air was worse than the worst of Glasgow. But here, within minutes of her arrival, the taxi was cruising through this place of broad, quiet streets, and houses lost among trees.

She had expected Burgo, but it was Margaret who met her at the station. "He couldn't change his duties round," she explained. "But he'll come down after eleven. Meanwhile we can have breakfast. Did you eat? You look marvellous. I can never sleep on those trains. I'm always afraid of waking up in Texas, which I'd hate—have you *seen* how *tall* the girls are there? Oh, hush my mouth!" She stopped, but only to breathe and laugh. Then she grabbed Catherine's arm and hugged it to her. "Oh, Cath! I'm so glad you've come! You are staying for good, aren't you? You'll never go back to that horrid place and those *awful* people?"

"Hey . . ." Catherine began.

"We'll have the apartment to ourselves. It'll be real hunky! Burgo's hardly ever there, of course. For him it's just a place to change shirts and write letters to you. Oh, boy—will I be glad that's over! A letter a day—whew! And him endlessly asking, 'What d'you think she's doing now? What's she thinking? If I say soandso, how will she take it? Would this make her jealous? Does that make me sound arrogant?' I tell you . . ."

"You mean you helped write those letters?"

"Oh! My darling! Let me tell you, I've spent so much time becoming Ontario's leading specialist on the subject of Miss C. Hamilton, I haven't wefted a warp, or flocked a block, or dashed off a simple little thousand-dollar dress since Christmas!"

Catherine pulled a face.

But Margaret looked at her sternly. "Listen, hon. You may think you're a little old nobody—just Catherine. And I may think so, too. In fact, come to think of it, I do. But not Burgo. To him you're the sun and stars. He'd do anything to win you away from Mystery Lover. Who is he, by the way? Burgo refuses even to guess. But my hobby now is psychology so I'm pretty certain it was Ed. Am I right? The Sheik of Micah? You know how we're supposed to long in secret for a really handsome rapist? I do, anyway."

Catherine had to laugh then. "There was no mystery lover."

"You just pretended there was? Clever thing! I didn't reach that chapter yet."

"But why did you help write those letters, Meg—if you disliked doing it so much?"

"Loyalty, I guess. Also, I secretly hate him enough (that's in Chapter Three: Siblings) for me to want him to marry you."

Catherine stared at her wide-eyed.

"Sure!" Margaret insisted. "You're obviously going to *adore* him. Which will be bad for him. His ego's big enough already. You know all about the ego and the id, I suppose. I'm for the id. She's my favourite. I think we ought to be able to exercise our ids the way men build muscles, don't you? I want to start a mail-order College of the Id, like the piano lessons. Can't you just see the ad: 'He laughed when my ego lay down to play . . . but then my id took him over!' Oh yes!" She clapped her hands. "Keep your eye on auntie!"

Catherine laughed, but a worry at Margaret's new kind of humour began to nag her. There was a decadent, frenzied edge to it that had not been there previously.

After breakfast she calmed down and showed Catherine that she had, in fact, been working hard since Christmas. She flipped through her notebooks and sketchbooks with a kind of offhand pride; Catherine had to keep on pushing a finger in to hold a page open. Otherwise it would all have been a blur. She was surprised to see no "simple little thousand-dollar dresses" there at all, but plenty of truly simple slipovers and day dresses—the sort of thing you could get in a 45¢ pattern from Butterick. There were drawings of Norman Hartnell court dresses and chic Paris model gowns, but they were in a separate notebook, where, too, she jotted down little sketches copied from magazine photographs—Mrs. Harry Brown, Lady Diana Cooper, and the Duchess of Argyll at Ascot, England—that sort of thing. These little drawings were so lively that Catherine laughed with pleasure to see them.

"I'm good, aren't I," Margaret said. "I know I am because I hardly ever go into college but they look at my work and say okay."

"Well, you obviously work very hard."

The fashion wasn't even half of it. There were books full of weaving designs and a few samples. And a whole folder of sheets of printed-textile designs.

"They're so clever with chemicals now," Margaret said. "You know you can get bleaches that bleach only certain families of dyes. So you can mix a bleach with, for instance, a bright yellow from a different family of dyes and print it on jet-black cloth so the bleach knocks out the black and the yellow takes its place! So you can get perfect yellow dots and lines on black without any risk of bits of white showing at the edges."

Her seriousness on her subject fought and beat her tendency to wise-crack all the time. Catherine saw how understanding her teachers were, to let her work alone at home. It was good for her. Too many people would kill that seriousness in her.

In the middle of it all Margaret suddenly asked, "D'you love him, Cath? Burgo. You have come to say you'll marry him, haven't you?"

"I didn't tell your parents that. Not an absolute promise, anyway."

"No. But . . . well, have you? He's really gone on you."

"I think so, Meg. It's hard to tell. I mean, there's love like in stories, where it comes like lightning, like a flood, and a girl's just swept away by it. And then there's love like this, where we've known each other for years and gone swimming and had picnics and danced and lived in the same house, like family. And it's crept up slowly. Besides, I'm not a girl any longer. I don't sweep away."

Meg laughed. "My! You've really got it bad, eh?"

Burgo came around eleven, as Margaret had promised. When Catherine saw him walking up the front-garden path her heart began to thump vio-lently. She thought, *I ought to remember this moment—every bit of it. There's the man I'm going to be with the rest of my life. We're going to make children together.* Yet, apart from her hammering heart, everything seemed so ordinary.

"Hey, Cathy!" He stood, unusually shy, at the door. She was amazed to realize he was nervous, too. He held his hat in his hands but did not hang it up.

"Hello, Burgo. Were you on duty all night?"

The air seemed to oppress him. "D'you want to go for a walk?" he asked.

"Aren't you tired?"

"Come on. Let's go up on the scarp."

Margaret already had Catherine's hat and coat—and galoshes—ready. "Make *hay,* gal," she said, and ducked a blow that Burgo did not aim at her.

The escarpment was over a mile away. They talked about Goldeneye, the journey, her first brief impressions of this part of Ontario, Margaret . . . they didn't even get to the subject of his letters until they were up in the thin belt of maple woodland on the edge of the scarp.

To reach it they crossed the railroad, which ran along the foot of the scarp. At the point where they crossed, a wooded gorge cut into the sheer face of the bluff. It began to twist almost at once so they couldn't see very far up it.

"There's a small river up the end there," he said. "A wee burn. But it makes a waterfall that is actually taller than Niagara itself by several feet." Then he pointed to a vantage right above them, at the angle where the gorge began its cut into the scarp. "But that's where we'll go first. The view from there is really something. You can even see my room at the hospital."

She took his arm and dawdled enough for him to understand he was helping her up the path. He wasn't big-boned, but he was tall—and tough, in a wiry sort of way. Pulling her along at his side was no effort. She liked to feel that lean strength at work. From time to time she glanced at him. This was, after all, her first chance to look at him as a husband. She began to realize what a lot of nice things there were to him.

His eyes, for instance. They were set deep beneath his dark eyebrows, which lent them mystery. They could stare at you keenly and yet seem shy; they could sparkle with laughter and yet go on being coolly observant; they could look hard, even furious, and yet suggest he was on the brink of concessions. If you tried to read Burgo by his eyes, you were lost.

His lips were always that slightest bit into a smile. When he really smiled, his top lip jutted out like a shelf and twisted oddly to his right. Last Christmas, Catherine had tried to imitate it in front of her mirror; all her efforts produced a cross between a drunken leer and a downright sneer. But Burgo made it so genial that she understood why any group of people always enlarged itself to include him when he strolled up. She had noticed that last Christmas, too. Even more, she had seen how, when he merely entered a room, those who looked around to see who had just come in automatically stood a little taller in unconscious invitation.

Wherever he went he *mattered*. Not for anything he had done, or said, or achieved (not yet, anyway); but just for what he naturally was. That was the best thing about him.

"Look at that view!" she said when they reached the spot. Someone had built a low stone wall for security. The rock fell sheer for over a hundred and fifty feet.

"I am," he said, not taking his eyes off her.

She smiled. "That's where we were, down there. We must have looked like ants."

A toy train skimmed westward beneath them. The line seemed to have been transplanted from the prairie for it ran poker-straight to the vanishing point. Toy-train noises, diddle-dum, diddle-dah, floated up to them. She did a slow traverse of the valley with her eyes, knowing it would end on him.

"You described this in your letters," she said.

"Ah, yes. My letters. That was a nasty trick."

"Oh, I hope you won't stop. Now that . . ." She paused.

"Now that what?"

Her eyes rested on him then. "You tell me, darling," she said. Her voice trembled.

"I could never tell you." His hands rose and gripped her below her shoulders. "And I could never finish telling you." He pulled her slowly to him until he could take her head between his hands.

A gust of wind took off his hat, but he did not even start; it must be plummetting and spinning slowly down. Her mind's eye saw it lodge among the scrub on the ragged scree at the foot of the cliff. The breeze tousled his dark, curly hair. He ought never to wear a hat, she thought.

He lowered his lips to hers and it was like no kiss she had ever experienced.

She parted from him enough to say, "Aren't you worried I may have Marfan's Syndrome?" He grinned and kissed her again, this time with his tongue on her palate. But then he began to laugh—and so did she—and they had to stop.

"What changed your mind?" he asked.

She looked at him archly. "Changed my mind about what, Burgo?"

"Why, about . . . " He hit his forehead and took her in his arms again. He was going to be facetious about it but seriousness overcame him. "I love you, Catherine. Life without you would be . . . I can't even think about it. Will you marry me?"

She had not expected herself to cry. She had no idea why the tears began to well up in her eyes. "Oh, Burgo. Darling, darling Burgo. Why didn't I say yes at Christmas?"

"I'm glad you didn't—now."

"I love you." She buried her face in his chest and wiped away the tears. He bent and kissed her hat. She tore it from her and let it follow his.

"Come and see these other falls," he said.

When they were back on the woodland path, walking up the western edge of the gorge, he repeated his question. "What changed your mind?"

"Fram," she answered. "The old Irishwoman who married Midge Laframboise. I don't know if you talked with her much at Christmas?"

"Mostly her medical condition."

"She's marvellous. I don't think I did change my mind. I think she just made me see sense."

He paused. "That's an interesting difference."

"What? Difference between what?"

"Men and women. Fram was really being a mother to you, wasn't she. I don't think a man would take advice from his dad in that situation. But a mother is the first one a woman'd turn to."

Catherine had a sudden memory of her mother. It was not like most of her memories, a picture. She could call up a picture of her mother anytime. This was different. It was how her mother really was. The smell of her, the sound of her movements, the warmth of her nearness, the quiet firmness of her voice, the unwavering light of her guidance.

Suddenly, too, she understood how Fram had worked her spell. She had slipped under all Catherine's armour of wilfulness, her self-destructive love for James, her inability to see any path out of the wilderness, and—what? She hadn't become Catherine's mother, not even momentarily; but she had provided all those qualities. She had become what Burgo had divined—the essential thing that mothers are *for* at such moments of crisis.

"Except Meg," Burgo added. "She wouldn't turn to Mom."

Catherine knew he was really saying that one day *she* might have to do for Margaret what Fram had done for her. The thought was too fragile to transfer in so many words.

"Don't worry," she told him.

He snorted. "If she was your sister, wouldn't you worry?"

"She is my sister." She stepped out a shade more briskly. "Tell me about our life. Tell me what we're going to do. But first"—she stopped and pulled him to face her—"tell me again."

"I love you," he said. "And I love you. And I love you."

Her stomach fell away inside her and she suddenly realized how easy it was going to be to forget James, and Ed, and all her awful, awful past. James had been right to say he was not the great love of her life—only the first.

19

The Cypress Hills in southern Saskatchewan, between fifty and ninety miles north of the border with Montana, are a summer paradise. They have all the good points of the prairie plus a few of their own—like not being plagued by flies, and like having trees and bluffs to break the force of that endless, steady breeze. In Burgo's case they had the further advantage of a cabin owned by P. J. Hanafy, his physiology tutor and the man who sold him his Model T.

P. J. Hanafy obviously knew more about metabolic pathways than hill roads. His map lost them twice before a man staking out a lynx directed them. Catherine would gladly have abandoned the search two hours earlier and slept under the stars. But Burgo was determined to get them there—which he did at close on three in the morning. Burgo's middle name was Determination. He even carried her over the threshold. But it was the last, desperate play of an exhausted body.

"You want a meal?" she asked when he made the second trip, with their bags.

His bloated eyes lit up. "You would? If I wanted one?"

She nodded, fighting a yawn.

He fell on her. She wilted. They propped each other up. "Greater love hath no woman than that," he said.

Somehow they stood upright again. "All I want," he added, "is an apple and bed."

When they were in bed he sidled over to her and put an arm across her shoulder. "You know what's supposed to happen now?"

"Yes. I know what's supposed to happen now."

"Well, it isn't going to. Not tonight."

She gave what would have been a giggle if it hadn't also been a yawn. "Greater love hath no man than that," she said.

He laughed. "Cath?"

"Mmmm?"

"We're going to have *the* most marvellous marriage!"

"Mmmm."

She woke just past noon. He still slept soundly. She lay beside him and stared into his face, ignoring the double five o'clock shadow, appraising him like sculpture. She realized she had never seen him asleep before—lying down with his eyes closed, yes, but not asleep. And there was a difference. When he was awake there were always muscles at work, drawing in his skin. His eyes were never at rest. But now, with everything relaxed, she could see, for the first time, the cherub features she had sometimes seen in James. She shuddered and shook her head, as if to dislodge the thought. She wanted Burgo unalloyed, no memory of James behind him.

She forced herself to slip from the bed, wash, dress, and cook their breakfast-lunch. The smell of bacon woke him. She saw the disappointment briefly in his eyes. "One egg or two?" she asked.

"Neither," he drawled. "You."

"I'll do two."

"Don't I even get a kiss?"

With the frying knife still in her hand she leaned down and kissed his bristly lips. Her breasts hung over him. His hands stole up and caressed them. Their tongues met.

She had to tear herself away. "They'll burn," she said.

That brief intimacy, her loving response, reassured him. He stopped trying to joke-seduce her back into bed. Instead he sat up, scratched his hair and beard, and passed his tongue over his teeth. "Yeurk!" He flunked his own inspection. "I need new muscles. How do those guys in the love stories get away with it!" He rose naked from the sheets. "But first we eat, ja?"

She was glad she hadn't known he was naked. "Where are your pyjamas?" He was "an hairy man." Ed and James had been smooth.

"Waal, ma'am, I sort of woke up in the night and saw how fair you were, and how unfair I was, denying myself to you like that, so I shucked them off and . . ."

He appeared to be building it to a climax. "And?" she prompted.

"And went right back to sleep. What are we going to do after breakfast?"

"We're going down to Whitewater and do some shopping." She spoke in prim tones uncomfortably close to Fiona's. "And then we are going for a hike. We aren't going to waste this glorious sun."

But he saw the glint in her eye. "Perish the thought," he said grinning.

After they had got in their supplies they set off on their hike; it was midafternoon. They took only oranges and chocolate to eat, and rugs to sunbathe on. In the best P. J. Hanafy tradition they got lost almost at once and re-emerged on the road down to Whitewater. A man who was freshening the paint on a DON'T LIGHT FIRES sign put them straight. Burgo gestured at a finger of a hill, pointing south and running out toward the prairie and the American border. "Is there a stream out there? Or a spring? We want to walk two or three miles, take a drink from a running stream, and stroll back again."

"Vacationers, huh?"

"Sort of."

"Honeymooners?" He was grinning at the thought.

"Convalescents," Burgo said earnestly. "We were both pretty sick this spring. A nasty attack of virgo-intacta. Both of us."

"Oh, I'm sorry." Honeymoonitis was obviously public domain; true sickness was private. "I hope you're better."

"Very nearly. A single day, in country like this, and weather like this, could see us completely cured."

"A few hours even." Catherine squeezed Burgo's hand.

"Well, there's as pretty a running stream as you could hope to see out there. Two miles, if that. It breaks over a rock and falls into a little pool.

You'll hear the sound. Just keep on south, work upward, a couple of benches, and you'll hear it. If you get lost, go right up on the plateau and you'll see where the trees follow the line of the stream up the hills."

Burgo had meanwhile noticed a stone chimney sticking up out of some secondary-growth aspen and dogwood. He asked what it was.

"Nobody knows," the man told them. "Some say it's a relic of Mexican-Spanish days, when they smelted silver there."

"Is there silver hereabouts?"

"Not that I heard of."

They thanked him and set off. When they were out of earshot, Burgo laughed at this information. "It has to be wrong," he said. "The Spaniards were never up here. I'll bet that's the relic of a Métis house."

When the man had described the stream, Catherine had pictured the little waterfall behind Beinn Uidhe, surrounded by granite boulders and heather. But it was nothing like that. The stream here rose just a few yards above a fault in the rock, over which it fell about eight feet to a shallow pool, waist deep and pebble-floored; it ran through the heart of a small, thickly wooded dell surrounded on both sides and above by open tracts of spear grass and some variety of wheat grass.

Burgo spread the rugs out in a patch of sun. Then he stood and took her in his arms. For a long while they stared each other out, arms around each other, pelvises tight pressed, swaying slightly. His smile was like a challenge; but it was also hesitant, asking her something undefined. She felt it was all happening too pat: walk—find lonely spot—spread blankets—spread selves—make love. So when he let her go, expecting her to lie down, she skipped away to the poolside, raced out of her clothes, and dashed into the ice-cool water—straight under the giant, massaging fist of the waterfall itself.

He sauntered over and sat on a fallen trunk, watching her. She liked the feel of his eyes upon her and though, when she faced him directly she kept her pubic hair below the water line and put her hands up to wipe her face, hiding her breasts in the process, she found ways to show herself off in between.

"I hope you're enjoying yourself," she said at last.

"I'm enjoying you more. After all, you had your turn this morning."

She splashed him, carefully missing. "I don't think you know what sort of woman you married, Burgo."

"I was just about to turn that very thought into a complaint, ma'am."

"You don't think I'm strong enough to come out there and throw you in, clothes and all."

"No, ma'am, I don't."

So she came out and did it, clothes and all. He went in with a great roar and surfaced, spluttering. They splashed around for a bit, then he peeled his clothes off and threw them, sodden, onto a rock. She climbed out, picked them up, and went to spread them to dry. Then she sat down on the rug, legs parted, braced body-up to the sun and let its heat caress her.

A shadow fell cool upon her. She opened her eyes and saw his shrivelled button of a penis, lost in its hair. She pulled a sad-comic smile and looked up at his face; then she saw his eyes—the love in his eyes—and she was serious, too.

He knelt between her parted legs. She lay back, blinded by sun, arm over her face. He put his hands on her stomach and hips and began to caress her. When they reached her breasts she gripped his arms and pulled him onto her.

"Oh," he murmured, "your body has the most gorgeous fragrance. It's like cinnamon."

She put her hand violently over his mouth. "Don't!"

"What?" He squeezed the word out sideways.

She took her hand away. "Just don't talk."

"Oh!" He smiled, thinking he understood. Then he lowered himself upon her.

Would she ever be free of James? Only by loving Burgo so much and giving herself to him so absolutely that there'd be no room for anyone else. She put her arms around him and clung to him with desperate strength. She felt his erection growing; it *grew* into her. And her climax, later, was like no other she had ever felt. The difference was that she knew they were starting a baby. That throbbing wasn't like Ed filling a rubber bag he'd pushed inside her on a trunk of gristle. It wasn't like James, moistening a handkerchief on her belly. That pulsation of Burgo's was filling *her;* it was like the first heartbeats of a new little life.

Weeks ago they had talked about starting, or not starting, a family, and she, not without some silent misgiving, had said firmly that she wanted to start right away. Now she was sure she had been right.

They made love again in the evening, and that night, and yet again late the following morning. By then they were both sore. But she hugged herself warmly and contentedly around all his seed, knowing how it would quicken her.

Until this moment she had never truly been a woman; she had never felt that special status which comes when a man centres his life on her and sets out to build his whole future in common with hers—and when she, likewise, puts him at the very centre of her being and can think nothing important unless he is part of it. By the same token, everything of which he was a part gained absolute importance, including herself. She was somebody. She was special.

"Do you like Goldeneye?" he asked one day.

"I'm like Ruth. Whithersoever thou goest . . ."

"Gee, I hope you mean that, Cath. Because I don't think Dad and I are cut out for a partnership. I'll manage this summer okay. I mean, we won't fall out too disastrously. Dad has this dream of making the hospital a centre for traumatic and orthopedic surgery. He wants it so much, he'll get it, too. He'll make it true. But I'm no surgeon. Never in a million years. So—er—we won't be living in Goldeneye."

"Where instead? In Saskatoon?"

"You don't seem too cut up, I must say."

What could she tell him? "Your father is now the biggest threat to our marriage. Never take me back there to live!"? What she said was, "Wherever you'll be happiest, I'll be happiest with you."

"I didn't get a chance to tell you this before the wedding. But on my last day at MacNair, when I collected the keys of this place from P. J., he offered me a post as demonstrator in physiology, in his firm, with tenure in five years."

"Firm?" she queried.

"Well—team. That's what they call a team at MacNair."

"And tenure?"

"It would mean I could be fired only for serious crimes, like seducing any new nurse before P. J. got the chance."

"No danger of *that!*"

He grinned. "Not from where I'm standing."

"Where will we live? In the apartment?"

"Same avenue. About two hundred yards farther up the hill. I've got my eye on a house there. Of course, we won't buy it until you've seen it and okayed everything. But I think you will."

"Did we walk past it on the way up to the escarpment?"

"We must have done."

Pictures began to flicker in her inexhaustible memory. "Was it set back more than the others, on a sort of extra mound? Brick below, white clapboard above?"

"That's the one!"

"Circular window over the porch? Ugly floral curtains?"

"Right! You're amazing."

"I like it," she said grandly. "Buy it. But not those curtains."

"Okay. Consider it done."

"Are you joking?"

"Of course not."

"But surely we don't have money for that? Do we?"

And so he told her how he had taken his grandfather's legacy of two thousand dollars when he came of age and begun investing in stocks and bonds. He explained how one could buy, say, ten thousand worth of stock on a five-percent margin, which meant all you had to pay out initially was five hundred dollars.

All! she thought.

Then, when the price rose, you could sell out and keep all the profit. Not just five percent of it. All of it! Of course, if the stock fell, you stood all of the loss, too. But stocks just weren't falling. The whole world was about to take off on one unprecedented and unstoppable rush of prosperity. They were right on the crest of that wave. Anyone with just a little money could buy space up there and get carried forward to unimaginable wealth. "In the next five years," he promised her, "that two thousand will be two million."

"Impossible!" She laughed.

"Not at all. I told you how you can lay out five hundred to get ten thousand worth of stock? Well here's the thing, you see. When they rise to twenty thousand, the banks will lend on the difference—a full ten thousand dollars on that stock. Actual folding money! So you can go out and put down more margin on more shares and take more loans. And so on. It can't lose."

"Why isn't everyone doing it?"

He grinned. "Everyone is."

She decided it was too far over her head. All she cared about was that they'd have their own house and could fill it with their own babies. If his cleverness made all that possible, then it was marvellous.

She felt warm and loved and content, and not lonely anymore. She felt *together,* not only with him but with herself.

PART THREE

1929~1931

20

Burgo sold the Cadillac in Toronto that Monday morning. The papers were still shouting: PANIC SELLING DELUGE GOES ON . . . MILLIONS MORE SHARES FALL . . . PRICES STAMPEDE . . . WILD SCENES . . . AVALANCHE. There was a restrained glee in the reporting; the losses were not yet felt too widely. The story was part serious, part silly-season. One reporter began his column with Pudd'nhead's well-known joke: "October, this is one of the peculiarly dangerous months to speculate in stocks. The others are July, January, September, April, November, May, March, June, December, August, and February."

Burgo could have driven to New York quicker, but he needed the cash more. He had bought most of his stock at rock bottom, so there was no panic to sell, even after the falls of last Thursday. Now, on Monday, the market looked like steadying, so he was still sitting pretty. However, the market was volatile, so maybe it was time to cash in and sit back a while. But one of the lessons of last Thursday was that no one outside Wall Street knew what the hell was happening; the tapes had slid hours behind the market. People were selling at what they thought was a hundred, say, and finding their true acceptance was at eighty. And worse might happen. They could see what looked like a falling market on the tapes, sell at bottom, and then, hours later, realize that the market had actually been rising.

So Burgo felt he had to get his stock certificates into his own hands and go to New York, where he could personally watch the market and decide what to do. His broker warned him that the only outfit that never makes money on the markets is a one-man band, but he brushed it aside. "Sell now while you're just a little ahead," the man said. But he refused.

He went nearly thirty thousand dollars in debt to the bank to meet the calls and get physical possession. But the stock was worth four times that, even on Monday's quotations. He left enough scrip with the bank to cover the loan, and caught the first express to New York. He put the cash from the Cadillac sale in his pocket so that, come what may, he and the family wouldn't starve.

To avoid worrying Catherine he told her he had to go down and "settle a little problem over Margaret." It was credible enough. Margaret, who had lived in New York for the past year, had recently lost a job in the fabrics department at Bloomingdale's (for being drunk), and now seemed to be having trouble holding down another at a wholesale merchant of trimmings and notions. Catherine would worry, of course, but it would be on Margaret's behalf. If he told her the truth, she wouldn't sleep for fear of what might happen to her and the two children—Kelvin, now three and a half, and baby Madeleine, not yet three months old. As for himself, he could just about stay together. But then he was the one who was, if only partially, in control.

He bought all the papers and settled down for a long, dispiriting read. But even before they reached Buffalo, on the border, the outlook had lightened from black to very dark gray: U.S. Steel was holding, and so, too, were Woolworth's, Paramount, and AT&T; they had slipped, but nothing much. And they were the "bankers" in his portfolio.

A man sitting opposite, who had watched him read through all the financial reports, said, "Them New York Jews had it coming to them."

"I don't know," Burgo answered. "It seems to me that a man who keeps his head could actually come out of this still smiling."

"You Jewish?" the man asked suspiciously.

"Next best thing—Scottish."

The man shrugged uncomprehendingly. "You could be right," he said glumly. "If there is a way out, them schlemmies'd know it. But I sure hope you're wrong. For once."

It was gone midnight before Burgo found Margaret's apartment, three floors up in a house on West Tenth near Bleecker, in Greenwich Village. A bleary "Who is it?" greeted his third rap on the door.

"Police," he said. "Open up." It was a joke from her student days.

"What?" There was wide-awake panic there. She must have forgotten.

"We got word you was harbouring a heap of dangerous dress designs in there."

"Burgo?" She was remembering.

"Drop your scissors and come out with your safety pins up!"

"Christ!" she shouted. "Drop your pants and come in bent over!" She opened the door.

They hugged each other. She was wearing only a long dressing gown, artistically cut (if the purpose of art is to reveal) from a Macrae tartan blanket. Then she mock collapsed in histrionic relief. "Never pull that joke in this city," she said. "Certainly not in this house. And you could've called —you have the number."

"It's a bit of a panic I'm afraid, Meg. This Wall Street business."

"You mean *our* Wall Street? Here? In little old New York? Down near the bottom of Broadway? Is it famous at last?"

He laughed. "The one and only."

"Is something happening there? Should I know about it?"

He checked to see if she was joking and decided she wasn't. For one thing she was too tipsy to hide such tricks from him. "Well," he said. "The girl who so recently bored the world to death over the gold standard and the League of Nations *has* changed."

"Oh, I'm still pretty close to both," she contradicted. "Now I worry about the rye standard and Geneva lace. The thing is, Burgo, I kind of have company." She nodded toward her bedroom.

"Oh."

"Okay. I'll give him the Bronx welcome. You stand over there with your back to the door."

As she led the "company" out she said, "That's my brother," meaning it as explanation. Burgo, taking it as an introduction, half turned, and saw why she had made him face away. The company was older than their father, he was fat, ugly, and bald. His hat had seen better decades and his clothes would be lucky to see next week.

"He's the kind you can humbly ask to scram," she said when the man had gone.

Burgo was appalled. "He's the kind you ought never to ask anything else of."

"Except a job." Her eyes were defiant.

"Oh, Meg. Is it *that* bad?"

"No, it's worse now. I just lost it."

"But . . . what job is worth *that!*"

"The ones they keep specially for women. Specially in the garment trade. And how's my favourite sister-in-law? And the babies? And the car? And how much did your lawn cost you last year? Are you still in touch with the real world, Burgo?" She giggled and sat down heavily. "Questions is hard work."

He came to a decision. "Listen, Meg. You're not well. You'd better come home and stay with us for a while. You can dry out, and I'll fix you with a job at the university, and then later—"

"What job?"

He thought furiously. "We need a medical illustrator. Someone who can work fast—over the surgeon's shoulder. Cathy can help you with the anatomy—"

"Surgeons?" She wrinkled her nose. "Blood? Cadavers?"

He saw he'd get nowhere that night. "Sleep on it," he said. "We'll talk about it in the morning."

They talked about it so long the following morning that he didn't get to Wall Street until after ten. Margaret still hadn't agreed to go back home with him. But she had accepted the fare and a few dollars on top, just in case something went wrong and he couldn't get back to her that day.

When he reached Wall Street, he saw at once that everything was wrong. In fact he saw it just seconds before he made the turn from Broadway. Trinity Church was open and had turned into a place of gloomy pilgrimage. Even men who were obviously Jewish were using it—simply because it was the nearest place of prayer. One such group went in as Burgo watched, self-consciously tapping one another on the shoulder and miming *Take off your hat!*

The Stock Exchange itself was unapproachable. Police and security guards ringed the entrance while their colleagues made repeated drives to clear the street—a lost battle against the grim crowd that waited . . . for what? Did they expect the fabric of the building itself to start crumbling symbolically? Or did they hope brokers would appear on the ledges and start jumping? Burgo felt the hopelessness of his slow struggle through those crowds.

It was a man in front who gave him the idea. He had pushed this fellow a bit harder than he intended. The man turned round, ready for a fight; but then he saw Burgo's bag. "Let the guy through," he began to shout. "He's a doctor. Let the doctor through!"

Burgo blessed the habit that had made him bring the bag along. He hardly needed to shout, "Let me pass, please. I'm a doctor!" more than a couple of times; the crowd did it for him. A doctor on some emergency errand was as dramatic as anything else they'd seen so far.

As he drew near to the front, he began shouting, to cover himself. "I'm the doctor. Where's the accident?" Miraculously, a policeman took him up: "Here, doc! He's over here."

There really was someone down. Heart attack by the look of him. Pallid. Sweating. Clammy. Thready pulse.

Burgo forgot his errand. He loosened the man's collar, got his head on one side, checked his tongue was clear of his throat, and then raised his knees.

He looked up at the policeman. "Where's the Stock Exchange medical office?" he asked.

The cop jerked a thumb over his shoulder at the Stock Exchange. "In there," he said. "We sent in, but they may not come out."

"Why not, for God's sake?"

"Doc, you wouldn't believe the tricks guys have been pulling to get through them doors!"

"Well, this guy's pulling no tricks. He's dying. He's dead if we don't do something. Do you know where there's a stretcher?"

"I do." It was one of the security guards. He was already running.

While they waited, Burgo prepared a digitalis shot and gave it to the man. "Funny," he said conversationally to the policeman (implying *You and I, we see death too often to be awed by it*), "I was coming here about a job. Starting next week. Looks like I already started."

"Next week!" the cop said. "There ain't no next week, doc."

But he made no attempt to stop Burgo from going in with the man when the stretcher came.

The medical department, though well equipped and staffed, was overstretched already that day. The director wasn't too pleased to have a patient brought in off the street. "He can go to Bellevue as soon as we can get an ambulance through that mob," he said. Bellevue, widely (though wrongly) thought to be a mental hospital, was well able to cover this sort of emergency.

"You short-handed today?" Burgo asked.

"You are a doctor, I take it?" an assistant asked. "Only some people..."

"I know. The cop at the door told me. Yes, I am a doctor, Burgo Macrae, Faculty of Medicine, MacNair. I'm willing to help out if you want."

They accepted him.

When the director had gone, the assistant, whose name was Joel Kahn, asked what Burgo had been doing in Wall Street, anyway. Burgo told him. Kahn looked far more serious than he did over a little thing like a heart attack. "Listen, Macrae," he said. "If you've got shares, you really ought to unload. Didn't you see what was happening out there on the floor?"

"No. I was watching our man there."

"Well, just listen!"

There was a steady roar from the trading floor, just beyond the door.

"That's not how it usually sounds?" Burgo asked.

"That's the noise of rich men dying, man. Death by a thousand cuts. Just before you came, the super told me they've wiped off two billion already today. Two billion, in—what?" He checked his watch. "Half an hour. That's over a million a *second*. Listen—you thought last Thursday was bad!"

"But there must be a rally, surely? It can't just go down and down."

"Can you afford to pay your margin calls *and* sit tight twenty years? Like Helena Rubinstein and the Morgans?"

Burgo shook his head.

"Then you can't afford not to dump what you've got for what you can get."

"All of them? What about U.S. Steel?"

"That's what started it today. The super said over half a million shares in U.S. Steel were dumped in the first three minutes."

"Oh, my God!" A sick knot began to curl in his stomach. He should have sold last week. He should have ignored Margaret and run here today. His shares should have been trading during those first three minutes. "How do I sell?"

"You got all your certificates?"

"Right here." He took the folder from his bag. "They're listed there."

Kahn let his eye run down the column. "It would help," he said, "if I had a few hundred bucks. Not for me, you understand. But it's the only thing that's talking out there today."

Burgo gave him two hundred and fifty.

"You cover for me," Kahn said, and slipped out into the chaos.

Burgo stayed all day, not merely to keep his word but to keep busy, too —to keep his mind off the appalling thing that had happened to him—and, of course, to Catherine, Kelvin, and the baby. The broker Kahn used had done his best, but it was nowhere near enough. Burgo was wiped out. Worse, the stock he had left as collateral with the bank was worthless. He was down the hole—way down, twenty-five thousand dollars down. Last Friday—yesterday even—he could have sold and come out well ahead. Now the bank would call in the loan. And there would be twenty-five thousand dollars he couldn't repay.

And he had stayed up in the Village arguing with a sister who was a lush!

No, that wasn't fair. *He* had come to New York, thinking he could do something smart—still make a fortune—stay long in bulls and short in bears! Bulls! In this feast of toreadors?

There was scant satisfaction in creeping out to the edge of the trading floor from time to time, watching mature men scream the vilest abuse at one another and even throw punches.

"Adrenalin's bullish!" Kahn said gaily, standing beside him. "You realize that practically every man in sight is ruined—or reduced to splinters of what he was this day last week?"

"Some of them treat you that bad, eh?" Burgo asked.

Kahn chuckled. "Does it show? Not me, actually. My old man." He breathed in through clenched incisors. "No, but some of them had it coming. There's a man I'm sorry for." He pointed to Post Twelve, nearby. "Mike Meehan. He put millions into radio."

"Someone must be out there making money, though."

"Only commission on sales. To make money today you want an office away from here. Plus a staff of fifteen, open lines to Paris, London, Chicago,

Los Angeles, a mind like a library and a calculating dervish in one. And a year behind you of dreaming about a week like this, every which way."

Burgo nodded with reluctant, disgusted envy. He left when the closing gong rang at three. He didn't even bother to go back to the Village. The shirt and razor he had left there weren't worth the hindrance. He had to get back to Dunedin and break the news to Catherine.

At Poughkeepsie a man joined the train with a piece of history in his hand: the last foot or two of that day's ticker tape. It finished: TOTAL SALES TODAY 16,383,700 GOOD NIGHT. Another passenger worked out that each one of those sales represented a loss of more than six hundred dollars.

A hell of a lot more than that, Burgo thought, *if you bought on margin.*

21

"Who's a naughty daddy then? Yes! Who's a naughty daddy?" Catherine shifted Madeleine to her other breast. Then, noticing the rolling, puckered eyes that meant wind, she raised the baby onto her shoulder and began patting and stroking her back. The child's arm got twisted between them. She pulled it out and arranged it less awkwardly. The amazing tightness of baby skin, so waxen firm and yet so soft, never ceased to amaze. Her own skin had already lost that fine bloom of pregnancy and was once again showing its twenty-nine years. Nothing much to be sure, but decided crow's feet ("laughter lines" as Burgo insisted); and the folds from the corners of her nostrils down to the edges of her smile, which were once single and sharp, were now narrowly twinned in places and looked as if drawn by a palsied hand ("and it's very obvious," Burgo said, "to anyone with a two-fifty-power microscope!"). All right, one had to look closely to see it; but she did look closely.

"Yes," she told Madeleine, "he could have called us from Aunty Meg's and let us know. He could have called. He's a naughty daddy."

It was equally true that she could have called Margaret's; the fact was, she had been afraid to learn what it might be this time. Often it seemed to her that one of Margaret's misfortunes was to have a brother rich enough to rescue her, start her off again, and keep word of it from their parents. Fiona would soon sort Margaret out. Burgo's kindnesses were not what that girl needed.

There was a huge, wet burp at her ear. "Oh, wasn't that good! Doesn't that feel better now!" She settled the baby back at her right breast and began to hum the Selkie song, Maddy's favourite. These feeding times, even the one in the small hours, were the best moments of the day—not even the clever paediatricians at the university could take them away from her.

The theory was that cuddling and hugging could do untold psychological harm to babies. Dr. Grantly Dick-Read, the world expert on all aspects of child rearing, was set hard against all such mollycoddling. One dreadful afternoon when she had been out with Kelvin in his pram and he had cried, and she had unthinkingly picked him up to cuddle him, the wife of the dean of psychology had actually come running down the street, shivering with anger. "If you took a butcher's knife and cut his face open, you'd do less harm!" she had screamed at Catherine. Nowadays she had to take Kelvin and Madeleine up to the gorge and go deep along muddy paths into the woods before she dared pick either of them up for a good hug.

Even to nurse her babies at her own breast was considered eccentric and old-fashioned. All the leading medical opinion was that it was unsanitary, unscientific, and psychologically negative. Breast milk had dozens of chemicals in it that scientists couldn't analyze. And even those they could were suspect; no exact functions could be assigned to them. And the whole composition of it varied so much from mother to mother, and even from feed to feed. How much more scientific it was to give a baby something whose formula was known and controlled, which could be guaranteed never to vary, and which could be fed at a guaranteed set rate in measurable quantities, from guaranteed sterile containers that took *hours* to prepare and so gave Mother a chance to show her guaranteed true love for her baby. Contrast her with the ignorant, lazy creature who flopped herself down any old where and fished out a breast.

"I just enjoy it so much," Catherine said—an answer considered to be in faintly bad taste.

Besides, she thought, how can any single rule apply to all babies, when each one is so different—even in the same family? Kelvin would go off to sleep whether it was quiet or the house was falling down all around him; but Madeleine needed noise. Sometimes Catherine had to switch on the vacuum cleaner and set it beside her cot before she would sleep during the day.

Today, though, was not one of those times. Maddy obviously decided to sleep without any greater artificial aid than the occasional passing vehicle. Catherine laid her in her cot, tidied away a shawl and a pair of little knitted bootees, and then went from room to room just straightening things.

She loved this house. It had taken four years to transform it into their home, but the result was worth the effort. Each room had the simplicity she had always wanted. There were no patterns anywhere. The walls were all in smooth washes of pale, neutral tints. The carpets were in plain, muted colours and so were the curtains. Here and there hung drawings by Margaret and some abstract etchings by a painter Margaret said was one of the all-time greats; but he hadn't signed them and Catherine had forgotten his name. Also under Margaret's influence she had begun to study printmaking, part-time, at the college. There she had done some abstract prints that Mr. Thomas, her teacher, judged "not very adventurous, but most satisfying for all that." Catherine herself did not consider them "art" because they had cost her none of the suffering that Margaret said was indispensable to the creative act; they were, quite simply, decorations made to suit her own home —which they did, perfectly.

Other university wives at first thought the place much too austere. But then Madame Meyerhof, wife of one of Canada's leading authorities on art, had seen a set of Catherine's prints at Mr. Thomas's home and had come to visit her and Burgo. Word came back from Montreal that she thought it was one of the most tasteful homes she had ever visited. After that, Catherine, who was the last to hear the opinion, was surprised at how often she was consulted in matters of taste in general and decor in particular. People were kind enough to say she could do it professionally. Thanks to her there was a rash of garage sales in Dunedin, at which a couple of tons of Victorian and Edwardian rubbish proved mostly unsaleable, eventually ending up on the town dump.

Margaret's explanation of the phenomenon was that Catherine had never been anything but a peasant at heart and she therefore had a quarter-century start over any woman so unfortunate as to be middle class and educated.

Catherine finished her tour of the house, filled with satisfaction at her luck in being married to such a good and clever man as Burgo—good because he let her taste have absolute sway at home, and clever for being able to afford it (for artistic simplicity is not cheap). She went into the kitchen to make a cake. The kitchen was the only place over which they fell out, she and Burgo. He would keep buying her gadgets she didn't want and wouldn't use. The electric eggbeater was an example. She hadn't asked for it, and he was always exasperated when he came into the kitchen and caught her beating eggs the only way she considered proper—with her fingers.

That was the way she beat them today. In the midst of it, Burgo walked into the house. She ran to kiss him, full of guilt, hiding her egg-drooling fingers behind her back. Then she saw his face and stopped.

"Oh, Burgo dear! What's the matter? Is it Margaret again?"

"Isn't Meg here?" he asked absently.

He couldn't look her in the face. That had never happened before. When she saw that she grew afraid.

"I thought that's why you went to New York."

He nodded. He looked exhausted. She went and swilled her hands, all thought of cakemaking abandoned. "Did you see her?" she asked.

"Yes. But that wasn't . . . oh, God, is there any coffee?"

"Burgo! What's the matter? What is it?"

"I didn't sleep on the train. And then I walked from—"

"The train! What's wrong with the car?"

"I sold it."

Suddenly she was afraid to ask any more. "Look," he said. "I'll take a quick shower. You make that coffee. And then I'll tell you everything."

When he'd gone she tried to remember the last time he'd walked into the house without kissing her or asking after the children. There never had been such a time. She told herself there couldn't be another woman, but the air was full of bad promise.

He was fresher, cleaner, when he came back, but even more glum. "Sit down, Cath," he said. "Have a coffee, too. I'm afraid I've got just about the worse possible news a man could bring home."

She was sure then that he'd lost his job. She prepared to offer what support and cheer she could.

"We're broke," he said. "We've lost all our money."

"Oh no!"

"Yes. I'm afraid we have."

"But how?"

"This stock market crash. We're not the only ones, of course. There must be millions—but that's no comfort. In fact, it's going to make things even more . . . even harder."

Now that the truth was out, she didn't think it half so bad as the vague, partly articulated fears that had possessed her before. She gave him an encouraging smile—not so broad as to seem insensitive, but broad enough to show him he was making too much of it. "Burgo, darling! It's dreadful, I know. But we can soon be up again. You've always got your salary. And I can be as thrifty as the—"

He was shaking his head. "If that was all," he said. "God, I wish that was all. You're the most wonderful wife in the world, Cath. God knows I've done nothing to deserve you. . . ."

"Burgo!" Every time she tried to get close, to share this disaster and face it with him, he drove a wedge between them. Her panic began to return.

"The fact is," he went on, "we're in debt, too."

The word "debt" was especially chilling to her. The Free Kirk version of the Lord's Prayer runs, *Forgive us our debts as we forgive our debtors.* Debt was not mere misfortune. It was trespass. It was sin.

"How much?" she asked, dry in the mouth.

He buried his head in his hands. "Twenty-five thousand dollars."

She was stunned. The words echoed and re-echoed in her mind but could find no meaning. Money represented labour to her, and she was still the woman who had been prepared to work a year or more to repay a hundred-fifty-dollar debt. And what did Burgo say? *Twenty . . . five . . . thousand!* That was more than ten years' salary.

"But we never had that much money, Burgo. How can we owe it?"

"In a way we did," he tried to explain. "If I'd sold all our stocks last week, we'd have had more. Then we could have repaid the bank and met the margin calls and have had enough left over for an economic holiday in Europe next summer. Instead I went to New York and sold them yesterday for a sum that left us owing . . . well, I can't say it again."

"But we'll be in debt for the rest of our lives." She was too numb to feel the full shock. It was still mere words.

"Oh no!" His sudden confidence filled her with absurd hope. "Not a bit. Five or six years could see us free of it and beginning to climb again." He saw the happiness returning to her and had to add, "I'm not saying it isn't an awful hole I've put us in. But it's not going to take a lifetime to climb out."

She did some rapid figuring, and it came out wrong. "But, darling, even if we don't spend anything, that's twice what you earn."

He nodded. "Right. That's exactly it. We have to spend zero—or as near to it as we can. And—yes—I have to take two jobs. It's going to be impossible, of course. With this crash there'll be millions—tens of millions—looking for just one job. Any job. And I've got to find two. And two damn good ones. But I'll do it."

Despite the gloom behind what he said, the confidence with which he said it gave her heart. "*We'll* do it," she corrected. "You've no idea how thrifty I can be. We can sell all our gadgets. I can do everything by hand. And—" His face stopped her. "Why not? What now?"

"It's way beyond that, honey. If we just ate two cups of rice a day for the rest of our lives, how much would that produce?"

"But it all helps. What more can I do? Just tell me. I'll do anything to keep us—our home—all of us—together. We've got to stay together, darling."

Again he buried his face. "I don't know how I can break this to you, honey. Or how I can ask you to do it."

"Just ask. I'll do anything."

"We have to sell this house. Like I sold the car. We have to sell every-thing. Even some of our clothes."

She was silent a long time. Mentally she was walking—floating, rather —from room to room, each one so recently brought to that perfect sim-plicity which was *her*. Each one a bit of her. Sell it! He was asking her to sell bits of herself. All that was primitive in her shouted a rebellious *No!* Rather sell herself. But a more rational Catherine already understood that it had to be.

"What is it anyway?" she asked aloud. "Only bricks and wood and plaster. We'll have it all again one day. Even better. As long as we're to-gether." She smiled. The notion, once she bit on the bullet, wasn't so dread-ful—as long as they were together. "We'll take a little cold-water flat in Selkirk, and I can go out to work. . . ."

Once more he was ahead of her, closing doors and putting up *No Entry* boards.

"What now?"

"None of this can look forced, Cath. It's all got to look as if my trip to New York paid off—as if I just saved us by the skin of our teeth. The sale— you and the children going away—that's all got to look as if something else is the cause."

"Going away?" She was horrified at the cool way it came out. "We're not going away."

"Oh, Cath! I hate doing it. But that's the way it's got to be. I can't see any other—"

"Well, maybe *you* can't. Let's see what two minds can do, shall we?"

"It's no go, Cath. I spent all last night looking at it from every—"

"After spending all the previous night sobering up Meg, no doubt—and all yesterday trying to sell our stock. Very nimble-minded you must have been! Come on now, Burgo. We have to save ourselves together." He was silent. "We have to," she repeated.

"Okay." He sighed, the deepest, weariest sigh. "Here's how it is."

"No. Here's how you see it. I'll tell you how it is."

"How it is!" he insisted. "There's no chance of paying this off by my taking the usual sort of night job—taxi driving, telephone relief. Not even doing night calls for other doctors. I'd need to stand in for half a dozen. No —I have to find a second job that pays even better than the university."

She started to object but he outspoke her. "I haven't the details worked out yet, of course. But that's it. I've seen others do it. God, I wish I were in psychology—it's such a fake anyway. Look at Jack—he makes twice his salary at weekends and vacations as 'advisor' to a string of ad agencies—and he told me himself, he makes up half his concepts as he goes along."

"But you'd hate yourself if you even tried. . . ."

"I know. I'm just envious," he said. But she saw he didn't mean it. He would do any paying work, however shoddy or intellectually degrading, to make money.

"I have to invent something, or discover some need—or do both—and bring them together. Something new, for which there isn't any fixed rate."

"What?"

"I don't know yet. Oh, if I did! But I know it's out there. I'll find it."

"And I'll help."

"Cath, I wish you could."

"I will. You know you don't even need to—"

"No—I mean, *could*. I have to hold the faculty job, of course. And I have to do this other one evenings . . . weekends . . . vacations. But how could I hold the faculty job if you and the children are here in some grimy little hovel or if we're trying to live in a trailer!"

"Where are we then?"

"Back home in Goldeneye, of course. That would almost explain itself to people. I could—"

"Home!" She was angry now. "This is home. To us. To Kelvin, Maddy, and me. Here! Not your parents' home."

"But I've already—"

"I don't mean this house. Not even this town. But *here*. This . . . space where we are. Where you are. You and I—we are a home. Our home. Not Goldeneye."

"But it has to be, Cath. Just for a bit. Just for a few years. I can drop hints about problems back home. Make it look—"

"You said it again. You keep calling Goldeneye 'home.' It isn't even *your* home anymore. We are your home. That's what I'm trying to make you see."

"We'll have a home again one day. In five years."

"You've never really thought of this as home, have you. It's simply been a . . ." She shrugged.

"That's not fair, Cath."

"And now you're saying we're just a burden. We'd be in your way."

He shook his head but said nothing.

"Well—aren't you? You want us out of the way while you save the family single-handed. I've never heard anything so. . . . If a family can't pull together and get itself out of trouble. Well . . ."

"I'm asking you to do the hard part, Cath. I'm not just saying that. I'll have the easy part—working all the hours I can. Burying myself in work. Burying my guilt, too. But I'm asking you to go away from everything you've done here—give it up—and go back ho— I mean, to Goldeneye and behave as if everything were normal. That's hard."

"I can't argue with you, Burgo. You sign the cheques—and that's what it would come to in the end if I insisted. But I do know you are wrong. This is the most important thing that's ever happened to you and me. If we can't save it and beat it together, then we've failed. *We*, I mean. You may succeed. I know you will. But *we* will have lost something."

"I don't blame you for feeling so bitter, Cath. But when it's over we'll look back and you'll see I am right." He glanced at his watch. "I wish I knew what happened to Meg."

22

They got half as much again for the house as they expected, and far more than any other house on the street would fetch. Catherine decided to take nothing but their clothing and bed linen. Everything else—everything she had built up over the last four years, all her prints and drawings, even Margaret's (and the anonymous world-beater's)—would stay as part of a whole. To break it would be to mar her own work to no purpose. Their next home would be different and would have its own different things hanging on the walls.

Thanks to this decision, the competition to buy the Macrae home in a "walk-in, hang-your-coat, and start-to-live condition" was fierce; it was, after all, the home that Madame Meyerhof had praised so extravagantly. The extra price they got for it enabled Burgo to lop a year off his estimate of the time it would take to climb back to solvency.

"It's all your doing," he said, to cheer her up. "Because you made it such a wonderful place."

Curiously enough, that was when she needed "cheering up" least of all. Once she had decided to sell not just the house but the home, too, there was a satisfaction in doing it so well. She had often wondered how a painter (and there were several among their friends) could bear to part with a picture after so much soul had gone into its making. Now she understood. The parting was not difficult. It was the decision to part that was hard; once it was taken she had actually become eager for the sale and had conducted all the business side of it with a keenness that surprised Burgo.

And when he told her that the good price was all her doing, she sprang on him her idea for the saving of the family—together.

"We'll move to Toronto," she said. "You can drive to the university each day, and I'll design people's homes for them. I'm sure Madame Meyerhof would help. I believe she was trying to get me to think about it when she came here. Meg says she was."

Burgo certainly did not reject the idea out of hand. In fact, he even asked her what it might cost to set herself up in such a business. But when, after consulting Mr. Thomas, she told him, he said they couldn't afford that much to start with. Perhaps next year . . . ?

"I'll borrow it from James. He knows a good investment . . ." she began. She had it all worked out.

It was an unfortunate choice of phrase, of course—"good investment." She was so mortified that he hardly needed to raise his voice above a whisper when he said, "The one thing we are not going to do—the one thing, the only thing, I forbid—is borrowing from the family. We are going to get out of this alone, by our own efforts. In the meantime," he went on more briskly, "it would do no harm for you to get up a portfolio of imaginary interiors like Meg's fabric designs, to show around when—and *if*—it becomes possible to do it professionally."

These words ought to have cheered her, even though the immediate prospect was so negative. But something in his manner conveyed that he did not really mean it. Next year, she knew, there would still not be enough to spare—nor the next, nor the next. Until they were so close to solvency that her own contribution would be trifling.

It was a very bitter Catherine who carried Madeleine and shepherded Kelvin into the taxi when they left that home-no-longer-home. She did not even turn her head to look back. Burgo was not coming with them to Goldeneye. He said he had too much to do, but she knew he couldn't face his parents. Over the past couple of weeks she had come to accept his reasoning —that if she and the children stayed east, they would have to keep up a certain style in order to support the play for jobs he was about to make. They could never afford it. Therefore she and the children had to go back to Goldeneye for a time. Their absence could be explained by vague hints of "problems" back there, delivered with a calculated mixture of embarrassment and reticence. But now that the actual moment of departure had come, she began to feel betrayed. No matter *what,* she kept telling herself, nothing was worse than this loss of each other. Not bankruptcy, not poverty, not even starvation, as long as they were together. This comfortable taxi ride to a comfortable train, taking them to a comfortable exile with amenable people was wrong; she had a sense of being ushered out of life.

They were about to make the corner when another taxi pulled into the road, passed them, and then nose-dived to a halt, peeling gravel. Margaret jumped out and ran, tiptoe and spindly, toward them waving her purse. She was wearing a fur coat and several hundred dollars of dress and accessories. She grabbed a handful of bills and thrust them through the door that Burgo had just opened.

"Darlings!" she cried, fresh as a stick of celery. "Marvellous news!" To Burgo, who only provisionally accepted the money, she said, "I didn't need it, honey." Then, back among the decibels: "I'm going to get married! Well —may-*be!* Anyway, all your worries on my behalf are over. I'm off to Paris." Then the situation took hold of her. She saw the whole family in the cab— and their heap of luggage. "What's this?" she asked. "Holiday? Where are you all off to?"

Burgo got out and walked her a short way up the street. First she listened, then an argument developed; Burgo hushed her, spoke some more, then, grimly white-faced, she went back to her cab.

"Is she not even saying goodbye?" Catherine asked as Burgo climbed back in.

"She's coming down to the station."

They drove on in silence while Burgo counted out the repayment of his loan exactly from the confused handful Meg had given him. He put it in his billfold and gave the surplus to Catherine. "Give it back to her. She says she's going to Goldeneye with you."

"But what about Paris?"

"Paris!" he said scornfully. "You still believe everything she tells you! Frankly, I'd be much happier to know she's safely with you and Mom and Dad. The last thing we need now is a bout of Margaret up to her usual tricks."

When they pulled up outside the station she turned to him and said, "Don't come in."

"What?" He was surprised. It was so unlike her.

"It'll make it seem so final, darling. We've said our goodbyes already. If you just drop us here, it'll be just as if we could all be back tomorrow."

He gave in. They kissed briefly inside the car, and again outside, while the driver and porter got their bags together. Then he climbed back into the car and waved until he was out of sight. By then Catherine and Margaret had their backs to him, walking into the station. She didn't know why she had insisted on parting outside; it was a spur-of-the-moment feeling that had prompted her.

As soon as they were settled, even before the train pulled out, Catherine took Maddy to the rest room for a feed. And a heavy feed it was, too; they were almost into Toronto before she rejoined Margaret and Kelvin. Madeleine gave a comatose burp that landed a small gobbet of curdy milk half on herself, half on her mother's lap.

Margaret watched Catherine deal with it, fascinated and repelled. "You're actually fond of those revolting tiny things, aren't you Cath," she said. "Me, I'm with Good King Herod."

"One more will be quite enough," Catherine said absently. Then her own words struck her. The thought behind them belonged to those days of long-ago happiness—last month. There would be no more babies for her. The knowledge brought a physical pain with it—a knife turning slowly in her. No more babies! Maddy the last? She clutched the child to her in a futile gesture, wanting to make the most of her every minute.

"How about that crumb!" Margaret said. "Not even taking you to Goldeneye."

"He has a lot to do here, Meg."

Margaret laughed. "Well, that's a token defence if ever I heard one! Okay, hon, I won't press you. But I only heard his account of it. You tell me how you see it."

Catherine hadn't meant to tell her everything. Only the facts, not her own feelings about splitting the family up like this. But the shock of realizing that Madeleine was probably her last baby made her too bitter to hold back. Out it all came.

"Well, you're not going to stay in Goldeneye, are you? Turn into a rutabaga?"

Catherine shrugged. "The prairie's a pretty good place for youngsters, Meg," she said. "They certainly wouldn't resent a childhood in Goldeneye."

"But *you?* I'd resent a childhood anywhere my parents resented living at. Looking back, I mean. Even if it was a paradise at the time. You're not going to bring up monsters, are you? I mean, they'll have feelings for you one day."

Catherine laughed. It seemed so odd that Margaret, who certainly was not noted for her sensitivity to the feelings of others, should be the first among them to make this point. She realized then that she had not, until now, actually tried to picture herself back there in Goldeneye, separated from Burgo, feeling estranged from him in her heart without actually being so, her life, her home, all she had done these last four years and more, all brought to nothing, wiped out—the phrase that was on everyone's lips was so *exact*.

Also there was James. This would be no home-for-Christmas sort of picnic, where they could eye each other amusedly, and even flirt a little, in the safety of gone-tomorrow. She and he would be together again, living and sleeping under the one roof, for . . . how long? a year? two years? even three? And with Burgo away? A thousand here-todays? She'd never hold out, and nor would he.

When Burgo had first said about going "home" to Goldeneye, the thought of James had been the least of her worries. Now, with everything else behind her and only Goldeneye ahead, it turned into her greatest.

Meg broke into her thoughts. "So you *are* just going to take it!"

"What else is there to do, Meg? We have no money at all. Not a cent. I have to stay. And work my keep."

"When you could earn ten times as much designing interiors? You're crazy!"

"Burgo won't allow it."

Margaret parodied her: "Burgow wown't allow it! Well, *fffff* Burgo!"

"Meg!" Catherine blushed for Kelvin, who noticed nothing, and Maddy, who slept on.

"Christ, Cath! If you knew how restrained I'm being." She grinned at a sudden thought. "Anyway, he won't be able to keep you at Goldeneye. My guess is he's going to have to bring you back here every six weeks . . . two months. He's going to need you."

"And me, him," Catherine said, blushing.

Margaret detected the embarrassment and said, "Well, that too. But I didn't mean that. I meant he's going to need you socially. He probably doesn't know it yet, but he will."

"How d'you mean, Meg?"

"Way of the world, darling. The sort of work he's looking for—he won't get it without mixing with politicians, the Chairman of this, the Hon. Sec. of that, and the Treasurer of the other. And it'll be dinners and dances, and the wives will say, 'Is it true you're married, Dr. Macrae? Is Mrs. Macrae—er—all right? How come we never seem to see her?' Muttered hints won't go too far with those pearl-'n-powder pompadours!" She nodded with satisfied confidence. "My dear dumb brother will be sending for you, Cath. Don't you worry!"

"But I've nothing to wear. I kept my mink, that's all. Everything else, all my gowns, I took to Toronto and sold."

"I'll send you all my Paris castoffs. Don't you worry about that. You'll have a new dress a month—the latest, too."

Catherine laughed, thinking it a joke. "Tell me about Paris—not that I'm going to believe it, mind you. Are you *really* getting married?"

"I don't believe it myself yet. I'm supposed to be on tomorrow's sailing from New York, but I'll catch next week's instead, now. Or the week after. Eurk! A transatlantic crossing in December!" She shuddered as if she'd done the crossing in every month, and December had always proved the worst. Then she brightened. "But Christmas in Paris! Won't that be wonderful?"

"Who's the lucky man—if I have the right word?"

"Oh, he's lucky all right. It's not every fat, bald, impotent, eighty-year-old homunculus with halitosis and a tic—and dandruff, imagine that, being bald *and* having dandruff—who gets a glad yes from a sweet, good-natured, loving, passionate, beautiful twenty-four-year-old virgin like me."

"Oh, Meg!" Catherine laughed and was shocked, both. "What's the truth, now?"

"Being a prince helps, of course."

"Only a prince? Still, times *are* hard."

"And a millionaire."

"Well, I can see how that helps."

"Remind me to see what books Dad has on poisons. His name's Mucchiobelli, or something ghastly. That's another thing I'm going to change. Belly! Huh! I like a man with guts, but that's ridiculous."

Catherine supposed that Margaret had found a job at last with one of the Paris fashion houses. This fooling around with the idea of a millionaire prince was her way of devaluing it. Margaret had inherited a strange variant of Fiona's pessimism. She had to devalue all her dreams, in case life got there first.

23

When Catherine had told Burgo that "home" was not so much a place as the togetherness of the four of them, she had really meant the two of them. The children had been included as a matter of course; she did not realize how great their contribution was. She did not know how much Kelvin and baby Madeleine did to make a home. Within a week her ignorance was cured. Goldeneye was not the place Nurse Hamilton had haunted; it was a new home.

To be sure, many things had not changed. Fiona still swiped at James every chance she saw—and those she didn't at once see were certain to be nudged by James more centrally into her field of view. Catherine understood why Burgo and Margaret had laughed so warmly at it when they came home for Christmas that time—it was pleasure at the sheer endurance of their parents. She now felt it, too.

Margaret left for Paris the day after their arrival—but not before she had had a long, earnest talk with Catherine about producing a portfolio.

"Lord help me, but I almost believe her this time," James said.

Fiona laughed at this naivety.

No one said anything about Burgo's and Catherine's tragedy for a week or more. Then Fiona said, "I'm sorry it had to happen to you, Catherine."

"It" was the betrayal, the kick in the face, that every woman had better expect from the men in her life.

"So soon, you mean?"

Fiona laughed grimly. "That's the size of it, dear. I imagine I ought to feel some responsibility, as he's my son. But they're all the same, sooner or later." She heaved a sigh that was meant to add conviction but did not. "Better sooner, I suppose."

Catherine actually began to wonder about the etiquette of the situation (who had more right to denigrate a man—his mother or his wife?) before her anger boiled up and she had to fight to contain it.

"I don't blame Burgo, Fiona," she said, trying to keep a light tone of unconcern in her voice. "He didn't set out to harm us."

"They never do. They just can't help it. Nor can we."

That puzzled Catherine. "Nor can we what?" she had to ask.

"Help ourselves. We can't help being so loving and forgiving. It's our nature."

Catherine looked to see if this was some rare moment of self-parody on Fiona's part. But it was not. Because she was half ready to laugh, she was wrong-footed and could think of no reply. James had said, once or twice, that Fiona, though she seemed so single-valued and predictable, was actually one of the most complicated people he knew. Every now and then, Catherine had a glimpse of what he meant.

"Even having their children for them," Fiona added.

"But surely you wanted Helen and Burgo and Margaret, too?"

Fiona shrugged. "James wanted them, anyway."

"You did, too," Catherine insisted.

"Once they were *there,* I suppose. Once they existed. It was a duty then."

"And a pleasure." Catherine smiled, bringing her face close to Fiona's, forcing her to agree.

"Sometimes. But it's always a duty."

"Well, I say it's almost always a pleasure. And, thank heavens, that helps us forget it's also a duty—goodness, how dull!"

"Forget! Yes!" Fiona sighed.

"Anyway, your duty's done. They're all grown up now."

Fiona was silent a moment. Then she asked, "Do you actually *want* to live, Catherine?"

Catherine laughed nervously. "Of course I do."

"Of course?"

"Yes."

"You mean, it's not a choice? It's an 'of course'?"

"No, I don't mean that."

"Even these last few weeks when everything's come to nothing—even then, it never crossed your mind?"

"What?"

"That you'd be much better off not being alive?"

"Not for one second. Not at the blackest moment. And anyway, Fiona —the children."

"Ah!" Fiona saw a feature that coincided with her own internal landscape. "Duty, you see. There it is!"

If Fiona had not changed, nor had James. In public he was as jovial and demonstrative with her as ever, but in private—well, there *was* no "in private." He avoided all possibility of it. She longed just to talk to him, to unburden herself of so many things she could say to no one else. But he developed an uncanny knack of never being anywhere she might "accidentally" find him on his own. If anyone went with him on his visits, it was always Miss Welland, the new regular nurse.

The pains he took to avoid Catherine's undiluted company were the clearest possible sign that his feelings for her were as strong as ever. From time to time, in rare, unguarded moments, her eyes would meet his and read their ancient longing—the same as stirred within herself.

At last the day came when Miss Welland was poorly and James had to make a visit to Hawk and would need a nurse along. He talked of cancelling it.

"But for heaven's sake," Fiona chided. "Take Catherine!"

He fought and lost the rearguard. They set out in the cutter, at a brisk trot behind two of his best ponies, right after breakfast.

The snow was packed hard, ridged by wind, melted and refrozen, scored and polished by the traffic. Here and there lay horse dung, deceptively fresh but hard as cannonballs and welded, it seemed, to living rock. This was the road she and James, and her two little cousins, John and Ian, had taken during her first week in Goldeneye, that same day when she first drove a car— and first met Ed and Renee. They passed over the frozen Goldeneye River, where she had bathed in almost boiling water that day—her first day with Ed, or with any man. Such a lot of firsts. And such a lot of her life to be rooted in this short stretch of prairie. Today it looked particularly bleak. The sky was as close to an unrelieved gray as it ever could be in those parts, promising neither snow nor sun. The land was one almost featureless snow-field. And the wind, of course, poured relentlessly from the northwest, neither buffetting nor falling slack; a machine could not have kept it steadier.

The wind, and the necessity to keep well wrapped, made conversation difficult—which was as well, for now that they were alone together they had both become unaccountably shy. By midday they were through with their calls. After dinner with the storekeeper and his wife, whose baby they had just inoculated, they set out to return to Goldeneye. James telephoned home first but there were no other calls and no emergencies.

Just outside the town they came to the crest of the ridge—Hawk Ridge— and the turn. James glanced at her and raised an eyebrow.

"Let's just have a look at the old place, eh," she said, avoiding his eye.

Without a word he headed the ponies northward. In fact, she had little hope of seeing the soddy again, thinking that the driveway from the road would be under eight or ten feet of snow. It was a way of making a decision —or, rather, of not making one. If the driveway was blocked, they'd turn about and go home. If it was cleared . . .

It had been cleared down to the same height as on the road, and recently, too.

"Does someone live there now?" she asked.

He shrugged his ignorance.

Halfway along the trail, as it wound through the windbreak of trees, they saw a young man walking toward them. She had not seen him since her wedding, when he had just turned fourteen; now he was rising nineteen, so she did not at once recognize her cousin John—not until he called out her name and greeted them both.

"You've not come visiting me, I hope," he said.

"Well, there's a right prairie welcome!" She laughed.

"I'd rather you thought me inhospitable than have you see the way I live."

She wondered if he had a woman there. He had grown tall and good-looking, with the same auburn hair as her own—maybe a touch lighter—and pale freckles over a skin-and-bone face as delicate as a woman's. But his frame and his lithe, easy walk were those of a man.

"Are you living here now?" James asked.

"Just till Christmas. You see I fixed all the shingles on the new house?"

"I didn't notice," Catherine told him. The "new" house was the one Murdo had begun building out by the highway. Only a part of its frame was up when he died. "All by yourself?"

When he was slightly embarrassed he scratched the back of his neck exactly as Murdo had done. "Ed said we should have a building bee with all the neighbours. Renee said there's an outfit in Saskatoon who send carpenters and plasterers all over. I said I could finish it myself so it got to be sort of a challenge."

"And you've won."

"Yep. Now it's got to be sort of a hobby. I'm cutting frets to put over the windows and the gables. She's going to be the prettiest house in Saskatchewan. Care for a look?"

The house was just a shell, of course, but now the roof was on he could start boarding the joists and partitions. Catherine wondered how many other men would start putting the decorative frets around the windows and gables before they had the floors in; she admired that instinct in him. And, naturally, she thought of the home in Dunedin she'd just had to sell. She'd love to do a decorating scheme for this place.

"I'll give you a cup of coffee back in the soddy if you'll just promise to shut your eyes to the state of the place," he said.

When they got there they saw what he meant. Dirty clothes lay everywhere. If he'd had more than one set of dishes, there'd be dirty piles of those everywhere, too. Much of the room was taken up with his foot-treadle fretsaw. There was sawdust over, in, and under everything.

"What are you living on?" Catherine asked. "Apart from sawdust."

"Oh, coffee, beans, biscuits, corned beef, jam . . ." The list petered out.

"Eggs?" she asked.

He hit his forehead. "Clean forgot! There's a pail of eggs in there. Say—thanks!"

She looked around again and sighed heavily.

He laughed. "I told you to shut your eyes."

When they'd finished their coffee, she and James went back to the store in Hawk and returned with a few provisions—apples, oranges, meal, lentils, and so on. Then James went home alone while Catherine stayed and washed and baked and cleaned up the place, returning to Goldeneye by train the next morning. She enjoyed a long talk with her cousin that evening, and really got to know him for the first time.

He was going to start farming his father's section in partnership with Ed, running both places as one enterprise; hence the work on the "new" house. His young brother, Ian, would join in when he left school.

"And a woman to manage it?" she asked.

He scratched the back of his neck. "Working on that, too." But he'd be drawn no further.

She strung a washing line across one of the unused bedrooms. The wet clothes, which were only hand-wrung, froze almost at once. In that condition they took several days to dry, for ice evaporates more slowly than water. She came back the following week and ironed whatever he hadn't simply pulled off the line and onto himself. Once again she cleaned up, did some more washing, and left him a shelf of pies and cakes.

From then on it became a regular weekly affair. Every Thursday she'd go over to Hawk, and John would meet her off the train and take her back on the Friday. Fiona said why didn't she take Kelvin and Maddy and move in for a couple of months; when those two grew up it would be something for them to say they'd gone through a Saskatchewan winter in their great-uncle Murdo's soddy.

She toyed with the idea for a while and even said she might try it after Christmas. But before then she turned against it. John was a good-looking young man and, even with the two children there, they'd be in each other's company too often and too long to be safe. If there was a big blow, they could be together, night and day, for a week or more. She knew herself well enough by now. And she knew him. He might be diffident but he was also normal. She saw that look of attraction and admiration in his eyes. While she visited only once a week he began afresh from the same baseline each time, and each time drew no closer than the accidental touch while taking a cup or plate from her. But if she were there all the time, his admiration would soon turn to hunger.

Besides, there was something pleasant in knowing the attraction between them existed and yet also knowing it would never develop into something more serious. She was making a home, she was looking after a man, she was talking with him about all sorts of things, from the most general to those that bordered on confession, she was even flirting with him a little, and yet it was all safe. It was a game. Her sense of her own virtue was not threatened.

Oddly enough, it made things easier between her and James, too. The very fact that they had made that turning off the Goldeneye road to go back to the old soddy, to risk a visit to that place, with all its associations for them, was like a silent acknowledgement that they were prepared to risk restarting their affair. At an emotional level it had never ceased. She would always be somewhat in love with James, and he with her. But there had been no intimacy since the night she had said "six weeks." Now, without resuming that intimacy, they both knew they were at least prepared to do so.

The knowledge somehow reduced the tension between them, and the power of the compulsion they had both been resisting. James no longer avoided her company and they made quite a few visits together; Miss Welland did not enjoy driving around in subzero weather and was more than agreeable for Catherine to take her place.

Once Catherine reminded him of the time he had said that for her to receive him was a mere peccadillo, but for him to lie with her, to occupy her love and deny it to husband and family, was a heinous crime. "What would it be now?" she teased.

"A peccadillo," he said mildly, not rising to it. "No more than the merest peccadillo."

24

Margaret was right. When Burgo joined them for Christmas, almost the first thing he said was that he needed her to come back with him. He had found his second job—or so he hoped.

"I actually had it that first day." He laughed. "I even told you—and neither of us saw it! Remember I said I couldn't make enough money doing night relief for another doctor? I'd need to be half a dozen, I said. That was it! Half a dozen."

"I still don't see it," she told him.

"Look—Selkirk has eight doctors, right? And if you take the surrounding places—Dunedin, Missaqua, and so on, out beyond the escarpment—there's another six. Fourteen doctors in all." He turned to James. "What would you give for a guaranteed undisturbed night, Dad? Every night."

James saw his drift. "I'd be called out myself if it was really serious, eh?"

"Sure, but everything from hangnails to whooping cough—you could sleep right on."

"Och, I might give . . . ten dollars. A week." He was trying to be encouraging.

But Burgo's face fell. "I'm hoping that in Ontario you'd give twenty. If not, I haven't found it."

"Weekends, too?"

"That's thirty dollars."

James looked even more dubious. "They won't all join, of course."

"Naturally. I'd expect half to be signed on by the end of this year. The rest to join in dribs and drabs."

"Even if you had half now," Fiona pointed out, "that would only bring in about ten thousand dollars a year. And you'd have another night locum to pay out of it. You couldn't do it all yourself."

Burgo grinned then. It was the argument he had been waiting for. "Selkirk is the sprat to catch the mackerel. And the mackerel is Toronto. Next Christmas you'll see. We'll be sitting down here discussing the transfer of all we've learned to the big city—more than two hundred and fifty doctors! Medicine gets out of its horse and buggy and enters the Radio Age!"

The night of his return, exhausted though he was, they made wonderful love—twice. And again in the morning. There was a greed in them both for something beyond mere sex. It was a hunger for the reassurance it could bring—that what they had lost was trivial compared with what they retained.

It did not entirely work. Burgo was different. He had not even retained parts of himself. There was a new eagerness in him to be back east, to be putting his Night Call scheme into practice—which automatically meant being away from Goldeneye, away from her, away from the children. He did his best to hide it, of course, but she knew every gesture, every flicker of his eyes. She saw that when he pretended to have a deep, professional interest in the work his father was doing in his hospital, he was actually miles away.

When Burgo had gone to work at MacNair, in P. J.'s firm, that first summer of their marriage, he had recruited a young graduate classmate to go to Goldeneye and work with James. Fortunately the two men suited each other perfectly. Jay Wilson was exactly the sort of younger colleague James needed. He was respectful of the old traditions but he was good enough at modern medicine to teach James a thing or two. Together they had begun to develop James's lifelong ambition to achieve something in the field of restorative surgery. They had some impressive cases recuperating in the hospital that Christmas.

"We're beginning to get one or two orthopedic patients, as well, now,"

James told Burgo. "Here's a woman who had one leg shorter than the other. Broken thigh in childhood, badly set. We broke the femur again, pulled the ends apart and packed it with a mixture of her own bone and chips of cadaveric bone to stop scar tissue invading the space."

"Cadaveric bone?" Catherine said, thinking it was really Burgo's part to show interest.

"Yes. It gets digested down, of course, as her own bone replaces it, but by then it's served its purpose. Look at her X-ray here."

Even Burgo was impressed with the clean lines of the re-formed thigh-bone.

"The trick is," James said, "to begin stressing it from the moment it knits. And keep increasing the stresses, week by week, so that the fine structure is laid down in a natural way. Otherwise the cancellous part of the bone doesn't organize properly. That's where Jay is so good—he can work out stresses to within an ounce—not so, Jay?"

"Within a gram, actually," Jay corrected.

"Isn't it marvellous what they're doing?" Catherine asked Burgo later.

"Very good. But it'll never be more than a hobby. This is only a *cottage* hospital, after all. Jay should learn all he can here and then come back to MacNair. He could *be* someone there."

The day they left Goldeneye to return east, he for the year, she for a week or so, Margaret's first letter came from Paris. Wrapped around it was her first "castoff"—a pale turquoise georgette evening dress, extravagantly embroidered with a flower motif in gold and silver thread. The hearts of the flowers were of openwork embroidery in primrose- and apricot-coloured silk and there was an apricot-coloured underslip in satin.

When Catherine tried it on she was surprised it fitted perfectly across her shoulders, where she was a good inch broader than Margaret; the waist was only slightly shaped, so differences there hardly mattered. The side panels, cut on the cross, flared out beautifully with every swish of her walk. Margaret hadn't forgotten the accessories either. There was a gold-spangled evening purse and a dainty pair of gold kid court sandals lined with white kid. They all looked hardly used.

Burgo was delighted. "Now let anyone hint we're broke," he said. "You look like a queen."

The letter explained the mystery of the expanding shoulder:

Here's my first castoff. I'm ashamed to be bored with it so soon—but you should see the ones that didn't get away! I'll tell you about it first because it's the most boring part of this letter. It's a Delon creation, copied, naturally. I tell Igor it's original so he gives me full price and then I get them made up by a wonderful little lady in the Rue Joffre and pocket the difference. Igor? I gave up the Belly man. Igor's a Russian count. White Russian, of course, though he's actually pretty swarthy. So you could say I'm in the White Slav trade. (I only put that in pour tourmenter mon cher Burgo, actually you'd be amazed how proper it all is. I was, anyway.) And this little lady leaves extra-wide seams in the shoulders. If you look real close at this one, darling, you'll see where I had her take the yoke off and let out each of those shoulder gathers a teeny bit so it will fit you. Fear not, dear Cath, your great stevedore deltoids will fit every rag I toss out of my carriage windows at you.

I don't think waists will be a problem for several years yet. (My God, I *hope* not! Why am I always making unintentional jokes on that topic?)

I have a very pretty little apartment out at Beaugrenelle, near the Bois, which is where every nice girl aspires to live. I dream of going for strolls in the Bois but haven't yet done so. Also of going over the river to Sèvres, but I haven't done that either. Nor climbed the Eiffel Tower. Nor been to the Exhibition at the Grand Palais. Nor been to see Sacré-Coeur, though I have stood in its shadow to see where all the great Modern Artists hung their canvases and, sometimes, themselves.

What have I done? The Louvre. I have *done* the Louvre. Wrong! I have done two galleries—in ten days. In ten lunch hours, I mean. Because I am, naturellement, a working girl. I work for M. Delon himself. Those hours and hours of Extra French are sure paying off, even if these Parisians find my Quebec French a bit quaint. (Quaintbec? No.) So are those terrible months in the New York rag trade. I only had to mention Bloomingdale's! Of course he wrote for a reference—but guess who did the translation when it came back! The French for intoxicated is *sobre,* unreliability is best rendered *véracité,* impetuous comes out *docile,* and pert is *disciplinée.* Hell—I even wanted to hire myself when I read it.

The point is, even grand Hauts Couturiers like M. Delon (who is *not* safe to be with after hours, despite what the girls here say) have heard the clink of the Mighty Dollar and are stunned to discover what Bloomingdale's, Butterick, Sears, and even our own T. Eaton will pay for paper patterns with magic names like Delon on them. I handle all that correspondence and sort out all their second thoughts, afterthoughts, and etc. I haven't yet found a really good French equivalent for "cheap clothes for fat old women." The English translation would be "inexpensive gowns for the matronly figure," but that isn't much help. Matronly is *d'un certain âge* in French—and that ain't hay.

More soon. Hug Kelvin and Maddy for me but please, please wipe them clean first. M.

"At last I think Meg's found herself," Catherine said.

"Looks like it," Burgo allowed.

"In Paris."

He grinned. "I can't be right *all* the time, honey."

By the end of that week back east, which travelling time turned into almost two, she had come to know an entirely new Burgo. She had never sat in on his lectures, nor seen his clinical sessions; she knew him only as a husband at home or on holiday—an off-duty man. What she saw now was a revelation. It wasn't just the amount of work he had done—the information he had gathered about the practices of his potential clients and the financial arrangements of the scheme, down to the price of the last postage stamp—Burgo had always been a worker. But she had never seen him as a *salesman*. There was no other word for it. Not a travelling order-clerk with a suitcase, to be sure; but a man with an idea and a passionate conviction in it—in both its commercial promise and its social value. He really saw in his Night Call service the seeds of something much bigger—an organization that would, for part of every day, provide the entire first-line visiting medical service for a whole city the size of Toronto. It was bound to have profound effects on the pattern of medical services in general.

Naturally, he was careful to keep these grandiose aspects of the scheme from the doctors he saw that week, but the vision fired his enthusiasm and added some lustre to the smallest, most mundane points he made. He began by taking Dr. Peace, the doyen of Selkirk's general practitioners, and his wife, out to dinner. Catherine's appetite vanished when she saw the prices on the menu; some of the dishes cost almost a dollar *each*. But to watch Burgo, you'd have thought they still had all those thousands of dollars to be carefree with. At one stage he actually confessed that the stock market crash had hurt him—he'd even had to trade in the Caddy. But the Peaces took one look at Catherine's "Delon" dinner gown—and remembered her mink—and smiled polite disbelief. Burgo didn't press the point.

In fact he thought they had no hope of signing up this particular doctor; they approached him first because he would have been mortally offended if they had not. Burgo was astonished then to see that Peace was actually nibbling at the bait. Catherine saw it too. She was sure the man was on the point of laughing—again politely—at the very idea; but he had then caught his wife's eye. She was interested.

To give her a chance to speak, Catherine had thrown in a general remark about the somewhat rarefied medical atmosphere up at MacNair and how keenly Burgo was looking forward to seeing "the sharp end" of his field (the phrase was actually James's).

"Sharp!" Mrs. Peace laughed. "At three in the morning. It's the 'end' all right, but 'sharp's' *not* the word for it."

Afterwards Burgo told Catherine her intervention at that point had been a stroke of genius. He said they made a great team.

"I said that before you exiled us."

That annoyed him. "I'm not opening up that again, Cath. This week will strain the bank's patience as it is. I cannot fathom why they're being so understanding—unless they're genuine in saying they have faith in this idea."

"Well, what other reason could there be, darling?"

"They must be desperate, too. If they jerk the rug out from under everyone, they'll be pulled down as well. They must have looked around and picked those most likely to succeed and decided to back them. But it doesn't run to buying the home we need to match the sort of business we're trying to do." His anger had gone. He took her hand. "I knew I was asking you to do the harder part, Cath. I still don't doubt it. And one day I'll make it all up to you. But right now I've got to add to your burden by calling you here when it suits the business and sending you away when you've done your part. I hate me for it. I think you're someone, really someone, not just to do it but to do it so well as you did tonight."

And that was the story of their week. They lunched or dined most of the doctors and partnerships in the Selkirk area. The more she saw of Burgo, selling his idea, the more she marvelled that in nearly five years of marriage she had never noticed this side to him. Superficially he was as genial and unflustered as ever; but behind the twinkle in his eyes was a nimble watchfulness, alert every second to catch some fleeting emotion in another's face—a clue as to what should be stressed and what played down. It was wrong to think of the doctors they met as "victims." Yet there was that aspect to it. They came to those meetings suspicious and distrustful; they left, many of them, wondering how they had managed all these years with you-scratch-my-back-I'll-scratch-yours arrangements. Even those who didn't join, or said they'd wait and see, were visibly impressed. Burgo certainly knew all their problems.

When it was time for her to leave they actually had nine of the district's practices—including, at the last minute, Dr. Peace—signed up—two more than Burgo had expected to be in it at the end of the first year. He was over the moon and said it had all been Catherine's doing. She was exhilarated, too. They *were* doing it together, even if she played only a small part, and only from time to time.

But, on the train back to Goldeneye, the thrill of it did not last much beyond the Ontario boundary. And Goldeneye itself, despite the lure of her children, despite the companionship of James and Fiona, despite all her happy memories of the place, came to seem more and more of a Siberia. She knew then how keenly she wanted to be with Burgo, helping him—helping *them,* actually—to climb out of the hole they were in. How much, too, she resented his freedom to do it all on his own.

That surprised her. She would not have believed herself capable of such resentment. When things had been going well she had not, even for an instant, thought of herself as any kind of provider. Even when Madame Meyerhof had tried to "fish" her, it was Margaret who had had to point it out. Catherine herself had not even been aware of the hints being dropped so heavily. So why, now, did she resent being excluded from the role? Because of what she had helped Burgo achieve during that week?

It was even worse the next time she went back east, seven weeks later. This time there was no dining out in restaurants. This was return-match week, when they were entertained by the participating doctors in their own homes. It was Burgo's idea, for "a relaxed, informal get-together, part-social, part-professional, to review their initial experiences and apply early correction where necessary."

While the professional part of the discussion took place, Catherine and the lady of the house usually retired to the sitting room. And there, inevitably, her opinion was sought on this or that aspect of the decor. "I'm so bored with these drapes, my dear. What sort of replacement would you advise? . . . What colour for this wall? . . . I'm not too sure about this picture . . . I just happen to have the pattern book here—could you possibly spare a moment . . . ?" And so on. Her still-intact home in Dunedin had been proudly and relentlessly shown off by its own owner. No one had forgotten Catherine Macrae, whom La Meyerhof had so extravagantly praised.

One doctor's wife even told Catherine she ought to take it up on a regular basis. She would certainly have made more money that particular week than the two hundred dollars Night Call had grossed. That time the four-day journey back to Siberia was twice as heavy to bear. At least she had managed to spare one afternoon and, later that week, the best part of a day, going around the stores in Toronto, collecting samples and looking at the latest lines. And Burgo had allowed her fifteen dollars to get brushes and colour and paper for her portfolio designs.

But she was a slow burner. All that year the tensions of frustration grew within her. Time and again they would rise to intolerable levels, only to be soothed by another wildly funny letter from Margaret in Paris—always with a ravishing "castoff" wrapped around it—or by a call from Burgo. She lived for those summonses and grew almost frantic for the touch of him on the interminable journey east. As soon as she arrived, usually in the early afternoon, she would race him up the stairs (he had a two-room flat over the Night Call office), tear her clothes off, and make greedy, insane love until it was time to stagger down to dinner.

But for all its frenzy, it was not lovemaking as they had once known it—an act that rose to a natural peak out of their days and nights together. These were climaxes without foundations. She saw how important was the mere act of being together, living together, spending, say, twenty-three sex-less hours out of every twenty-four in each other's company, gossiping, reminiscing, planning, quarrelling . . . sleeping. What they did on those visits was meant to be love—it ought to have been love, for they had not stopped loving each other—but it lacked all those everyday preparations whose importance is not noticed until they are withdrawn. It was not love finding itself in their sex; but sex looking frantically for love. Burgo noticed the difference less than she did.

Once, while on the train to Ontario, she had felt her longings beginning to mount up and she resolved that this time—just to show Burgo and to convince herself—they would not make love at all, but enjoy a truly romantic time together, doing everything else that lovers might do—everything but that.

"Okay," Burgo said lightly. "I think that might not be a bad idea. I want you to look at some figures anyway. It's going very well."

Twenty minutes later they were in bed, locked together, gasping with their first exhaustion. And she had been the one who had shivered the way upstairs, tugging him urgently behind; he had followed, grinning and damnably smug.

To all her other reasons for wanting the four of them to be back again as a family was added this, the most important of all: their love and their sex life were being eased apart. It did not diminish their love, but it made sex far too important. She began to consider it as something in itself, with a mental compartment all on its own. In their years together it had been marvellous and stirring and important at its moments, and no more than a blurred memory of warmth in between. But now she found herself thinking about past occasions, and even *planning* future ones, with a sharpness that almost tore out her innards.

So when Burgo joined them that Christmas (to be greeted by Maddy with "Who man?"), she was more than ever determined that this next year would see her move back with the children to Toronto and begin to work professionally as an interior designer. She already had a good portfolio of sketches. The drawing was weak but the colours and textures made up for it. She sent one to Margaret, who sent it back with the comment that she was beyond doubt the Douanier Rousseau of Interior Design.

Margaret also sent her a marvellous Christmas present—a duplicate copy of *Les Trésors du Louvre,* which (though it looked new) she said she had picked up second hand on a stall in the Rive Gauche. On the same stall she had picked up a translation of Charles Lamb's essays that had marginal annotations—which later turned out to have been scribbled by Lord Byron. She had paid a few sous for it and had resold it for eighty dollars.

One puzzling thing about the *Louvre* book was that it bore a sales sticker from a Chicago bookstore inside the cover. She mentioned this in replying to Margaret, pointing out the extraordinary coincidence that Hymie Amoils had given her the original book in Chicago—and was still there, no longer a student, of course, but a conservator, at the Art Institute. (Catherine knew as much because she and Hymie still wrote to each other very occasionally.) Margaret replied, six weeks later, with yet another castoff to add to Catherine's distended wardrobe, saying that the coincidence was even more fantastic than that. She'd done some sleuthing and discovered that the copy she had bought had actually been sold to the bookseller by no less a person than Hymie A. himself. Disconsolate with unrequited love for the bonny Scots lassie whose company Fate had decreed he should share on that memorable day so long, long ago . . .

There was eight pages of it—pure fantasy, embroidered with such a wealth of realistic detail (some of it most improper) that Catherine cried with laughter, even on the third reading.

But that was much later, long after Christmas, when she really needed a laugh.

That Christmas, Burgo told a delighted family that Night Call (which he still regarded as only a pilot scheme for a much bigger operation in Toronto) had managed—with the savings from his salary—to pay off a quarter of their debt. The bank was delighted; successful new ventures weren't too thick on the ground that year. One of the directors had told Burgo personally that if he had one more good year like that, they'd consider putting up working capital to a degree sufficient to absorb the remainder of his debt—in effect, transferring it to Night Call Ltd.

Later, Catherine showed him her portfolio and told him how keen she was to go east again, be a family once more, and make it all possible, not by being an extra burden on him but by working. Now that Maddy was well weaned onto solids, it would be so much easier.

He saw that by "keen" she meant "desperate" and grew scared. His own beautifully constructed plan of recovery was being knocked sideways by this impetuous charge of Catherine's. "It's taking on two risks in one year, honey. It really would be asking for trouble."

"I know it's *not* a risk," she insisted.

"Sure. And so do I. If I had the money, you wouldn't even need to ask. I'd be falling over my own feet to invest in you. But it isn't me you have to convince."

These easy superlatives—the high-flown promises she could never call— depressed her. Through them she saw that Burgo was, in fact, determined to do it all on his own. He would actually dislike her, and himself, if her contribution threatened to become in any way substantial, a match to his own.

How could she convince him that, even if she made a thousand times more than he did, it would pose far less of a threat to their love, to her sense of their "belongingness," than this forced separation and the distortions it was creating? She did not even try; she knew he wouldn't understand what she was driving at, much less agree.

"Hell, Cath," he grumbled, "it can't be so bad. I'll come back here more often this year. And the prairie's a fine place for Kelvin—and for Maddy when she's a bit older. And you can't say it's weakened our marriage. I feel we're stronger than ever. I know I never loved and appreciated you enough when things were easy—certainly not a tenth of what I do now. I think you're the finest wife any man could hope for. I worry about the children, of course—but then, as I say, you needn't come east so often this year. I'll come back here a bit, when time allows. So they won't forget me."

She had never felt so desolate. Even her lifesaving trips to Ontario were to be curtailed. She made one last try: "I could ask James to loan me the money—not to us. Just to me."

He was furious then, and refused even to discuss it.

Just before he went back she said, "If you won't let me be with you and help, as I know I can, will you start another baby with me?"

His exasperation impaled her. "Oh, Cath! Don't keep asking these impossible, ridiculous things, eh? My life's hard enough without adding this fear that you're going to pieces back here. Don't be a burden, huh? Play your part and I'll play mine."

The next few months were the most miserable of her life—rendered even more so by the feeling that Burgo was more than half right. She *was* asking for the moon. He was, and ought to be, the breadwinner; it was her place to rear the children here in what was, after all, a beautiful home. Just think of all those poor out-of-work people living through this dreadful winter in tarpaper shanties, shivering from one dole of soup to the next. Think of the struggle the farmers were having—which she knew about at first hand now with her weekly visits to Hawk Ridge. And then think of Burgo, clever enough to hold down his post at MacNair and build a new business no one had thought of before—all from a starting line that was twenty-five thousand dollars behind the field. Wasn't she the selfish one— when she ought to be on her knees thanking God daily for all her blessings?

But the undeniable logic of these self-inflicted pep talks did not reach to the core of her hurt, which was somehow bound up with the way her love and her sexual needs were being forced ever wider apart. It threatened all the morality she had ever learned—and morality, for Catherine, was no dry matter of theology, it was a feeling. A good feeling. But now the feeling was gone, everything else was being opened up for questioning.

Where were the clear, simple lines of her childhood now? When, for instance, did her proper wifely longing for Burgo's body shade over into the impurity of carnal lust? If the difference between sin and grace was so stark, surely the division should feel like the switching off of the sun. How could anyone fail to notice it? And Margaret obviously traded favour for favour with a sequence of men; she did not exactly flaunt the fact in so many words, but she managed to squeeze it in four-foot letters between lines that were a quarter-inch apart. Once, in Catherine's view, that would have damned her utterly—even one such transgression, let alone a string. But now—could she honestly say that Margaret was damned? It was all much more complicated.

And these, she had to remind herself, were the grand old certainties of her faith; the items in the soul's balance sheet that no sinner, standing face to Judgement, could even have questioned. What then about the areas that had always been ambiguous? What of her wish to join her husband as pro- vider? Was it a sinful denial of God's plan for men to work and for women to make homes and babies? Or a holy desire to use a faculty He had given her?

Why had He given it? To test her? But which way? Was it virtuous to use His gift or to deny herself the pleasure of it?

She took down her Bible and opened it at random, looking for an augury. It read: *There will I make the horn of David to bud: I have or- dained a lamp for mine anointed.* Oh, yes?

Her eyes traversed across the page: *Surely I have behaved and quieted myself, as a child that is weaned of his mother: my soul is even as a weaned child.*

It wasn't meaningless; but it was no help. More and more these days, when she turned to God's kingdom, she found He had slipped across the border into the Land of Yes-and-No.

Thought did not end her confusion. It bred more. And confusion, in turn, bred resentment. She looked after Kelvin and Maddy. She stopped her cousin from turning into a pig. She helped out in the cottage hospital and the practice. She loved a man who lived on the far side of the moon; he loved her back and was working his guts out for her—but across all that distance what good was it? There was no core to her life anymore. Home was here, love was there, the family was split, and sex was nowhere. They were the four walls of her life and they just didn't meet any longer. She felt utterly devalued. What was she *for*? She longed for someone—anyone—to tell her.

She also began to long for James. After all, she loved him, too, and he was not on the far side of the moon. Her desire reached such an intensity that she knew it was only a matter of weeks before she would be begging him to come and lie with her again. He could sense it, too.

She waited for a saving letter from Burgo. He wrote often but never to say come to Ontario, and she was too ashamed of her own importunity to suggest it. When her longing for James grew desperate she toyed with the idea of seducing her cousin John—not only because he was so good-looking but also to quell the fire that was consuming her. Her relationship with John was expendable—or shallow enough to survive the experience. Also his admiration was now very frank; he'd be more than grateful. He'd make her feel wanted, all right. That led her to the simplest idea of all—just offer herself to the first handsome man she met. Go to Saskatoon or somewhere like that where she wasn't known. He'd be doubly appreciative, because he'd have no call to expect it at all.

At that point she realized how muddled she'd grown. If she could do that with just any stranger, even a handsome one, the thing she was looking for could hardly be erotic—that is, to do with *love*. It had all become mixed up with her sense of her own worth and purpose, or lack of it. She had no measure of her own value any more and she was throwing herself back on the most primitive one of all—in her thoughts, anyway. Thank heavens it was only there.

25

Burgo did not write until April. She was on the point of leaving for Ontario when another letter came for her. It had a Chicago postmark. She wondered if it was from Hymie; they still wrote each other from time to time. But the hand that addressed the envelope was not his, nor was the return address. She opened it eagerly; anyone who took the trouble to write to her won her eagerness. It ran:

Dear Mrs. Macrae:
I think you are Maggie's mother? Or sister-in-law maybe. Anyway, you're about all whom she writes and your name is the same. I am her friend, we live in this same place. . . .

Only then did Catherine take in the address. A high number on Lake Shore Drive. It rang no bell. But there must be a mistake, surely. Meg was in Paris—she'd only just written from there. She'd never have come back to North America without dropping by, or saying so. And why Chicago, of all places?

Miranda would slay me if she knew I was writing you, tho I know she is too worried. It's your Maggie. She has a problem. I mean a Problem. She's a case. I'm not going to write too much, which I can't anyway, but I think if you can you or some family should get over here right quick. I don't mean it's bad yet, but I know the signs, see. And believe me. We're all sposed to be alocoholics even if only a bit. But Maggie! And this place won't ever cure her. When you come, or whoever does, should call first and speak to Miranda, who I will tell before. And not use the front door but round the side.
I'll just sign Maggie's Friend.
Miranda will be mad to lose her but you have rights. She can't hold Maggie just so as you insist.

On the train east Catherine had the best part of four days to exhaust every possible explanation of this puzzle. Was it a hoax? A joke of Margaret's? A case of mistaken identity? Or had Margaret developed her usual drink problem, been thrown out of France and, too ashamed to get in touch, gone to this home for alcoholics in Chicago? Nothing added up, but there was the annoying little fact that wouldn't go away—the *Louvre* book had looked new, and it bore a Chicago sales sticker. Yet it had been mailed in Paris early in December.

She showed the letter to Burgo at dinner that first evening. His response astonished her. "Oh, godfathers!" he said. "Isn't that *all* we need!" He saw her face and added, "Well—there she was, safely remote in Paris. And here we are, just beginning to steam. And suddenly she's in this alcoholics' home in Chicago."

"But she's your sister, Burgo."

"So's Helen. But Helen's no trouble."

"That's how people are graded these days, is it? How much trouble they give *us!*"

Now he was surprised. "Yes!" he affirmed. "Wouldn't you say we'd had enough lately? Wouldn't you say it's reasonable not to want more—and to be annoyed when a sister dumps a fresh heap of it on us? Did you show the letter to Mom, or Dad?"

"Of course not! Good heavens, Burgo—have you lost all—"

"Mom would cope. You should have shown her." He rose, wiping his lips. "Sit tight. I'll call her now."

Panic began to edge in. Catherine had no idea she and Burgo would ever be such poles apart in a matter so close to both of them. "If you do, Burgo, I'll turn right round and go back. Via Chicago. Tonight. I only came here because I knew—I was *sure*—you'd want to come, too."

He inhaled sharply and then gave a slow grin. He was seeking a way to turn her wrath. "But you waited until after we'd gone to bed, eh!"

She blushed and tried to change the subject. "What does the letter mean?" she asked. "Where it says Miranda is too worried. Why *too* worried? Too worried for what?"

He looked at it again. "No, there should be commas there. That's sloppy-American. The way kids say, 'You are, too, fat!' You've heard that, surely. It means Miranda is also worried. Or indeed worried."

"Everyone is, it seems—except her own brother."

His good humour thinned. "Her own brother of twenty-five years! Don't leave that out. Twenty-five years. I've had a bellyful of Meg—belly and craw." He chopped his own throat with his hand. "She's stuck here if you want to know. And I'd love nothing more than to spit her out."

"Burgo! For heaven's sake! Stop talking like that. Come with me now. To Chicago. We must help her." She looked at him tensely. "Will you? Come with me?"

"No! No, I will not! The last time I saw her drunk—or the morning after—I was sitting in Greenwich Village, pleading with her to take the fare from me and come home. Two goddam hours!"

"Burgo!" He had never used such awful language.

"I mean it, Cath. Two goddam hours. While our debt rose—I don't know what. Twelve thousand dollars? I was too sick to find out. But thanks to the loss of those two hours, I now have to work—*we* now have to work—*two years!* Two years, Cath. Two years apart from each other *extra.* That's what her last binge is costing you and me. Think of that every time you leave me here and go back to Mom and Dad. Next Christmas could have brought us together again. But it'll be two more years—and all thanks to my darling sister's fascination for the bottle! You still want to go and help her?"

Though she understood Burgo's bitterness, she already—even in the heat of it—began to feel something like contempt that he could not rise above it.

"You don't offer or withhold help, Burgo, on some kind of scale like that. How much the person's damaged you or done you good. Not to family. Not to a sister. And not to a sister who's in such a bad way that a total stranger thinks she has to write and tell you."

"You go on and on, helping and helping, until you're bled dry, eh?"

"*Yes!* And beyond."

"Then you're a fool, Cathy. I never thought you one, but if you really believe that, then you are. I've given more help to Margaret than— My God!" he suddenly exploded. "And she didn't even need it last time. Remember that? She came and flung it back at me the day we left Dunedin for good. She didn't even use it! *That's* how much she needed our help. And now you expect me to drop everything and scoot to Chicago! Jesus! Two years more of *this*—and she didn't even need it. Now try and tell me you're not a fool."

She sat silent. Bitter and resentful. Had he always been so small-minded, this man she had married? Had she just never seen it until now? Or had the work of this past year diminished him? And all his other good qualities—his genial wit, his confidence, his way with the world, his tolerance of her ideas when they did not coincide with his, his devotion to their children . . . were all these subject to the same limits as, she now saw, curtailed his compassion and generosity? Could they be exhausted, one after the other, by overdrawing on his stock? How close were they now to the final double line?

"No matter what I say, you're going, I suppose," he said.

She nodded.

"And you want the fare and then some?"

Another nod.

"And if I say no, you'll ask Dad to wire it?"

"Yes. I'll go tonight. I was going to leave it until tomorrow."

He drove her, mostly in silence, to Buffalo, where she was in good time for the last train of the evening to Chicago. Their goodbyes were surly and bleak. He still thought her a fool. To her he was less than half the man he had always seemed. Neither view was one that could easily mend. Catherine cried herself silently to sleep in the Pullman.

They were through Detroit before she went along for breakfast. This was the route she had taken with Hymie, almost twelve years ago. Nothing looked familiar—or, rather, everything, the whole North American scene, now looked so familiar that nothing equated with the strangeness she had seen that day. Even the endless length of the train now seemed normal.

Of course, she remembered, she hadn't done a great deal of window gazing this part of the journey; she had been too busy talking with Hymie and looking at *Les Trésors du Louvre*. This time she had brought Margaret's new copy with her. As soon as she got the letter she knew she'd be going to Chicago and she thought there would be a chance of meeting Hymie again, so she had packed the book.

Back in her seat she took it out and leafed through it yet again. It was a new edition but the economical French publisher had reused most of the plates from the earlier one. The Breughel was there, *Les Mendiants—The Beggars*. She remembered with amusement how she had thought the painter's name was Breugel MDLXVII. She remembered, too, all the things Hymie had told her, which had then seemed like revelations. How a painting could have many different values imbedded within it, all at the same time, all intended by the painter. That had been the first moment of her life in which she had seen how different values—even contradictory ones— could exist, deeply imbedded, in one and the same thing. *My, haven't we grown!* she thought. Where could she look today for a single, clear-cut, hundred-percent value? Even her bitterness at Burgo didn't blind her to the fact that he had some right on his side—much less than on hers, of course. But some.

Forgetting that she was told to call Miranda first, she went straight to a cab. It was twilight. When she gave the address to the driver, he looked at her twice, up and down, and said, "Side door, huh?"

"Yes." What was all this about "side door"? Was the front for drunks only? "How did you know?"

He laughed. "How did I know!" He looked at her again. "You Canadian?"

"Yes."

"How did I know that? Some things you just know."

She couldn't see any connection between the two. "You seem to know the place, anyway," she said.

They drove past the Art Institute. She recognized its Greek outline and thought of Hymie thinking of her every time he looked out of his window into the park.

"Uh huh. Every cabdriver in town knows it."

"Oh. I pictured it as just a house. Is it a big place then?"

"Oh, it's a house all right." Again he laughed. "They say it's the only house between here and Seattle that Al Capone don't control."

She'd heard of Al Capone—a mobster who sold bootleg liquor. "I should just think not!" she said.

"No," the cabbie agreed. "That Miranda, she can roll a forest of logs. She's got wires go right down to Washington." He sniffed. "Capone never liked it. Now it looks like curtains for him."

"Oh?"

"Yeah. Tax evasion! Can you beat that!" He glanced at her sidelong. "I don't suppose a lady like you 'ud know them Capone houses?"

"We don't have the same kind of Prohibition in Canada."

"No?" He frowned, puzzled. "Well, I guess there is a *kind* of connection. But they're awful places. Two-dollar turnstiles and the guy says, 'Pick up your soap and towel. Booth Twenty-eight. Clip the card.' You can't even choose. And it's fourteen minutes from then. Fourteen! Not fifteen. Not a neat quarter-hour. Fourteen." He shook his head as if still not quite believing it himself. "What sort of mind got it figured down to fourteen minutes!" Again he gave her a sidelong glance, this time with a grin. "I guess you don't go on no fourteen minutes, huh?"

Catherine, more than somewhat bewildered, said, "Time's important to everyone."

"Well . . . I guess. Yeah. I guess it is." He seemed at a loss for a further conversational gambit.

They went past Lincoln Park, out onto Lake Shore Drive. It was two lifetimes ago. But she wondered about the fat man—did he still waddle out late at night?

"Those are grand houses," she said.

"Wait till you see Miranda's! Are you married, lady?" As soon as he asked the question he seemed embarrassed at his own boldness. "I mean— seeing them rings and all."

"Yes. My husband's a doctor, a medical doctor."

"In Canada?"

"Yes. Near Toronto."

"Tough, huh? I guess times is tough there, too."

"Indeed. No one's finding it easy these days."

"That's right." He wet his lips and dashed her a furtive glance, wondering if this conversational lode, too, might not give out as suddenly as the last. "Tell me now, lady, this kinda interests me. How does a lady like you, doctor's wife, living how many thousand miles away, how do you even get to hear about Miranda's? And then fix up to go there? I mean, I can see you don't want to go to no house in Canada, right?"

At last Catherine understood the man's strange manner and bewildering questions. He thought she was going to Miranda's for a cure! She laughed. "You think I'm going to be *admitted* there!"

"If you ain't, lady, you're wasting your money and my time. Besides"— he licked his chops and made comic eyebrows—"from here I'd say you needn't worry none. About admission."

She laughed. "I don't. I'm not seeking admission at all. I've never had *that* problem. I'm just going there to . . . to see a friend. That's all."

At last the cabbie understood Catherine's strange manner and bewildering answers. This was no pro tryst but an assignation. That was something new for Miranda's—assignations. "Ah *hah!*" he said. "I had you all wrong, lady. Gees, I'm sorry and all about that!" With relief he pointed at an imposing turn-of-the-century house, its towering façade writhing with carved stone of baroque magnificence. "That's it. That's Miranda's." They pulled into the carriage sweep and stopped.

Catherine's heart fell as her eyes took in all that opulence. "I'll bet she charges!" she said.

"It's fifty bucks just to go inside. That's why I never did."

"Also, I guess, you don't have a problem."

He laughed weakly.

She paid him the fare and overtipped him a quarter. She had brought her bag with her, thinking she and Margaret could check in at a small hotel or bed-and-breakfast. The cabbie carried it to the side door for her. As he left he turned and asked, as if compelled to it, "Lady—ain't you at least gonna put them rings on some other finger?"

"Of course not!" Catherine looked at her outstretched hand and laughed. "Why on earth should I?"

"What an extraordinary man!" she said to herself as he climbed back into his cab.

"Dames!" he said to himself as he drove away. "And a doctor's wife, too!"

In the gathering dusk the world was growing cold. She rang the bell. The sound reminded her she ought to have called first. It was too late now. And, anyway, Maggie's Friend had said she'd tell Miranda. The door opened, and there, in silhouette against the low-wattage warmth of a long passage, stood a young woman in old-fashioned maid's costume—a severely cut dress of black down to her ankles and a white lace apron and bonnet.

"Good evening. I'm Mrs. Macrae. I think the proprietor of this establishment is expecting me?"

She could not see the maid's face, but she felt sure the woman looked her up and down as the cabdriver had done. "She said nothing to me about it."

"I'm . . ." She paused. She had been about to say "Margaret Macrae's sister-in-law." But perhaps Meg had booked in under a false name. "I'm Maggie's sister," she said. "Is Maggie here still? It's her I've come about. I was sure your . . . er . . . the lady of the house knew."

The maid laughed. "There's twenty ladies of this house, honey." She stood aside. "Come in if this is on the level. Only I'll warn you now, Miranda don't like to be hustled. If you're hustling for work, forget it."

Catherine entered. "I'm not. I just want to see, er—I don't know her surname—Miranda, your employer, about Maggie."

The maid took her to a small room at a bend in the passage—a glass-sided booth, in effect, created out of a widening of the passage. "MacKay, was it?"

"Macrae. Mrs. Macrae."

The maid shrugged in bewilderment and left her. Catherine looked through the lace curtains at the passage. She was clearly in a no-man's-land between the servants and the posh part of the clinic, or home, or whatever they called it. A little aslant from her was a door to the kitchens—and grand kitchens they obviously were. Whenever a porter came in or out with sides of meat or tubs of vegetables from the scullery, she caught a glimpse of several chefs and lots of silver and cut glass. And she saw a sommelier step out of a service elevator with a trolley of wine bottles, venerable with dust.

That surely was a new cure for alcoholism! She remembered the cabbie's sarcasm. Perhaps Miranda only pretended to run a clinic and was really in competition with Al Capone. That fitted, too!

The room she was in was like a doctor's waiting room—a few chairs, a worn ottoman, and a table piled with old comics and magazines.

She picked up one of the magazines, took it to the ottoman, sat down, and opened it. A second later it was hurtling across the room, and she was sitting bolt upright, shivering with shock. Her heart began pounding. What an extraordinary, revolting thing for anyone to leave lying about!

But behind that immediate reaction was a growing unease. She approached the table again.

All the magazines were like that. Horrible! How could people—decent-looking young girls, too—so degrade themselves, even in private, never mind with a photographer there—and knowing it was going to be put in magazines and sent out everywhere, to places like this?

Places like this?

What places were "like this"?

She backed away from the table, swallowing hard, holding both open hands tight to her mouth, thinking she might vomit. Thinking, too, what a blind idiot she was. That bewildering conversation with the cabbie—he must have thought she was coming here looking for work. So did the maid. Her face—her whole body—burned with shame at it. And Margaret . . .

Poor Meg! was her first thought. Her only thought. She must go to her at once. Take her away. What did the letter say? "Miranda won't like it. But she can't hold Maggie. Just insist on your rights." Something like that.

She sat down again on the ottoman and waited. She tapped her fingers. Then she went over and picked up the magazine she had flung down. She leafed through it, carefully this time.

Who would enjoy looking at such things? They were nearly all pictures of women, so it must be men. But what sort of men? The sort of men who came here. Men who . . .

Poor Meg! Oh, poor, poor Meg!

There were footsteps in the passage. Catherine wanted to shrink into the upholstery. A young woman, even less at ease than Catherine, peeped through the door, glanced around and, seeing the room empty, slipped swiftly in; then she reversed her vigil, darting nervous looks up and down the passage. When she was quite sure the coast was clear, she relaxed and smiled. Catherine smiled back. The woman looked too obviously decent to be—well—one of Them.

"Miranda?" Catherine asked.

"My! No!" The woman gulped and fanned her face at the very idea. "Are you . . . ah . . . I'm Maggie's Friend. Miranda's making out she's mad I wrote. But that's only so's it don't get like an epidemic with the others. Okay? I mean, she *knows* Maggie's got to go." She tipped an imaginary glass to her lips.

"Bad?" Catherine asked.

"It was. But she's real good right now. I mean, she *can,* you know. But one more time, and—*pff!* Miranda knows—only she can't have us writing off all over like I wrote you." She smiled. "You are taking Maggie—I mean, that's why you're here? Please?"

"Of course I will. Where is she? Can you bring her here?"

"No! Miranda's got to give you the third degree first. I mean Miranda *cares.* She won't let Maggie out to just anywhere."

"Oh! Well you can tell Miranda that 'Maggie' is very dear to me. And I intend to take her home with me. Especially—well—*now.*"

"Good. Because, like I said, one more time and—*pff!*"

After a pause Catherine asked. "Do you . . . I mean, what do . . ."

The woman smiled. "Indeed I do. I work here."

"And Maggie?"

"Yep. It ain't no disgrace. Not these days. And not *here.* This is the highest-tone house in America, you know. I mean we are the cream. We got tycoons and big pols and diplos and movie stars. If I go to the movies, I know what they all look like, head to toe. And big-time preachers. Boy!"

"Oh." Catherine was surprised to feel something very close to envy stirring within her.

"I mean a Young Lady here, she's like a princess. And if she saves, if she's Scotch, she can walk out a princess. Even Maggie, now—and she's no scrimp—she's got a heap. That's the danger. That's why I wrote you. She's got to have someone watch her how she spends it. Not"—she drank another imaginary glass—"you know? Gee, I'd better go. Miranda'll be here any minute. Not a word, huh? She'd *strangle* me." She suddenly adopted an entirely different voice and posture and said, "It's been a great pleasure meeting you, Mrs. Macrae."

She just made it to the elevator.

A large woman with steely gray hair, her green eyes flecked with steel, her vast body held together by steel-ribbed corsets, came down the passage. Instinctively Catherine rose, such was the woman's dignity. Miranda beyond a doubt.

She sailed into the booth, stared at Catherine with eyes that seemed to plumb the depths of her, and then broke into a smile of bewitching radiance. It might have been so rarely produced that Miranda herself was actually a little shy of it. This hint of vulnerability as those firm lips quivered gently, revealing now more now less of those perfect little pearly teeth, softened Catherine toward her.

Miranda inclined her head at the table and its offensive display. "A shock, isn't it, my dear." Her voice was refined, too high-pitched for her bulk.

"It certainly is, Mrs. . . ."

"I don't suppose you ever saw such things in your life."

"Certainly not."

"No. I didn't think so. Mrs. MacKay, isn't it?" She held out a hand.

Even if Catherine had resolved not to shake it, she could not have refused a gesture that so perfectly combined grace with command. "Macrae," she said, almost apologetically.

"Mrs. Macrae. I knew, of course. I just thought you might prefer to use some other name. We don't get too many respectable women visiting here—only nuns collecting for charity. The place fascinates them—or maybe they think we're a soft touch. Have you eaten, may I ask?"

"I thought I would collect Meg—er, Maggie—and we could eat downtown."

"Well, I promise not to spoil your appetite, but I usually enjoy a small cold collation at this time of day and I was so hoping you would join me?"

"I'd really rather collect Maggie and go, thank you."

Miranda's smile no longer trembled. "You don't take my meaning, Mrs. Macrae. It wasn't actually an RSVP kind of invitation. I look after my young ladies. I have no intention of allowing you to 'collect' Maggie, as you put it, until we have had a talk." She was sailing back into the corridor before she finished speaking, leaving Catherine no choice but to follow.

The stairs at the end of the corridor led up to a small door beneath the grand sweep of a marble staircase. Catherine had a hasty impression of spirally twisted marble pillars soaring to a dome whose lights showed the very last of the dying day, eclipsed by a brilliant brass chandelier of rococo richness. Matching flambeaux ringed the walls. The restlessness of it all was enhanced by potted palms, displays of peacock feathers mingled with fronds of lacquered pampas grass, and turkey carpets. It was a compendium of everything that Catherine loathed in interior design. She had never imagined there to be a moral element in her dislike; but here it was. How else could one decorate such a house?

Miranda said, "Letty, the maid who let you in, she thought you were looking for work here."

"I'd scream every time I saw this."

Miranda turned in surprise at the violence of Catherine's words, then saw her eyes sweeping over the walls and decorations, saw the sneer on her lips, and said, "Well—that's a new one."

Her room was to one side of the great wrought-iron entrance doors. To the other side a footman in powdered wig and livery, straight from Ruritania, stood ready to answer coded rings. He was checking results in the *Daily Racing Form*.

The cold collation was salmon mayonnaise or tongue with Russian salad and out-of-season strawberries. The only drink was champagne.

"I'm glad your invitation was so pressing," Catherine said.

Miranda's smile was a reward in itself. But reward for what? Catherine wondered. There was something about the woman that made you want to please her.

Letty served them both and withdrew.

"I wasn't really seeking your opinion of the decor," Miranda said. "I'm sorry you don't like it. I understand you are something of an expert in that line."

"Meg told you?"

"I've had a long talk with Margaret. I don't think of her as Maggie anymore, somehow."

"Tell me, Miranda"—it would never feel right to call this immensely dignified woman by her Christian name—"has she been here long? Has she been here all the year—all last year, I mean?"

Miranda chewed her mouth empty, slowly, never taking those reptilian eyes off Catherine. "Let's talk about Margaret and you," she said as if they had been discussing something quite different. "When I mentioned work here, I was looking for your response to that idea—not the decor. Let me ask you directly: Would you care to work here? Be one of my young ladies?"

Catherine breathed in sharply but Miranda interrupted. "Think now, before you answer. I'm not asking it for your sake but for Margaret's. She's the one I care about, not you. So think. Are there *any* circumstances in which you would?"

"To save the life of my child, I suppose," she said. It was the only acceptable answer that occurred to her.

"Ah! So the 'Never! Never!' that you were about to cry out is, in fact, qualified?"

"I'm sure any woman would, to save her child."

"Only that? Suppose your husband, or a parent, needed an operation you couldn't afford? Not a lifesaving one, you understand—just to be cured of a lot of pain."

"He's a doctor himself. He'd be treated free."

"But you get the point."

Catherine nodded. "All right. That too."

"Good! I like you, Catherine. Your moral instincts are there, but you're no fanatic. Try this. You have a kid brother. The school says he's the brightest they've seen in a long time. He wants to go through medical school. Your family has no money. And—"

There was a knock at the door. Miranda shouted, "Come!" A young woman with bright red hair and sharp features entered. She smiled pleasantly at Catherine and said hullo. Her clothing was modest and tasteful but ruined by the most awful pair of vermilion-coloured stockings. "I can't, Miranda, I just can't!" she said, pointing a leg.

Miranda looked at it and shook her head in agreement. "That's what he sent? Let's see the rest. My God—what a color!"

The woman plucked up her skirt and showed a whole range of exotic lingerie in the same dreadful scarlet. "I can't." She turned to Catherine. "What do you say, honey?"

"I say it goes with the decor but not with you."

Miranda laughed. "Pay her no heed. Take it off. I'll tell him that even for him there are limits. He'll be here soon."

"Oh, thank you so much, Miranda!" She threw her arms around the madam and hugged her. "The quality's appalling, too."

"That's the other thing." Miranda escorted her to the door, holding her by the arm. "That girl," she told Catherine as she returned to the buffet, "is keeping her mother in a home for incurables and putting a kid sister through college. They think she's a fashion buyer at Marshall Field's. Can you see yourself doing that?"

"I don't know. If I wasn't married . . . if I didn't love my husband . . . I don't know." She didn't want to know.

"Fine. Well, it begins to look as if Margaret's in luck, having you as a sister-in-law, Catherine. Let's try the next hurdle, shall we?"

Catherine opened her mouth and shivered at the sting of the champagne. "Very well," she said. It was like one of those quizzes in *The Saturday Evening Post*—except for its subject matter, of course.

"All right. The decision is made. Your sister needs that operation and you're going to see she gets it. You come to me. Ask for a place. I say yes. In fact, I say I have a partner for you right away. You've no time to think. No time to back out. I take you to him, I introduce you, and I leave. It doesn't happen like this, of course, but I want to know what's going through your mind at that moment. What are you thinking?"

Even in her own mind Catherine was avoiding the issue. What she was actually thinking was, *What answer does she want me to give?* She knew it had some important bearing on Margaret's leaving this house. She took one look at those hard, unwavering eyes and decided it would be unwise to tell anything but the truth. "This man," she said. "Is he distinguished? Is he handsome?"

Disappointment showed in Miranda's face. "Ah, that would be important, would it? Or are you trying to imagine yourself-as-you-are-now instead of yourself-with-a-bright-brother? Or sister? Try!"

Catherine did. She shut her eyes and tried to imagine herself in that other situation. She didn't see the man. All she saw was the situation.

"I'm here because of my brother. I think of my brother. He's sick. I turn and smile at the man."

"How? How d'you smile?"

What would Meg say? "Ravishingly!"

"Go on!" Miranda was trying to keep the approval out of her voice.

"I'm thinking I must get his money."

"Get?"

"Well—earn."

"It's an important difference, my dear. How will you earn it?"

"By doing all I can to please him." For the first time she began to think about the man—about the *actual* situation. The man was eager for her.

"Do your all, eh? How much is your all worth?"

She remembered the cabbie's "fifty just to enter," and said, "A hundred dollars."

"Not a dollar less?" Miranda kept on the pressure.

"Not a cent less!" Somehow the catechism had become a battle; she was filled with a fierce kind of joy.

"Very well. He pays you. In tens. Here comes the first one. Can you see that ten dollar bill? Feel it in your hand?"

"Yes." Her hand tightened on it. Her neck tingled. It was becoming real. The man was so eager he'd give her all that, just for . . .

"There's another. Another. Another. Five. . . . Six. What are you thinking now?"

"I'm wondering . . ." She faltered. The man's eyes gleamed. He was longing for her. His hands trembled. His breath shivered. She had caused all that in him. And she was *worth* all that to him.

"Say it."

"He doesn't even know me. He's never met me. But here he is giving me a hundred dollars. Just to please him."

"And do you?"

"I'm smiling at him and I'm caressing him—or whatever he wants. It doesn't matter. I just do it."

"And what are you thinking?"

She was thinking that when this man went there'd be another. He'd see her. He'd look her over. There'd be that same gleam in his eye. And his hand would tremble with excitement, too. And his breath would shiver, he'd want her so much. And he'd value her so highly, too. And then another. And another. Every day. She was wondering what it would do to her to be wanted so much and so often—to reduce all kinds of rich, distinguished, powerful, respected men to that one, quivering state of longing. Yet give nothing of herself. Nothing real. How could so little of her be worth so much?

"Well?" Miranda prompted.

"It isn't me doing it. But that's what he wants. He's paying me *not* to be me, not to tell him about my brother, and how sick I was yesterday, and my headache. He doesn't want *me*. He's paying me to step outside for a while and lend him the leftover bits." She opened her eyes and gazed straight into Miranda's cool, penetrating stare.

"Are you on the level, honey?" Miranda asked quietly.

"Level?"

"You're not fresh stock."

Catherine frowned.

"You've done this before."

"No." When she saw Miranda did not believe her she added, "I swear it." Then she blurted out, "What's it really like, Miranda?"

Miranda believed her then. "It's whatever you think it's like. It's narcotic. It's anaesthetic. It's heaven. It's power. It's a yawn. A vacation. A death sentence. A reprieve."

"But for *me*. You've seen them all. You must know. What would it be like for me?"

There was a hint of alarm in Miranda's voice. "Listen, honey, I didn't mean to start this. I thought you were some bluenose religious lady. I just wanted you to—"

"I understand what you wanted. Don't worry. That's all right. But just tell me—"

"Calm down, will you! Drink some of that."

Catherine took a gulp and gasped again at the sudden, stinging release of bubbles.

"You never once thought about it?" Miranda asked.

"Never."

"I didn't think there was a woman born who hadn't even *thought* of it." Her eyes narrowed. "Why didn't you?"

"I don't know. I just never did. Not for money, anyway."

The shrewd appraisal went on. Miranda's eyes never left Catherine's, even when she ate. "Well, you're right about me, honey. I have seen them all. And I do know. And I know about you. I know that if you can go from never having thought about it to where you got just now—just through a piece of make-believe—you could be one of the greatest." She tapped her skull. "That's where you've got it. The only place that's important." She gave that vulnerable little smile again. "What d'you say? You want to give it a try? Just one night?"

Catherine licked her lips, but her tongue and mouth were dry. Why didn't she say no? Why didn't she shout it?

"This is *the* most exclusive house in North America, you know. *La crème de la crème.* No riffraff here. Just gentlemen of the highest civilization. Interesting men. Men who can talk."

All those different men . . . all trembling for her!

"Tonight you could have the chairman of a big Senate committee, two millionaires, a big movie producer, the president of one of Chicago's biggest corporations. . . ."

And for nothing! It wouldn't even be her—not really her—doing it.

"It's sixty dollars minimum, you know? And for something heavy it goes up to a hundred. And you get to keep half, plus tips. You could clear a hundred fifty every day."

But then all that money and admiration wouldn't be in honour of her either. They'd be paying and admiring a fake, their own fantasy creature. In a way, they'd be paying and admiring themselves. "What about Meg?" she asked.

"What about her?"

"She's my responsibility."

Miranda smiled. "How very noble of you, honey. It's not a bad life, you know—not here. Distasteful, of course, but so is . . . er . . . nursing, wasn't it? At times, anyway. So is clerking and waitressing and stenographing—and taxi dancing."

"I ought to take Meg."

"Good food. Beautiful clothes. And you keep yourself oh-so-nice. Hands soft as a baby's. And the other young ladies are nice."

"No. I must go to Meg."

"And it honestly isn't hard work. Not nice sometimes, but not hard."

Catherine stood and set down the empty glass. "Is Meg upstairs?"

"I guarantee you if you stayed here a year—exert yourself a bit, no vacations—you'd leave with over sixty thousand dollars."

"Really, Miranda, it was all just make-believe. I couldn't. Where's Meg?"

Miranda sighed and shrugged theatrically. "Well . . . if ever you change your mind, honey . . ."

Catherine laughed. "Sure!" She almost convinced herself she had merely toyed with the idea.

Miranda became all matter-of-fact again. "You know about Margaret? You know what she is? A bomb. That's what. She's a time bomb. But you can handle her now, Cath. You can take her from *here,* from a house like this, and you can handle her. Because you understand yourself a whole lot better, I think."

Catherine nodded.

Miranda went on: "Margaret doesn't know *who* she is. She's a basket of dolls. Life size. *Twice* life size. You never know what Pinocchio is going to come jack-in-the-box at you next time you lift the lid. You know what you're taking on, I guess?" She laughed an aside. "It's more than my customers here did, I may say!"

"I've not seen her in over a year. A year and a half. All I've had is her letters from Paris—or pretending to come from Paris, I suppose."

"I have friends there—*naturellement.* They re-mailed everything. I do a lot of re-mailing for my young ladies."

"You do a lot of everything for them."

"I love them, Catherine." Her tone was completely matter-of-fact. "Not soft love, you understand. Not sentimental. But old-woman-in-a-shoe love. I don't despise one of them. I don't think of them as so much meat or stock. I'd defend their value—as people, as professionals—against any other calling. So I don't want Margaret going out to live among people who know what she's been and who think she's dirt forevermore and who'll make her feel—"

"Never!"

"I know, my dear. I know it now. But I had to find out, didn't I? I couldn't just accept your word for it." She rose and, taking Catherine's arm, led her to the door. "You know her mother, of course."

"Yes."

"I can form no picture of her. And that's significant." They went back into the hall, where the footman was helping an elderly gentleman into an art-nouveau elevator. It rose at a snail's pace. The old man spotted them and called a greeting to Miranda.

"Are you going to expire on us tonight, Andrew?" she shouted back.

He saw Catherine. His eyes lit up and he grinned. He poked his cane toward her. "Not while you freshen your posy with such flowers!"

Miranda turned an amused gaze on Catherine and said quietly, "It could still be arranged. And he's a marvellous lover—quite the favourite here."

Catherine laughed impatiently. She wanted to see Margaret again and take her home to Canada. But she smiled at her would-be lover and blew him a kiss.

Miranda said, "Oh, and Andrew—there's only two things I really frown on. Bad money. And bad taste."

"No red stockings?"

"No red stockings."

"I think I will expire—just to spite you."

Miranda laughed and resumed their walk.

"Margaret's mother. I was saying I couldn't form a picture of her. In fact, I can form too many pictures. Margaret's talked about her so much." They went through the door beneath the great staircase and began the descent to no-man's-land. Miranda went on talking. "There's a time in every girl's life when she needs to find out who she is—as distinct from the person everyone else has always assumed she'll be. I think Margaret spent that time trying to become her mother. And then suddenly it was too late to try to be herself. The moment had passed."

"That's very pessimistic," Catherine said.

"I mean the moment when it could be done easily. Now it'll have to be done the hard way." She turned and paused, staring at Catherine. "And you know who's got to do most of it."

"Yes." Catherine understood what had been meant by being gentle and hard at the same time; it was in Miranda's very eyes.

Catherine had one last question to ask. "Are most of your young ladies supporting their family? I mean . . . sick brothers and things like that?"

Miranda understood she was really asking about any reason Meg might have given; she paused awhile and gave it some thought.

To fill the silence Catherine added, "She's been sending me clothes, you know. Expensive clothes and things."

At last Miranda said, "Most of them'll tell you they're looking after someone. That's only natural. But I think why a lot of them do it is they don't really know what it's for. They can't fit it into the rest of their lives. So it just sticks out there on its own. In the end, charging money for it is the only thing that makes sense—I mean the only thing that ties it back in with the rest of life. It's the only way they can get themselves back together. Everyone needs to know they're valued somewhere for something. Sixty dollars, folding money, is a pretty unequivocal valuation set beside an I-love-you and a yawn and a snore and where's-my-lunch-pail."

"But it's a valuation on a fake," Catherine pointed out.

Miranda gave her a playful push. "I changed my mind about you, honey. You're *too* good. You turn out and square up so fast there's no time for a trick in between." When she saw Catherine's hesitation, she said, "You've been pretty close to it yourself, I guess?"

Catherine nodded. "Without exactly realizing it."

"I believe that, too." She looked about them and said in a hushed voice, "I turned out once myself, you know."

It was a display of genuine naivety. Catherine was moved by it. The vulnerability she had glimpsed once or twice was there laid quite open. Miranda sensed it, too, and shuddered in vexation, mostly at herself, as if to say "Now see what you've done!"

The suitcase had been removed from the booth. "It'll be in Margaret's car," Miranda said. "And so, I hope, will Margaret. We said our goodbyes already—she and I."

So, Catherine thought, *I was expected.* It was a house of falsehood all right.

Just before the door Miranda grasped Catherine's arm. There was a new urgency in her voice and grip. "Like a lot of young ladies who come here," she said, "your Margaret is a child still. She's a young girl in a grown woman's body. She needs grown values. You can give them to her, Catherine. There's no doubting that. So don't let anyone *de*-value her, now. And keep her busy, eh? Keep her mind busy. Don't let her evaluate herself until you've put something there for her to notice. Be proud of. And *you* be proud of her. Be proud even of what she's done here. It wasn't easy. Especially for her it wasn't."

They shook hands. Suddenly Catherine didn't want to go. She wanted to stay in the maternal warmth and security that seemed to hang around Miranda. *Values,* Miranda said. She had them! Here, in the last place on earth where Catherine would have considered looking for values to put in place of the grand old certainties that no longer fitted, here she had found them: the values of love—not the kind of love that was sold above, but the old-woman-in-a-shoe kind, always on offer below, to be earned, not bought.

"I'll write and let you know what happens," she said.

Margaret did not get out of her car—a classy and powerful Kissel White Eagle with the top folded. Catherine saw her, sitting tensely behind the wheel, drumming on it with her fingers, starkly but dimly revealed by the light that spilled from one of the scullery windows.

It needed little intuition to divine that Margaret was terrified of this meeting. Catherine hurled herself over the passenger door and threw her arms around Margaret, giving her a fierce hug. "Oh, Meg!" she cried. "Meg! It's so good to see you again. We've missed you so much!"

Margaret began to laugh, a wild, hiccuppy laugh, close to tears. When she was calmer she asked, "What do they think of all this at home? What did Fiona say?"

"They think Miranda's is an alcoholics' clinic. Thanks to whoever signed herself Maggie's Friend. She truly was a friend. Even I thought it was a clinic until I was inside the place. I had a *weird* conversation with the cabbie who brought me here. He thought I was coming here to work."

Margaret's laughter was more controlled this time. "You! Work here!" she said with a patronizing smile.

Catherine swelled pugnaciously. "I'll have you know that Miranda just made me an offer. She even picked me out a . . . client?"

"Partner. They're Miranda's clients—our partners. Who?"

"A distinguished and handsome elderly gentleman called Andrew."

"Andrew van Hyssen! Oh, he's sweet. He was my first, too. I was so nervous. And he couldn't have been nicer. And when he came I was so pleased. 'My body works! My body works!' I kept singing to myself. I was so happy I gave him a second one free. Miranda was mad. How did you make out?"

Catherine punched her playfully on the shoulder.

"Careful!" Margaret warned. "That's your next dress I'm wearing."

"Let's go."

"Don't I shock you, Cath?"

"Not a bit."

"Be truthful now. Not a *bit?*"

"All right. A bit."

Margaret smiled triumphantly. "You wait." She fired the starter. The car gave a wroughty roar as it throbbed to life—a hundred and twenty-six horses bottled up in eight straight cylinders. But she pulled away so slowly Catherine was sure she'd had more than one reprimand about scudding the gravel.

"*Adieu, Château de l'Amour Facile!*" Margaret called as she drove past. She grinned at Catherine. "My alma mater, you know. Within whose shady portals I passed the happiest lays of my life."

Catherine laughed. She was beginning to see the shape of the immediate future—which was simply to let Margaret talk and talk and talk it out of herself.

"There's a lot of wisdom in the old folk sayings and proverbs, Cath," she went on as they reached the street. "Like *Too many cocks spoil the brothel.* Now that is profoundly true."

Catherine's hopes of a modest little bed and breakfast were soon passed over: "I've been bedded enough and I never eat breakfast. No—we'll stay at the Madison—Chicago's ritziest. One night of indulgence, eh? Is it worth a lifetime of shame? I'd say it's a fair trade, wouldn't you?"

They took a suite at the Madison, had deep foam baths in tubs that were gilded shells such as Venus might have bathed in, and ate oeufs en cocotte, sole Colbert, and crêpes Suzette in the suite. Catherine was then mentally prepared for bed but Margaret grabbed her up and said, "Come on. Let's go out and soak some jazz. Did you hear of Gene Krupa?"

"No."

"Bix? Bud Freeman? Benny Goodman?"

To each Catherine said no.

"Then come and live! I can't imagine where you've been."

They did not get back to the hotel until two-thirty that morning. By then Catherine was almost dead. She had thought it a dreadful thing to do—two women, going alone to a jazz club. But Margaret had been marvellous. She had a way of brushing off men that left them feeling they were great fellows. Then her ear drums had been blistered out of her by raw trumpets, wailing clarinets, rasping trombones, and drums that sounded as lethal as cannon. But the music! Visceral. Primitive. Mind-numbing. At times she had forgotten who or where she was; she and Margaret had melted into a finger-clicking, hand-clapping, foot-stomping mass—swept away in a roaring welter of rhythm, buoyed up by soaring and strangely poignant melody.

Margaret, looking as if she'd just stepped from a night's deep slumber, was still humming "High Society" as they returned to their suite. Then it was a second bath in the gilded scallop shells—during which Catherine fell asleep and was wakened with a cold rain of ice from the champagne bucket.

Then they half-sat, half-lay in their twin beds, sipping champagne while Margaret talked and talked. She wanted to know nothing of Burgo or the business, nothing of Goldeneye, nothing of Kelvin and Maddy. She had two thousand experiences to scale. And it all poured out—far worse than anything Miranda had led Catherine to expect. Margaret unpacked self after contradictory self, opinion after opposite opinion. It had been the happiest time of her life, her partners had been princes among men, she was only leaving because of Miranda—she was a pig, the other girls ("Young ladies!" she sneered in parody of Miranda) were better than sisters, but some partners were shit, the food was magnificent, she was leaving because she'd had all she could take, if it hadn't been for Miranda, she'd have left long ago, Miranda was as good as a mother—better (God! If only Fiona could have been like Miranda), the other girls didn't appreciate how lucky they were, she felt nothing but contempt for her partners—*partners!* That was a good one. Enemies! Greedy eyes, greedy fingers, greedy jacks. And the vile food. All those enemies, self-important bastards thinking you just lived for them and their squalid frenzies. With some girls it was true. Cows!

"Men! They can't see that cause and effect are different. If I fill a man with lust, he puts it back on me—thinks I must be full of it, too. You'd think they'd learn, wouldn't you? What else are all those gorgeous naked marble ladies in museums for? I'll bet they think the Venus de Milo lost her arms twitching for those ten million men who passed through the turnstile and couldn't take their eyes off her."

It was near dawn before Margaret reached the temporary salvation of this bout of humour. The accidental excursion into the art world must have reminded her of the *Trésors*. "Hey," she cried, startling Catherine out of a doze, "doesn't your Hyman Amoils live here? Aren't you going to see him?"

"Not this time, Meg." Catherine yawned. She had, of course, intended looking him up; but with Margaret in this condition it was out of the question.

"Because of me?"

"Because of everything. I had a fight with Burgo over all this. He thought I should have told Fiona and left her to come and get you. Mercy! Just think if I had!"

"Don't! But don't change the subject either." She was suddenly quite calm and normal again—whatever "normal" was with her. "You go ahead and see your Hymie. Tomorrow—I mean, today."

Because she said *your* Hymie, Catherine, who had meant to dismiss the whole idea again, said instead, "Not without you, Meg."

Margaret grinned. "Attagirl! Ask him to dinner tomorrow night. We'll dine at the Lafayette—you've not tasted escargots until you've tasted theirs."

"I've not tasted escargots—period."

"Even better. And don't worry about me, hon. If I can get a little high, like last night, and just let it pour out, like . . ."

"Like all night!"

"Like all night—I'm a kindergarten teacher for weeks after. Hey—did you hear about the kindergarten teacher who worked at Miranda's and said to her partner, 'I don't care if it takes all night—you're going to stay here and keep it till you get it *right*!' Anyway—don't worry—I won't disgrace you with your Hymie."

"He's not *my* Hymie."

"Of course not. Now if you don't mind—I'd like to get some sleep. This is my bedtime."

Margaret was as good as her word. Watching her at dinner that night, holding the most erudite conversation with Hymie about Savonarola, the Jesuits, the Counter-Reformation, and the destruction of the humanistic triumphs of the Florentine Renaissance, it was impossible to equate her with the rambling, tipsy woman who had robbed last night of its sleep.

Hymie had not changed much. He was not so youthful, of course; and at thirty-five his hair was "just beginning the long republican march" ("away from the crown," he explained diffidently, in case they didn't get it). He had also married—and brought his wife, Rebecca, with him. She was eager to see this girl, now woman, who had made such an impression on Hymie that he still, twelve years later, tore open her letters even before he looked at long-awaited replies from Bartoldi, Hausmann, Foster, and all the other luminaries of European art.

Rebecca was a dark, short, pretty woman, "fat enough to keep him warm," as Margaret said afterwards.

Margaret dominated the table, but not in a way that anyone could have objected to. She was their hostess, after all—she made that clear from the outset. It was obvious to her that Hymie still carried a torch of a kind for Catherine. It was probably only a stage property in his own self-drama (she knew a lot about men's self-dramas now), but would Rebecca realize that? Margaret drew a lot of potential fire that evening—fire that, if it had gone Catherine's way, would certainly have burned Hymie after.

Toward the end, Catherine shyly produced the new edition of the *Louvre* book and explained, or gilded over, what had happened to the first. Hymie agonized a long time over what to write in the new dedication and eventually put "To Miss Catherine Hamilton with respect from her friend Hyman Amoils, Chicago, 1919; and to Catherine and Margaret Macrae with love from their friends Rebecca and Hyman Amoils, Chicago, 1931."

He'll pay for that "love," Margaret thought.

Hymie then shyly confessed that he, too, had had an accident to her sprig of heather. The glance he gave his wife and the grip she took on her glass showed that a certain amount of gilding over was involved here, too. Only last year he had written to the postmistress at Strath, explaining why he needed a replacement sprig of Beinn Uidhe heather—and would she arrange to send it?

"He sent her a *ten* dollar bill," Rebecca added.

Catherine wondered what sort of a tale Mistress Menzies, postmistress at Strath, had concocted out of that request.

When they parted they said goodnight or au revoir, as if they might meet again very soon; but just as they reached the revolving door Rebecca turned and waved.

"Goodbye!" she called as the door whirled her out into the night.

Meg laughed. "I hate women, don't you?" she said.

26

Catherine's original plan had been to bring Margaret (whom she had expected to find a trembling, penniless alcoholic) back to Burgo at Selkirk and discuss with him what to do next. As soon as she discovered that Margaret had not only the car but a little over forty thousand dollars, as well as a wardrobe fit for a travelling princess, she realized that some other plan would have to be made.

"How were you going to explain it, Meg?" she asked.

"I'm not ashamed."

"Of course not. But that isn't the point. You're going out to do some other kind of work. With people. You have to take account of their—"

"Okay, okay!" Margaret cut in. "I embezzled it. It was a political contribution. I have charitable status. I got mistaken for a state highway and everyone just threw money at me. Pick a card."

"Be serious."

"Mom and Dad must already realize I don't always sleep alone."

"You know, Meg, I don't think they believe you. They're convinced it's all fantasy. They think you're pretending to be Tallulah Bankhead."

"They *know* of Tallulah Bankhead?"

"And Noel Coward. Newspapers do eventually reach Goldeneye. You're going to have to go into some kind of business. Don't you realize that? It's going to be at least nineteen forty before you can admit to having all that money."

"Work? I only know one kind of work."

"That's not true."

"The other wasn't work. It was failure. And that is true."

"It was a failure because you weren't your own boss. The only thing you can ever be, Meg, is your own boss." Catherine spoke the first words that came into her mind. Only after they were out did she realize they probably were profoundly true. Not only of Meg but of Burgo, too.

Margaret's silence confirmed it—or perhaps she just liked such a flattering idea. "Right," she said.

The following evening they were in Minneapolis, taking turns at the wheel all the way. Her encounter with Miranda—and the outpouring of Meg's subconscious—showed her how close, in spirit at least, were Meg's case and her own. What was Miranda's phrase? Squaring up. If Meg was ever to square up properly, she wouldn't do it in Goldeneye, where James just joked with her and Fiona made her feel useless. And she herself could not stay there either. She understood things so much more clearly now, and saw the direction in which she had been drifting. Both of them had to get away from Goldeneye; that was the starting point of all thought about their future. On a practical level, too, Meg had to do something that, in the fullness of time, would adequately explain her new wealth. That would be impossible in Goldeneye.

But what? And where? And how to explain it to Burgo? The problem was insoluble.

Thought of Burgo reminded her that he was probably expecting her and Meg in Ontario. They stopped and sent him a cable to say they were heading for Goldeneye. Next evening they were at Minot, North Dakota, where they ought really to have gone north into Saskatchewan, through Regina and Saskatoon to Goldeneye. Instead, next day, they set off on a thousand-mile detour across Montana, to Chinook, where they turned north through the Buttes, making for the Cypress Hills, where Catherine and Burgo had spent their honeymoon—a lifetime ago it now seemed.

It was no sentimental journey, though that was the reason both Margaret and Catherine agreed on between themselves; both of them knew they were postponing the return to Goldeneye until they had figured out some kind of programme.

At Whitewater they put up at a "hotel" which, give or take a telephone or two and an electric lamp or twenty, could have featured in any cowboy movie. The following day was warm for spring and as near windless as it gets in those hills when the sun beats down on them. They decided not to press on at once but to rent a couple of hacks from the livery stable and take a pack lunch out into the hills.

"Mustn't it have been marvellous when this was the only way to get around here!" Catherine said. "The car is a terrible destroyer."

The way led out of the one-street town over a bridge on the White River, where Catherine caught the first tang of wolf willow, made volatile by the sun; its heavy musk revived for her so many past confusions. A path branched off along the coulee, winding up by a series of ridges into the hills. It led past a derelict stone chimney. Catherine remembered it and knew where they were.

"A man told us that this was where the Spaniards once smelted silver," she said to Margaret. "That's the local legend."

"We're not taught any real history, are we? What does school teach any of us that has any bearing? All our history was Greeks and Romans, and Magna Carta, and Wolfe at Quebec, and a line or two about John Mac-Donald. We weren't really taught to believe in ourselves or Goldeneye. D'you think eventually everyone'll go back to Europe? Or will there be an exam and they'll only take the best of us back?"

They laughed. "I never think of myself as Scots now," Catherine said. "Only Canadian. I could never go back. I'd be so out of place."

"You don't know. It might have changed, too. Where's the Hamiltons' old spread? Och aye—I remember it. Just out there past the White Heather Radio Station and the Wee Dock and Doris' All-Nite Diner."

They stopped in a grove that Catherine remembered well, in an old burnout, high up on the bench. Kelvin was conceived there. She thought of the third child, who would not now be born—a boy, of course. Sometimes she felt him at her breast, where no baby would ever suckle again. She saw his large, boy's head and tousled hair where, instead, there would always be a space. It was easy to work out who she *wasn't*.

The place was carpeted with harebells and wild anemones, barely moving in the breeze that soughed through the Alberta spruce, silver birch, and aspens, stretching for virgin miles around them. The sound of the waterfall came from nearby.

The lonely beauty of the place and its nostalgic associations contrasted so starkly with Catherine's present miseries that she soon found herself telling Margaret all about them. Before long there were tears in her eyes. They flowed almost independently of her story—that is, her words were not interrupted by sobbing. But in the end the tears won. She turned on her stomach, buried her head in the wheat grass, and let them flow.

Margaret was much less affected by it than Catherine might have expected. She sat close and patted her perfunctorily a couple of times; then she delivered a stinging slap on Catherine's bottom and said, "Brace up, kid. We'll think of something. Let's go find that water. Don't you just feel like a skinny dip?"

They raced out of their clothes and stood beneath the waterfall with a great deal of shouting and yelping. It was mountain cold, and heavy. They jumped and twisted until their skin was so chill and numb they no longer felt its touch. Then they came out, scooped up their clothes, and raced back to the clearing to lie in the sun and dry. The sudden warmth after that icy cold was soporific; they both fell asleep until, two hours later, the shadow of a lodgepole pine fell across Catherine and she woke, shivering again.

But their clothes soon had them warm.

"Now I'll burn and peel," Margaret said crossly. "You have that unnatural Scandinavian skin that never burns. You're so suspiciously lucky."

They broke out their lunch packs. Margaret cracked her hard-boiled egg on Catherine's head. She, deliberately not reacting, said, "The mosquitoes are out early this year."

Margaret said, "Wouldn't it be nice to be kids again?"

"No!"

"I'd like to live in a log cabin. Right here. God, look at it! This is one beaut of a country, Cath. Wouldn't you like to live in a little cabin right here?"

"All alone?"

"Sure." She paused, screwing up her face for a little concession. "Well, maybe just the Lafayette next door. And that Gene Krupa crowd over there. But *nothing* more than that."

"Well, don't wrap it." Catherine laughed. "I'll slip it on right away."

Margaret punched her arm with delight. "Hey, sister! You've got the makings of quite a mensch, you know that?"

They ate in silence. Then Catherine said, "Would you like to do that, Meg? I'm sure we could find a cabin here to rent. We could go back to Goldeneye, collect Kelvin and Maddy, and come back here. We could stay all summer. How about it?"

"On what money? I mean, how do we explain it?"

"It wouldn't cost much. And you must have made something in Paris."

"That's what I bought the car with—and it's only half paid, anyway. That's the story."

"Of course." Catherine sighed. "I'm not thinking, am I!"

"You may not be. But I have been. I like this lodge idea, though. That's what we'll tell everyone we're doing—coming here. Pretend we've sold the car. And that'll give us five months to get started in Toronto."

"Started? At what? And why Toronto?"

"So that when Burgo does move Night Call there, we'll be able to rent him the office. I just want to see his face!"

Catherine relished that prospect, too. "But 'we'? What are 'we' meanwhile?"

"We are unique. We not only sell inexpensive gowns for the matronly figure, we also sell expensive decor for fat old women's homes. Tonight we'll find a friendly storekeeper in Whitewater, maybe even an actual cabin, rent it until September—it couldn't be more than fifty bucks—tell him how to relay mail and calls (and I'm Saskatchewan's expert on that, believe me)."

"And if Burgo decides on a surprise visit?"

"That's easy. Mr. Aardvark—or whatever he's called—says, 'Gee mishter, sure is a shame. They went east yesterday. Said they was gonna surprise someone. You want the keys?'" She grinned at the cleverness of it. "To-morrow: Goldeneye. Collect Yeurk and Yeurk and head east. Find a place in Toronto. Train to Selkirk. Tell Burgo about the cabin. And catch the Cypress Hills train—except we get off at Toronto."

"Why not simply tell him the truth?"

"You know why. He'd only say no."

"I could tell him your clinician in Chicago advised it—say he told me you ought to run a little shop of your own. And I'll look after you. And James is lending the money."

"You're no fun anymore, Cath. Don't you want to do it *without* Burgo? Show him you're someone even without him? Don't you like secrets?"

Catherine felt the challenge, but not in Meg's terms. Meg obviously thought there was a thwarted Interior Designer inside her sister-in-law, longing for this chance to get to work; but all that Catherine wanted was to pay off the debt and get the family together again as soon as possible. More than anything she wanted that other baby. If there *was* a thwarted Interior Designer in there who could help—well and good. But *it*—the designer—had better get used to being thwarted again once the job was done.

"I suppose so," Catherine allowed.

"Anyway, darling, I'd go crazy here. One more dawn chorus like yesterday's and I'd open up a gunshop and *give* the stock away. And if I went to Toronto on my own, I'd end up *under* the wagon. And my way is best because there's nothing for Burgo to turn down so that's what we'll do."

Catherine shrugged. "Okay."

That night, Margaret, while climbing into her bed, said, "It's fine without men, isn't it."

Catherine agreed reluctantly. "For a time."

Later, when the lights were out, Margaret said, "You're right. I'm going to *have* to have men in Toronto, Cath. I love the bastards too much."

27

Catherine realized how bad a liar she was going to be the minute they reached Goldeneye. Fiona produced a letter that had arrived the day before. It was from Margaret and had been mailed in Paris only ten days earlier—at a time when Margaret was, presumably, already at the clinic in Chicago. It clearly called for an explanation but her mind simply went blank—which, too, was how she felt in the space where her stomach used to be.

But Margaret just picked up the letter with a fond smile and said, "Silly woman! That's Madame Dutourd, the concierge. I threw it away before I left—she must have found it and mailed it on."

It even convinced Catherine until she remembered.

Everyone was so glad to see Margaret and to find she was no alcoholic wreck that they forgot the letter. Later Catherine asked Margaret if she had expected it.

"No, I'd forgotten." Margaret laughed.

"So you hadn't prepared that story."

"Heavens no! Life would be one long nightmare if I had to prepare stories at that level." She saw the shock in Catherine's face and said, "Don't worry, kid. Reality's just a gestalt." She tapped Catherine's forehead. "Most of it exists only up there, anyway."

Though it cost them another week they went back to the Cypress Hills, to the cabin they had genuinely rented until September, and indulged Kelvin and Maddy in a brief romance of the back-to-nature life. They also took snapshots for the album.

"Burgo's bound to ask how they like the cabin, what do they like doing best, things like that. We don't want it all to come apart on two little words like 'What cabin?' do we?" Margaret said.

They also left canned foods and things that wouldn't perish, sheets, sets of wilderness clothes, books . . . all the things they would leave if they had truly gone east for a surprise visit.

"See! It's not a 'tangled web' at all," Margaret said. "What a lot of progress we've made since the good old days. Of course, they only 'practised to deceive.' We deliver the master performance."

It took five days by car to Toronto, driving back via Chicago and Detroit, where the roads were better. Business in Toronto was so depressed they could have their pick of downtown sites. Their need for some secrecy, however, led them to rent a house with a small showroom ground floor in Yorkville, a block north of the city's smartest shopping artery. They interviewed a number of women to look after the children, clean the house, and fix a midday meal. Catherine herself would see to the evening meal—or that was the plan. They picked a Mrs. Rennie, a widow with a grown daughter, a quiet, watchful, reserved woman whose strong body and work-lined hands made all the claims for her that others made for themselves with their mouths.

They left the children with her when they took the bus to Selkirk to see Burgo. At his request they didn't bring the children—"I won't have proper time to devote to them and they'll only get unsettled." Margaret said they were all staying with Patricia Dole, a college friend in Toronto, who could look after them for the day and bring them to the station so that she and Catherine could take a through-train west from Selkirk. Margaret went to see other old college friends for an hour or two while Catherine and Burgo mended fences the only way open to them nowadays—in bed. It did not work except in the most mechanical way. The cause of the rift between them (which they had studied to ignore) was too great. She could not participate. Part of her simply lay there and watched herself and Burgo become clients of each other's urges.

Later he said he was delighted to hear Margaret was not nearly so ill as "Maggie's Friend" had led them to believe, and glad, too, that her clinician in Chicago thought this holiday in the Cypress Hills would do her good.

"And she'll be company for you," he said.

There was an edge to this throwaway remark that made her ask what he meant.

"These are the make-or-break months for Night Call, Cath. I don't know how I'm going to find time even to sleep. We now—just while you were away in Chicago—we now have every doctor but one in this area signed up. So I have all that to organize. And now, last week, Hector MacIver from the physics department—remember him? They have that Victorian house up on the scarp?"

She nodded. They had stained-glass windows above the stairs; she remembered that, but not the MacIvers themselves.

"Well, he thinks he can squeeze a radio transmitter-receiver into the trunk of a car. I have a version of it downstairs. I'll show you. We have to build that and test it. I think it's the answer to all the problems of transferring Night Call from an area like this to one with over two hundred doctors. Radio cars. So there's one hell of a lot to do."

"You mean you won't be coming to the cabin?"

He put his head on one side and smiled persuasively. "In the Cypress Hills? In these circumstances? With all those associations?"

She wished he had somehow spoken those words in just that way before their lovemaking.

"What're those glass things?" Margaret asked when she returned and Burgo was showing off Hector MacIver's new, experimental car radio.

"Tubes," Burgo said. "Radio tubes. Every radio has them. Thermionic emission tubes, if you want the full—"

"Thermionic *what?*" Margaret's eyes shone with sudden fascination.

"Emission."

"My God! I had no idea radio was all so visceral and Freudian, Burgo. Tubes! Emission! At last I understand why we have to turn them off overnight—a nocturnal one of those things would be pretty embarrassing to have to clear up next day." She tickled the radio. "Hey, cheeky!" she said.

"Same old Meg!" Burgo tried not to smile.

He drove them down to the station and once again Catherine asked him not to come inside—to say their goodbyes out here. She gave the same reason as before, but this time it was to conceal the fact that they were to walk straight through the station and come out in the bus plaza, where they would board a bus for downtown Toronto that would put them off in Yorkville. Her faltering relationship with Burgo, and her deception, made her actually glad to see him go. But it was no victory.

Burgo had written himself out of her life. He hadn't meant to and he'd have been shocked to hear it. He never would have understood it, though. When she and he headed a family, she had never once doubted herself or questioned her own purpose; it was all too self-evidently around her. But now that he had broken it all up he had made himself irrelevant. He was no longer a yardstick of her value; his ambitions did not even touch her reasons for existence. No matter how high his motives nor how hard he drove himself, its connection with her was too abstract to mean anything.

Now she was frightened and alone. When she had agreed to try this little business in Toronto with Meg, it had only been in order to get the family together again even quicker than Burgo had predicted—not just for the sake of speed but so that she could say: "See—I did my bit, too."

Things weren't quite working out like that. Burgo wasn't "doing his bit." Or not like a man pushed to the bottom of the heap and struggling to get back. He was loving it. Ruin had liberated him. He was discovering that this was what he had always wanted to do. He had jumped out of the frying pan and into his true element—the fire of competition and success.

Why had she not seen it on earlier visits? Because her longing to get the family together again had been so overwhelming. She hadn't even questioned whether or not he shared it. But why did she question it now? What was different now? Was there some of that same excitement in her—was the thwarted designer just beginning to get a whiff of that same fire? And was Burgo only a mile or two ahead of her on the same path, away from a nice, modest little house in an unpretentious suburb of a quiet town?

No! It must not happen. She must not spend her life running away from every home she made. One was enough. And one more was all she wanted. If it took her the rest of her life, long or short, she would not be diverted. She would get back her home, get back her family, and get back Burgo.

She did not know whether to bless Meg and her scheme, because it had made these matters so clear, or to curse her for making the alternatives so enticing. She felt irritable now—both eager and reluctant to get going.

"You oughtn't to talk smut in front of Burgo," she told Margaret when they were safely Toronto-bound. "He'll worry now about corrupting Kelvin and Maddy."

"Cut it out, Cath. You're becoming the car-ride home from every party I ever went to." She parodied Fiona: " 'Well! You were pretty lively to-night, I must say!' And all I did was try to organize a snow-boot shuffle or a bicycle ride up Mount McKinley." She brightened then and returned to the here-and-now. "But just guess what *I* found out this afternoon! I didn't go see old college friends. I went to see a Mr. William Sturton, direc-tor of brother too-busy-bee's bank, to tell him I saw an opportunity to ar-range a thirty-thousand-dollar collateral for Night Call Ltd. when and if it makes the big leap. Told him I was Caligula's sister, of course. And *he* wasn't to be told of it."

"And?"

"And he just smiled and said it wouldn't be necessary. I said what did he mean and he said Night Call has all the backing it needs already. So I said Burgo sure didn't know that. And he said that's right, I wasn't the only one with that idea. I said tell me more and he said he couldn't but Burgo could be mighty proud of his family."

"James!"

"Well, no odds are quoted on Helen and Arthur."

"James!" Catherine smiled. "He's been behind us all the time."

They called themselves MaCaBu Creations–Dress and Decor—literally. They put out no shingle, printed no letterheads, no cards. They just *called* themselves MaCaBu.

Margaret offered near-copies of Paris and New York model gowns, made to measure—at least, that's what she called them. In fact, they were mostly her own designs, Paris-inspired. Catherine offered to redesign the ladies' homes—if they wanted.

Neither of them had the slightest idea how to start, let alone run, a business; it was very slow to pick up. If they had been dependent on it for an income, they would have bitten their fingernails to the quick, and the pieces would have scratched their backbones on the way down. As it was they read a lot, played with Kelvin and Maddy a lot, went to the movies, and slept late.

But then, about midsummer, their lack of business knowledge combined in a special way with the psychology of their potential clients to turn MaCaBu into a success—small at first, but it grew steadily. They had never advertised, for instance, because it had never occurred to them—after all, Burgo had never advertised Night Call and he was the model at the back of their minds; also, they couldn't put their real names in print like that. One client, who happened to peep through the empty showcase window and was intrigued enough to enter, asked why on earth she'd never heard of them, and why they'd never advertised.

"We've never found it necessary," Margaret told her airily. "Vulgar puffs in the press wouldn't cut much ice with *our* sort of people. Word of mouth, you know. Word of mouth."

She was improvising, of course, as Margaret so often was; but it just happened to strike the right chord in the woman, who was the wife of the chairman of an international insurance company—and who, when her new gown was admired at the next Guild ball, professed surprise and said, "But *surely* you know of MaCaBu?"

She was not the only one, of course. In a small, big-city set like that it didn't need too many people to say, "But *surely* you know of MaCaBu?" while others said, "They're not in the book," and others replied, "Well, of *course* they're not in the book!" before everyone not only knew of MaCaBu but was also rather glad that they were not in the book.

Business was never sensational. But for two people working out of their own home, who carried next to no stock, who subcontracted everything from paperhanging to buttonholing, who spent nothing on promotion, threw no trade parties, employed no staff, they did well at first, and then very well. So much so that by December they were looking back on the "halicon days of May," as Margaret called them, and trying to remember the last time they had seen a movie or finished a book.

"If I hadn't already made a home of my own," Catherine said. "If I didn't have a family—I'd quite enjoy this."

"Go on," Meg said. "It's fun."

"No. It's just irksome."

In all that time, Catherine "came east" to see Burgo only once, at the end of September—and was so distressed that she almost went back on her resolution and almost asked Margaret to pay off his debt secretly and let the fur fly. He was a skeleton of his former self in every respect but one: the business. He lived for Night Call alone, it seemed. Even his lovemaking was grudged; he satisfied her (at a physical level, anyway) but was unable to reach his climax. "Out of practice," he said with a grin—almost a grin of relief. "Not to worry. If we're patient and grown-up about it, it'll all come back together one day. Quite soon, I'd guess. Maybe even next year . . ."

Next year! Catherine thought.

But he was already excited again. Not by her. Not even by her body. Not about this distant vision of potency. But—of course—about Night Call Toronto, as it was now to be called. NCT for short.

The business had devoured him. His heart was now a construction worker for NCT.

During November two of her letters, re-mailed from Whitewater, were unanswered. They had by then "moved," because of the snows, to a non-existent cabin near town. If they had really been staying in the Cypress Hills, she would have walked down into town and called him but she could think of no way to disguise a Toronto call as one from Whitewater. The other thing would be to "come east" a few days before he was due to go back to join them in Goldeneye for Christmas; she was worried enough to do that.

Margaret was to take Yeurk and Yeurk, whom she now more often called Samson and Salome (from their respective love of destruction and the dance), back to Goldeneye while Catherine went down to Selkirk. The situation she encountered was far worse than anything her fear had led her to imagine.

Burgo had a broken leg, which he ought to have been resting for the last week. He had not rested a single hour. Since yesterday he had developed an abscess on his lower left wisdom tooth. He was deaf on that side. When she told him he must go and see their dentist and then come back to Goldeneye at once and put his leg up all over Christmas, he said it was absolutely impossible—utterly out of the question. He was due to have dinner with the chairman of the Toronto Chapter of the Canadian Medical Congress, in Toronto, that evening. He *had* to make that meeting. It was vital to the very survival of NCT. Nothing would keep him from it.

He was living on codeine and some new drug called Prontosil. He was so constipated he couldn't walk straight.

Catherine, seeing that nothing would deflect him, took charge of those things he would allow needed attention. She called Wendell Craig, their dentist, who, fortunately, worked only two blocks away, and begged him to come round quickly with everything necessary for an emergency extraction. He was there in ten minutes. Burgo wouldn't take gas or an injection, not in any circumstances; he needed all his faculties. Catherine, who held his hand and fought back her tears all through the grisly business, could feel his pain through the agonized strength of his grip. His eyes bulged in their sockets. His breathing was strangled. His pulse went to over two hundred. It was the first time she saw anyone physically *leaking* sweat; it started out as if from countless miniature springs under his skin. How he came through without a heart seizure she could not understand.

Yet the moment it was over, he began to recover. Wendell, who was in a fair sweat himself, packed the cavity with absorbent cotton soaked in codeine (onto which Burgo later dripped a few drops of adrenalin, to stem the bleeding). Burgo's pulse fell back. No more sweat beads started where she wiped his skin. He worked his jaw a couple of times in all directions and at once began to speak normally. "Now, why didn't I think of that!" he said, giving that characteristic grin of his and squeezing Catherine around the waist. "Now, honey. Friend or enema?"

When Wendell was gone she gave him the enema, which soon had the desired effect—except that the straining made his nose bleed. He came out of the bathroom cursing, for he had only just changed out of his sweaty shirt into this, his last clean one.

Catherine thought that would settle it. He couldn't go to this dinner with the chairman. A few minutes later she was on her way to the shops to buy him two new shirts and collars. Nothing would keep him from that dinner. She drove him, his nose plugged with adrenalin-soaked cotton, to the city and marvelled as she felt him revive with each passing mile. He was a zombie, possessed by NCT. It breathed life and warmth into him.

Her heart almost stopped for good when she saw the chairman's house. It was one she herself had recently decorated. Burgo, thinking she didn't know her way about the city, had said, "Left here . . . right here . . ." instead of giving her the address straight out. If he had done, she would not have been able to control her agitation.

But would he have noticed? He said he was sorry she couldn't join them, but he didn't turn and wave to her as he limped up the path on his crutches. Where did that energy come from? And that indifference to pain? He was a doctor, too; he knew the risks of not resting that broken leg. What bit of his mind overruled all that?

She drove back to Yorkville, certain he was, this evening, going to uncover their deception. Even though, professionally, she called herself Kate Hamilton, it wasn't much of a disguise against Burgo. Margaret was not, in fact, taking the children to Goldeneye until tomorrow. She came to the door white-faced.

"It's you!" She gulped with exaggerated relief. "My God! When I saw Burgo's car with all that radio junk . . . Hey! Will it pick up CBS—can you get Paul Whiteman? Wouldn't it be divine to drive out along the lake shore with jazz all the way?" Then she saw Catherine's face. "What's up, hon?"

Catherine told her then, everything that had happened—including her certainty that they were now unmasked.

Margaret was not too worried at the prospect. "At least we've got good news for him, kid. I went through our books while you were out and—"

"What books?"

"Well, you know what I mean. I put all the receipts we've issued in one hatbox and all those we've been given in another and weighed them and you know what—they weigh about equal!"

"Meg!"

Margaret giggled. "No. I added them up and—truly now, no fooling— we're about eight thousand dollars to the good. I couldn't believe it."

Catherine couldn't believe it either. She redid the arithmetic and added in a lot of expenses that Margaret had considered to be "domestic" rather than "business." Too, she took off a thousand to allow for lost items, forgotten expenses, "depreciation" (which, to her, was just a word that Burgo had used a couple of times), and luck. It still came out just over five thousand eight hundred ahead.

"Wasn't I right to insist on our charging so outrageously?" Margaret crowed. "Or, wasn't Miranda right?" she corrected herself, remembering whose experience she had been relying on. Miranda had once said to her, "The only difference between you and a twenty-dollar showgirl is forty dollars. The *only* difference. But if you act four *hundred* dollars, no partner will ever see it."

"What are we going to do with all that money?" Catherine was awed at what they had achieved.

"Buy stock in NCT, of course," Margaret said. "We're not just going to *give* it to Brother Dracula, I hope?"

"We'll need to think about that, Meg. If the miracle happens—if he hasn't put Kate Hamilton and me together—we won't say anything for the moment."

She had given Burgo the number of MaCaBu, saying it was Patricia Dole's, Margaret's college friend. He called at eleven, said everything was wonderful, wonderful, wonderful, and asked her to collect him five minutes ago. He couldn't wait to get back to Selkirk.

The miracle had happened.

"What sort of a house is it?" she asked as they drove away. "What's it like inside?"

"Very nice," he said. "You'd have liked it, I think. But you could do something ten times better."

"I hope you said what a beautiful home."

"I say that to everyone. Even Hector MacIver and his stained glass."

All the way back to Selkirk he sparkled with that evening's achievement. It was the last big hurdle before NCT could begin operations. Nothing could stop it now. He'd resign from the faculty in the new year and start at once, after Easter. He was vibrant with the delight of it—and could still hardly believe that something begun so offhandedly as a part-time job to pay off a debt should have developed into an organization that could yet change the course of medicine in Ontario. She waited for him to say that the stock market crash of two years ago was the best thing that could have happened to them. He just managed to hold back from the idea. But he believed it. She knew that.

Back at NCT's office in Selkirk she helped him up the stairs, taking as much weight off his broken leg as possible. His hand, over her shoulder, found her breast. He began to caress her there, urgently, on the edge of pain.

"Burgo!" She laughed.

"Thank God you're here, Cath!" he said. His voice was trembling.

They did not even get inside the room. He forced her up against a wall and began to tear down her pants.

"Burgo!" she repeated. But he could hear she was more delighted than shocked. Her resistance was conventional—soon not even that.

It was crude, urgent, and quick—over even before he was out of breath. "Damn!" he said. "I think my nose is bleeding again."

And it was. She was so busy soaking up the blood and putting salt on the stains on his shirt that she forgot to douche.

But as soon as they were in bed, he began once more—as ardent as he had been on their honeymoon. This time, because of the cast on his leg, she had to do the work. It almost made up for their eight months apart, ignoring the disastrous September encounter.

"Thank God you were here tonight, Cath!" he repeated. "In all this time I haven't cheated you with any other woman—nor even come near it. I even began to wonder if all that sort of thing wasn't over—especially in September! I thought it might all have . . . transferred—all the energy—transferred to the business." He laughed. "But tonight! I almost raped you in the car on the way home. I was so full of it."

"What was that on the stairs then if it wasn't rape?"

"Bliss!"

Once again she forgot to douche immediately. Later she remembered—and decided not to, anyway. He didn't notice. She felt both mean and justified.

She was glad he was able to be her husband again—though on that night at least, she was little more than his champagne bottle, long held over in bond, and finally uncorked for the celebration. But, as she got older, she noticed that their motives seemed to matter less than what they actually achieved. Motives grew more complex, less easy to call good or bad.

Back in Goldeneye she asked Margaret, obliquely, about the subject. They had all gone skating on the rezavoy, including Kelvin, who was going to be another Margaret, and Maddy, who was going to be at least as good as her mother. The children got tired first and Jay took them home, together with Burgo, who was now chained to a wheelchair but who wanted to make the most of every precious minute with the children. The two women stayed to enjoy a second cup of chocolate and maybe skate some more.

That was when Catherine shyly asked Margaret how much she knew about impotence. Margaret mimed an imaginary bookshelf in front of her. "Enough to fill all these," she said modestly. "Are we worried about the functional kind?" She grabbed a good handful of nonexistent volumes but then put them back. "Or psychological?" She riffled a fingernail along the remaining three dozen spines.

"Psychological, I guess."

"Well! Where do we begin? Let's begin at your end. We are, I hope—and then again 'hope' may not be quite the word—we are talking about my brother?"

"Not about him *now,* but in September. And not really impotent. It was just that he couldn't . . . finish. And now—well, it's very different."

"And you relate it to the turning of the business tide?"

"So does he."

"Uh huh!" She fished down one of the imaginary books and mimed a search through it so well that Catherine almost heard the pages turning. "Got it," she said at last. "I knew it was here somewhere." She even shifted slightly to get a better reading light on the "page." Catherine felt like a child again—the pleasure of being read to aloud. She suddenly realized how rich life was around Margaret and how much she'd miss her if they were ever separated.

"Listen now. This is good." Margaret pretended to quote: " 'Cinderella (twenty-three), a Young Lady in an exclusive North American house, reports that one of her partners, a noted physician, was caressing her left breast when his whole demeanor suddenly changed. He had detected what he later described as "the unmistakable *thrill* of mitral stenosis"—a heart ailment that causes the blood to gurgle or sing in a characteristic fashion on its entry to the heart, and from which, indeed, Cinderella was found to be suffering. . . .' "

She laughed and raised her eyes from the imaginary page. "Hey, it's like Jimmy Kellerman finding Marfan's Syndrome in that nurse, isn't it! I never thought of it until now."

"Did that really happen?"

"Oh, sure. Burgo dressed it up a bit. Anyway, this goes on: 'From our present point of view the interesting feature to emerge is that the doctor's sexual excitement vanished within seconds of his making this discovery. The professional within him asserted itself at once. Not even the undoubtedly powerful sexual urge could withstand it. The mitral thrill, one might say, triumphed over the sexual thrill.' "

She pulled a sour face and pretended to consult the spine of the book: "Who is this jerk? Remind me to avoid everything he ever wrote." She grinned at Catherine, ending the charade. "Does that—if you'll pardon the phrase—*cover* it?"

Catherine laughed. "In a funny way I suppose it does."

"I don't know any other way. The whole subject's pretty funny."

Catherine frowned suddenly. "That wasn't you, was it? I mean, you don't have mitral stenosis?"

"No, but it really happened okay. The girl's name was Cindy. As for your sudden return of wedded bliss, I'll tell you a funny thing that did happen to me. Two or three times. And to all the girls. You'd get some partner who'd only want to talk. He'd pay the full amount and then just pace the room. Maybe his arm round you. You could be his daughter. I mean no groping or anything. And he'd talk all about some big deal he'd been cooking up for years. And tomorrow was the big day. Tomorrow he was in the world series. And then he'd just thank you for listening and maybe kiss you on the forehead and go."

She shook her head slowly and gave a faraway smile. It was the first genuinely tender memory concerning those partners that Catherine had ever heard from her.

"If they failed," she went on, "you'd never hear from them again. But if they succeeded, wow! They'd be back next night and nothing was too good for you. I never enjoyed going with any partner—you know what I mean. Not enjoyed, like that. But those came closest. Because they were suddenly somebody. And they had come back, swelled with triumph, come back to tell *you*. To share it with *you*. Out of all the world, all the people they knew, they came and shared it with you. That's bound to make you feel somebody, too, isn't it? I guess every woman likes to be made something of by a man who's a somebody. Even a Young Lady, huh?" She picked out the chocolate dregs on her finger and licked it. "God, I'm randy suddenly. What d'you think of Jay?"

But Catherine hardly heard her. Without knowing it (or did she know it?) Margaret had suddenly put the whole jigsaw puzzle together. And it was so simple: NCT mattered to Burgo, deep, deep down, in a way that MaCaBu would never matter to her. *Could* never matter to her. It wasn't simply that NCT meant so much to him; NCT *was* him. The whole thing had progressed far beyond the original point of honour—the restoring of the family and its vanished fortunes. It had become a kind of life dedication. She saw now that she could never tell him the full story of her part in MaCaBu. It would hurt too much.

On their way home she explained all this to Margaret, who listened skeptically. "Are you going to be the doormat forever?" she asked.

"Meg!" Catherine was scandalized.

"Well, it's true, honey. Listen—you've done a great thing this year. We both did, but I'm talking about you. You went ahead and did, in your way, exactly what he did in his. And you looked after a house and two kids as well. Three, if you count me. And you made as much money as he did. So why this urge to play gopher and get your head down?"

"Because it's his *life.*"

"And it's not yours?"

"Not to that degree. Look, I saw him with a broken leg, an abscess on his tooth. And that terrible constipation. I saw him—with all that—getting ready to go to a business dinner. And blood all over his shirt. I still don't know how he did it. But don't you see . . . doesn't that prove what it means to him? And I just know he'd be terribly hurt if it ever came out, what I've done this year. So we'll say you've done it all, okay? I just washed the dishes and the floor."

"But that's falsehood, Cath. You can't make a new start on a falsehood."

"I have to. Now promise me. I know you. We'll do what I say—falsehood or no."

"He doesn't deserve it. He doesn't deserve you."

"Promise, now!"

"He ought to know. He ought to learn to value you."

"Promise, Meg!"

"Well . . . *fuck* him!"

"Meg! It's my marriage. My family. That's what I did it for. I know it doesn't mean much to you, but to me it's everything. Promise now!"

"Okay."

"Say it."

"Promise."

But, as Catherine ought to have known, Margaret was just not the person to be able to hold herself to such a promise, even if she had meant it at the time.

On Christmas Day, when they all opened their presents, there was a giant parcel for Burgo, shaped like a four-foot-long dog's bone. It was a hoax—at least that was the way it seemed as he unwrapped layer after layer of nothing but paper.

Catherine watched Margaret's face, but not until Burgo neared the end of the unwrapping did she receive any inkling that this was how Meg had chosen to break her word. Then she became certain of it.

"Meg! No!" she cried out.

"Yes!" Margaret was itching with delight.

"You promised."

"It'll be okay. You'll see."

Catherine turned to Burgo, who had stopped in surprise. "Don't," she said. "Don't open it."

"Why ever not?"

"Just *don't*. Please!"

When it was clear he was going to do as Catherine asked, Margaret seized the remains of the parcel, shook it to shreds, and retrieved the envelope that fluttered to the ground. She held it to Burgo. He looked at Catherine and then refused it.

"Please, Meg," Catherine begged.

"I'll be all right, kiddo. Trust me." She tore open the envelope and took out a handwritten note. " 'The directors of MaCaBu Creations have pleasure in presenting the enclosed cheque for five thousand eight hundred dollars to Night Call Toronto, Ltd., and cordially offer free office space and a transmitter site at their Yorkville Headquarters.' There!" She grinned triumphantly at Burgo, then at Catherine. She passed him the envelope.

He grinned at Catherine. "Don't be so serious, darling," he chided. "I can take a joke. What is it? Bank of Toyland?" His eyes fell on the Bank of

Toronto cheque as he spoke. All colour drained from him. He looked up angrily at his sister. "Cathy's quite right," he said sharply. "You could go to jail—writing cheques like this." He passed it to James for him to see. But James had caught nuances that Burgo had missed. He looked shrewdly at Margaret and Catherine, waiting.

"Oh, Meg!" Catherine sat down and buried her face in her hands, not in tears but in sheer hopelessness.

Burgo, catching his father's mood, and puzzled by Catherine's behaviour, stared back and forth between the two women.

"Just present it," Margaret challenged. "See who goes to jail."

If only he weren't in that damned wheelchair, Catherine thought. She could run outside, screaming or something, and he'd be sure to follow.

"Where did you get that much money?" he said in angry disbelief. He turned to his father. "Is this your doing?"

Catherine suddenly shouted: "Shut up! Everybody!" Maddy began to cry. "You too!" she yelled.

Maddy, still crying, ran to Fiona, who picked her up but didn't take her astonished eyes off Catherine. Everyone was looking at her.

Catherine walked through the big double doors to the adjoining dining room. "Jay," she called over her shoulder. "Be an angel and wheel Burgo in here, will you? I want to talk to him alone." She did not dare to look at Margaret; she wanted to tear her hair out.

As soon as they were alone Burgo began to speak; but she laid a finger on his lips. "Hear me first," she asked.

He was silent.

"The money's there," she said. "It's not a gift. It's intended to buy stock in NCT, if you're selling. I'll tell you how it happened. It has nothing to do with James."

The harm was already done. She could see that. No matter what the explanation, they—she and Margaret—had poached his demesne. They had cast a five-thousand-dollar shadow over his achievement. Nothing could undo it. He had held the ace of trumps but the moment he played it she had called "Snap!" and played its twin.

She made the best explanation she could of it—the impossibility of keeping Margaret occupied in the Cypress Hills, the return to drinking, the desperate trip to Toronto where they invested her last penny in MaCaBu Creations—"We even included you from the beginning, you see. And boy, how we've needed you! Do you know what Meg does over money? She gets out the kitchen scales and puts the bills in one pan and our invoices in the other and sees if they tip in our favour. If they do, we're solvent."

But how could she, Catherine, ask him to get involved when, as he said

himself, he didn't know how he'd find time to sleep? Couldn't he see what a
fix she'd been in? Margaret going to pieces in the cabin—her only hope
was to get involved in a small business somewhere, in fashion, which was
the only trade she knew—and that meant a big city. Yet they couldn't worry
him about it. They'd *had* to deceive him. And she felt so miserable about it.

She knelt down and leaned against him, to force him into comforting
her.

"So it's really just Meg's money," he said. "Why all the fuss? It's very
nice of her, of course, but we must refuse it. Don't you agree?"

Catherine laughed bitterly. "We almost called it CaMaBu, you know.
Or BuMaCa. But how right we were with MaCaBu—me playing pig in the
middle!"

"You're not suggesting we take it, Cath?"

"We're a partnership, Burgo. Meg and I. We're partners. The cheque is
only a symbol. We already have the money. You already have your office, if
you want it."

He considered that. "Yorktown, eh? Not bad."

She congratulated herself on deflecting him. Let the rest come out slowly
over the months.

Then he said, "But about the money, Cath. Okay—legally it's what you
say. But Meg's the one who's earned it. She should keep it. I mean, all you
did was wash the dishes. That's not two thousand dollars." He patted and
stroked her back.

Suddenly she saw how ridiculous she was being, kneeling beside him,
listening to his complacent, patronizing, ignorant sentiments.

She rose, shivering with fury, mostly at herself. "Christ! You smug . . .
shit!" she said. Additional dialogue by courtesy of Meg.

Burgo's eyes went like saucers. He forgot to breathe. At last he croaked,
"Cath!"

"All I did was wash the dishes? Yes, I washed the dishes. And yes I
brought up two children—you remember them? And yes I went out and
made three thousand dollars—and yes I've a damn good mind to leave you
guessing how!"

"Cath!" He gulped. "You never used language like that before!"

"You never riled me like that before."

"Riled you! After all that I—"

"You think you're the only one who's had it hard? You know what I
think? I think you had a party. I think these last two years were the best
years of your life."

"Oh!" He was getting angry, too. "You think it was fun! Slaving night and day. Some weeks I went three days without sleep. Not one hour. If you think that was—"

"I don't *think,* Burgo. I know. I've built up my own business this year, too. I started from nothing. Now it's the best in Toronto. And I looked after Margaret. And the house. And Kelvin and Maddy. So don't tell me about hard work. But I'll tell you. I could have done it all with you there, beside me. I could have shared every day of it with you. Because that's another thing I found out. It's *fun.* Isn't it! It's about the best fun there is. And that's what I'll never forgive you for, Burgo. You cut us out of *your* fun."

She hadn't meant to say all that. She hadn't even thought it to herself, not in so many words. She didn't know she was so angry until it all came blurting out.

Burgo was nodding, his lips pinched in a tight, bitter smile. "Fine thanks, I must say. After all that. It's a fine thank you."

"You don't want thank you's, Burgo. You don't want rewards, because you've been getting them every day. And you've been keeping them all to yourself. Well that's over now. You're going to have to share NCT with us and we're going to share MaCaBu with you. We're going to be a family again, *Daddy.* Right from now."

"You're going *on* with it?"

She smiled, surprised at how calm she had become. "Yes, Burgo. We're going on with it. I confess I hadn't intended to. Until today I thought of it as a temporary career, just to help us out, instead of idling away in the Cypress Hills. But now it's more than that."

"And if I told you I didn't want you to? If I said I'd prefer you to give it up?"

She almost exploded again—except that some very cool, observant part of her mind kept her in check. *He* wasn't being naive now; there was something very calculated behind that question. She had never before been angry enough to realize she had such a faculty for coolness inside her. "I'd take note of it," she said. "I daresay I won't be designing people's homes forever. It would colour my decision about when to quit."

"And if I ordered you to right now?"

"Are you? Is that what you're saying?"

"No, I'm saying *if.*"

She smiled. "I won't answer *ifs.* You just go ahead and do it, my darling. Make it an order, if you really want to know the answer."

He began to wheel himself toward the door. "Well, let's not spoil everyone else's Christmas. We've got a lot to talk about and a lot to think about. Come on and join the others with me."

She sat tight. "In a mo." When he reached the door she let him struggle with it and then she offered him the first hint of an olive branch. "Burgo? If I really had been lying around in the sun all these months, would you honestly think more highly of me?"

He sniffed and avoided her gaze. "As I said—we both have a great deal to think over." He tried then to devalue her decision. A cunning gleam came into his eye. "Of course," he said airily, "it would *look* better from my point of view if you did carry on." But he hadn't enough self-assurance to stay and see the effect of this jibe.

She was still smiling after he had gone. She'd go on working at MaCaBu until the new baby got big; but she'd tell him that in her own good time. Meanwhile, she was thinking she could afford to be quite generous, now that the truth was out between them—and now that she knew she was his equal.

PART FOUR

1939-1942

28

The British Embassy Rolls purred away, its broad tyres crunching the gravel; the loudest noise in the house was the ticking of the old grandfather clock on the halfway landing. In the garden, the children were screaming and laughing. Burgo came from his study, deep in thought.

"I got tea all ready," Catherine said.

"Oh. I'm sorry. They, er"—his mind wasn't on her and tea at all—"apologies. Tend their apologies."

"And what did they want? All I got was their names. Air Commodore Allardyce and Flight Lieutenant Something."

"Neeve. He's Allardyce's aide. And Allardyce is head of the Medical Branch of the Royal Air Force."

"Just passing through? We might as well have tea. It's a pity to waste it." He nodded.

"Just passing through?" she repeated, taking two of everything off the tray.

"I'm not supposed to say. Yet."

"Is it good or bad?" She carried the depleted tray through to their dining room.

"I don't know." He followed. "There is going to be a war, isn't there?" He spoke as if his next words were conditional on her agreement.

"How many more conferences, bits of paper, and invasions can there be? Is this one of your milk days? Or lemon?"

"Milk. I guess Canada would be involved if Britain and France were. I mean, it would be the Empire and dominions all in it together."

"Is there any doubt of that?"

"No." He put the cup down to cool. "Of course I said I'd think it over. But what's to think about?"

"Think what over?"

"I'm not supposed to tell even you—so here's a good start! Our English friends have offered me a temporary commission in the R.A.F. Never call it *raff*, by the way." His grimace showed that he had done exactly that.

She was afraid to ask if the offer also meant going to England. Instead she said, "What is temporary?"

"Duration of the war. A year or two at the very least. Of course, I'll get leaves back here and I'll wangle trips whenever I can."

"What d'you mean? England? You have to go over there?"

"I'll be based there. The job they're offering me is to organize all their emergency medical services. I'd have the rank of group captain, which is like an army colonel. I'd actually be in the Royal Canadian Air Force, but permanently attached to the R.A.F. They seem to think my experience with NCT is some kind of qualification. Plus the fact I can fly a small airplane. Or *aeroplane,* as they say."

His tone implied that they were fools to think so. "You can do it," she said. "You could do anything like that. Anything that needs organizing. And to do with medicine."

"Only if it's . . . I mean, I only ever worked in a commercial environment. The military mind . . . it's different. But I was saying—I'll be based in England but the work could take me anywhere. I mean, where's the war going to be? Europe? Africa? The Middle East? *Canada?* Who knows?"

"They understand it means all five of us going over?" she asked and hung on his answer.

He grinned and squeezed her arm on the way to picking up his cup. "Good try!" he said.

Grant came in through the patio windows and stood holding the curtain, kneading it.

"Don't do that, Grant, there's a honey. They've just been cleaned. Has Kelvin been nasty to you again?"

Grant nodded. It seemed to have nothing to do with him. They might be discussing another boy called Grant.

"And is Maddy on your side today, or his?"

"His. Who was that man in blue?"

There had been two men in blue but even Grant, she realized, had noticed that one of them was far more important than the other. "They were new friends of Daddy's."

"Kelvin sat on my face and made a smell."

"Oh, you are disgusting. Both of you. Have you fed the rabbits?"

"No."

"Well, go and do it. It's your turn."

He was about to argue but she said, "Go on!" so fiercely that he obeyed.

"They are disgusting," she repeated. "Last night they had their tooth mugs in the bath, turned upside down, catching wind from their bottoms. They're obsessed with breaking wind. They think it's so funny. Kelvin starts it."

Burgo chuckled. "Golly. I remember doing that." He was quickly serious again. "This war will be very different from the last 'show,' as Allardyce calls it. It's going to be very mobile. Also over very quickly." He emphasized the last point to her.

"I don't mean we'd all have to travel to England together," she answered. "I'll take a month or so to settle everything here. But I can manage all that. We'll follow you over."

He was shaking his head, a sad look in his eyes.

"Burgo, we are not going to be separated again. We are *never* going to be separated."

"It's out of the question, Cath. Look, I'll be home just as often as . . ."

"Separation is out of the question. That was a promise."

"We never thought of war."

"We thought of everything. Honey, if your friends in blue could *guarantee* we'd all be taken prisoner, or raped, or anything like that, I'd still say we're a family and we belong together."

"Not in England. It's a theatre of war, or will be. And a war that's going to be even more horrible than the last. Air bombers day and night. Civilians will be in it just as much as the forces. And gas. And germs. And how about if our side loses? Cath, I just can't believe you want to risk bringing our children into the middle of all that."

It was a strong argument, but he put it with a force that came partly from within himself and that had nothing to do with abstract logic. There was an excitement in him. That air commodore had touched some nerve. Burgo was now the warrior the night before the raiding party, the hunter looking over his spears, shivering to limber up his muscles. The abstract argument was necessary to *him,* to release him from civilization and its ties.

In how many homes in Europe, she wondered, was some variation of this scene being enacted day after day? How many mild-faced men in knitted cardigans sighed their abstract regrets and dreamed of the companionship of fellow hunters and their nightly shows in the *theatre* of war?

She said: "Even Canada's not safe—you yourself said so just now."

"In a world war, honey, nowhere can be absolutely safe. But what are the chances of Canada's being overrun by Hitler? Compared with England's chances?"

She shrugged. "All I know is that it's better for families to be together than to be separated. Even in bad times. We both know it. And I mean *know* it." She tapped her breast. "Anyway, what's England to us? Why should we sacrifice? Of course they're desperate now. They've done nothing about Hitler except feed him small countries—and now they're astonished how big he's grown."

"I understand, Cath. You're naturally upset. But when . . ."

"Don't tell me I'm upset. You're patting me on the head."

"You'll see what's best, when you think of this war and then imagine Kelvin and Grant and Maddy in the thick of it."

But he did not realize how many times a day a mother conjures up such possibilities. She waves her children off to school and sees the truck that could run them over. "Be careful crossing the road, now!" she calls. Her boy gets his first roller skates one Christmas, and she sees the slope down which he'll plunge helplessly. "He'd better not go out on the street until he's perfect," she says. Dad says, "Let's go to Niagara," and she can already see the tousled blond head of her little girl arcing over that shimmering ledge of green water, falling free into the white, obscuring mists (and it happens to several every year). "Keep a hold now," her mind's voice practises while she packs the picnic.

She was a veteran of every imaginary disaster—except separation. That could never again be imaginary.

Next day she went into Toronto to see Margaret, whose shop, Marguerite, was now right on Yonge Street and was one of fashion's honeypots in Ontario. MaCaBu had died with the birth of Grant.

"Look at that," Margaret said, pointing to a rakish black hat with a long feather—and an exclusive label prominently hung on its stand. "Mrs. Ganly was in here just now and she said, 'If that's exclusive, why is it so cheap?' So I told her it's because we buy in such vast quantities. And that satisfied her! It must be the way I tell them. D'you think I'd even make out in politics?"

"Business is good, then?" Catherine asked.

"I just cabled the hot-cake shop saying, 'Why don't you give up?' "

There was an edginess to her humour that Catherine had almost forgotten. Since making a success of her shop she had become—even Burgo had said it—"almost a responsible citizen." She still got tipsy from time to time, but never scandalously. "I may not know how to hold my liquor," she once said. "But I do know where." Her humour softened over those years. It lost its keen, self-slicing edge. She was less sheer fun to be with—but also a great deal less nerve-racking.

"Is that the same Mrs. Ganly who lives on Highlawn Avenue?" Catherine asked. "Just a few doors down from us?"

Margaret nodded. "Just a few *acres* down from you. She says you had a pair of interesting visitors yesterday. In a shiny motor."

Catherine looked quickly round and took her sister-in-law a few paces away from the nearest other person. "That's supposed to be a secret."

"Sure!"

"It is, honestly."

"So they disguise up in bright blue suits and one of them drips scrambled egg all down the peak of his cap, and they come out on a Sunday afternoon in a Rolls-Royce with diplomatic plates and a Union Jack where every sensible person carries a radiator thermometer or a nude. And it throws all your neighbours right off the scent. Mrs. Ganly swears it was a perfectly ordinary Freemason muscle squad collecting overdue subscriptions. I'll have to sit down and think about it for several weeks before I even begin to realize it was a couple of English air force men come to ask Florenzo Nightingale to prepare the injections for Hitler—when they get him. Secret, huh!"

Catherine laughed and scratched her head. Now she didn't know what to do. She had come in to talk about the affair, of course, but in hypothetical terms: "Burgo and I've been discussing the war and the chance that he'd be called up and having to go to England . . ." and so on. Now it would just be too transparent.

"You'd rather not talk about it?" Margaret asked. "Go ahead. Be different. Be the only person in Toronto who isn't."

"Is it as bad as that?"

"It will be by noon. Give her and your other neighbours a chance."

So Catherine told her.

"I hate to say it," Meg said with relish, "but the jerk's right for once. You can't take them to England, hon." She saw Catherine's mouth set in a stubborn line and went on, "I agree with you in one way. It is just remotely possible that Russia and Japan may simultaneously decide that Walt Disney really has gone too far this time. And they may come stomping down through the prairie and mess up his palette. I mean, if I was Russia and Japan, that's the first thing I'd do. But I have to admit it's much more likely that Hitler wants to get his bit of paper back from that sweet Englishman with the gray hair."

Catherine failed to smile.

Margaret sighed. "On the other hand, I also know what can happen to families when mom and the kids are supposed to be living out an idyll in the mountains while Dad is all alone down there on the plains, popping aspirin and washing the blood out of his shirts. I do remember."

Catherine smiled then. "That's it."

"I can't imagine Toronto without you, darling. I've had every man worth having within fifty miles and there's still too many days each week."

"Take up flying," Catherine joked. "Burgo'll lend you his plane. He hardly needs it now. He said it's one of the few things that've kept him sane." A thought struck her. "Maybe this war's come just in time for Burgo.

That's an awful thing to say, I know. But maybe it has. I think he'd mentally used up everything NCT had to offer some while back. He can't wait to start this new thing."

"Maybe men need a war every couple of generations."

"Well." She grinned. "Burgo's got one now. I hope he doesn't push for two."

29

They sold NCT and the house on Highlawn Avenue. Margaret bought the plane. The proceeds plus their savings came to just short of a hundred thousand, Canadian.

The plan—Burgo's plan—was for her to take the children back to Goldeneye, at least for the first year or so of the war. After which, he implied, all their choices would suddenly become wonderfully fluid and open again. They'd see how the war was going and they'd probably all be able to live together again. England might be safe. Or he might find he could do his particular job even better from a base in Canada. And pigs might sprout wings and fly.

But even Catherine was now in two minds about following him to England with the children. She had had a waking dream, a daymare, in the small sleepless hours one morning. Her first picture of a house in England had been characteristically North American: two centuries old, built of mellowed stone, clad with Russian vine, and set like a jewel in some green and bosky valley. But her fantasy had brought her and Burgo home to this place, after some R.A.F. celebration—one night toward the end of the war—and they discovered it reduced to rubble, the children buried and burned with it.

"A German bomber, ma'am," a British bobby said. "It must have sneaked in."

"We thought we'd seen the last of them," his colleague added.

And there, among the smoking timbers and charred stone, she had suddenly seen Grant's teddy bear.

It did not help for her to tell herself the whole thing was so wildly improbable as to be absurd. She had seen that terrible destruction; it had been real. She knew it was ridiculous, yet she had touched that teddy bear and smelled the wet smoke in it.

Now she was at war with herself. The rational part of her told her that this imaginary scene was nonsense—implying she should ignore it and go. But the same rational element also suggested that she was only imagining such nonsense in order to blot out much more reasonable objections to taking the children to England.

Her emotions were in an identical turmoil. They dwelled on the imagined horror—implying it was a visionary warning she should not ignore. But they also longed for the wholeness of her family—especially after Burgo sailed for England. She longed for him as husband, as the children's father, as lover, as friend. A hundred times a day she had occasion to turn to him—to fix a drink, or a bicycle, to share a thought, or their bed—and there was only a space and a silence. A yearning.

The train journey back to Goldeneye filled the longest five days of her life.

At Winnipeg, Grant, who had been notably subdued all the way, wrote a postcard and asked her to send it.

"Dear Mr. Hitler," it read. "People think you're going to start a war and have daddies sent away everywhere. Please say you won't and tell everybody so they can send my daddy back here again because I want him and love him very much. Yours respectfully, Grant (age 7, nearly)."

Not being sure of the address, or even the spelling, she wrote: "Herr Hitler, Berchtesgarden or Berlin, Germany," and mailed it.

Grant cheered up at once. She noticed how quickly he fell asleep that night. His worries were over. Hadn't they always taught him that the best way to get anything was to ask for it nicely?

And what about his disillusion, later?

All the big, common-sense arguments said *stay in Goldeneye.*

All the little vibrations of her family said *join Daddy.*

"I'm so glad you're through with that nonsense about going to England," Fiona said. "I have a feeling that Burgo is going to make a big mark for himself in the R.A.F. and it'll be so much easier for him if he's sure you and the children are all safely here."

Later Catherine felt that if ever there was a precise moment when she decided to go to England, it was during that welcoming speech of Fiona's. Then and afterward Fiona managed to imply that this desire to be with Burgo was nothing but lust. Nor was Fiona alone. The Calvinist tradition was strong throughout the prairie: Catherine, who shared it, was especially sensitive to its pressures.

And there was James. There would always be James.

"Helen would like you to go down to California and stay with them," he said to her. "Now that Wendell and Eva have flown the coop, and Cameron's about to, I think she misses the presence of children."

"D'you think I should go, James?"

"You and Helen always got on quite . . ."

"I don't mean to California."

"Ah."

"Don't say ah like that. It means you're going to be all bedside manner and no prescription."

"There will be work for you here."

"You sound like my father. An Dóiteán was always saying, 'Get some work into your hands, girl.' What sort of work?"

"Your sort of work. This hospital is already the centre for reconstructive surgery in the whole province. And the way the medical board is talking of investing, we look set to become the main centre for the entire west. We get cases from Montana and Alberta, even now."

"But that's marvellous for you. I didn't know that. I'm so out of touch with nursing, though."

"I was thinking more of physiotherapy. We have training facilities here. Did you never think of wanting to be a doctor?"

She laughed, it was so absurd.

"You have the mind for it," he persisted.

"And three young children, James."

"That's an interesting objection."

"In what way?"

"It suggests that when you no longer have three young children . . . ?"

"But it's never crossed my mind."

"No. I thought it hadn't."

She laughed. "What would Burgo say?"

James smiled. "Aye. That too."

"It's ridiculous even to think of it."

"You would need several exams before you could apply to a medical school. Zoology, chemistry, mathematics, physics, English. You could take them one by one or two at a time. It would be a good way to fill a war, Catherine." He raised his eyebrows. "And I would help what little I might."

Ridiculous or not, his matter-of-fact recital of these milestones made her think of it seriously for the first time. She remembered how, almost twenty years ago now, she had studied first aid and anatomy and simple physiology, and how enjoyable it had been—her room, the desk, the coal-oil lamp, the peaceful dark, and the textbook full of new facts and ideas. Opening it had been like breaking the cellophane round a box of chocolate. Every time.

But she remembered, too, James's help, and the love it had kindled, and then the desire. It had taken five years for her inhibitions to be overcome. Now such inhibitions as she had (and she was not sure even of that) would not survive five days.

Before the week was out she had booked passage from Halifax to Liverpool for herself and the three children. Burgo had given her power of attorney, so she did not need his express consent to take them off Canadian soil.

Fiona was livid and predicted every kind of disaster. She was so mad she even denied herself the pleasure of one final picnic at the rezavoy. James, Catherine, and the children went without her.

She and he sat on deck chairs in the shade of the haystore while the children romped in the water.

"Fiona certainly knows how to make one feel guilty," she said.

"The guilt is there already," he answered. "She merely fans it."

"Well she surely knows how."

"It is a kind of love." He measured her with his eye before he added, "You cannot understand how love, for her, for many people, is felt only as a kind of tension. Have you noticed how, when I draw near to Fiona, she will stiffen? Sometimes even retreat."

Catherine was uncertain about admitting that she had noticed.

"The casual observer, now," he went on, "would take that as a sign of loathing in her. But it's not. Not at all. Just the opposite. She's one of Calvin's masterpieces, dear Fiona. She fears surrender, which her flesh is forever urging her to make. That tension is the true measure of her love. The harder she fights, the harder it grips her."

Catherine looked at him in surprise, having always supposed those feelings dwindled in middle age and would be nonexistent in people's sixties.

"How did you escape this Calvinist scourge?" he asked.

She reached over and grasped his hand, raking her nails over his open palm. "I was taught by the most wonderful lover a girl could ever hope for. But that's why I have to go to Burgo. You know that, don't you."

"There's enough passion in you, Cathy, to build and destroy a hundred of the folk hereabouts. And they know it. And envy it. That's the envy you feel. I say ignore it. And ignore them."

"And go to England?"

"Was that ever really a choice?"

His sadness so moved her that she fell to her knees beside his chair and put her arms around him. That gesture did far more than the mere possession of shipping tickets to persuade her she really was going to England. Without the certainty of that coming separation she never would have dared this intimacy.

Her ear was close to his lips. She felt the shiver of his breath and sensed it in his body. She hugged him tight. Old reflexes claimed her, too.

"Buried," he said, barely above a whisper. "It is buried. Yet read the gravestone. *It doth but slumber.*"

She released him and, seeking employment, began to set up the trestle table and lay out the picnic. He rose to help.

"Is Fiona quite well?" she asked. "Sometimes she looks very tired."

"Aye, but tired of what? Of me? Of hiding her own true feelings? She hides so many levels of them. And what *are* her true feelings? They are as . . . as incandescent as Elinor Glyn. I suppose no one's heard of her now. In her inmost heart, Fiona lies on a tiger skin, 'a rose between her lips, not redder than they.' She hides it even from herself." He raised an almost clenched fist and groaned with frustration. "Och, the waste of people in the name of God and John Knox! What a power she would be. But in her outer heart she lies on a polar bear skin, an icicle between her lips, not colder than they." He laughed at his own fantasy.

"Do you mean that one day she won't be able to hide from herself any longer? And then she'll break down?"

He shrugged. "Flesh is the most enduring stuff we know." He risked taking her arm. "But that's the danger for her." At the word *danger* he laughed. "You would not avoid the war here, Catherine. You would merely change the nature of its threat to you. You would not be safe." He was serious again. "And nor would I. So I say yes—go to England."

"And you really mean it?"

"I do."

They left from Halifax, Nova Scotia, on August 23, the day Neville Chamberlain told Hitler that this time Britain was serious. It wasn't like the Ruhr, or the Saar . . . Hungary . . . Austria . . . the Sudetenland. This time, really, honestly and truly, cross-her-heart, Britain meant it: Hands off Poland!

Before they sailed she put through a call to Burgo to tell him what she had done. She had refrained from calling him earlier because, if there was a lightning way of revoking a power of attorney, he would find it. Until now she had been calm, but as she heard the clicks and buzzes of the international circuit, her stomach fell away and her heart began to beat violently. Then she began to shiver. Then to sweat. When they finally reached the Air Ministry switchboard it was all she could do to stop herself from slamming the earphone back into its cradle. Her relief was immense when the operator came back and said, "Group Captain Macrae is out. Will you speak to his secretary?" But her voice still trembled while she told the woman the name of their ship and her expected date of arrival in Liverpool.

Just to be sure, she sent a cable, too.

They stood on the afterdeck of the little cargo ship that was to carry them to Liverpool and watched the summer-green hills of Halifax, the last of Canada, slip away.

"The decks are going round," Catherine said and laughed, remembering the childish misunderstanding on that emigrant ship, twenty years ago.

But, for Kelvin, the decks *were* going round, swimming in his tears. He was saying goodbye to all he loved, to his country, to Canada. No one had ever hated England so much as he, at that moment, hated her. "Goldeneye," he whispered to the salt-eaten teak of the handrail. "Goldeneye . . . Goldeneye . . ." The very name held everything that was precious to him: days on the endless, open prairie: the sluggish, alkali rivers of high summer; the crisp, blue snows of winter; the winds you could tuck yourself into and lean on. And because Goldeneye was his youth, its name embraced all the haunts of his youth, even the red oak and maple woods of Ontario. He knew he would never see them again. He had never felt such misery.

30

Halfway across the Atlantic they were "diverted" to Southampton. Catherine thought it an odd choice of word. To her, a diversion was a movie or a book. On the last morning of the voyage she came up early on deck only to be confronted by a group of islands that looked astonishingly familiar. These were the silhouettes that had burned themselves into her memory while she stood on another deck, in high fever, all those years ago. This was not England at all; it was her native land.

Scotland! She had thought all those feelings were dead; she knew she was now as Canadian as maple syrup. But the name and those majestic humps, rearing from the ocean, caught and held in a mighty stillness by the

September sun, took her unawares and filled her with visceral grandeur. The nape of her neck tingled. "Scotland!" she murmured.

Jimmy the One, the First Officer, who was also a Scot, joined her at that moment. "Aye!" he said. "You ken it well." He had befriended the children and spoiled them shamelessly all the way over. They reminded him of his own bairns, he said. At least he'd cajoled and shamed Kelvin out of his mawkish homesickness.

"I was seeing it the once," she told him, hearing an ancient lilt creep back into her voice, overlaying the Canadian. "But I was travelling the other way." She pointed over the stern. "The other airt, I would have said then."

He nodded. "The heart is Highland," he said. "Did you not hear we'd been diverted again? It's the war, we may suppose."

"Has it started?"

"Mr. Chamberlain's to speak this morning."

When Catherine realized they had been diverted to the Clyde, she was certain they would actually dock at the same jetty in Greenock from which she sailed in 1919. But it was not to be. They steamed past it, more than a mile upriver, and made fast nearer the heart of the city. But Greenock marked another milestone in her life. The jetty where the *Hector* had lain was broadside to them as Neville Chamberlain's curiously unhistoric tones, relayed over the deck tannoy, were telling the world: "I have to announce that by twelve o'clock today, no such assurance had been received at our Embassy in Berlin, and that this country is, accordingly, now at war with Germany."

She squatted among the children and pulled them to her. "You hear that? The war has started. You understand?"

Grant began to cry. It hadn't worked. Hitler had ignored his postcard. He must have made some mistake in the writing of it. And now it was too late to try again.

The announcement of the war had one immediate effect on her plans. As soon as she realized they were making landfall on Clydebank, she had half decided to take the children up to Beinn Uidhe to meet their grandfather. She would cable Burgo and let him know, to expect them in about a week. True, An Dóiteán had never answered her annual letters, telling him all her news and enclosing photographs. He might even be dead, for all she knew—though surely, since her return address was on every letter, someone would have told her. He was probably still angry and hurt; but he couldn't resist his grandchildren, she hoped.

Also it would be a way of postponing the meeting with Burgo—a meeting she was now beginning to dread more than anything in her life. She would rather relive all her worst moments than add this new one to them.

But the announcement of the war ruled out any kind of a detour. She had to get to Burgo as soon as possible.

The air-raid sirens were sounded soon after—a doleful wail that seemed to tense the very air above the city. More than the prime minister's sombre words, more than poor little Grant's baffled howl, that one-note dirge impressed on her from every angle of the bright sky what a terrible mistake she might have made in bringing here these three trusting, dependent little things—away from those thousands of miles of security, freedom, and plenty—to this little island, which, though it might not yet know it or feel it, was already under siege.

Her guilty eyes began to search the quays along Clydebank for the figure of Burgo. She was convinced he would be here and would forbid them to land. Too late she had discovered that their ship was due to sail straight back to Canada as soon as it had fresh cargo. Perhaps the war would alter those plans. That was her only hope.

They made fast and, sure enough, a figure in R.A.F. blue, wearing an officer's hat, was the first to bound up the gangway. Her terror turned him into Burgo until he was close enough to say, "Mrs. Macrae, I take it?" and offer his hand. "I'm Flying Officer Windle. Movements officer."

He felt her trembling and misread the emotion in her face. "Sorry," he grinned. "You were expecting the group captain?"

She nodded, not yet trusting her voice.

"Well, if wishes were deeds, I'm positive he'd be here. He's called my office five times a day to make certain there'll be no hitch in the arrangements."

"Arrangements?" It didn't sound like her own voice.

"Yes. Your movement to London."

"Oh."

"Why? Where did you think you were to go?"

"I . . . I don't know. Nowhere. I thought we might be sent straight back to Canada."

"Oh, well, that's not what I've been told. The group captain told me you have a quarter at Queens Langley."

"A quarter?"

"An R.A.F. married quarter. A house. Your own house. It's called Gideons." He gave her a slip of paper with the address: *Gideons, near Queens Langley, Herts, Telephone: Queens Langley* 2. "I've made your travel arrangements to get there." He referred to his clipboard and became all businesslike. "I can't stay, I'm afraid. There's a lot on, as you can well imagine. I've managed to bring a lorry so we'll get your heavy trunks and things to the station. Here are your warrants. You're booked on overnight sleepers to Euston in London. Times are all written down here. I made them second class because they have two bunks per cabin. First has only one—not really for children, is it. You only have to go down the road from Euston to Kings Cross and take a local train out to Queen's Langley. You'll be met there and driven to your quarter. What've I left out? Oh yes—we have an arrangement with the Great Northern Hotel, by the station. They know you're not staying the night, but you can use a room there and have high tea. Just sign the chitty, no need to pay. You have English money? Good. The banks are all shut. Sunday. Everything's shut. I wouldn't be surprised if they chain the swings in the park. Remember, if you pick up any Scottish banknotes a lot of places in England won't take them. Banks will, though. I think that's everything. Any trouble, just ring my office. Number's there on the docket. And my name. Flying Officer Windle. Someone'll sort it out. I can't give you a lift into the city. Sorry and all that. I'm going on to another dock. But you'll get a taxi easily enough. Ask for a receipt. Get receipts for everything. You never know. Welcome to England, Mrs. Macrae. Toodle-pip!" Moments later he was back with his electric flash of a smile. "I mean Scotland, of course. Do forgive me." And he was gone.

Overwhelmed with relief she marshalled the children down into the lorry and went straight to the hotel, where she tried at once to get a call through to Burgo. But the operator told her that the trunk lines to London were fully taken with government and military traffic; she hadn't a hope of a line. She explained their situation and he said he'd see what he could do toward evening. They took lunch in the hotel and then went out for a walk.

She had forgotten how small everything was. The trains were like models. The cars on the streets—what few of them there were—seemed like toys; and they still had bug-eye headlamps on stalks. And the way the traffic came from the wrong direction kept her constantly on edge, fearing a momentary forgetfulness on the part of the children. Their wanderings brought them to a park. They went in to see if the swings were chained, but couldn't find any swings at all. They bought tea and rock cakes, most of which they fed to the ducks. Catherine heard a passing couple talking about them. "Americans," the man said. "Probably waiting for a boat," his wife replied. "I 'speck they'll all be gaein' hame, noo." Wisdom was universal.

The children wanted her to buy some comics. A series of brief encounters with strollers sent her looking for a newspaper *kiosk,* where she was to ask for comic *books.* She began to realize how much she had either forgotten or, in her Highland youth, had simply not needed to know. The only open kiosk proved to be at the station, where she bought an armful of *Film Fun, Tiger Tim, Beano, Dandy, Girls' Own, Hotspur, Rover,* and *Wizard.* The last four were more like the penny dreadfuls she remembered—acres of text with a few illustrations. The others were all drawings with characters speaking in balloons.

"What are they all saying, Mummy?" Madeleine put *Oor Wullie* in front of her—a story in which Our Willie and his friends filled their balloons with Glaswegian as broad as his name. She could make nothing of it. "I thought you were supposed to be Scotch," her daughter said crossly. But she stayed with *Oor Wullie* for the opportunities it provided for loud complaint.

"Are we going to where you came from?" Kelvin asked. "Are we going to see our Scotch granddad?"

"Not this time, darling."

Maddy's complaints grew quieter and less frequent as she and Grant became absorbed in the extraordinary world of *Desperate Dan, Lord Snooty and His Pals, Big Ego, Pansy Potter, Corky the Cat,* and *Meddlesome Matty.* Kelvin, meanwhile, was lost in *Rover* and *Hotspur,* a world of public-school boys, private detectives (who were overgrown public-school boys), and soccer heroes (who were overdeveloped public-school boys).

Catherine, glad of the children's absorption, read with them in increasing amazement. The world revealed in these "comics" was insane. And none of the (presumably) adult people who compiled them seemed to feel any need to explain away or remedy the insanities. The children read on, unperturbed by anything but occasional unfamiliarities of language or slang. They simply accepted a street gang led by a twelve-year-old lord in a top hat and Eton uniform; a fat, cowardly, greedy, lazy, scheming, shortsighted school boy who was also a hero; and all the rest of it. It was just a new kind of normality.

She had then an intimation that she, who had lived the first half of her life in this country, was actually going to find it harder to adapt here than Kelvin, Maddy, and Grant, who were scarcely eight hours landed.

She tried one last time for a line to Burgo, but without success.

They all slept soundly on the train, whose swaying motion seemed normal—unlike the land, which, after those days at sea, had developed an uncanny habit of heaving and tilting. Once or twice the train stopped out in the country, and imagination conjured every distant roar into the drone of bombers; but nothing came of it. At those moments she was acutely conscious of their lack of gas masks. Everyone in Glasgow had been carrying them, in tough little cardboard boxes slung over the shoulder by a cord.

The porter at Euston told them it was the oldest station in London and one of the oldest in the world—more than a hundred years. With its great

Greek arches and classical vaults it seemed more like two thousand years. He then spoiled it by saying he hoped it would get bombed to bits; it needed rebuilding from scratch.

At Kings Cross they had no time to put a call through to Burgo. Their train was about to leave. They sat in the restaurant car and wolfed down a vast English breakfast while first the north London suburbs then the manicured rural fringe of the city slipped by.

Later, when she knew the line well, she was astonished at the triviality of the things that lodged in her mind during that first trip. From that day on she could never picture an English railway station in her mind without seeing at least half a dozen enamelled advertising boards, all painted in a caramel colour, all bearing in black the legend *Virol* and, beneath it, in much smaller type, *Convalescents need it,* or *Growing boys need it,* or *Nursing mothers need it,* or *Strong men need it* . . . the variations were endless. Virol, she later discovered, was a kind of Bynomalt.

One place alone stuck in her mind: Welwyn Garden City, Home of Shredded Wheat. It seemed more North American than English, not merely because no other town so proudly announced a commercial connection (and with a breakfast cereal at that), but also because of the newness of the whole place, and the feeling that the houses had all been designed in the same office. She wondered what they were like inside—full of suits of armour, maids in black with white caps and aprons, and golf clubs, like every other English home?

She remembered her first train journey through America and Canada. They, too, had been foreign countries; but she had looked at them with the eyes of a child, or of a naive stranger, to whom everything is remarkable— and therefore to whom nothing is especially remarkable. Now she looked around her with the narrowed vision of an adult and failed to see the wholeness. She envied her children their unclouded eyes.

"It's quite like Goldeneye," Kelvin said, looking out at the rolling, wooded hills that stretched away from the line once they were out into the open country north of London.

Catherine was surprised at the comparison. She saw no similarity. But then her mind's eye stripped away the hedges that crisscrossed the slopes and valleys, and it turned the beeches and oaks to aspen and blackbark birch— and she knew exactly what part of Goldeneye Kelvin meant—the Little Hills section on the far side of town from James's badlands. That vision was precisely what she envied in them—to see things without being told.

31

No one from the air station was there to meet them at Queens Langley. She considered phoning the adjutant, but the stationmaster found them a taxi and she realized that would be quicker. Gideons was about four miles from the station. It stood halfway up the side of a hill, which was crowned with a dense and ancient beechwood. The house was approached by a winding, unsurfaced lane that promised endless wipe-your-feet battles with the children and their friends. Below the lane was a field that bottomed out in a wide, shallow stream. Cows stood in it, floating lazily on their own reflections, moving only when goaded too far by the flies. When the taxi stopped, the silence was immediately filled by skylarks, pouring down their melody over the stubble and the still-leafy woods. Nothing more remote from the war or thoughts of war could be imagined. The house was covered with roses and Russian vine, and it was Georgian, exactly as in her waking nightmare. She thought, *I must find a phone, I must call Burgo.* Reassuringly a pair of telephone wires ran along the valley and up to the house. But no power.

"No hydro," she said.

The taxidriver, whom she now knew as Mr. Perry, looked blank.

"Electricity."

"You have your own generator," he told her.

He seemed to know the house well—certainly well enough to go straight round to the kitchen courtyard, to the outdoor lavatory, where, on a nail on the back of the door, he found the key to the house.

Catherine looked around her. The yard contained a car chassis, a broken laundry mangle, several outhouses bordering on dilapidation, some fretful chickens, two bored cats, and a weaned mongrel puppy who sneezed and wriggled an awkward path toward them, his hind legs constantly overtaking his front ones. Catherine guessed he was part-spaniel and part-dachshund (or sausage dog as the children soon learned to call it).

"Timoshenko!" Madeleine cried out in delight, as if she had known the puppy from birth. She had heard the name on the radio and had vowed to give it to her first pet, whatever its sex or species. And Timoshenko he was, from then on.

Inside, the house did not live up to the promise of its outside. It was drab. She had barely taken in that general impression when the phone rang. For a while she couldn't find it. The bell was ringing in the hall but she had to follow the cable to a cupboard on the halfway landing before she located the instrument itself—an upright model with the earpiece hanging from a lever to one side.

It was Burgo. "How are you?"

"Fine," she said and held her breath.

"And the brats?"

"Fine."

There was a silence.

"You're mad at me," she said.

"Not really, Cath."

"You are."

"A bit." He lowered his voice. She guessed he was not alone in his office. "But also proud. A bit of both. Or a bit of mad and a lot of proud."

"You're only putting a brave face on it."

"You've got about ten hours left to believe that. Then I'll convince you otherwise."

"D'you mean it?"

Grant, standing at her side, looking up into her face, saw her smile for the first time. He smiled, too. She saw him and asked, "You want to speak to Daddy?"

She held the phone down to him but he grew suddenly shy and ran away. Laughing now she put the thing back to her ear.

"Sorry I wasn't at Euston, darling," he was saying. "I had hopes, but there's just too much doing here. I'll hear all about the voyage tonight. Did transport meet you at Queens Langley?"

"No. We took a taxi."

"Well there's another cockup. Was the taxidriver called Perry?"

"Yes. He's still here."

"Good. Hold on to him. You'll need him. Now listen. Time's short. If you look in front of you, on the first shelf, you'll see two telephone directories. Between them I've left some money—ten pounds, which is plenty—and a list of what to do first."

While he was speaking her eyes wandered over what could be seen of the house from where she stood. It was a dismal survey. "Darling, have you been living here?" she asked.

"Heavens no! It'll need a month of your touch. It's awful, isn't it. But—as everyone's saying now—there's a war on! I'll see you tonight."

"Say you're not mad again."

But he had gone.

The list he had mentioned was formidable. She was to go back to Queens Langley, to the bank, the police, and the town hall, where someone from R.A.F. Welfare would give her their ration books, identity cards, and gas masks. "She (it will probably be a W.A.A.F.) will also gen you up on our fuel allocations, the blackout and A.R.P. in general, and anything else that occurs to her or you—including, no doubt, her opinion of my brother officers on the station. Lean on her all you want, honey. Use her. That's what she's for. Toodle-pip!" In a much more hasty scrawl below he had added, "How could I forget! There's an 18-yr-old girl, Oenone (no kidding!) Braithewaite, coming at 1:30 each weekday. Her pay is 9s.6d. a week. She wants to come the full day for 19s. but I said I'd leave the decision to you. She *says* she can do anything in the house or garden, scrub, cook, sew, or hoe. Sounds too good. Also remember she is the village's eyes and ears on us. She's been feeding the pets. Aren't they cute!"

Nothing about schools. It wasn't like Burgo to forget that. Perhaps Queens Langley had only one school. Or maybe the R.A.F. had its own educational arrangements.

It was now midmorning. She decided to stay out here until after lunch, when the Braithewaite girl would turn up and she would leave the children with her. Mr. Perry helped her haul the trunks upstairs. Then she made him a cup of tea and asked him to come back at two.

Timoshenko did a puddle on the linoleum. She pressed his nose in it and put him out. He seemed to think it was a game.

The two boys did not even want to help. She could sense that. But, though she felt they ought to, she hadn't the will to battle with them and with this dreadful house. So, as a token, she made them go around and open all the windows, on the promise that they could go out and explore as soon as they had finished. It was not so easy a task as she had imagined; the windows were all of the sash type and most of them were either stuck to begin with or managed to get stuck somewhere during their vertical slide. Kelvin was handyman enough to find a mallet and a screwdriver and, with them, to persuade every window but one (which was painted fast) to open.

The house was much quieter after they had gone. She sent Madeleine out to find where the hens were laying and to bring in any eggs she discovered. Timoshenko did another puddle, this time in the hall. He still thought his training was a game.

By lunchtime she had washed, cleaned, and dusted two bedrooms. The difference was barely noticeable. And that helped her to pin down exactly what was so dispiriting about the house. Its drabness—its sheer awfulness—lay not in dirt or flaking paint . . . not in anything that could be chased away with a mop, pail, or brush; it lay in the very fabric of the house—specifically, in its furnishings.

Whoever had rented this house to the R.A.F. had obviously removed all their own furniture and replaced it with the cheapest secondhand rubbish that would meet the service's minimum standards. It was all cracked veneers and wobbly legs. Nothing matched. Springs sagged, joints groaned, backs leaned, arms rocked, and upholstery bristled with a fuzz of horsehair. It was an anonymous collection of orphaned furniture; those pieces had not grown up together, and no one had ever cared for them. Was it too late now? She looked at the wardrobe, jazzy passé, at the bed, a sagging hulk of veneered lath, at the dressing table, built for the comedy stage—and she knew no amount of love and polish could rescue them. And here, amid these waifs of wood and chrome and glass, she had condemned herself to live for . . . what? "The duration."

Madeleine came in with a dozen eggs. One smelled bad even through its shell. They put them all in water. Three floated and two made brief, tiptoe lurches toward the surface. They threw those away and hardboiled the rest. She was peeling them under the tap, eyes down, when the window darkened. "I'll get some lettuce," a woman's voice said, just as Catherine looked up.

She had the briefest glimpse of a broad face and gentle eyes before the woman turned and walked away toward a walled garden. She must be Oenone. From the back she had that wide, heroic build popular with certain "realist" painters and monumental sculptors. Her dark hair, confined in a broad green sweatband, was bobbed almost to masculine length—a style Catherine thought had vanished ten years ago, along with two-foot cigarette holders.

She returned a few minutes later bearing an earthy armful of green and red—lettuces, a cucumber, radishes, tomatoes, and what she called spring onions, though Catherine knew them as scallions.

"Second crop," she said. "Better than the first this year. I'm Nono Braithewaite, by the way. You'd be the group captain's wife, Mrs. Macrae."

She offered a dry-earthy hand, which Catherine shook.

Her voice was deep and musical. And Catherine had not been mistaken in that brief glimpse of her eyes; they were a gentle, deep brown, as watchful and unchallenging as a gazelle's. Altogether it was a fascinating face. Catherine knew of several Toronto painters who would already be running for their sketchbooks and charcoal, eager to capture this rare and spectacular blend of bulky strength and exquisite delicacy. Her lips were so finely chiselled as to seem unreal.

"You found what was in the larder, did you?" she asked. And, not waiting for an answer, went to what Catherine had taken to be a broom closet and returned with some cold game pie, a loaf of homemade bread, a pot of butter, and some cheddar cheese.

Catherine looked at this bounty in astonishment. She'd been told all about rationing. Nono saw her reaction and laughed. "Pity those who live in towns, eh!" she said.

"Is this your butter, Nono?" Catherine asked.

"No. It's yours." She looked at it critically. "I made it, mind you."

"But from what?"

Nono frowned. "From milk, of course. From your cow."

"We have a cow?"

Nono went to the window; Catherine followed. "That cow. Jessica."

A small, placid Jersey stood in the shade of the farthest hedgerow, which bordered the steeply sloping hillside. "Is that our field, too?"

Nono nodded reassuringly. "Four acres! Four acres and a cow—that was the cry in this country years ago." She turned and went back to slicing the bread. "Yes, that's your four acres, Mrs. And I think you'll keep them, unlike some."

"What d'you mean, Nono? Will some people not keep their land?"

"Well, there's talk of these War Ags—that's War Agricultural Something-or-other, don't ask me—these War Ags will take over bits of parks and tennis courts and such for growing things—veggies and fodder and the like. But I reckon that hill's too steep for anything but what it is—pasture. So I'd say you're safe."

"Who milks her?"

Nono laughed. "Well, she don't milk herself, Mrs.!"

They called the boys, but there was no reply.

"Probably up in Gideon's Wood—that's all along the hilltop. There's a gang of men up there turning the old water tower into a fire-watching point. They'll be all right."

It was such a glorious, Indian-summer day that they took the lunch out to a table in the orchard and sat in the dappled shade of the fruit trees, loud with skylarks, drowsy with the murmur of bees from half a dozen hives that stood against a nearby wall.

"We have bees, too?" Catherine asked.

"I'll introduce you after we've eaten," Nono promised.

They ate awhile in silence, until Catherine became uncomfortably aware that Nono was staring at her intently. She turned to face that deep, searching gaze. "I'll bet you know a lot," Nono said.

"Er . . . in what way?"

The girl stood and walked with statuesque grace, out of the orchard and up the grassy path to the house. Moments later she returned with an ancient school satchel, which she put on the bench beside her as she sat again. From its depths she fished a torn, leatherbound book: *The Nature of the Universe—Lucretius* was blocked out in faded gold on the spine.

"I'll bet you can understand a book like that," Nono said.

She drew forth another. *A New Model Universe—Ouspensky.*

"Or that," she said.

Another: *The Mysterious Universe—James Jeans.*

"Are you interested in astronomy?" Catherine asked.

"They're so different." Nono ignored the question. "I don't see how three books on the same thing can be so different. But they are."

Catherine leafed through the Ouspensky book, dipping here and there. It might as well have been in ancient Greek for all she grasped.

"See now!" Nono said admiringly. "You can read it just like that! Sometimes I spend half an hour on one sentence and I still don't get it." She sighed at the unfairness of things.

"It's not my sort of book at all, Nono." Catherine felt a fraud. "Why d'you read them if it's so difficult?"

"Well, we've got to understand these things. I'd like to understand everything. I buy every book in Langley market, off of Mr. Slocombe, that says *Universe* in the title. He keeps them for me. Because that's everything— the universe. Everything." After a few mouthfuls she added, "Do you know, Mrs., some stars are so far away that we can see them before we were born!"

"I don't understand that."

"Exactly! No more do I." Nono's voice was full of relief. "But isn't it marvellous? I get goose-pimples all over thinking of things like that." She pushed a knot out of the wooden tabletop and hammered it back with her great fist—a blow so gentle that nothing rattled or stirred. "I understood it more when I read it," she added.

When they were carrying back the remains of the meal, Nono said, "D'you think there's a God, Mrs.?"

Catherine closed the gate with a swing of her hips before she said, "Yes, of course there is." She wondered why she had even hesitated.

"There's a heck of a lot don't think so," Nono told her. But she spoke as of a strange and faraway tribe.

The taxi came before Catherine could be introduced to the bees. She returned to Gideons, as Mr. Perry informed her the house was named, after five o'clock, exhausted with form filling, signings in triplicate, and explanations of rationing, local schools, the blackout, fuel regulations, the A.R.P. (or air raid precautions), the R.A.F., daylight saving, and military security. The house, for all its drabness, seemed so welcome a haven that she almost forgave its owners their taste in furniture.

Nono had a scrumptious casserole of rabbit going on the stove. Maddy had made a hutch for Timoshenko. And Kelvin, helped somewhat by Grant, had cleared the outbuildings to produce a pile of "salvage" and a bonfire.

"Don't light that until tomorrow," Catherine warned, still full of her blackout and A.R.P. lecture.

When they had eaten and washed up, and sent Grant up to have his regulation four-inch bath, Nono reminded Catherine she hadn't yet met the bees.

"Can't it wait? At least until tomorrow?"

Nono was shocked. "They'll never work for you, Mrs.," she warned.

So Catherine had to go out to the orchard again, where, feeling extremely foolish, she greeted each hive and introduced herself.

Nono took Catherine for an ignorant townee until the moment came when the girl said, "Well, I'll just milk Jessica, Mrs., then I'll be off home."

"Good heavens," Catherine replied. "What must you think of me! It's way past your going-home time, my dear. You slip along now. I'll milk her."

A disbelieving Nono hung around until Catherine, wearing an old teacloth bandanna, buried her head in Jessica's flank, tucked the pail at a slant under the large, low udders and made the metal ring with the swift jets of milk. As the milk rose and the note deepened, Nono said, "Well!"

"There now! Didn't think I could, did you!" Muscles she had not used for almost twenty years—or not in just this way—rippled back into action, forgetting nothing. She was exultant.

"Well I never!"

Catherine told her how during the first half of her life she had milked their little Galloway cows twice every day—and bled them every week in winter.

"Bled them!" Nono had never heard of that.

So Catherine paused in her milking to show Nono the vein in Jessica's neck—the vein that, in her father's cows, she used to open each week and draw off a cupful of blood to mix with the oatmeal for the haggis.

"I'm surprised the cows could stand it," Nono said.

"Oh, they couldn't. By the end of winter they were so weak they couldn't rise. We used to draw them out to the fields, lying on . . . you'd call them sleds, I suppose. Wooden sleds made from old fishboxes and driftwood spars. It was a job for seven or eight neighbours going round all their crofts pulling the exhausted cows out to pasture."

"And then they'd stand up?"

"No. They'd graze what they could, lying down. Then we'd drag them on a few yards. It was a week or ten days before they could stand properly. But come the end of summer they'd frolic like lambs."

Nono, who thought she had seen poverty here in Hertfordshire during the early thirties, was impressed.

They turned Jessica back into her pasture and carried a pail and a half of rich, creamy milk down to the house.

"It must be four gallons," Catherine said. "Our milk was never so rich, either."

"Three gallons," Nono said. "That'll give you more than a pound of butter."

They brought the milk into what had once been the lamp room and boot room of Gideons. Nono turned on the tap to the washboard cooler and tipped the milk into the top reservoir. It ran down over the corrugations, through a cheesecloth filter and into a small churn. A wooden-barrelled butter churn stood over against the window. "We'll add tomorrow morning's milk to this," Nono said, "and then churn it. Don't take long this weather." She lifted out the filter and held it to the fading daylight. "That's got out the horns and tails, anyway," she said and washed it under the tap.

This return to the simple things of life—the vegetable garden, the bees, the cowshed and dairy, the food that was all grown, trapped, or shot within view of the kitchen window—filled Catherine with an immense satisfaction. They were a million miles from Highlawn Avenue and worries over the precise mixture of grays they needed for the living room. Not that she would now accept the tawdriness of the present interior; but the place had its compensations.

"If your boys can stick some tiles back up over that middle shed, we could shift all this lot over there," Nono said.

"What'd we do with this room?"

"Make a nice place for a living-in maid," Nono said artlessly.

Catherine ran for cover. "We'll have to talk to my husband about that, Nono."

"Shall I come at eight tomorrow morning, Mrs?"

"Yes. We'll do the shopping. You can show me round—see that people don't try to cheat us."

Nono was gone before Catherine realized she had no idea where the lighting set was or how it worked. Judging by the feebleness of the lamps, the batteries must be pretty low. With the help of a flashlamp she followed the cables out through the back door, round the wall of the yard, and into the garage.

From its very appearance she knew it was going to be a brute. It wasn't made for the job. In fact, as she later discovered, it had been cobbled together from a large lawn-mower engine driving two magnetos taken from wrecked lorries. There ought to be an exhaust-valve lift somewhere but in the semidark she couldn't find it. She almost tore her arms out at the roots trying to start the thing. In the end she gave up. Only as she returned to the house did she realize they had no blackout curtain anyway.

There was the noise of a car coming up the lane.

Burgo!

All her terror returned. His good nature this morning, his letter—even his acquisition of this potentially splendid quarter—it was all a ruse to lull her until he could face her and vent his fury.

She trembled as she scrubbed the grease off her hands. It suddenly seemed sinister that the car showed no lights—a camouflage-dull shape, scrunching the gravel of the drive and rolling to a halt on the carriage sweep. A gibbous moon was just rising above Gideon's Wood, shedding enough light to reveal that the man who stepped from the car was, indeed, Burgo.

She stepped back into the deeper shadow of the porch and cracked her fingers. The cold light carved his face into cruel highlights and anthracite darks. Imagination gave his unseeable eyes a vengeful glaze. Why, if she feared him so, had she come halfway around the world to meet him?

She saw two swift images of fantasy. In one he was about to kill her; in the second they were naked, locked together, he in her, and she was drawing from him all his anger, subduing him. Fear was a sudden aphrodisiac.

"Daddy!" shrieked three ecstatic voices as Madeleine, closely followed by Kelvin and Grant, shot past her and hurled themselves at the familiar figure in its still-unfamiliar uniform. He staggered under the weight of them, striding like a beleaguered colossus toward her.

Her fear passed as quickly as it came but it left behind a certain tension. "Did you eat?" she asked.

They kissed briefly, arching inward over the youngsters. He had shaved in the last hour; she knew the soap.

"I ate in London. I could use a pink gin."

"I didn't get any liquor, I—"

The children's enthusiasm swept him indoors. "No liquor!" he complained over his shoulder. "What did you *do* all day?"

It was a joke but in her state she would have taken any remark, even a comment on the weather, as a kind of reprimand. "I'm sorry," she called after him.

Her words were lost amid the children's babble. He swept them upstairs and settled Grant and Maddy with a story. Then he had to admire (and make technical comments on) Kelvin's drawings of Spitfires and Hurricanes, Wellingtons and Wellesleys, before he could grope his way back down the creaking stairs to Catherine.

"You're sorry?" he said, showing he had heard. "No. I'm sorry."

She leaned against him and cried, as quietly as she could. For a long time they stood in that embrace. She could feel his heart beating. She could feel his erection. But there was no way of knowing his real thoughts. She began to wonder if she had ever known his real thoughts about her or any of the important things. Sometimes the way he looked at her was like an audit.

When she was calm he said, "Let's go for a walk."

"Not upstairs?"

"That bed creaks like a Red River wagon."

"Oh? Experience?"

"Foresight."

The word jogged her memory. "I'll just get my coat," she said and ran upstairs to slip in her diaphragm and cream. She left her panties and stockings on the carpet and came back with two blankets as well as her coat. The action, and her nakedness under her light skirt, had such an effect that she wanted to cast caution aside and make love right there in the kitchen.

But he already had one foot in the yard and was holding the door open for her. The moonlight was bright enough to hurt.

Damn him, she thought. *He knows how I feel.* She handed him the blankets as she passed.

"We're getting old," he said.

She did not answer.

"Or wise." He took her arm to slow her down. "We call that a bomber's moon now. Poetry in camouflage."

"It's just midafternoon in Goldeneye," she said.

He chuckled. "They don't know what they're misisng."

"I couldn't have stayed there, honey."

"I know."

"Are you really not mad? I know how it looks to everyone else, but they didn't live through nineteen-thirty—or not my nineteen-thirty."

"Sure. I know." There was a small haystack inside the gate to the four-acre field. "Here?" he suggested.

The moon made it too public. "One of the children might follow us out," she said.

"Terrible for them to discover we love each other."

"Let's go up to the woods."

She climbed ahead of him, exaggerating the sway of her hips.

He said, "You may have to put up with a bit of flak at the station—mainly, I would think, from other officers' wives."

"What's flak?"

"I mean pointed remarks. Maybe not. We'll go down for cocktails tomorrow evening. Get out your prettiest frock and air it. No jewelry. *Whooo!*" He panted. "Either we get a new bed or I'm going to wangle a posting to Norfolk."

"What's Norfolk?"

"Flat."

They were both out of breath as they reached the fringe of the wood. For some reason she now wanted to prolong this moment before they lay down together. She turned and faced the valley. The house was like a darkened ruin. This was brick country—red bricks, purple-brown tiles; the farms and cottages, even in this bright moon, were no more than dark-russet smudges in the blue-black fields, set among copses of deep viridian. The river was a spill of silver, fixed in its meanders.

Behind her Burgo spread the blankets in a small clearing among the bracken, not five yards into the wood. There was silence. She heard Jessica belch up a cud and start chewing. Burgo was walking toward her. When he was right behind she began to turn to him but his hands on her hips held her. She leaned into him and closed her eyes. His arms went around her and began exploring . . . caressing. She reached her arms back around him; he was naked.

He eased her blouse out of her skirt and undid the clip of her bra. Then with cruel slowness—showing just how well he knew her—he began to undo her blouse, raking the backs of his nails over the skin each unbuttoning laid bare. His lips found her ear. His tongue curled around her lobe, then wriggled, ten degrees hotter than her skin, down to her neck.

She longed to turn and clasp him, bury herself in his arms; but he felt the beginning of every such move and gripped her until she relaxed again. "Burgo?" she pleaded.

He cupped a hand under her chin and ended her begging with a kiss. Her blouse slipped off her shoulders. His hands eased her bra forward and went down around her breasts. Now she must turn. It was too tender to bear. But his embrace was still a prison.

She unbuttoned her skirt. It slid down her to the ground. She began to turn to him but his gentle hands were suddenly fierce, holding her where she was.

"Burgo?" She tried to turn to him again.

He said nothing, but his hands took a new and even stronger grip on the ridge of her pelvis. His fingers clenched tight the soft flesh at the edges of her stomach, clamping it to the bone. He was turning it into a battle of wills.

"Honey," she complained.

He pulled her against him and folded his arms around her. She was pinioned in the grip of a machine as he thrust himself into her. She stopped fighting. Her lips went up to his. Her hands went back onto his loins and pulled him, pulled him, pulled him. He eased his grip. His hands strayed over her, as gentle as they had been fierce. There was no landscape but his face, no sky above, no ground beneath, no warmth but theirs, no life but his in hers. And suddenly their longings were squandered.

She shivered. "Cold?" he asked.

Not wanting to talk yet, not trusting her voice, she turned him, putting him side-by-side with her, and walked him to the blankets. The moon was now so brilliant she was glad of their concealment. She cuddled against him. "Oh, I missed *you*," she whispered.

He kissed her. "I love you." Between kisses he added: "And I'm glad . . . you insisted. . . . They're still furious. . . . How could one explain this . . . to them?"

She did not like the suggestion that such a love as theirs needed justifying to the Air Ministry. At this moment it was the war that ought to be justifying itself to their love. She said no more but went on kissing and caressing him until they were excited enough to make love once again—this time more conscious of their abilities, less victimized by their yearning.

The chill, reaching through the blankets to their no-longer-vigorous bodies, stirred them back to the world about half an hour later. She tried a third, token arousal of him, but to no avail.

"I can't understand it," he said, puzzled. "I was fine at the rehearsal this afternoon."

She punched him playfully. "You and Meg!"

When they were dressed again she huddled the blankets around her and they set off down the hill. A vixen yapped a farewell from the wood. Jessica watched them incuriously. "Tell me about the work," Catherine said.

"That's a question we're all learning not to ask, honey. But I can tell you I shall be off to France with the B.E.F. next week. For your ears alone."

"To fight?"

"You could say that. I have a feeling our first set battle is going to be against the British army, or the high command thereof. They and the French think it'll be more or less like the last shindig—except the trenches will be permanent palaces like the Maginot line and the Siegfried line. We think it's going to be a bit more mobile than that. We're working on plans for flying surgeries and flying ambulances. But keep it under your hat. Don't even tell anyone I'm in France."

Once again he was putting their love on the defensive—with the war in the judgement seat. Yet already this relegation to some outer court of everything personal and human—and the corresponding central elevation of the war and its demands—seemed less unreasonable than it had earlier.

"D'you like this house?" he asked.

"Not the interior."

"But the house?"

"Why d'you ask?"

"Well, it's not actually an R.A.F. hiring. I rented it directly from the woman who owns it—the Honourable Mrs. Law. She's the daughter of Viscount Roche, who lives over near Whipsnade."

She laughed. He spoke as if he'd been here years and knew them all. He went on. "The point is, she had a lot of money tied up in Germany. She's on her uppers at the moment, I think. She hasn't a stiver, as they say. We might be able to pick the place up for a song—a few thousand dollars— no more than five."

"Oh, I don't know, Burgo."

"That's with four acres of pasture, five acres of woodland, a half acre of garden, fishing rights on a quarter mile of the river, the house, the out-buildings. . . ."

He obviously wanted it. "How long are you going to be attached here at Queens Langley?" she asked.

"For the duration, as far as I know—but that may not mean much. I could be a week in France. Or a month. Or a year. Or I could go to the Mediterranean—or to Scotland. What I mean is I won't be fixed. But I'll often be in London—that's pretty gen. And this house is probably safe from anything except a really incompetent bomber, or one who has to dump his load and vamoose."

"Why'd you say 'this *house*' like that?"

"Well, it's a couple of miles from Queens Langley and a couple of miles from the airfield, and—well, there's another hush-hush target *that* way we're not supposed to know about. I mean the area isn't the safest in England but this house is about the safest you could get."

She pondered this in glum silence. "You mean Queens Langley isn't safe? The town?"

"It has a munitions factory. And the airfield. And there's the Vauxhall plant at Luton just a few miles away. It's the sort of thing raiders like— plenty of secondary targets if the main one's too hot." After a silence he added, "Naturally, it'd be safer in the Scotch Highlands or the Welsh hills, but then you might as well be in Goldeneye. Surely you expected something like this?"

"I'm thinking of the children at school in Queens Langley."

"Well," he said, and paused as if assembling quite a speech. But all he added was, "We have to face that."

As they crossed the courtyard, he said, "If the interior bothers you . . . well, of course it bothers you. It's awful. Go down to Harrod's or Maple's or one of the big London stores and buy exactly whatever you want. Don't be afraid to splash out. Make this the home you've always wanted."

Imperceptibly but swiftly he had edged them beyond the point where the choice, to live here or not, was hers.

"It wouldn't seem right," she said. "Extravagance in wartime."

"The war won't last forever, hon. And we don't know what we'll be doing after it. I'm going to make a lot of useful contacts over here. And when we've won, a lot of important people are going to feel they owe me one, for responding to their call so quickly. The British are marvellous like that. They don't forget obligations. So a good impression made here, now— well, you could say you were already building the postwar world. *Our* postwar world, anyway."

"Burgo!" She was half amused, half shocked, thinking he was just trying to fabricate reasons to allow her to indulge herself.

But he went on, with all apparent seriousness, "That's business, Cath. It's opposites. Thinking about opposites, simultaneously, all the time. How can I take this guy's last penny? How can I let him steal back enough to walk out of here with dignity—and live to be useful to me one more time? Opposites. That's what business is."

"Are you doing this job so as to help England in her time of need? Or to feather our own nest?"

"Those aren't contradictory aims, honey."

"All right. But which comes first?"

"Both." He laughed. "When I hear the band play the R.A.F. march-past or 'God Save the King,' I get that lump in my throat and I'm helping England. But when Allardyce introduces me to the president of the Royal College of Physicians or some such dignitary, I wouldn't deny I hear the heavy clatter of feathers falling on our nest."

This conversation—in fact, everything he had said since leaving the top of the hill—gave her the feeling she was being manipulated; not just now, but ever since her arrival in Glasgow. He was humouring her. She was no longer his wife but a problem—a small difficulty that had to be faced for a small part of each crowded day.

At once she felt guilty. He had a big, important job in a war that could save civilization. Of course she was unimportant—at the moment anyway. She'd just have to adjust to that fact. It wasn't peacetime any longer.

But this common-sense reflection did not appease her anger at being treated in that way by him. And so her guilt grew.

32

"Three children!" said the Honourable Mrs. Law, as if the number were almost unique. "How nice."

Her only connection with the air station was that her family once owned the land over which it now spread. She behaved as if no change of ownership had occurred. This officers' mess was hers, the gentlemen in it her guests; and they, being indeed gentlemen, behaved as if they were (except that her drinks went on their bill, Catherine noticed). She accommodated herself to this reversal without a blush. It might almost have been a kind of rent.

At that moment she was giving Catherine the sort of verbal frisking that upper-middle-class English ladies are groomed to give from kindergarten up. The questions are harmless enough—where are you living, have you got any children, do your people live nearby, and so on. But the answers are attended to with an ear as discriminating as a cat's, backed up by a mind with more pigeonholes than the Central London Sorting Depot.

The choice of words, the degree of information volunteered, the nature of the counterquestions—all were charged with significance. Catherine's Canadian accent was full of unwelcome ambiguities for the Hon. Mrs. Law. Indeed, at one point they both foundered in mutual misunderstanding—

when Catherine counterquestioned with, "And do you have children, Mrs. Law?"

The older lady looked at her askance. "Well hardly these days, my dear."

"Oh," Catherine said in embarrassment. "I'm sorry."

They were saved by the commanding officer, Wing Commander Staples, who explained that the Canadian *do you have* is, in English, *have you got,* whereas the English *do you have* means *are you in the habit of.* . . .

"And remember," he added with a twinkle at Catherine, *"bathe* and the world bathes with you. *Bath* and you bath alone."

"Your children," the Hon. Mrs. Law interrupted. "They would speak . . . er . . . with a Canadian accent?"

"They are Canadian," Catherine said.

The Hon. Mrs. Law nodded sympathetic agreement at this sad fact. "Then I think it is most sensible of you to be sending them away to Bedford. The English farm labourer and the provincial tradesman are the salt of the earth, God bless 'em. And so are their children. I'm inordinately fond of 'em and shan't hear a word said against 'em. But they're not the most cosmopolitan and enlightened tribe, don't-you-know. In a local school your three would have been ragged unmercifully as the litter of a group captain. What would have been done to 'em as Canadians into the bargain, I shudder to think."

"Bedford?" Catherine asked.

"Yes." The Hon. Mrs. Law's eyes brightened. She sensed she was onto something here. But she went on. "It is Bedford, isn't it? You're so wise to send them to public schools. God knows our English public schools are detestable hothouses of bigotry and narrow-minded conformity. . . ."

At this a cheer went up from a knot of young officers nearby.

"It's true!" she asserted, glaring furiously at them. "But they are at least accustomed to hearing the odd colonial accent without laughing. And to seeing the odd Hottentot face." She smiled. "It is Bedford, isn't it? Don't tell me I was misinformed. I've passed the news on to several others already. I hope you don't mind—I feel something of a proprietary interest in you and the group captain as it's my house you're living in."

"With that awful furniture?" Catherine said. "Surely that's not yours."

The Hon. Mrs. Law was taken aback—but only momentarily. She laughed. "You're quite right, my dear. It's dreadful, isn't it. I have the original furniture, of course. Not bad stuff, most of it. Chippendale and things, you know. If it were of any interest to you. . . ."

Catherine had been staring across the room, trying to catch Burgo's eye. He saw her at that moment and winked. She hooked a finger at him and turned smiling back to the Hon. Mrs. Law.

"We're interested in more than the furniture, Mrs. Law. My husband's interested in buying the whole place—house and land. He's very rich, you know. If I were you, I'd take him for all he's worth."

Again the Hon. Mrs. Law showed an exemplary command of her own astonishment. Catherine had found the entrée—the usual one for North Americans—to English landed society, for the next words the Hon. Mrs. Law spoke were, "You must come and have tea with me one afternoon next week, my dear. When the children are off your hands. There are some friends I'd like you to meet."

Burgo joined them. "I'm glad you're getting along so well," he said. "Can I freshen that glass?"

"Allow me." Wing Commander Staples had watched the exchange with fascination. "How about you, Mrs. Macrae?" He accepted her glass, letting his fingers rest too long on hers; he had hardly taken his eyes off her all evening.

"I won't have another," she said. "And if you'll excuse us, I want a word with my husband." She took Burgo's arm and led him away. "And that word," she said, "is Bedford."

The argument began in the car on the way home. She said, "What was that awful woman talking about? Sending the children away to Bedford?"

He said, "Why did you come to England, Cath? I mean I know why you came, but—what was going on between your ears? What did you expect?"

"Where is Bedford?"

"Surely you knew about modern war? The dislocation it causes . . . the uprooting. Refugees?"

"And why does Mrs. Law know about it—and all her friends—and I don't?"

"How do I know how she knows? Maybe she has a young nephew who teaches at the school."

"So it's true!"

"You didn't answer my question: What was in your mind? What did you expect over here?"

"They are not going away to school, Burgo. Over my dead body."

He cleared his throat, letting the silence tell her she had not exactly picked the most fortunate phrase in the language.

"We must find another way," she added.

"Queens Langley school is closing. And the infant school. The laugh is that the government is going to evacuate several thousand children to guess where—Canada!"

"There must be another answer. Anyway, what makes me mad is that you just went ahead and did it."

"Yes, I'm sorry about that," he said, adroitly making this the substance of the argument. "I ought to have waited. In an ideal world we would have time to wait. The war turns everything into an emergency, though."

"God, you just wriggle in and wriggle out. 'Yes, it's my fault, no it isn't, it's the war!' That's what you're saying. Hogwash! You went ahead and did it without me because you knew I'd never agree."

"That, too," he said.

"You are so damn smug."

"It must appear like that. To you, anyway."

"What's that supposed to mean?"

He was silent awhile, as if gathering to himself all the reasonableness and all the calm in the world. "I don't think you really tried to imagine what it would be like over here. Not the day-by-day situation. You thought *back,* to nineteen-thirty, not forward. You thought—"

"You suddenly know a hell of a lot about what I think! Well, I think husbands and wives should decide things *together.*"

"I quite agree, honey. But first they have to be on the same wavelength. They can't decide together if only one is thinking about today—nineteen-forty—and the other is stuck about ten years back."

"Well why didn't you tell me as soon as I got here?"

"Don't think I'm trying to blame you. Those years were terrible. It was terrible to lose everything like that. Home and everything—especially for you. I know how important—"

"Why did I have to hear about it from that ghastly woman?"

"I know how important home and family are to you. Well—to both of us, of course, but especially to you. So naturally I don't blame you."

"Will you cut out all this flannel and soft-soap and answer me!"

"I didn't tell you because I know you. You're a tigress when it comes to fighting for home-and-family. And a tigress isn't a thinking human being. I just hoped that even a day or two of actually living here and seeing the sort of preparations that are being made—gas masks, air-raid shelters, evacuation, blackout . . . all that—I hoped it would just alert you a little to reality. The way things really are." He tried a persuasive little laugh. "Honestly, Cath, how would it have been if I'd said, 'Hello darling, welcome to England, lovely to be all together again, and by the way I've fixed for Kelvin, Maddy, and Grant to go away to a nice safe school!' You'd have blown . . ."

"Grant!" The name hit her like a physical blow. Never for one instant had she imagined they were talking about sending him away.

"Of course Grant. He's as precious to us as the other two, isn't he? He's as much right to be safe as—"

"Grant is only seven, Burgo."

"And he's going to a boarding school where they start at six. So he's a year late in starting. He'll be with a hundred boys between six and ten years old. He won't feel—"

"It's grotesque! It's horrible!"

"It's England. It's the way they do it here."

"No, Burgo. Absolutely not. I just will not have it."

"The nearest infant school is at Croxley. You want him to cycle six miles a day? On these dark country lanes? In the blackout? And all the cars without lights? There's no school bus goes that way."

"Okay, we'll get a house in Croxley, so he can walk."

Too late she realized that in saying this she appeared to concede the case for sending Kelvin and Maddy away.

"You think I didn't try? Not that I had a great deal of time. But I lit a few fires under a few people and I tried. There's no house to rent or buy nearer than Gideons."

"Then we'll build one. Or buy a trailer and I'll live in it. . . ."

"Cath! Can you hear yourself?"

"Can anyone hear me," she said bitterly.

They had arrived home. *Home!* She looked out at the dark pile of buildings and pictured it empty of children, and empty of Burgo most of the time. It was the most odious, drab place in the world.

"I know you didn't expect it, darling," he said. "But that's only because you didn't really sit down and think before you came. But you won't feel so bad after you've seen the schools in Bedford. The children will be very happy there."

"I am never going to Bedford."

"We're fixed to go on Saturday. By train. It's only thirty miles. Honestly, you'll feel very different then." He put a hand on her thigh and gave a squeeze.

"Damn you!" she yelled. She almost fell out of the car in her haste. "Damn this country! Damn the goddam war!"

She ran upstairs and locked the bedroom door against him. All night she lay awake trying to shut out of her mind the realization of what she had done in coming over here.

33

The train crawled at last over the River Ouse and into Bedford Midland station. "That's where you'll row in summer, if you're an oarsman," Burgo told Kelvin. "Otherwise you'll play cricket."

"Will I row a boat?" Grant asked excitedly.

"When you get to Upper School. Down in the Inky you play cricket."

"Inky" stood for "incubator," the preparatory school for six-to-twelve-year-old boys.

"And me?" Madeleine asked.

"I don't know what the girls play in summer," Burgo said. "Tennis, maybe?"

He smiled at Catherine. She smiled thinly back. What else could she do?

Their taxi drew in through the school gates just as the great clock on the science building showed noon. The main building, Gothic in inspiration, Victorian in its making, was an impressive pile—all angles and crannies, with battlements and towers, crowned by a central spire—once bright copper, now with a patina of green.

A bell rang as they entered the school. The building came to life with boys changing classrooms for the last lesson of the week, for Saturday was a schoolday. The uniform was sober enough—black shoes, gray trousers, black jacket, white shirt, black tie, gray pullover. Catherine noticed one boy had a blue tie. He stopped another boy from running and took his name. After that she saw several boys with blue ties, all obviously in some kind of authority. Two senior boys, lords of the earth carrying malacca canes, before whom crowds parted and fell to silence, had not only blue ties but brown shoes as well.

Even without these obvious marks of status Catherine would have known they were in a hierarchical world from the way the boys' eyes invariably travelled first to the sleeves of Burgo's uniform and the four broad rings that encircled them—and then the respect with which those same eyes rose to look at the man! It was almost tangible.

They came to a place where there was a choice of doors. For a few moments only they were forced to stand like a bunch of tourists; then a blue-tied boy took charge, with a "May I help you, group captain? My name is Cullen." A short while later he was showing them into the head's study. "D'you play football?" he asked as Kelvin filed past. Kelvin, a little taken aback, said, "Sure." Cullen nodded and smiled: "Good man." Catherine saw how Kelvin swelled with pleasure. It seemed almost like a conspiracy to entice her family from her. There was something familiar about Cullen; she'd almost swear (except that it was impossible) they'd met before.

The conspiracy lasted the rest of the day. The head, a Mr. Maybrace, was a short, stocky man with bristle-filled ears, white side whiskers, a penetrating stare, and a habit of discharging his words with a clipped precision as if he were in permanent competition for a prize in drawing-room oratory. He spoke of the school, its age, its traditions, its emphasis on producing the all-round man. He talked to Kelvin and Grant in a kindly enough manner but every question went right to the heart of its matter, and their replies had to be pretty full before he was satisfied and moved on. Catherine could not deny he was an impressive man.

At length (though the interview lasted only ten minutes, she was later surprised to discover) he said that Bedford would gladly accept both boys. In normal circumstances Kelvin would have had to take the Common Entrance examination but they'd waive that requirement; they would, however, like him to sit the exam, simply in order to help them place him in his appropriate set.

"How typically English!" Catherine said afterwards. "We'll waive the exam but we'll ask him to take it nonetheless!"

Cullen was still waiting outside. He showed them around the main school, and Memorial Hall, which housed a debating chamber and a library bigger than Catherine had seen in any Canadian school. It must have held over ten thousand books. The debating chamber was lined with tall blue plaques framed in gold on which were written the names of those Old Bedfordians—and they were several hundred—who had died in the First World War. On the side nearest the school, most of the plaques were blank. "We'll start filling those now," Cullen said cheerfully. "Most of the seniors here can't wait to join their regiments. A lot of the masters are joining up, too. I'm off soon, myself."

He pointed out the science block and chapel, the open-air swimming pool and gymnasium, the woodwork and metal shops (where the lathes were already turning out handles for stick bombs and small spares for armoured-car engines), the art building, fives courts, rifle range, the cricket pavilion, and the path to the "Inky."

"I think you'll be having lunch with Mr. Bevis in Burnaby—his house," he said. Then, turning to Kelvin, "That will be your house, Macrae. I'm in Talbot's, which is next door almost. So I'll come and collect you at half past two and show you all these other places."

Burnaby, the boarding house, was just outside the school gates. The exterior was pretty enough, with lilac and laburnum trees (long past flowering, of course), and with roses climbing the walls. But inside, the world was spartan indeed. The housemaster, Mr. Bevis, was a wiry, muscular squeezer of arms and a clapper and dry-soaper of hands. He was annoyed at being forty—just too young for the last show, he said, probably too old for this. He'd written to his old regiment but they had asked him to wait; he hadn't much hope of being called.

There were forty boys in the house. Lunch was about to be served. The Macraes ate alone, en famille, in the private part of the house; but Mr. and Mrs. Bevis ate in the boys' dining room—all scrubbed deal tables and bentwood chairs. The meal was cottage pie and reconstituted peas followed by jam tart and custard. Months later Kelvin told them the real names for these dishes: "Meat stodge, green sheep—er—dung, abortion pavement, and . . ." But he coloured, and refused to tell them how custard translated.

The dormitories had only beds, chairs, and chests of drawers. No carpets. No pictures. The beds were all of black-enamelled tubular steel. The blankets all red. "It creates an *illusion* of warmth." Mr. Bevis explained.

The four most senior boys shared the only two studies. The remaining thirty-six lived in The Barn, or common room, whose ceiling was at that moment being reinforced by stout steel pipes to make it suitable as an air-raid shelter.

"We're not expecting bombing raids here," Mr. Bevis reassured them. "Bedford's only industry is schools—there are thirteen in the town, you see. But one has to be ready, don't-you-know."

The changing rooms smelled of male sweat, the lavatories of carbolic.

Catherine was attracted by the spartan simplicity of everything. Often enough in Toronto she had wondered if they weren't spoiling their children simply by bringing them up in a rich North American suburb. Burnaby House was more simply furnished and had less privacy than many a Canadian prison—yet some of the boys here probably came from the famous stately homes of England. Except that Kelvin would be away from home, and in a strange land, she saw no harm in his coming to a place like this.

They took their leave, having noticed Cullen waiting in the street outside. He showed them around all the buildings he had only had time to point out that morning. The place was a world to itself; everything a boy needed was there.

"Except beer," Cullen said. "We have to go into the town for that."

They thought he was joking but apparently boys over eighteen were allowed beer.

"Is there any sort of boy you'd advise parents not to send here?" Catherine asked. "What sort of boy is most miserable?"

"Most of us are miserable at some time, ma'am," he answered. "I wouldn't send an artistic boy here, I suppose. Not unless he was good at fencing or swimming or something."

"I can see sport's important here. Are you good at it?"

Cullen grinned. "I'm rotten at everything, Mrs. Macrae. But I'm saved by fencing. It's the only thing I'm even slightly good at. I'm in the house and school teams. So I pull my weight there and sort of oil out of everything else. Every few months they have a brace-up campaign and I have to turn out in running togs for a cross-country. But generally I slide by. I pity the weeds who aren't top-hole at something. They have to sweat like billy-oh at everything—that's four hours of major sport, four of minor sport, and seventy-five minutes of physical jerks every week. And twice that if you're keenee." He looked down and saw Grant staring at him open-jawed. "Well, young 'un"—he ruffled the lad's hair—"what are you, eh? A keenee? Or an oiler like me?" He laughed without waiting for a reply. Catherine's feeling she had seen him before, somewhere, was growing stronger.

He didn't simply talk about the school but asked about Canada and told them something of his own home in the West Country. He asked Burgo about joining the R.A.F. and the qualifications for becoming a pilot. But for the "sirs" and the "Mrs. Macraes" he kept throwing in, he might have been an adult already, so easy and natural was his conversation.

At the miniature rifle range the shooting team was at practice. The regimental sergeant major, a regular Grenadier, saw Burgo's uniform and came to attention with a thump that shook the earth. His salute was the most aggressive flourish Catherine—or Burgo himself—had ever seen. "Carry on, sar'major," Burgo said in the best Ronald Colman tones.

"*Sah!*" the man's roar blistered the air.

Then he noticed Kelvin's envious gaze and shrewdly offered him the chance to bang off five rounds.

Catherine's heart began to thump with anxiety for her son. She just prayed he'd hit the target. He certainly looked coolly professional as he lay down, splayed his feet, snaked the sling around his arm, found the point of balance, checked the chamber, put one up the spout, and took aim. The R.S.M. watched, too. There was a subtle change in his manner.

Kelvin loosed five well-aimed shots—breathe in, breathe half-out, aim, first pressure, squeeze. Then he eased springs, and laid the rifle down.

"Good lad," the R.S.M. growled and, checking that all the other rifles were bolt-open and grounded, sent Kelvin forward to bring back his target.

The rifle wasn't zeroed for him so the five shots were off centre. But they all fell within a quarter-inch circle—and that was what counted. The R.S.M., who had been ready to make some joking comment, studied the target in silence. "Well, son," he said quietly, "we shall have to pay your dad to send you 'ere, shan't we."

Kelvin tried to look as if no one could be more surprised than he to see the result of his shooting. "It's probably the only thing I'm even slightly good at, sir," he said.

Catherine caught Cullen's eye. A suppressed smile passed between them. Then Cullen winked at her in a way that was far from schoolboyish. And suddenly she knew where she had seen him before—twenty years ago, at Micah. For Cullen was the reborn image of Ed Kirby as he had been then. She blushed. He saw it and gave a little grin of tight-lipped triumph. That was Ed-like, too.

Their impressions of the Inky and, later, of the Girls' High School, were just as favourable. Catherine actually caught herself planning the purchase of uniforms for all three children—what she would buy here, what she'd ask Meg to send from Canada.

She saw then what insidious power there could be in blind social pressures—especially at times like this, times of emotional upheaval; and time of war, when the urge to be like the rest of the tribe, to pull together, is overwhelming. For most of the day she had been among people to whom it was the most natural thing in the world to send children away from home at the age of six. And now that she herself had seen those children, who were boisterous, happy, rudely healthy—not at all the homesick, Dickensian, pinch-cheeks she had expected to find—she was actually considering sending hers to join them!

Only when they were all back on the train and Kelvin, Maddy, and Grant had settled to a game of three-sided battleships, did her true feelings come back to the surface. They were a *family*. They belonged together.

"Well?" Burgo asked. "Impressed?"

They went out and stood in the corridor. "Of course I'm impressed," she said. "But that wasn't the point."

"They'd all be very happy there."

"They'd all be very happy if we went to live in Tahiti. There's a thousand ways to make them happy, Burgo. But I don't think any of those schools are for us and our children."

"What choice do we have? Queens Langley is going to—"

"Is there an air station near Bedford?"

"Cardington. Why?"

"Forget Gideons. We'll take a house here in Bedford and you can get your group transferred to Cardington."

"Talk sense!"

"You said about getting a transfer to Norfolk the other night."

"That was a joke and you know it. Hell, Cath. This is a war. I'm in the armed forces. I can't badger the Air Command to rearrange the war to suit my wife and children."

"You can do anything you want, Burgo. You have done all your life. If you've wanted something bad enough, you've found a way. It's just that you don't want to."

"War is different."

"You never wanted us here."

"Well at least your memory is still normal."

"Christ, Burgo! Don't you start patronizing me."

Grant opened the compartment door. "Dad. Maddy says you can, too, put a submarine right against an aircraft carrier."

"Tell her she's wrong. You have to have deep blue sea around every vessel."

"Nyaa!" Grant's sneer was nipped off by the closing of the door.

"Or," Catherine picked up the thread, "we can find some other nearby school. You didn't look. There must be some other way. They don't have to go to boarding school."

He answered wearily. "In the end it comes down to a decision made by someone who is still able to think with his head and someone who can only think with her guts."

"Who the hell d'you think you are? What sort of talk is that? Do you—"

The door slid open and a furious Madeleine cried, "Dad? A submarine can have the same deep blue sea as a ship, right? You don't need two deep blue seas between them."

To hear Burgo answer you'd think he and Catherine had been discussing the weather. "No, honey, of course not. All you need is one deep blue sea clearance between any two vessels."

"Nyaaa!" Madeleine turned back to her brothers.

"They're not leaving home, Burgo," Catherine said, trying to regain her calm. This whole argument had gone wrong. Somehow she had failed to reach the main point. But Burgo had got her so mad, and so confused, she'd forgotten what it was.

"It ain't your decision, Cath."

"It isn't even *ours.*"

"It could be, if you would only think straight. Since you can't it's got to be mine. Our kids are going where the education is best. I told you I thought the prairie was best of all. You wouldn't have that. So now they're here. And they'll go where it's best here."

"I have no say at all. I'm just nothing. And what about them? They may have an opinion, too, you know."

"They are children. And you're acting like one. Even at the best of times, childish opinions count for very little. In wartime—nothing."

"Damn the war."

"You chose to bring yourself and them nearer the heart of it."

"I chose to keep our family together."

"Tough."

She put her face inches from his. "Well . . . *shit,* Burgo!" she shouted.

She turned and walked off down the corridor, but the partition door separating the first from the second class was locked. She was trapped. Burgo had gone back into the compartment. She stood alone, leaning where he had leaned, feeling the warmth he had left in the teak handrail, and she watched a bleak, gray dusk settle over this loathsome country.

She found it incredible that they made love that night. It began almost as a rape, for she hated Burgo now. She hated his arrogance. She hated his financial power over her. His calm assumption of correctness—his patroniz-ing manner, which said, *Well, that's settled finally, and you'll come around to my way of thinking when you stop being so emotional*—his maleness.

So when he reached across the bed and tried to ease her toward him, she went stiff with anger. She could have fought him but she resolved in-stead to lie there as dead to him as possible. How could he not feel those waves of hatred! How could he lift her nightdress and pull apart her thighs in the face of her utter unresponsiveness? Where was his pride?

She lay as slack as a corpse. She even tried not to breathe.

And then her body rebelled. Her goddam body! It began to take his part against her. The ice in her mind could not stop the sudden thump of her heart. The numbness of her spirit could not still the twitch of her hips. She stood by in powerless fury as her body began a long-familiar writhing, thrust to his thrust. Even her breathing slipped beyond her control. Her brain heard her gasp to him, felt her angry nails dig deep into the rippling muscles down his back, listened to her snarl as he bit her neck and shoulder to make her stop. Flushes of heat and pain warped through her. Sweat sprouted where he lay heaviest. He stabbed her through and through, a steel machine.

"God damn you, Burgo!" she shouted in her ecstasy as he throbbed within her, giving little screams of *oh* and *oh* and *oh* that shattered her ears. Then for the first time that dreadful day she burst into tears. And so did he. He wiped his cheeks into her hair and kissed her ears, bringing her back to a second spasm.

But it solved nothing. It merely shut one more door in her soul. She had thought of going back to Goldeneye, to keep at least the four of them together. Now she knew she did not dare—or her body did not dare. If anything, she hated him even more for this slavery.

He rolled over and away. In the dark she heard him pull off a rubber—so it had been no spontaneous act on his part. More like a proclamation: *From the Occupying Power—Achtung!*

"They'll be home twenty weeks every year," he said out of the blackness.

She said nothing. She knew how quickly childhood slipped away, how precious each moment was. It did not matter how long or short this war might be, something had been filched from her that could never be given back.

Ten days later, after a nightmare anti-spree of buying uniforms and sewing in name tapes and getting schoolbooks and hockey sticks and football boots (and using up all their clothing coupons), and arranging extra coaching for Kelvin in Latin, she drove them up to Bedford and left them at their respective schools. The hardest part had been to act jolly with them, to pretend that Mummy and Daddy were united. She was amazed at their acceptance of what was going to be a traumatic change in their lives. They were far more sanguine about it than she was, inwardly.

Little Grant nearly broke down when the moment came for parting, but she reminded him it was only three weeks to his half-term exeat and then they'd all be together again, and he went off cheerfully enough.

After a dismal lunch at one of the hotels she went for a stroll along the river bank. The Ouse suffers a change of level in the town, falling over two weirs almost a mile apart; between them there is therefore an upper and a lower Ouse. The upper is an urban river, stately, broad, and man-made, flanked on the town side by a stone embankment, with a carved balustrade, and geometric gardens. The lower, which Catherine chose, is a rural traipse among aspens and willows, through meadows whose grass is flattened by lovers all summer long.

She picked a slow, careful path beside the ragged bank, nibbled by ancient floods into minute clefts and bays. Otters—or perhaps they were water rats—launched themselves ahead of her, leaving semicircles of ripples to be plucked downstream. Cloying fronds of weed, hidey-homes of stickleback and tench, swayed in the dark beside her feet. Only a little farther out the surface was misted and then silvered by the clouded sky. A patter of rain-drops spread a mesh of that silver over the intimate depths and greens be-neath her.

So gentle. So restful. It promised a peace that had vanished from her world. It promised an end to slavery, an exit from this box canyon of her marriage. Its simplicity called her down.

But the idea was a conceit of her brain—she knew that. There was no moment when she seriously entertained this notion. She needed no images—not of her body dragged from the reeds, half-spilled over the next weir; not of her bewildered, shattered children; not of a life-penitent Burgo—she needed none of these to hold her back.

She had, she realized, a lot of fight left within her.

But as she walked back, hatless in the gathering storm, even that realiza-tion did not stop this day from being the most miserable of her life.

34

There is a method of dipping ice cream in batter and frying it in deep fat, so fast that it can be served with a hot, crisp exterior and a still-frozen heart. And that, with due allowance for the slower chemistry of human emotions, is how the cold of Catherine's misery survived the heat of many subsequent hours (not to say days and even weeks) of happiness. Years of such happi-ness would have been needed to melt it; and those were the very years that were being denied her—stolen from her. The family years.

But there was plenty to keep her occupied and to prevent the misery from overwhelming her. MacTavish, Burgo's batman, got a load of tiles from a derelict pigsty on the perimeter of the flying ground and fixed up all the outhouse roofs. Catherine acted as his labourer and they spent many hours talking about the Highlands. He was from Loch-na-Beiste, only thirty miles from Strath, and had often poached down as far as the waters that An Dóiteán had legitimately fished. He knew her father well. The man's temper and stubbornness were a legend still, though he must now be sixty. He still farmed Beinn Uidhe and fished the sea at its foot. MacTavish said he'd find out more on his next leave.

A lot of the work at Gideons he did in his spare time, saying it was better than boozing in the canteen or walking around town kicking tin cans. He would take no money for it but was well paid in cups of tea, cakes, hot baths, and cigarettes; and once or twice Nono sponged and pressed his trousers for him.

When the outhouses were weathertight again, they filled them with all the dairying and beekeeping equipment out of the old lamp room. Then Nono moved up from the village and became a "proper living-in maid." Catherine bought her a secondhand wireless of her own so that she could listen to the serious talks, which she complained she could never listen to at home. But Catherine noticed that privacy soon palled. Nono and she spent many evenings together cleaning eggs, knitting comforts for the troops, making butter, roping onions, sterilizing seed pots, bottling honey and pears and jam—and listening to "Variety Band Box" and "Music Hall" and "Monday Night at Eight" and other programmes far removed from the "serious talks" category.

The extraordinary war-that-was-not-a-war, the phoney war, as one American living in Britain called it—a name that soon caught on—did not bother them as it bothered many others. They were not desperate to "have a crack at Jerry." Few A.R.P. wardens ever came their way to shriek "Put out that light!" at every little flicker of a candle. And the privation of the war hardly touched them. They were so well off for honey, eggs, and butter that Nono was able to operate a thriving barter for meat, bacon, corn for the chickens, flour, and almost everything else they needed. Catherine felt guilty about this until the vicar called one day—a tall, shrewd, grinning hedonist with two daughters who, Nono said, had initiated half the boys in the village in the tent on the vicarage lawn where they slept every summer because the vicar was a fresh-air fanatic. He puzzled and enraged the incumbents of neighbouring parishes who could not understand how his choirstalls were packed to overflowing with angelic little boys while theirs were depleted by the general decline in church attendance. He did it, Nono said, by making sure that a choirboy's weekly pay never fell short of the price of ten Woodbines, a cheap and popular cigarette.

Nono spilled these beans as the vicar, the Rev. Leach, was wheeling his bicycle up the lane. So Catherine was less surprised than she would have been when the man declined her invitation indoors and asked her to show him the walled garden instead, where he made an extraordinary proposition.

"I'll come straight to the point, Mrs. Macrae," he said. "There's already a nasty black market in the village. I'm afraid of it. I'm afraid not only of what it'll do to our souls but for the divisions it'll cause. There'll be murder done before too long, if things go on as they are."

Catherine, hoping her blush was not too obvious, said, "It would be difficult to stop, vicar."

"Oh impossible!" he said, cheerfully rubbing his hands. "Oh, yes! Utterly. Quite impossible—as, indeed, you know. You're in it yourself."

"Oh." She was at a loss.

"Yes. I don't propose to stop it. I propose to run it. I consider it the Church's duty to—ah—muscle in and take over the black market." Then, seeing the shock in her face, he added, "I shall, naturally, put the proceeds toward the Village Hall Enlargement Fund. I've spoken to Constable Bentham and he's happy enough with the idea."

"And where do I come in, vicar?"

He gestured at the garden and the high wall about it. "Here, Mrs. Macrae. You and I have the only two substantial walled gardens in the neighbourhood. Between us we could produce enough to drive out every other operator and corner the market. Will you help? We could, if you wish, devote part of the proceeds to the welfare fund at the air station?"

Thus Nono's freelance black market was put on a regular, charitable basis, and with police approval, too.

Their war effort did not end there. She and Nono took an occasional turn at fire watching from the converted water tank up in Gideon's Wood, and Catherine joined the local V.A.D. and refreshed her knowledge of practical nursing.

Often she thought of James's suggestion that she should study biology and those other subjects as a good way to "fill up a war." It made her smile. Even a phoney war, once it got going, needed no filling up.

Every now and then, but not so frequently that she counted as a regular, she went over to the mess at the air station for cocktails. She would have gone more often if it hadn't been for the Hon. Mrs. Law, who seemed to think that Catherine, as the wife of a group captain, ought to spend more time organizing and less time actually doing things. The other drawback was the wing commander, who kept trying to flirt with her. But everyone else was good company.

She was astonished at their youth, their seriousness, their impeccable manners, their reserve. They reminded her of Cullen, those self-possessed, unaffected boy-men. Surely they were the very best type of young manhood: decent fellows with all their lives before them, who would yet die for that intangible blend of country, duty, and freedom. Nothing—not casualty lists, not newsreels, not dispatches from war correspondents—nothing could bring home the monstrous waste of war half so effectively as the silent absence of familiar faces, week after week. Often on her way home—in the early days, anyway—she would quietly weep at their passing, at the thought of the women they might have loved, the families they might have reared. Later such deaths, though far more common, were less individually remarkable; they simply added to the general sadness of the times—those deliberately jolly, those determinedly extrovert times.

Paradoxically, because it fashioned a new yardstick, a monster yardstick, of suffering, it enabled her to bear her own deprivation better, though, since that sort of pain is not relative (in that the woman who has lost a brother-in-law does not cheer up the moment her neighbour loses a brother), it did nothing to diminish her sadness at the loss of her family as a family.

The worst moments in Catherine's life came when it was time to take the children back to school after their exeats and holidays. To watch them, first Madeleine, then little Grant, then Kelvin, walk away down the paths to their respective houses; to see them turn and wave dutifully, already in spirit among their peers, self-conscious of this affectionate display; to endure that ritual with each of them, at the beginning and middle of each term, or almost twenty times a year, was heartrending. Often the tears would run down her cheeks on the drive home and again when Timoshenko, sniffing around inside the car, refused to accept she had left them behind.

Burgo believed that, except at those particular moments, she had overcome her sorrow. The children had settled well. They enjoyed the all-embracing world of boarding school. They said they appreciated home much more than they used to, and they certainly seemed to get on together better than they ever had done before. Their end-of-term reports were average to good. Maddy and Grant both lost their Canadian accents and came home talking like little English ladies and gentlemen—though they returned to school with the twang of North America restored. Later they grew adept at switching at will. Kelvin picked up an English vocabulary but kept his native accent; a curious effect of this was that when he said "biscuits" and "sweets" instead of "cookies" and "candy," it sounded wrong —like a pretend-Canadian who hadn't done his homework.

The amazing adaptability of the children made it harder for Catherine. If just one of them had rebelled, it would have given her some focus for her own deprivation, and for the anger she still felt. Time and again they deceived her in that way. "I hate school," one or other would say. "It's lousy . . . rotten . . . *shent* . . ." The adjectives would fly, freighted with small hopes for her. But moments later they would be laughing at something they and their friends had done; and it would turn out that what they really hated was the pudding they got each Tuesday ("curdled snot" or some such) or a particular senior boy or girl who was too "hell's keenee."

Burgo spoke little of his work (which was a hard restraint for him to practise) but he had thrown himself into it with all the zest that had once gone toward the making of Night Call in Selkirk; many of the periods of leave he "chose" to take were, Catherine knew, enforced by his seniors against his will. In that atmosphere of almost universal sacrifice it would have gone quite against the grain of her character to parade her own sense of deprivation. But its suppression was not its death; the vacuum left within was not filled by the mere business of her life.

Throughout 1940 the news was almost uniformly bad. The outlook grew steadily more bleak. By midsummer, Britain stood alone against the Fascist powers. The Luftwaffe now had hundreds of new airfields in occupied Holland, Belgium, and Northern France, hundreds of miles closer to the airfields and factories of Britain. From thenceforth, the air battle was on. The army, defeated in France and evacuated with great heroism at Dunkirk, was in no position to counterattack. The navy was fighting the U-boat battle out in the Atlantic. Only the R.A.F. stood between Britain and the Wehrmacht. For months Burgo was a fleeting visitor, often too tired to do anything but sleep. Sometimes Catherine missed his visits altogether, for when the night bombing of Germany began in early July, she was often on duty in the station hospital—not doing dramatic things with the wounded who limped home, but taking over mundane tasks so as to release the fully trained staff.

In every way it was her busiest time. She and Nono were taking honey almost daily from one or other of their hives, now numbering eight. They also took swarms, aiming at an apiary of sixteen hives before winter. They had electric-fenced almost half of the four acres and saved it for hay, which they now had to scythe, turn, and gather by hand. Often they were out at sunrise to get in a few extra hours before breakfast.

Early one evening, in the middle of the long dry spell that August brought, they were both out in the field, stooking the hay, when they saw the figure of a young officer on a bicycle coming clattering up the lane. He arrived at the field gate before she was halfway down the slope. He waved and shouted, "Hello, Mrs. Macrae!"

It was Cullen. Her heart sank. The last thing she had time for now was entertaining schoolboy soldiers on leave. Then it occurred to her he might have news of Kelvin.

"I hope I'm not intruding," he said as she came closer.

"Not at all, Cullen," she answered. "Are you posted to this area? You're Second Lieutenant Cullen now, I see."

"Such is the scarcity of officer material." He laughed. "Do call me Ian, if you can bear it." He leaned over the gate, saluted casually, and shook her hand. "Alas, I'm not posted here. I'm on embarkation leave, with an aunt who lives in Queens Langley—my people are in Singapore. So I thought I'd pop over and see you. You don't mind?"

"Of course not. How did you know we live here?" He was very hand-some in his uniform—boyish without being a boy. Now he looked even more like Ed.

"Your address is in the school list. Is the group captain around?"

She laughed. "Don't you know there's a war on?"

He looked at Nono, still stooking the hay. "May I lend a hand? I have done it before. Also"—he shot his eyebrows up and down like a seducer in a melodrama—"I have a bar of chocolate."

"You should have said that first. We'll allow anyone with a bar of chocolate to help with the hay." She slipped the bolt on the gate and pulled it open. "I'll get another bottle of cider. It's rough cider, not sweet, if that's all right?"

"I have been known to drink it."

"There isn't another hayfork. You'll have to manage with the yard fork. There's dungarees and an old pair of tennis shoes in the cowshed. Keep that handsome uniform for breaking the young girls' hearts. When are you off?"

"Tomorrow afternoon."

"Oh! You haven't much time."

His eyes did not leave her face. "No. I haven't," he said solemnly.

She laughed as she crossed the yard to the house, but there was a slight tremor in her hand as she reached a cool bottle down off the pantry shelf.

Ridiculous, she thought. But he was very handsome—and he knew it. Just like Ed.

It was much easier work with the three of them. They could all build the same stook, he from the centre, Nono from the left, Catherine from the right. After fifteen minutes, when the sweat was streaking down from his collar and out from his armpits, he took off his shirt. He must have done a lot of his field training in the sun these last few months, for he was marvel-lously lean and bronzed. It was a great pleasure to both women to see the muscles of his chest and shoulders, so well developed by his years of fencing, rippling in the evening sun.

They finished the entire harvest before it set. He threw two stooks to-gether and they spread themselves side by side, Ian in the middle, with the hill at their back and, shining almost horizontally at them, a monster, golden sun just sinking over the opposite rim of the valley. He undid the bib of his dungarees and bared his chest, letting the sweat run down it, snaking clean rivulets among the harvest dust.

Cider had never tasted so good as at those moments, when tired muscles relaxed and the aches of long, repetitive hours could be eased. The chocolate, too, was marvellous. It was weeks since either of the women had tasted it; all their sweet ration, and their sugar ration too, went to the bees (a ruse for avoiding having to ask for the special beekeeper's sugar ration—which would have entailed giving up most of their honey in return). They sweetened everything with rose-hip syrup, which was not rationed.

"Did you see much of Kelvin before you left, Ian?" Catherine asked.

"I kept an eye on him, from a distance. The fourth and the sixth lead pretty separate lives, you know. But he's a fairly average fellow. Knows how to rub along. Doesn't get cocky. I had a word with Cray, his fagmaster, and he seemed pleased enough. That's one reason I came here tonight—to put your mind at rest on that."

"Oh. That was kind. But why?"

"Well, you looked pretty glum that day."

"Dear me. I was trying to hide it."

"I know."

"The worst thing, the thing that took longest to get used to, is being out of touch. If he was at school nearby, I'd know about air raids and things. I'd know if he was all right."

"There's lots we don't know about," Nono said. "That sun could have snuffed out or blown up and we wouldn't know anything about it for eight minutes. That's how long it takes for sunlight to reach us, going at three times ten and a baby ten centimetres a second."

Silence fell at this news. "Eight minutes, eh!" Ian repeated, to fill it.

A late-evening breeze just managed to stir the topmost leaves of the trees, like distant laughter. On the hillside there was only the drift of the warmed air as it rose sluggishly, heavy with the hay scent.

"I'll miss the Canadian fall this autumn," Catherine said. "Last year we were too busy with buying school uniforms and moving in. This year I'll miss it. The colours are beyond anything you've ever seen. There's an oakwood near Thousand Islands that's just hundreds of acres of vivid scarlet and crimson."

"Everyone talks about what they're missing because of the war," Ian said. "I think we've all gained a lot, too. Don't you, Miss Oenone?"

"Me?" She was flustered at being consulted. She didn't mind contributing facts, but opinions were something else. "I suppose so. Yes, I suppose I've gained." She didn't say what.

"The whole country's gained. We're all much more together. Queens Langley used to be torn in two by class differences. People couldn't bring themselves to talk to each other. That's almost gone now, thanks to the war." Halfway through delivering this opinion he lost interest in it. Probably, Catherine thought, it was something his aunt had said, and when this present conversation had called for an adult-sounding statement he reached for it.

With a zest more genuine to his youth he aimed an imaginary rifle at some rabbits who had ventured out into the bottom of the field farthest from them. "Pah! Pah!" He loosed both imaginary barrels at them and said, "Missed!"

"We have a shotgun if you want," Catherine told him. "A real one. Only a four ten, but it kills rabbits."

"Where?" He was interested.

"In the hedge there with the rest of our things. We always bring one out—in case of enemy parachutists, we say, but actually for rabbits. D'you want to bag a couple?"

He looked at the darkling sky. "The light'll be gone by the time they come out up here."

"There's a field just over the brow of the hill, with good cover coming through the wood. If you don't bag at least two there, you shouldn't be going off to war. I'll show you if you wish?"

She made it a challenge.

"Lay on, Macrae!" he said.

"And you'll stay and have a bite? I won't call it dinner."

"If I manage to bag one. Thank you. Otherwise I don't think I could look Miss Oenone in the face—adorable though hers is."

Nono was captivated by him. She gathered up all she could carry and ran down the hill in great bounds, eager to prepare something special for this special young man. When she was out of earshot Catherine laughed. "You waste no time," she said. His eyebrows questioned her. "You know!" she insisted.

The gun was loaded but broken. He unloaded it and slung it over his shoulder. At first Catherine led the way through the woods but he soon came to her side and slipped his hand through her arm. She made herself not react.

"Remember that day you came to Bedford?" he asked.

"Very well."

"D'you remember I winked at you?"

"Sort of."

"You blushed."

"Did I?"

"You know you did. It's extraordinary, isn't it, how we build on such little things. If you had taken offence, or looked bored, or just laughed, I'd probably have forgotten it."

"It might be best," she warned. "Even now."

"I don't know why I did it, except that you seemed—you *are*—a very beautiful woman. But even so, I'd never done that sort of thing before. And the fact that you blushed opened my eyes to possibilities I would never have dreamed of."

"Listen!" Catherine stopped and faced him. Half of her was amused at his cool presumption. Half of her was excited.

"Oh I don't mean you *intended* it that way," he said before she could speak. "I'm sure you didn't. But ever since then I haven't been able to stop thinking of you." He put a finger to her lips. "Please? Just listen to me. I don't know if I can make sense of it, but just listen anyway. It's all tied up with the war. With thoughts of going off to battle. You know how we read *Morte d'Arthur* and things like that, and we laugh. Sir Galahad and pure love, romantic love and peerless ladies. When we're snotty little fifth formers, we read all that and laugh. But when I began thinking about joining my regiment and going away to fight, I remembered it all, and I didn't laugh. That sort of perfect, romantic love, it's all tied up with the nobility of sacrifice, isn't it. Only politicians talk of liberty and patriotism. We need a more personal ideal."

Catherine nodded solemnly. She wanted to say, "Me?" but was afraid that an unintended note of scorn or patronage—or even laughter—might creep into her voice.

"Only it doesn't stay romantic. In poetry, maybe. But not in real life, not with me. The question is, does that make it impure? Dirty? Do *you* think physical love is impure, Mrs. Macrae? Is it something dirty?"

"No," Catherine said. She knew she ought to be . . . what? Offended? Upset? At the very least she ought to back away from this danger.

But it didn't feel like danger. He was so serious, so young. It would have hurt him so much not to take him seriously, too.

"We were talking just now about the things we miss, because of the war. I didn't say what I miss. If I die, my last regret will be that I'm still— can you say a man's a virgin? That I won't have known the *feel* of love. I could pick up a floozie in London tomorrow evening, but that wouldn't be it."

In the twilight gloom he was a darkening shadow against a dark lacing of leaves. She could just see his eyes. She reached her hands up to his head, running her fingers through his hair. He shivered but made no move toward her. She pulled herself against him, her lips against his.

Her seizure of this initiative gave him a jolt. He grew tense and even pulled himself a fraction away from her before some contrary force inside him thrust him against her once more, bearing her back against a sloping tree.

It was the merest pause, measured in objective time, but in it Catherine lived an age.

She knew it would be wrong, but that did not really bother her. She had reasons enough to flood that corner of her conscience. Burgo. Revenge. The war. Her loss. Ian's need. Her answering warmth. The opportunity. His youth. Memories of Ed. His handsomeness. Her age. The flattery of it. Her *need* to give. It would be so easy.

But three small ghosts clustered around her, too. Kelvin, Maddy, and Grant. They had been here, with her, so often in the flesh she could not banish them now; their pressure, though incorporeal, was no less compulsive than his ardour.

Would it threaten them if she found room in her life for an elemental sex, uncomplicated by love or loyalty? She felt she had so much love to give and so little time to give it in—such small windows in her life to squeeze it through. Was there not room in so wide a sea for one small island of untreated affection?

Even to ask the question was to state the doubt. And she had too much love for those three shades, for the home she kept for them at the heart of her, wherever they were—and too much love for Burgo even—to risk discovering the dangerous answer.

The decision came as Ian pressed her against the tree. It was not a conclusion, not the result of an exercise in logic; it came like a piece of instantaneous self-knowledge. She knew she could not let him have her. At once, the whole of her body began to rebel. It thrilled to his touch. Waves of longing for him urged *yes* upon her. She ached with the intensity of her yearning. Her sex was a shout of rage at being cheated of all that was so close, so hard, so ardent.

An extremity of shivering overcame her. Then something pulled the insides from her, her blood, even her breath. Its force was so cosmic and, in a curious way, so external, she hardly recognised it as an orgasm. Only when its second wave took her, and its third, did she know it. She laughed, though the noise escaped from her like a sob. Her body had cheated itself!

Ian took his lips from hers, from her neck, from her ears, from her cheek. "Are you . . . is anything the matter?" he asked. He saw her tears.

Inside her it still felt like laughter.

"Oh, Mrs. Macrae!" He kissed her tears, savouring them on his tongue. "Oh, I'm so sorry. I didn't mean . . ."

She pressed her lips to his, to stop him talking. They went on kissing for a while, but each kiss was a farewell. Without a word from her he knew he had already taken the best of all that she could give.

"I don't want to go," he said.

She left the ambiguity alone. "If Oenone doesn't smell a rabbit, she's bound to smell a rat."

As they picked their way through the wood, she behind him now, she was filled with exultation. In a literal sense she had done the moral thing; but in every other way she had been his joyful adulteress. She, too, had taken the best of him.

They were lucky. His dark-accustomed eyes saw the field as bright as day. He swiftly brought down two good-sized rabbits. One was killed out-right. "Are we poaching?" he asked as he finished off the other over the toe of his boot.

She laughed. "Don't say you are worried about *poaching!*"

He blushed.

"No. It's Ralph Perry's land—the father of the taxi driver. We give him honey, every now and then."

"It's not my night for breaking commandments, is it!"

"Not so far."

The sound of the shots had brought Timoshenko up from the house, barking furiously. Now he caught up with them and, wearing that idiotic, mongrel grin of his, led them proudly back through the wood as if he had organized the whole expedition.

When they passed the sloping tree against which they had lain he sighed up a light laugh and asked, "How can it all be so normal again?"

She sighed, too—but inwardly. For his youth.

"I love you, Mrs. Macrae. I adore you. Every bit of you is so precious to me, I'd do anything for you. Tell me not to go tomorrow and I'll desert."

"My orders are different," she answered, determined not to play to his solemnity. "They say you're to go out, wherever you're going, and cover yourself with glory."

It was exactly the right thing to say. He saw he would get no response to his mawkishness (which, of course, he took to be the height of courtly love) and her indication of the paths of duty and glory offered him a way out—a very British way: "I'll probably make a giddy ass of myself," he said complacently.

She laughed. "I'll never get used to that word."

"What word?"

"Never mind. There's Nono, wondering who shot who. Or even whom. She's a marvellous girl. Don't you like her?"

"I've never really noticed her."

"You should."

They left the rabbits hanging in an outhouse.

Crossing the yard he hit his forehead with his hand. "I know what she meant now! 'Three times ten and a baby ten'! Of course!"

As soon as he was in the kitchen he looked around and his eyes settled on the old school slate, where they wrote reminders. The nail squeaked as he wrote: $3 \times 10'^\circ$. He turned to Nono and said, "Three times ten to the tenth. That's how you say it."

She repeated it several times and asked what it meant.

"Three times ten times ten times ten . . ." He went on, shooting a finger up at each *ten* until all ten digits were raised. "Three with that many noughts after it. Ten noughts. Thirty thousand million. Americans call it thirty billion."

He did not even glance at Catherine when he said "Americans." She saw what he was doing. He had at last looked long enough at Nono's face to really notice it. Most men glanced at her and dismissed her as a big lump of a girl. Few saw her exquisite—but so unfashionable beauty. Renoir, the painter, would have seen it. And Maillol, the sculptor. Now Ian Cullen saw it, too. And he was simply talking in order to give himself the excuse not to stop looking.

Catherine slipped upstairs itching with hay dust. When she came back down, strip washed and changed, Ian was explaining eclipses with the help of two apples, the candle, and a Ping-Pong ball. And he was still looking at her all he could.

Nono's dinner was a feast. They drank more rough cider and became merry—the stage where anything, even the chiming of the clock, can cause a fit of giggles. Catherine staggered to bed for fear of dropping off to sleep in the kitchen. She had just gained the foot of the stairs when Ian came tumbling after her along the passage. "I say, Mrs. Macrae, thanks most awfully. For everything," he said. Then he giggled.

She leaned over and pecked him a chaste kiss. "Don't keep Nono up too late. Every day is a long day here in August."

"I won't," he promised and went back to the kitchen, still giggling.

She thought of some lines by Frances Cornford, which she had heard on the wireless that morning:

A young Apollo, golden-haired,
Stands dreaming on the verge of strife,
Magnificently unprepared
For the long littleness of life.

But they suddenly seemed unfair. No one was prepared for that.

Next morning she was awakened by a footfall on the gravel. She went to the window and, by the light of a vast, setting moon, she saw Ian Cullen, spruce again in his uniform, wheeling his bicycle out through the gate. He paused. She thought he saw her and she hid her nakedness behind a curtain. He raised his hand—to blow a kiss, she imagined; instead he saluted.

Birds were already singing in the dawn that was masked by Gideon's Hill. She pulled on a dressing gown and went down to Nono's room.

"Was he here all night?" she asked.

"Are you angry, Mrs.?"

"No. Just worried. Was he?"

"Yes."

"Did he sleep with you?"

"Yes."

"You know what I mean, now? I don't mean . . . just sleep and snore."

"I know what you mean, Mrs. We loved up, if that's what you mean."

"Did you take precautions? Or did he?"

"He put out the light."

Catherine sighed. "I mean not to have babies."

"I wouldn't mind having his baby. I've got nought against babies. There's a lot of men's babies I wouldn't mind having. Only no one ever asked."

At that time of morning, after such a night, it seemed an entirely reasonable answer. Only by effort of a still torpid intellect did Catherine manage to say, "Think now, Nono. He might not marry you. He might even . . . not come back. You and a baby. Alone in the world."

"Would you turn me out of doors?"

"Of course not. But we could be posted anywhere. And when the war finishes . . . Anyway. Think now. It may not be too late. There are things we can do."

"I'm not having any of that. You mean needles, like Jinny Welland. Now she can't have none at all."

"No! I mean now, this minute. Wash it out. With warm soapy water. We could wash out his . . . what he left you . . . his seed."

Nono thought a while. "Reckon I'll chance it. Leave it to God, eh? If there is a God. We still never found that out, did we. Maybe we will now."

"How?"

"I dunno."

"Exactly. Nono. That about sums it up, doesn't it! You don't know. I don't know. Oh God! I feel so responsible for this."

Nono looked at her as if that was about the most surprising thing Catherine could possibly have said.

35

By November there was no doubting it. Nono was pregnant. When Catherine told Burgo he was furious and wanted her thrown out immediately, but Catherine dug her heels in and, for once, she won. Nono stayed—but only on the quite unworkable condition she have no contact with Madeleine.

"And who once sneered at the Air Command for believing in sympathetic magic!" Catherine taunted him. "I've never seen a medical book that claims pregnancy's contagious."

"There's a lot of it going about," he said. It was his usual joking manner, but underneath it he was angry.

That Christmas, while foraging for sticks in Gideon's Wood, he had a serious talk with Madeleine on the subject, which left her more bewildered than enlightened.

"I don't know what Daddy's worried about," she said. "I'm never going to get married anyway. It all seems a stupid waste of time to me."

Catherine left it there. Most things were "stupid" in Maddy's eyes. She seemed to need to prove her superiority over everything and everyone. When the wireless announced a victory, she would say, "And about time, too!" For a defeat she'd say, "Well, what did they expect?" No snippet of criticism escaped her ears. She'd come back from shopping in the village with Nono and unload a whole budget—"That vicar wants his head looked at. . . . Guess whose wheelbarrow was outside The Lamb and Flag last night—*again*. . . . Honestly, I think it's time they disbanded the Home Guard . . ."—all of which was fourth-hand opinion, overheard.

It would be understandable if Madeleine herself were inadequate in some way, at her schoolwork or at games. But she wasn't. Far from it. She was good in class; if she weren't so slapdash and lazy, her reports said, she'd be the best scholar they had. Instead, she used her brilliance merely to help her get by. It annoyed Catherine, who had had to work hard for her own little learning; all waste annoyed her. "Perhaps if you applied yourself more at school, you really would be superior to everyone, honey," she told her daughter. "Then you wouldn't need to keep showing it in this very childish way. Nobody thinks you're the least bit clever to keep shouting things at the wireless and bringing home every malicious bit of tittle-tattle."

Burgo, of course, took Maddy's part. "A girl doesn't need to be clever," he said. "That's Meg's trouble. Too damn clever. Look at Helen—not a thought in her head and happy as the day's long."

"But Maddy's reports—" Catherine began.

"Yach! A lot of dry old maids—all their geese could be swans, I'll bet. Anyway, mothers and daughters never did agree. That's a rule of human nest building."

When Catherine thought of the fearsome complexity of human relations and experience that Gideons had witnessed since they moved in— when she thought of the tangling of her own emotions and ideas—and then compared it with these facile nostrums of his, she seethed with anger. Did he know nothing? Did he not even want to know? Was his own part in the war—a war being waged by hundreds of millions of others—was his tiny part so important that he could not be bothered to find out what was happening right here around him?

Were all men as uncaring about their wives' real wants and feelings? James wasn't. Fiona could hardly have done more to alienate and exclude him, yet he persisted in understanding and even in loving her. Why did Burgo have to be so opposite? Just because she loved him and responded to him with as much passion as he could wish for, he assumed that *all* was well. It was like living inside a coarse story. "Keep telling them they're beautiful and give them all their joystick their little cockpits can take . . ." she had once overheard Wing Commander Staples say to an admiring group of pilot officers.

Then one day, one marvellous early summer day in May 1941 (though it was, coincidentally, the day the House of Commons was demolished by the Luftwaffe in the heaviest raid to date on London), the doorbell rang and, when Catherine answered it, there stood Meg. And not just Meg, but Meg in the uniform of a sergeant pilot; and not just Meg in the uniform of a sergeant pilot but, standing a little behind her, almost blotting out the daylight, a tall—a seven-foot-tall—full-blood American Indian, also in the uniform of a sergeant pilot.

"Am I right for Shangri-La?" Meg said. "Those peasants in the village weren't sure."

"Meg!" Catherine shrieked and hugged her. Then, unable to contain her delight, she swept her out past her grinning companion and danced around on the lawn.

"Hey, Cherokee!" Meg shouted breathlessly over her shoulder. "I plumb forgot to warn you about that British reserve."

When her delight had run its course, Catherine said, "Oh, have I missed you!"

Margaret was caught a moment between flippancy and seriousness. "I missed you, too, kiddo. Come and meet Cherokee. Don't ask him what the weather's like up there. He's heard that one."

"How d'you do, Mrs. Macrae." They shook hands. "I'm delighted to meet you at last. I've heard so much about you from the sergeant here."

"My heart sinks! But what are you both doing here?"

Meg answered, "Oh, just waiting around in case someone says 'Sherry?' —you know how one does."

They left their bags in the hall and went into the drawing room for drinks. But Catherine, too restless to sit, or even just stand, took them out to the lawn again.

"Seriously," Catherine said, "why are you here? How did you get over?"

"Oh, we had Canada up to here, so we just put on this disguise, went down to the nearest R.C.A.F. base, and hopped on the next plane. Seriously? That's our job. They let women fly the planes over to England. Women and injuns. Right, Cherokee?"

"Right, sergeant!"

"And how d'you like England, er, Cherokee? Look—if I'm going to call you Cherokee, you're going to call me Catherine. Or Cath."

"I like it fine, Cath."

"He likes it fine," Margaret confirmed. "He asks for whisky here and you know what? No bartender has ever refused him."

Cherokee underlined her joke by throwing out his vast chest and beating it like Johnny Weissmuller doing Tarzan.

"I think we could almost have lunch out here." Catherine led them into the orchard. "That's Nono."

Oenone was up a ladder, pruning the apple and pear trees, which were in the first flush of blossom.

"Looks like she once said Yes-yes," Margaret said. "Ought she to be up that ladder?"

"She's fine. She always leaves the pruning until blossomtime. It fills the house with flowers and it doesn't seem to affect the harvest. I didn't ask how long you can stay?"

"A couple of days."

"Marvellous. The children'll be sorry to have missed you."

"Why don't we drive up and see them after lunch? We've borrowed a car. We left it at the end of the lane. I suppose they're free on a Saturday?"

"Free to play football and hockey. But that's a marvellous idea. You'll slay them, Cherokee. You'll turn Kelvin and Grant into overnight heroes."

Nono provided her usual banquet. Margaret, even though she knew all about it from Catherine's letters, was impressed. "Cathy's told me how fantastic you are at everything, Nono. I didn't believe it till now. My God, is there anything you can't do—apart from not being able to get into last year's girdle, I mean?"

It was lost on Nono. "I can't seem to get the hang of polarized light," she said.

"How's that? *What* light?"

"Polarized."

"Sure," Cherokee said. "Polarized light."

Margaret gripped her head as if she had a sudden migraine. (In fact, she was trying not to laugh.) "Gee, I wish you hadn't said that, Nono. It bothers me, too. I've been fighting it in secret for years."

But Cherokee, who was, in fact, a physics major, made it so clear that even Meg was momentarily interested.

"She's priceless," Meg said when they were all in the car and Bedford-bound.

"To me she is," Catherine replied. "She is my sanity." She turned to Cherokee, who was driving. "I'd better know your official name," she said. "To introduce you around."

"Sure. In fact, I'm not a Cherokee at all."

"That's just the code name of the first plane he ever crashed," Margaret threw in.

He took every one of her jokes with a wry smile and a little shake of his head. "I'm a Cree," he said. "To the air force I'm Sergeant Jones."

"Tell her your Indian name. Tell her what it means."

"Tishe-ton Wa-ka-wa Ma-ni." He grinned. "It means The Hawk That Hunts Walking."

"Isn't that cute? You know how Indians get those sexy names? They get named for the first thing the papa Indian sees after they get born—the minute he steps outside the papoose, or whatever those smelly tents are called."

"Tepees?" Catherine offered.

"Yeah, tepees. I must write that down one day. So that's how they get called Sitting Bull or Running Cloud or Crazy Horse. The first thing he sees."

"Isn't that nice!" Catherine was delighted. "It's such a shame when good old customs like that die out."

"Not around old Cherokee they don't. Right?"

"Right, sergeant."

"He's got six kids, all named that way. Shall I tell her?"

"You tell her, sergeant."

"It's the story of his life. He called them Heap Bottles, Hole in Tar-paper, Rat Rat Rat, Running Nose, Social Security Check, and Sex-Crazy White Man."

If Cherokee had heard the joke before, he'd heard it with a different list because he laughed so much he had to pull over to the side of the road. "Oh, isn't she something!" he said to Catherine when his laughter was exhausted. "Someone should write it all down. Last night she told me jiving is an arthrodisiac. How about that!"

"Ah ah! Bedroom secrets," Meg warned.

"Are you married, Cherokee?" Catherine asked.

"Gee, honey!" Meg was scandalized. "That's a hell of a question to ask a man with six kids."

"No, ma'am." Cherokee jerked his head toward Margaret. "She won't let me."

They had tea with Mr. and Mrs. Bevis, the housemaster and his wife; to them Meg was simply bewildering. Somehow the talk got around to the old debate of one-sex schools versus coeducation. Margaret said the Golden-eye school had been co-dead rather than co-ed, but a boy had once sat beside her in class when she was thirteen and she'd let him peel a Band-Aid off her ankle. The Bevises were still bewildered even after Catherine had explained that a Band-Aid was like Elastoplast.

"You let a boy peel an Elastoplast off your ankle?" Mr. Bevis said, utterly lost for meaning.

"Oh, don't remind me!" Margaret buried her face in shame. "It was even worse than that. It was flesh-coloured!"

"I think Miss Macrae is gently pulling our legs, my dear," Mrs. Bevis said with a dutiful smile.

"The creeps!" Margaret complained afterward. "What made us con-descend to take their rations? He's the only guy I ever met who speaks in semicolons. Did you *hear* them?"

The children were overjoyed to see their Aunt Meg again, and, of

course, were mightily impressed with her new friend, Uncle Cherokee.
There was an argument between Kelvin and Madeleine (who had leave for
the afternoon) over whose school they were to be shown around, since there
wasn't time to do both. Margaret settled it with a promise that next time
she'd make it a special visit just to the Girls' High.

"And bring Uncle Cherokee?"

"She couldn't stop me," he said.

Their jocular mood gave way to something more serious the moment
they entered the main school. The B.B.C. Symphony Orchestra had been
evacuated to Bedford for the duration, to avoid the blitz; it used the Great
Hall for its rehearsals. That Saturday they were practising Beethoven's
Eroica. Kelvin put his finger to his lips and led the party tiptoe along the
top gallery, where the instruments were far enough away to blend perfectly,
and the ceiling too close to give an annoying echo. They stood there, en-
tranced, bathed in magnificent sonorities, far longer than they had intended.

Kelvin took them next to the Memorial Hall, where he told them
something Cullen had omitted to mention on his conducted tour, almost
two years earlier. The word REMEMBER was carved above the door—
meaning, of course, "Remember these valiant dead." But the school prefects
(or monitors, as they were called), with characteristic gallows humour,
had chosen that doorway as the site of the chair over which the victim of
a school beating had to bend. Kelvin described the ritual in loving detail.

While he was speaking, Catherine's eye was distracted by a notice board
to one side of the door, not three feet from her. There, in alphabetical order,
neatly lettered in italic script on slips of card that could be juggled around
to accommodate new entries, were the names and school dates of those
killed in action in this present war. The first name she saw—or was conscious of seeing—was I. F. Cullen (31–40). She stared at it for several seconds, not believing it, not *wanting* to believe it: I. F. Cullen (31–40). At
last those dreadful words were all she could see. Needles of black dizziness
swirled around them. I. F. Cullen (31–40).

"Cath! What is it?" Meg had noticed.

"No," Catherine said. "No."

Meg's arm went around her. "Honey?"

"No. Oh no. Oh no."

Meg looked at the board, saw its purpose. "Who is it, darling?"

Kelvin came between them and the board. He saw the name at once.
"Cullen," he said.

He turned and put his arms about her; Meg dropped hers. Kelvin, now a fraction taller than his mother, held her. "God, how rotten! I didn't know, Mummy. I didn't know. I'm so sorry."

Catherine lowered her eyes to his shoulder, turned inward to him, and wept.

It was soon over. She cried more in shock, for grief is slower to take hold. She accepted Kelvin's handkerchief and blew her nose. "I'm sorry." She blinked around with a watery smile. "It was so unexpected. He was so nice to us that day we first came here. I even said if our boys turn out to be like him . . ." She almost broke down again.

"Kelvin," Margaret said, "why don't you take your brother and sister and Uncle Cherokee down to the rifle range where you've had all those triumphs? Your mother and I will just take a turn or two around one of these greenswards or whatever you call them, and we'll meet up in about twenty minutes, huh?"

When they were alone, strolling on the grass, Meg said, "But that's not all, is it, Cath honey?"

"Cullen is the father of Nono's baby. Or he was."

"Oh . . . God! Poor kid!"

"She had no hope of marrying him. She knew that. I've said, a couple of times, 'Let's write and tell him.' But she wouldn't hear of it. Funnily enough, I don't think she wanted him to know. I don't think she wanted to share the baby with him. Does she even think of it as his, I wonder?"

"Will this mean no pension or anything like that? Who'll support her?"

"God—Burgo will be even more mad now. He was all for throwing her out last November."

"My brother is an asshole."

They crossed a gravel walk onto the Lower School playing fields.

"I didn't tell you everything, Meg," Catherine said.

"No?"

"No. That evening poor Cullen came out to see us—well, he came to see me. Don't laugh, but he came on purpose to seduce me."

Meg didn't laugh. "And did he?" she asked.

Catherine tapped her breastbone. "In here he did."

Meg's eyes took in the gesture and then fell—meaningfully—about two feet.

"Damn nearly there, too!" Catherine said.

"What did he look like? Was he handsome?"

"You remember Ed Kirby? Over at Micah?"

"Do I!"

"He was the image of him."

"So who could have blamed you?"

They reached a goal post. Meg grasped it and swung around, reversing their direction.

Catherine asked, "D'you think one can love two men?"

"In *that* way?"

"In any way. In all ways."

Meg snorted. "My problem, you may remember, was keeping the tally down to only two."

"I'm serious."

"Okay, Cath. You tell me—can you love two men? You should know."

Catherine lost her innards for a moment. "You mean Ian Cullen?"

"I mean you and Dad."

"Oh, my God!" She swallowed. "Does Burgo know? How did you know?"

"Because I've got a naturally dirty mind. Also—you remember me—I'm sentimental. I like happy endings."

"Does Burgo know?"

"Would it worry you?"

"Well of course it would. He'd kill me."

Meg laughed. "Ergo Burgo don't know. Or right now you'd be swopping earthly memories with Ian Cullen. Even earthy ones. Anyway, how little you understand your lord and master!"

"Why?"

Meg surveyed her awhile. "I guess you're old enough," she said at last. "Men aren't all the simple creatures we like to imagine. I mean because we can all pull their eyes over our wool, we think oh they're easy. But they ain't. Especially my big brother. You know when he first started getting interested in you?"

"He said it was that summer, the year before we married. That summer after you went away to art school."

"Right. But I can date it to an exact conversation—during which I let slip the fact that I thought Dad was sweet on you."

"You said that?"

"Of course, I didn't imagine there was any heavy stuff. I didn't imply that. And I'm sure Burgo didn't take it like that, either. But I'm also sure that's when he really started to get interested in you. Riddle me that, you Freudian scholars."

Catherine looked at her suspiciously. "Are you joking now, Meg? Is this a legpull?"

"You don't believe me? Ask Burgo then. I'll say one thing for that Oedipus fellow—his heart was in the right place. He loved his mother, didn't he?"

"Fiona knows. I think she guessed at once. After that blizzard—that's when it happened, you know. I thought we were going to die. I thought James would die and never know I loved him, so I kissed him. And then, when we didn't die—well, there was no taking back that kiss. But Fiona knew at once. She's never shown it, mind."

"Oh, she wouldn't. Some women are natural Mormon wives. It's a pity they changed that law, I think. My, but aren't we a weird family? Only Helen's normal, if *anyone* in California can be called normal. Is it still going on—you and Dad?"

"It doth but slumber."

"Oh good."

"I never felt I was cheating Burgo, and I honestly don't think I did. It's two very different kinds of love, you know. Loving Burgo is like . . . like always being at war. There's no peace. But loving James is all peace. Even without 'heavy' stuff as you call it. I mean, that's the least important thing."

Meg looked at her in surprise. "Well! Welcome to our weird, weird family. I think you just graduated, right?"

"Right—sergeant. Hey, I like Cherokee."

"Me, too. We keep each other out of trouble."

"Are you . . . 'walking out' as they say?"

"Lying in. I guess it's the same except it's the version for thirty-year-olds."

"Are you going to get married?"

"What for? I'm thirty-six. I'm not going to have kids. Besides, he's ten years younger. It's only a wartime thing. He'll get a squawk of his own one day."

"Squaw."

"Wannabet? Why don't you have 'a wartime thing,' darling? It's not that difficult, men-being-what-they-are-thank-God."

"It wouldn't be me."

"Because of . . . God?"

"No."

"I thought not." There was another pause before Meg added, "Wasn't it marvellous when whatever happened you could say, 'This is God's will. He has visited these awful things on me for a purpose'? And you could pull on the hair shirt singing. *O be joyful in the Lord?*"

"You never did!"

"I mean you. I often think the pioneer sodbusters were like all of us when we're young. I mean, what a terrible life they had, really, from one point of view. They came with nothing. Just hammers and nails and axes and seed and the plough. And a team. And those places like near Winnipeg where they had to cut hundreds of trees and bust up all the roots. I mean, the sheer labour. The sweat. Yet they could sing *O be joyful*. And now look at us city slickers. We've got everything. It's all there. Decaying. Used. Secondhand. Tenth-hand. Breaking down. Dirty. You can't trust it. You can't trust anyone. It's too complicated. You don't understand it. No one understands it. And that's just like us as we get older. It's what we're like inside. If only we could go on pioneering ourselves all our lives. There should be places we could get our brains cleaned. Put lightning through them or something. Can you imagine that? A world full of people who couldn't remember a single damn thing to cry over! Creepy. Did you ever look deep into the eyes of a man who's had a lobotomy?"

"You're incredible, Meg. You talk in jokes and riddles and yet you end up saying more . . ."

"You want it straight? Well, straight is there's no going back from complication to simplicity. Cherokee has this psychiatrist buddy. He says nine out of ten women have this fantasy where the doorbell goes and they answer it and there's a handsome, smiling young man who forces his way in and oh-so-gently, oh-so-beautifully rapes them. He ties them with soft, silken cords on swan's-down beds and presses grapes between their lips and gives them wine from jewelled goblets. And you know what? This dumb-cluck psychiatrist thinks it's a *sex* fantasy! Men are sex mad."

"It isn't?"

"Of course it isn't. It's a symbolic daydream. The young man is Life. Those women are just acting out what life does to us every day. Life is a handsome, smiling rapist. He has a gentle way with the silken cords, and he knows every trick to pull with those gifts of wine and fruit."

"Are you glad you're a woman, Meg?"

"With men like Cherokee in the world? How can you ask! Be thankful for big mercies." She put an arm around her sister-in-law and gave a squeeze. "But go find one of your own, huh?"

36

From then on Margaret and Cherokee were fairly frequent visitors to Gideons, bringing with them a shower of silk stockings (later nylons), candies, bananas, maple syrup, rye whisky . . . whatever the current short-age might demand.

Toward the end of 1941, Burgo made a brief visit home to Goldeneye. As James had predicted, the hospital was now one of western Canada's leading centres for the study and treatment of traumatic bone and joint lesions. One of its great advantages lay in the hundreds of miles of un-polluted prairie all around. Exposed bone is acutely vulnerable to infection. At the slightest hint of it, all they had to do was open the windows and it blew away. No second infection blew in to replace it. Few hospitals in Britain could boast such a facility *and* the kind of expertise James and Jay had acquired. Burgo now wanted to make Goldeneye *the* centre for the long-term reconstruction of R.A.F. and R.C.A.F. personnel with smashed bones and joints. The plan was to handle each patient's acute crisis in Britain, stabilize the condition, then fly him (or, more rarely, her) over to an airfield in eastern Quebec, and then on to Goldeneye by whatever means seemed best—train or plane. Within two months the system was brought into operation. It had been no wifely exaggeration when Catherine had said that if anything in the medical line called for organization, Burgo could do it.

But something was happening to him. That early-wartime eagerness was tarnished. He came home more often—still not *very* often, but more than before. And now, when he unwound with her, he was full of gripes about the Air Command, the Air Council, the Air Ministry . . . Group . . . the Joint Services *this* and the *that* Liaison Committee. They sprouted like nettles on an old dungheap.

She asked him why he was losing his enthusiasm, and he blamed the war. She might have believed him if she hadn't seen it all before, in the early 1930s, when NCT was well established. As soon as the firm reached more or less its mature size, he had begun to fret. The hurly-burly of build-ing it up had been a daily tonic to him; but the grind of keeping it going, and of developing those bits of the organization that can pardonably be neglected in pioneer years, was like a slow death.

When she had angrily accused him, that Christmas back in Goldeneye, saying that the years after the crash of 1929 had been the happiest in his life, she had spoken a profound truth about Burgo. Now she saw it happening all over again. Burgo had been on top of the world when war broke out. He was an achiever and there was everything to play for. The top brass had been too panicky and too busy elsewhere to bother him much. And in any case, all they wanted was results, which he delivered every day.

But now the war was settling down. Its new bureaucracy was well dug in. Committees were reaching out and absorbing all the one-man bands. Procedures were being standardized. Interservice routines had to be harmonized. Burgo had done his work too well, for he had, in fact, eliminated the essential need for a person of his abilities and calibre. He wouldn't see it that way, of course; he'd now start to defend his empire against the invading hordes of bureaucrat-barbarians. And he would lose.

There was nothing Catherine could do but wait, and go on with everyday life as well as she could.

Burgo's batman, MacTavish, went on Hogmanay leave in 1942 and returned with the news that An Dóiteán had married again—a schoolteacher called Wilkie, Miss Imogen Wilkie, who had come to Strath school at the age of nineteen the year after Catherine had left for America, and who still taught there. So the new stepmother was a year younger than her stepdaughter.

"And she's not unlike yourself to be looking at, mistress," MacTavish added. "She took a terrible go of the flu last summer, but she's a hell of a hardy. And now she is for being a right bonny one. And An Dóiteán himself is ten years younger, they are saying."

A week after this news Catherine had a letter.

My dear Catherine (if I may so call you, being your stepmother),

Do not be surprised at this. Your father married me last autumn but it was not until your Christmas letter and photographs came that An Dóiteán was getting out the old sea chest where he has all your other letters, going right back to 1919! I have spent the last two weeks reading and rereading them until I think I know your life as well as he (and he can quote every letter as if it were Scripture, and give the year!).

And then I asked him would he reply or I, and what sort of news did he usually send you? And only then did he tell me he was never replying at all! Not even once! So I told him I thought that was a terrible thing, and how good you were to go on writing like that and never be hearing a word from him. And how you must have missed all the news of your home and your own people.

But where to begin? With your home, of course. Your father is in bonny health. No one will believe he is sixty-two this year. His life is little altered from when you shared it, except, I suppose, a few more comforts around the house. The yard is drained, so the dirt is not walked so much indoors. There is talk of the electric but he says he will not have it. I miss it less than I believed I would, so we will see. No one here has it yet but they brought it halfway from Strath for the new knitting factory and Angus Pine's joinery, which is now his son's, young Angus that was at school with you. It would be little cost, they are saying, to bring it on to every house. But such matters are not quickly settled here on Beinn Uidhe, it will put no surprise on you to read.

Bando and Ewan the Graves died this five years. Young Peigi has the old place but she does little good with it. Your father and I would be keen to buy her away.

There were three ministers since your time, the Rev. Gunn, the Rev. MacCullough, and the present one, Rev. Sandy Bain. He has a "guid pulpit souch," as they say, but your father and I have our private doubts as to the soundness of his theology. He is a weathercock who will blow one day to the cold blasts of fundamentalism from Loch-na-Beiste (which always was primitive in its purity) and next day will almost ask the Lord to wait outside while he delivers the Kirk's social message to the Youth Club and the Factory Social Institute. What will be the next of it!

A few weeks ago he spoke on the matter of religious hysteria but, when your father pressed him on the business of the Pentecost and the Apostle of the Gentiles, he swung right about and said that the tradition and theology and practise and discipline and ethos of our Church (he is something of a lawyer, you see, and covers every approach) can accommodate the subjective and even the imaginary experience of the Lord. But we are not satisfied! He is also weak with those who take strong liquor.

These four years that went past have seen an increase in our population, after many decades of decline. Well you did to leave in 1919. Your father was many years in admitting it, but I knew it in 1921, when almost every single and able young man in Strath who did not die in the Great War was leaving on an emigrant train to Glasgow. A black day it was. I thought all my chance of marriage went with them that hour. And for most of my life this was a town of old men, and old maids of all ages. But the Lord has dealt mercifully with me at last.

Only young Angus Pine and Oh-Kay Macaulay are here from the young men with whom you were at school. Oh-Kay is these many years a ghillie for His Grace of Sutherland. And Huey MacLintock failed in the depression in 1930 and his wife died of T.B. (his cousin, I think she was). They were near you in Canada, so perhaps you already know this. He came back here and was found drowned one morning by your father. It was in the burn on the far side, beneath the overhang of the rock where there is a waterfall.

So now you have all our small change. I know the travel is not easy in these days, but if you can come here to see us it would give me, but more important to you I'm sure, it would give An Dóiteán, such pleasure. Long ago he forgave you. More recently he forgave himself. It was the harder luxury for him to endure, but he has survived it well. Please come if you can. After your many fine letters you will be no stranger to us, and I, I'm sure, would soon be none to you. There is the telephone at Pine's Joinery. The number would be Strath 3.

Yours sincerely, Imogen Hamilton

She had underlined her first name. Catherine replied at once to say she would love to come as soon as she got the chance but, the war being what it was, she couldn't say when that might be. Meanwhile she'd start writing more often than her previous once or twice a year. Strath was in a restricted area of the Highlands, but she was sure she'd get a permit easily enough.

She liked the sound of Imogen, an upright, God-fearing skeptic with a quiet drought in her humour. "It was the harder luxury for him to endure . . ." Well she knew An Dóiteán! How much was merely hinted at in this letter—how much more could be discovered only face to face? As soon as the war permitted, Catherine would go back to Beinn Uidhe and find out.

One fact alone revealed in the letter filled her with disquiet and diminished her general desire to go back. It was the finding of Huey MacLintock's body in the burn. Drowned. As if that business nearly twenty-five years ago had been unfinished business. Drowned at the very place where she used to bathe to avoid An Dóiteán's spying eyes. Drowned where Huey had kissed her for the first and only time, and herself wet beneath her clothes, which stuck to her skin and might as well not have been there (how well she understood now what had so baffled her then). Drowned where An Dóiteán had burst Huey's head open and held him below the waters until the life almost left him. No one had shouted. She had not screamed. Death was in silent harness with the waters, and her grim father held the reins.

She remembered how she had climbed the overhang, slithering in the cold burn, until she was poised right above his head. There she had launched herself at him, lithe as a panther and as strange to mercy. She tasted her father's blood where she bit, saw it mingle with Huey's in the rushing water. Then she waited to be killed herself.

Instead he turned, while Huey was nudged away by the flow and beached on the pebbles, where he floundered and crawled off into the heather. An Dóiteán turned and, trembling like his own anemic cows in spring, eased her from him and held her to him and caressed her with his great, deadly, loving hands, and wept upon her with bewildered anger; the riptide of his passions had swept him far from his familiar coastline, whose barren mountains rose beyond the treacherous reefs of God fear.

All that spring and early summer the unanswered—and perhaps unanswerable—questions hung over her, adding to her general unease. At last she decided she must go and face it. Face him. She arranged to visit Beinn Uidhe immediately after the children's summer exeat at the end of May. The permit was granted. The ticket was bought, the sleeper booked. It was done.

She looked forward to the exeats more than the holidays. They were too short for the children to become quarrelsome. The business of growing up, too, was reducing their tendency to fight among one another. Kelvin, now over sixteen and a "junior option" at school (the junior grade of boys allowed to wear blue ties and order the black-tied boys around), was too grand to compete with Grant, now rising ten. He became a tolerant, lordly lion to Grant, whom he treated as a playful cub. Madeleine, now almost thirteen, began to draw apart from them. She was more likely to be found with the two women, salvaging sheets or shirts by sewing on patches, polishing the glorious old rosewood and mahogany furniture with which her mother was slowly refilling the house, dusting the chicken shed against red mite, carrying water out to Jessica, or rescuing Timoshenko.

Timoshenko had needed rescuing ever since he discovered bitches. He could smell a bitch in season five miles against the wind. At such moments his eyes developed a monomaniac glaze. He lost control of his lower jaw, which went into a shaky kind of rigor. And he whimpered without mercy until he was let out for his share. The trouble was that his particular ancestral mix of spaniel and sausage dog was typecast for a comic rather than a romantic role; he was Larry, or Curly, or Moe, desperate to play Rhett Butler. Catherine had once seen a bitch cross the water meadow below the house, in the usual way of bitches, sniffing furiously at every thistle and dandelion, utterly (or seemingly) oblivious of the tail-wagging, hard-breathing, tongue-dripping pack just two yards behind her. Not a mongrel among them could have pawned his pedigree for twopence, yet they turned

on poor Timmo as if he were the Wandering Jew with the plague. They
didn't offer him the dignity of a stand-up fight but simply nipped him and
scraped grass divots at him. He retired, a mass of punctures and blood scabs.
Yet, for that missing Clark Gable touch he substituted sheer persistence—
not for nothing do we say "dogged." By evening he had enjoyed his share,
and at greater leisure than his hasty predecessors, whose excitement often
betrayed them into having one another rather than wait out their turn.

Time and again Timoshenko would crawl up the lane in the last stages
of mortal exhaustion, looking as if only two months of intensive nursing
could save him. Two hours later he'd be limping off again, harried over the
fields by that genital tyranny. Sometimes he would lose the scent, or be
nipped and pissed on by other dogs beyond even his capacity for humiliation: then he would merely sit and howl until the police or a neighbour telephoned Gideons to say "that creature of yours is at it again." Then one of
the women, or Madeleine if she was home, would have to cycle in to
wherever it was and bring him back in the handlebar basket, baring one
fang in a haggard, idiot grin.

And his persistence paid off. A satisfying (from his point of view if
from nobody else's) number of puppies in the area began to show that
same idiot grin, those same ludicrous ears, that characteristic brindle colouring, and the body whose length seemed to have strayed beyond design
limits.

On the last afternoon of that summer exeat, Catherine and Nono were
working among their bees. Nono's new baby, called Ian after his father,
was asleep in his pram just inside the orchard gate. Catherine thought that
Madeleine was down in the village, collecting Timoshenko from yet another escapade; she also thought Grant was indoors taking an old wireless
set to pieces, while Kelvin was up in Gideon's Wood, shooting gray squirrels.

In fact, Madeleine had told Grant she thought Kelvin had gone up
there to meet Thelma Perry—and wouldn't it be fun to spy on them? The
pair of youngsters had crept up the hill, out of sight, on the far side of the
hedge that marked off the four acres. When they drew close to Kelvin,
Grant had slipped off his shoes and, in his gray school socks, had begun to
stalk his brother the way Cherokee had shown him only a month ago.

The first Catherine knew of this was when Maddy came screaming out
of the wood and ran full pelt down the field. She was halfway, and still
screeching, when Kelvin appeared at the edge of the trees and shouted.
The words were indistinct but there was no mistaking their urgency. Madeleine stopped, breathless.

Catherine turned to Nono. "Go and telephone the air station," she said.
"Tell them to send an ambulance and a doctor. Quickly."

It had to be something to do with the shooting. She had heard the bang, and had simply taken it to mark the death of a gray squirrel. She wanted to run up the hill at once, but she forced herself to think. What would she need? Gunshot wound? She prayed it was "only" a wound. Tourniquet. It was all that occurred to her. Tourniquet. She had on a head scarf. That would do for one. And there was an old woollen scarf in the cowshed. She ran and collected it on her way to the field gate. Crossing the yard she scooped up half a dozen kindling sticks chopped and left there by Grant just before lunch.

"Pick them up and bring them in. Don't just leave them lying there," she had said to him three times.

Would his disobedience now be the saving of his life? With all her heart she hoped it was nowhere near so serious.

Halfway up the hill she had to stop and draw breath. Maddy hurtled into her arms, howling and shivering with terror. "What is it?" she asked the child. She couldn't answer; only a strangled gurgle emerged from her throat. She howled again. Catherine, her breath recovered slightly, made to go on but Maddy gripped fiercely. "I must go, darling. Come with me?" She shook her head vehemently. "Then go on down to Nono. Do as I say now." Not too reluctantly, but still crying, the child ran down the hill.

Kelvin had gone back into the wood. He returned just as she gained the edge of the trees.

"What is it?" she gasped, breathless again. "Is it bad?"

"I thought he was a squirrel. All I saw was a bit of gray."

"Is it bad?"

They were running side by side.

"It looks awful."

Even at the time she was astonished at their coolness. For all the things people would have done in the movies—screamed, wept, hugged each other, said, "There, darling, don't crucify yourself"—there simply was not time.

Catherine almost did break down when she saw Grant, lying motionless and covered in blood in the undergrowth. He looked dead. But a quick check showed that he was breathing still, rapidly and not very deeply, but breathing. Mercifully he was deeply unconscious, probably because he had lost so much blood.

A tourniquet applied ten minutes earlier would have saved a great deal. The buckshot had taken him in his right leg, mainly the foot, which was just a pulp of gray wool and blood. An unlucky pellet, or several, had punctured the femoral artery—the limb's main vessel—just at the point where it turns from the front toward the back of the thigh. Two large veins were ruptured in the same region. That was where most of the blood loss had occurred. By now the ruptured artery had gone into spasm and very little more blood was escaping. But any attempt to move him might open it up again.

"We've got to try and get him down to the house," she said. "I've already sent for the ambulance."

"Piggyback?" Kelvin offered.

"No. We'll make up a stretcher. D'you know anywhere where there are saplings? Ready cut? Has anyone been cutting saplings? About five feet long? Five or six feet?"

"There's some iron pipes by the old water tower—the salvage they never collected."

"Go get a couple. And bring some blankets, too. You remember where the spare key is hidden?"

"He's not going to die, is he, Mummy? He's going to be all right?"

"He won't die, dear. It isn't nearly as bad as it looks." She wished it were true.

When he had gone, she knelt beside Grant and twisted the scarf around his thigh, using the heel of his discarded shoe to make the pressure point. When it was tight, she eased his jacket off him. It would be needed for the stretcher. He was so loose-limbed and vulnerable. She took off her own jacket as Kelvin came running back with two iron pipes and the blankets. She pushed the pipes through the sleeves of her jacket, then of Grant's. Kelvin, seeing what she was at, took off his own and added it to the others. They laid the makeshift stretcher beside him and put a blanket upon it before they eased him over on top.

Catherine checked the tourniquet and folded the spare half of the first blanket over him. They put the second blanket on top.

"Gentleness is more important now than speed, darling," she told Kelvin. "We'll carry him down quietly and steadily. You lead."

As they emerged into the field they could hear the distant, urgent ringing of the ambulance bell.

"I can still see the squirrel I thought it was," Kelvin said over his shoulder. "I'd still swear it was a squirrel."

"Save your breath, dear. You mustn't reproach yourself. That would be silly. It would be like saying you meant to do it."

"I'd give anything for it to be lunchtime again."

"I know. I know that feeling so well."

She had to give him something to do. The ambulance was bouncing up the lane as they came into the yard.

"I'll go to the station hospital with him," she told Kelvin. "You get on the telephone to the Air Ministry in London and keep pestering until they put you on to Daddy. Tell any lie you like. You can even say Grant may be dying as long as you get through to him. Then tell him what's happened and where we are. All right?"

"You're pretty marvellous, Mummy. I was so scared I almost—"

"We'll talk later, darling. You stay here by the phone, okay?"

"Okay."

Nono was beckoning the ambulance backward into the yard. The nurse ran past her toward the stretcher.

"He needs plasma, quickly," Catherine said. "Where's the doctor?"

"There's only me." The nurse ran back and banged twice on the ambulance side. It stopped at once. She opened the door. The driver ran to relieve Catherine. "No," she shouted. "Take the boy's end." Kelvin transferred his grips and ran into the house.

Catherine caught sight of Madeleine's chalk-white face at the kitchen window. She put on a cheerful smile for the child. "It's all right, darling. It's going to be all right."

Madeleine smiled wanly back. Despite everything, Catherine was aware of a fleeting disappointment that passed across Maddy's face. Aside from her anguish something in her had been relishing the drama.

They put the makeshift stretcher directly on the proper one. The driver shut the door and climbed back behind the wheel. They were off again.

Everything for a plasma drip was there, but only a doctor was allowed to use it. Catherine, trained in a more self-reliant nursing tradition, squeezed between the nurse and Grant and, over her protests, set up the drip. She'd answer to Burgo for it, not to anyone in the station's chain of command. The nurse shrugged away all responsibility, lifted the blankets, and checked the tourniquet. "When was that applied?" she asked.

"About ten minutes ago."

"Try easing it off slowly."

"The femoral artery's punctured." She pointed at the spot.

The nurse made a quick decision. "Leave it, then," she said.

At the station no one queried the drip. They took X-rays and began to cool the leg with ice. They now gave blood instead of plasma. They also cut and bathed away the tattered sock, strip by strip. It needed no X-rays to see that the foot inside was fairly shot to bits. Catherine had meanwhile scrubbed up and, gowned and masked, slipped into the theatre, where she arrived just before the X-rays.

The surgeon, a friend of theirs called Freddy Colère, snapped them up, still wet, onto the screens. But he hardly looked at them. He hardly needed to, for they simply confirmed what everyone could see—that the foot was smashed beyond surgical repair, that the lower leg was touch and go, but that the thigh, except for the fairly shallow wound that had severed those blood vessels, had only two or three pellets, lightly imbedded.

"We'll have to amputate," the surgeon said. "Either at the ankle—if we can find it—or just below the knee. How's the blood pressure?"

"Responding," a colleague said.

"We'll need consent. Is Mrs. Macrae still outside?"

"I'm here, Mr. Colère," Catherine said at his elbow. Everyone spun round to look at her. "And I'm afraid I can't give my—"

"How dare you!" the surgeon shouted. "How dare you come in here?"

"I'll leave if you wish, sir," she said quietly. "There's nothing I can do at the moment. I wanted to be here if the patient regained consciousness." She deliberately used the impersonal language of the ward diary.

Immediately the surgeon felt the implication—that he was the only one around here who was behaving emotionally. "I'm sorry, Cath," he said. "But we must amputate. Surely you can see that?" He gestured at the X-rays.

There was a knock at the door. Through the circular window could be seen the head of an orderly, unsterile. The theatre sister went and pushed the door open a crack. The orderly muttered briefly and left. "Group Captain Macrae is on his way here from London," the sister repeated.

Catherine almost collapsed with relief. The decision would not be hers. "He'll be here in an hour, Freddie," she said. "You'd never forgive Sandra if she gave such a consent when you were only an hour away—would you."

"We could borrow a bit of vein and patch up this artery," the other doctor said. Catherine couldn't recognize him.

Colère came to the decision. "We'll do it under a local," he told them. "If he comes around, we'll give him some morphine. What's the blood pressure?"

"Hundred over seventy. Still improving. He's had the best part of two pints, including plasma."

"Poor little chap," Colère said. It was a test. He watched Catherine closely. "Okay, Cath," he went on more briskly. "Stay by him. I suppose you'd only go quietly mad out there. Check his breathing and pulse. Watch his eyes."

At that moment she loved Freddy Colère.

It was "minor surgery" by the book, but the anastomosing of a smallish artery buried in muscle and sinew, traumatically ruptured, and in spasm is a ticklish job—especially when the finished "embroidery" has to be leak-proof against a full arterial pressure. Colère and his unknown colleague worked with a skill born of too many recent emergencies.

"He's all right for antitetanus?" the doctor asked.

Catherine nodded. "He had one last autumn."

"We'll boost it. No harm."

"Has he ever had penicillin? Hardly." Colère asked and answered the question.

"No."

"Well, we'll start giving it as soon as this is patched."

The sister nodded and went to the theatre medicines cabinet.

Grant began to stir just as the last few stitches were being made. They decided not to give him morphine until he showed signs of actual pain. But he still was unconscious by the time Burgo arrived. Before that they had removed every pellet in the thigh and lower leg.

Burgo came into the theatre scrubbed and gowned. The doctor in him outgunned the father—that is, he looked at the X-rays before he looked at Grant himself. His eyes briefly dwelled in Catherine's; she saw them soften and knew exactly the tight, grim smile he was making behind his mask. He asked a barrage of questions that brought him up to date on Grant's condition and the treatment he had received.

When he looked at the broken-up foot, Freddy Colère said, "We have to amputate, sir. As you can see."

Burgo turned again to Grant's foot, pinched the toes, watched how long it took the dimples to fill out again. "There's just a chance," he said, more to himself than the others.

Colère drew breath to speak, but Burgo ignored him. Catherine had never seen him in a professional setting like this; he radiated authority without seeming to try. She was more glad at that moment than she had been for years that she had married him and no other. "Cath," he said, "go home. Now. Go and pack for yourself and Grant. One change of clothes and something warm. Furs." More generally he added. "There's one of these new modified B-17s flying from Blackbushe for Gander and Montreal tonight. With about twenty patients for reconstruction. I want him"—he stabbed a finger toward Grant—"among them. Ambulance, driver, doctor, nurse, and room for Mrs. Macrae. There's two doctors on board. Hand over to them. Well, Freddy. Can do? Only got an hour here."

"Wilco, sir," Colère said. They were already bustling as Burgo swept Catherine out. The car took them to Gideons still in theatre overalls and boots. On the way she told him, step by step, all that had happened.

"I think you did marvellously," he said. "If we save this foot, it'll be largely because of the way you acted so promptly."

"We will save it, won't we, darling?"

She saw his eyes assessing her, dashing every hope. "I'm afraid the chances are very small, love. But away from Goldeneye, none at all. His only hope is there, with Dad and Jay and their team." He bit his lip and then said carefully, "You could be away a year, you know? It could take six or seven operations. Spread over that long."

Panic seized her. She hadn't thought of that. She wouldn't have time to say a proper goodbye to Maddy—and poor Kelvin. And the whole house would just have to be left to Nono. She'd never cope, not with the baby as well. Who else could help? Would Fiona come over? That's what grandmothers were for—crises like this. Or could she possibly ask Imogen, whom she hadn't even met? It was only for the school holidays, really. Perhaps she could come back for those? Beg a lift on one of Meg's or Cherokee's flights? She knew that wartime rides over the Atlantic weren't exactly dished out like bubble gum, but perhaps Burgo could pull a few strings? It was only two months to the start of the long summer hols.

Oh, that split-second of miscalculation in Gideon's Wood! It was going to change all their lives. None of them would ever get back to where they might have been if it had never happened.

"Can you stay tonight, Burgo? Stay, and take Maddy and poor Kelvin back? We must—"

"Of course, honey. Of course I will. I'll see Bevis and Maybrace. Explain everything. They must keep an eye on Kelvin. And you—you write to him often. And as optimistically as ever you can."

"There he is now."

Kelvin was waiting at the foot of the lane. Catherine jumped out of the car, which went on up to the house with Burgo. He had some urgent telephoning to do.

"Well?" Kelvin asked her.

"They were going to amputate his foot but Daddy said no. I'm going to take him over to Canada, to Granddad and Uncle Jay. They'll be able to save it. Isn't that marevellous?" She linked her arm in his.

"When?"

"Now. I'm leaving now, darling. As soon as I can pack. Daddy's wonderful. He can arrange anything."

"I want to come, too. Can he arrange that?"

"Oh, darling—you can't. It's an R.A.F. plane. Daddy's having to pull every string he can just to get *me* on board, too."

"I don't want to go back to Bedford."

"Why not?"

He didn't answer. Raindrops began to patter on the overgrown hedge-row around them; she hadn't even noticed how the sky had clouded over.

"You're so happy there."

"I was."

"But this won't have changed that. You mustn't let it." She squeezed his arm. "It's done, Kelvin honey. It's done. And those people at Goldeneye are going to undo it. There's nothing you can say or think or feel is going to change it. What you must do—"

"Not even pray?" he interrupted.

She was nonplussed for a moment. "Well, of course, that goes without saying."

"Hm."

"What d'you mean 'Hm'?"

"It usually does, these days—go without saying."

"What you must do is go back to Bedford and do everything even better—school, games, everything."

"Officer Training Corps?"

"No one doubts you're feeling awful. Everyone'll know it's probably even harder for you than for your brother—gorging himself on ice cream and popcorn and steak and all that California fruit. You're going to have the hard time. You've just got to show what the Macraes are made of. You've got to rise above it."

"I'm never going to shoot a gun again. Not even on a range at targets."

"You know what they do to a pilot after a crash?"

"Send him straight up again. But . . ."

"Exactly. For your own sake you ought to go right back there and kill yourself a gray squirrel."

Again he was silent.

"Won't you do that?"

He pursed his lips and shook his head.

She sighed. "I can't force you."

At the gate he turned silently and threw his arms around her. "I'm sorry," he whimpered. "I'm sorry."

"I know, dear. Today is the worst day. Each day from now on it won't be so bad. You'll see."

Nono was marvellous. She'd manage everything, she said. Mrs. wasn't to worry. The vicar would arrange for extra help out of doors; she'd cope with the rest.

Her farewells to them all were painfully brief—though in their present misery, she realized, brevity was a mercy. Before the hour was up, she and Burgo were back at the station watching a now conscious Grant being lifted into the ambulance for the two-hour drive to the airfield. Their farewells, being public, were very stiff-upper-lip. Burgo called her "old girl" and told her to be good; she told him to look after himself. They both felt the most dreadful fakes, and had to say everything they really meant with their eyes. Their farewell kiss would have passed any censorship board in the world.

Thirty-six hours later she and Grant were in Goldeneye.

PART FIVE

1942-1945

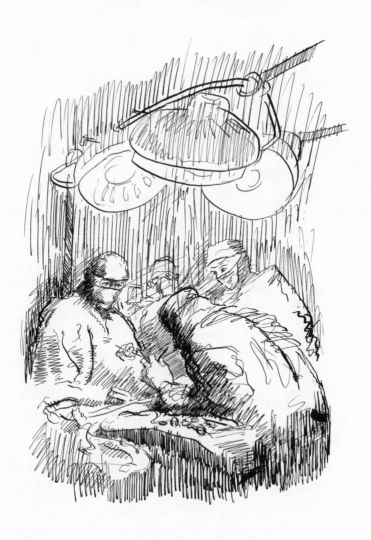

37

The summer was well advanced before Jay could be sure that the reconstruction schedule for Grant's foot was working. The bones below the ankle would never be much more than a fused mass, and the ankle itself would possess only a small degree of movement, depending on how well the reconstruction went. The important part was not the downward, or "tiptoe," movement, but its opposite, which lifts the ball of the foot clear of the ground when the leg swings forward. Grant would always walk with a limp. If they couldn't restore that facility for upward movement, he would have an ungainly and tiring limp into the bargain.

Grant was a little hero about it. A lot of the time, especially after each operation, he was in considerable pain. They explained to him about the dangers of morphine addiction and he kept off all pills until the pain went beyond his limits of endurance.

The real family problem was back there in England, with Kelvin. The optimism in Catherine's letters did nothing to lighten the darkness that had settled on his spirit. At first everyone had thought he was just depressed—and understandably so; they thought, too, that his self-accusation and bitterness would soon pass. So more than a month went by before his masters and fellows realised that a permanent change had come over Kelvin.

He refused to put on his O.T.C. uniform and said he wanted to be registered as a conscientious objector; there were a few such in the school, even at the height of the war. They were put in the "Pioneer Corps"—a civilian band disguised under a military title, as a sop, no doubt, to the generals and brigadiers whose names spattered the Old Boys' register. And while the rest of the Upper School drilled and studied for the War Office "Certificate A" (which would later excuse them the first six weeks of basic military training and let them leapfrog over all the state schoolboys who joined the colours), the Pioneers swept up leaves, rolled the cricket pitches, carried duckboards, laid cinder paths, painted the pavilion, weeded the gravel, and did all the other menial work that was fitting to their degraded status.

Burgo was naturally furious when he heard of it. He went roaring up to the school and shouted at his dumbly defiant son until even the most blimpish and chauvinistic of his fellows felt a touch of sympathy. Mr. Bevis was more understanding, though no less firm. He spent many evening hours wrestling with Kelvin's doubts and scruples. When he failed, Mr. Maybrace took over. Kelvin spent three successive Sunday afternoons at the Chief's own house, but his conscientious objections were only strengthened, being tempered by so many strong and heated challenges.

In the end, because Burgo absolutely refused to sign the papers that would have made Kelvin's objections acceptable to the school, he was, technically and in fact, in plain defiance of school rules by refusing to put on his uniform. Normally he would have been stripped of his blue tie and returned to the ranks of the untouchables. But, quite coincidentally, something happened that made such a move by the school authorities impossible; they had a face to save, too.

The Head of the School at that time was a boy called Groves. Kelvin greatly admired him. One Saturday, after end-of-week assembly, Groves whisked him off to the Head of the School's room and began talking about the slackness that had crept into school life lately and the need for a general bracing up all round. There were rumours of smoking in the park, and of boys going to the motion pictures at the cinemas in the town. Others were even drinking in public houses, it was said, and placing bets with bookies' runners. Then Groves pounced: "You must know several people who are breaking the rules in this way, Macrae. I want their names."

Kelvin stalled, but to no good. It was his duty—distasteful and unpleasant though it might be—to report those he knew. All the imperatives of schoolboy loyalty were the other way, of course. Many of these lawbreakers were, or had been until recently, his friends. Two were school monitors. One was the head of his own house. Another was a dayboy called Tree whose parents lived only a few hundred yards from the school; often he had been there for afternoon tea. He was keen on Tree's sister. The ramifications were endless, the clash of loyalties fierce.

In the end, because Groves was who he was (and Kelvin was who *he* was), there was no contest; friendship yielded to duty. Later Kelvin was horrified to find that, instead of roping in, say, twenty Junior Options and getting them all to inform, or at least to confirm previous information, Groves had asked only two—himself and a boy called Singh. They therefore carried the full odium of the informer.

And there was, of course, a fearful stink. Blue ties and brown shoes were whipped back off boys like live rounds after a day on the firing range. Worst of all, three of the four house monitors at Burnaby lost their rank— and the private study that went with it. Among the three boys promoted in their stead was Kelvin himself! He tried to refuse it. He tried to resign his blue tie. But there simply was no mechanism to allow that.

Soon people began to say he had turned informer not out of his much flaunted conscience—his oh-so-wonderful conscience—but to keep the position of Junior Option, which his refusal to wear O.T.C. uniform would otherwise have caused the powers-that-be to strip from him. But now, how could they take the blue tie away from someone who had done such splendid dirty work for them?

The Chief (for it was, of course, his decision at the last) was in a dilemma. Fortunately, the summer holidays intervened. The ten-week break might bring many changes. So nothing was done.

Kelvin and Maddy spent a lot of that summer at Beinn Uidhe. As soon as Imogen heard of Grant's accident she had written to Catherine suggesting the arrangement, not only for this but for every holiday until Catherine and Grant returned to England.

But Catherine was disturbed when, in August, she had a letter from Imogen, who was obviously torn between, on the one hand, not wanting to distress Catherine in circumstances where Catherine was unable to come over and sort matters out and, on the other, keeping silent and thereby letting a tragedy build up beyond any possibility of sorting out.

In a nutshell, Kelvin had got himself into a dangerous mood—one in which he actually seemed to welcome martyrdom. "There is something about him that cannot wait to get back to school, where he can take up his self-imposed punishment once again," Imogen wrote.

She took him on long walks, over the rocks, up and down the foreshore, or away through the heather. Many times they rowed around the bays, setting and lifting the lobster creels. Slowly she had got him to admit just the faintest possibility that he might actually be welcoming all this misery as a punishment for what he had done to Grant. But he still claimed, most vigorously, that his abhorrence of war and killing was not solely due to his having accidentally shot his brother; he had been feeling that way for a long time. In fact, it had begun to dawn on him back in 1940, when the *Empress of Britain* and the *City of Benares,* both laden with hundreds of children being evacuated to Canada, were torpedoed by U-boats and sank with few survivors.

"I told him," Imogen wrote, "that if he was sincere in his objections to war, he ought to be asking you and his father to send him to a Quaker school. He had heard of Quakers, of course, but did not know they are all conscientious objectors, nor that they have schools of their own. I said, 'Well, now you *do* know. And if you persist in wanting to go back to Bedford, *we* will know it's more because you want to be a martyr than anything else.' I hope I did right, Catherine, dear. It seemed to me that he was in a most dangerous state of mind, and might go back to Bedford and do *anything*. I'm afraid for it.

"I'm afraid, too, that the Group Captain is in no mood for reasoned discussion. I have tried, but the telephone nearly fused! Perhaps Mr. Bevis or Mr. Maybrace? They seem good, sensible men from all Kelvin tells us. An Dóiteán is no help, of course. 'The boy must abide by his principles,' is all he says. 'He must go back and face them that persecute him.' But what else would he be saying—the man that he is?"

Imogen had copied out the full list of Quaker boys' schools from the book in the reference library. "The only one I know anything about (and little enough it is) would be Ackworth School, which is in Yorkshire. One of my boys at Strath was there before. He seems well enough grounded and is willing for the work. But one robin does not make the winter, nor two swallows the spring. I mention all this, Catherine dear, as I think it wiser to be too anxious and be mocked for it than to be too complacent and be my own self-accuser for what might happen."

Even before she had finished reading the letter, Catherine saw that something had to be done at once. For the next two days she tried to get a transatlantic circuit but was constantly elbowed to the back of the line by "essential" traffic much of which was, no doubt, generals and war correspondents filing orders for whisky and nylons. Meg just didn't reply to her Montreal number. In the end, Catherine ran Cherokee to ground and, finding he was taking a Liberator over the next day, got him to promise to relay a message to Burgo first thing.

But it wasn't Burgo who called back. It was Cherokee himself, with the embarrassing news that Burgo was actually in North America at that moment—in Washington, D.C. She spent most of the following day on the phone, calling just about everywhere she could think of and that her apologetic respondents could suggest—the embassies, the War Department, and every air force base within a hundred miles.

She found him by pure fluke. Someone suggested the Walter Reed Hospital. And a surgeon there just happened to have met Burgo at dinner the night before and just happened to remember that he said he was seeing a man who was lobbyist for the ethical drugs industry, but he couldn't remember the man's name.

Then she was shunted around Capitol Hill for a dozen and a half calls before she got the lobbyist's number. She tried it. Yes, Burgo had been there but they'd gone on to some evening meeting. Great reluctance to be more specific. Would his hotel number do?

So she finally got to him after midnight, blessing and cursing Ma Bell. He was far from pleased. And when she recited the day's chronology—to show him how important she had considered it to get in touch—he hit the ceiling.

"Oh, that's just swell, Cath! Now everybody knows where I wasn't today. And I'll bet they're already asking where I was. Gee, when you snarl a thing up, you *really* snarl it up, don't you!"

She swallowed her anger. "I'm calling about Kelvin."

"What about Kelvin?"

"Burgo—if it's not air force business, then what *are* you doing in Washington?"

"Collecting feathers."

"For your cap or your nest?"

"Not so sharp, Cath. What about Kelvin? Except that he's a pain in the ass, which I already know."

"Honey? Have you been drinking?"

"What about Kelvin?" Even at her end it came out as a scream.

"I think I'd better call you tomorrow. I don't think you're in any state to talk right now."

"Fine," he said and hung up.

She was so fuming mad it took her hours to get to sleep. She called him at seven, Washington time, next morning. He had already left the hotel for some appointment but they expected him back that evening. She left a succinct message with the clerk, which she also backed up with a cable: FIX FOR ME TO RETURN ENGLAND SOONEST.

He must have called in to see if he had any messages, because at ten that morning he was through to her. "What's all this about going to England, Cath?" he asked at once. "Is this what you were fretting over last night?"

She wanted to say, "Oh, you can remember last night, can you?" but she counted down her anger.

"Cath? Are you there, honey?"

"I'm here. And I want to go to England."

"You got me worried last night, sugar. After you hung up I got a circuit to Scotland, to that woodwork place, Strath three? They're working shifts, thank God. They promised they'd call back—collect, of course—if there was anything the matter with the kids. And so far there's—"

"It's not that, Burgo. There's nothing wrong that way. But I've had a letter from Imogen and she's worried about Kelvin's mind. The state of his mind."

"Kelvin hasn't got a mind. He tipped it all away and filled the space with stubbornness and self-will."

She was so horrified she didn't know what to say.

"I know what Imogen wants. Send him to some other school. You tell her nix. He's going back to Bedford where he'll just have to sweat it out."

"Sweat it out, Burgo? What sort of language is that? We're talking about our son."

"He picked this fight. No one forced him. Well, now he's not going to run away from it. No son of mine is going to—"

"Burgo! What you say may be perfectly true. But I have to talk to him. I have to see for myself. I can't sleep for worry. I must go back to England."

"I wish you wouldn't keep saying that, Cath. There's no need. Take it from me. I wish you'd just . . ." He paused.

"Keep my nose out of it?"

"Sorry, someone handed me a memo here. I haven't much time. I was saying I wish you'd just try to keep calm. I know it's tough, being so far away, being out of things. But Kelvin's going to sleep in the bed he's made. No argument. So—no need for you. Okay? How is Grant? The last X-rays looked really good."

"Burgo—please fix for me to go to England. Please?"

"Oh, the British would just love to work off their obligations to us so lightly! 'We helped your wife back and forth like a Yo-yo, every time one of her darlings sneezed!' Nix, honey. I'm saving it for the big one. Now look, I've just got to go. . . ."

She was so mad she slammed the phone down on him. She tried Meg's number but there was still no reply.

All through lunch Fiona smiled a sour, I-knew-it smile. No one could tell her about men and arrogance and betrayal and folly . . . and *men!* Strangely, if it hadn't been for Fiona, Catherine might really have grown to mistrust and finally to dislike all men.

James watched her toying with her food but said nothing. It was a blistering summer day with a hot wind off the ocean of wheat. Every window in the house and hospital was wide open. Broad sunshades stretched over rustic seats and trestle tables where sat servicemen who were "amputees" and "rehabilitees" to the committees that consigned them here but who became people the moment they arrived. They read paperbacks, listened to the radio, whittled sticks, played poker, sketched, winced at phantom pains, or slept and dreamed of flying again.

Catherine and James walked among them. Every so often James would stop and ask this one or that some question about his recovery—could he do so-and-so? . . . did it hurt? . . . had that clicking noise stopped? And so on.

"Do you know every case?" she asked him when they had passed the final group and were walking beyond the lawn-sprinkled zone into the badlands.

"Every case—and the man behind it. I can look at any one of them and see just where each damaged muscle and tendon finishes—and where we're aiming to get it finally."

"Are you okay? The heat's not too fierce?"

He chuckled. "There's not much left to dry out in this old carcase."

"Oh, James. I should have married you. I should have stayed in love with you. I mean in love *only* with you. Get angry if you like—and I shouldn't say it, I know—but you deserved a loving wife like me. It's Burgo who deserves a wife like Fiona."

He was silent.

"Are you angry?" she asked.

"No. It's true. Could you still sleep with me?"

"Yes!" She hugged him and laughed, to hide her desperation. "Oh, yes! Now if you want. Or anytime."

"Then I'm glad Burgo's not here."

She did not know quite how to take his remark.

Again he chuckled. "You think I'm actually suggesting it? No, I'm glad he's not here because one half of you would arrange for it to happen by sheer accident. Dear me, what a shock! But only after the other half had already arranged for Burgo to accidentally see it."

"Do I hate him so much?" She sighed. "You—you must think we're all out-and-out bitches. And who could blame you!"

"It's not worth my energy to deny it. But you're wrong, Catherine."

"Burgo's changed. He's not at all the man I married. All right—so everyone changes. But he's an entirely different person. Losing everything in twenty-nine. That's where it started. He caught business like a disease."

"He always had it."

"No! Not like he does now—and ever since then. Before that he was always just interested. But since then it's become a mania. He'll go three days without sleep to pull off some deal. He'll work and work and work. I've seen him work until he's groggy. Until his nose just bursts out bleeding. And then he'll sleep a few hours, wake up, write something, pace around, cross out all he wrote, write something else, stumble back to bed. He's like a lunatic. He wasn't like that when we got married."

"Oh, but he was," James insisted. "Inside he was."

"Thanks for the warning."

"Would you have heeded it?"

Catherine had to think back. "No," she admitted. After a pause she said, "I wonder what he's doing in Washington? I suspect he's being kicked upstairs."

"How's that?"

"I think the R.A.F. is a bit tired of Burgo." She felt him stiffen. "No—that's too harsh. They're tired of the Emergency Medical Services being run as a private show. And there are some very clever organizers at Air Command who are finding things for Burgo to do in Washington and Tangier and so on—and they quietly take over little bits while he's away."

"Surely he realizes?"

"Sometimes I think he doesn't care, you know. If they took it all away, they'd have to give him something new, and he'd really rather like that. Burgo likes *starting* things. Anything new—except this new business with Kelvin. What d'you think, James? Am I making too much of it? Should I stay here or go back? You've read what Imogen said."

"Is it really important to you?"

"I don't think I can rest until I've seen poor Kelvin and had a talk with him."

James grinned wickedly. "Your husband isn't the only one around here with any influence, you know."

"Can *you* get me back?" She was delighted.

"Back and forth and back and forth . . ."

"Like a Yo-yo!" She laughed.

"I wouldn't put it quite like that."

"Burgo would. How can you do it?"

"You're a practical nurse. You're a V.A.D. We're not ferrying over any more acute cases these days. You're exactly the nurse we're looking for to sit and hold their hands on the long, boring flight over from England. And there's no shortage of planes going the other way."

"I could go back with Meg, or Cherokee!"

"To name but two."

She threw her arms around him. "Oh, James! Dear James—you're such a darling!"

He unpeeled her from his neck. "Steady the Buffs!" he said. "You'll shatter all my resolutions."

She knew exactly what he was talking about. "Anytime," she told him seriously. "I mean it. What I said back there. Just ask. Burgo's not the only one who's changed."

38

Catherine faced the return to Beinn Uidhe with deep misgiving. Yet, as the little Highland Railway train wound its way among mountains and over moors she had not seen for nearly a quarter of a century, the very sight of them impressed on her what that span of years now meant. She and that naive, frightened Catherine Hamilton whose path she was retracing had so little in common.

It was the sort of day on which clear blue skies darken, shed rain, and brighten up once more, a dozen times an hour. A blustery day with shoals of white horses far out to sea. There was either a storm brewing or one just past, for the branch line to Strath was flanked with gulls. As the engine chugged along, each thrust of its piston delivered a nudge in the back; the birds rose, wheeling and screaming, to settle in its wake with a swank and a swagger.

At last the train breasted the final shoulder of land and began its descent to Strath. The little town, nestling scrappily at the very gullet of the bay, with Beinn Uidhe rearing to the south and the long flank of Cragaig tumbling seaward to the north, seemed as it had been in 1919. Only the wireless aerials slung between the chimney pots were new. Then, bit by bit, the eye caught other novelties—a house here, a terrace there, and the Gothick hydroelectric, self-consciously perched halfway up Cragaig. But for these a sad stagnation would have overwhelmed the spirit. Her last glimpse of the bay before the train pulled into the maw of the station showed the Gunn brothers' trawler nosing among the rowing boats, taking on board the shellfish and small catches of the line fishermen. What day was it? Wednesday. Yes, Wednesday had always been the Gunns' day. Was An Dóiteán out there, handing up his lobsters and mackerel? She and the town had reversed the role of Rip Van Winkle.

MacAuley's taxi was new, or it had been six years ago. The same James MacAuley whose ponycart had taken her to Strath when she ran away now took her back to Beinn Uidhe in his Morris Cowley. He remembered that day and (knowing of her return as soon as Kate Menzies, the postmistress' daughter, had spread the word) had waited at the station to be sure of the chance to remind her. She had forgotten one thing—the way a Highlander's eyes rummage your clothing and baggage for tags, labels, and other marks of quality: a guide for any scale of fees for all possible services. MacAuley did it now; even his teeth watched her and joined in the audit. If she had answered all his prompts (they were not exactly questions), he would have known her life as well as she by the time they reached the narrow, un-surfaced lane that led through straggling banks of gorse and heather to the croft.

Several folds of land away she saw Kelvin and Madeleine come a-running. "I will be getting down here," she told MacAuley. He rocked the car back and forth in a six-point turn and left her in a swirl of dust. As if on a cue, a dense, brief shower came to settle it. She stood in the lee of a gorse-bush watching the dry surface suck up the puddles as the heavy leading edge of the shower swept away inland. Moments later the entire shower was half a mile off. The sun was too high to strike a rainbow but it turned the black of the rain to white, making it seem as if a curdled milk was falling slowly to the earth.

"Mummy! Mummy!" Madeleine bolted into her embrace and hugged her fiercely.

Kelvin slowed to uncertainty as soon as he came in sight; he halted a dozen paces away. She reached an arm toward him over Maddy, who was saying, "Oh, you are so lucky to have lived here when you were young. And Grandpa's wizard!"

He shuffled forward, with a wry grin that reminded her at once of Burgo—the same peaked lip and watchful eyes. "Hullo, Mummy. Let me carry that bag."

"Aren't you going to give me a hug?"

He obeyed awkwardly, looking around first. This embarrassment was new, but was not, she felt, to do with his recent trouble; it was simply part of growing up. Sadly—but with a sadness that did not break in upon her smile—she wondered how long it would be before he could once again give her a good, unself-conscious hug.

"Sorry about all this," he said.

"No need," she told him. "The important thing is to make some defi-nite decision."

His pinched lips said he had already done that, but he did not voice the thought.

"Daddy sent a telegram," Madeleine said.

"Shut up," Kelvin cut in. "I was going to tell her."

"What does it say?"

Kelvin put down the bag and fished the telegram from his breast pocket. It read: DECIDE NOTHING UNTIL I ARRIVE THURSDAY.

"What do you think?" he asked.

The words, "It looks as if we're winning," begged to be spoken, but she did not want to set it in the terms of conflict, or not so openly. "We'd better wait and see," she said. Then, spotting the weariness in his face, she quickly added, "We can talk about it by all means."

Down on the foreshore she could see the sheep, grazing the seaweed between the tides. When the waters rose they would retreat to hollows and shallow sand caves in the dunes. How often had she strolled down there under their baleful gaze. When Burgo, then a fledgling lecturer at MacNair, had spoken of the terror of a hundred pairs of eyes, all fixed on him, the image in her mind had not been of students—not of people at all—but of those silent, steam-breathing sheep staring from their sand bunkers at anything that moved. Their wet misery and vile diet had helped to alleviate her life here, just by offering the comparison.

"Is An Dóiteán at home?" she asked. "Your Grandpa?"

"I can speak the Gaelic," Maddy said.

"He was down to send off the lobsters," Kelvin told her.

"Listen: *Ciamar a tha sibh? Is mise Madeleine. Thoir pòg dhom.*"

Catherine laughed. It seemed centuries since she had heard those inflections. "And do they?" she asked.

"Do they what?"

"Give you a kiss. That's what that last sentence said—*Thoir pòg dhom.* 'Give us a kiss.' Didn't you know?"

Maddy blushed; obviously they had told her it meant something else.

She saw him walking up from the low cliff on a path that would intersect hers and the children's at the croft. The red hair was undimmed—and unmistakable; it bobbed among the heather like a challenge.

They were met, a hundred yards out from the house, not by An Dóiteán but by Imogen. Catherine could see at once the similarity MacTavish had mentioned. She had the same height and build as herself, the same colouring, the same neat, determined firmness of gesture. She glanced at her two children, almost guiltily wondering if they had noticed.

"You're gey welcome, Catherine dear," Imogen said.

Such a greeting she herself might have given had she stayed here. She kissed her stepmother's cheek.

"It will put strangeness on you to see it all," Imogen said. "After so many years."

"So little has changed."

"And why should it!"

Catherine laughed. "Aye—why indeed."

Madeleine caught the new-old halfway inflexions in her mother's voice. "Did you use to talk like Imogen, Mummy?" she asked, fascinated.

Catherine raised her eyebrows.

"I'll not be called Grannie," Imogen explained. ("By children of a woman older than I," she might have added.)

Catherine turned to her daughter. "And you, honey, used to talk Big-C Canadian. Believe it or not."

An Dóiteán had made a detour and came on them from behind one of the outbuildings. "Is it yourself, Catherine, *a nighean?*" he asked, stretching forth both hands. Always an impressive figure, he now had the grandeur of an Old Testament prophet.

"Aye, Father," she said. She accepted his embrace and felt the forgiveness in it. He gave a sigh of relief, held her off at arm's length, smiled, tossed his head, and finally released her.

Until this moment she had been afraid; she had feared that if he lost that knot of fierceness, that raging intensity which fired him, he would become a pathetic shambles of a man. She was afraid he had no way of mellowing. Now she saw her fears had been groundless. He had mellowed without softening; the strength remained but the imprisoning rage had gone. His eyes burned as fierce as ever, but they were no longer cruel. Catherine smiled her involuntary congratulations at Imogen, who, with time her ally, had wrought this transformation. Imogen smiled and nodded back. She understood. They all understood. And the half-dozen words that passed between Catherine and her father had little enough to do with it.

"I was away to the Gunns," he said.

"I saw. As the train came into Strath I saw. I knew you would be there." She looked at the buildings around them. "I knew it would all be here. That's a bonny breer upon the corn."

It was a homecoming of which she might have dreamed, but for which she would not have dared to hope. That night, alone, in the dark, straining her ears for every familiar groan of the old house and keening of the winds around it, she caught the rhythmic creak of lovemaking from their room. But Imogen did not cry out in pain, nor sob when it was over. Nor did An Dóiteán fall to his knees in the aftermath, damning his soul and begging God to curse him forever.

Was it strange that none of them had mentioned Kelvin's problem, which was, after all, her reason for being here at this particular time? Burgo's telegram had embargoed the subject for all of them, it seemed.

She slept profoundly.

"Get some work into your hands, girl!"

The gruff voice woke her instantly and transported her back half a lifetime. Then Madeleine laughed and the spell was broken. "Oh, Grandpa, you're so *neat!*" she said.

Catherine relaxed and smiled: An Dóiteán as a tourist object! That was something.

"Take that in to your mother," he commanded. There was the rattle of a teaspoon on china.

"She may not be awake yet."

"It is time."

"I'm awake," Catherine called out.

Madeleine came in with not only the cup of tea but a digestive oatmeal biscuit, too. Behind her was An Dóiteán with a can of hot water.

"The march of civilization!" Catherine said.

"The march of the seasons," Maddy corrected. "It's winter again, see!" She drew back the curtains on a lashing of rain. A dark gray blur of low clouds scurried inland, following the gulls.

"Did you hear the bangs in the night?" Madeleine asked.

"No."

"I thought it was the lifeboat maroons," her father added. "But they say it was a German airplane, laying mines. One of them exploded and he crashed."

"Kelvin's gone down, looking for wreckage," Maddy said.

The silent but inexorable cooling of a can of hot water in a cold bedroom is like an alarm clock that cannot be switched off. In this house to lie in bed five seconds was always a luxury; hot water to wash in was so luxurious as to be quite unheard of. Now they balanced each other out—the more of the first, the less of the second. Eventually the thought of a lukewarm wash dragged her from her bed into the August-winter day.

After breakfast she put on oilskins and went out in search of Kelvin. The constancy of little things pleased her—the random bobbing of the heather and the shivering of the long, pale cliff-top grasses in the pluck of the wind; the exact lie of the rocks and shoals; the point on the path at which two remote and tiny islands came into view from behind the promontory of Cragaig; and the even lower point where, on turning round and looking back, the slopes of Beinn Uidhe and Cadhabeag made a perfect V, with the chimney of the farmhouse at its throat—all these were just as she remembered them.

And the same sheep (or so it seemed) stared in the same incurious way from the same holes along the dunes as she walked toward the point of Beinn Uidhe. Halfway there she saw Kelvin picking his steps over the rocks and sand toward her. He had some shattered piece of an aircraft in his hand. "I'm pretty sure it was a Heinkel," he called out.

When he drew closer she was aware of a strange diffidence in him, a tension. She put it down to a conflict of dignity—the man in him apologizing for this boyish excitement.

"Is there any more there?" She made to go on, toward the headland.

"No." He threw away the scrap and took her arm, turning her back. "Just some oil. It's very blustery. Let's go this way instead."

Over the roar of the wind and sea, amid the drumming of the almost incessant showers on their oilskin hoods, they talked for the best part of an hour. He said nothing that she had not already divined from his letters—and Burgo's and those from the school and from Imogen; but she understood how deep his belief and resolve now went.

"I can't be intellectual about it," he told her. "Anyway, I think a schoolboy intellectual is a bit of a fraud, don't you? All secondhand opinions. I can't give you biblical quotations, or lines taken from great thinkers. All I have is a conviction that to kill is wrong. I couldn't kill a German if he were standing in front of me. So how can I justify to myself any other way of doing it? Dropping bombs or firing torpedoes and so on." His voice wove itself in and out of the wind and rain. "Could you kill anyone?" he asked.

"If it was to save you and Grant and Maddy, or anyone I love."

"I don't believe you could. Not when it came to it. You'd imagine his wife and children, or his parents. You wouldn't be able to. You only think you could. Really you're on my side."

She heard the certainty in his voice and began to dread the arrival of Burgo.

He came that afternoon by the same train as had brought her the previous afternoon—it was, in fact, the only passenger train of the day. The weather had brightened. Sporadic showers swept up the tail of the storm. Catherine and Kelvin set out after lunch to meet Burgo halfway from Strath—Kelvin because he was spoiling for this fight, Catherine because she could settle to nothing until it was done.

They met him in MacAuley's taxi where the road ceased to hug the edge of the bay and turned inland for the croft. He sent MacAuley on with his bag and got out, saying, "Ten o'clock tomorrow, right?" It was redundant. The 10:20 was the only outgoing train of the day.

Kelvin hung back, giving his parents time for a brief, public kiss—the sight of which in his rearview mirror nearly put MacAuley in the ditch. Then father and son shook hands.

"Wild enough the day," Burgo said, scanning the clouds.

"At least the rain has passed," Kelvin answered.

There was no warmth in either part of this exchange—as Burgo showed in his next words: "I guess you're pretty pleased to have gotten us all travelling umpteen thousand miles just to—"

"Burgo!" Catherine cried out in dismay. "If you take that tone—"

"Okay!" He rounded on her. "I'll start on you. I thought I made it pretty clear I didn't want you to come over here."

She smiled sweetly. "I was posted. That's war for you, honey."

He obviously had no idea what she meant. But, sensing he would gain no advantage by pursuing it in front of Kelvin, he dropped the matter and turned again on his son. "Surely you can see . . ." he began.

But she interrupted him. "Burgo—why not begin by asking instead of telling? Ask Kelvin to explain his point of view."

"I know his point of view. I didn't come in on this thing halfway. Like some. I'd even go so far as to say I think his point of view is perfectly reasonable. Let's walk, eh?"

Kelvin and his mother were both puzzled at this last statement as they turned to thread their way, Indian file, along the low cliff that skirted the dunes and rocks of the foreshore. She led. Burgo brought up the rear.

"It's perfectly reasonable," Burgo went on, "to shoot your brother accidentally in the foot and then to take against guns for a while. Anyone can understand that. What isn't reasonable is to prolong that very human reaction and perversely elevate it to the status of a . . . a new morality."

"*Aaargh!*" Kelvin in his frustration made as if to clutch at the sky and pull it down around them. "It has *nothing* to do with Grant. Nothing. Nothing. Nothing! How can I get that *clear?*"

"Not by screaming."

"Okay. Let me just say it, for the hundred-millionth time. My objections to war have nothing to do with what happened up in Gideon's Wood. They—"

"It's just a terrible coincidence!"

"From my point of view it couldn't be more terrible."

"Just *listen* to him, honey," Catherine called back. "Don't keep chipping in like that."

"You agree with him, I suppose."

"Then you suppose wrong. I do not agree with him. But at least I listened."

"For heaven's sake," Kelvin shouted, "don't argue over me. I'd rather . . ." He hesitated.

"What?" his father asked. "Fight? Join up?"

"Yes," Kelvin snapped, but his tone hinted he had been going to say something else.

Burgo smiled. "These celebrated conscientious objections are beginning to sound interesting. Or interestingly flexible."

"It's really very simple, Dad. It's a simple conviction. I could not kill another human being. If I had a gun and you put a German in front of me, I could not kill him."

Burgo chuckled. "You could if he drew a bead on you."

"That's what Curragh says. He's a master. He lost a leg in North Africa. He says it's the only reason men really fight—because they're there and have guns in their hands."

"That's British understatement."

"I just know I couldn't. I'd never be able to stop seeing him as a person."

"A German! A person?"

"Yes!"

Burgo saw it was an unprofitable line and dropped it. "Look, son"—his tone was more conciliatory now—"you're only sixteen, huh? Normally this conscientious objection business wouldn't come up for another two years. Normally you wouldn't get your call-up papers until you were eighteen and a half. It's only because of the Bedford O.T.C. that we're having to consider it now. Right?"

"All right." Kelvin was wary.

"I'll make a bargain with you, son. Are you prepared to bargain?"

"I won't bargain away my convictions."

"And I wouldn't want you to. But also I wouldn't want you to be so stiff-necked, *now,* that you couldn't even admit the possibility that those convictions might change between here and nineteen forty-four. You're not that pig-headed are you?"

"I doubt if they will." He was even more wary now.

"Exactly!" Burgo was triumphant. "Doubt! That's exactly what I'm talking about—doubt. I promise you now that if by the time you're eighteen and a half—when you're due for call-up—if by then you are still of the same mind as you are now, I'll not oppose you."

Catherine turned and stared at him aghast. What hostages he was giving to fortune! Never had she seen Kelvin look more suspicious.

"Better," Burgo added, grinning at the effect of his promise, "I'll back you to the hilt. There now. What d'you say?"

"And meanwhile?"

"Meanwhile? Just don't burn any of your boats. Do nothing irrevocable. Admit there is some doubt. Stay in the O.T.C. Eh?"

Kelvin was silent—and thoughtful. Remembering how passionate he had made his convictions seem that morning, Catherine was astounded he did not at once rage with angry rejection.

"After all," Burgo went on, "what does it mean? Running around the school playing field throwing fireworks at each other and shouting 'Take cover'! What sort of challenge is that to anyone's principles! All I'm asking is that you save it for the real challenge—the real army—the real war."

Still Kelvin was silent. Catherine sensed in him the disappointment of the cheated martyr. He gave a baffled laugh. "It can't be that easy," he said.

Burgo winked triumphantly at Catherine. She turned to their son. "Don't for one moment imagine he's going to leave you alone!" she warned.

He looked at her and then at his father.

"I most surely am not," Burgo confirmed. "I am going to fight for your intelligence, son. No preacher ever rassled over a sinning soul the way I'm going to hold a mission over your—"

"No!" Kelvin suddenly flared up and backed away as if he sensed he were already in some kind of trap. In doing so he led them off the path and down a shelving ledge to the rocks. Below the rim of the cliff they were somewhat sheltered from the wind, for though it was blowing off the sea, the great mass of Beinn Uidhe forced it to rise, leaving a pool of calm where the foot met the waters.

"Oh, but I am." Burgo spoke more quietly now that he didn't need to compete with the roaring of the wind. "You say you can't kill another human being." They leapt from the shelf onto the sand and headed for a nearby bar of rock. Sheep galloped frenziedly away and then stood at a mistrustful distance, panting. "I'm going to show you that no German comes into that category."

"Burgo!" Catherine protested. "That's just un-Christian."

"You think so? You know nothing! The only human German is a traitor or"—he laughed at Kelvin—"a *German* conscientious objector!"

"That's a terrible thing to say," Catherine persisted.

Kelvin took her arm—to calm her, she thought. He walked slightly crabwise, leading them at a diagonal across the beach.

"Terrible?" Burgo asked. "You come and talk to Jules Tisserand, one of our surgeons at Group. One of our best. We got him out of Occupied France before he went mad. Me? I don't know how he's still sane."

"We've all heard atrocity stories, Daddy."

Burgo stared at him awhile. "Oh, but you haven't. You have not. Jules was taken in by the Gestapo, who suspected him of helping the Maquis—rightly, as it happened. They also thought he could lead them to the Maquis hideout—wrongly, as it happened. But that didn't stop them torturing his thirteen-year-old daughter to death before his eyes."

"Burgo!" Catherine cried. She felt Kelvin's clutch on her sleeve. "Don't!"

"The boy must know the choice he's making. He must know what sort of fight his precious conscience won't let him join. He must know what wizard chaps he cannot bring himself to kill. Nine days they took over it, lad. Nine days they burned and skinned and shocked the life out of that thirteen-year-old girl. Think of her as Madeleine, son, because they'd do the same to her. Think of those nine days."

Catherine looked at her boy, expecting to see in his face the horror she knew was showing in hers. Instead she saw a mask of cold malevolence. Burgo was destroying something as precious to Kelvin as this French surgeon's daughter had been to him. "Burgo! Leave it!" she said.

"I'll leave it," Burgo promised grimly. "Just so long as Kelvin understands that sometime in the next two years, when he's got his reasons good and ready, he's going to meet Monsieur Tisserand and tell him why he can't kill the men who did that and—"

"They didn't do it," Kelvin shouted. "Not *all* Germans."

"Any one of them in uniform is fighting to defend those who did. The guilt is not divisible. But don't tell me. Come and tell Jules."

"No!" Kelvin broke from Catherine's steadying grip and ran ahead. She thought he would leap the rock bar but something caught his eye and stopped him dead in his flight. Something on the ground. Something just beyond the outcrop.

"What is it?" she called, beginning to run toward him.

"Stay back," he cried halfheartedly.

Burgo ran, too.

Even before the shape began to register she knew it was the body of the pilot of the aircraft that had crashed last night. He lay beached hard against a straight limb of rock, carried by the storm beyond the reach of the later tide.

Burgo did not hesitate. "German," he said, crouching beside the body and going through the motions of checking for a pulse and an eye reflex; the man had obviously been dead for at least ten hours.

He was blond, in his early thirties. A handsome man with beautifully sculpted features—an Aryan advertisement.

"Bomber pilot," Burgo added, beginning to search the man's pockets.

Something about the flying suit must have marked him off from fighter pilots. The black colour of the waterlogged leather stressed his blondness poignantly.

"Beck. Henrich Beck. Married. Three children." Burgo passed up the man's identity disk and a wallet containing a snapshot, taken in happier days. Catherine looked at the children—orphans as they now were—and felt an impulse to tears. She glanced back at the pilot. His helmet had been pulled diagonally across his head, allowing some of his hair to escape. One blond lock, dried by the wind, shivered in the breeze. Almost alive.

Burgo finished his search of the pockets and rose with a small handful of effects. "We must inform the police," he said.

"Oh, come on, Daddy," Kelvin mocked, "you can do more than that. Let's get in some practice, eh? Why, I'll bet this is the first German in uniform you ever saw. So how's this!"

He lifted his foot and, before either of his parents could stop him, drove the heel of it with full force into that perfect face. Even he was surprised at the crunch it made and the mess it left.

Catherine screamed. Burgo shouted, "Kelvin!"

But Kelvin, after that momentary pause, was shouting "Torturer! Rapist! Swine!" and stamping again and again on the ruined face.

Burgo's fist took him at full swing and left him winded, sitting on the sand, yards away. Burgo knelt beside the corpse as if he could do something to help. Catherine was crying but could not cover her eyes nor take them off her son and her husband.

Between gasps Kelvin said, "I'll see your French surgeon, Daddy—on condition you go and find Frau Beck when this war's over and tell her why I had to do that. Tell her how her husband skinned Maddy. Then I'll leave a letter telling *my* son why the eldest Beck came gunning for me. And who'll tell his son why mine killed *his* Vater? And where do we stop, Daddy? You don't know." He began to get up again. "You want me to avenge the death of your surgeon's daughter? Don't you understand about getting your own back? It never *is* your own. It's always moved on. Don't you see?"

This time Burgo's fist crushed his son's nose. Blood flowed at once.

"Stop it! Stop it! Stop, for God's sake!" Catherine yelled at both of them.

But Kelvin had already stopped. Above the streaming blood, through brimming eyes, he stared at his father in something grotesquely like triumph. "Now we know what was really hiding under all the sweet reason," he said, almost conversationally. "Might is right. Whose side does that put you on, Daddy?"

"Go wash your face," Burgo told him. "Sniff up some seawater. Stem that blood."

"Yes, *sir!*"

"Come on." Catherine tried to sound conciliatory without giving the impression that she approved of anything Kelvin had done.

They went down to the exposed rocks, where the spray off the angry sea struck like rain. There, out of earshot of Burgo, she said, "You knew he was there, didn't you? You found him there this morning."

Kelvin, rinsing his nose, said nothing.

"You steered us here. Deliberately." She almost told him he had planned it to the last syllable and movement, but she could not bear to lay such a thought between them—in case it was, indeed, true.

"You should try being sixteen," Kelvin said.

"What do you mean?"

"Facing him. And people at school. All their arguments. All their confidence."

"But darling—you mustn't meet it with deceit."

He laughed. "That's a very prewar sentiment, you know. We no longer call it deceit. We call it Information, or the real griff, or pukka gen stuff. Total war is total war. And it's total. Everywhere. Pick up any pebble on this beach and you'll find it underneath, playing someone's national anthem."

She sighed. "I don't understand any of this. Why don't you just do what your father asks?"

He smiled so pleasantly she was ready to forget all that had happened— to excuse it as the behaviour of an overwrought boy. "Of course I will," he said. "I've got his promise, now: He'll back me when it counts. He's right about O.T.C. It means nothing. Throwing fireworks and shouting take cover! That just about sums it up! I don't mind doing that." It was a Kelvin she had never seen before.

That was not the last of his surprises for the day—nor the last of the horrors he was ready to inflict. He and Madeleine were sleeping in camp beds in the hayloft. Each evening, after the nine o'clock news, he gave her ten minutes to go over and undress before he followed. This evening he lingered on, listening to his father and grandfather. Around nine thirty, sunset, they lighted a candle. He toyed with the wax, pulling slivers of it from the side and melting them in the flame. This fidgetting annoyed Burgo, who told him to go to bed. Instead of obeying at once Kelvin—in a level, conversational tone—asked: "D'you think I'm maybe a coward, Daddy? D'you think I just don't want to fight? Too scared?"

Burgo, a little taken aback by the easy tone as much as by the thought being voiced, said, "Why, no, son. I don't believe I do."

"It would be a reasonable assumption, though."

An Dóiteán, sitting opposite, nodded agreement and watched his grandson intently. Catherine and Imogen, carrying out the enamel cocoa mugs, caught the merest hint of a shrill edge on Kelvin's voice and paused in the doorway.

"Well, just to prove it," the boy went on. "Just so you can never say it, even if you do think it . . ."

While he spoke he grasped his left wrist firmly in his right hand and laid both elbows on the table, completing an upright triangle with his forearms—all of this with lightning speed. Equally swiftly he swung his open left palm into the candle flame.

It seemed an age. In fact it could only have been a couple of seconds before he began stamping and yelling at the intensity of the pain; yet still he kept his hand there against a reflex jerk like a mule's kick.

Catherine was appalled that neither of the watching men made a move. It was left to her, screaming her son's name, to run back to him and sweep away the candle. Simultaneously she began to rain down ineffectual blows on Burgo's head and shoulders and those of her father. "Damn you, damn you, damn all you *men* . . . !" she shouted.

Imogen put her arms around Catherine from behind and stilled her. The men tolerated rather than accepted this rebuke; even through the intoxication of her own anger and distress she could sense they were excited at Kelvin's self-imposed ordeal. The lad had done something they hoped they would have the courage to do—and equally hoped they would never be brought to test. The spontaneity of it only added to their admiration.

Catherine ran from the house. She could take no more of these male games. Imogen stayed only long enough to find the boracic powder; then she ran after Catherine, carrying her stepdaughter's coat.

The storm had passed, leaving a fine, clear sky with just a few shoals of high cloud. The sun had set but the whole western skyline was a blaze of orange rising up into a deep red, which fell away to purple over Cadha-beag. Catherine was a pale, bobbing shape up on the shoulder of Beinn Uidhe, where the path led around to the burn and the waterfall. Imogen called her name. She stopped and waited for her to catch up.

"You'll need this." Imogen handed over the coat.

"Thanks. I was so boiling mad."

"I noticed!"

They walked on in silence, passing out of sight of the house, over the shoulder and down to the waterfall pool. A dryish summer had reduced it to a trickle; today's rain had done little more than recharge the ground.

"I used to bathe here," Catherine said.

"Bathe?" asked Imogen, for whom the word meant "swim."

"I mean bath. I used to bath here. Soap and water—you know."

Imogen pretended to shiver. "Even in winter?"

"Aye. Even in the snow. I couldn't for the life of me do it now, but it seemed nothing very unusual then."

"You were well sheltered anyway. Was there no bath below?"

"The burn is so clean. I liked its freshness."

"Aye. There's that all right."

They sat side by side on a granite outcrop and watched the pool turn lazily. The stink of violence still hung on the air. Catherine knew that Imogen was thinking of Huey MacLintock's body floating there; she herself was trying not to picture that much earlier violence, the last time she was here at this spot.

"He's your father's grandson," Imogen said. "An Dóiteán is a proud man this night."

"He's Burgo's son, too. They'll both be happy—all *three.*"

"But not you?"

"It's a bad time to ask, Imogen."

Imogen nodded.

Catherine could not leave it there. "This morning, before Burgo arrived, I thought Kelvin was really taking trouble to explain it all to me—all his thoughts. But he wasn't. Not a bit. He was only practising. He was just using me. I think that's all we're for—to be used and then used up." She laughed. "Oh dear! I'm beginning to sound like Fiona, Burgo's mother. I'm sure she's said those words a hundred times."

"You don't suppose you're a wee thing on the hard side, Catherine?"

"Not hard enough. I'll never be hard enough for them. Listen—let me tell you about being hard." She described then what Kelvin had done that afternoon. Imogen was horrified—even more so when Catherine told her that it must have been planned.

"It sounds so unlike Kelvin, or the Kelvin I know," she said.

"And the Kelvin I know, too. But what else can I think? It doesn't matter if he planned it in detail or only vaguely. Both are horrible to contemplate. And suppose he didn't? Suppose it was all spontaneous?"

"That's even more horrible—in a different way."

"They are so . . . *ruthless.* Both of them. And secretive. They tell me nothing. Or only what they absolutely can't avoid telling. I still don't know why Burgo was in Washington last week. And I suppose I never will—unless he wants to cast me for some minor role in his drama. *His* drama, mark you. That's the really awful thing, Imogen. They've destroyed all my trust. You may hear raised voices tonight, because Burgo's leaving again tomorrow and I've got to have certain things clear between us." She stood and walked to the water's edge, looking down at the rippling embers of clouds touched red by the last of the long-vanished sun. "Not that it ever will be clear. That's why I say they've killed all my trust, those two. If Burgo is pleasant and forthcoming, I won't be able to stifle the suspicion it's because he wants me for a new part."

"And if he goes into a rage?"

"Perhaps he's really angry. Or perhaps he's afraid I'm drawing too close to some discovery he'd prefer me not to make."

Imogen laughed softly. "It's no different from your father."

"Oh, it is, Imogen. Pardon me—unless he's greatly changed. He's only like that about himself. His own beliefs and . . . and passions. I wouldn't mind that. I can understand it. I'd call it human. But with Burgo—and now, it seems, with Kelvin, too—it's about business and careers and being top dog and doing the other man in the eye and *winning*. There's no morality in it apart from winning."

"What they call the law of the jungle."

"Aye. But the worse of it is they don't inhabit the jungle. They *are* the jungle."

Imogen touched her arm hesitantly and then withdrew. "Oh, Catherine," she said, bewildered.

"Maybe it's just this awful war," Catherine said more brightly, as a way of turning the conversation. It was not offered as a serious belief.

They went back to their rock seat.

"D'you sometimes wish you'd stayed?" Imogen asked. "D'you wonder what you might be doing now if you had?"

"I'd be a crofter's wife." Catherine laughed. "I'm sure of that. It took a year of being independent in Canada before I realized that life offered *choices!* Until then I was looking for the prairie equivalent of a croft to be a wife on. I hope you teach all your children life has choices. Especially the girls. We're born too willing to give and submit and be used. It's our eyes that need opening."

"There is a theory that the purpose of education is not to fit people for society but to unfit them. It is not looked on with much favour by the Kirk or the people."

"Would it unfit them?"

"To teach them they have choice? Me? In this society?" Imogen gave a laugh whose bitterness surprised Catherine. "You have no idea what it's like to grow into an old maid, have you, Catherine. An unused, unwanted woman. I began with *choice,* as you may call it. Choice ideas of a choice husband. And then for twenty silent, despairing years I watched them wither. In the end there wasn't a wreck of a man for miles I'd not have wed. I'd take anyone. I thought An Dóiteán *was* anyone—until we married and I saw what marvel had happened to me. You don't know what despair is like. Despair that must keep quiet, and go on smiling, and go on being thankful, and give body and spirit to forty children, year upon year. Despair that can never cry its rage nor drink its own oblivion. But you'll maybe understand why I'm not minded to speak of choice to wee girls of fourteen. Not in these parts."

"I'm sorry," Catherine began, not knowing how to amplify.

But Imogen laughed and clasped her arm with genuine warmth. This time there was no hesitation. She did not withdraw her hand. Together they began walking back to the croft. "No need to be sorry," Imogen said. "If you'd come with your grand talk of *choice* last year, before I married your father, I'd have clawed your eyes out. Now . . ." She did not pursue the thought. "Anyway," she went on, "choice is the lesser half of life."

"And the greater half?" Catherine asked, fearing a reheated sermon.

"Relationships," Imogen answered. "Family ties. Friendships. Feuds. Love. Hate. Belonging to a community. Relationships like that. Life can be rich in them too, even when it offers no choice."

Naturally Burgo told her nothing of importance about his trip to Washington—nor about anything else. He even made his evasiveness seem like her fault. "I saw a lot of people who just may one day be useful to us," he said. "But if I add that they were mostly in and around the pharmaceuticals industry—I know you. You'll go leaping at once to the conclusion that I'm getting interested in pharmaceuticals. And then you'll be thinking that's where we'll be after the war."

"And where will we be?"

"I don't know. That's my point. It's all feelers. It's all fluid. It may even be a million miles from medical things. But you hate that sort of uncertainty, Cath. So I try not to share it with you."

"That's not true, Burgo. *You* hate revealing anything until it's too late even to make the smallest change. You always did. I'd actually love to share all the uncertainty. Talk it over with you. Maybe even resolve it with you."

"You *say* that."

"And I mean it."

"Okay, maybe it's me, then. If I spelled it all out to you, explained everything—well, even putting it into words could make it more definite than I want. Possibly it's a defect in me to prefer it as a kind of muddle of maybe-ideas. That's how I work. You know that."

"I know that."

He seemed to have forgotten the words that had puzzled him earlier that afternoon: "I was posted here"—her explanation for being this side of the Atlantic. Later she was sure he hadn't forgotten them. He had displayed his anger as a threat, and then he had left the threat hanging between them—so that if he seemed to forget it, she was supposed to be relieved and not go poking around too much. He was treating her not as a wife but as a tactical problem in his business, a person to be manipulated as he would any other. It hurt. It was the worst kind of rejection.

"You want to make love?" he asked.

"No."

"Okay, honey. Good night."

39

By the following spring Grant's ankle was as good as surgery was ever going to make it—which was not very good. He had just enough movement to lift his toe when walking; but the corresponding action—rising on tiptoe—got locked almost as soon as it started. He had no spring in his stride.

"We could operate again," Jay said. "There's really no end to the amount of fiddling we could do. But let's not kid ourselves—we're never going to restore more than twenty-five percent of function. The sort of minor changes we could achieve now by surgery he could just as easily achieve by adaptation. I'd say that's where we've got to concentrate now."

"Can he go back to England?" Catherine asked.

"Lord, no! Don't breathe a word of this to James, but I'm coming round to the belief that the surgery is the less important half of what we do here. We also try to achieve a proper adaptation to loss of function—partial loss, I mean. The human frame is so infinitely adaptable we have to teach the one right way and suppress several dozen wrong ways. If not, Grant could end up twenty years from now being treated for migraines—when what's really wrong is the tension in his thigh and hip muscles!"

Naturally, Burgo had to be consulted on this decision not to operate further. By now America was in the war in strength. The probing, preliminary bomber raids of 1942 were evolving into massive daylight attacks on targets deep into Germany. Unfortunately there was then no fighter with that sort of range to cover them and though U.S. pilots were highly trained to fly tight formations, and though their planes had powerful 0.50 calibre guns, the losses soon began to mount. Burgo was too deeply involved in air force work to come personally to Goldeneye, even though he made a brief trip to Washington that spring. He called from there.

"What sports, if any, will he be able to follow without disability?" he asked Jay. He had, of course, seen the X-rays and followed each report.

"Swimming," Jay said. "Riding. And he'd have very little disability at golf."

"Tennis?"

"Ah! Well, he could get by. No suburban needle matches, but he'd get by."

"Screwing?"

Jay laughed. "You want to talk to him yourself about that?" he asked.

Burgo laughed too. "Sounds a pretty good schedule to me, Jay. Hey— you know the latest joke, about the difference between a 'skedule' and a 'shedule'?" He pronounced it the American and English ways.

"No?"

"The only difference is that a 'skedule' works."

"I'll just bet you're popular in London."

"All I do there is think them up. I come over here to tell them."

"We often wonder why you come."

His letter formally agreeing to Jay's therapy for Grant came the following week. In it, too, he told Catherine the true reason for his being there. Telling her was a breach of security but he had grown more flexible lately; he trusted her to burn that part of his letter, which was on a separate sheet.

The fact was that the R.A.F., which had had several years' experience of flying sorties over Germany and France, believed there was no way for unescorted bombers to escape destruction except by night. Luftwaffe fighters were just too good. The British Air Command had tried to impress this upon General Arnold, the U.S.A.A.F. chief, through official channels, but Arnold was determined to carry on with daylight missions, because they were far more accurate than the R.A.F.'s night raids. Word came back to Churchill that the R.A.F.'s well-intentioned warnings were simply playing into the hands of those in Washington who wanted to soft-pedal the European half of the war and throw all the muscle they had into the Far East. From then on Churchill flatly vetoed all official warnings about daylight raids by unescorted bomber formations. Let the Americans fight the air war any way they wanted, just as long as they fought it. So now the warnings flowed at all sorts of unofficial and informal levels—"among them," Burgo wrote, "myself. Why me? Because I'm North American and therefore a kind of Trojan horse. Because I'm Medical Branch and therefore have no tactical axe to grind. And because, I guess, the Air Command suspects I'm as devious as *you,* Cath darling, know me to be!"

So the Air Command had found a useful way of kicking him upstairs— and, in the process, had raised him to the rank of air commodore, with a welcome increase in his salary.

Catherine, too, became a regular transatlantic traveller, going east with the deliveries (not always Meg or Cherokee) and returning west with amputees and rehabilitees who were about to become people again. She had hoped in that way to keep in touch with all the scattered elements of her family and home but, inevitably, they remained on the fringes of her life. It was not satisfying, but in the context of the war it was satisfactory. Many women never saw their husbands again; some lost home and family overnight.

The war numbed people. You got used to taking orders. You got used to loss. Someone lost an arm and you cheered him up with a joke. Someone else got blinded, and before you could say how sorry you were, he made a joke about it. Whatever you were doing, however important it seemed to you, there was always a bigger priority out there, above you and beyond your control. In the end, you always submitted. Submission became a virtue. Cheerful, willing submission. You hardly realised you were doing it.

All that summer Grant swam in the creeks and at the rezavoy and rode James's ponies, building up his partly wasted muscle. On his way to the Rockies for a holiday he took part in a small stampede in Alberta, which had a few junior events. There he won nothing but the admiration of those who knew why he limped. He took a bad fall from one of the horses and knocked out both upper front teeth. Jay, who was travelling with him, put the teeth back in their sockets at once and held them fast with plaster of Paris while he got Grant to the dentist, who wired and cemented them properly so that they actually grew back as firm, living teeth.

"He stood there in the dust with the blood streaming down his chin," Jay wrote to Burgo. "I guess he was as close to tears as he ever has been. But if this last year has taught him anything, it's taught him how to accept pain. He leapt back up on that bronco (because his left foot, you know, now has all the spring of both feet combined) and didn't the crowd roar! One man behind me said, 'Hey, that's some kid!' I guess you'd have every right to boast of him, Burgo. He's a fine boy."

This letter arrived while Catherine was in England. She was proud of

Grant, naturally, but the tale also made her feel it was time for the boy to leave Goldeneye and come back to school. There was an attitude out there on the prairies which turned such heroics into the full measure of a man— of manliness. It had its good side, to be sure. But it had its ugly side, too. She had seen supposedly educated men—no: *genuinely* educated men—at MacNair, behaving in a most uncouth and vulgar way because of that concept of manliness.

Of course, it existed in all males and all male societies. Young boys the world over probably grumbled that cleanliness and combed hair and brushed teeth were cissy. But on the prairies, where endurance and bravery and indifference to pain were often essential to survival, those qualities had become especially enshrined. In the wider world it would do Grant no good to become infatuated with them.

He had once told her, with amazement, of the school cross-country run in which great slugs of boys, who you wouldn't think could run a hundred yards, came back from the ten miles of mud and woodland, well down the field, "knackered and absolutely shent." And yet, he said, they were cheered and patted on the back like heroes. Not sarcastically but with real admiration. Just because they *tried*.

It was time to get him back to that school, and that school of *thought,* where playing the game was far more important than winning it.

She got a flight with Meg the first week in August and took Grant straight up to Beinn Uidhe, where Imogen coached him in some of the subjects he had missed. She could do nothing with his Latin, where he was now almost four terms behind; that would need extra coaching back at school. But he was well up again in arithmetic, history, and English by the time he went back.

Kelvin was not in Scotland that summer. The school—like several others in Bedford—was endowed by a fund created in the seventeenth century by Sir William Harpur, who had owned Howbourn fields, now the site of the inner-London district of Holborn. He had left the fields to a charitable educational trust, the Harpur Trust, which now collected the rents of a whole district of London. Part of that endowment went to Bedford School. By way of return, the school's charity was the Holborn Boys' Club for the less privileged boys of the borough. Both Holborn and the club had suffered badly in the blitz. Kelvin and several other boys spent most of that summer making good what damage they could.

The Air Ministry—or Burgo's part of it—was, as it happened, also in Holborn, just two blocks from the club. So father and son got to see quite a bit of each other. Often they strolled across Kingsway of an evening and dined at the Holborn Restaurant, a vast Edwardian establishment housing no fewer than fifteen separate restaurants under its roof, as well as three Masonic temples and numerous private banqueting rooms. Large parts of it were shut for the duration; the rest served what Kelvin said was indistinguishable from school meals. But the atmosphere was something yet again. The improbable survival of this pile of fading grandeur, at the heart of the war-wearying Empire, was in a strange way part of what they were fighting for—or so it seemed to them both.

At other times Kelvin went on long, solitary walks through central London—down to the City and East End, over the river to Waterloo, westward to Soho and the West End, south to Westminster. There was bomb damage everywhere, some of it fresh, for, though the blitz was over there were still frequent raids on London, a few of them heavier than any the city had experienced in 1940 and 1941.

It was an aspect of the war Kelvin had missed in Bedford and the Highlands. Newsreel and newspaper shots of bombed buildings, or even whole streets, could never convey the scale of destruction—not as those walks revealed it. He began to understand how difficult it was to stand aside from modern war. His flight of fancy—that total war was to be found under every stone on the beach at Beinn Uidhe—was, here in London, the sober truth. Every stone that lay in the streets and on the sites of ruins was there because of total war. Where could anyone stand aside from the tornado or the blizzard?

From their conversations Burgo was aware of these changes in Kelvin. He kept expecting the boy to declare that his conscientious objections were at an end, but Kelvin never did. Then he looked at it from the boy's point of view and asked, Why should he? What was to be gained? No decision was needed for at least a year; why declare himself now when silence kept all avenues open? It was an argument he could appreciate—even admire. Kelvin had a businessman's instinct. Even the way he'd managed that face-to-face on the beach at Beinn Uidhe . . . it had been crude and he'd gone way over the top, of course. What he'd done had been unforgivable—except that the idea behind it had been sound. All he needed now was a little finesse, a lot of experience, and all those awkward corners whittled round and smooth. Time would do it. Burgo was well content to wait, now he saw how the lad was shaping. Many a son had been ruined by an overeager father.

It was Catherine who worried him now—and had ever since the start of the war. But the root of it went way back beyond that, back to 1929. The loss of her home then had made her completely irrational on the subject of home-and-family. She would do anything—even self-destructive things, or things that were self-defeating—to protect and preserve them as she imagined it.

For himself, he'd been bored stiff with NCT after five years. His own inclination would have been to sell it off and go into some other business. But he knew how much he owed to her and the children so he had gritted his teeth and stuck it out, until the war changed everything. By then he thought she had calmed down again and was able to take a more reasonable view of "home and family." But no—that terrible demon had driven her to bring the children to England and try to re-create something that the war had made impossible. A moment's thought (if only she were capable of it) would have told her it was impossible.

A wiser husband would have met her at the quayside and sent her right back. But such wisdom must first kill love and then stifle human understanding. He loved her too much and understood her too well to have done such a thing. Even so, she blamed him for having to send the children away and for marooning her between school and airfield.

She also said he didn't confide in her or discuss things. Instead, she complained, he tried to humour her and manipulate her. But how could he do what she wanted? She measured everything by that one yardstick: home-and-family. In most people's lives, home-and-family was just one element among many; it had to learn to be flexible—give and take, like everything else. Like one child in a big family. But for Cath it was an only child. A sacred thing. Everything else had to yield to it, adapt to it, serve it.

So he was in a fix. Either he accepted her completely unbalanced viewpoint and applied it to his own life—come bankruptcy, come padded cell—or he quietly and unaggressively went his own way and hoped to nudge her gently into following him. It was no grand strategy but it was the only way forward that he could see. He must be getting better at it, though. She was a lot easier to nudge these days. And much less complaining. Perhaps as the children got older, she'd relax and begin to understand that life was meant to be something more than a domestic obsession.

Still, she was owed a favour or two. Not by him. It wasn't his fault the war had messed her life up so much. But he was her husband, and he loved her dearly, so, whether he owed her or not, he'd do her that favour. When the war ended and he could go back to doing whatever he liked, he'd take a year off and just spend it with her. She'd have the home that was now denied her. Even if the children were away at college by then, he'd help her rebuild that home-thing which was so precious to her.

Then, when it was all together again, maybe he'd be free to go out and do . . . whatever men are supposed to do. Build an empire, or something.

40

In the winter of 'forty-four, coming up to Christmas, Catherine took a party of rehabilitees over to Goldeneye. She hated being away during the children's holidays. Usually Group was very understanding and arranged her roster to coincide with termtime; but there were occasions, like this, when it was unavoidable. They knew she had the fall-back of Beinn Uidhe and that Goldeneye was family, too. In later years she often wondered how different all their lives would have been if she had not been the one to make the trip to Goldeneye that Christmas.

They had intended to refuel at Montreal and go on to Saskatchewan by air. But the forecast was bad so it was decided to send them by train—four extra days, not allowing for mishaps. These rearrangements always upset the men, for whom travel was in any case acutely uncomfortable. However, grumbling was itself the universal therapy of the war—"democracy's secret weapon," Burgo called it; and there was, fortunately, time to cable ahead to the welfare ladies in Toronto, who came to the train laden with books, jigsaw puzzles, and decks of cards. Then Catherine saw the amusing perversity of human nature. One man, a Wing Commander Hickock, who had fretted all the way from Montreal for something to read, put the novel he was given on his bunkside cabinet, took out a pad of writing paper he'd brought with him all the way from France, and started to write a letter home! At least, it was amusing once Catherine had become inured to the fact that their fretfulness over trivial things was often their only way to redirect their frustration at the useless pains they were undergoing.

Hickock interested her because his fussiness was genuine. He'd have been that way even if he hadn't lost one leg, below the knee, and looked set to lose the other unless Jay and his team could do something about it. He worried about whether the signalman had switched the tracks the right way. He worried about whether the drinking water was sterile, "because what they take on for the engine and tender isn't, you know." He worried whether the cretins in his section (he had been in charge of a large pay office) weren't snarling up half the R.C.A.F. pay and home allotments. When Catherine wiped some spilled orange juice off the floor with a paper towel, he said, "I hope you burn that right away." And then, moments later, he asked, "Is the stove safe where you do it?" When she straightened a paperclip to poke a dime out of a fissure where it had fallen, he called, "Be careful, Mrs. Macrae, those things can prick your fingers." When he played poker, he fretted endlessly and drove the other players mad. "Tell me again, now—what beats three-of-a-kind?" was the sort of thing he'd ask. But when they at last reached Goldeneye, he was somehow a couple of thousand ahead —in chips, naturally; Catherine wouldn't allow gambling for money (or not openly).

Normally she helped around in the hospital until her return flight, or more rarely ship, to England came up. But this time, with Christmas so close, she stayed in the house and helped Fiona.

Almost at once she knew something was wrong. Fiona was so tired all the time; and her skin had a dry, creamy—almost yellow—colour, as if she had recently had jaundice. Catherine actually asked, but that wasn't it. Fiona was on the verge of saying more but held her peace—with some effort.

On Christmas Eve she finally told Catherine, who had spent part of the afternoon decorating the wards—"as if these twenty-foot drifts of snow all around didn't already make the place Christmasy enough!" She was laughing.

"They'll have all the fun over there, as usual," Fiona said. "Don't feel obliged to stay here with us, Catherine dear."

Catherine put an arm round her shoulder and gave a big squeeze. "Fiona!" She chided, grinning to force her to grin. "Doesn't that recording ever wear out?"

Fiona laughed grimly. "D'you want to hear something funny? D'you want a big laugh? A new record, too?"

Catherine was serious again. "What's the matter?" she asked. "Something's wrong, isn't it?"

"Who was it always said, 'I can die anytime now'? Who said, 'Once the children are gone, there's nothing left for me to do or be'?"

Catherine was at a loss what to say, for it was, of course, Fiona herself who had said those things. Often.

"Well, the laugh is," Fiona added, "it's not true. Now that it *is* true—it isn't! How about that!"

Catherine was trapped between understanding and not wanting to understand—or not wanting to show it.

"Don't tell James I've told you, my dear. And don't tell any of the others. But I want you to know, so that it won't be such a shock. So you can be ready to help them. Especially"—her lip trembled and she turned half away —"especially Margaret."

Catherine touched her arm gently. She felt distressed enough to want to hug her, but Fiona was not the huggable sort.

Fiona stiffened even at the touch; she permitted it just so long and then drifted to the far side of the kitchen table where she sat down, putting its wooden expanse between them. Catherine took the seat facing her. Fiona pulled the ham to her; she had scored its hide, ready for baking. Now she began to stick it with cloves.

"They write it down," she said, "in a strange, cabalistic tongue. And they lock the paper away. They think I don't know where the key is, and that I can't look it up in Quain or Dorland." She stared her daughter-in-law square in the eye and said, "They call it neoplastic hepatosplenomegaly."

Catherine was well-enough trained to give a little smile and nod sympathetically, as if Fiona had said, "I've had quite a few headaches lately." But she knew it was a death sentence.

Fiona smiled. "Well done, dear," she said.

"You could live for years yet."

"Six months."

"Are you guessing that?"

Fiona shook her head slowly. "When it happens," she said, "don't let them call Meg, or wire her. You break it to her. *You* be there. Go and find her, wherever she is, tell her and stay with her."

"She's a big girl now, Fiona."

"Promise!"

"Of course I will."

"Is the oven up yet?"

Catherine looked at the thermometer. "Nearly."

"You've seen a lot of people die, Catherine. We both have."

Catherine nodded.

"Have you ever thought how you want to go—when it's time, I mean?"

"Don't dwell on it, Fiona."

"It should be quick. And natural. Like an animal. We were all animals once. I don't want to go full of drugs."

"Of course not," Catherine said.

Fiona came as near to taking up Catherine's hands as she could bring herself. All her pleading was mute, in her eyes. "Don't give me soft, professional answers, dear. Please! Talk to me."

Catherine was acutely uncomfortable. "James is the person to really—"

"James is a *man*."

"He happens to be the man who loves you, Fiona."

"How does that make it any easier?"

Catherine did not anwser.

"After telling him for years how glad I'd be to die? After taunting him with it for so long?"

"Why did you?"

"Why do we do anything? We do what we have to."

Catherine nodded.

"You're the only one I can talk to about it, Catherine."

"I'm the only one who's here, you mean."

"No . . . the things we both share."

There was a pause before Catherine said, "Oh, Fiona, what a mess it is."

"You must help James too. Afterwards."

"He'll be shattered, even though he knows."

"That's why I'm telling you. Or asking you."

Catherine looked at the thermometer again. "It's ready now." She picked up the cloth and opened the door before carrying the ham to the oven. "There." She looked at the clock: six fifteen.

Fiona hadn't moved. "What is life?" she asked. "Did you ever wonder that when you nursed the dying? My body's dying. I can feel it sometimes. It's a quality all its own, you know—dying-ness. But *I'm* not dying. Not *me*. On the contrary, I'm free. For the first time in my life I feel . . . liberated. I won't see another fall. But that made last fall the *first!* It was the first fall I'd ever truly seen. Everything's like that now. It's all the last. So it's the first, too. In the beginning, when I learned about it, I thought I'd take all the money I could raise and just get on a train, and then another train, and another—stopping off in between. A day. Three days. However long I felt like. Just travelling and resting, until. . . ." The memory dwindled to silence.

"Until you woke up in some strange hospital surrounded by—"

But Fiona waved her to silence. "It wasn't a practical dream, dear. It wasn't serious. And then I realized I could do it all here. I've never discovered Goldeneye, or the prairie, or this house. Or James."

"Doesn't that make you happy?"

"No!" Fiona almost shouted. Then she dropped her voice. "It makes me want to live. That's what I'm trying to say. I don't care what's happening to my body. I don't want to be dragged down with it. Dragged. Drugged. I want to get out of it while I still can. I want to go on."

Catherine was shocked. "That's blasphemy, Fiona."

Fiona laughed in genuine surprise. "Lord, Catherine—you haven't changed at all, have you! In all these years, and all that's happened—you're untouched."

Catherine smiled. "I'll stay here, Fiona," she promised. "However long you need me. Six months. A year. It doesn't matter."

Fiona seemed not to hear. "All the people who ever died," she said in a wondering tone. "All those millions. They must have wanted it, too. Every one of them must have felt her *self*, or his self, as keenly as I do. They must have longed to survive their bodies, too. Why haven't we heard from them? Why haven't they come back and told us exactly what to do?"

"Why don't we hold antenatal clinics for unborn babies?"

Fiona considered this answer. "Oh, I hope you're right, Catherine," she said at last. "I hope that's it." She smiled then and busied herself. "There's one thing I want you to know, Cathy dear."

"Oh?"

"You remember how I felt about your taking the children to England?"

"Oh that. Well—"

"Let me say it. I was wrong. And you were right."

Catherine gave a little laugh. "And just as I've come around to the opposite view! I think I did a terrible thing. Every time I remember it I'm so ashamed."

"Oh no. You—"

"I think Burgo was marvellous to accept it the way he did."

"The thing is—"

"He had every right to . . ."

"The thing *is*," Fiona insisted. Catherine was silent. Fiona, surprised, forgot for a moment what she had been going to say. "Oh yes—the thing is you never know how long you've got. So you have to. While you've got it. You were right. You had to do it, and so you did."

"But it was a trial for Burgo. I tried him sorely, Fiona. And he was marvellous. He bought a house. A beautiful house. And he got the children to a safe school, only thirty miles away. I hated him at the time. But he was right. The children have thrived. And he did it all. On top of working day and night at his job, he did mine, too. Your son is a wonderful man. All your children are."

Fiona insisted. "Don't blame yourself. You did the right thing and Burgo knew it. That's why he behaved like that."

The following morning, just as it was growing light, Catherine was awakened by a gentle but urgent knocking at the door, she called," Come in."

It was Jay. He slipped into the room and leaned against the door. Then he seemed at a loss for words.

"Merry Christmas," Catherine said. "Or even Happy Christmas! Which side of the Atlantic am I?"

"I think you'd better get dressed," Jay said. "And go and wake James."

Catherine was suddenly wide awake. "Fiona," she said.

He looked surprised.

"What's happened? Not so soon, surely?"

He gave a shocked little laugh. "You *knew?*"

"She told me last night."

"So she did it deliberately."

"Did what? Jay! Is she . . . are you saying Fiona's dead?"

He nodded. "Out there in the snow, beyond the hospital. What were *you* talking about?"

"Her illness. It doesn't matter now. Oh, poor Fiona."

But Jay, suddenly waking to the fact that Catherine was preparing to dress, had bolted.

She found him outside on the landing, unable to be still. "D'you think I should tell James? It's rotten to put it on you."

"Go down and start making some coffee, Jay. And put a call through to Ottawa. Burgo's in France. There's no hope of reaching him direct. I'll call Helen and Arthur later."

"And Margaret?"

"I'll do that, too. Did you bring . . . I mean—you said 'in the snow'?"

"I left her just where she was. I covered her with a sheet. I thought James ought to see. Or ought to have the choice."

"What does it look like happened?"

He shrugged. "She was wearing furs. Coat, gloves, boots. And a thin nightdress. It looks like she went out, lay down, opened the coat . . . and froze to death. She's almost smiling."

"Natural. Like an animal."

Jay was uncomfortable. It was not the expected comment.

"That's how she said she wanted to go. Last night. She told me. But I didn't know she meant so . . ."

"So literally?"

"No. So soon."

James was only shallowly asleep. He stirred and turned as she entered. She sat quietly at the bedside and looked at him.

Her other father. Her teacher. Her other lover.

What would he do now? How would he take it? He had seen so much of death. Would that make it easier?

She knelt and kissed him. His breathing stopped. He came awake. Joy was in his face. Then guilt. He turned to look at Fiona's half of the bed and, seeing it empty, did a mime of relief, collapsing on his back, hands behind his neck.

Now she did not know what to say. Between the trite and the cryptic there was only silence.

"To what do I owe this pleasure?" he asked the ceiling.

She gripped his arm. Her eyes swam and prickled with tears. "James?" It didn't even sound like her voice.

She felt the tension growing in him. "Fiona," he said sharply. It was exactly as she had said it to Jay.

"Yes."

He turned to the empty half of the bed. "Och, woman! Woman!" he cried. He raised his fist and brought it down on her pillow; but at the last second he stayed the blow, turning it to a gentle nudge.

"How?" He was still looking at Fiona's space.

"She walked out and lay down in the snow."

He fell back on the pillow and exhaled. It was as if his life went out of him in the same breath.

"She told me last night," Catherine said. She stroked his hair, now almost all silver. That and the act of speaking helped to calm her. "About her illness. I think she was also trying to tell me about this."

"Never." He was absolute.

"When I said I'd stay as long as was necessary, as long as she needed me, there was a look in her eye—just for a second—as if I'd . . . made up her mind about something. I think it was this."

"She wouldn't incur the obligation!"

"Oh, no, James. Don't let's think of it like that. She wanted to be sure I was here. That must be it. For your sake and Meg's. She must have thought, suppose it happened at Easter, with me in the Highlands and Meg halfway over the Atlantic. She saw this way would be better. It was a *good* thought, my darling."

"Aye, aye. You have the truth of it. That was the way." He sat up. "Have they brought her in?"

"Jay thought you should decide."

"I will see her then." He rose and dressed.

The cold was intense. The breeze, though light, was keen. It bit with a dry scorch. They walked in silence the path she must have trod, her last.

Jay eased the sheet from her face. It was more at peace now than Catherine had ever seen it in her lifetime. Her immediate thought was: *Meg must see this.*

James responded to it, too. He knelt beside her, his knees shielded behind his long fur coat, and smoothed the graying hair from her alabaster brow. "There," he said. "There, there!"

Instinctively, no signal passing between them, Catherine and Jay turned and left him. "I'll get someone to help with the stretcher," he said.

"You've got me," she told him.

A few minutes later they laid her out in the mortuary. "Can you keep her just like this?" Catherine asked. "Can you keep that look of peace? Meg ought to see it."

He said he'd try.

"Don't let any of those morticians near her. No make-up. No powder. Nothing like that. Meg must see how genuine it is." Her thoughts turned to the problem of first locating Meg, then persuading her to stay where she was for four or five days while the train lumbered eastward, then breaking the news, then the best part of a week coming back. Why was this country so damn *big*!

Jay had a better idea. One of their patients happened to be an air vice marshal—their first and only one of the whole war. After Jay had spoken to him he spent most of that Christmas morning on the phone—as a result of which a Dakota would be standing by from first light next morning at the Montparnasse R.C.A.F. Air School, just forty miles down the railroad toward Edinburgh. It would fly Catherine to the MacIver airfield outside Toronto and would wait there to bring back herself and Margaret.

It dovetailed perfectly. Margaret was flying back to Montreal tomorrow, having ferried over a Mosquito just before Christmas.

Catherine lay awake a long time that night. At last it seemed ridiculous that convention should keep her and James apart at this of all times. She slipped on her dressing gown and carried her alarm clock, set for six thirty, along to his room. He was awake, too.

"I hadn't the courage," he said as she put down the clock and slipped out of her dressing gown. "I was sampling loneliness."

He lay on his back. She kissed him and cuddled herself against him. He remained passive.

"It is quite different from being alone," he went on. "She's gone. It is not true we live on. Only memories live on, and they are but the wake of the ship." After a silence he added, "The dead are not at peace. They are not at anything."

"She said last night how the illness made her feel. She knew she was something different from her body. She could feel *it* dying, but not *she*. She and it were not the same."

"There is no peace in life. And none in death." He chuckled grimly. "Surely that was obvious to the very first man who ever considered it. Yet we persist in our craving: Peace in our time. Peace on earth. Grant us peace, O Lord. *Requiescat in pace*. Peace be unto this house and all who enter in. The peace of God which passeth all understanding. Go in peace. Why? Why is this our most persistent delusion?"

"I don't think Fiona was deluded."

"No! She knew that peace is war carried on by other means."

"She knew the pain and the decline that lay ahead of her. She said she didn't want to be dragged out. Dragged and drugged, she said. She understood it very clearly."

He digested that in silence, and then answered, "Understanding. It's the root of the problem. It has the wrong geometry. Life is a line. Understanding's only a point. An infinity of points can never form a line. I understand loneliness. My mind knows all its points. The understanding of it is *now*." He glanced at the luminous face of her alarm clock on the bedside table. "At ten minutes to one on this day of Saint Stephen. But the living of it—living loneliness—is not now more than it was five hours ago or will be five years hence. We live on long, dumb marches. We understand, briefly, and probably wrongly, only as we pass the mileposts."

"Don't be pessimistic, darling."

Briefly he played with one of her curls. "Spoken like a true Canadian," he said.

"Tell me about Fiona. How you met. How you came to Goldeneye. How you settled here."

They were still talking at three, when Catherine went down and fixed them some coffee. Then came a point at which they passed all need for sleep; they were as refreshed and alert as if they had slept eight hours. They were still conversing when her alarm went off, though by then they had long since ceased to talk of Fiona. Catherine was describing her return to Beinn Uidhe and her new relationship with her father.

She even told James of the fight between An Dóiteán and Huey MacLintock, and of the coincidence that Huey should have drowned in that same place more than twenty years later.

"Imogen doesn't know that," she said. "The only other person I ever told was Meg."

"And what did she say?"

"She said it confirmed her belief that Life had been to see *Hamlet* once too often since 1905."

James laughed. "You know that was the year she was born?"

"Yes. I worked it out—weeks later. A lot of the things she says are like that. Delayed-action bombs. Don't you think she could write a marvellous book? That strange blending of comedy and despair—she must use it."

"She does. Oh, but she does!"

41

MacIver airfield began its wartime life as a fighter school, but it wasn't long before people realized the place was an ideal collecting point for aircraft made in North America and destined for Britain. There they did their final commissioning flights before the ferry pilots—people like Margaret and Cherokee and a few hundred others—flew them to Gander, Newfoundland, for a refuelling stop and then set out on the 3,600-odd nautical miles to Britain. And to MacIver they returned, either for their next plane or for a spot of leave. Catherine landed that evening at half past seven, having lost two hours on the clock from Mountain Time at Goldeneye. There was a further hour to go before Margaret's plane was due to land. Obviously after a flight of close on nine hours the Dakota crew wasn't going to turn around and go back that night. She fixed to meet them again around eleven the following morning.

Then, after arranging two overnight beds in the sick bay, she went up to the watch-tower and waited. She was in her nurse's uniform. No one questioned her. This was one of the world's most transient airfields and the war had taught her the value of a uniform.

Thanks to a good tailwind, Margaret's plane was nearly twenty minutes early. Catherine, now down on the tarmac, saw her picking a way through freezing slush. She scanned every face carefully; they all looked exhausted.

Except Margaret. She looked awful. She already knew something. Catherine could tell.

Margaret reacted with that peculiar, urgent, unsmiling delight people reserve for friends at times of distress. "Cath!" she called, and came running, leaving her flying gear and valise in the freezing puddles behind her. "Oh, Cath, isn't it just awful! Thank God you've come." She hugged her fiercely.

"How did you get to hear of it?" Catherine asked.

"How did *I* get to hear of it? I knew right away. But how did *you* know? They're still saying there's hope and he may just have ditched and people have survived weeks and . . ." She broke down at last. Through her tears she said, "I just know he's dead."

Catherine digested this awhile. "Cherokee," she said flatly.

Margaret went on crying. Then, with delayed comprehension, she stiffened. "Of course Cherokee." She pulled away and turned Catherine toward the light from the watch-tower. "You mean you didn't . . . you weren't . . ."

Catherine shook her head. "Let's get your bags and go in. There's a plane to take us back to Goldeneye tomorrow. We'll stay here tonight."

"Tell me!" Margaret shouted.

Catherine picked up her bags and began walking. "Come in where it's warm," she said. "It's turning too cold out here."

"It's Dad, isn't it!"

"It's your mother, honey. I'll tell you when we're inside."

"She's dead. You don't need to tell me. Oh, *boy!*" She stamped her flying boot on the frozen slush and shook both fists at the dark skies. "Wasn't it e n o u g h!" she shouted, prolonging the last word and making it ring out over the flying ground.

They got a lift on a jeep to the sick quarters, which were on the far side of the administration buildings. Meg sat silent all the way. Catherine, holding her arm, could feel the tension.

They had two beds in an empty four-bed bay. "The doctor could give you a shot," the nurse suggested.

"Better still," Meg said, unpacking a bottle of Scotch, "send him in here and I'll give *him* a shot."

Behind Meg's back Catherine made a soothing face at the nurse, meaning *I can handle this,* and nodded toward the door. "There's the buzzer if you need me," the woman said as she left.

Catherine told Meg then, everything—her conversation with Fiona on the night of her death, the way she had looked when they found her, how James and she had sat up all night (as she put it) talking about it, and all that James had said.

"He's too calm about it, and much too abstract," Catherine told her. "I wish he'd just let go. I'll stay around until I'm sure he's okay."

For the first time Meg came far enough out of the shell of her grief to look at Catherine. "Oh darling," she said. "You've had the worst time of all, I'll bet. Let's get some sleep, huh?"

"You want that shot?"

Margaret glanced at the Scotch. "Maybe."

"The shot would be better."

"Okay."

The doctor offered Catherine one, too, but she was already half asleep.

The flight back was cold and bumpy, but far preferable to an eternity on the train. The funeral was delayed two more days to allow Helen to get up from California. The coroner certified no objection to burial. He took formal evidence of death, cause hypothermia, and adjourned *sine die.*

Margaret was drunk at the funeral. No one noticed in church, except Catherine, who was right next to her; but when they went out to the grave-yard it was obvious. A chinook had blown since the day after Christmas and all but the deepest drifts had melted and even dried away, so there was no easy excuse for Margaret's fall. Catherine helped her up and led her away down the path to the waiting cars. She took her home while everyone else went on to the mortuary, where the dead were entombed until the thaw.

On the way she said nothing, but Meg said it for her: "How can I? Go on ask me. I'll tell you—it gets more and more difficult until by now it's well-nigh child's play."

Catherine parked in the doctors' section, round the back of the house, near the hospital. The front approach, she thought, was too conspicuous. Un-fortunately it was such a bright, warm day that the glass doors of the so-larium were open and several convalescents were out on the patio. Among them was the fussy little paymaster, Wing Commander Hickock. He watched the approach of the two women and his face curled in disgust when he saw that Margaret was drunk. "You won't let her throw up all over me, will you?" he asked loudly. "This is my own personal blanket, you know."

An extraordinary change came over Meg. Catherine thought she was trying to make herself heave, just to teach Hickock a lesson; actually, she was trying not to laugh while she turned up her black veil. "Wild Bill!" she cried when she had succeeded.

He looked at her in surprise and then broke into a broad grin. "Mother Macree! You didn't tell me you were *that* Macrae. I mean"—he pointed at the house—"this Macrae."

Meg giggled. Looking at his missing leg, she said, "They sure cut you down to size!"

"Meg!" Catherine was scandalized.

Initial shock changed to delight in other faces on the patio; not a man there who hadn't longed to say some such thing to the paymaster since he had arrived.

But Hickock was not at all put out. "Yes, Virginia!" He laughed. "There *is* a Santa Claus."

Meg lurched down and kissed him.

"And she drinks Scotch." He fanned his wrinkled nose but this disgust was ersatz. "Where's Cherokee?"

"He bought one. Last week."

"Oh! Too bad. Well—you have a right to that Scotch, old thing. See you around."

Margaret steadied herself and gave his shoulder a squeeze in the same movement. "Don't run away," she said.

Behind them he gasped the tail end of a laugh.

"Did you meet him over in England?" Catherine asked as they went indoors.

"Never saw him in my life," Meg answered. She refused to be drawn beyond that.

Yet "Wild Bill" was the saving of Margaret—and she of him. It proved impossible to treat his other leg. After they took it off, almost as soon as he came round from the anaesthetic, he asked to see Catherine. Puzzled and intrigued she came to his bedside. "If old Doc Macrae could just be a little more stricken," he said, "a little less self-reliant, a little more in need, it could do wonders for your sister-in-law."

If he had been anyone other than who he was, this advice, however well meaning, would have struck her as impertinent. But he was so obsessive and so frankly concerned that Catherine had to articulate the excuse for his butting in. "You knew her quite well over there?"

His reply was characteristically oblique: "A lot of people want to call me Wild Bill—obviously. But they take one look at me and they think *nyah!* I can see it in their eyes."

"But she does call you Wild Bill."

"She's the only one."

"You *want* to be called Wild Bill?"

"Sure. Wouldn't you? If you were a man and stood five four and had practically zero-twenty vision and got breathless fighting your way into a pullover and made your living as an accountant?" He paused. "I just realized. I'm not five four any longer. I'm down to three ten in my stockinged kneecaps."

Suddenly Catherine saw the affinity between him and Margaret. That was exactly the sort of thing Meg would have said. It was the same when the doctor later told him they could make his artificial legs longer than the ones he had lost. He said, "You mean at last I get to look over the convent wall?"

Catherine passed on Wild Bill's suggestion to James. But there was no need to put it into practice, because Meg began to spend a lot of time with Wild Bill himself and much less with the bottle. Both continued to be very cagey about how or where they had met, or what sort of a relationship they had had.

Margaret got a compassionate discharge—in fact, she never put on uni-

form again. As soon as it was clear that the work of looking after her father
and her renewed friendship with Wild Bill were enough to keep her sister-
in-law out of trouble, Catherine left Goldeneye for England once more.

By then it was clear that the war in Europe was all over bar the winning.

42

Catherine had feared that V.E. Day would be an anticlimax. True, the
children had a special exeat, and Burgo was actually home on leave, but the
end of the war had been so long in view that this formal mark of it was in
danger of being swamped under the burden of everyone's expectations. But
she needn't have worried. The mere fact that all the family was together, if
only for two days, was enough to flesh out the public and official symbolism
with which the occasion had become invested. It was not necessary for them
to *do* anything special in order to confirm how special it was.

What they in fact did was suitably Anglo-American. They watched
Maypole dancing on the village green. Then they went to the movies, to the
Odeon in Queens Langley, where they saw Anton Walbrook in *Dangerous
Moonlight*. In the dark Catherine shed a few unnoticed tears for those splendid men, young and not so young, who had flown out on missions from
which they had never returned—and, of course, for poor Cullen, the magnificently unprepared. Then they ate a frantically dull meal at the British
Restaurant, where one of the table-tidying women told Grant, who complained about the stale bread, "Don't you know there's a war on?" Then
they went back to the village, where the effigies of Hitler, Goering, and the
late Benito Mussolini were burned on a vast bonfire. And so to bed.

Next day they turned their first cut of hay. The line of them—Burgo,
Madeleine, Grant, Nono, Kelvin, and Catherine—working steadily up the
hill, with the morning sun creeping up to its zenith, symbolized peace in a
stronger, more universal setting than anything they had seen or done yesterday. Young Ian, Cullen's memoir, romped in the turnings with Timoshenko,
veteran of a different, more eternal war. From Gideon's Wood came the
call of a cuckoo. Two young lads walked up the right-of-way at the far end
of the four-acre field, which, Catherine had recently discovered from the old
tithe map at the vicarage, was called Gideon's Stye; no one knew why, and
the name had dropped out of local use.

"That's my cousin Harold Hillier and young George Bennett from Langley Green," Nono said. "They go and pick up cigars from round the American Forces Club in Langley and they smoke them up the old water tower. You should see what those Yanks throw away. It's chronic."

Madeleine, now a knowing fifteen, hinted darkly, "They're not the only ones to pick up things down there!"

She missed the smiles that passed between Catherine and Nono. Catherine was taken back in memory twenty years to when Margaret had been every bit as brash and would-be knowing as Maddy now was.

As for Kelvin, his conscience had never, in the event, been tested. He had registered for military service last summer, at the age of eighteen and a half, but, since he had already begun his medical studies, the authorities had deferred his call-up. He had stayed on at Bedford to take Distinction Papers in zoology and chemistry and sit for his First M.B. He was deputy head of the school; everyone there said that if he hadn't kicked against the pricks back in 'forty-two, he'd be Head Boy by now. He and Burgo whiled away the haymaking by challenging each other to lists of nerves, arteries, enzymes, embryonic segments, hormones, vitamins, analogues and homologues . . . any subject in which either of them felt sure enough of himself to challenge the other. For the purely anatomical lists they had to banish Catherine to the other end of the haymaking line, because she still remembered enough to beat both of them, much to Kelvin's surprise.

Grant, now twelve and in his first year in Lower School, passed the time by driving Madeleine to fury guessing all the unlikely boys with whom she might be in love.

After lunch, when they had worked right across the Stye, they took their hayforks and went over the hill to help Ralph Perry with his first cut of hay. They had almost finished when Burgo did a double take on the "tractor" Ralph was using to pull a swath turner along the gentler part of the slope, where hand turning was not needed. It was actually a car chassis —a rolling, motorized car chassis. And the radiator was shaped like a house in end view.

Ralph saw his interest. "Marvellous old things weren't they—in their day."

"*Is* it a Rolls-Royce?" Burgo asked, keeping the excitement out of his voice as well as he could.

"It was, squire. One of the first. Belonged to a maharajah, that did. He ran it over here. Never took it to India. Only did half a dozen trips—Ascot, Goodwood, that sort of thing. We bought it and got Mulliners to turn it into a hearse for us. Very classy work that brought in. Viscount Roche, the eighth viscount, grandfather of the present one, he went his last mile in that. Then it ended up here on the farm. Never stops. Marvellous motor. I don't think they ever made a better. We've owned four or five over the years."

"Be fun to restore it, what?" Burgo said.

Ralph laughed. "Yeah. Be what you'd call a full-time hobby."

"Exactly. It'd keep an unemployed ex-air commodore out of mischief."

"No denying that." Ralph's whole manner changed. He sensed an offer in the wind. "I'll bet Rolls-Royce still carry all the spares for it. And the drawings. Connally's would do all the upholstery. There's lots of specialists who could do the things you couldn't."

"Oh, no! The fun would be to do it all yourself, down to the last nut and bolt."

"Well—takes all sorts, they say. Are you making an offer, squire?"

"Twist my arm and I might go as high as"—he looked guiltily at Catherine—"ten pounds?"

She laughed in disbelief. It wasn't so much the waste of good money— forty dollars on a heap of scrap like that!—the real puzzle was to understand Burgo's game. If she knew him, he had no intention of rebuilding the dreadful old thing. So why would he waste ten pounds on it?

"Ten quid?" Ralph begged an unseen audience of angels to share this joke. "A tenner for a Rolls-Royce!"

"A heap of junk, Mr. Perry. A rolling heap of rust."

"Nevertheless, air commodore, a Rolls-Royce. I couldn't part with it for under forty. I've got my eye on a nice big tractor. A Fordson Major. Bloke wants a hundred quid for it. I couldn't let this go for a penny under forty."

In silent amazement Catherine listened while Burgo was hustled up to twenty-five pounds for something she wouldn't have valued at twenty-five pence. "I'll come over and collect it tomorrow," he said when they shook hands on the deal. "I must clear some space in the garage."

On their way home through the wood, actually as they passed the tree where she and Ian Cullen had leaned, she said, "What *have* you done?"

He chuckled. "You've no idea, have you."

"Have *you?*"

"And nor has old Perry. That was a forty-fifty horsepower long chassis Rolls-Royce of 1911."

"No!" Catherine's delight was sarcastic. "I thought it was much older!"

"Laugh away. D'you know its other name?" He prompted: "Silver . . .?"

"Fool's silver?" she suggested. "Silver Mug?"

"Silver Ghost. The Rolls-Royce Silver Ghost. I have bought us a legend."

Next morning Catherine took the youngsters back to school while Burgo went over to Perry's to collect his "bargain." He still had not returned with it by the time she got back. It was well on to afternoon teatime when she heard a commotion in the lane outside. She reached the window just in time to see Burgo approaching the front gate. His head rode along the hedgetop. And behind him, about ten yards, Ralph Perry's head rode along the hedgetop too. And behind him, another ten yards, his son Tony Perry's head also rode along the hedgetop. And about six yards behind him, the other son Bob Perry's head brought up the rear. Whatever vehicles they were on, two of them had no silencers.

Burgo turned into Gideons' drive on his Ghost chassis. Ralph Perry followed on a chassis that, give or take different arrangements of binder twine and baling wire for holding the working parts together, was identical. Tony Perry followed on a third variant, towing his brother Bob on something even worse. Not even in their heyday had those cars been parked with a greater flourish nor regarded with more hand-rubbing pride than Burgo now showed, first in directing them, then in turning to Catherine.

"They saw you coming!" she said. "Every junk dealer in the district."

"Nope. They're all Perry's—or were."

"I don't want to hear any more, Burgo. Just . . . just . . . just give me a year, will you?"

He looked back at the four chassis. "Bit longer than that, love," he said. "That's three Silver Ghosts and a Phantom I."

"And I'll bet you got them for only a hundred pounds!"

His grin told her he'd done *much* better. "Ninety-nine!" he crowed. "You don't really think I'd pay three figures for a heap of junk like that, do you!"

"In real money it's still four hundred dollars."

"You want real money?" He jabbed his finger at the lined-up rust. "There's real money. You wait."

When the Perrys had taken their cheque (made out to "cash," of course), drunk their tea, eaten their cake, and gone—"Like three dogs with six tails," as Catherine said—she asked Burgo what he was really going to do. They were still outside in the yard. It was a warm, early summer's day. He sat on the tailboard of one of his purchases and patted the space beside him. She took off her apron and spread it before she complied.

"Until yesterday," he said, "I had no idea what I was going to do—only what I was not going to do."

"And that was?"

"And that was rush into business." He patted the chassis. "You know how these people are so successful? Rolls-Royce? You know how they make the best in the world? Money? Research? Being firstest with the mostest? Not a bit of it. Rolls-Royce never pioneered a thing in their lives, not in cars, anyway. They let someone else have the headaches. They wait and watch for two or three years. Then they pick the best system and they go to whoever makes it—Delco-Remy, Borg-Warner, Lockheed, Lucas . . . whoever—and they say, 'We like this system of yours and here's how we want you to improve it: We want you to make this part thicker, more bearings here, uprate this drive fifty percent, double the number of securing bolts' . . . and so on. And the system manufacturer catches his breath and says, 'That's going to be expensive!' and Rolls-Royce says, 'So?' And that's why they are the best: They wait; they watch; and then they improve. And I'm going to take a leaf out of their book."

"In medicine? I don't see how."

He drew a deep breath. This was the hard part. "D'you really think I'm a doctor, Cath? Honestly?"

"Of course you're a doctor."

"No. I'm really a businessman. That's what I'm cut out for. I tell you— I was ready to sell NCT back in thirty-six. I only stayed with it because . . . well, because of my other responsibilities. You and the children."

Catherine had a terrible sick feeling. She hadn't thought much about what Burgo might do but she had never dreamed he had been toying with the idea of starting from scratch again.

"I figured we'd go back to Canada," she said. "When will you be demobbed from the air force?"

"Well, since I volunteered, I had a gentleman's agreement that I could go as soon as hostilities ceased. I knew, or thought I knew, I'd be busting to get out into some new business. It's true there's a little show still going in the Far East, but I don't think the Medical Branch is so short of permanent officers they want to send temporary—. Anyway, I'm hardly medical these days. More political. And there's nothing more temporary than a high-ranking war-commission officer with his fingers in political plum puddings the permanent boys would like to taste! I guess I could go when I want."

"You see I thought that with Kelvin taking First M.B. and Maddy doing her School Certificate and Grant not yet in the Upper School—all of them at the end of this term—well, it seemed ideal to make the break and go back home. Kelvin could stay, of course, if he wants to go to London or Edinburgh."

He fretted with the damaged wood of the tailboard, tearing off slivers. "It's logically compelling," he said at last. "But it scares me. The thought of Canada scares me. I know that North American buzz. That zip feeling." He snapped his fingers. "Come on, come on! Git or get got! Hustle! It really scares me."

"And you think you couldn't do it!" She was scornful.

"No! I know I could. That's the whole point. I couldn't avoid it. The pressure! But it's not what I want. It's not the Rolls-Royce way. I thought that as I have *months* of leave saved up and my demob leave on top of it, we've got the best part of a year on full pay. Plus my gratuity. I wanted to take a year off and stay here with you and just do nothing."

Her heart leapt up at the words. It sounded marvellous. A daydream come true—except that she would never even have dreamed it because Burgo wouldn't have considered it.

"When I say 'do nothing,' I mean gardening, walks, reading—just think of all the books we bought to fill the leisure we never had!—and going away, a week here, a couple of days there, discovering this country. We don't know England at all, do we. Suffolk . . . the Yorkshire Dales . . . the Cornish Riviera . . ."

It still sounded heavenly. "Okay," she said.

"Except that I'd be carried away by men in white coats after two months. You know me."

She returned to earth. She knew him.

"Hence . . ." He patted the chassis.

"I'll come and read to you while you work," she said. "I'll get out all the guidebooks to Suffolk—the Yorkshire Dales—Cornwall."

"We'll do all that, too, Cath. I promise. All those other things. But I must have a purpose as well."

She stood, half-appeased, and walked away to where her eye could take in all the junk that now filled their yard. "But this is *four* purposes, Burgo. I *do* know you. You're going to out-Rolls-Royce Rolls-Royce."

"I couldn't just leave a Silver Ghost chassis, with a working engine—I couldn't just leave it rusting in the corner of some field."

"Four chassis."

"Okay—four. Could *you?*"

"Very easily!"

He rose and walked to her. He stood behind her and folded his arms around her body, resting his chin on her shoulder. She knew exactly the look that was on his face—that soft, proud look he had given Kelvin and Maddy and Grant when they were each newborn.

"Try and think of it," he murmured, "as a hobby to last a lifetime. On and off."

"Something like marriage, eh?" she said.

PART SIX

1945-1960

43

In the year after the war, Catherine and Burgo saw quite a bit of England. They saw Budleigh Salterton, where Burgo heard there was a retired admiral who had three spare Silver Ghost wheels. They saw Wolverhampton, where there was someone who was a wizard at nickel plating. They saw Lowestoft, where lived a retired upholsterer who remembered doing the seating in one of the first Ghosts. They saw Dollis Hill, in London, where there was a forge that still made springs for Rolls-Royce. They saw Wormwood Scrubbs almost weekly when Burgo went to the Rolls-Royce London Service Depot to pick up this and that.

Catherine divided her days between the garden and the garage, helping Burgo with the restoration. They entertained and visited very little. The coming of peace turned their world inward and made them content with themselves—and more than content. Catherine was happier than at any time since the first years of their marriage.

But she knew they could not go on forever like this. The nearer the day drew when the Silver Ghost was restored to its original glory, the nearer loomed their decision about their real future. Even so, she was afraid to discuss it with him because the here-and-now was so pleasant and she wanted it to last as long as possible.

It was Nono who made the decision imperative. Bob Perry had become a frequent visitor to Gideons. At first it was to marvel at the restoration of one of his old wrecks, but more lately it was to court Nono. An aunt of hers, who had owned a small but thriving chain of beauty salons, had died and left her a few thousand. Catherine supposed Nono would give up domestic service then, but instead she asked if she could buy Gideons and the land. Bob Perry wanted to marry her and they had plans to go into nursery gardening. There was to be a New Town at Stevenage, and other towns nearby were to be enlarged, and all those new houseowners were going to be looking for plants to stock their gardens; it could be a real money maker, they thought.

The postwar decision could be put off no longer.

That evening Catherine brought the bedtime drink of cocoa out to the garage, where Burgo was fitting the nickel-plated headlamps onto their upstands.

"There!" he said proudly. "Didn't she need them!"

Catherine agreed. "She looked blind before."

"I think even Jack will be impressed."

Jack Walker was a newly acquired friend in Queens Langley. He had
spent the war in various Rear Workshops, repairing everything from tanks
to HQ lawn mowers; without him the restoration of the Ghost would have
taken the lifetime Burgo had once joked about. He was now busy making
his first fortune in hydraulics, stripping war-surplus units of every size and
fitting them to agricultural and site machinery as if Archimedes had only
just announced, "Give me a pivot and I'll move the world."

"What about Nono and Bob?" Catherine asked.

"What about them?"

"You know what about them."

"I don't know what to do."

"I want to go back home," she said. "I miss Canada."

"I know."

"More and more each day."

He sighed and nodded, sipping his drink.

"Don't you?" she asked.

He gestured at the car. "This has been a way of not asking that."

"Nono needs a decision. And I think we owe it to her not to linger
over it."

He turned to the car again as if it might save him from the necessity of
that decision. She drained her mug, set it down, and came and put her arms
around him from behind. "Haven't these days been wonderful?" she said.

"The best. But they've been a kind of holiday. I mean, a holiday from
life. We couldn't always live like this."

"But we could get pretty close to it."

"How's that?"

"I know one should speak no ill of the dead, and I know Fiona was always charming and pleasant to me, but she wasn't to James—"

"I don't see the connection," he interrupted.

"This. Suppose she had been. Suppose Fiona had been a tolerant, easygoing, sweet-natured person like me. . . ."

Burgo cleared his throat, heavily.

"If you contradict," Catherine warned, "I'll tear your eyes out and never
talk to you again. If, as I say, Fiona had been like that, wouldn't James's life
and hers have been pretty much the sort of life we've led these last months?"

He thought about it and then allowed that it would.

"So!"

"You mean I should go back into medicine! And into general practice?"

"Don't you owe it to yourself? Or at least to *us*? You've proved, even to your own satisfaction, never mind the world's, surely you've proved there's nothing you can't organize effectively, either in the hurly-burly of peace or the lunacy of war. You don't want to spend the rest of your life proving it all over again, do you? Don't you owe yourself these simpler pleasures?"

He drained his cup and set it down on the flat of the mudguard. Then he turned to take her in his arms, holding his hands so that they would not touch her. She looked at them, saw they were not very dirty, and said, "It's all right, these are going in the wash."

Snug in his embrace, she said, "Well?"

"Go back to Goldeneye?" he asked.

She chuckled. "Whithersoever thou goest . . ."

"But you'd prefer the prairie?"

"I'd prefer anywhere we can be together, like this, and be part of a community, and not try to change the world or . . . make a million or anything." She hugged him fiercely. "Just be *us*."

"I'll finish the Ghost first. By June, I'd say."

"That would give us time to go back to Canada, find somewhere, and get Maddy and Grant into their new schools."

"And Kelvin?"

"He's old enough to decide for himself surely. My guess is he'll still choose Edinburgh. His heart's set on it now. Of course, I'd prefer him to choose MacNair. But . . ." She shrugged and smiled. The pain of parting was not yet. "What do we tell Nono?"

"Nothing. We let her ask us twice more, so that she's the one who's doing all the pressing, then we say . . . what? Three thousand?"

"But she's a friend."

"No friends in business, dear."

"And three thousand is ridiculous. No one wants these big houses nowadays, with the impossibility of getting staff."

"That's for her to say, not us." He grinned.

Eventually the sale was agreed at £2,500, which Bob Perry paid in notes damp from hiding places beneath floorboards, crushed from chair seats, dusty from old cupboards, or smelly from the mart, or sacks, or his mattress. It was Burgo's poor, unworldly solicitor who gained an undeserved reputation as a secret war profiteer when he paid them into the bank.

The Silver Ghost took its final polish early in June, just as Burgo had predicted. It was—even Catherine, whose initial skepticism had taken so long to wither, had to admit it—magnificent: one of the finest cars ever built. It didn't quite pass the penny-on-its-edge test with the engine ticking over, but there were moments when they came to a halt at crossroads and Catherine was deceived into thinking the engine had cut out.

They splurged their petrol ration on an end-of-term journey to Bedford to collect the two youngsters. It wasn't the done thing to turn up there in posh cars. Usually parents with Rolls-Royces borrowed modest Standards or Fords from poor relatives when they visited the schools. But a thirty-five-year-old Rolls-Royce was old enough to verge on the permissible. It was certainly admired, and Burgo had to take every boy in the house, and a couple of nostalgic masters, round the Block—a two-mile circuit of the streets bordering the Upper School playing fields.

Grant laughed and smashed his fist into his open palm. "I've just realized—I'll never have to run around the Block again!"

"They made you run all this way?" his mother asked. "With your foot?"

"Why not?" Grant bristled while she kicked herself for letting her surprise show like that.

The Ghost was admired even more a few evenings later, when Jack Walker returned from a big war surplus sale in the north and, as a thank you for all his help, Burgo and Catherine took him and his wife out for a grand dinner (or as grand a dinner as could be managed within the 7s.6d. legal limit that was still put on all off-ration meals).

At the end of the evening, when they dropped the Walkers off at their home in Queens Langley, Jack tipped them a wink and beckoned them toward his own garage.

"I know it's only the moon compared to your sun," he said apologetically, "but I can't resist showing you."

He swung open the door and there, Bayard Red on Tudor Gray, with a gold stripe, gleamed a brand-new Silver Wraith.

"Hey!" Burgo said. "Lookit *that!* Are they back in production?"

"Not . . . properly," Jack said. "But I'm pals with one or two of them. You know how it is."

Burgo laughed. "With you, you old sod! I know how it is."

Of course, they had to go for a short spin. They felt like the king and queen in state.

"Went right up to Warrington and back in her last week," Jack said. "Got into top at the end of our avenue and didn't get out of it for two hundred and fifty miles. Like sitting on whipped cream all the way."

"And all from hydraulics, eh, Jack?" Burgo asked.

"Every last nut and bolt."

Catherine often wondered how different their lives might have been if

Jack Walker had taken delivery of his Wraith just one month later, while they were halfway back over the Atlantic.

Or even if Burgo had not asked that last (and, as she came to see it, fatal) question.

44

Away from the wet areas Northern Ontario is beautiful country—rolling hills, farmland, woods of maple, willow, and birch, with purling streams and patches of forest and lake. By the forties it had been long enough settled, for the most part, to have lost its untidy, ramshackle, pioneer edge—but not long enough, or prosperously enough, to have become pretty, or even graceful, like much of New England.

Driving through it that summer Catherine saw a score of places where she was sure they could settle happily for the rest of their lives—century-old communities that had long weathered and effaced the scars of their newness. But Burgo found something wrong with each; usually it was something intangible, so it was hard even to discuss. Catherine began to suspect he didn't really want this new life at all—the country doctor who messed around with old Rolls-Royces on a summer Saturday, the not-so-big fish in a very small pond. She told him so.

"Don't you miss England, Cath?" he replied.

"What's that got to do with it?"

"You see! I knew you did."

"I miss the woods," Maddy said.

"And fish and chip shops," Grant chimed in. "Oh! Three penn'orth of each and a scoop of scrumpy bits!"

"There are woods here," Catherine pointed out.

"I want beechwoods."

"I cried when we left Southampton," Grant confessed.

"I wish we'd only rented Gideons to Nono and Bob," Maddy went on. "I'd like to think it's always there."

"You can always go there, anytime. Nono'd love to have you. You know that."

"It isn't the same. And I wish we'd been to London more often."

Catherine turned to Burgo. "Now look what you started. And you weren't even answering my question."

"Which was?" He smiled.

"You obviously don't relish the thought of life hereabouts. So what *do* you want?"

"Oh, yeah." He scratched his head, let a silence grow, and then turned back to her. "And yet you do miss England."

"I'll miss you more when I'm through strangling you. Look, let's kill this thing, once and for all."

"These dumps don't even have proper cinemas," Grant said.

"You shut up," she told him. "Once and for all, as it happens, I don't miss England. And nor am I going to. I'm glad we lived there, and I'm glad it was in the war. I don't think people over here had that sense of all-in-it-together and sharing danger we had over there. But peacetime England, even in lovely Hertfordshire, was drab. You can't deny it. So I'm glad we're home. All right, everyone? Is that clear?"

"This isn't home, Mummy," Grant said. "This is the east."

"You were born in the east, only two hundred miles from right here."

"Three hundred," Burgo corrected.

"What do you call a proper cinema?" Maddy asked.

"Two, three, what does it matter?"

"Continuous performances," Grant explained. "Even so, the east isn't home. The prairie's home."

"Canada's a dump," Maddy said. "England's civilized. All my friends are there."

"Don't interrupt your brother," Burgo told her, surprising not only her but Catherine, too.

"What's so great about the prairie?" Maddy asked Grant. "The cinemas there don't have continuous performances."

"They do so. How do you know, anyway?"

"I shouldn't *think* they do."

"Will you shut up about cinemas," Burgo cut in. "Let the boy talk about the prairie. Why d'you like the prairie, Grant?"

"I like the prairie, too," she answered. "Better than *this*." She looked around in elaborate disgust.

"Okay." Burgo softened. "You talk. What's so great about the prairie?"

Catherine burst into laughter. "Burgo! You—you puppetmaster! Why not come out and say it—*you* want to go back west!"

He was all wide-eyed innocence. "I haven't decided anything. And I don't want to decide anything until I know how everyone else feels."

Still laughing, Catherine turned to the youngsters. "Do you buy that?"

"Sure," Grant said at once.

"Provisionally." Maddy felt she owed her mother some support.

"Well, sooper-dooper." Burgo rubbed his hands. "I guess we'd all like to see the prairie again. Before we decide."

"And then the Maritimes, and Quebec," Catherine added. "And the Rockies, and Vancouver Island. Oh, and Loon Lake! Let's not leave out Loon Lake."

"Perish the thought!" Burgo laughed.

"Until we're all so punch-drunk with choice we say, 'Whatever you want, Dad!' Isn't that it?"

He pointed an accusing finger at her and grinned. "If you can't take a joke, you shouldn't have joined up."

"Joined what?" Grant asked.

"It's an old R.A.F. saying, dear." To Burgo she added, *"Very* old."

"But what's it mean?" Grant persisted.

"For the love of Mike!" Maddy said.

Catherine explained: "If a man lost an arm or a leg or was blinded, people said, 'You shouldn't have joined up if you can't take a joke.' It was just a saying. There were lots of them in the war."

"I shouldn't think it's much of a joke being blinded or losing an arm or a leg."

"Oh, for the love of Mike!"

Later Burgo said to Catherine, "Goldeneye is turning into quite some place, you know. When Dad fought for it to be the C.N.R. divisional town all those years ago, I don't think even he knew what he was starting."

"Meg says there's even a problem with prostitution. That's how big it's getting."

"All the farm agencies are there."

"You think there'd be room for another doctor?"

"Sure," he said. "And even if not . . ." He let it hang.

"What then?"

"Well, we'll cross that bridge when we come to it." He kissed her. "Tell you what. Why don't you go to Toronto and look over all our furniture— the prewar lot and the stuff from Gideons, if it's come yet—and I'll take the brats to Goldeneye and scout around. You sell whatever we don't want and either come on west and join me, or go visit old friends and I'll come back and pick you up."

It was too reasonable a dovetailing of their activities for her to refuse, but she had the strongest sense of being manipulated. She picked over their furniture in half a morning and fixed for the sale of the surplus during the other half. She was one day behind Burgo in arriving, unheralded, at Goldeneye. It was a day too late.

45

"Just tell me what was wrong," Catherine asked, "with the idea of being an ordinary country doctor and having a home life."

"Northern Ontario was—" Burgo began.

"Forget bloody Ontario. What was wrong with the idea *here?* You can't say there's no room—with two partnerships dying to have you join them."

"How did you know that?"

"I called James, remember?"

"Well he's wrong. They don't want me. They want a Macrae, because Dad's such a big wheel in provincial medical affairs. And especially now that he's bought the *Inquirer*. And the Masons and Elks and all that. But that's not what I want. I don't want to be here on his coattails."

"Burgo, that's ridiculous. You're the air commodore who organized the entire emergency medical—"

"Not here, honey. I'm James Macrae's boy. Always will be."

"Then let's climb into the car and head west until we meet people who say, 'Who's James Macrae?'"

Burgo grinned but said nothing.

"Why not?" she persisted. "Now we come to it, don't we! It's not Northern Ontario *or* Goldeneye. Or points west. It's not places at all. I don't even think it's the thought of being a doctor again. It's the very idea of a quiet, modest, normal, ordinary life. Am I right?"

Trapped, he sighed and avoided her eye. "If you really want to know—it was the thought of becoming like Mum and Dad used to be."

"Me! Like Fiona?"

"No—me. And you like Dad."

"Burgo! If you said you were afraid you might die of starvation or . . . or Nieman-Pick disease, I'd believe you more."

He grinned. "Well, I was coming to that."

"So what's the real reason?"

"The real reason is I remember Jack Walker and what he's been able to do in one year with hydraulics, and I keep thinking of all the farms and machines we have out here, and all the sites, now, next year, the next hundred years."

"And you also keep thinking of new Rolls-Royces."

"Sure. That helps."

"And the fact that you know less about hydraulics than I know about—"

"About Nieman-Pick disease?"

"Right."

He laughed. "Well, Cath, it isn't decided yet. Nothing's irrevocable. But at least come and look at the site for the factory, huh?"

"What site for what factory? Burgo—you've only been back here one day."

"Come and see."

"No, I want to wait for Meg to get back. Or until James gets up."

"He'll be okay."

At that moment they heard James's laboured breathing and footfall on the stair. Catherine ran outside and up the stairs to meet him, three at a time. He groaned.

"Darling! Are you all right? What's this? Have you got arthritis?"

He dropped the pretence—for that's all it was—and held wide his arms. When she hugged him, he lifted her off the ground with a strength that belied his seventy-six years.

"Oh, James, I'm going to divorce that man and marry you. Your son is impossible."

He put her down. "I need time to think that over," he said.

"And I want it in writing," Burgo called up.

"Twenty-one years of trust!" Catherine sneered. "Our China wedding's behind us, did you know?"

The lightness of her tone masked the heaviness inside. Burgo was not going to settle for the quiet life. She knew exactly what it was. He had said it without realizing it, a few minutes earlier: "I'm James Macrae's boy— always will be." In the wider world he was the Dr. Macrae who'd changed the shape of medicine in Toronto. He was the Air Commodore Macrae who'd organized the emergency services of the air force. But here he was still James Macrae's boy. He must have sniffed it in the air within minutes of stepping from the train. And minutes later he must have resolved to turn it all upside down, so that in years to come people would say, "You've heard of Burgo Macrae? Well, James was his father."

She didn't need to speculate on it. As soon as Burgo said "Nothing's irrevocable," she knew there was no going back.

"Did you hear about Meg and Wild Bill?" James asked as they went on downstairs.

"I was keeping it," Burgo cut in. Then, to Catherine, "Wild Bill got a partnership with some accountants in Saskatoon."

"So they move out," James said, "and you move in." He gave her arm a squeeze. "And I get to eat some real cooking again."

But she was disappointed. "I'll miss Meg. She's one of the reasons I wanted to come back to Canada."

"They'll only be half a day away," Burgo comforted her. "We'll get a light plane and you can learn to fly. Then they'll be even nearer."

"Men like you planned the pyramids," she told him.

He winked. "And found the slaves to build them."

Days later, when Meg and Wild Bill had left for Saskatoon, and Burgo was back east, talking to old friends and bank presidents, Catherine said to James, "It's going to be the early years of NCT all over again. Between one change of shirt and next we won't see him."

"Would you prefer the later years of NCT then?" James asked.

"What do you mean?"

"Well, well! How short is the human memory. I remember, just in those years before the war, a very unhappy Catherine complaining about a very bored and underoccupied husband. Your dream of a Burgo who can do a passable imitation of me—as a domesticated animal and small-town bigshot —was only ever that: a dream."

She did not want to accept the truth of it. "Why did he just hide up all last year, then? I mean the Burgo you're seeing now is just so different from. . . . We had a marvellous year, you know. I thought he was so happy. I thought he'd at last come to realize what—you know—simple pleasures there are in an ordinary home and an ordinary marriage. I thought, when I suggested a nice little country practice in Northern Ontario, I thought he'd jump at it. But he was only pretending."

The word "pretending" came as a revelation to her. "That's it!" she said. "Somewhere inside Burgo is the real knowledge of everything he wants from life. Everything he wants to do. Everything he wants to be. And he won't admit it. Not to me and not to anybody."

"To himself?" James asked.

"I sometimes wonder even about that. But everything we see—it's all pretence."

"All?"

"Mostly."

"But that's true of everybody, Cathy. At times."

"I wouldn't mind. If only he'd take *me* into his confidence. Or even consult me. I mean, if he'd said, 'Cath, I'd stifle to death in a small-town practice. I want to do something in industry. Something big. Will you come along with me,' I'd have said yes. But that's the one thing he'd never do. I'm not a partner to be consulted. I'm a tactical problem to be manoeuvred around."

"But he even courted you like that, before you married. So you can hardly complain."

She sighed. "That's my real trouble. I never had a clear idea of what I wanted. Burgo has a clear idea, but he keeps it to himself. I don't. So I just drift. I'm a pushover, James."

"Cathy . . ." He was troubled.

"I told Imogen once that I grew up without knowing we can *choose* in life. But now I wonder if we can. Or if I can. I didn't choose to run away from Scotland. The alternative was just too ghastly. I didn't choose to work at Ed and Rennie's. It was just the nearest thing to a croft I could find. I didn't choose to become your nurse. Where else could I have gone? Did I choose to marry Burgo—with you pushing and him laying siege? And when we lost everything, he said *go* and I tamely went. And Meg dragged me into MaCaBu with the strength of her little finger. The only thing I ever *chose* was to go to England in 'thirty-nine. And that was wrong."

With a trembling hand he gripped her arm. "It was right. You know it was right."

She threw herself against him and clung tight. "Oh James! I should have waited. I should have married you."

He stroked her hair and kept silence.

"Why is Burgo going back to all his old tricks? Darling, I feel so alone, suddenly."

"You are not alone."

"Take me up to bed."

There was a long pause before he said, "You are sure?"

"Otherwise there will never be any ease or peace between us."

And so they resumed a relationship that for the past twenty years "did but slumber." For her it was like finding an old photo—the kind that makes you say, "Lord, how I've changed!" In that sudden confrontation her body remembered old ways that were now the ways of people so different they were almost aliens. She was comforted to realize they had suffered no loss—only a change.

She was comforted and no longer alone.

46

While Burgo was back east he sent the three Rolls-Royce chassis on to Goldeneye, still in their crates. But the Silver Ghost he uncrated in Montreal and
set off on a headline-grabbing journey across half the continent. At that time
it was still a much easier car ride the long way round, through Detroit and
Chicago, south of the lakes. But he took as his slogan *Canada all the way!*
and slugged it out across Ontario and Manitoba. The gesture (and, to be
sure, that car) caught something in the postwar mood of the nation so that
by the time he arrived in Goldeneye, two adventurous weeks later and just
in time to lay the car up for the winter, there were few Canadians who had
not heard of his journey and, more important, did not know that he was
staking his considerable all on Golden Power Hydraulics, as he called the
new firm.

Orders arrived ahead of him; so did less concrete but no less welcome
expressions of interest, requests for literature . . . meetings . . . interviews
. . . work. Salesmen were on the doorstep or the phone all hours of the day.
Until his triumphal return, Catherine bore the full brunt of that North
American hustle and zip he had once told her he feared. Now she understood why. The urge to be doing, responding, deciding, calling back, con-
firming, was almost overwhelming.

Time and again her stomach went queasy with the adrenalin as she
caught herself thinking, *I've forgotten something . . . I've left something
out . . . there was something I had to do . . . what's next, what's next?*

"And that's what Burgo actually wants," she marvelled to James. "For
himself. He wants to feel that tightness, that compulsion. All the time."

"And you don't understand it?" James asked.

"I do not!"

But she was wrong. When Burgo came back and took over, just for that
first day or two, she did miss it. An uneasy flatness had crept into her life; a
pall of anticlimax overshadowed the hours. Soon, however, a more easeful
normality returned and she was glad not to be part of that hurly-burly. But
she never forgot that, just for a day or two, she had understood what Burgo
had known would be missing from life as a country doctor. It helped over
the months when Burgo was hardly ever there but was risking, alternately,

frostbite and welding burns in the plant, a mile away on the northern edge of town.

Whenever she watched a hydraulic shovel at work, she could see its seduction for Burgo, quite above and beyond the question of profit. Its action was slow, relentless, and seemingly irresistible. And even when the shovel came to a halt—against a great boulder, say—it didn't shriek and whine, nor strip a train of cogs in an orgy of twisted metal, nor smoke and burn out. It suffered none of the failures associated with other forms of power. Instead it went on pushing away silently and steadily. And nine times out of ten there'd soon be a little hair-crack in the clay around the boulder, which would widen to a rift until the stone turned into a plaything for the shovel.

In a way, hydraulics and Burgo were made for each other. In a way, hydraulics *was* Burgo.

In the best Rolls-Royce tradition, he had decided to concentrate on just one product and to make it the most robust and best-engineered thing available. The front loader and the liftable buckrake were then unknown on standard farm tractors, though there was a gantry affair that worked off the power winch; it had never caught on because the gantry had to be lowered to get the tractor through most garage doors. Burgo saw that hydraulic cylinders could replace the winch cable and do away with the gantry. But he forgot the other Rolls-Royce precept: Never be first. And his hydraulic front loader was a kind of first. It took longer to get it right, and then for it to catch on, than he had feared even in his most deliberately pessimistic forecasts.

There came a point where they could no longer go on simply manufacturing for stock. The stock filled the yard and spilled out along the roadside. Then they began to take on any jobbing work in welding or bending, just to make ends meet. Finally they were even doing repairs, a glorified form of blacksmithing; it hardly paid the wages. The bank was getting edgy and suppliers were reaching the four months' credit line, the traditional limit to their patience.

Burgo grew depressed in a way Catherine had never seen before. "There's nothing I can *do*," he complained. "If there was, I'd be doing it already."

James offered a loan but Burgo, as ever, wouldn't even think of it.

"The real mistake," he complained to Catherine, "was coming back to Goldeneye. This is just the wrong place. We should have gone somewhere bigger."

"Well, why didn't we?" she asked. There was a bitter edge to his voice, as if he blamed her.

"You know why."

She thought she did—so that Goldeneye would realize James Macrae was *the* Burgo Macrae's father. But she could hardly taunt him with that at such a time, so she said nothing. He seemed to take her silence as a kind of guilty acceptance of his unspoken censure—for what she could not guess. Returning to Goldeneye had been much more his idea than hers.

It almost broke her heart. When things were going well, he was so wrapped up in success that she could hardly get near him. And now things were so bad, he still wouldn't let her share it. She knew exactly what fears and self-torment he was going through. Her distress was no smaller than his. But he could share neither.

The business was saved by a heavy snowfall. Burgo, the supreme opportunist, saw his chance. He challenged the regular snow-clearing teams to a contest—their snowploughs against his front loaders.

"Of course, we can't possibly win," he told Catherine and James. "But that isn't the point."

The margin by which they lost was so small that, a week later, more people remembered the boast that a Goldeneye Front Loader could lick a regular snowplough than remembered his actual defeat. Even the snow teams were impressed, for the loader could go places the snowploughs couldn't; the town ordered two. Several other communities followed. It got the firm off the hook, though not out of the hole.

Then came an oilman from Alberta. He wanted a mobile unit that used hydraulics to fold, bend, crimp, or guillotine steel sheet, or angle, or tube. Burgo and his best mechanic worked three days and nights, round the clock, and came up with a unit that would also punch holes and slots of any shape. It had been intended as a one-off but the oil people were so impressed they ordered a dozen—one a month.

Burgo saw at once that the Universal Steel Fabricator, as he called it in his patent application, would be useful in garages, on big sites—anywhere that steel was fabricated. By that spring he had an order book it would take five years to satisfy at present rates.

"We desperately need more capital," he said.

"Back to the banks?" she suggested.

"With our present sales figures? And existing liabilities? They'd just laugh at us."

"Even with that order book?"

"Orders can melt like spring snow. Besides it's really only my word."

"Then why not take all your books down to Saskatoon and see Wild Bill? Then it would be his firm's word, too. And their respect carries far beyond the province."

Halfway through her suggestion she saw him switch from rejection to acceptance. "Hey, that's not a bad idea. Maybe this time next year I'll be glad I thought of it."

He left the books with Wild Bill, intending to return the following week. Two days later his brother-in-law was on the phone, asking him to come back right away.

"Trouble?" Burgo asked.

"I hope I can say they're all behind you."

They met not at the office but at home. Meg was out getting her hair fixed so they had the place to themselves.

"Did you write your assessment?" Burgo asked even before they were through the door.

"No need." Wild Bill grinned enigmatically.

"What d'you mean—no need? I can't go back to Bank of Toronto and—"

"Bank of Toronto! What for?"

Burgo raked the ceiling with his eyes. "Well, not many people know this, Wild Bill, but they do a wizard lamb kebab there. And their soufflés! It's worth the four-day trip. Don't tell Cath."

Wild Bill laughed and spread out some of the papers. "I guess you could get by with an injection of a hundred thousand, Canadian."

"You see, you did know."

"It just so happens I have such a sum—or Meg and I do—and we want to—"

"Oh, no!" Burgo cut him short. "No family charity, thanks. I already turned down Dad. Thanks all the same."

"Then you did him a disservice. I think this is the best investment opportunity I'll see in my lifetime. I'm certainly not writing the report that'll enable you to walk out of here and raise the wind in Toronto. When you go, you'll take me with you—or the bit of me I value and love best. My wallet."

Burgo stared at him, almost convinced; but at length he shook his head. "It's too easy to say something like that, Wild Bill."

"I mean it."

"Sure. Don't think I don't appreciate it."

"Listen, you idiot—"

"There's only one way I'll believe you."

"What?"

"Do what you said back there. Come in with me. Not just your wallet, but *you*."

"I can't just do that."

"If you believe in this venture so much, you're worth even more to it than your wallet. The head you have for money."

"It's out of the question, Burgo."

"You see! I knew you were just being kind. Where d'you get that sort of money, anyway? We always did have our suspicions about Pay Section."

"Most of it's Meg's, actually."

"Meg's? Where the hell did she get it?"

"She sold Marguerite's for around a hundred thousand."

"Never!" Burgo gave a wild laugh. "That dump? A hundred grand? Did you ever see it?"

"It was pulled down."

Burgo was lost a moment in thought. "Never a hundred thousand. Half that—just maybe. She must have had some other racket, too."

"Well, it was nearly ten years ago—a lifetime with the war and all. Does it matter?"

"I guess not," Burgo said.

But of course it did matter. Catherine had been a part of that setup. It mattered very much.

47

Within days Wild Bill decided to throw in his lot with Burgo. Like a second cup of kerosene on a reluctant fire, this second injection of capital was all that Golden Power Hydraulics needed for it to blaze into growth. Within a year it became the biggest employer in Goldeneye. Within two it had agencies throughout the west and into the bordering American states.

For most of that time Burgo was far too busy to remember his doubts and curiosity about the origin of Meg's money. At first it had been the unbelievable gift horse, whose mouth it was unwise to inspect too closely. But then, as fortune grew more familiar—so much so that it almost seemed part of the natural order of things—two memories kept recurring to him. One was the scene he had burst in upon at Meg's apartment in Greenwich Village, twenty years ago: the fat ugly man whom Meg had passed off as a potential employer. The other was something Catherine had said at Christmas two years later—that Christmas she and Meg had presented him with a cheque for over five thousand dollars; apart from exhibiting an unprecedented coarseness of language, Catherine had said, "I've a damn good mind to leave you guessing how we earned it."

Of course, MaCaBu had existed and it had evolved into Marguerite; and Cathy had designed people's homes. He'd met the people and seen the homes. But had there been nearly six thousand dollars in it? And in copies of Paris frocks? True, women were crazy about what they'd pay to get a fashionable interior—or exterior. Almost as crazy as men who'd pay small fortunes for a few moments of . . .

He couldn't voice the thought, but its shape was there. A business friend in Chicago had told him of a house called The Verandah, the most exclusive house in North America. It had closed in the Roosevelt administration, but the simplest transaction there had cost sixty dollars. Sixty dollars! And at the height of the Depression, when good-looking girls could be got for no more than two.

These memories, and Meg's unexplained wealth, began to obsess him. When he and Catherine made love, he found himself wondering about her. *Why* had she thrown out that taunt about how they'd earned it? Cathy would never think along those lines naturally. Meg would, of course, in her Tallulah Bankhead moments. And Cathy had been with Meg most of that year.

But had there been men? Could Meg have had men and Cathy not? Six thousand dollars in savings would imply at least six hundred men, probably more. In nine, ten months? Two or three a day? Not too much for one, and not many for two.

At first, when he veered away from such thoughts, at least while he was in bed with Catherine, it had been because he feared what it might do to their relationship. Specifically, he was afraid that suspicion and disgust might make him impotent toward her. But no thought is harder to exclude than suspicion. And like disguises like. Whenever their lovemaking drew to its climax he could not suppress the thought that those same gasps and wriggles and sighs might once have been counterfeited for cash.

He was astonished then to discover that such thoughts had the very opposite effect to impotence: they excited him to a new pitch. He would never have believed it of himself. He cringed for shame at the discovery. But at those particular moments, and increasingly in between, he almost exulted at the thought of all those possible predecessors. Their shadows lay beside her, filled the bed, crowded the room; their very presence was like a mute but roaring applause. He had suppressed his thoughts for fear of hating Catherine. He released them only to discover he disgusted himself—and that his self-disgust was a powerful aphrodisiac. Often on his way home from the factory, or from sales meetings all over the west, he would imagine she had spent the day entertaining men. "No, no, *no!*" he'd tell himself, screwing his eyes tight in anguish and shaking or thumping his head to dislodge such dreadful notions. But nothing could prevent them from flooding back; and then the hours would drag until bedtime.

In time, Burgo's intellect managed to rise above his obsession. He still could not prevent himself from imagining Cathy in whorish settings, but instead of cowering in disgust at himself he groaned inwardly, with the sort of weary tolerance that good parents learn to practise on petulant infants, as if to say, "Oh Lord, are you at *that* again!"

He saw that whatever was at work within him, it was not a suspicion of Catherine; he didn't truly believe her capable of such behaviour. She'd starve to death before she let anything like that happen to her. So would Meg. It was all talk. Meg might have had a rich lover—even two or three over those years. But that was the extent of it. These fantasies he was having were just a kind of sexual game he was playing, solitaire. They said nothing about Catherine, or Meg—but they spoke unpleasant volumes about himself.

Only when he reached that new pitch of understanding did he feel secure enough to ask Meg directly for the truth. *Had* MaCaBu and later Marguerite really earned $100,000?

"Nope," Meg said simply. Then hooding her eyes, pinching her mouth to the vamp size of her childhood days, and doing a Mae West with her hips, she intoned in a gravel voice, "I woiked in a whorehouse."

"Be serious," he told her, hiding his excitement at this artless (or, if true, oh-so-artful) confirmation of his thoughts.

"Okay, I'll be serious. So what business is it of yours?"

"The money happens to have been invested in my business."

"Our business. But that's what you're really asking about, right? The thing that turned *your* business into *our* business. Money."

"In a way."

"Not in *a* way, darling. In *your* way. How long before you slip-slide around to the real question, Burgo?"

"What are you talking about—'real' question?"

"Something's bothering you. Tax? You're worried about having to explain my nest egg to the tax gatherers? You're going to sell us out and you want to explain my investment to whoever's going to take my place in your new scheme?"

"My God, you must have a low opinion of me. I never realized."

"Huey Long never bothered about such things. Why should you?"

"I should have known better."

"You see! There's always something we *can* agree on."

He inclined his head, seeming to accept defeat. "I'm not inquiring into how you got the money. Your life is your life. I really just wanted to feel sure that if you did have a bundle, you had it already when Cath joined up with you in MaCaBu."

"Because her life isn't her life? Is that it?"

He laughed. "I deserved that. Okay. I had no right to ask."

"And I'll quote you on that. You had no right to ask and I'm under no obligation to answer. But, if the spotlight's going to be turned on Cathy, then I will. Someone's got to love that girl."

He turned to her, absurdly hopeful.

She laughed. "Not now, dear boy. Impetuous, foolish creature! I'll find a way, though. You'll see."

This exchange and its concluding promise had one surprising effect on Meg—surprising even to herself. Catherine, Wild Bill, and just about everyone she knew were always telling her, "You ought to write a book, Meg." She'd heard it so often that her, "Yeah, yeah, sure!" was now an automatic response; they were all so positive she could write one of the funniest books ever. She tried it once but discovered only how intimidating blank paper can be, and how permanent is the written word. A funny spoken remark lay on the air, and then on the inner ear, for just so long; it had a dying fall; then it was gone forever, leaving her life wonderfully unencumbered. There was always room in the air around her for more. But a page just got filled up with words and then it held them forever. It devoured and never disgorged—like an endless constipation. It was the visual equivalent of a car with its horn stuck. Also, spoken words, even if not quite right, could be made to seem right with an appropriate gesture or inflexion of the voice. The written word, shorn of such props, had to be just right. None of hers were—in her own opinion; they all seemed just a little off target. She knew she would never write that book.

Then came her promise to Burgo, and by some obscure process it unlocked the will that had once made her try those few dispiriting pages. She began again, only this time she wasn't working for an unknown, unknowable, future reader; she had an audience. But it sustained her through only a few dozen pages—by which time she had forgotten Burgo and was remembering the awful, screaming permanence of each written word. Then at the top of the next blank sheet she scribbled:

> Though I'll never eat my words,
> I shoot and cannot hit.

Poor page! Although you eat my words,
You hoot and cannot shit.

And it all went away in a drawer for years.

48

By the fifties Golden Power Hydraulics was established as one of the country's leaders in hydraulics applications. Their main outlet was still in agricultural and site machinery, but they had important contracts in military,
petroleum, and general industrial areas, too. Over those years of growth
Burgo and Wild Bill had only one serious disagreement, which was when
Burgo, without a word of consultation, lifted an entire design team from an
American rival and put them to work on new applications for GPH—
specifically, a whole range of tractor-mounted hydraulic implements, from
backhoes to logsplitters, powered by an amazingly efficient pump working
off the PTO shaft.

It wasn't that Wild Bill was hurt; he was scared that Burgo could do
something so big without any discussion. The fact that the team and its
products were outstandingly successful was neither here nor there. In a way,
its success only made matters worse; Burgo thought it justified what he had
done and that Wild Bill was a curmudgeonly stick-in-the-mud for not admitting it. Wild Bill was scared that an unrepentant and self-satisfied Burgo
might try it again.

So when, in the spring of 1950, Burgo did the proper thing and called a
full board meeting to discuss certain changes he thought it was time to make,
the promise was good. But all that was revealed by their discussion was how
wide a gap separated their two business philosophies. Burgo was a grab-the-
hot-iron man; Wild Bill was for consolidating what they had before em-
barking on any new expansion. The hot iron that Burgo wanted to grasp
was pneumatics—as close a cousin to hydraulics as they could possibly find.
The arguments for it were strong—compressed air was a big industry in itself, and a well-established one. On top of that there were all sorts of new
industries in which gases were pumped, stored, compressed, rarefied, or just
moved from process to process. Hot, corrosive, radioactive, supercold, or
supervolatile, they all demanded new knowhow. Burgo feared that if they
didn't get in on the act now, while it was still forming, they could be excluded forever, or be forced to pay an extortionate entry fee later.

Wild Bill conceded all those arguments but stuck to his basic position that the breakneck expansion of the last few years had created strains in the organization, muddle in the executive ranks, imbalances in their investment, and all the other ills of hasty, heady growth. To take on more now, without attending to their present deficiencies, would be to invite disaster.

Burgo, knowing how much money would be needed to finance his ambitions, and knowing, too, that the eastern money-men would listen more to Wild Bill than to him, fumed at his impotence. The argument dragged on into the summer. It was still unresolved by the time Burgo and Catherine left on their vacation to Hawaii—an often promised and often postponed trip that even Burgo hadn't the nerve to put off one more time. Not in their silver-wedding year.

For three weeks, as they worked their way up the islands, from Hawaii to Maui to Molokai to Oahu and Honolulu, Burgo behaved like a good tourist. They swam, rode, played golf, hunted wild goats and deer, shot miles of movie, ate roast pig and washed it down with papaya juice, climbed volcanoes, spotted celebrities, and did everything that thousands had done before them and would do after. But by their last week, which they spent on Kauai, he began to fret over the indecisions he would soon be facing again. They sailed off Poipu beach, marvelled at the sea fountains erupting from the lava tubes, stood awestruck on the rim of the Waimea Canyon, went screaming down the natural water slide at Waipahee, and walked up the Hanalei Valley, the legendary birthplace of all the world's rainbows; but through it all she would catch Burgo withdrawn into himself, no doubt churning over future arguments with Wild Bill and those who agreed with his caution.

Their last day was also to be the highlight of their vacation. The main highway circled the island north and west from Lihue, the chief town; but on the opposite corner of the island the two arms of it failed to link up. On their first day they had driven to one of the ends, the Kalalau Lookout, where the dizzying Kalalau Valley, plunging four thousand feet in less than four miles, gave the highway engineers every excuse for not going on another ten miles and completing the circuit. Catherine, looking through the binoculars at the sea from that point, had said, "No one can get down to those beaches—and I'll bet they're the best in all Hawaii."

Burgo hadn't left it there, of course. That same evening he had chartered a helicopter to take him and Catherine there on their last day, putting them down in time for the 5:42 A.M. sunrise and lifting them off just after the 7:53 P.M. sunset; for the whole of that time they'd be out of sight, sound, and reach not just of civilization but of any other human being. They would be Adam and Eve and the last couple on earth.

For the dawn hour they huddled around a fire and reassured each other it was going to be a wizard day. On the embers they cooked a breakfast of pineapple fritters and bacon steaks, washed down with champagne—the first time in their lives they had had champagne for breakfast. It, and their early start, made Catherine drowsy. The sun was well up by the time she awoke. Burgo was farther along the beach, indulging in his only seaside pastime: dam building as a prelude to dam busting.

It had long since ceased to annoy her that he could never rest. When they were first married and went out on picnics he would lie down for about ten minutes, no more. Then he'd spring up and say, "Okay, I've done that. What's next?" Now, on all their picnics, he carried a little trenching tool, a combination shovel and pick, and if there was any running water within miles, he'd start constructing an elaborate system of dams, canals, diversions, spillways, overflows, levees, and aqueducts.

He was naked. She was hot enough now to shed her clothes, too. The surf was too huge for her to do more than paddle and roll in its dying fringes. Farther along the beach, just below Burgo's hydraulic playground, the stream he was damming had formed a small lagoon, newly laid bare in the receding tide; there, in water a little too warm for her taste (which, in these matters, was still Scottish), she splashed around in safety—until Burgo burst one of his dams and sent torrents of red-muddied water down to her.

She ran out by the clear end and stood full-face to the sun, letting its heat reach through the wet until it felt like a scorch. Goaded by it, she strolled up toward Burgo. The two white ostrich eggs of his untanned buttocks made the rest of his skin seem even darker than it was. She looked down at her own breasts, pale, veined, and milky against her golden tan. Would they burn and peel in this sun? It was tonight's worry, or tomorrow's.

"Is it more fun building up or breaking down?" she asked him.

"Building up, of course." He laughed. "But check with me again in half an hour when it's dam buster time."

"It's going to be roasting by midday. I'm going to move our stuff into that grove of palms. Shall I get lunch ready now?"

"Or what?"

"Or not." She smiled provocatively.

"Okay. First ve eat, ja?"

She went away laughing. "You'll never change."

The grove mingled the hot shade and the cool sea breeze to perfection. She had just finished setting out their lunch—though not opening the food boxes—when Burgo called excitedly to her.

It was one of the best systems he had ever built. The huge upper dam, helped by two natural abutments of living rock, was brim full, the lower dams and waterways invitingly empty.

"Crude or subtle?" he asked.

"Subtle."

He drew one finger through the sand at the top centre of the upper dam. A spurt of water leapt forward, out and down over the rough-sand slope, darkening it, smoothing it, vanishing before reaching the foot. More water was right behind, pulling more sand in its train. It also disappeared into the dryer bottom slopes. The sand at the foot started to glisten; the vanished water was reappearing. The roughness fell inward to a gleaming smoothness. The smooth sand began oozing forward. The collapse ran progressively back up the stream, enlarging its course.

In the beginning a finger could have stopped it—like the Dutch boy-hero who saved a town. Now a whole hand could not. From then on the collapse rapidly gathered momentum—trickle to babble, and babble to pouring stream, a rushing river in miniature; two men could not have stopped it.

She watched Burgo intently; he had eyes for nothing but this now unstoppable catastrophe. He stood on the fringe of the cataract and let it swirl and roar past him. When the water looked like overwhelming the second dam he ran to the farther end and made a breach. But the torrent, contemptuous of his aid, forged straight ahead and ruptured the wall immediately below the gap in the first dam—a gap now almost three feet wide.

Next it was forced to divide, and subdivide, and subsubdivide through a network of channels. "That's pretty," she said. "You never dug anything like that before."

"I'm testing a theory of mine about fluid biassing—where a small side current can switch a big main current from one channel to another." He watched it awhile, poking his shovel in various small channels and noting the result on the larger channels adjacent. "Disappointing," he said.

"It doesn't work?"

"No, it does. Perfectly."

"Well, why should that be disappointing?"

"Because I already knew it would work. So I learn nothing new. We only learn when things start to behave unexpectedly."

Soon the rush of water had destroyed the delicate interlacing of channels, leaving some high and dry and scouring others to switchbacks of water, sand, and mud. Within ten minutes the little river had re-established itself and nothing remained of the upper dam but a few large boulders Burgo had rolled or thrown down first to mark the line of it.

"When we retire," he said, "I want it to be on a hillside near a stream. We oughtn't to have sold Gideons."

She linked arms with him. The sun, the breeze, their isolation, and their nakedness were stimulating. "We could retire right here," she said. "Build a house on the little hill there, with Trader Vic's next door, and a little jazz club down here."

"Why on earth?" he asked with a laugh.

"Otherwise Meg would never come and visit."

"Oh, sure. It sounds like her prescription." He sighed. "Yes—Meg and Wild Bill."

"Isn't this marvellous, darling," she said. "And aren't you wonderful to have fixed it all."

They stopped. He took her in his arms and they kissed. They ran their hands over each other. His erection grew, pulse by pulse, against her excitement.

"Crude or subtle?" he asked again.

She ran her lips and breath over his shoulder, his neck, his ear. "In that order," she murmured.

Crude was where they stood, feet braced apart, straining at each other on the sand; subtle was when he lifted her in his arms and carried her to the grove, where the blankets were already spread.

She awoke at two, ravenous. He was sitting beside her in his underpants, hunched over his knees, staring out to sea. She reached over, snapped the elastic gently, and said, "What's this? Did a serpent come by?"

"Touch of ballsache," he said ruefully. "Too much employment."

"Oh, isn't she a wicked woman!"

He turned and lay beside her, half on her, with one hand on her breast. He moved it onto her shoulder but she lifted it back onto her breast. "Insatiable," she said.

"I love you," he told her.

"And I love you."

"It's twenty-five years, twenty-five days, and nearly twenty-five hours since we made love for the very first time, just like this, after a dip, in the open air with the sun shining."

"I remember."

"If only we'd known then what we know now, eh?"

"What do we know now?"

"Well—for a start—what a big mistake it was for me to have anything to do with medicine. That's been a stinking red herring dragged across our lives, at MacNair, at NCT, and in the war. I've only got my life straight these last five years. And half of it's already squandered."

"Oh, Burgo, that's not true. That's twisting everything. Aren't you starving?" She sat up and began to ease the lids off the boxes.

There was chicken, neat's tongue, chippolatas, and salad in the coolers, with cheesecake to follow. "Was there ever a better century in which to live?" she asked. "And a better continent than North America? Look at us. We live better than the ancient rulers of world empires."

"If we'd got married in 'twenty-two, with no nonsense about a career in medicine, we could have been big enough by the crash to have weathered it and the Depression. We could have made a fortune in the war. Talk about empires? We could have bought this beach, this whole coast, just on a whim."

"How awful, Burgo. Anyway, how can anyone buy a place like this? How d'you buy solitude and a gentle breeze and desire like we still feel?"

"I wonder if Kelvin's making the same mistake? Perhaps, now he's qualified, before he gets caught up in medicine—in 'the career structure,' as they call it now—perhaps he should just take out a year and see what he thinks of business."

"But he knows already. He hates it."

"That's just his English education. Business is a dirty word over there. You see, there's another thing. If we were really big now, we could expand over there and wipe the floor with the English. They're forty years behind us. The Americans working over there are just printing money."

"Burgo?" She was worried now. "Don't try and distract him. He wants to be a doctor. He chose it. He's much more like James than you."

He shot her an oddly uncertain glance.

"Just as you're much more like Fiona's father than your own—or so she always said."

"A year either way is neither here nor there—as we know very well, honey. He isn't even married, either."

"Just don't! Okay?"

"Anyway, James isn't such a bad businessman. All that property he bought quietly over the years, all his investments, and the *Inquirer*. I tell you, we've a way to go yet before we're as rich as he is."

"If Kelvin wants to follow that trail, he'll do it his own way."

Burgo's sigh seemed to accept the argument. "I wish Wild Bill wasn't so cautious," he went on.

"If he weren't, the banks wouldn't listen to you with half such respect."

"We're getting big enough now for banks to listen with respect with or without him."

"Are you thinking of splitting?"

"Of course not. Perish the thought. He's a buddy."

"No friends in business, honey," she quoted back at him.

"He's the exception. But I'd just like to ginger him up a bit. He'd be fine in a hundred-million-dollar company. But no company ever got that big without taking risks—just the sort of risks he's turning down right now."

"He'd say that no company ever went bankrupt so easily as by taking such risks, though."

"That's absolutely true. How else do you keep the adrenalin flowing?"

"James's way?" she suggested.

He laughed and kissed her with chicken-greasy lips. "Oh, Cath, you have such a brain, you know. You shouldn't just be on the board. You should have an executive job with us. Remember what a team we made in Selkirk, starting Night Call there?"

"Let's give it a try," she said, not seriously.

"I wouldn't let you within ten miles."

"Whyever not?"

"Because you'd take Wild Bill's part nowadays. If I'm going to have people as sharp as you about me, I want them on my side. Maddy and Grant, maybe, when they're through with college."

"Are we all allowed to have wants?" she asked.

He smiled at her but said nothing.

"I want more times like this," she told him.

"Discussing the business, you mean?"

"You know what I mean. We've only taken this vacation because it happened to be our silver wedding and even you hadn't the nerve to call it off yet again. And yet it's been a time we'll both remember forever. I want more of them. I want the man I love, the most wonderful man in the world. I want a *life* with him. Not the heel of a life."

"Cath . . ." Her intensity troubled him. He wanted to soothe her.

"Yes, *you*. I told you. I'm insatiable for you. A few long weekends each year and a month of paradise like this every five isn't enough." There were tears in her eyes now. "Oh, God, why did I start this! It's impossible, I know."

"Cath!" Miserably he picked up a piece of driftwood and threw it down the beach. He stood and walked away.

She got out the cheesecake and divided it.

He wandered to the sea's edge, turned, and came back with a little more purpose in his stride. "It's not impossible," he said as he took his slice of the cake. "Listen to this. It's impossible to reconcile your wants and mine at the same time. Obviously. No—that's wrong. It's wrong to call them 'your' wants and 'mine' like that. I want the same as you—more of a life together.

And surely you want the security of money, plus the satisfaction of knowing there's a good achievement behind us?"

"I'd say GPH is already a good achievement, Burgo."

"But *nothing* to what it could be."

She laughed with a hopeless kind of humour. "But you'll always say that. If we do what you want—expand into pneumatics—and become the Rolls-Royce of the industry, you'll be drumming your fingers on the table, the chair, the dresser, the mattress—just like now—and saying we ought to expand into mining equipment, or air conditioning or some equally logical extension. I mean, whatever size we are, you'll always say we could be a lot bigger. You always want everything bigger."

Grinning, he reached over and caressed one of her breasts with the backs of his fingers. "Not everything. Some things reach a perfect size and stay there."

"You don't get out of it that way."

"Okay." His hand dropped. "Try this way. We can't satisfy both our wishes simultaneously. And we can't satisfy yours first and mine after. You couldn't let go. And the world of business wouldn't wait. So let's try it the other way. Give me ten years. We'll set that limit to it. In ten years we'll be sixty. Time enough to fulfil your wishes then. What do you say?"

"I worry about letting go. You say I couldn't. Could *you?*"

"In ten years? I may be damn glad to."

"And then again you may not."

"It's the sort of bridge we can't cross here and now, honey. What do you say? Shall we give it a try?"

"Or what? Are you offering a choice?"

"I always offer a choice, you know that. I never force anyone. You're absolutely free to choose to give it a try here and now—and for the next ten years."

"Or?"

"Or go away, think it over, take all the time you want, and *then* choose to give a try."

She laughed. "That's a Burgo-style choice, all right!"

"Well, you shouldn't have joined if you can't take a joke. Come for a walk?"

"I'll have a nap first."

She lay in the dappled sunshine, feeling its heat steal slowly up her left side, drift across her, and fall into the shadow to her right. From time to time she opened an eye to a squint and saw Burgo dwindling to a point far away to the east.

She expected to fall asleep but instead she found herself reliving the discussion she had just had with him. It was the first time in years she had dared to talk about the things she really wanted. Dared? Was it really a matter of daring?

No. She had to admit it. "Bothered" was a more apt word. It was the first time in years she had bothered to talk of such things.

And how mild she had been! How unassertive. Could Burgo be blamed if he now assumed she was completely happy in *his* chosen way of life?

Eventually the heat lulled her. This special day and her life had a lot in common. Both came by courtesy of Burgo. Both were set apart from reality, which was visible but beyond reach. Both were so congenial that most people would think them a kind of paradise. Both were warm—soporific, even. Was she not baying the moon to ask for more?

It was after four when she awoke, hot again. The sun had slipped below the smallest palm of the grove and lay full across her, fetching out a light sweat. She sat up into the grateful breeze and stretched. Burgo was nowhere in sight. She called his name. There was no reply. She stood and walked the full depth of the beach; only one set of footprints, made on his outward journey, was visible. He was not.

She went up to the little lagoon and cooled off again. Then, looking inland, she saw smoke rising from a point about a hundred yards into the "jungle" above the beach. For a moment she wondered who it could be before she realized that it could, of course, be no one but Burgo. A short while later he reappeared in the pine grove and waved to her. He began to gather their things.

She got out and rolled in the dry sand, covering herself in it; she loved the itching-scouring sensation of it falling off when it dried.

"Didn't you hear me call?" she asked when she was nearer.

"Burgo hear," he said. He had gathered everything up except the empties. Laughing, she ran to relieve him of the rugs, cushions, and their clothes.

"Cathy good," he said. "Burgo good. Burgo build home. Cathy see. Cathy like." He led her into the bush.

"Heap pretty tepee?" she asked.

He groaned and slumped. "Tarzan and Jane, you dumb cluck! 'Heap pretty tepee!' My God, what's the point of trying!"

"Why did Tarzan not answer when Jane called?"

"Tarzan home not ready. Surprise not ready. See! Jane like!"

Surprise was the word for it. He had hacked and woven a desert-island hut out of saplings and palm fronds. A fire crackled merrily, its flames eclipsed by the sunlight, in a ring of stones before the open doorway.

"Oh, Burgo! It's beautiful! How did you do it?"

"You see them do it in movies, or, rather, you see the hero hack down one leaf and then it's fade-out-fade-in and the hut is built, and you think 'oh, yeah!' But, actually, it's not too difficult. D'you know what was the best help?"

"What?"

"Remembering the weaving patterns Meg had to learn when she was at Selkirk. There's a pure hopsack weave of saplings under that." He took the rugs from her and spread them inside. "When the fire's down a bit, we can barbecue those ribs."

She threw herself on top of him. He turned over. She pinned him down and began to kiss him.

"What did you cover yourself in all that sand for?" he asked.

"Me Girl Friday," she said.

"Well! It beats having a headache, or an aching back, or being tired."

"Beast! When did I ever say any one of those things to you?"

"In fact, I'll bet you've found the original put-off. Womankind's first. Hubby comes home from the dinosaur hunt and says, 'Okay, what's in it for me?' and wifey grins and says, 'Sand!' Go on—the little river's just to the left there. Wash it off."

"First ve eat, ja?" She giggled, enjoying the sensation of being both available and untouchable.

They had finished the barbecue and the fruit and were just about to make love when there was the faint but unmistakable beat of a helicopter in the distance.

"Damn these tropic sunsets!" she cursed, and began to dress in a panic; civilization's values had invaded their Eden, borne in with the rising throb of the aircraft.

Burgo laughed as he watched her. "It'll keep," he said in a lordly way. "In ten years' time I reckon it will be just about perfect."

49

"But Dad does have a point, Mummy," Kelvin said. "He does regret having studied medicine and having been sidetracked by it for twenty-five years. And all I'm doing is giving up a year, one year, just to be sure I'm not making the same mistake."

"But you've done six years' training, darling. What about that?"

"So did Hopkirk, who qualified with me. He's going to explore the Ruwenzori Mountains for a year. Everyone says splendid. No one says what about those six years—and they were paid for by the British taxpayer in his case."

"But he's probably wanted to do it all his life. And you certainly can't say you wanted to go into business all your life, can you now."

"Anyway, Dad says a medical qualification is very useful in business. Other businessmen are either obsessively healthy or worried that they're unhealthy. But he can make both kinds feel uneasy inside thirty seconds, either by just looking at them or—if that doesn't work—asking, 'Pardon me, but were your fingernails always that colour?' or some such question."

"Oh, that's your father all right. Turn anything with a joke. Only it's your life he's turning. What exactly does he think you'll be doing?"

"Running my own show."

"No, dear. That's what he *promised* you. But what are you *really* going to do?"

"It's true. Wild Bill won't agree to branching out into pneumatics. So Dad has taken an agency for Bernoulli and Co. They're a Vancouver firm who've been in pneumatics about ten years. He's forming his own little company, quite separate from GPH. And he's giving me forty-nine percent of it. And I run it. Look, Mummy, suppose it doesn't work out. I can still go back to medicine, and I'll be a much better doctor for it. Most patients are in business, one way or another. How many doctors can claim to understand business from the inside—to *know* the life at first hand?"

But Catherine was only half listening. She was realizing that Burgo's generous "gift" of forty-nine percent of the new company was a way of building a Trojan horse. Kelvin would make a success of it—puppetmaster Burgo would see to that. Then Wild Bill would overcome his caution and agree to a merger. And Kelvin's share in the little company would dilute Wild Bill's in the big one—maybe by only four or five percent, but enough to break the present deadlock holding. Then, with Kelvin at his side, Burgo would be unstoppable.

And so, indeed, it turned out. Within the year Kelvin was as obsessed by business as Burgo. He threw himself into the pneumatics industry as if he were actually inventing it, just as Burgo had once thrown himself into Night Call, in Selkirk, when he truly was inventing it. Their only relaxation was the restoration of the next vintage Rolls-Royce chassis on which they had decided to build the Limousine-Landaulet body, with the shallow scrolls on the doors.

This time they had professional coachbuilders, panelbeaters, and upholsterers to do that side of the work; but the mechanical and electrical side, and the paintwork, they tackled by themselves, with, of course, the resources of GPH and Golden Dynamics, Kelvin's outfit, to back them.

To call it relaxation was a misnomer. During those hours in "Phoenix Hall," as they called the site of their labours, they discussed the business and the future endlessly. Catherine helped at first, as she had helped with the restoration of the Ghost. But she had to stop. She could not bear to listen to Burgo, slowly and surely twisting Kelvin's mind away from medicine and his chosen path. Burgo could make business sound as challenging as philosophy, as exciting as sport, and as rewarding as art. Kelvin, brought up in the English tradition to think of business as grubby, dull, and beneath a gentleman's dignity, was bowled over, of course. Even Catherine felt herself getting caught up in its challenge and excitement—which was, to her, another reason to reduce her hours in Phoenix Hall. When she taxed Burgo with turning Kelvin's life upside down, he pointed out that Kelvin was, after all, almost twenty-six and quite old enough to strike out for himself. Also, he reminded her, she had given him these ten years; she couldn't step in now and try and run them for him.

She saw then how *blanche* was the *carte* she had given him in that Burgo-style catchall of a promise.

Within two years GPH had re-formed as Golden Power Dynamics; Wild Bill capitulated to commercial pressure and agreed to the merger.

"It isn't just this battle he's won," Catherine told Wild Bill when he and Meg came round to dinner one evening, Burgo being away east. "From now on he calls the tune at GPD, you realize."

Wild Bill was very relaxed. "I realize."

"Why did you do it?"

He laughed. "Hell, Cathy, I thought you, of all people, would understand why."

"What's that supposed to mean?"

"I mean all of us who go into partnership with Burgo hold out just so long. But in the end he makes it so impossible we all simply yield. We see there's no future to be gained in resistance. It's like those dams he builds when we go on picnics. *We* are those dams—we who try to resist him. At the right moment he strokes a finger across us—and all that head of pent-up energy does the rest. We cave in, and he is streaking away down the valley as if we'd never said no. I tell you, I've built my last dam. From here on I'm trying to imitate the water turbine. The jolly miller's wheel."

"He was right about pneumatics," Meg added. "We were wrong."

Wild Bill did not demur. "Burgo is the biggest asset any firm could have. But he's going to need more and more people like me to organize behind him and to firm up the quicksands he likes to skim over. I think I had my role wrong all these years. Now we're getting it right, we'll really start cooking with gas."

"He's just abdicated," Catherine said angrily to James, when their guests had gone. "He's merely putting a good face on it."

"Everyone abdicates in the face of Burgo," James answered. "Sooner or later."

"You believe I have?" she asked.

"You believe not?"

She could not answer. She had abdicated, long ago. Now she sought for nothing new—only to conserve as much of the old as possible: the family. The children's sense of family. And James. He was no mere lover. He was a part of everything. (A substitute for everything? she wondered, but shook away the thought without pursuing it.) And Burgo. She took what there was of him and she was grateful. They all followed in his wake and scavenged for crumbs; Burgo's crumbs were as big as others' cakes.

All the same, she thanked the heavens that Maddy and Grant, who were, respectively, reading English and Economics at MacNair, were beyond the reach of the business.

50

"It's the chance of a lifetime," Grant said. "Anyway, if it doesn't work out, we're both qualified. We can find work easily enough."

Catherine, looking into his eyes and seeing there the fevered light she had so often seen in his father's, knew she had lost; it was futile to offer any further argument. But, like him, she had to persist. "You're qualified, right enough. There never was such a qualified family. The head of it could now be one of the leaders of the nation's medical profession, but instead he's selling deep freezes. The eldest boy is a qualified doctor who spends his days with pneumatic door closers and paint sprayers. The daughter took a degree in English and stayed on to take another in journalism. The youngest is an economist. And what do they want to be? Short-order cooks!"

Maddy laughed. "It's a bit more than *that*, Mummy. We think we've found—"

"We *know* we've found," Grant corrected.

"Yes, we know we've found a cottage industry that could boom to factory size inside five years."

"Less if Dad will guarantee this schedule of loans we've worked out."

"Wild Bill said it's the best prospectus he ever saw. We know exactly how firm we want each steppingstone to be before we trust our full weight to it," Maddy said contentedly.

"Look, darlings, it was fun, I know, cooking for people and catering for their parties. And it was a good vacation job—"

"More than good—it was stupendous."

"—but it isn't the real world."

"The money was real enough. We didn't cost you and Dad a penny last year," Maddy reminded her.

"And"—Grant grinned like a man breaking the ultimate secret—"we earned something more than just money—both of us. We earned diplomas in French cuisine."

Catherine collapsed. She hadn't known they were as serious about it as that.

"Everyone's getting freezers now," Maddy went on. "And even if they don't, they rent a cold vault."

"And what do they put in it when they've used up last season's venison?" Grant asked.

"*Cuisine Glaciale,*" Maddy answered. "That's what we want to call our new outfit."

"Good name, eh?" Grant asked.

"I thought of it," Maddy said.

"Does this double act go on all the time?" Catherine asked. "Or am I getting the dress rehearsal for the performance you'll be giving your father?"

They exchanged glances. "We kind of hoped you'd maybe like to have a word with him first," Maddy said.

"Me? Why?"

"Soften the ground," Grant explained.

She laughed, a shade bitterly. "But don't you understand—your father's going to leap at the chance."

"Is he?"

"You mention the word 'freezers'—it's the twenty-four-karat word for nineteen fifty-four, by the way—and in three years you'll be working for him."

"Oh, but we don't want that."

"You want his money."

"No. Only his guarantee."

"He's a Venus's-flytrap, darlings. He lures in people like you, with the Macrae surname, and then he devours you."

"Oh, Mummy!" Maddy laughed persuasively. "Kelvin's *happy.*"

"Is he? As happy as he was before 'fifty-one? Ask him. He's treading this same road ahead of you, remember."

"He isn't." Grant was very firm. *"Cuisine Glaciale* is going to be *our* outfit. No one else's."

She abdicated. "Go and see him. You don't need a pass from me, or any letter of recommendation. But make sure you sup with a long spoon."

"Am I wrong?" she asked James later. "They're grown-up, aren't they? I mean, they talked themselves into this. It wasn't Burgo, like with Kelvin."

"Will you not content yourself?" he answered. "Think of your own youth. Who could have lived your mistakes for you?"

She nodded, grudgingly.

"And as for warning you—what language could they have used? What were your mistakes, anyway? What action taught you so little you'd gladly undo it?"

"None, I suppose."

"Think, too, of the life they've had. First Dunedin, then here, then Toronto, England, the war, away to school, Inverness, Grant back here for a year, then all here except Kelvin. And now you expect them to settle to—"

"But Burgo only ever had *one* home—and he's the worst of the lot."

"Exactly! We don't know how anything's going to turn out. If the greatest poet who ever lived can say of his own work *perhaps it may turn out a sang, perhaps turn out a sermon,* how can we lesser mortals expect to know what our own even more wayward creations will be?" He stroked her hair. "I wish you could be more accepting. You worry me when you're like this."

"How?"

"I'm afraid you'll get like Fiona, except that she was always like that. She ended up predicting disasters as a way of avoiding the sort of disappointments you're now torturing yourself with. Don't you trust your own children not to make fools of themselves—or, if they do, to know how to mend matters?"

She squeezed herself into his embrace, shivered, and kissed him. "Why can't I talk like this with Burgo? I only have to say two words and he's already assuming I'm just out to criticize."

He murmured into her hair. *"But to see her was to love her, love but her, and love forever."*

"What does Burns say about loving two men?"

"He says plenty about loving a dozen lasses."

"Aye! Or a hundred. But it's not the same, is it." She smiled up at him. There was not an inch of that now wrinkled face she did not know by heart and adore. She knew he was thirty years her senior and, in the order of things, would die before she was even old. Sometimes, as in moments like this, when she needed him so much, his mortality lay almost on his skin.

Echoing her mood he said, "One day there will be no one but Burgo to talk to."

"I can't even think of life without you, James."

"It would be wise to start. It's only sixteen years to my hundredth birthday. After that I'll have to think seriously about drawing up my will."

She smiled, but only because his humour was like a command. In reality the prospect of his death terrified her.

51

Cuisine Glaciale was such a success within two years that even Burgo, the coach on the sidelines, couldn't believe it. He had to go east for a month and check the operation for himself. The evening after he left, Kelvin turned up unexpectedly at Wild Bill's and Meg's.

"Did you eat?" Meg asked. "We're on our way out."

"Where to?" he asked.

"Doctor's House. It's our bridge night. Come, too. We'll play poker."

"I wanted to talk to Wild Bill about— Do you have to go right now?"

Wild Bill came in as he was speaking. "What about?" he asked. "Company business?"

"In a way. I just wanted to say that if Dad comes back with some wild notion of absorbing Maddy and Grant's business, I'm going to quit."

"You have a new job?" Meg asked excitedly.

Kelvin, taken aback at this easy acceptance of his bombshell, said, "No, of course I haven't."

"Well, don't quit until you have one," Meg told him. "Remember—a bird in the hand, er, can't shit on your head. Or whatever."

"I think you could take it a bit more seriously, Meg," Kelvin said grumpily.

"Come and tell your mother." Meg was unrepentant. "She's the one who could really do with cheering up."

"That's enough, Meg. Are you serious, Kelvin? Well, of course you are. You want to talk about it?"

"I am being serious," Meg insisted. "Kelvin, honey, if you really want to hurt your mother, just leave her to go through your pockets and find the airline ticket."

"She doesn't go through my pockets anymore," Kelvin answered scornfully. Then he grew worried. "Does she?"

Meg took a fistful of her own hair and tugged at it, screaming gently.

Kelvin laughed. "Never kid a kidder, eh? Well, I'm only kidding you. Except you're not really a kidder. You just make quips all the time."

Meg shrugged. "It's the same rule—never equip a quipper. But seriously, come and tell your mother. She'd be hurt if she found out she was the afterthought."

Kelvin came and they played poker. When they stopped for waffles, he announced, as if for the first time, that he would be leaving the company if Burgo came back with any grand notion of branching out into frozen foods on top of all the existing chaos.

"Oh!" Meg said excitedly. "You have a new job?"

"No!" Kelvin was annoyed he couldn't add that she knew damn well he hadn't. "It's just a threat."

"Oh, just a *threat*," Meg echoed. "Well, take a bit of advice, as one kidder to another, kidder. My favourite brother, Il Magnifico, isn't going to take any threat too seriously unless it's backed with an alternative salary and starting date."

"I'll make him believe it without that."

"Pardon me, dear nephew, you will not. Let me tell you—in case you hadn't noticed—just how unstoppable my big brother is. When Death the Reaper slices him off at the ankles, he'll be three weeks buried before he wakes up to how serious things are suddenly looking for him. No, on second thoughts, I take back my advice. Don't line up one job. Line up three."

"Would you go back to medicine?" Catherine asked.

He could see the idea pleased her. "Probably. Yes. Certainly." He smiled at her, glad she was taking it like this—and glad, too, he had followed Meg's advice.

"In Toronto?" James asked.

"In B.C., I think, Granddad. I've grown very fond of Vancouver."

"You and I could outvote him," Wild Bill cut in.

"Sure. But could we face the consequences?"

"And if he gets back your voting stock, could I?"

"May I ask what's wrong suddenly," Catherine said, now that she was recovering from the first surprise. "It's sudden, isn't it?"

"Outwardly, I guess. But up here"—Kelvin tapped his skull—"it's been going on ever since he merged my little pneumatics agency into the business. Even that little acquisition, you see, isn't digested yet. Not properly. And yet look how it's gone on since. From pneumatics we made a perfectly logical extension into compressors. And from compressors there was another perfectly logical extension into freezers. And from freezers, no one can deny, it's perfectly logical to launch into *Cuisine Glaciale*. We take bigger and bigger bites of the market but we never pause to digest anything. I'll bet we're the only company our size on the whole continent that has a door with a shingle on it saying 'Legal and Marketing Department.' I've seen visitors grinning with disbelief, but we've all grown so used to it we've forgotten how it happened in the first place."

"Oh," Wild Bill said, "that was when Adrian Barry left to join—"

But Kelvin stopped his ears with ramrod fingers. "Don't," he cried. "I couldn't bear to hear it. And I'm sure it's tremendously logical."

"We may be jumping to conclusions," Meg said. "It's not certain he's got any designs on *Cuisine Glaciale* at all."

Kelvin turned to her. "Before he left he said to me, 'That name, *Cuisine Glaciale,* is worth ten thousand dollars alone. And the mind that thought it up is worth ten times that.'"

Meg nodded glumly. "It's certain," she conceded.

"Vancouver's no distance at all by plane," Catherine said happily.

"Don't." Meg's sudden anguish was theatrical.

"Don't what?" Catherine asked.

"Don't build castles in Spain. Or even in Capilano Canyon. There's one player who has yet to join this cast. Let's wait for Act Two before we decide whether or not to walk out on the show. We don't even know if it's tragedy or comedy."

"It doesn't matter what Dad says. If he's going in for a further bout of expansion, I'm leaving. He won't talk me out of it."

"Why not stay and fight him?" Wild Bill asked. "I don't mean just voting a flat no to everything. But we could use our voting muscle to press things slowly into shape."

"It's too late, Wild Bill. A couple of years back, maybe. If I'd had more business savvy. But he's run too much line off the reel since then. He wouldn't even feel us playing him." He turned to Meg. "Your style is catching." He laughed. "Now I'm almost taking it as lightly as you."

"Oh, I don't take it lightly, Kelvin," Meg told him, picking up the cards again. "On the stage, tragedy *happens to* people. It's over inside three hours. And we breathe again and clap hands and shout *Author!* But in real life, down here in the basement, it *becomes* people, instead. It's lifelong. There's no curtain call, no whipping off the mask, no 'see you tomorrow, my darlings!' And we are naturally too ashamed to cry *Author!*—we self-made characters." She laughed but no one else joined her. "Jesus! Hark at me!" she added. "I knew it was a fatal mstake to start writing again." She began dealing face up. "First one to get the bastard with the axe, okay?"

52

"But you *promised*," Catherine almost shouted at Kelvin.

"I didn't promise." He felt about six years old again, excusing himself in this way. "Not in so many words. I didn't say, 'I promise.' "

Catherine merely stared at him, as disappointed as if she had caught him stealing pennies.

"I didn't," he insisted. "What I meant was I'd get out of here. I'd leave Goldeneye. I'd leave head office. And that's what I'm doing."

"You think so? You'll still be part of the business."

"But I'll be away from all this chaos."

"Far enough? You think London's far enough?"

"I'll have my own office. I've got my own brief. And I'll be able to run it my way."

"But you were so positive. Whose idea was it, anyway? Yours or his?"

"He came out with it right after I told him I was quitting."

"I'll bet he thought it up as he went along."

"I don't think so."

"Well I do."

"He's always wanted to do business over there in England. You know that. He thinks they're a pushover."

"He's a world expert on pushovers. I think you're running away. I think you should stay here and fight for—"

"Is this the same mother," he asked in rhetorical amazement, "who only six weeks ago wanted me to get out altogether!"

"Getting out is one thing. Getting out is all right. But you're not doing that. You say you know there's a lot that's seriously wrong with the business. But you're not staying to try and put it right. Oh no! You're running away to London to make matters worse."

"How d'you work that out?"

"You're going to do the very thing you criticized your father for doing —you're going to take yet another bite at yet another market, which you know very well is not going to be properly digested either. Just like all the rest."

He sighed. "It won't be like that. I wish you knew more about business. You'd see how I'll be able to keep it quite separate."

"Yes." She was bitter. "I wish I did know more about business. I'd go into that office every day and put it straight—do all the things you and Wild Bill ought to have done."

"Oh, look, Mummy, there's no great Freudian clash going on here. If I were all Oedipal about him, I'd stay and fight it through. We'd have a real classic father-and-son stand-off. But no one can feel like that about Dad. He's worth ten of any other man. I love that guy. Being on his team is like being one of the original four musketeers. I'll never regret these five years with him. So I'm not going to stay and cloud the memory of them. Talk to Grant. Maybe he will."

"Or Maddy."

"Yes. Even better. He's scared of her."

"What?" She was incredulous.

"Sure. And of you. He's scared of all women a bit. I guess I shouldn't tell you this. It's putting a terrific weapon in your hands."

"I don't believe you."

"He told me. He said we never know what you women are thinking. Even women never know what women are thinking. So that's one frightening thing. And the other is that you seem to have an instinctive knowledge of how things ought to be—and then making them so. You have the nursery wallpaper chosen before we've even proposed. He says you probably had the entire Mesopotamian banking system all worked out long before the first man decided to give farming a whirl. And that's more power you have over us because, without thinking, you can come out with things like, 'Don't say that word,' or 'Sit up straight,' or 'Never wear blue,' and we catch ourselves beginning to obey automatically. We actually have to stop and step outside the situation and shake ourselves and drink cold water before we can tell ourselves, 'No—she's wrong,' and then do whatever we know is right." He laughed. "So, yes, maybe Maddy *is* the one." He looked at her less confidently as he added, "Or . . . you?"

"Me?"

"Yes, Mummy. You're the only one who happens to be married to him. You can't go on fighting proxy battles, using your children, forever."

She stared at him, dumbstruck, while he opened a drawer and fished inside. He pulled something out and threw it on her lap. It was an airline ticket. "For me," he said, "it's as easy as that. Maybe I'm not excessively proud of the fact. But it is a fact. My guess is that Maddy and Grant will say the same if they get as fed up as I was. They'll just buy a ticket someplace. We love him enough to say goodbye without a fight and without any bitterness. But that way isn't open to you, is it."

That final throwaway question of Kelvin's would not leave her alone. He could not possibly guess at the dissatisfactions within her. When they had been boiling openly—all those years ago—he had been far too young to see them. And now they were buried so deep beneath the sediments of middle age that even she could forget them for weeks on end.

Yet inadvertently he had stirred them. The corrosive sublimate was at work again in those depths. Its first by-products were merely whimsical. She remembered James's suggestion of twenty years ago that she might study medicine. But what had been absurd then was now embellished with two further decades of that absurdity. Nevertheless, she wondered if she might not study pharmacy. She also thought of asking James for some kind of job on the *Inquirer*.

These particular stirrings came to nothing. But the acid, she knew, went on biting. She knew that she would not go on forever the way she had tamely gone since the war. And she knew, too, that her instinct was right. She would never find her way by seeking it *inside* the life that Burgo donated to her; it must be outside. And even if medicine, or pharmacy, or reporting were not the way, she had to get an independent toehold on something out there.

53

"I've got the plane for the day," Meg said. "I thought I'd fly down to Regina. Want to come?"

"I'd love to, Meg," Catherine told her, "but I'm going out to the rezavoy with James to see to the ponies."

"Nurse Marchant can do that."

"I'd rather do it myself."

"Burgo'll catch you one day," Meg warned. "Speaking of which, or whom, wasn't he supposed to be back here today?"

"He called and said he had business that would keep him over in Toronto."

"And I called Maddy and she knew nothing about it. Nor did Grant, because she asked him. And Maddy knows *everything* that happens in the Toronto office."

"Oh," Catherine was puzzled. "That is strange."

"Burgo is up to something. I'm sure of it."

"Like what?"

"Who can tell? Most businessmen live in fear that the competition will run circles around them. Burgo, I'll swear, lives in fear he'll wake up one day and find that the guy who just ran circles around him was, in fact, himself. Hey, did you finish Orwell's *1984* yet?"

"Last week. D'you want it back now?"

"Sometime. The reason I asked was d'you remember that bit where after Winston has been brainwashed he hears an Inner Party speaker attacking the enemy and praising their ally. And some assistant passes up a slip of paper telling this guy that things have switched, and the crowd he's praising are now their enemies, and the lot he's attacking are their new allies. And the speaker goes on talking without a break in the flow, and he completes the sentence, switching the names of the ally and the enemy, without the teeniest little jolt to the grammar or the syntax. Remember?"

"Oh," Catherine laughed. "Guess who!"

"The fantastic thing is, Orwell never once met Burgo. Or did he? It's kind of hard to believe he didn't, don't you think?"

"I've been aware of a sort of mood lately," Catherine said. "I asked him if—now that the Frozen Food Division is going so well, and Maddy and Grant are so pleased with things—I asked if he's about to shake everything up with another gigantic merger or acquisition."

"And he said perish the thought. I can just hear him. And by the way, Maddy and Grant aren't at all pleased. But that's another story."

"He said the only possible expansion now would be to freeze hell over."

"That's pretty definite. The trouble is he's only ever that positive when he's lying."

Catherine wanted to ask her what she and Maddy were up to. They had both made flying visits to New York the previous week. Catherine had heard about them only through a third party. But, she thought, it would keep.

She wondered, too, what Meg meant by saying that Maddy and Grant were dissatisfied; but that, too, would have to keep.

Around midday the sun came out. Catherine and James drove the cutter to the rezavoy in a light whose clarity and brilliance hurt the eyes. She wore dark glasses but he never would; he sat hunched beside her, squinting out through eyes narrowed to reptilian slits.

"You look grim today," she said.

"Burgo should be back. He said he'd be back."

"You weren't relying on that, surely?" She laughed.

"And you shouldn't be so jovial, Cathy. That's how you always end up with the worst of both worlds. He thinks you're happy. Maybe you even fool yourself. And so he gets away with murder."

She felt a brief impulse to tell him that she felt herself changing lately, but it was still too tender a growth for such exposure. By contrast, she needed no effort to be the sort of Catherine he was criticizing. After all, it was precisely how she had gradually turned into that sort of Catherine—by making no effort.

"It's that or weep. I don't suppose anyone ever gets all they want. You didn't. Nor have I. We're half-a-loaf people."

"What did you want?"

"If there had been no Fiona. If I had married you."

"When there wasn't, you did. Everything but the ceremony."

"The ceremony's important, though. And the family. That's what I expected with Burgo, I think. A doctor, a university lecturer, a nice, modest house in the nicest little town in Ontario, with the lake, the woods, the scarp, and all that beautiful tame-wild country round there. And then the children. One, two, three. Wouldn't it have been a lovely life—but for greed?"

"Greed?"

"That's what it was. Burgo wanted a fortune, too."

"Och no, woman, it's more than that with Burgo. If he'd stayed in medicine the books by now would list Macrae's Syndrome, Macrae's Test, the Macrae Suture . . . something like that. It's more than simple greed."

"I always used to be afraid of making a mess of my life. I didn't realize how easy it is, especially if you make all the right choices and do all the right things. I feel guilty now for being dissatisfied. Here we are with . . . what? A million dollars? Two million? Burgo says both. A hell of a lot, anyway. Much more than anyone could reasonably want. Yet it gives me no feeling of security. All the security I have comes from living with you in Doctor's House. You know Burgo wants to build us a new house across town, in Little Hills? He asked me to 'sound you out' about moving."

"Which you, being a dutiful wife, are now doing?"

"It's an awful urban ranch-house he has in mind, split-level, sliding glass walls, patios all around. Helen saw the sketches and said there's a million of them in La Jolla alone. Awful, awful, awful! But there I go. How many women wouldn't give their eyeteeth for such a house, and a husband who's made a million or two? So when I say I want something different, isn't that a kind of greed, too? That's what I mean by feeling guilty. I'm either guilty for the mess I've made or I feel guilty for being so greedy and ungrateful." She hugged his arm. "Thank heavens for you, James. And An Dóiteán. If I hadn't got you here, and if I hadn't been able to get away to Scotland these last two summers, I think I'd have walked out on it all."

"Or you might have fought more for yourself!"

They had reached the hay barn at the rezavoy. He reined in. The loose ponies came galloping up in a haze of splintered snowcrust, iridescent with hints of rainbows; their breath wreathed them in pallid steam. She helped him lug out the day's ration of hay bales. The well water, heated still by the little wind generator, melted the ice in the drinking troughs. They argued all through these chores, each accusing the other of doing too much, she reminding him he was eighty-nine, he reminding her she was only thirty years younger, which at their age was nothing.

They sat on unbroken bales and watched the ponies jostling and filching hay from one another.

"Still makes a profit," James said. "Fiona never believed it. She thought I cooked the books."

"I can't imagine you doing anything that makes a loss, dear."

"Would you really walk out on Burgo?"

"Probably not. Running away is for when you're young. Where would I go, anyway? Besides, he gave me his word he'd retire at sixty. That's only two years. Time enough to run away then—if he goes back on his promise."

"Or stay and fight him."

She laughed. "Kelvin said something like that, before he left for London. Why, after sixty years, should I suddenly turn myself into a fighter?" Vanity made her add the correction: "Fifty-nine years, anyway."

"You don't regret marrying him though?"

A stallion pony crept boldly into the shed and snitched a wisp of hay no more nutritious than the hay he was trampling. *How like a male,* she thought.

"Do you?" James prompted.

A mare did exactly what the stallion had just done.

"Regret is such an elastic word," she said. "We had an R.A.F. officer at Queens Langley whose deepest regret was he'd never be public hangman. He was serious, too. The war was a good time for madmen."

"You're evading the question, woman."

"Did you regret marrying Fiona?"

"Every day! But only for a few minutes."

"The same, I guess. We musn't get cold."

"I'm fine. I don't feel it. We die a bit at a time, you know. Didn't Fiona say something like that to you?"

"I forget. Anyway, I'm cold even if you aren't."

"Have we still got any of that Gideons honey Nono sent?"

"One pot."

"Let's go back, and do you make some oatcakes, the way you can make them, and we'll gorge ourselves, eh?"

"All right. We must leave a bit for Meg, though. I promised." She rose to unhitch the two draft ponies but he clutched at her.

"I still love you, Cath."

She squeezed his hand; it was chill. "Aye. Aye."

"You're the finest woman I ever knew."

"Aye."

When she had unhitched the ponies she turned back to him and said, "Come on."

He tried to stand up. He looked at her in bewilderment, as if she had just said something in an unknown language. Then he fell backward onto the haybales, eyes closed.

"James!" Alarmed she vaulted the bale they had sat on and knelt beside him. "James—darling—James—" She went on speaking while, more by reflex than by thought, she loosened his collar, got his head on one side, raised his feet, and did all the other proper things for a heart attack. His pulse was thready, his brow damp and cold.

"Oh, darling, darling!" She lay beside him and kissed his mouth. "Oh, James, don't die. Please don't die. Please! I love you so much."

Briefly he opened his eyes. He muttered something.

"Don't talk. Don't try and talk, darling. Just hang on. Just . . . ."

She could sense his agitation more than see it. She fell silent. His eye opened again. "How it began!" he said. He even tried to chuckle.

She fought with herself not to cry. A crying woman is a bad nurse, he used to say.

What to do? Wrap him up, cover him with hay, and go and get help? Or try and move him? She'd never carry him, not even the few yards between the cutter and the haypile. Then she saw the bed of the cutter was just the same height as the bale on which he lay. Would it back over the dirt floor?

After some difficulty she got the two ponies to back it the right distance. Then, using a pole as a lever, she inched the cutter sideways until it was broadside to the bales and hard against them.

Fifteen minutes later she had James, still unconscious, under intensive care in his own hospital. Then she called the Toronto office. Burgo wasn't in but he was expected back at any moment. She told his secretary the news and then called Helen in California—who said she'd catch the next flight to anywhere in or near western Saskatchewan.

As soon as she hung up, Burgo was through to her, making her wonder if he hadn't been there all along.

"Burgo?"

"Honey."

"I'm so sorry, my darling. But thank heavens they found you."

"I'm flying to Chicago in an hour. I ought to be gone five minutes ago. How is Dad? I mean . . . is it really . . . you know?"

"Jay seems to think so."

He paused. "What d'you think?"

"Well, obviously, I think you ought to catch the next flight west. Why? I mean, surely you are coming?"

"I don't think I can *today,* sweetie."

"But Burgo . . ."

"You see, I have this meeting scheduled for tomorrow morning in Chicago. There's people coming from Washington, and L.A., and from M.I.T. It's taken months to set up. I'd hate to . . ."

"James is dying, Burgo."

"Well, *is* he? That's what I was asking you. Obviously, if it's life and death, I'll cancel and come home. But if it's going to be one of those three-reelers, I mean, I can be there tomorrow evening. That's for certain. What d'you think?"

"I think I'm not going to stand here negotiating your father's possible death with you over the telephone."

"Tell you what, honey." He was actually suggesting a bargainer's compromise! "I'll fly to Chicago as arranged. I'll be in our usual suite at the Palmer. You have another talk with Jay and if it really is bad, cable me there and I'll come on. Okay? By the way, I asked one of the girls here to get in touch with Grant and Maddy. Have them stand by."

Catherine laughed.

"What's so funny?" he asked.

"Well, they'll come, of course. Ask them to stand by and they'll come. Ask you to come, and you stand by!"

"I got to go now, honey."

And he went.

She didn't even bother to consult with Jay, but cabled the Palmer in Chicago at once, telling Burgo to come on home without delay.

She and Meg sat with James all night, taking turns to catnap or watch him. He did not recover consciousness.

But he came around briefly the following day when Helen arrived, followed shortly by Grant and Maddy. "Burgo?" he asked.

"He's coming, darling," Catherine promised. "Everyone's coming. You'll have quite a party when you're well again."

He seemed easier after that.

Nurse Marchant took over for the afternoon, letting Meg and Catherine get some sleep.

He asked for Burgo again that evening. By then he was obviously fading.

"Why the hell doesn't he show?" Margaret hissed at Catherine.

She slipped out and called Chicago. "Mr. Macrae left word he'd definitely charter a plane from here to Goldeneye this evening," his secretary said.

Catherine returned to James's room just as Jay was leaving. Her eyebrows framed the question she could not quite put into words.

"It's so hard to say," Jay answered. "He's certainly weaker then yesterday. But he always had the constitution of an ox—as we all know. If I peeped in the Book above and saw a date next week set against his name, I'd accept it."

"As long as Burgo gets here before he goes."

"When d'you expect him?"

She shrugged. "Now? This evening? Before midnight, anyway."

"I'd say it's odds-on." He smiled reassuringly.

She was half reassured.

Burgo's plane—his own Cessna 407—touched down just after eleven that night. They all heard it. James opened his eyes and seemed to locate Catherine.

"It's Burgo," she said. "Burgo's come, darling. Now we're all here."

He closed his eyes again, for the last time. She was sure that was the moment the life went out of him. He neither breathed nor moved again. Within the minute everyone else in the room was aware of it. Nurse Marchant felt for his pulse. Her eye caught Catherine's. Catherine gave a barely perceptible shake of her head. The nurse casually let go, appearing to be satisfied. It deceived no one, but that was not its purpose. It was an open sign of a conspiracy among them to pretend that he lived until Burgo came into the room.

Catherine seethed with shame and anger.

Burgo took an age—though it was probably less than fifteen minutes—

to come across town. He slipped quietly among them, nodded briefly to each, and came at once to the bedside. Everyone except Catherine withdrew then.

Burgo nodded with resignation. "Too late," he said.

"Ten minutes too late! He's been asking for you all day." She threw herself on the bed beside James and put her mouth to his ear. "He's here, my darling. Burgo's here. Can you hear me? Darling, darling James? Burgo's here. He *did* come."

Perhaps it was the futility of this gesture, perhaps it was some elemental bodily memory of the years of nights when she and he had lain so, in fact or in waking dream—she collapsed in bitter sobbing. Burgo did not touch his father but her. He gripped her shoulder lightly and gave a gentle shake.

"Don't you *touch* me!" she shouted into the cavern of warmth between her and James's body. She squirmed as far as she could from Burgo, and as close as possible to James.

"There was a power of attorney and a patent assignment," Burgo began to explain. "If they hadn't been signed on American soil, we'd have been weeks running to and from the consulate."

She sat up then and turned upon him, drab with defeated anger. "I don't care if your damn business was folding all around you. He died asking for you, Burgo. How to get that fact through your thick hide? After eighty-nine years of life your father died asking, 'Where's my son?' You were all he wanted."

"Well!" She could see he was angry but was trying to appear otherwise. "It wasn't always so, was it, Cath!"

"What's that mean?"

"Don't imagine I didn't know about you and him. Before we were married."

She laughed, an angry, bitter, helpless laughter.

"Mom told me. That Christmas I proposed to you."

"You think that was it, Burgo? You think it ended then?" She knelt, curled over James and cradled his head. Rocking gently, she went on speaking, more to herself than him. "This man was my real lover, all my life. When we were broke and you sent me back here to this house—he was my lover then. And in the war. And ever since. His last words to me, yesterday afternoon, his last words were *I love you, Cath*. And mine to him, the last words he heard this side of death, were mine—*I love you*." She kissed his still warm brow. "Oh, James, darling, how am I going to live in a world without you?" She turned to Burgo and said quietly, "My life has ended with his. What have you got that can take his place?"

It hurt him. She could tell. For a moment she was moved to relent—to retract what she had just said. If only he would show his hurt openly. But he never would—not to her. All he said was, "Come on, Cath. You mustn't say such things just for the sake of trying to wound me. I'm sorry I was late. Truly I am. But there's no call to say things like that."

She realized then that in her own mind she had paced this as a short bout of anger—a flare-up, a few harsh words, and then a reconciliation of kinds, or at least a standoff. Now she had an intimation of it as something much bigger. The moments just gone, moments that now could never be recalled, were going to mark a permanent change in their relationship. Her love for James had always been an extra; it had never challenged or taken the place of her love for Burgo—quite the contrary, in fact, for it had sweetened the times of bitterness and made that greater love the easier to sustain.

How could she make Burgo see that now?

The mere question brought all her anger back to the boil. No! He was not going to get away with it so lightly yet again. She was not going to say, *Well, that's Burgo . . . you know Burgo . . .* and then play along as ever.

There was a rare feeling of hardness in her as she said, "Time to tell the truth, honey—whether it hurts or not. And the truth is James was my anchor in this house and in this town. Every time you've cancelled a home-coming, or put me off, or stood me up, or just plain ignored me—and got away with it—your release came by courtesy of James. Now *you* think about that."

There was a knock at the door. Burgo called, "Come in."

Nothing happened. He went and opened it. Nurse Marchant stood there. "Will you call me when I'm to come and lay him out?"

"I'll do it," Catherine said. "You don't mind, do you?"

"No, of course not."

Catherine couldn't bear the thought of anyone else performing that last service for James.

The interruption had broken the tension between them at its peak. She looked at Burgo. He looked away.

"Don't worry," she told him. "I won't let us down in public. But don't imagine things can ever be the same between us. Or if they can, you've got to do the work. I mean you've got to work at it *now,* Burgo. And you've got miles to run before you get where this man was."

54

With all the family there except Kelvin they did not wait the traditional three days; James died just before midnight and was committed to the winter vaults thirty-five hours later at eleven in the morning. All of Goldeneye—and half the prairiefolk for a hundred miles around—were there; some of them Catherine had not seen for more than thirty years, when she and James tended them and their families. Everyone had a warm and grateful memory of him to share; the character of the occasion subtly shifted from a mourning of his death to a celebration of his life.

The celebratory mood persisted—even strengthened—among the family when they returned from the cemetery. Margaret, sensing how close to collapse Catherine was, acted as hostess in Doctor's House. The elegance of dinner that evening surprised Helen, who remembered her kid sister as an indifferent cook at best.

"Maddy taught me the secret," Meg said, bright-eyed. "It's the cooking sherry. You're supposed to slosh it over the *food*. I never knew that. They ought to put it on the bottle. Or in a book somewhere. Talking of books . . ."

"This is very civilized," Burgo said of the béarnaise.

"We're all civilized these days," Meg picked him up. "The war taught us about being cosmopolitan and stuff like that." She turned to Wild Bill. "When was the last time I threw up red wine and the fish course in the same heave?"

"Last week," he said evenly.

"Yes but *apart* from that? Anyway," she chided him, "you always said, before we got married, how much you appreciated my cooking."

Wild Bill smiled all round and nodded his agreement. "Sometimes I'd get so hungry trying to cook for myself I'd go to my shelves and take down books she'd borrowed and returned—just to get the smell of the coffee and sauce she spilled over every page."

"Talking of books . . ." Meg tried again.

"No." Burgo said. "Let's talk of real estate. Does anybody know what's in Dad's will? How did he leave this place, Doctor's House?"

"I think he just left everything equally," Helen said. "Mind you, that was ten years ago, when we talked about it."

"So." Burgo pulled a face. "We each own a third of the house, a third of the *Inquirer,* and a third of every other property. Oh boy! What's a third of a pony amount to?"

"A quarter-horse," Meg said. "Everyone knows that. Ask a difficult one."

"Did you ever see his will?" Burgo asked Catherine.

"No," she said. "Young Mr. Jeffcott has it."

"Wild Bill did all Dad's books," Meg volunteered. "Which reminds me . . ."

"Would we think of selling this house?" Burgo asked. "We three who own it?"

"No!" Helen and Catherine were in unison.

"Well, not sell," Burgo said. "But Dad's been blocking the westward spread of Goldeneye with this toy ranch of his. There's a demand for housing tracts here, and we're ideally placed to meet it. What I'd like to suggest is that we form a company and develop it ourselves. Sell it a bit at a time."

"No!" This time Meg joined her sister and sister-in-law.

Burgo looked at the three women and laughed helplessly. "Can you imagine the first poor guy who invented the wheel? Can't you just hear what the womenfolk said when he trundled it into the village!"

"What makes you think a man invented it?" Maddy asked.

"All the women I ever met. They're designed to say no. They are *programed,* as we will all soon learn to say."

"Well, if I have a voice," Maddy answered, "I'd hate this place to be sold. So count me in."

"You were never out, darling. But it doesn't matter, actually. Even though we could probably raise a lot of money on the place—"

"And you just happen to have a contract in your briefcase!" Catherine sneered.

"Not quite." He remained amiable. "Even so, we can get by without."

There was a pause and then Wild Bill said, "Meaning what?"

"Meaning what would everyone say if I told you we've had an offer of close on ten million for Goldeneye Industries in all its glorious richness and diversity?"

There was a concerted gasp.

"And that, before we're through bargaining, I estimate the bid will close at something nearer twelve?"

They began to laugh at the impossibility of it.

He's going to retire, Catherine thought. *He's going to keep his promise, after all. That's what he was fixing in Chicago.*

At once she felt awful at the hurtful things she had blurted out to him on James's deathbed. Would he understand? Would he forgive her?

"Do we get sold with the business?" Grant asked.

"Who's offering?" Maddy put in, more to the point.

"Frigorifico," Burgo told her. Then to Grant, "That's up to you. D'you want to stay back in the past, or join the future?" He looked at his son, then at Wild Bill, and grinned. "Come on, girls—it's not that difficult. Really it isn't. I'm not talking just about our future, but everyone's. What's the next revolution?"

They began to guess: TV . . . jets . . . space travel . . . an end to all disease . . . mascara that doesn't run . . .

"Bigger!" Burgo said to each. "What do all businessmen use? What do they operate on? What flows across every desk in business—and government —every kind of administration? What's the commodity?"

"Information," Grant said.

"I told you!" Burgo was triumphant. "I said to myself, in a couple of minutes Grant will be there. It took me months, but you're there"—he snapped his fingers—"like that!"

"Sell information?" Wild Bill asked.

"Nope. We sell, or we lease, the ability to process it. I think leasing is the better tax deal—but that's a technicality. These computers are going to offer ways of handling information that just make the mind boggle. . . ." And he went on to tell them of the researches he'd been making into the subject, from time to time, over the last few months.

"And," he went on, "it just so happens that while I was in Chicago talking with Frigorifico, I met someone from Honeywell who's on the point of going over to IBM, and he—"

"Oh!" Meg said. "Your kind of guy, all right!"

"Only not so loyal to family and friends as me," Burgo told her. "He says there's a stack of money waiting for people who are smart enough to get into computer leasing."

"What's Doctor's House and the land worth?" Catherine asked.

"As tract housing?" Burgo turned to her. "Given careful development and an orderly release of the land . . . why, a million? Maybe a little less. Over twenty years. But as it is? Thirty thousand. Could be thirty-five. Why?"

"I'll buy it," Catherine said.

Everyone heard the needle in her voice.

"Sure." Burgo turned to Meg and Wild Bill. "I thought to call this computer-leasing firm DataLease Dominion, or DLD."

"Sounds like an insecticide," Meg said.

"Never mind what it sounds like. If you join, it would mean your moving to New York. I don't want to start in Canada and then expand south. I want to start with an eastern–North America operation and expand west-ward as soon as we can manage it. It's a hundred-million-dollar company, Wild Bill. Just tailor-made for you. We wouldn't find that kind of money anywhere but Wall Street."

"I'm serious," Catherine said, "about buying Doctor's House."

"Consider it done, honey," Burgo said edgily.

"Talking of New York," Meg said—and this time her whole manner insisted on a hearing—"I may have forgotten to mention that a book of mine is being published there soon, by no less a firm than Hebel. So why don't we all talk about that instead? Tell me, Helen, what did you think of it?"

"Think of what? Your book?"

"What else?"

"I haven't read it. I didn't even know you'd written one. I thought all that was just a sort of standing joke. I don't know the first thing about it."

"So what? We don't know the first thing about computers. That didn't stop us talking about them."

Helen laughed.

"Come on! You're not *that* provincial, even in La Jolla. Since when did we sophisticates let a little thing like not-having-read-a-book stop us from talking about it?" She grinned brightly around. "I know! I'll tell you what it's about and then you can pretend you've read the reviews. And then we can talk about it. Just for an hour or two. Nothing heavy."

Catherine said, "Without making any promises, honey, we would like to hear what it's about at least. And when we can see a copy?"

"And if it really is going to be published!" Burgo added.

"Oh, there's a contract," Wild Bill said.

"I didn't write it to be published," Margaret cut in. "Heavens forfend! Mine were the very highest motives: fun and therapy. Just like any old Hemingway."

"Is that true?" Burgo was impressed. "You've really got a contract?"

"Magic word, eh, Burgo?" Margaret grinned.

"What's it *about?*" Helen insisted.

Margaret looked for aid from the heavens. "God, you're all going to loathe it. It's a romance. A real woman's book. It's about . . ."

"What's it called?" Helen asked.

"Men Who Have Known Me." She challenged them with her eyes.

After a silence Burgo said, "It doesn't exactly trip off the tongue."

"The first chapter," Meg offered, like a consolation prize, "is called, *Never argue with a man who's got you covered.*"

Burgo nodded and gave a prim, glassy smile. "I'm beginning to guess what it's about," he said.

"It's about this sweet, innocent virgin. I did her entirely from memory, too! And she goes to work in the ritziest whorehouse in North America, except that I've moved it, along with just a few hundred acres of Lake Michigan, to Las Vegas. That was for the sake of realism, you see? And then—this is the clever bit—then I've moved Las Vegas to the Gaza Strip, right in the middle of the Suez War. That was to bring in a bit of symbolism. They say that part of the world is the cradle of civilization, so this book is one of those cradle-to-grave sagas. And that takes care of comedy, too. So it's got everything. Romance for the women. Realism for the men. Symbolism for the critics. And comedy for the kids. How can it—"

"And sex," Burgo added.

"And sex for the birds. How can it lose!"

"What's it really about?" Burgo asked.

"I just told you."

"Really?"

"And truly."

"And it's under your own name? Which I have the honour to—"

"Ha haaa!" Meg pointed an accusing and jubilant finger at her brother. "Got you!"

"If it doesn't worry Bill, I don't know why it should worry me."

"Yet it does! *Eppur si muove!*"

"Well—are you?"

"Sleep easy, brother dear. I'm calling myself Margaret Meek. It started as Margaret Meek Rae, geddit? I have a friend who said that tested out quite well when she straw-polled it with ten Manhattan bookshops." She grinned at Maddy and then stared at Catherine, mimicking her wide-open mouth and eyes. "You thought books just happened, didn't you, honey! Not anymore. They've become a weird form of merchandise that opens down the side."

"Why did you drop the Rae?" Catherine asked.

"Bob, my editor, he vetoed it. He says Margaret Meek is better. People will vaguely believe I'm an anthropologist—and that's very smart. He says you've no idea what crap people will swallow as long as they think it's written by a genuine anthropologist. And especially a woman anthropologist. Why don't I get the typescript and read it to you? No one's going anyplace in the next five or six hours, are you?"

"I guess they wouldn't agree to publish if it was too awful," Burgo said. "Though you can never tell nowadays."

"Can I quote you?" Meg laughed. "I'm desperate for good endorsements like that."

Just as the clan was breaking up for the night Maddy said, "I have two announcements, which might as well come now as later. The first is that Kelvin has resigned, as of this week. The second is that, as of next week, so have I. But, in view of this new development, I'm willing to—"

"You *what?*" Burgo stared at her icily.

"Oh-oh!" Meg rose to her feet. "I just remembered—my bubble gum is double parked." She left, dragging Wild Bill reluctantly away with her. Helen went, too.

"Just what do you mean?" Burgo asked when he was alone with Catherine, Maddy, and Grant.

"Exactly what I said. I'm going to head the copywriting section at Cowsnofski-Waterfield, on Madison Avenue. With a piece of the action. That's what I've just been fixing."

"Behind my back."

"Dad! Even *you* go behind your own back. What were you doing in Chicago?"

"Working for all of us. Securing all our—"

"Don't!" Maddy said in a choked-back scream. "Don't say the word *future!*"

"I'm the only one who faces it."

"Oh boy!" Maddy slumped in defeat. She looked at Grant. "You're going to go on working for him? You're out of your skull!"

"You mean you're going to live in New York?" Catherine asked.

"I'm afraid so, Mummy." She squeezed her mother's arm. "I tried. God knows I tried."

"Listen, honey." Burgo was all conciliation and understanding. "I know I'm not the easiest man to work for . . ."

"Hah!"

"All right. I'm the most difficult man in the world. But I do have this knack of knowing the tides and currents. You can't deny it."

"You need it, Dad, because your other favourite trick is fixing to steer a two-acre log jam—which is also your very own creation—down the rapids. No! What am I saying! *Up* the rapids!"

Grant laughed. Even Catherine laughed, though, what with this news and her bereavement and tiredness and Burgo's unforgivable behaviour, she was not too far from tears.

Burgo, discomfited, said, "Well, we always knew you had a way with words."

"So, now, do Cowsnofski-Waterfield."

"It's not too late, honey, is it? This computer thing really is big. I mean we're talking hundreds of millions. More."

"Oh, God, Dad, this is the blank wall I've faced every day of the last three years. The fact that you are right—I don't doubt that—doesn't make you any the less impossible to work with, you know."

At that point Catherine slipped quietly into tears. She stood and walked to the door. "I'm going to sleep in the spare room tonight," she said. "Goodnight."

"What spare room?" Burgo asked, thinking she had forgotten they were all taken.

"The one that's *now* spare," she said.

Maddy ran to her. "Mummy. I'm sorry."

"Now," Burgo said. "You see!"

"Don't you dare!" Catherine told him. "Don't you dare use me."

When she was alone in that bed she wondered what on earth she was going to do now. Burgo had finally broken up the family—the last of the life threads that bound her here. He had not intended it. He had simply caused it, just by being what he was. In the same heedless way he had started this new business. He obviously had no intention of keeping his promise. And now that everyone was leaving Goldeneye, she thought, what was there to detain her?

Silence.

The bed seemed to float. An intimation of freedom? The sensation frightened her. She clutched the pillow to her and whispered for James. "Stay with me, my darling, wherever you are. Stay with me a while yet."

55

Next morning young Mr. Jeffcott came and read James's will. It was not as Helen had said. The *Inquirer* was left to an independent trust to benefit the town. Near three-quarters of a million in property and money was divided equally among the three children, except for a handful of bequests to old friends and colleagues. But the remainder, Doctor's House and its land—Burgo's coveted housing tracts—was left to Catherine, with a reversion to the surviving grandchildren on her death.

"Now you're *someone*," Meg told Catherine when they were driving Helen to the airport at Saskatoon.

"Yes," Helen said. "A woman of property. How does it feel?"

Catherine breathed deep with satisfaction; she *did* feel different. "James knew what Burgo would try to do. I'm sure of it."

"It's like giving you a shield." Meg chuckled.

Catherine remembered James's almost-last words: *Or stay and fight him.* The gift of the house and land was like a shield.

But not a sword. To fight you needed a sword as well. James had not given her that.

On their return trip she asked Meg if she and Wild Bill were really set on going to New York. Wouldn't they stay with the old firm, Goldeneye Industries, and go on living in the town?

"Golly, I'd love to, honey," Meg answered. "I'm going to miss you. But New York is just too tempting. I know Goldeneye has turned into quite a town, but it's still a town full of farm folk and they scare me. Everything bucolic scares me. Even the chickens. My God, when I was at Doctor's House those hens took one look at me and curled up and died of diseases that had never before gotten closer than Hawaii. You're different. I mean, you know that cows don't give milk when you crank their tails up and down." She peered anxiously at Catherine. "You *do* know that, don't you?"

Catherine laughed.

Meg went on: "And when you took over at Doctor's House those hens just lay on their backs in ecstasy and farted eggs like tommy guns. You belong here, and I belong in New York. Like Archimedes said, 'Give me a Saks charge account and I'll move the world.'"

When she saw Catherine's disappointment, she added, "Sorry, darling, but I'm a hedonist right deep down to the bottom of my skin—and I don't go much deeper than that."

"Tell me about your book," Catherine said. "Is it really what you said?"

"Sure. Did Burgo ask you to find out?"

"I haven't seen Burgo except for the reading of the will this morning."

"Oh. Like that, huh?"

"I don't know what to do, Meg."

"You're not breaking up?"

"I don't think so. But we're not much for togetherness, either. I get the feeling he doesn't greatly care."

"Oh, he cares, honey. I think your trouble is he doesn't believe you'll ever *do* anything. You know what I mean? I mean *do* anything."

"His stove has a hundred back burners and I'm the pot on the smallest of them all. I know that."

"The only time he's ever asked me anything about you since you got married was when he found out I had so much money to invest and he suspected MaCaBu had been a front for a bordello in which you and I were Les Girls."

"He asked you outright? That?"

"Does Burgo ever ask anything outright? But he asked, okay."

"What did you say? I hope you left him guessing. God, sometimes I wish I had taken Miranda up on her offer. She was serious, you know."

"I promised I'd give him the answer one day."

"And did you?"

"That's what *Men Who Have Known Me* is all about."

"Oh, Meg! You mean you want him to know? I nearly had a fit last night when you said something about a whorehouse on Lake Michigan."

"Yes, I want him to know. Just like you wish you'd taken up Miranda's offer. It's the same music."

"Even so. You're virtually telling him you worked in that place."

"The whole world's a whorehouse."

"Is it?" Catherine asked. "I don't think so."

"How would you know? You only know the whole world."

Catherine chewed on that. "I think your whorehouse was better than the whole world."

Meg laughed. "Gee, I am going to miss you." When Catherine did not make the expected response, she said, "What are you thinking?"

"I was just remembering something Burgo once said to me, when we were in Hawaii. 'We only learn from things that behave unexpectedly.' Something like that."

Meg laughed. "For *things* read *people*." She shot a swift glance into the back of the car. "Somewhere in all that mess behind you is the original manuscript, if you're interested."

Catherine rummaged and found it, a tattered heap of papers, scribbled over in many hands, inks, and pencils, coloured and plain.

Chloe had pouting, wet lips [it began], as if someone had just confiscated a flute from them and she had not yet adjusted. They burned a purple-red, as if a bee, or a white Anglo-Saxon Protestant, had stung them—which, in a sense, he had. A seventy-dollar sting; for Chloe was one of the Young Ladies at . . .

"You don't think it reads too much like *Rebecca of Sunnybrook Farm*, do you?" Meg asked. "That's where I'm cribbing most of it from, especially the plot. I'm hopeless at plots."

"Who is B. B.?" Catherine asked, pointing to the initials at the end of a handwritten marginal note.

"Ah, think what happiness the world owes to those with double initials —William Wordsworth, Charlie Chase, Alcoholics Anonymous, Margaret Meek. . . ."

"And Brigitte Bardot. But that's not *this* B. B., right, sergeant?"

"Right! God, I haven't thought of poor dear Cherokee in years. But this B. B. is the most powerful name in New York publishing. The only man who ever said *who?* when Walter Winchell called—there's another, by the way. We're an army, and Bob Benson is our leader. That's B. B."

"The Bob who changed your name?"

"And my life. Talking of New York, honey, we'll be settled in in no time. Come on down if you want to get away. Stay as long as you like."

"Away!" Catherine echoed. "With you gone, and Maddy gone, and Kelvin, and James dead, and Burgo and Grant in the east most of every week, it's Goldeneye that's *away* these days."

56

Some time back, Burgo had bought a quarter section in Little Hills, a mile east of Goldeneye; it was there he intended to build the "dream" house Catherine had described to James. All he had built there so far was a three-hole golf course. The level fairway between two of the holes doubled as a private landing strip. It was from there that Burgo flew east before Catherine got back with Meg from Saskatoon. He had expected Grant to go with him but at the last minute Grant declined, saying he'd stay and have a word with his mother. Wild Bill, too, wanted to see the lawyer and have another talk with Meg.

When Burgo's Cessna was a dwindling speck, Grant turned to Wild Bill and said, "My clubs are in the clubhouse."

"Mine, too," he answered.

The "clubhouse" was the tractor shed that housed the aircraft.

"Join me for a couple of rounds? It's not that cold. Winter rules?"

"I'd be delighted." Wild Bill had developed a golfing style that compensated pretty well for his two artificial legs.

The snow had been ploughed from the landing strip and swept from the greens at each end. The "rounds" could only be out-and-back, between the two holes.

"Well, here's a how-d'ye-do," Grant said as they teed off.

"Yes." Wild Bill looked guardedly at his nephew. "Have you decided what to do?"

"In what way?"

"Stay, leave, or stick with your father."

"What about you?" Grant asked.

"I asked first."

"It rather depends on you."

"You mean if I join this new company, DataLease Dominion, you will too?"

"That would be a start."

Wild Bill's second stroke brought him onto the green. "That for a birdie," he said. "What d'you mean, 'for a start'?"

Grant sliced his second into a drift. Wild Bill laughed and said, "You play like a cripple! What a pair."

Grant's smile was grim. "We're a pair, all right. And we'll end up as real cripples"—he tapped his forehead—"unless we do something."

"Like what?"

"Like force Dad to build this new business properly. So anyone can run it. I mean without him Goldeneye Industries is just a can of worms. Frigorifico must be mad, or desperate, to offer twelve million. Or ten. And what a typical Burgo-Macrae spread of vagueness there is in those two figures." He chipped a new ball up onto the green in two.

"It'll be twelve million without a doubt," Wild Bill said. "Frigorifico needs our tax liabilities badly enough to pay that much." He sank his putt in one. "Ten dollars on the next hole?"

"You're on. I might have guessed it would be something like that, where Dad's concerned."

"What's your worry, Grant?"

"Last night I had a long talk with Dad. About the things that made Kelvin fed up. The things that forced Maddy to quit."

"Ah. Creative chaos!"

"That's Dad's description."

"And yours?"

"Plain fucking anarchy." He teed off and got a good lie right in the middle of the fairway.

Wild Bill's eyebrows shot up at this sudden improvement in his golf. "My! It's easy to see what motivates *you!*"

Grant laughed. "Not really. I just don't like bad organization. I can't understand Dad, either. He rescued those Rolls-Royce chassis because he said he couldn't bear to see them being misused. But that's exactly what he did with the business. The dynamics is pure Rolls-Royce but the mechanism! It's all baler wire, chewing gum, and Band-Aids."

"Did you tell him that?" Wild Bill's shot landed a little behind Grant's, and left of the centre line.

"I tried to get him to see how much more successful we could be if only we organized. But all he said was, 'I know what *you* want. You want a business bureaucracy. Full of grades and reporting structures and echelons and responsibility charts—until even *we* have to take a year off to study motivational psychology.'"

Wild Bill laughed. "And then he got all eloquent and starry-eyed about the future? And suddenly it was too late to go back and pick up the old threads and respond to his arguments? Yeah! That's your father."

Their second strokes brought them up within easy distance of the green. "It isn't funny, Wild Bill."

"No. I don't laugh either. I'm the man who left a twenty-thousand-a-year partnership, teamed up with your father, and is now worth . . . what? Four, five million? I don't laugh, Grant."

Grant put his ball within inches of the hole. "Bad luck," he told himself. "And you're right not to laugh," he added to Wild Bill. "Because with proper organization your stake could be ten times that. With Dad's flair, your head for money, and my ability to organize, you know goddam well we could be brand leaders in this entire hemisphere. Hell—in the world, given a little time. Yet you're happy with four million! I just don't understand you."

Wild Bill overshot into the snow beyond the green. He seemed unconcerned. "What are you thinking?" he asked.

"The same as you."

"Oh?"

"Yes. I'm thinking that this time we mustn't let Dad foul it up. He must, of course, have a free hand at building up DataLease Dominion. He's a genius at that. But we must be right there behind him, every step he makes. You sew up the finance, good and tight. And I'll button up the organization." He tapped his ball home, one-handed, for a par four. "He won't stand a chance." He chuckled.

"That's ten I owe you. Double or quits?"

"As you like."

"Mind you, Grant, I won't go along with anything underhand. No stabbing in the back."

"Of course not." Grant was one big smile. "Mind you, once or twice we may have to let him feel the point of the dagger pressed hard between his shoulder blades. You know how sometimes he just will not take a hint. But stab him in the back? Perish the thought!"

57

Burgo came home that weekend, and the next; but they were grisly times. The truths Catherine had blurted out in her grief and anger now lay between them, sour, huge, indigestible. Before he left he told her that Data-Lease Dominion was going to take up a lot of his time over the next few months and he probably wouldn't be coming home much.

"Night Call, all over again," she said.

He shrugged. "You won't believe it, I know. But I'll swear it's true. I want to retire. I want to keep that promise I made you. So I want to work like hell and leave with something worth owning. Maddy and Kelvin are going to eat their hearts out."

Her weariness almost felled her. "Who are you trying to fool, Burgo! With six million? We could retire tomorrow. Grant isn't going to thank you. In another year you could drive him the way Maddy and Kelvin went."

"Not him. Not Grant. He's a fighter. A stayer. And he's a winner, like me."

"Well, you'll have all summer to count your winnings, Burgo. Because I'll be staying with Meg."

"New York in July and August?"

"Don't you worry about us."

"Okay. But I think you could worry about *us,* Cath. You and me. And one of the things you might worry about is how, all our married life, I'm the one who's been forced to bear the burden of all the important and unpalatable decisions. When we were hit in the crash of 'twenty-nine, you wanted us to stay together even if it took twenty years to climb out of the hole. You wanted to do the self-indulgent, emotional thing. I know you wanted to do it for the sake of the family. You've always made the home and the family a kind of god. Everything must bow down to it. You've never been able to understand that sometimes—especially in hard times or dangerous times—the best interests of the home and the family are served by subordinating them. It's a hard thing to do. But that's what sorts out the grown-ups from the kids. You never grew up that way. It was always me who had to make the hard, sensible decisions. You've always resented that, I know. It was the same when the war came. You did the easy, emotional thing and followed me over there—instead of doing what hundreds of more mature and disciplined wives did, which was to keep the home and children where it was safe. As a result, our two older kids don't know if they're English or Canadian and are too confused to be able to pick a straight path in life. . . ."

"Bullshit!" Catherine, who had intended to say nothing, was too riled to let this last monstrous charge go by. "They knew exactly what they wanted in life until *you* got to work on them."

"Only Grant, who came back here to Canada, to his true home, for that one vital year—only he has come through it with any purpose." He was relentless. "When it came to sending the children away to school, again you wanted to do the self-indulgent, emotional thing, and again I had to make the hard but rational decision on my own. And now it's the same story. You want the easy, emotional indulgence of retirement. It's left to me to make the hard but entirely rational choice—to leave behind us something of which our whole family, for generations to come, can be proud."

"God! How you twist things!" she began, thinking he had finished.

But he pressed on, ignoring her. "Think of that while you're away, Cath. All your life you've done the easy, self-indulgent thing. You've left the hard choices to me. But I have been right. And you have been wrong."

"Are you through?" she asked.

"For the moment."

"May I speak? Will you let me speak without interrupting?"

"Go ahead."

"I didn't leave any decisions to you. You kept them to yourself. Never once in all our marriage have you involved me in a decision you haven't already taken. Even before we were married, you *told* me I was going to marry you. Of course, that was very flattering to me. And I was in a pretty mixed-up mess and couldn't think straight. But it was a big mistake— letting you get away with that. And then, when we did marry, you let me think I was marrying a doctor who was going to practise in a prairie town. Only on the honeymoon did you tell me about MacNair and the teaching job. You'd known about it for weeks, of course. You'd even accepted it. But you didn't tell me. And you know how I love the prairie."

"You said whithersoever thou goest . . ."

"Don't remind me. I've been pretty nice to you, Burgo. Too damn nice. You walk all over me and I'm the one who feels guilty and starts apologizing!"

"Walk all over you?" he sneered.

"I mean exactly that. In fact, I mean bulldoze, not walk. You make decisions and then bulldoze them all over me."

"I don't know how you can say that."

"I'll tell you exactly how I can say that. Or you tell me. Disprove me. Tell me *one* time—one single time in all our thirty-four years—when you came to me with a big decision *not yet made?* When did you ever say, 'Cath, honey, here are the facts. Now what do *you* think *we* should do about it?' Just tell me *one* time and I'll withdraw everything I've said."

"The reason I didn't should be pretty obvious."

"Not to me."

"All those decisions involved a threat of some kind to your god of home and family. They simply weren't discussable. You wouldn't have considered them. I had to go it alone."

"Burgo, you're fooling yourself. In the first place, you behaved like that even before we were married. I've just told you that. And in the second place, it isn't just me—it's everyone. Look at this decision to sell the business —whom did you share it with? With Grant? With Maddy? With me? With Wild Bill? Do we all have gods that make us unfit to share your plans? And going into computers—who did you share that decision with?"

"Everyone."

"Sure! *After* you'd taken it. There's a pattern, Burgo. You don't have friends. You don't have partners. You don't have children. You haven't even got a wife. We are all just tactical problems in the way of your solo drive toward personal fullfilment. We exist only to be persuaded, cajoled, outmanoeuvred, or bulldozed into agreement. And if all else fails—we are to be cheated. But never consulted. Never, never that."

Her words reached him, she could tell. But they were only a pinprick in his sense of self. There was still an I-know-better gleam in his eye.

"Are you walking out on me for good, Cath?" he asked.

"I don't know."

"D'you hate me?"

"No. I still love you."

"Can I come and see you in New York?"

"On business trips, you mean?"

"No. I'll finish whatever business, fly home to Toronto, and turn right round and go back to New York. Keep them quite separate."

She grinned.

"Okay," he said. "It's amusing but it's also serious. That's exactly what I'm talking about. In your world these things *can't* be combined. Business and family—mix them? Perish the thought. They can't yield a little to one another."

"When did your business ever yield!"
"Can I come and see you in New York?"
"Why not."

58

Men Who Have Known Me was one of the successes of the fall of 1959. Critically it vied with *Henderson The Rain King, The Mansion,* and *Advertisement for Myself*. One critic said, "Margaret Meek is the Norman Mailer of the Canadian boondocks."

"Which, by my reckoning," Meg retorted, "places me slightly to the coy side of Doris Day."

It stayed on the best-seller lists for nearly five months, alongside *Exodus, Hawaii,* and *Lolita*. United Artists bid $250,000 on the movie rights, and won. The paperback rights cost Bantam a cool $75,000. Meg gave a few interviews that had producers trembling and executives sweating, until the reactions began to come in. Then she had to ration her appearances as what was oddly called a "guest" on various shows. On radio she stood up well to Groucho Marx; a lot of people thought she actually won. Meg was finally in her element.

Catherine was at Meg's side throughout those months. She saw Burgo often—in fact, more than she would have if she had stayed in Goldeneye. She intended to see him but not to sleep with him. It didn't work. Her body—as always—overruled the intention. Their lovemaking was fierce, like a battle.

In coming to New York the only thing she had left was home—*her* home. His home was everywhere. He could make a home in an airplane seat. Here she was even more available to him. It would not do. She had to give him a real shock. And herself.

When Meg was commissioned to do the libretto of *Trick or Tryst?* a Broadway musical loosely based on her book ("And when I say *loosely* you should see the costumes," she told people), Catherine decided it was a good time to move on. Burgo expected her to go back to Doctor's House, which she did, but only to pack for a long visit—an indefinitely long visit, she told him—to England. She'd spend Christmas with Kelvin and his wife, Caroline—and their baby daughter, Emma—in London; then she'd go on to Gideons for a while, and then go up to Beinn Uidhe. Or maybe Beinn Uidhe first, then Gideons.

"Can't you even say roughly when you'll be back?" Burgo asked.

There was something odd in his manner. He did not speak like a worried lover, a man who feared his marriage might crumble; but more as if he were *eager* for her to go away for a while. There was a contained excitement within him.

He was there only two days of the seven it took her to pack and make all the other arrangements. He was loving, tender, warm, good-humoured, good company—all the things he had ever been to her at his best. And underneath it all he had not budged an inch. She might as well never have spoken. Did he even understand what she had said?

She thought she had the explanation of his secret excitement when it was time for her to leave. He had recently finished the reconstruction of the last of his Rolls-Royce chassis, the Phantom I. Naturally he was far too busy these days to do any of the work himself; this had been a professional coachbuilder's job from first to last, except for the final polish, which Burgo had applied himself. It was now the monarch among aristocrats. Even Burgo's new Silver Cloud (which he affected to despise, calling it the "Silver Detroit") paled beside it. For it was not the standard Phantom I body but the classically elegant Roi des Belges coachwork that had been copied in this restoration—the car that had swept the crowned heads of Europe around their realms in magnificent silence and luxurious comfort. And it was in this, one of the most beautiful cars ever built, that Burgo had arranged for her to be driven to the airport at Saskatoon. Jack Walker's down-to-earth description, "like sitting on whipped cream," had never been more apt.

The surprises didn't end there, for, instead of joining the scheduled domestic flight to Toronto, where she would change to the scheduled international flight to London, she was swept out to a waiting Boeing 707. Feeling like a fraud, but looking like a queen, she was ushered on board. This, then, was the real cause of Burgo's excitement. The Phantom I had been a mere hors d'oeuvre.

Seats in the forward section had been removed to make a stateroom containing a bed, a sofa, easy chairs, and a table, all bolted down yet arranged so casually as to seem like a corner of Doctor's House. The impression was enhanced by the fact that the bedcovers were identical to hers at home, and so were the upholstery, the carpet, and the curtains. Later, when she sat down to dinner in lonely pomp somewhere over Newfoundland, it was served on the same Coalport Indian Tree pattern porcelain they had at home. The wine was poured into an Orrefors crystal goblet, also identical to those she had chosen for her own dinner table. On the walls were flambeau vases full of flowers that probably came from her own hot house, having been carried to the airport an hour or so ahead of her. Next morning at breakfast the boiled egg had *Our Own* handwritten upon it, and the honey was a jar with a printed label reading *Sweetened for you by Gideons bees.*

She saw then that Burgo would never change. Like a snake he would wriggle out of his old skin and grow a new one. And with the cunning of the legendary serpent he would stare aghast at the old one and say, "Faugh! How could I ever have gone around looking like that!" And somehow the passion and sincerity of this declaration would blind everyone to the fact that the new skin was identical. Did he even blind himself that way?

And this showmanship with the car and the plane! It was now the only language in which he could communicate to her the things that were important to him—the language of Big Money. (Later she found that it was not at all as flamboyant as it appeared. Two days after the special 707 put her down at Heathrow it took off again, still under charter to DataLease Dominion, full of computer programers, systems analysts, and their wives, all being brain-drained to America. But by then the message had registered on Catherine: Burgo would never change.)

What was she to do, then? Leave him for good? Live out her days alone, an itinerant visitor of her children, in-laws, and friends? Or accept him, accept that he could not change now, accept that she had married him as he was and should stay with her choice to the bitter end?

Either end would be bitter.

59

The pleasure of being in London again lessened the urgency of her problems, especially now she had money enough to enjoy it all. Kelvin had the post of clinical physiologist at one of the big private clinics in the Valley of the Shadow of Death ("the medical term for what you laymen call 'Harley Street,'" he told her. "Formerly known as 'Butchers' Acre'"). This being England, he had been appointed not merely on merit, and not even mainly on merit; it counted far more that his wife, Caroline, was a cousin of the Duke of Aumerle. That same kinship had secured them a spacious flat in one of the Nash terraces overlooking Regents Park, less than half a mile from the clinic.

It sounded idyllic. One of London's most coveted apartments, the home of a fashionable doctor, his aristocratic wife, and their gifted, precocious two-year-old daughter. There, however, all pretensions to elegance ceased. In her earliest letters home Catherine wrote, "Caroline is the sweetest, but not the tidiest, of persons." That was in the days when Caroline was obviously making an effort; but even then Catherine could not help noticing what Caroline laughingly called "filth packets" in corners, under carpets, and behind sofas. Within a month or two, Catherine was saying that her daughter-in-law, though still the kindest, jolliest, *nicest* soul imaginable, was beyond doubt a slob. "She calls herself—cheerfully—a *slut,* but I don't believe she means by it what we would mean."

By that time the home was back to normal—Caroline's normal. Their bedroom floor was a sea of clothing. When Kelvin needed a clean shirt (which was not every day, his mother shuddered to notice), Caroline wandered around, picking up shirts at random, sniffing them, and eventually choosing one that smelled of half-rinsed-out soap; she ironed the collar, the cuffs, and the front down to the third button, before she gave it to him.

At last Catherine could bear it no longer. When Caroline and Emma were away for a long weekend, and Kelvin on duty at the clinic, she took every bit of clothing down to the launderette, washed the lot, ironed what she could on the roller iron there, and brought the rest back to do at home. Nono came up on the Monday and they spring-cleaned the flat from top to bottom. She was no stranger to the flat. She came up to London almost every month now, and always called on Kelvin and Caroline before catching a late-evening train to Queens Langley. Ian, now eighteen and his stepfather's chief help in their nursery garden, came too that day, to lend his muscle. He was, at first sight, astonishingly like his father, Cullen; it gave Catherine quite a wrench to see him. But as she got to know him better, she saw he had none of Cullen's easygoing superiority and public-school charm. In its place, he had Nono's gentleness and intensity.

"He's a fine boy," she told Nono when Ian was outside, filling up the dustbins.

"And you wanted to wash him out of me with soapy water, eh!" Nono teased. "Remember that night?"

Catherine laughed. "That's not fair. I only asked if you wanted to do that."

"He's all right," she agreed. "He and Bob get on well. And that's the main thing. The one I'm sorry for is little Emma. Here, what's all this about never saying *no* to a child?"

"Oh, it's the latest fad. When I had mine it was wrong to pick them up and cuddle them. Now it's all the rage, and what you mustn't do is discourage them or thwart them in any way."

"Without a word of lie, Catherine, I've seen things here as would make your hair stand on end."

"I know!" Catherine relished the chance to get all her frustrations off her chest. "The other day poor little Emma had her gumboots on the wrong feet and she was hobbling around in agony. So of course I took them off and put them on the right feet, and Caroline was furious. 'Oh,' she said. 'That's the first time she's almost put them on by herself. I do hope you haven't discouraged her forever!' I ask you, Nono!"

"Poor kid! It must be like trying to live inside a jelly. All she wants is something hard and fast. Here! Did you know she's got a degree in bacteriology, Caroline has?"

"Yes!"

"You could have knocked me down with a feather. I always thought they were *against* germs, bacteriologists."

"Still . . ." Catherine now felt a little guilty at discussing her daughter-in-law like this. "She's got a heart of gold."

"I agree there. But it's like I said to Bob—she'd give you the shirt off her back. But would you want to take it? That's my point."

Later Catherine asked her about God, if she'd ever sorted out that problem.

"Oh, yes," Nono said. "I don't think there is one."

"Why not?"

"I don't think there's room. What can God do that the universe can't do on its own?"

"You don't go to church anymore?"

"I go to the Planetarium."

Nono and Ian had gone before Caroline came back. Looking around at the utter transformation of the place, Catherine began to get cold feet. But Caroline was delighted. "You're an angel," she cried. "An absolute *angel*. Of course, I'll never keep it like this."

Nor did she.

By way of reward Kelvin and Caroline took her out to the theatre and dinner the following Saturday. Catherine chose *A Man For All Seasons* because it sounded vaguely as if it might be about a man like Burgo. And in a way it was, except for the ending. Burgo would have talked himself out of being beheaded.

Afterwards, at the Cafe Royal, Kelvin finally broached the subject that had obviously been bothering him ever since Catherine had turned up.

"I heard from Maddy the other day," he said, searching his pockets. "Damn! I put the letter out to bring, and forgot it. Anyway, she wonders if you're going over for Meg's first night."

"I'm sure Meg has told her I'm not."

"Oh?"

Their eyes dwelled in each other's. He looked away first. She smiled. "You're so like Burgo at times, Kelvin."

"Meaning?"

"Maddy knows I'm not going. Meg must have told her. So what really happened is that Maddy has asked you to pump me and find out more. Why don't you come straight out with it?"

"Okay. It's Dad, isn't it? You're avoiding Dad."

"Kelvin!" Caroline was shocked. "It's none of our bloody business, mate." She smiled apologetically at Catherine.

"I don't mind, dear," Catherine told her. Then to Kelvin: "*Avoiding* isn't quite the word. I gave him one or two things to think over, in the few spare seconds he can carve out of his obsession with DataLease Dominion. And I'd rather not distract him until he's thought good and hard."

Kelvin's eyes sparkled. "An ultimatum? From you to Dad? I say!"

She winced at the word. "We're not the United Nations. It was just one or two things to think over."

"You're not splitting?"

"On the contrary. I hope he's going to retire and then we'll be together more than ever."

Kelvin laughed. "Dad will 'retire' in exactly the same way he 'relaxes' on a beach. If you retired to the North Pole, he'd buy the local ice cream concession as a challenge."

"If he talked it over with me first, and if we both agreed on it, I wouldn't mind that in the least."

He reached across the table and squeezed her arm warmly. "You did it!" He was triumphant. "You finally did it!"

"I finally did it."

"Mind you, it's only the beginning."

Her smile did not fade. "I hope so," she said.

60

Catherine stayed in London until a month before Easter, when she had a sudden hankering for the Highlands. She went up on the overnight train.

The Atlantic put on a spectacular display. The harbour mouth at Strath was closed, but the sea hurled itself at the salt-logged timbers and rose in flat, angry sheets of fabulous beauty and malevolent strength. Boats moored in the inner harbour, in the lee of its supposed protection, nudged one another nervously. The wind that created these monsters found a momentary lull, and Peter MacAuley, who had inherited the family taxi business, was confident of getting through to the croft.

But even the abated gale rocked the car. When it turned inland, the blast scooped it forward, allowing the engine almost to idle up the gradient. At the house Imogen stayed indoors until Catherine, having paid the fare, was ready to brave the short dash from interior to interior. "Young" Peter tucked himself hard into the wind, carried her bags into the porch, and left them. They let him go before they opened the inner door.

"It's getting up again," Catherine said.

"Aye," Imogen agreed. "We must expect it at the equinox, to be sure. Do you bar the door or it'll blow down."

Catherine obeyed. Out at sea the waves were lifting to break but, before they could curl over, the wind hoisted them on its back and hefted them bodily at the mountain. The shutters were all closed on the weather sides. The water smacked against them like solid shot.

"That porch is a great improvement," Catherine said. "It's cut the draught right down."

"Aye, and so is the electric," Imogen added. "Away and warm yourself now."

Catherine was less sure about the electric. She remembered too many nights when the gentle light and warmth of candles and oil lamps had banished the howling demons who swept in off the ocean. "And how is my father?" she asked.

"Not altogether well. He has a wee thing of a chill these days that went past. Och, but he's hardy yet. He's asleep now—what else is there on a day like that! I'll make us some tea."

"Just in the hand," Catherine said. While it was drawing, she walked around the house renewing old memories. By now nothing remained that had been here in her time, over forty years ago. Yet, in a sense, nothing had changed. And that was not merely because the same simplicity was everywhere; more important, the way of life itself had hardly altered. The kitchen that was also dining room and living room still lay at its heart. The little parlour to one side was still for special, awkward, nervous occasions. The bedrooms would not have made a trawler master homesick for his cramped cabin. The only structural change had been to knock a doorway through to the shed, converting it to a bathroom-washhouse. The washing machine was now an electrical version of the machine Catherine had marvelled over during her first week in Goldeneye, but the bath was still a galvanized-steel tub that hung on a six-inch nail when not in use.

"There's been a revolution here," Imogen said, joining her and handing her the cup of tea. "No more wet slippers and thistle pricks in the ankles when you go 'round the back' at night. See?"

She indicated another small porch that had been built out from the bathhouse door, to one side of which had been added a brick privy. A new Elsan set gleamed in its dark interior; but it was still little more than a shed with a bucket.

"You're so lucky, you know," Catherine told her.

"Lucky?"

"Yes. All your world is here. Between here and Strath. Your friends are your neighbours. And even people you don't like are your neighbours, too. The kirk, the shops . . . everything you need—it's all here. Only an earthquake or some almighty disaster could remove it."

"Ah," Imogen was dismissive. "The simple life!"

Catherine felt an impulse to explain. She even drew breath to begin. But then she thought, *No. I must not bring my problems to this house. I must forget them while I am here.*

"My life is the simple one," she said. "Sometimes it's so simple, it's absolutely empty."

"But not Burgo's?" Imogen guessed.

Before Catherine could answer, there was a call from her father's bed.

"Isn't he in fine voice!" Imogen said. "I'll take him a cup of tea. Go away in to him now."

An oil heater burned low in the corner of the room, beside the door, giving it a more ancient smell than the rest of the house, which was overlaid by synthetic pine from some disinfectant. The curtain was drawn. The gloom and the smell from the heater gave her a sense that time had gone more slowly in here than elsewhere in the house.

"Hello, Father." She bent and kissed him. The dark darkened even his wrinkles.

"Is that another year?" he asked.

"No. Two. I missed last year, remember? James died. Listen to the gale! It's getting up again."

"And Burgo?"

"He's too busy—as always."

"We'll maybe play Monopoly after our tea."

Catherine saw the mental connection and laughed.

"Sit you here," he said, patting the bed. He moved to give her room and the exertion made him cough. She hauled him upright and slapped his back —that huge back on which he had slung hundredweight sacks and made them seem no more than feather cushions. She noticed he had an electric blanket on the bed.

Imogen came in with the tea and a plate of digestive biscuits. Catherine helped him into his dressing gown.

"Look at him, then," Imogen said. "The Caliph of Baghdad!"

"The electric Caliph." Catherine laughed.

An Dóiteán smiled uncertainly and covered the pause by dunking his biscuit in his tea. He never knew exactly how to respond to either his wife or his daughter when both were there.

Though their talk was inconsequential it filled Catherine with an immense joy. The small talk of this small pocket of the Western Highlands would always be special to her.

When Imogen cleared away the tray, she said she'd be out to the byre for the milking.

"Oh, let me," Catherine begged. "I'd love to milk again."

"D'you mean it?"

"Aye, of course."

"Then do it tomorrow for me, and I'll slip in to Fort William and get a few little extras."

"Not on my account. Please—nothing extra on my account."

An Dóiteán's hand soothed hers and patted it. "You'll not stop her, girl," he said.

And so it was arranged.

The storm blew itself out during the night. The next day was dry and blustery, with low gray cloud scudding inland, driven by a wind whose force seemed much gentler at ground level. The glimmer of dawn exaggerated the speed of the clouds. Catherine was up and about at first light. She did not like the new electric lamps in the byre, but everything else was as she remembered it. The cows were even better, for prices since the war enabled hay and cake to be fed over the winter, when the milk premium was higher. The eight milkers and their followers were, of course, no longer cut for their blood.

She put on her father's cap, backwards, with its peak down over her neck, clutched the bucket aslant between her ankles, and buried her head in the soft, pregnant flank of the first cow. The beast was tense, as they always were when a new hand was on the teat; but shortly the creature relaxed and began again to chew its hay. She was accepted; she was home.

After lunch An Dóiteán got up. The wind dropped further and the sun came out. He was restless indoors and went out, just to move some hay, he said. She watched him manhandling the bales and marvelled that he was in his eighty-first year. When he did not return she went out to seek him, and found him sitting on a bale to the south of the byre, in a pocket of warm sunlight, out of the breeze. He was reading a book. She bent to look at the title, expecting to see a scripture commentary or a collection of sermons. But it was a novel—*And the Cock Crew* by Fionn MacColla. Her father held the spine up to her with a smile.

"The leopard has changed his spots," he said.

"And enjoys it?"

"Aye. I never was in Sutherland. And reading this I'm glad of it."

"It was a hundred years ago, and more."

"That's not long. Not here."

"I know several people in Saskatchewan—my age—whose grandparents had been in the Sutherland evictions. To them it was ancient history."

"Then they left the anger behind them, here."

"Do you feel it? In yourself?"

"When I read, aye. I feel it in the book and then it is in myself. It makes me feel my life is imagination and the book is real."

"You're right about the leopard and his spots. You have changed."

"Aye." His gaze went out to the horizon, to the shape of the world he had seen every day of these eighty years gone past.

"Would you like to start all over again?" she asked.

He nodded. Now he was not simply scanning the horizon, he was avoiding her eye.

"Do you still believe in God?"

It was more daring than anything she had ever said to him. Thinking it too plain, she added, "As you used to, I mean? Is it the same?"

He looked at her then, unreadably opaque; he neither nodded nor shook his head. "I don't," she said. "Not in the same way."

He pointed to the bale beside the one he occupied. Still speaking, she seated herself on it. The hay was warm through her skirt. "I never told you,

did I, about my first two weeks in America? Where I stayed. I was still quite
ill when I landed. Or not ill, but weak. The nurse who'd nursed me on the
voyage was a Roman Catholic."

No reaction.

"The only place she knew for me to stay was a convent. Can you
imagine how I felt when I found out?"

"Aye."

"I believe that was God telling me I hadn't even begun to see His
purpose."

"And now?" he asked. "Is it clearer?"

She shied away from a direct answer. "So many of the things that have
happened to me seem to have been like that."

"Many?"

"Yes. For instance, I always thought my purpose—never mind God's
purpose—but my purpose was to be a good wife and a good mother. Yet
when I was both, it all got taken from me. And it was not given back until
I disobeyed my husband and went out and worked like a man. So how can
we ever know?"

"Was that the worst?" he asked. "Was it the hardest test of your faith?"

"No. There was worse."

"Did you ever think the whole world was not God's creation but the
Devil's? That God himself did not exist but was a cunning lie put about by
Satan as his most fiendish torment—so that we, thinking we are God's
chosen people, would deny ourselves the only pleasures to be found in all
eternity. I mean the pleasures of this world. And then, when we would be
ushered in to Judgement and would raise our eyes to the Seat, thinking to
see God, and hoping for mercy, we would see only the Prince of Evil, laughing at us and saying, 'Your chance has gone. Now you face eternity among
the tortures of the damned.' And down you would go. From that place all
paths would lead to the infernal depths."

The bleak despair of his vision suddenly caught at her. "You surely
never believed that?"

"For twenty years," he said.

"After I left?"

"Aye."

"Oh, I'm sorry! Father? I'm so sorry." She took his nearer hand between hers and warmed it on her lap. Their eyes met, saying much that
could not be said in words.

"What restored you?" she asked.

"You ken fine what restored me."

"Imogen."

"Aye. Imogen. And that power. If it is the Devil's, then God has deceived us. If it is holy, the Devil is mocked. Even the harlot may mock the Devil—or so I now believe."

Catherine's eyes were pricked almost to tears. It was a Highland version of the insight she had gained at Miranda's all those years ago. Had An Dóiteán achieved it then, too? Had he gone on some tortured mission, to Glasgow, say, and fallen—only to rise again in this epiphany? Did their lives, his and hers, run some strange parallel?

"And so I will tell the minister," he added.

"You will do no such thing!" she said with some spirit.

He chuckled. "Not yet," he agreed.

"Not ever. You argue enough with them as it is. Imogen tells me in her letters."

He nodded, smiling in satisfied agreement.

"And Huey," she said flatly. "Huey MacLintock. What of him, now?"

The smile faded. Once again his eyes sought the horizon—the conformable shapes of the Hebrides. "Aye," he said in apparent agreement with her speculative tone; he matched it precisely: "Which of us killed him, I wonder?"

The way he turned the question dried her mouth. Now she could only stare at him.

He looked at her, put his head on one side, and smiled such a quizzical, knowing smile. Suddenly she saw in him all that he had in common with James—all that James's ten-year lead had concealed or distorted.

"You did not think it could be you?" he asked. "Yet you thought it could be me. And we are of one flesh and blood."

"I was not even here."

"But that could be *it!* You were not here!"

"He was no longer a young boy, Father."

"When do men cease to be young boys? Was it not perhaps a young boy who chose to drown the forty-year-old MacLintock at that place?"

"*He* chose?"

"He. Or the Lord. Or the Devil. It was between the three of them."

She was easier after he told her that. There was a pause. Then she said, "Imogen doesn't know about Huey. I could feel that from the way she wrote when you were just married. In the war. Her first letter to me."

"She does not know."

"Does she know why I left?"

"Do you?"

"Aye, I do. D'you think I was wrong?"

"It was God's will."

"You mean, an opinion would be blasphemy?"

"It has been for the best."

"It was for the best then. From the beginning it was always for the best. There would have been murder here if I had stayed. Aye—or worse."

"Yon doctor, James Macrae, did you lie together with him?"

She considered denying it. She tried to think of the implications of telling the truth. In the end her hesitation was answer enough.

"Aye." By then the word was superfluous.

"You knew the peril of damnation? You knew how it would damn you?"

"Of course."

He started in surprise, as if he expected her to say more. When she remained silent, he echoed her, "Of course? Is that all? Do you not also say you know God is merciful? Wherefore redemption if we may never sin? 'Of course'? Is that all you say?"

With a guilty smile she nodded.

He fixed her then with the strangest grin. She had expected anything but that—anger, shame, disappointment, disgust—anything. Instead he stared at her with a broad smile on his face; and the smile was a blend of pride and satisfaction. Behind it was something less easily named. Was it envy? Or a certain sadness? That smile—all that it said, all that it hinted— she never forgot.

He went on. "Imogen says you are not pleased with the simple life?"

"I am not discontented." She meant it in a religious sense, which she knew he would understand; in the everyday sense, of course, she was, precisely, discontented.

"You are Dives and Lazarus in the same flesh. Some people think those are names, but Christ never named anyone in his parables. 'Dives' is Latin for 'Rich Man.' And 'Lazarus'—d'you ken?"

A long-forgotten prelection, or sermon—she must have been only eight or so at the time—came to her aid: "God has helped."

"Aye!" He was pleased. Was his mind, too, busy reinventing the kirk and the people as they had been on that day, half a century ago? "God has helped," he repeated. "So do not despair, Catherine, *a nighean*. In the end you will get all you want. Blessed are the meek, for they shall inherit the earth!" and he laughed.

She never thought she would hear him quote the Gospels in irony—as if he were hinting that God had enjoyed so many jokes against man they could justly savour this one on Him.

61

Before the rhododendrons fell she was at Gideons with Nono and Bob. Though she had seen it before, the steep field behind the house, Gideon's Stye, still surprised her. It had been terraced to provide nursery beds for tens of thousands of shrubs and young saplings. The lie of the land was not changed at all; but its character had been altered completely. There was now no spot where she could say to herself: *Here Cullen sat with Nono and me and planned our seduction . . . here I led Burgo up to the woods on our first night in the house . . . here Kelvin and I carried Grant down to the ambulance . . . here we made hay on the first day of peace.* All those places had gone.

And a good thing, too, she thought.

Nono was the only person she could talk to about Burgo. Inside two weeks there was nothing left to tell; Nono had it all.

They were standing out among the beehives, taking the first good lot of honey and extracting the surplus queens, when Nono said, "You always thought it was Cullen who talked me into letting him stop all night and loving me up. Didn't you now?"

"You mean it was the other way round?"

"With me, yes. Not with you, though. He talked you into it."

"What d'you mean?"

Nono grinned. "You needn't pretend, Cathy, love. He told me. Him and you. Up in the wood up there, before he shot those rabbits."

Catherine thought swiftly. What was to be gained now by putting the lie in Ian Cullen's mouth? "He told you?" she asked.

"He told me. Not but what he needed to. I knew what he was after the minute we saw him cycling up the lane. That's all young men his age ever want off us. Either to do it or to talk about it. I thought he was going to talk about it with you and do it with me."

"He was only practising with me. With you it was the real thing."

Nono put her head on one side and gave a smile of weary tolerance. "Oh Cath! Why d'you say a thing like that? You know—that's all your trouble. You're too bleeding soft."

"It's the truth."

"Maybe. But you'd say it even if it wasn't. If Cullen was the biggest love of your life, you'd still give him away to me like that."

"But where's the harm?"

"Where's the *harm!*" Nono's agitation communicated instantly to the bees, one of which stung her hand. Catherine used her long fingernails to tweak out the sting without squeezing the poison sac. "Let's finish this," Nono said, "and then I'll tell you where the harm is."

On the way back up the orchard she linked her massive, gentle arm in Catherine's and said, "The harm is exactly what you've been telling me, love. I'll bet you think you couldn't possibly live without Burgo. Come on, be truthful now. I'll bet that's behind it all."

"It'd be very lonely and very bitter."

"You think so?"

"I know it."

Nono sniffed skeptically. "What's it been like this year? Or this time you've been in England?"

Catherine was silent.

"Lonely?"

"No . . ." Catherine said reluctantly.

"Bitter?"

"But then I knew I'd be going back to him sometime."

"Ha haaa!" Nono gave a shriek of triumph that startled all the birds in the apple trees. It was as if she had trapped Catherine into a fatal admission. "You see! That's always at the back of your mind, isn't it. There's always this idea—you're never going to leave him. Not *really.* Not forever. And that's how you never give yourself a chance."

"I don't understand that," Catherine said.

"You mean you'd rather not! I used to cry for you, Cath. Honest. The way he'd go and do things all off his own bat and he'd only tell you when it was too late to change anything. And the way you just let him!"

"Not always."

"Oh, sometimes you'd argue a bit. But it was the same in the end. You let him get away with it. Honest. I used to cry."

"Well!" Catherine was at a loss for words.

"When you rang me from Canada and said you were coming over, alone, and you hadn't fixed any time for going back, I thought to myself, 'She gone and done it at last!' I said to Bob—you ask him—I said, 'Three cheers! Old Cath's done it at last!' And now you stand here and say you knew all along you'd go back to him! Can't you see, love—it's like smothering a baby the moment it's born."

Catherine gave a weak laugh of embarrassment.

But Nono was relentless. "I tell you, Cath, until you can face Burgo, with your hand on your heart, and say, 'I don't need you. I can live without you. I've got friends out there. I've got a whole life of my own waiting out there!'—until you can say that and mean it, you haven't got a snowball's chance in hell. And even when you *can* say it, you'll still only be just about his equal. And to beat him you've got to be more than equal, a lot more, because he's been at it sixty years, see?"

Catherine laughed with joy then. Nono had done the one thing she herself had never been able to do, and would never have done on her own: She had forced Catherine to question *the* fundamental assumption of her life and love with Burgo—that she could not live happily without him. Until now that very belief had ensured its opposite; because of it, she could not live happily *with* him! Nono was born understanding the paradox it had taken Catherine sixty years to fathom: that for any woman to live happily with a man, she had first to be certain she could live just as happily without him.

She wanted to go up to Gideon's Wood and shout it to the world. If James's bequest of Doctor's House had been her shield, this new gift of insight from Nono was her armour. But still she had no sword.

62

About three weeks later she had a call from London. It was Bob Benson, Meg's editor. They had met several times last summer in New York and when she had said she was coming over here, he said he'd call her if ever he was in London, too. She hadn't actually believed him, so it was a double surprise. "As a matter of fact," he said, "I have some things to tell you that I think you ought to know."

Intrigued, she was early for their meeting, in Stone's Chop House, between Leicester Square and the Haymarket. His favourite place, he said.

He walked in as if he were there every day. She noticed that the confidence of his manner induced the outer and inner doormen to treat him as if, indeed, he were a regular. With their quaint, olde-worlde aprons, their cutaway coats, and coloured bowler hats, they had slightly intimidated her.

He located her as soon as he was relieved of his own coat and hat. "Cath! How super to see you!"

He did not try to talk like an Englishman but he observed the local vocabulary and custom scrupulously, like a game—but an important game and one that deserved to be played well.

They drank sherry in the lounge while they waited for their table, though she knew that in New York he'd have gone directly to his table and ordered a Manhattan; sherry would have killed him. He referred to the doormen in their "bowler hats" not "derbies."

"I love this place," he said. "To me it's the center of London. It's where everything changes. A quarter-mile *that* way is sleazy Soho. A quarter-mile *that* way, The Mall, Saint James's, Carlton House Terrace, the Horse Guards. That way—books, opera, theatres. That way—the best of Old England, handmade sporting guns, handmade shoes . . . Fortnum and Mason's. And they all circle this place without actually meeting and mingling. This place is something yet again. It's eighteenth century. Can't you see Doctor Johnson holding court here?"

Catherine laughed. "And I thought you'd crumple if you ever left Manhattan, Bob! Meg told me you believed Montreal and Toronto were just telex codes. And she once had to argue with you an hour before you'd accept that ships which ventured beyond The Narrows didn't actually fall off the edge of the world."

"Talking of Meg," he chuckled, "you know she's started in on a sequel?"

"No! What's she calling it?"

"As a matter of fact, she's working on it up in Goldeneye right now. I'd love her to call it that: *Goldeneye*. But she's holding out—probably rightly—for *Sons Who Knew My Daughter*. And what about this?" He fished a cable from his pocket.

It read: FIRST CHAPTER TITLED QUOTE NO MAN IS CONTINENT UNTO HIM-SELF ALONE UNQUOTE STOP SAY YOU LOVE IT ME LIFE MONEY EVER MEG.

"And you do?" Catherine asked.

"Right. It's a misquote, of course—a mangled misquote at that—but I'll ride with it."

"Did you cable her back? It's going to be an expensive book."

"No. I remembered you have telex at your place. So, for the same price, I sent her this."

It was a whole page covered with line after line of laughter: HAHAHAHAHA. . . .

"You nurse her a lot, Bob."

"Oh, but she's worth it. I'm not speaking commercially. I mean in every way. She's—" He sought for a superlative. "Do you know Dorothy Parker?"

Catherine shook her head.

"She was 'Constant Reader' of *The New Yorker*," he prompted.

"I've read some. She digs up bad books and pokes fun at them—or she used to, rather."

"That's her. And that's the best of her. The short stories are full of a cloying self-pity which ruins them. You find yourself saying, as you read them, 'Oh, what would this woman *be* if only she could stop rattling her broken heart like a charity-collection box!' And the answer, of course, is Margaret Meek! She is what Dorothy Parker could have been." He pulled a face and thumped the arm of his chair gently, in a Lee J. Cobb parody, adding: "And *would* have been if I had edited her!"

He put on half-moon glasses and stared at the menu as if he were seeking out misplaced semicolons.

"I want very little," Catherine told him.

"I'm so glad you said it." He grinned. "I never know how to—without sounding like that awful character in that Somerset Maugham short story. You know the one?"

"The aunt who bankrupts her nephew in Paris by eating very little—Beluga caviar, asparagus, and out-of-season peaches or something?"

"That's the one. But what's the alternative? You end up looking like G. K. Chesterton. Would you like to order, by the way?"

"Thank you." She smiled. "As you're not a hard-up young writer struggling on a hundred dollars a month in Paris, I quite like the sound of caviar, asparagus, and a peach."

"Wonderful!" He laughed.

His conversation fascinated Catherine. He asked her a lot about herself, her family, her early life in Scotland and at Goldeneye—and, of course, about Meg. But again and again he would take the things she said and relate them either to characters in books or to literary people he knew. When she read a book it was to step, as it were, *outside* her own daily life. But for him it was quite the opposite: books, characters, writers, and real life all flowed together in what Nono called "a continuum."

Throughout the meal he gave no hint of the special news he had mentioned on the phone. Over the coffee she reminded him. It was the only time she saw him embarrassed. "I don't know how to tell you," he confessed. "Or, rather, all the way through my tale you're going to be thinking to yourself, 'What business is it of his? Why is he telling me this?' Well, I want you to know I do have a reason—in fact, I have two. But I want to keep it till last. So—bear with me, eh?"

Catherine fluttered her eyelashes and imitated Meg. "My oh my, Mr. Benson. You surely know how to get a girl all agog!"

He laughed and pointed at her. "That's very good." Then he was serious again. "I wish what I have to say was one-tenth as funny. It concerns

Wild Bill and . . . well—you'll see." He gestured for more coffee. "It all begins with one of those coincidences that are so common in real life, but which a good editor would never allow one of his authors to use. We—I mean Hebel, my firm—own a warehouse at Great Neck. When you fly into La Guardia, you go right over it. We don't use all of it now because we're transferring to another facility in New Jersey. So we've rented half the space out to a firm called Systems Leasing Corp."

"Really?" Catherine was intrigued. "They're a big rival to DataLease Dominion, you know—probably the biggest."

"I know. It so happens that we hold our own internal sales conferences out there rather than in Manhattan. There's more space. And it's more secure." He laid stress on the last word. "When I was there in January, it was like a scene in some Mafia movie. A great black limousine pulled right up to the door. A man got out, looked all around, and nodded at the two passengers—who literally *ran* across the two yards to the warehouse door."

"You must employ some interesting salesmen, Bob."

"Oh, they weren't ours. They'd come for what they must have thought was a very secure meeting with Systems Leasing. But I recognized one of them."

Catherine stopped breathing for a moment. "Wild Bill?" She couldn't believe it.

He nodded.

"Do you know the other one?" she asked.

"I didn't—until Maddy showed me a family photo."

"Burgo? My husband?"

He shook his head. "Grant."

"They're probably talking a merger." She swallowed her disquiet and put the best face on it for him.

"Whatever they're talking about, it's big. They came again in March, and Wild Bill came again last week. And those are just the visits I know about. I don't go there all that often. For all I know they come there every week."

"Probably merger talks, as I say. You've no idea how sick I get of the sheer cleverness of people in business."

"I hope I'm doing right to tell you."

"Yes. Why are you telling me? Unquote."

He grinned. "That was the other thing. You see, Cath—Maddy and I are getting married quite soon. Nothing's fixed, but—soon."

Catherine slopped her coffee in her delight. "But that's marvellous! She's a lucky girl all right. I hope you know just what you're taking on though, Bob."

"I think so. I think she's pretty fabulous; as a matter of fact I feel honoured."

"Does everyone know? Have you told Meg?"

"You're the first."

"Well, thank you." She suddenly reached across the table and gripped his arm. "But of course! Now I see your problem. You poor man. Your future father-in-law may be being cheated by his partners."

"That's it."

"And one of them is your future brother-in-law and the other is your favourite author's husband."

"Right! And with a wound like that, who needed the salt!" His mouth laughed but his eyes regarded her oddly.

"Is there something?" She fished out a powder compact with a looking-glass lid.

"No. It's just that you didn't include yourself."

63

Catherine's first instinct had been to call Maddy as soon as lunch was over. Then she had a better idea. She sent a cable telling Maddy her time of arrival at Idlewild, but nothing else. Next day she and a mountain of excess baggage were airborne and homeward bound.

"I think it's wonderful about you and Bob," she said as soon as they were in the taxi. "And you look so *well!* The prospect obviously pleases."

"Oh." She blushed. "I hope Bob behaved himself."

"Of course he did. What an odd thing to say."

"Well, I suppose you know he's terrified of you."

Catherine laughed. "What nonsense!"

"It's true. He says you're the most genuine, honest, downright, *real* person he knows."

"Oh, dear!"

"And he's afraid he'll come out with something just a little bit pretentious or . . . pseudo, or—oh, I don't know—affected. And you'd see right through it at once, he thinks."

"I don't believe you, Maddy. You're making it up."

"I'm not. And I'm not even exaggerating."

"Well! I shouldn't think he'd even know *how* to be affected."

"I'll tell him you said that. He'll love you for life."

"In fact, I was the one who felt a little intimidated."

"By Bob? For heaven's sake! Why?"

"Well—all the brilliant, gifted, great people he meets. You know he was over there to talk to Bertrand Russell? And Winston Churchill's son? And just before lunch he'd been talking with Laurence Olivier."

"Even so, I'll bet his meeting with you was the highlight of his day." Maddy suddenly hit her own forehead and bit her lip. "I forgot! Meg's been frantic to reach you. Can you call her as soon as we get in? I meant to tell you at the airport."

This exchange, with its heartening assurance that Bob had enjoyed her company as much as he had appeared to, came at exactly the right time for Catherine. Nono had told her she could have a rewarding life of her own out there—but that was just theory. Now, with Bob and Maddy, she realized that it was, indeed, true. Bob, who met all those great people, had enjoyed lunch with her—not because she was his future mother-in-law, not because she was his favourite author's sister-in-law, but for herself. She *was* someone in her own right.

She called Meg as soon as they reached the apartment.

"At last!" Meg almost screamed. "This new streak of independence is all very well, Cath, but wait till you see what it did to your phone bill since yesterday."

"What's so important?"

"How about: The world just ended?"

"It looks fine here."

"That's everyone else's world. I'm talking about yours and mine and DataLease Dominion. I've got Wild Bill here, in a terrible state."

"He's there? With you?"

"Yes. He keeps saying he's let Burgo and Grant down and all he wants to do is die. Jay's been wonderful. He's got him sedated to the gills. Burgo's on his way here now from Montreal. And Grant's coming up from Dallas. Can you make it tonight, Cath, honey? Everyone's going to need you. Not least *me*." After a pause she added, "Don't tell Bob I said me instead of I."

Catherine laughed. "I'll see what I can get tonight."

"Charter if you have to. Shall I fix it?"

"Give me half an hour."

"Hold on. I've found an American Airlines flight to Chicago. It gets in at ten thirty. I'll have one of the company planes standing by for you. Clear customs at O'Hare if you can."

"Okay, Meg. Is this really something? I know Wild Bill isn't given to imagining things. But—what does Burgo say?"

"Oh, it's real, hon. Burgo says it's just an annoying little technicality. But Wild Bill says it's the end. Anyway, Burgo'll be here by the time you touch down."

Catherine expected her to wind up to a goodbye; but there was silence instead. "Is there something else?" she asked.

There was a pause. Then the crackle of a sigh. "I promised not to tell you this, but I can't let you walk into it cold. You're going to hate it. Burgo has a surprise for you. He thinks you'll love it. But I know better."

"What is it? I like surprises."

"Not this one. I can't say more. Just hurry, huh?"

"Okay. Keep smiling."

"I am. It's beginning to hurt."

"And—Meg?"

"Yes?"

"I'm ready for Burgo now. I don't care what he's done, or what this surprise is, I'm ready for him."

She left most of her bags at Maddy's. It was the small, dark hours of the following day before she arrived at the Little Hills landing strip. Burgo was there to meet her. She fell into his arms. "I think I've been flying for a week," she said.

"Poor kid. Meg shouldn't have rushed you like that."

"It sounded important."

"Ah! Women love dramas—you know how they are!"

"You're cheerful, I must say."

"It's nothing. A technicality. I'll explain it in the morning. And then . . ." He paused.

"And then what?"

"No. That'll keep, too. Are you really home now, Cath?" He helped her into his Silver Cloud. The deep, soft hide of the seat enveloped her.

"If there's trouble," she yawned, "I'll stay by you. I needn't tell you that."

"That sounds only like a truce."

"Please, honey, I'm very tired. Don't start."

"It's just that after all this time away I thought you'd see . . ." He shrugged.

"See sense?" she suggested.

"No! See that we belong together."

"But I never questioned that. What I doubted was that I could lead a life apart from you, without being lonely and bitter. And now I've discovered I can. I've had a lovely year of it."

He was silent.

She grinned at the dark world outside. "What have you discovered?"

"I think I was . . . that is, I've realized you were right. I've been pretty awful to you at times. Not all the time. I mean, we've had good times, too, haven't we?"

"We've had marvellous times, darling."

"*But!* Yes, all right. There were other times, as well. Too damn many of them. But that's going to change, Cathy. I'm going to make it all up to you."

"How?"

"You'll see. I haven't wasted these months either."

64

Next morning, at breakfast in Doctor's House, the whole story came out.

"You remember last year," Burgo said, "when we raised that seventy-five-million loan? Well, the repayment was scheduled over ten years, but there was a teeny little clause in the agreement which said that if our debt-equity ratio climbed above a certain limit—I'll spare you the math—then the whole loan would become repayable at once."

"And that's what's happened?" Catherine asked.

"In a way. In a way."

"That's exactly what's happened," Wild Bill cut in. "And I didn't see it. I didn't stop it showing in the accounts."

"Like how?" Burgo challenged him. "How could you have hidden it?"

"I don't know. But I could have found a way. Hell—what are accountants *for* if they can't do that."

"If it's anyone's fault it's mine," Burgo said.

Catherine interrupted. "Can we just take it a step at a time?"

Burgo raised his hands, accepting the rebuke. "What happened was that I closed a big deal in California, with one of the universities. It was for ten million dollars, but part of the deal was that they got a hundred and eighty days' credit." He turned to Wild Bill and Grant. "It was the only way I could close the deal."

"Sure, Dad," Grant soothed him. "Nobody's blaming you."

"What was so wrong about that?" Meg asked.

"Nothing was wrong," Wild Bill told her. "If the hundred and eighty days had fallen entirely within our financial year, it never would have shown. But the last twenty days just overlapped into this current year. Even then—if I'd just had the savvy to get a proper commercial note or a bank guarantee!"

"But?" Catherine asked.

"But I didn't. So it had to show in the annual accounts as unsecured debt—which put our gearing above the bank's limit."

"Gearing?"

"It's just another name for debt-equity ratio."

"But," Burgo pointed out, "it was a purely technical overgearing. The university was a rock-solid, gilt-edged debtor. Even before the accounts were published the money was paid and we were back within limits. I don't think the bank properly understands that. But when they do, it'll all be ironed out. They can't possibly call the whole seventy-five million because of a technical overgearing that lasted less than three weeks, and which is already cleared up."

Grant, staring out of the window, gave a heavy sigh. "They didn't sound too accommodating to me, Dad. I explained all that to them and they were still . . . well—pretty cool."

Until that moment Catherine had assumed that this was some exterior catastrophe, which not only threatened the firm but had forced Grant and Wild Bill to put aside their treachery (if, indeed, that was what they had been engaged in) and pull as a team with Burgo again. But she knew Grant as Burgo did not. She knew the timbre of his voice when he was trying to sound innocent and was not; Burgo had been away, carving empires and collecting feathers, during all those moments. Now she knew, absolutely, not only that Grant and Wild Bill were traitors, but that this foreclosure by the bank was part of their plan.

"Just let me talk to them," Burgo said. "They'll sing a different tune then."

"You mean you didn't talk to them yet?" Meg asked.

"How could I—with my director of finance falling apart up here in Goldeneye! Bill, you've just got to get yourself together and come down there and talk to them with me. Hell, you know as well as I do they're just angling to reschedule this loan a little more tightly, or get better terms. They're not going to call it and bankrupt us, and get only fifty cents on the dollar! Come on, old buddy. We've seen a lot worse than this."

"I really think you ought to talk to them, Dad," Grant insisted. "They aren't playing your tune at all."

"I will, I will. As soon as this son-of-a-gun has pulled himself back into at least one quivering heap. You see if you can't talk sense into him.

Meanwhile, I want to take my favourite wife"—he opened his arms toward Catherine—"and show her my little surprise."

There was an embarrassed silence. No one could look at anyone else.

"You're all wrong," Burgo said. "She's going to love it. Come on, honey."

In the car he made her bend her head and look only at the floor. But she could tell from the passing soundscape that they were crossing the town, going back to the landing strip.

There was a slight jolt where they left the made-up road and went onto gravel. The broad tyres scrunched as they rolled to a gentle, slightly uphill halt.

"Okay. You can look up," he told her. "It's dead ahead."

A winding driveway led up the slope, between shrubs and trees. She seemed to be in a botanical garden. The grass was immaculate, finer even than the bowling-green lawns at Doctor's House. Sprinklers were at work everywhere, maintaining this feast of horticultural impossibility in the heart of the near-desert prairie.

"It's beautiful," she said. "But this is where your golf course was. It's ruined your golf course."

"I've called it West Gideon," he said.

She laughed and picked up his fantasy. "We can build a replica up—"

And then she saw it. Her arm fell back to her side. He had built it! He had gone ahead and built it—his awful, awful, awful, split-level, urban ranch house. She hadn't noticed it immediately because it and the garden cross-invaded each other.

"Isn't that something!" he said, rolling the car forward again.

"That does it, Burgo," she said. He had just handed her the sword—one-edged. "That's *it!*"

She opened the door and slipped from the car, which was still only crawling. She began to walk back into town.

"Hey!" he cried after her. "Cath!"

She paid no heed.

There was a sudden roar of the engine. She half-turned, in time to see the massive Royce yawing round on the immature lawn, spinning black divots against the sky. She did not pause, not even when he slowed to a half halt beside her.

"Hey, what's this?" he asked.

She looked at him. Even now she couldn't feel any hatred, only anger. And pity. "If you don't know, Burgo—if after all I've said—after all I told you about going ahead and doing things on your own—if it still hasn't sunk in, then there's no point in—"

"What are you talking about?" At tickover he just kept pace with her.

"There's no point. There's just no point."

"Are you talking about the house?"

"I suppose there never was a point. You just kept pretending."

"You didn't even look inside it."

"You just pretended enough to keep me going along."

"Inside, Cath. Your part. You didn't even see it."

Still not looking at him she said bitterly, "What did I miss? Do fountains play when the door opens? Does a robot cocktail shaker start to rattle?"

She heard the exasperation in his voice. *"Exactly* the opposite, Cath. You couldn't be more wrong."

"Oh, I suppose it's all just bare concrete and brick!" she sneered.

"Not *even* that. You should come and look. You really should."

Her curiosity was pricked. Against her better judgement she stopped and, looking at him for the first time, she asked, "How can you not even have bare concrete or brick?"

He grinned. She held back an impulse to hit him. "Just what I say. It's a shell. Walls, windows, doors, and roof over a hole in the ground. Sixty thousand empty cubic feet. From basement floor to roof, it's empty—not a floor, not a wall, not a door, not a stair. Nothing. It's for *you* to say. You design it."

She stared at him.

He laughed. "You don't believe it! You thought this leopard could never change his spots. But didn't I promise you that from now on we'd do everything together? And where better to begin than with the house we're going to live in for the rest of our lives? I build it. You design it. *Together*—see?"

She knew the heavy futility of it all but she could not help saying, "Together? *You* decide we won't stay on in Doctor's House. *You* decide we'll move over here to Little Hills. You landscape the place, dig a hole in the ground, and roof it over. *Then* you tell me about it. And goody-goody, I get to put the walls and floors and doors anywhere I like! And that's what you call doing everything together!"

There was a glimmer of understanding in his eyes—a faint scratch in the twenty-inch armour plate of his self-confidence. "So you're not even going to look at it?" he asked.

She set her face to stone and walked on.

"All right," he called after her. "So we didn't discuss it first, but it might be exactly what we would have decided on if we had. Did you think of that?"

She walked on.

"And you'll never know, because you won't even look at it."

Still she ignored him.

"Marvellous!" he sneered. "Here's my business falling around my ears but I take time out to show my wife a dream of a home in the middle of paradise—and she won't even look at it!"

Anger boiled within her but she held it.

"We could be bankrupt this minute, and what do you do?" He was shouting now. "You throw it all back in my face—a surprise it took a year to prepare for you."

She broke into a trot. She had to tap the energy of all the hatred that suddenly welled up within her.

The pitch of the engine rose slightly as he edged forward to pass her. She turned her back on him as he drew level. His voice was once again conversational—almost conciliatory—as he said, "A walk will do you the world of good."

The fat rear tyres fired gravel at her legs as he roared away.

"Christ, Burgo!" she yelled after him. "Just . . . get out, just goddam get out, get the stinking hell out . . ." Worse words hovered at the rim of her voice, but even that monstrous rage could not force their utterance. "Bastard!" she screamed. "You bastard!"

When she was sure he was out of sight she turned to look at "West Gideon." Even in her anger she had to admit he'd done it beautifully. The house was quietly unobtrusive, and the garden around it—a miracle of green —was exactly the sort of garden that, if they drove past it, she'd say, "Oh, I'd love a place like that!"

But this realization only fed her anger. If Burgo knew her well enough to make the place so exactly *right* for her, how could he fail to understand the necessity of deciding about it together—and before, not after? He could not possibly be so sensitive in one direction and so blind in the other.

The walk across town was made longer by the fact that she knew almost everybody she passed and had to share with them the news of her time away in New York and England—and catch up on the happenings in Goldeneye. It was gone midday by the time she turned into the gates of Doctor's House.

They must have been watching out for her. Burgo skipped quickly down the front steps only moments after she came into view; Meg stood anxiously in the doorway behind him.

By then Catherine had it all worked out—the bleak but Burgo-free life that lay ahead. He was to leave Doctor's House and never return. She'd see out her days there, alone except for her memories. He would not be welcome. Make a clean break. An absolute break. If he wanted a divorce. . . .

The words were assembling themselves in her head—until she saw his face. Then she knew something was wrong. Bad news in every line and wrinkle. It couldn't be to do with business—he'd be grinning and posing if it were that. This was personal, to do with family. To do with her.

The name of her father was forming in her mind's ear even as Burgo spoke it, so her outward shock was slight. But there was a rushing and a roaring in her ears, and a tingling weakness behind her knees. . . . He got a strong arm around her just in time.

"Is he . . . dead?" she asked.

There was a fleeting, unreal sense that all this had happened to her once before, exactly here, on just such a day, with Burgo's arm precisely where it was. She even knew, as he said them, what his words would be: "They say there isn't much hope. Kelvin is there on holiday. He rang. He said"—Burgo looked at her—"there's no hope. God, Cath darling, I'm so sorry."

She could only think how trivial the other events of this day now seemed. Divorce from Burgo . . . their multimillion-dollar bankruptcy . . . they became as nothing.

Until Burgo said, "I'll come with you, of course."

"No," she said, without thought.

He looked surprised and pained.

"Grant will represent you," she insisted. "You stay, you and Wild Bill, you stay and save the firm."

He smiled in reluctant triumph. "That's all taken care of," he said.

His smile persisted. She knew what was going through his mind. He was thinking, *See, the walk did you good. Didn't I say it!*

The implied patronage did not penetrate her numbness. "I'll pack," she said.

When she reached the foot of the steps up to the porch, Meg came forward and hugged her. "Oh, honey, I'm so . . . what can I say?"

"You can help me pack. Or *re*-pack. Thank God I didn't leave *everything* at Maddy's."

Everyone was glad of the activity. Grant demurred at first but Burgo grew so angry that he quickly gave in; he probably thought his plans were in ruins anyway.

When they were almost finished, Wild Bill came in. "I've laid on a company flight to Idlewild. You've more transatlantic choices from there. Let the New York office know your flight and if it doesn't connect to Scotland, I'll fix for a charter to be standing by at London. And a car at Glasgow."

She felt the incongruity of it. The vast wealth that would ease her way to Beinn Uidhe and the little croft that was her goal—modest to the border-lines of poverty: two worlds, two ways of living, between which she had hovered all her life, never settling. Even now there was no sense of impending farewell, not to either of them.

Everyone gravitated to her room in the end, because it was the centre of action.

"We've been slow, slow, slow!" Burgo crowed as he breezed triumphantly in.

Everyone turned to him except Catherine. "Listen girls," he said to Grant and Wild Bill. "We've been looking the wrong way. Those guys, they don't want a rescheduled loan. They want *in*."

"Preposterous," Wild Bill said.

"Absurd," Grant agreed.

Again that tone in her son's voice let Catherine know he was lying. She looked at him and could see it in his eyes. At that same moment Burgo was saying, "I didn't see it myself. It was something your mother said. . . ."

Grant looked at her, stung.

Burgo put one arm around her and gave a big-buddy hug—as if no cross word had passed between them. He kissed her neck lightly. "Play along," he whispered.

Her eyes never left Grant's. She shook her head, barely perceptibly, but he understood her denial and relaxed. She thought what an ineffectual conspirator he made; even she would have had enough savvy to go on pretending to be surprised. If he really were innocent, what cause had he to look either stung or relieved?

"I tell you," Burgo was saying to the two men, "this lady has a *head* on those shoulders. If I yield to anyone, it'll be to her."

She packed the last few items. "What did I say, honey?" she asked idly.

He laughed and punched her shoulder playfully. "What did you say? What *didn't* you!" He was instantly serious. "Listen you chaps, here's what we'll do about this crisis." They watched him, waiting. He waited until the tension was at break point. "Nothing!" he said. "Go fishing."

"Be serious," Wild Bill told him. "Suppose you're right. Suppose—"

"I *am* serious. And I am right. Don't you see! It's the very last thing they'll expect. It'll really get them worried."

Grant made a last stab at salvaging the conspiracy. *"You* could do that, Dad. And put it about that Wild Bill's in hospital—whereas he could secretly be back in New York and organizing—"

Burgo waved him to silence, squashing the words with his hands. "I'll take you and your mother to the landing strip. Wild Bill can telex those frauds, say we're all up here on a hunting trip . . . fishing . . . anything.

Ask why doesn't their president—Art . . . whatsizname . . . or that Howard guy who thinks he should be next Chairman of the Federal Reserve
Board—why don't they come up and join us and we'll sort the whole thing
out over a wiener roast."

Catherine had always warmed to Burgo-in-a-crisis. He came alive then.
She knew exactly what Kelvin had meant when he said that being on
Burgo's team was like being one of the original musketeers. Even now, in
the midst of her despair and anger at him, in the midst of her worry over
An Dóiteán, she responded to that cheery confidence—or, rather, she felt
herself automatically responding, like a child at the movies when the U.S.
Cavalry at last stream in toward the beleaguered circle of wagons. She took
a grip on herself and squashed it.

"And they *will* come," Burgo said. "Trust me. And when they do, they
won't be half so cocky. Meanwhile, I'll tell you at least five dirty tricks we
can play right now. I didn't just pick that bank out of Yellow Pages. Oh no!
I know a thing or ten about those sharks. We can kill Howard How'syour-
father's Federal Reserve Board ambitions stone dead just for starters."

"I'm ready," Catherine said.

At the landing strip Burgo found a moment alone with her. "I hope it's
all a false alarm by the time you get there," he said.

"Yes."

"I'll come if you like. If you want me."

"No. You save the business."

"The business can go hang. Hell—I should retire anyway, Cath. Say the
word and I'll drop it all and come along."

She smiled wearily. "You're safe saying that. I fold. I won't call."

He grinned, taking her meaning. "But you'll see me? I mean you'll
come back, no?"

For the first time she looked up at "West Gideon." Then she turned to
him. "I'm coming back. To Doctor's House."

He drew breath but then thought better of whatever he had been about
to say.

Finality was postponed, not cancelled. It *was* finality, and they both
knew it.

As soon as they were airborne Grant asked, "What did you say to Dad?"

Suddenly she felt herself a different person. She really was free of Burgo.
The last hold he had over her spirit was loosened. She answered as she never
would have answered before, "I told him we're through. I took one look at
that awful place he's built and I said, 'that's *it!*' So we're through."

It took Grant utterly by surprise.

Before he could recover she went on, "And I want to know what sort of plan you and Wild Bill have been cooking up?"

His surprise turned to alarm.

"This bank thing," she said. "You and he are in it to the hilt." When he opened his mouth to protest she silenced him by adding, "Darling, I was there while you grew up. I've listened to the way you tell lies and try to bluff from the moment you could talk. Not Daddy. He wasn't there. But I was. So don't try to deny it."

He was slightly relieved. "You mean Dad doesn't know? What *did* you and he talk about? If it really wasn't this bank thing, why does he pretend *you* gave the game away?"

"How do I know? When did he ever share that sort of confidence with me? Perhaps he wanted to say, 'Look girls! It's simple—it's so simple that *even* your dumb mother can see it.' Burgo has motives that would shock even himself. So tell me—what's the conspiracy?"

His eyes narrowed. "Are you spying for him?"

"It's to stop him, isn't it? You've let him build up DataLease Dominion and now you want to stop him spoiling it the way he spoiled every other—"

Grant laughed and shook his head. "Dad's right about you. You have a mind keen as mustard. Even if you are spying for him, I can tell you. He'd never believe it anyway. It was—it *is*—a plan to ease Dad out with dignity. Not out altogether. Just to the touch line. He's finished as a player but we want him for coach."

He explained it then. The bank was in on the plan, and so was Systems Leasing. So were some of the big stockholders. The strategy was to double the size of the firm overnight—make it so big, so suddenly big, that even Burgo would see it was too much for him to handle. Then he'd have to do the one thing he'd resisted all his life. Let in the Organization Men. That was the strategy. The tactics had already been revealed—let the firm default on some loan conditions. Only in a technical sense, of course; nothing to hazard the firm's true financial soundness. But something legally watertight. "So that the bank can insist," he said. "They really are going to call in this loan. Then, when Dad realizes they're serious, when he starts to sweat, when he pleads with them, then they'll say, 'Okay, but only if you merge with Systems Leasing.' And that's how we double the size overnight."

"Good," she said. "I want to help. Some way, any way—I don't mind how. My hand is *in.*"

Grant looked at her a long time—a long, ambiguous time. She saw more of Burgo in him during that scrutiny than she had ever suspected was there.

"It isn't vindictive, Mummy," he said. "We don't want to hurt Dad. We owe him too much, Wild Bill and I. Dammit, we love him too much."

She laughed, surprising herself at the harshness of the sound. "That's where he'll get you, then. Love! I'm a million miles ahead of you on *that* road. Let me tell you about love battles with Burgo. You're fighting. You're in the ring. He's doing badly. He's groggy. Then the lights go out—or thick smoke comes drifting in from nowhere. And when it clears, when you can see again, you're alone in the ring. And Burgo's in that *other* ring, which you don't ever remember seeing. And the umpire or whatever they call him is holding up his hand—Burgo's hand. And all the reporters and cameras are over there, too. And Burgo looks across and says, 'What happened? Where were you?' What I'm saying, darling, is that whenever you seem to win, he changes the fight. You need me. I'm the only one who really knows him."

Grant merely repeated himself. "It's not vindictive. It's not even to teach him a lesson." After a pause he added, "Anyway, this isn't why we're flying to Scotland."

65

It was a quiet such as was rarely known on that Highland coast. The sea was as calm as textured glass; in the inner reaches of the bay it was actually mirror smooth. Cormorants dived at their skyward-rocketing twins, meeting at the surface in a hushed bull's-eye of spreading ripples. The mewing of the gulls was edged with surprise that their lifelong accompanists, the wind and the sea, were absent. A mile out from the head of Cragaig, a school of dolphins made silent leaps—stark, astonished arcs of black against the golden lemon sunset waters. Far up Beinn Uidhe the kestrels were having a field day. The thermal, rising off the sunstruck hillside, was enough to keep them teetering precariously aloft but was too light to move the grass and heather in ways that might conceal the passage of small creatures.

Her limousine pulled into the yard. No one came to the door. She told Hamish, the driver, to wait while she let herself in. Grant had dropped off in Strath, where Kelvin and Maddy were staying. As soon as she was indoors she knew the house was occupied. She turned and beckoned the man in with her cases. She pointed to her room; he carried them there in silence.

Imogen came out. To Catherine she seemed ten years older. Both maintained their public poise while the man was there.

Catherine turned to him. "Come back the morn at nine, Hamish. Thanks for a smooth run—and sleep well now."

Hamish left them.

Imogen broke down. Catherine, tired and not too far from tears herself, put her arms around her and soothed her like a baby. "There now, hon. Don't be shy of it. Let it go. Just let it all go."

"He's done," Imogen sobbed. "Kelvin won't say it, but I can tell in his eyes. Oh, Cath, what'll I do? I can't live without him."

By now she was weeping too much even to stand. She slumped into a chair and sprawled across the table, her whole body racked with sobs.

Catherine sat and stroked her hair. Then she, too, began weeping—she hardly knew for what.

For the forfeit years of silence between her and that old man, now dying.

For the shy rediscovery of each other, when life had changed them both beyond any easy recognition.

For the profounder understanding whose seed had been sown only two months ago and which now would never blossom.

For youth, prepared for everything except itself, and now long gone. For the hopes that went with it.

For age, the hastener, which was loss upon loss upon loss.

For the long littleness of life.

Imogen went out to the washhouse, where she chilled her cheeks and eyes under the tap. Catherine followed and did the same. They smiled with bleary sheepishness at each other.

"They wanted to take him," Imogen said. "Dr. Melrose said he was to go into Fort William Infirmary. But I said no. He always begged me to let him die here, even if he died the sooner for it. He was only to go to hospital if there was more than half a chance of recovering. It's his wish. I have to abide by his wish."

She was becoming agitated again.

"Of course you do." Catherine soothed her. "I can hear him saying it. You're doing exactly what he wants." In a different tone she added, "Can he not speak himself?"

"He can't move. He's in a coma now. It was a stroke. Maybe several. Silent strokes, Kelvin calls them. He could open his eyes this morning. But now . . ." She almost broke down again, just managing to master herself.

"May I see him?" Catherine asked.

Imogen took her arm and guided her to the door. "I don't know if he can hear us or not. I talk to him all the time. About anything. I even read him the newspaper today."

"I'll talk to him."

His breathing was shallow. In that silent room on that silent day, it was the first and loudest thing she heard.

"Father," she called from the door. "It's Catherine. I've come to see you."

He did not stir. The north light lay on him like white paint; out of its glare his skin was as oak bark. She passed a hand between his closed eyelids and the light. Not a flicker.

She knelt beside the bed and kissed him. The brief rhythm of his shallow respiration did not change. With her lips close to his ears, her eyes fixed upon his majestic profile, too near to be focussed sharply, she told him all her news.

The light began to fail—the first intimation of the long summer twilight, which, at those latitudes, begins even before the sun has set.

Next she quoted from memory some of his favourite Bible texts—the Sermon on the Mount and parts of the Book of Proverbs. At the outset she deliberately misquoted, knowing that nothing would agitate him more and so be more likely to make him stir. But that adamantine calm remained frozen. She corrected herself and made no further errors.

Then an extraordinary thing happened. Later she reasoned it out as telepathy. A more ecstatic personality than hers would have called it a command from on high, a divine instruction. For that, indeed, was how it seemed: A voice within her head pronounced clearly the words *The Song of Solomon.* Why that book, she could not say. He had never read it to her or referred to it; and she had never understood why it was in the Bible at all.

But there was no gainsaying that clear injunction now. She reached his Bible from the shelf beside his bed and, turning to that book, began: *The song of songs, which is Solomon's. Let him kiss me with the kisses of his mouth: for thy love is better than wine. Because of the savour of thy good ointments thy name is as ointment poured forth, therefore do the virgins love thee. . . .*

There was no response from him, no change in the slow, shallow pace of his breathing, no flicker of his eyes. But she *knew* he heard those words. She knew they brought him the comfort of a God he had approached all his life; the God of Love, who is also the God of all the ambiguities, human and divine, ensconced within that word.

He died the following morning. At his bedside were his wife, his daughter, all three of his grandchildren, and Caroline. Kelvin and Grant went into Strath to tell the minister and the undertaker. Madeleine and Caroline went out for a melancholy walk down along the shore.

It was a day as calm as its predecessor. Again the kestrels rode the thermal off Beinn Uidhe, higher up, above the kiss of the morning sun. The dolphins had moved on but several gray seals were in the bay, basking on the rocks or poking their old colonels' heads above the water and looking this way and that, as if to say, "What have I missed?"

They missed nothing. They heard it before the two women. In fact, it was the sudden alertness of the seals that made Caroline and Maddy stop and listen.

"My God! What is *that?*" Maddy asked.

An intense, dolorous wail hung on the air. Like mist it seemed to have no source. It was joined by another. The two sounds wove in and out of each other, a wreath of sorrow.

"They're keening the dead," Caroline said, only half believing it.

"*Mummy* is?" Maddy could not even half believe.

"Look at the seals."

Their behaviour was extraordinary. Those who were basking, belly to the sun, waving a languorous flipper as a fan, rolled over and sat up. They had no doubt about the source of the sound. Those in the water came waddling onto the sand or rocks and sat motionless. All their noses pointed directly at the croft, and all their huge, dark eyes.

And the keening went on. An insistent, eldritch wail fetched up from the utmost depths of grief and despair. It reached out and united with all the past sorrows of this sad land. Ancient crofters, long dead, heard their voices briefly raised again in those notes; they spanned history, they abolished time.

The seals watched the croft, bonded creatures waiting for the order of release.

Maddy felt the bristles on her neck; her flesh crawled. "If you were superstitious," she said, barely above a whisper, "wouldn't you believe they were departed souls?"

"Let's go and meet the men," Caroline said.

The seals hardly marked their passing.

The car stopped at the bend. "Anything wrong?" Kelvin asked.

"Better park here and walk up to the house, darling," Caroline said. "Switch off a moment."

The silence returned; the grieving still upon it.

"They're keening the dead," Maddy explained.

The four young adults did not know whether to be moved or to make an embarrassed joke of it. They kept silent.

Kelvin let off the brake until the car had rolled onto the verge. Instead of walking directly to the house, up the road, they all set off along the cliff path, the way the two women had come.

"I wonder if Imogen will stay on now," Maddy said.

Kelvin was more direct. "It would be a tragedy if some stranger came in here."

"D'you think the old folks might buy it off Imogen?" Maddy suggested. "If she decides to go back into Strath."

"Or even if she stays," Caroline said.

"It would at least secure the place," Kelvin agreed.

"Hark at us!" Maddy laughed. "Talk about vultures!"

They all laughed and then, remembering the day, looked guiltily at the house. The keening had stopped.

"We'll give them a minute or two to gargle," Maddy said.

This time the laughter was perfunctory.

"Before we go indoors," Grant said, "There's something you guys ought to know." They all turned to him. "This could take a while, so let's go down to the shore and up that way."

As they walked he told them of his and Wild Bill's plans to ease Burgo upstairs, and how it had all probably gone sour, partly because he, Grant, was not there to take a hand, but mainly because of Burgo's uncanny ability never to fight on the obvious battleground with the obvious weapons.

"When I get back," he said glumly, "he'll probably have fixed things so that it doesn't really matter what the bank does. It'll all be somehow irrelevant."

"If he's really on form," Kelvin agreed, "he'll fix it so they march laughing through the door marked *Winners* and find themselves in the street."

"Mummy said something like that," Grant told him. "And another thing. I didn't tell you but somehow she found out about Wild Bill and me cahooting with Systems Leasing—God knows how, but—"

"Isn't it obvious?" Kelvin said. "Dad *knows*. How else could Mummy possibly know? She was over here."

"But I don't see how Dad could possibly know, either. We never met with Systems Leasing in Manhattan. We always went out to their warehouse at Great Neck, and—"

"Where?" Maddy asked.

"Great Neck."

"Does that mean anything to you?" Kelvin asked.

"Well . . . not really."

"It ought to," Grant said. "The first thing you see when you walk in is boxes and boxes labelled *Men Who Have Known Me*. It's where Aunt Meg's publishers warehouse their stock. The other half of the same building."

Kelvin laughed. "So maybe Aunt Meg found out and told Mummy! But if the bets are between her and Dad, I'd say it's no contest."

"But she was so vehement about him," Grant objected. "She can't be in this with him. She isn't that good an actress. She meant it. She really wants to hurt him. She wants to join with Wild Bill and me to hurt him. I told her it isn't like that."

"Either way, Dad knows. You have to reckon with that."

But Grant would not believe it. "It would finish him. He'd never understand our intentions. He'd see it as treachery. It would absolutely finish him. So he can't know." He turned to Maddy. "What do you say?"

She was uncharacteristically offhand. "I don't know. I'll talk to her if you like."

"Leave it to me," Kelvin said. "It'll round off a conversation Caroline and I had with her at the beginning of the year, remember darling?"

Caroline nodded. "At the Cafe Royal."

The funeral tea was held in the hotel. Kelvin, knowing how little his mother and Imogen had slept these last few days and how deeply they grieved, was surprised at how brisk they now were. That awful ritual around the grave, which to him had seemed mere mumbo-jumbo, climaxing with a moment of intolerable grief as the earth had thundered down to separate An Dóiteán from all above, had, as it were, ruled a line across their lives, starting a new kind of now, and founding a new hereafter.

The two women were not exactly cheerful, but they smiled, and their smiles were only a fraction short of cheerfulness. Though they talked of things other than the death and their sorrow, they did not avoid those subjects. When neighbours said An Dóiteán was a good man and had a good long go of it and had lived through storms into the calm waters of old age—and all the other simple and flowery things people say at such times—both Imogen and Catherine agreed and smiled. And were truly comforted.

On the way back Kelvin made the driver stop at the turning where the path ran down to the rocks and the beach. "Come for a walk, Mummy," he suggested. "There are one or two things I want to discuss."

Caroline laughed to hide her embarrassment. "That's a bit ham-handed, mate," she said.

Before Kelvin could respond, Catherine said, "I think it concerns you all. I tell you what. The sun's so nice, why don't we take hay bales out below the byre and have tea down there?" She smiled around. "Then you can all have a go at me."

"It's not that," Grant protested. "No one wants to have a go."

"Then I'm looking forward to it even more."

The young folk looked bewildered; here was a mother they didn't quite recognise.

When they were all in the suntrap below the byre, no one wanted to begin.

Grant said, "You should pave this over, Imogen. It'd make a swell patio. Barbecue over there . . ."

Maddy over-reacted: "And account execs all over the place! Knocking back martinis and telling each other how they treat their bodies like fine violins! You're out of your skull, Grant. That's not what this place is for."

"Oh no?" Grant began.

But Catherine cut in. "Let's deal with unfinished business, shall we."

They all stirred, and waited.

She went on. "Grant has probably told you about the conspiracy? Yes, I see he has. And you're wondering how I found out. And you're convinced it must mean that Burgo knows about it, too."

"He doesn't?" Kelvin asked.

She looked wearily at him. "Of course he doesn't. It would finish him. He'd never survive if he knew."

"So how do *you* know?"

"Pure fluke, darling. A chance remark of Bob Benson's. He—"

"I knew it!" Maddy said. "As soon as you said, Grant, that you only ever met Systems Leasing at Great Neck, I knew Bob was involved."

"Has Maddy told you her other news?" Catherine asked, ignoring her daughter's wide-eyed plea for silence.

"What?" the others asked.

"She and Bob are getting married."

"No!" They all stood up in surprise and grinned at Maddy, who hid her face in confusion. Caroline ran over and kissed the top of her head. "He's super," she said. "I'm so happy, darling."

Kelvin asked, "Are you ashamed of it or something? Why didn't you say?"

Maddy, red as a sunset, faced them, laughing. "I can't *bear* people looking at me and thinking I *belong* to someone. I *don't* belong to anyone. Not now and not after we're married."

Catherine felt an impulse to contradict; husbands and wives *did* belong. But the irony of it made her pause and then kept her ruefully silent. Imogen caught her eye and smiled a smile that said, *Ah youth!*

"What did Bob say?" Grant asked.

"I just asked him—after he told me about Maddy—if he'd seen you, or Wild Bill, or any other *family*. And he laughed and said he had—out at Great Neck."

"When was this—I mean, when did you see Bob?"

"I had lunch with him last week, or the week before. Dear me, I've lost track of time. Whenever it was. Of course, I thought it was some master-scheme of Burgo's and that you and Wild Bill were the messenger boys. My interest in the whole affair was so-big, I must admit." She held her fore-finger and thumb a crack apart. "Until I got back to Goldeneye and heard this thing about the bank. And"—she smiled at Grant—"heard your voice. You are an awfully poor conspirator, honey. I don't understand how Burgo hasn't seen through you, long ago."

"Are you going to tell him?"

"That depends."

"On what?"

But she hadn't yet worked out what it depended on. There was a great deal she hadn't yet worked out. Rather than admit it she changed the sub-ject—in the most dramatic possible way. "You ought to know—all of you—that when I go back to Goldeneye, I'm going to live at Doctor's House. Not West Gideon—*never* West Gideon."

"We warned him," Grant said, looking around. "Didn't we?"

They nodded. "What does Dad say?" Maddy asked.

"I told him we're finished." She smiled wanly. "But he probably doesn't believe it."

"And do *you?*" Maddy pressed. They were all alarmed now.

Kelvin cut in. "What'd you want from him, Mummy?"

"It's not our business," Caroline objected.

"Well, it's ridiculous to talk of splitting up at their time of life. Of course it's our business. How can we stand by and let it happen? We've got to establish what Mummy wants. And then—"

Imogen interrupted. "What does any woman want? I don't know about you young folk, but women of our generation. I'll tell ye what we want. A home. A family. A man. That's all your mother's ever wanted."

"And to help make the decisions," Catherine said. "Without that, it's just so much charity."

"Of course, hon. Aye, of course."

Catherine smiled at her children. "It sounds simple, doesn't it! I've never wanted more than those simple things—yet your father can't give them. There's just something in him that—"

"If he retired *now,*" Kelvin said. "Would that make a difference? If business was . . . all in the past?"

Catherine laughed. "And if the cows milked themselves, and the hens could butter their own eggs, and the fish leap into the pan!"

"But *if?*" he insisted.

"And if he never mentioned West Gideon again?" Maddy added.

"There's no point even discussing it."

"But *if!*" Kelvin and Maddy said.

"He wouldn't. He *couldn't.*"

"*If!*" the three young people shouted.

She shrugged. "Of course it would be different. But—"

"No buts!" Kelvin said. "Let's just leave it there. Don't let's—anybody—don't let's take up fixed positions." He looked especially at his mother. "And you say Dad probably doesn't believe you're leaving him? You weren't absolutely categoric?"

"No. I'm afraid I wasn't. I was just a hundred-percent positive—which, of course, he'd take to be the next best thing to capitulation."

"Well"—Kelvin shrugged—"let's leave it there. For the moment." He turned to Imogen with his best doctor's smile. "And now you, young lady."

Her eyebrows shot up but Catherine could see she enjoyed the banter.

"Can we talk about you? And this place? While we're all here?"

"What's to talk about?"

"Well, we'd quite understand if a combination of memories and the winter gales made you want to move back into Strath now. It's just that if you do, we'd like the option to buy from you."

"Or," Grant added, "if you'd prefer, we could buy the place now, giving you a life tenancy, and you could buy an annuity with the proceeds—enough to go on a sea cruise each winter."

Catherine thought her children had done quite enough in the way of rearranging the world for one afternoon. "Imogen is well provided for," she assured them. "Beinn Uidhe is hers to do with as she likes. No doubt she'll bear your wishes in mind, but she's obliged to do no more than that."

Imogen nodded.

They swallowed their impatience in the wake of their mother's finality. Silence washed back over them.

Maddy sipped her whisky and sighed. "I don't want to go back. I could stay here always." She turned to her mother. "Why did you ever leave, Mummy?"

She meant it half rhetorically but Kelvin took it seriously. "Yes. Why did you? I often used to wonder."

Catherine considered the question. Should she tell them?

She could repeat the facts, but could she conjure up the reality? Would they see Huey MacLintock's cheeky, adoring, freckled face? Would it be as dear to them as—in certain nostalgic moments—it still could seem to her? And if not, would they then understand An Dóiteán's passionate anger? Would they see him as a fiery red giant, not the ancient patriarch but a man in full vigour, only four or five years older than Kelvin now was? Could they, who today stood around his grave, be made to see that giant lift young Huey bodily above his head—on that selfsame spot—prepared to dash the life from him on that very gravestone? Could they, who knew the waterfall over the hill as a place to splash and romp and laugh, could they see the darkness of murder and death that still haunted it and her?

The facts would collapse under such a burden; they would be rejected.

"The times were hard then." Imogen filled the silence.

"Aye," Catherine agreed. "The times were hard then." She smiled. "But life was oh so much easier!"

She looked at Kelvin, who was a million miles away, and wondered what he was planning. What a *secret* family they were!

66

They went back via Montreal, where Grant was to take a car to Toronto, to DataLease Dominion's head office. Catherine intended waiting for a flight onward to Saskatoon. But as they came out of Customs, they were paged on the PA.

It was Burgo, calling from Toronto.

"Cath? I'm sorry about An Dóiteán. How are you?"

"I'm over it now. Over the worst, anyway. I'm over a lot of things."

There was a pause before he said, "Yes—er, can you come here with Grant? He didn't leave yet, did he?"

"He's here beside me. D'you want him?"

"I want you, Cath."

She did not answer. A terrible, weary foreboding filled her. If Burgo now laid siege to her, if he really tried, she wasn't sure she'd withstand it. Mentally she would. But it wasn't her mind that would let her down.

"Honey?"

"I'm still here. Tell me what you have to say."

"I want to see your face when I do."

"I'll bet!"

"I do. It's going to make you so happy."

"It? What's *it*? East Gideon? North Gideon? . . ."

He had the grace to laugh. "Nothing like that. It's something you really want."

"I doubt it."

"Come and find out."

She almost yielded. He sounded so eager and excited, so sure he would please her. But in the end that small, hard knot within her would not unravel for him. "No. You come. Come to Goldeneye and tell me."

"Cath! Have you any idea what—"

"If it's important, you'll do it. If it isn't . . . well, then we'll know."

She cradled the handset before she could weaken. Grant was livid. He had wanted to glean all he could of the current state of play. He picked up the phone again and put a return call through. Catherine, afraid that Burgo would simply use him, said, "Don't take any messages for me. Tell him I'll listen to him only in Goldeneye. Even then it will be with reluctance. I'll go now. And don't you come looking for me, either."

She held her cheek forward for a kiss. He was asking for Wild Bill as she left him.

There were over two hours before her connecting flight. She went for a facial. She was just paying for it when she was paged again. Her first impulse was to ignore it. The caller could only be Burgo. But then she told herself, *No! Think of it as one more chance to din your message into his brain.* So she took the call.

But it wasn't Burgo. It was one of the company pilots, in person. Burgo had sent a jet to take her all the way to Goldeneye.

It softened her feelings toward him—at least as far as Ottawa. But there the plane tilted left and the sun patches crept back toward the tail and then began to edge in through the starboard windows. She called the pilot. "What's happening, Sam?"

"I've had instructions to detour via Toronto, Mrs. Macrae."

"Any particular reason?"

"To take on one more passenger. No name."

She had to laugh. He was so predictable. "I suppose it's no good for me to say turn back—go on to Goldeneye, Sam?"

"It'd put me in a bit of a spot."

And of course there was no extra passenger to take on at Toronto, and of course there was an empty car waiting to whisk her downtown. But there the expected sequence was broken.

The DataLease Dominion building was full of bailiffs, tagging, marking, and listing everything. Burgo, who must have had spies looking out for the car, was there to meet her in the concourse. "Sorry about this delay, honey," he said. "We'll go back to the airport in just five minutes."

"We?"

"Yes. I'm getting out of this place. I'm leaving. I'm coming with you."

"What's all this?" She pointed at the bailiffs.

His look conveyed they were so familiar he'd almost stopped noticing them. "Bluff," he said. "It's called piling on the pressure. Any moment now they're going to wake up to the fact that they're pushing at an open door."

"Has Grant got here yet?"

"Soon. You overtook him."

"How's Wild Bill?"

"Better. He hadn't the guts for a fight. As soon as I told him I'd throw in the towel, he recovered."

There was something wrong. Burgo's words were those of a loser, but his tone said *winner* all the way. He was too smugly cheerful to be throwing in the towel.

"Are you really giving up?" she asked.

"That's what I wanted to tell you on the phone. I have retired. It's official. As from five P.M. today. Also I put West Gideon up for sale. That was an unforgivable thing to spring on you, Cath. I must have been mad. Or high. Now I've decided to quit—why there's Grant now. Let him hear this, too."

While they waited for Grant to join them, Burgo finished his last sentence. "Now it's final, I feel like I've really . . . I've rejoined reality. I feel like I've been high for years." Grant joined them but Burgo went on talking to her. "The relief! Never another telex. Never another all-night, all-ticket contest with clients or suppliers . . . think of it, Cath!"

"You'd better mean it, Burgo."

"Oh it's *you,* Mummy!" Grant laughed sarcastically. "What was it—engine trouble?" He turned to his father. "And you? Is this true? I called Wild Bill, but I still don't believe it. You're just bowing out?"

Burgo grinned, and again there was that unambiguous triumph about him. "I'm bowing out of DataLease Dominion, yes. The bank can have it. And Systems Leasing. Of course, whether they'll want it by the time they've got it is another matter."

Grant's face crumpled. "Oh, Dad! No!"

"Oh yes! You just watch their quotations over the next few days."

"But Systems Leasing—"

"Systems Leasing! That's not a company. It's a Kremlin. It was born with arthritis."

"Oh, Dad—this is every Friday evening of my *life.*"

"They want this company? Well, I'm turning it into a millstone, and I'm going to hang it round their neck. They want to swallow us? Well, let them swallow that!"

"Blood and thunder! Break out the Jolly Roger, eh!" He became serious. "I'm going to fight you on this. You might as well know—"

"No, you're not."

"I am."

"I'll tell you what you're going to do." He looked around and then swept them up the passage toward the fire-escape door. Safe on the little balcony beyond it—which he dominated like a captain on his bridge—he said, "Ever since January I've been putting together a new operation—something that'll make this outfit look like a dealership in empty Coke bottles."

Grant struck himself on the forehead. "Get me out of this nightmare."

"You're quick, Grant. You'll see it."

"Wild Bill didn't mention this."

"He doesn't know. I wanted you to be first. You'll see the logic of it and then you can talk him over."

"I know I'm going to regret this, but see the logic of what?"

"We've been fools, my boy. Shortsighted fools—just leasing computers and software, when we could be in it front to back. Span the market! Well, now we're going to change all that. This bank hassle couldn't have come at a better time. Just the push we needed! We're going for full vertical integration. We'll manufacture in Japan, assemble in Mexico, and we'll have bureaux right across America, Europe, the East! We, my boy, we three prairie hicks are going to challenge I.B.M.!"

"We?" Catherine queried.

"Oh you're still awake, are you!" Grant turned on her.

"To my own interests, yes," she said evenly before turning back to Burgo. "Who is 'we'?"

He grinned awkwardly. "Give me ten days, honey—ten days in Chicago to raise the last four hundred million—"

"Oh! So you weren't coming to Goldeneye with me?"

"In ten days."

Grant laughed.

"And I suppose West Gideon *isn't* up for sale?" she pressed.

"Of course it is. Would I lie? But no one's going to buy a shell like that. I was going to ask you, would you design the interior? You'd do such a wonderful job. And we'd get double the price."

"In ten days!" she asked.

Grant laughed again. "Sure! If he can put together a world empire in ten days, you can do an itty-bitty thing like design an interior!"

Burgo grinned at him. "Not me alone, son. *We*. The deal's already together. All but. We're going to Chicago just to dot the eyes and cross the tees. Then it's all yours. Yours and Wild Bill's and your team of bright young organization men. It's my farewell gift to you."

"Oh yes! And you? You'll be growing roses in Goldeneye? I *don't* think."

"I'll be taking your mother around the world." He turned to Catherine, for the reward of her surprise, her smile.

"Honestly, Burgo?" she asked. "You mean it?"

"Every word. I told you—I'm through with business. But I'm going out my own way. In my own style. I'll show that bank."

"The bank had a good position marked up for you," Grant objected. "An honourable position."

"Yeah!" Burgo sneered. "Honourable-Grand-Chairman-Emeritus-In-An-Iron-Mask-Available-Alternate-Sundays! I couldn't wait!"

Catherine laughed.

Grant rounded on her. "Well thank you, Mummy, for all your help. Without you, I'd probably never have got this trip to Chicago."

"My help! But you turned it down."

"What help?" Burgo's eyes narrowed. "How could you help Grant?"

She smiled a challenge back at him. "I was going to cut your ears off, darling. And you'd better be straight with me this time. The knife is still sharp."

He laughed. "Will you design that interior?"

"I can keep a bargain."

"I'll get a mobile home sent up there," he said. "Equipped like a full design studio. And so you can cook. Of course, the barbecue by the patio works already. And there's power and water—"

She put a finger on his lip. "Just leave all that to me, huh?"

She began to wonder whether it was going to be quite such an unmixed blessing to have a hundred percent of Burgo's organizing ability lying around the house a hundred percent of the time.

"Burgo," she asked. "Why this sudden change of heart? It's so total."

"Don't trust me, eh?"

"Would *you?*"

He sighed. "Kelvin called me. He made me . . . see things."

"It didn't occur to you off your own bat?"

"I'm sorry—no."

"Good! *Now* I trust you."

67

Three weeks on the nose he called her from Midway, Chicago. "We did it, Cath! We did it. Are you at West Gideon?"

"Yes. Oh, Burgo, that's marvellous news. And I'm so happy for you, too."

"For us, Cath."

"Yes. For us."

"What's the weather there?"

"Fine, dry, and warm," she said.

"I'll be with you in three hours. Let's have a barbecue."

"Burgo."

"Uh huh?"

"I love you."

"Me too. We're going to have a *wonderful* marriage."

"Is 'wonderful' different to 'marvellous'? I hope so. I didn't like 'marvellous' at all."

He laughed. "You'll see!"

She was lighting the barbecue and just beginning to scan the sky—hoping that tailwinds might have cut his E.T.A.—when Margaret came storming onto the patio. Her face was bruised with a flat-hand shiner from temple to jawbone, red-brown and promising purple. Wild Bill had come up to Doctor's House that day, for a long weekend with Meg, who was still labouring over *Sons*.

"Meg! Who did that?"

"Wild Shit Hickock."

"That's despicable."

"You should see his face—when he gets up off the floor."

"But why?"

"*Wild Shit Hickock* wouldn't be a bad title for a book, would it. The story of my divorce. And oh-so-much beside."

"Tell me what happened, honey. Sit down. D'you want some steak on that? I've got a whole pile here."

"Vodka on the inside of my bruises is better."

"Help yourself."

"I had to come. As soon as I found out, I had to come over, or I'd never face you and Burgo again, ever." She poured a good slug, saying, "Oh Bob, where are you when my adverbs need you so badly."

"He's in London with Maddy. She stayed on after the funeral. I'm convinced they're going to marry secretly over there."

"If you're going to be so literal all evening, I'll swop the glass for the bottle right now."

"Found out about what?"

The charcoal began to ping as the heat took a grip.

"About Wild Bill." She knocked back half the glass. "And Grant. I have some very unpalatable news, I'm afraid."

"I think I know it."

"Oh, you don't!" The rest of the tot vanished in one.

"About Wild Bill and Grant selling out to Systems Leasing?" Catherine said casually. "And fixing up for us to get overgeared? And making the bank take the blame for the merger and reorganization? And easing Burgo out? There, I think that's going to burn now. Stay and have a steak?"

Meg was so astonished she forgot to refill her glass. She sipped its emptiness and stared at it in annoyance. "You do know."

"Yes. Bob told me—when? In London."

Meg gave her insanity giggle. "Bob? My Bob?"

"The one and only. Systems Leasing share your publisher's warehouse. Bob saw Wild Bill and Grant arriving for several meetings there."

Meg poured another drink. "And you told Burgo? He knew all along? Oh boy!"

"I didn't tell him. That was the week the sky fell in—when I called you from New York? I was going to tell him, but then he seemed to cope well enough without knowing. So . . ."

"And you didn't tell him since?"

"I was going to, but it wasn't necessary in the end."

"Not *necessary!*"

"Well, I had a talk with Grant and he explained that it was all really a kindness on his part—and Wild Bill's—"

"A kindness!" Meg roared with laughter. "Oh darling—you are such a mixture of cunning and naivety, you know. Do you really believe that? I mean, you may have been born before Sigmund Freud walked across Brigadoon or whatever they call the gateway to Scotland, but heavens, Cath, you've lived with Burgo long enough now. Do you honestly believe Grant?"

"Yes. I do. I've no reason to doubt him."

"Cath—he's a *businessman*. He never sleeps. You know the type. He probably has five different explanations of everything, ready for all occasions. He just picked the most effective one for you." She laughed. "They see you coming, Cath. They know just how to use you."

"They?"

"Grant and Burgo. Both."

"You're saying it wasn't like that?"

"I'm telling you that Grant and Wild Bill have been plotting for centuries, right from before DataLease Dominion was born, they've been plotting to let Burgo build it up and then they'd squeeze him out and take over. This wasn't some panic be-kind-to-Burgo response when the big-bad-bank said get him out. They planned it all. Down to the timing of the last little telex."

"How are you so sure Wild Bill told you the truth?"

"Because I'm no peasant. I'm neither cunning nor naive. Just ruthless. If you want to know, I took away both his legs and beat up on him until it all came out."

"My God! Really?"

"Really! I don't believe that stuff about not kicking a man when he's down. It's always seemed the very best time, to me. I've still got both his legs, in the trunk of the car now. And the spare set is back in Brooklyn Heights."

Catherine tipped on a little more charcoal. It was damp. A ball of steam enveloped her briefly. "Don't tell Burgo, please, Meg. Never say this to him."

"I'd hate him to think I was party to it."

"He won't. He'll never know. D'you want me to do you a steak?"

"I want a bath, first. Is the water hot in the trailer?"

"Go ahead. Stay the night, too. The bed's made up."

They saved every drop of water at West Gideon; it went to maintain shrubs and borders that would have wilted in the naturally meagre rainfall. Catherine heard Meg's bathwater gurgling out into the storage tank beneath the patio just as Burgo's plane, the company's Gulfstream, came cruising into the sunset and put down on the landing strip. She plumped up the salad and went for fresh ice.

Burgo came running at her across the terrace, arms out like a winning candidate. "We did it! We did it!"

They hugged in an ecstasy Catherine had not felt for years. They were together again. Just him and her. For six months . . . a year . . . however long it took. Well, it was going to take the rest of their lives. She'd see to that. One way or another, she'd see to it. Once the business habit was broken, she'd see it never mended.

"Was that Meg's car I saw as we came in to land?"

"Oh yes, she and Bill have had a little fight. A bit worse than usual, I think. She's staying here tonight. Tell me again. Are we really going around the world? I just can't believe it!"

"Pour me a Scotch and I'll tell you. Where d'you want to go first?"

She poured his drink. "Samoa."

He laughed. "What's wrong with Paris?"

"Paris is a city. I don't want to go to a single city. I want to go to all the wild places—Samoa, Antarctica, the Gobi Desert, Katmandu. Samarkand. . . ." She gave him his drink.

"We have to go to *some* cities, Cath."

"No we don't. We're not even going to pack one suit."

"Just London, Paris . . . Rome . . . Tokyo. Places like that."

"No, Burgo, not even one place like that. I want this to be an absolute break."

He laughed awkwardly. "I can't just make an absolute break, honey. Not absolute. Not just like that."

"But why not?"

"Well—you see—I mean, this trip. It *is* for us. It is for you and me. But"—he cleared his throat—"there is also—"

"There is also *business* in it," she said bitterly. She ought to have known. "Wonderful" was going to be just the same as "marvellous." She ought to have realized. It was what Meg said: *They see you coming. They know just how to use you.*

"It won't be much, honey. I'll just be meeting people and looking at potential locations for our bureaux, going through the national and regional marketing surveys . . . that sort of thing."

Heavens, Cath, you've lived with Burgo long enough now!

"I mean Wild Bill and Grant will be doing most of the work back here. All of it really. I'll just be"—a little, insouciant laugh—"gadding around the world with you and taking out the odd day or two."

Grant and Burgo both. They see you coming.

"At least half the time I'll be with you. At least half."

They probably have five different explanations of everything, ready for all occasions.

He put his fist under her chin. "Cath? You surely didn't think I meant to drop the business absolutely, did you? I mean—you know what a sacrifice even this is. Say something."

Meg appeared. Her hair was in a towel-turban. She was in one of Catherine's kimono dressing gowns. Part Carmen Miranda, part Dorothy Lamour, Catherine thought. Miranda-Lamour—now, there was a conjunction!

Always kick a man when he's down.

Or up.

"Meg," Catherine said, "I think you'd better tell Burgo after all."

"What?"

"Tell him why you and Wild Bill had that fight. Tell him exactly what you told me."

"You sure?"

"What is this?" Burgo laughed uneasily.

"I never was more sure of anything in my life."

So Meg told him. She had the conspiracy in such detail that Burgo could not doubt her. Catherine watched him intently, noting every fleeting detail of his reaction.

She had expected him to argue, bluster, or ridicule his way through all the uncomfortable things Meg was revealing. But at moments like this he rarely did the expected thing. Once it became clear to him that this was no fantasy, he stood as tense and contained as a great cat, watching every movement of his sister's face and lips. When she paused, he sipped his drink —mechanically, not reacting to the afterburn.

He was eager to find contradictions, of course. Every now and then she saw the flicker of hope behind his eyes. But one by one those alternatives were closed off by some new detail of Meg's relentlessly circumstantial account, and then she knew that *he* knew he was cornered at last in a world that had ceased to be pliant and accommodating.

Surely he would now see?

He set down his empty glass and walked away to the far end of the patio, and then down onto the terrace.

"My God, I hope I did right," Meg said. "What changed your mind?"

"He promised me a world cruise. It turned out to be a business trip, with half-day excursions to the Grand Canyon and Pompeii."

"What's he doing now? What's going on in that mind of his?"

"That, Meg, is precisely what he hopes we are thinking. His first aim, in any crisis, is to thicken that smoke of uncertainty which always surrounds him. But it won't help this time. He's the only person left in there."

Meg stared at her in surprise. Catherine smiled back exultantly. She had never felt so confident as now.

He turned and began to stroll back. Catherine waited until he was just within earshot and then said to Meg—as if she thought she would not be overheard—"Now he's wondering if we're anxious and worried enough."

It threw Burgo; she could see it plainly. He had been about to say something quite different but instead he asked, "Did you know about this, too, Cath?"

"I heard about it tonight. From Meg. When she came over with that black eye."

"But why were you so cheerful? When you greeted me . . ."

"Because I *believed* you, Burgo. You'll laugh when I say I thought you had told me the truth when you said you'd set up this new venture and then retire. I thought, why spoil it for you? Why ruin your life? You'd finished with the business. I had your word on that. Cross your heart. It was over. It was the past. Why rake up the past?"

"My own son," he said.

It was obviously what he had intended saying in the first place. Now it came out limply, an afterthought. "And my best friend. My buddy. After all we've done together!"

"Done *how?*" Catherine pounced. "You didn't say *together,* did you?"

Looking at the exultation in her face, he understood how completely he had lost. All his instincts had deserted him. "And the bank," he went on, mechanically now. "And all the big stockholders."

It didn't even sound pitiful. It was an empty incantation, spoken with the wrong timing and in the wrong tone. Burgo was broken.

She poured him another whisky—neat.

He walked away from it, toward the trailer.

"Burgo?" Her voice was a schooling whip. "You're not planning anything foolish?"

He gave a wan smile. "Perish the thought," he answered.

She put a couple of steaks on the barbecue.

"He'll never work again," Meg said, aghast at what she had just seen.

"No." Catherine sipped the whisky. It burned. "He won't." She turned the steaks to seal them. The gorgeous smell of burning blood rose up to her. "It was better that way, Meg. You pitching, me catching. Now I can pick up the pieces."

"My God, Cath! You're a killer whale, you know that? Even better—you're the only killer whale that can go around with everybody saying, 'My, just look at that dinky little sardine!' How d'you do that?"

"Just mix with a dash of Burgo and shake gently for thirty-five years."

68

Burgo vanished. The shell of him still inhabited the house. Catherine could push it around anywhere she wanted. It smiled. It sighed. It talked. Mostly it slept.

The Big Deal crumbled in his absence. It had, in any case, been the usual mixture of bluff, hope, and realism. The original reorganization and merger of DataLease Dominion and Systems Leasing went through as planned—or plotted. Wild Bill—once Meg had given him back his legs— was president; Grant was chief executive officer.

When, after nearly three weeks, Burgo still showed no sign of life beyond that of a zombie, Catherine began to worry. It was Meg who suggested a complete break, for both of them. "Go and visit with Imogen," she said. And it was so arranged.

It was like travelling with an idiot son—someone you had to dress and steer and feed.

Imogen was delighted to have them. Loneliness was beginning to claim her once again. She said they were to stay just as long as they pleased; she said it often. At least once a day.

Burgo slept most of the time—in bed, in An Dóiteán's chair, in the heather, in among the rocks. Then he began to read science fiction—something he had always scorned before. Soon the place was littered with Azimov, Heinlein, Blish, Simak, and Bradbury. The problems of unreal and unreachable worlds fascinated him.

Then in August there came a sequence of scorching, breathless days. The three of them went on long, silent, easeful walks up over Beinn Uidhe and down around the headland. They became such familiar figures that the seals let them pass without a grunt. Catherine never mentioned the future. Nor the past. She simply waited.

At last he said the words she thought she'd never hear. He and she were out alone, walking up and over the hill.

"What are we going to do, Cath?" he asked.

She hid her exultation. "Finish our holiday here? And then go home?"

"Don't ask me. Tell me."

"No," she said. "We're not going to substitute my dictatorship for yours."

"Dictatorship!" He gave a humourless laugh at the word. After a silence he asked, "Do you really think of Goldeneye as home?"

She did not exactly understand him.

"Rather than here, I mean? Beinn Uidhe? Isn't this home to you?"

"Of course not."

"Oh." He seemed surprised, as if her answer put a stop to whatever else he had been going to say.

"You were born in Goldeneye," she reminded him. Then, to lighten the suddenly dour mood, she laughed and added, "Remember? 'Thy home shall be my home.' "

"There's a lot of opportunities here, Cath," he began.

"There's more in Goldeneye," she cut in before he could enlarge on that. "Just think of all the things that town lacks. All the things it needs. And why? Because men and women with vision—people like you—did what you've done all your life. They turned their eyes outward. Looked away and went away. Can you blame some of the young people, how they behave? The trouble they get into? Whether you think of it as home or not, honey, that town needs you."

He grunted.

A little while later he said, "Were you really that mad at me, Cath?"

"What year are we talking about?"

"You know what I'm talking about."

"I must have been," she began. Then, abruptly: "No! Why should I sweeten it? How d'you think I felt? You told me you'd finished with business. You were really and truly and at last going to bow out and cultivate your marriage for a change—for the first time in a long time. Mad? I tell you, you owe your life to a sixty-year habit of restraint on my part. Otherwise . . ."

"That trip could have been a hell of a lot of fun, though." He cleared his throat. "It still could be."

Deliberately she held her peace.

"What d'you say?" he prompted. "We'd have a marvellous time."

Still she did not react.

"Come on, Cath! Did you really think I could give up? Everything? Can you honestly see me idle for the rest of my life? How long would I last?"

Wearily she turned to him. "You're doing it deliberately, aren't you. You are deliberately refusing to understand."

"What?"

"Tell me—what do you think made me so angry? Be honest."

"Hell, Cath. You must have known I wouldn't retire."

"What made me mad?"

"I'd just curl up and die. You know that."

"What made me mad?"

"You know."

"I really think you still don't know. You still haven't understood, have you. It's all been a waste."

"All right. You wanted me to give up business. You wanted me under your feet all day."

"That's it?" she asked, peering into his eyes to see if he was fooling.

"Of course."

"You think I'm that stupid? You think I don't know the first thing about you?"

"Wait a minute now—what are you saying? Are you saying that wasn't it?"

"Heavens, Burgo—anyone who ever tried to spend half a day 'relaxing' with you on a beach knows you could never retire. Not like that. I never expected that. I didn't even want it."

He laughed weakly. "Then I'm at a loss. I'm utterly at a loss. What was it all about?"

She stepped quickly in front of him, facing him and blocking his path. She gripped his arms and said, *"Deceit,* Burgo. At the risk of repeating myself for the ten-thousandth time, it's about deceit. Telling me one thing and planning another. You know? Treating me as a tactical obstacle. That's what made me mad. It made me so mad that if you ever try it again, we are finished. Through. For the rest of our lives I want—"

"I know," he interrupted, trying to regain the initiative—or the illusion of it at least. "You want to be part of our decisions."

But she smiled and shook her head. "Wrong again, honey. Not 'part of' but 'party *to.*' I want to be party to every important decision we take from now on."

There was a moment of understanding in his eyes. It made her feel she might not be entirely wasting her life in continuing to press this point.

Their wanderings brought them to the edge of the waterfall pool.

"It isn't just Goldeneye, is it, Cath," he said.

"Not just Goldeneye what?"

"That needs organizing properly. It's the whole of Saskatchewan."

She smiled and began to undo the buttoned belt of her dress.

"People outside think it's all just wheat and prairie. But really we've got everything."

She undid her blouse and slipped it off.

"Mountains? We've got mountains. Hey—steady!"

She undid her bra.

"And lakes and sloughs—we've got the biggest wild-duck factory in the hemisphere. What *are* you doing?"

"Going for a swim."

"And deer. And moose."

She slipped out of the last of her clothes and rushed beneath the spout of the waterfall, tricing up to its flow like a trout to white water, tucking into it as she would tuck herself into a prairie wind.

"Soon," she shouted.

"What?"

"Let's go back soon." She bent and launched herself into the shallow pool, and from the water she called up to him, "Now d'you know what sort of woman you married?"

Smiling, he watched her. And then he answered, "I'm beginning to."